TAMI HOAG

DARK PARADISE

ISBN 0-553-56161-8

50599>

DARK PARADISE

TAMI HOAG

BANTAM BOOKS
NEW YORK · TORONTO · LONDON
SYDNEY · AUCKLAND

DARK PARADISE
A Bantam Book / April 1994

Grateful acknowledgment is made for permission to use lyrics from "Cry Like an Angel" by Shawn Colvin and John Leventhal. Copyright © 1989 AGF Music Ltd. / SCRED Songs / Lev-a-tunes. Used by Permission—All Rights Reserved.

ISBN 0-553-56161-8

Published simultaneously in the United States and Canada

Bantam Books are published by Bantam Books, a division of Bantam Doubleday Dell Publishing Group, Inc. Its trademark, consisting of the words "Bantam Books" and the portrayal of a rooster, is Registered in U.S. Patent and Trademark Office and in other countries. Marca Registrada. Bantam Books, 1540 Broadway, New York, New York 10036.

PRINTED IN THE UNITED STATES OF AMERICA

RAD   0 9 8 7 6 5

Author's Note

Inspiration comes from everywhere and from nowhere, from life and from dreams and from places that have no names. It comes most often in small pieces as tiny and bright as diamonds. I catch them when I can and hold them tight. I wish on them like stars and from them come the seeds of stories.

This book is the result of many small inspirations that came to me over the course of time. I have a number of people to thank for those diamond lights. Mary W., for striking a spark half a decade ago. Mary-Chapin Carpenter and Shawn Colvin, songwriters whose gift for touching the soul with words continually leaves me in awe. Philip Aaberg, Montana-born pianist who can transport me west with a handful of tender notes and the exquisite silences between them. John Lyons, cowboy and teacher of wisdom and patience. Sarge, old friend long gone from all but my memory and my heart.

Also, thank you to fellow Bantam author and agency sister Fran Baker for your generous donation of information on the life of a court reporter. Thanks, Don Weisberg, for the Feed and Read. Thanks to C.B. and M.E.F. for your spirited bidding in support of MFW and my ego.

Readers, I hope you enjoy this trip to Montana. It is a place of unique and spectacular beauty, at once tough and fragile, timeless and threatened, as is the American West itself. It is a place where the incredible, boisterous spirit of the frontier can still be felt, and where it can be felt slipping away like sand through grasping fingers. To all who would fight to save that spirit—natives and outsiders alike—I wish you success.

The streets of my town are not what they were
They are haloed in anger, bitter and hurt
And it's not so you'd notice
It's a sinister thing
Like the wheels of ambition at the christening

—Shawn Colvin, John Leventhal
"Cry Like an Angel"

Dark Paradise

PROLOGUE

She could hear the dogs in the distance, baying relentlessly. Pursuing relentlessly, as death pursues life.

Death.

Christ, she was going to die. The thought made her incredulous. Somehow, she had never really believed this moment would come. The idea had always loitered in the back of her mind that she would somehow be able to cheat the grim reaper, that she would be able to deal her way out of the inevitable. She had always been a gambler. Somehow, she had always managed to beat the odds. Her heart fluttered and her throat clenched at the idea that she would not beat them this time.

The whole notion of her own mortality stunned her, and she wanted to stop and stare at herself, as if she were having an out-of-body experience, as if this person running were someone she knew only in passing. But she couldn't stop. The sounds of the dogs drove her on. The instinct of self-preservation spurred her to keep her feet moving.

She lunged up the steady grade of the mountain, tripping over exposed roots and fallen branches. Brush grabbed her clothing and clawed her bloodied face like gnarled, bony fingers. The carpet of decay on the forest floor gave way in spots as she scrambled, yanking her back precious inches instead of giving her purchase to propel herself forward. Pain seared through her as her elbow cracked against a stone half buried in the soft loam. She picked herself up, cradling the arm against her body, and ran on.

Sobs of frustration and fear caught in her throat and choked her. Tears blurred what sight she had in the moon-silvered night. Her nose was broken and throbbing, forcing her to breathe through her mouth alone, and she tried to swallow the cool night air in great gulps. Her lungs were burning, as if every breath brought in a rush of acid instead of oxygen. The fire spread down her arms and legs, limbs that felt like leaden clubs as she pushed them to perform far beyond their capabilities.

I should have quit smoking. A ludicrous thought. It wasn't cigarettes that was going to kill her. In an isolated corner of her mind, where a strange calm resided, she saw herself stopping and sitting down on a fallen log for a final smoke. It would have been like those nights after aerobics class, when the first thing she had done outside the gym was light up. Nothing like that first smoke after a workout. She laughed, on the verge of hysteria, then sobbed, stumbled on.

The dogs were getting closer. They could smell the blood that ran from the deep cut the knife had made across her face.

There was no one to run to, no one to rescue her. She knew that. Ahead of her, the terrain only turned more rugged, steeper, wilder. There were no people, no roads. There was no hope.

Her heart broke with the certainty of that. No hope. Without hope, there was nothing. All the other systems began shutting down.

She broke from the woods and stumbled into a clearing. She couldn't run another step. Her head swam and pounded. Her legs wobbled beneath her, sending her lurching drunkenly into the open meadow. The commands her brain sent shorted out en route, then stopped firing altogether as her will crumbled.

Strangling on despair, on the taste of her own blood, she sank to her knees in the deep, soft grass and stared up at the huge, brilliant disk of the moon, realizing for the first time in her life how insignificant she was. She would die in this wilderness, with the scent of wildflowers in the air, and the world would go on without a pause. She was nothing, just another victim of another hunt. No one would even miss her. The sense of stark loneliness that thought sent through her numbed her to the bone.

No one would miss her.

No one would mourn her.

Her life meant nothing.

She could hear the crashing in the woods behind her. The sound of hoofbeats. The snorting of a horse. The dogs baying. Her heart pounding, ready to explode.

She never heard the shot.

CHAPTER 1

"*I*t started out as a bad hair day and went downhill from there," Marilee Jennings said aloud as her Honda crossed the border into Montana. She took a last drag on her cigarette and crushed out the stub amid a dozen others in the ashtray.

The line was a joke she and Lucy had shared time and again during their friendship. Whenever either of them began a conversation with that line, it meant the other was to provide the Miller Lite, the pizza, and the shoulder to cry on. Usually, they ended up laughing. Always they ended up commiserating.

They had met in a stress management course for court reporters. After two hours of being counseled not to attempt to resolve stress with cigarettes, liquor, and shop talk, they walked out of the meeting room and Lucy turned to her with a wry smile and a pack of Salem Light 100's in her hand and said, "So you want to go get a beer?"

The bond had been instant and strong. Not a cloying friendship, but a relationship based on common ground and a sense of humor. They both worked on their own, hustling for government contracts and working for a string of attorneys, taking depositions and doing the usual grunt work of transcripts and subpoenas and fending off amorous advances of legal beagles in heat. They both saw the kinds of ugliness people could resort to in labor-management disputes, and took down in the secret code of their profession first-person accounts of everything from the absurdities of divorce battles to the atroci-

5

ties of murder. They shared the common problems of their profession—the stress of a job that demanded perfection, the headaches of dealing with arrogant attorneys who wanted everything but the bill in twenty-four hours, then went for months without bothering to pay them. And yet, in many ways, they were as different as night and day.

Lucy liked the glamour attached to the people she worked for. She thrived on intrigue and dyed her hair a different shade of blond every six months because sameness bored her. She looked at the world with the narrow eyes of an amused cynic. Her insights were as sharp as a stiletto and so was her tongue. She was ambitious and ruthless and wry. She adored the limelight and coveted the lush life.

Mari still harbored the weary hope that people were essentially good, even though she had seen that many were not. Appearances seldom impressed her because she had grown up in a neighborhood where the phrase "all style and no substance" was the battle cry of most of the women as they ran to their BMWs, charge cards in hand, to race to the latest sale at Nordstrom's. She had no aspirations to fame or fortune and dreamed mostly of a quiet place where she could fit in unnoticed.

Their differences had only served to balance their relationship. They had shared a lot in those late-night beer and bullshit sessions. Then Lucy had come into some money, chucked her job, and moved to Montana, and while the bond between them hadn't broken, it had been stretched awfully thin.

The intervening year had been a long one. Mari had missed her friend. Neither of them was good about writing letters, and time slipped by between phone calls. But she knew the friendship would still be there. Lucy would welcome her with that same kind of casual amusement she turned on every other aspect of her life. All Mari would have to do would be to step out of her car, shrug her shoulders, and say, "It started out as a bad hair day and went downhill from there."

Her eyes darted to the rearview mirror, betraying her

as the tide of depression tried to rise again inside her. She frowned at the state of her wild, streaky blond mane. Who was she kidding? Her whole life had been a series of bad hair days.

While her two sisters had inherited their mother's champagne-and-satin locks, Mari had been given a tangle of rumpled raw silk with dark roots that turned nearly platinum at the ends. It was an unmanageable mess, and she wore it sheared off just above her shoulders in a bob that somehow never lived up to the description of "classic" or "stylish." Long ago she had decided her hair was a metaphor for her life: she was wilder than she ought to be; she didn't match the rest of her family; she never quite lived up to expectations.

"It doesn't matter, Marilee," she declared, leaning over to shove a cassette into the tape deck and crank the volume. "You're in Montana now."

Sacramento was just a dot on the map behind her. The life she had led there was in the past. She was officially on hiatus with no plans, no prospects, no thoughts for the future beyond spending a week or three with her old friend. A vacation to clear the mind and soothe a bruised heart. A pause in the flow of life to take stock, reflect, and burn the pile of business suits that covered the backseat of her Honda.

She buzzed down the car's windows and breathed deep of the sweet, cool air that rushed in. A wondrous sense of liberation and anticipation filled her as the wind whipped her hair and Mary-Chapin Carpenter proclaimed to feel lucky in spite of the odds. Life began anew right now, this instant. Glancing down, she fished the pack of Salems out from among the mountain of travel guides on the seat beside her, but she paused as she started to shake one out. Life began anew. Right now. Grinning, she chucked the pack out the window, stepped on the gas, and started singing along in a strong, warm alto voice.

The mountains to the west had turned purple as the sun slid down behind their massive shoulders. The sky above them was still the color of flame—vibrant, glowing. To the east, another range rose up in ragged splendor, snow-capped, the slopes blanketed in the deep green of pine forests. And before her stretched a valley that was vast and verdant. Off to her right, a small herd of elk grazed peacefully beside a stream.

The sight, the setting, shot another burst of adrenaline and enthusiasm through her. The trip to euphoria from near depression left her feeling giddy. She imagined she was shedding her unhappiness like an old skin and coming to this new place naked and clean.

This was paradise. Eden. A place for new beginnings.

Night had fallen by the time Mari finally found her way to Lucy's place with the aid of the map Lucy had sent in her first letter. Her "hideout," she'd called it. The huge sky was as black as velvet, dotted with the sequins of more stars than she had ever imagined. The world suddenly seemed a vast, empty wilderness, and she pulled into the yard of the small ranch, questioning for the first time the wisdom of a surprise arrival. There were no lights glowing a welcome in the windows of the handsome new log house. The garage doors were closed.

She climbed out of her Honda and stretched, feeling exhausted and rumpled. The past two weeks had sapped her strength, the decisions she had made taking chunks of it at a time. The drive up from Sacramento had been accomplished in a twenty-four-hour marathon with breaks for nothing more than the bathroom and truck-stop burritos, and now the physical strain of that weighed her down like an anchor.

It had seemed essential that she get here as quickly as possible, as if she had been afraid her nerve would give out and she would succumb to the endless dissatisfaction of her life in California if she didn't escape immediately. The wild pendulum her emotions had been riding had left her feeling drained and dizzy. She had counted on falling into Lucy's care the instant she got out of her car, but Lucy didn't appear to be home, and disappointment sent the pendulum swinging downward again.

Foolish, really, she told herself, blinking back the

threat of tears as she headed for the front porch. She couldn't have expected Lucy to know she was coming. She hadn't been able to bring herself to call ahead. A call would have meant an explanation of everything that had gone on in the past two weeks, and that was better made in person.

A calico cat watched her approach from the porch rail, but jumped down and ran away as she climbed the steps, its claws scratching the wood floor as it darted around the corner of the porch and disappeared. The wind swept down off the mountain and howled around the weathered outbuildings, bringing with it a sense of isolation and a vague feeling of desertion that Mari tried to shrug off as she raised a hand and knocked on the door.

No lights brightened the windows. No voice called out for her to keep her pants on.

She swallowed at the combination of disappointment and uneasiness that crowded the back of her throat. Against her will her eyes did a quick scan of the moonshadowed ranch yard and the hills beyond. The place was in the middle of nowhere. She had driven through the small town of New Eden and gone miles into the wilderness, seeing no more than two other houses on the way—and those from a great distance.

She knocked again, but didn't wait for an answer before trying the door. Lucy had mentioned wildlife in her few letters. The four-legged, flea-scratching kind.

"Bears. I remember something about bears," she muttered, the nerves at the base of her neck wriggling at the possibility that there were a dozen watching her from the cover of darkness, sizing her up with their beady little eyes while their stomachs growled. "If it's all the same to you, Luce, I'd rather not meet one up close and personal while you're off doing the boot-scootin' boogie with some cowboy."

Stepping inside, she fumbled along the wall for a light switch, then blinked against the glare of a dozen small bulbs artfully arranged in a chandelier of antlers. Her first thought was that Lucy's abysmal housekeeping talents had deteriorated to a shocking new low. The place was a disaster area, strewn with books, newspapers, note paper, clothing.

She drifted away from the door and into the large room that encompassed most of the first floor of the house, her brain stumbling to make sense of the contradictory information it was getting. The house was barely a year old, a blend of western tradition and contemporary architectural touches. Lucy had hired a decorator to capture those intertwined feelings in the interior. But the western watercolor prints on the walls hung at drunken angles. The cushions had been torn from the heavy, overstuffed chairs. The seat of the red leather sofa had been slit from end to end. Stuffing rose up from the wound in ragged tufts. Broken lamps and shattered pottery littered the expensive Berber rug. An overgrown pothos had been ripped from its planter and shredded, and was strung across the carpet like strips of tattered green ribbon.

Not even Lucy was this big a slob.

Mari's pulse picked up the rhythm of fear. "Lucy?" she called, the tremor in her voice a vocal extension of the goose bumps that were pebbling her arms. The only answer was an ominous silence that pressed in on her eardrums until they were pounding.

She stepped over a gutted throw pillow, picked her way around a smashed terra-cotta urn, and peered into the darkened kitchen area. The refrigerator door was ajar, the light within glowing like the promise of gold inside a treasure chest. The smell, however, promised something less pleasant.

She wrinkled her nose and blinked against the sour fumes as she found the light switch on the wall and flicked it upward. Recessed lighting beamed down on a repulsive mess of spoiling food and spilled beer. Milk puddled on the Mexican tile in front of the refrigerator. The carton lay abandoned on its side. Flies hovered over the garbage like tiny vultures.

"Jesus, Lucy," she muttered, "what kind of party did you throw here?"

And where the hell are you?

The pine cupboard doors stood open, their contents

spewed out of them. Stoneware and china and flatware lay broken and scattered, appropriately macabre place settings for the gruesome meal that had been laid out on the floor.

Mari backed away slowly, her hand trembling as she reached out to steady herself with the one ladder-back chair that remained upright at the long pine harvest table. She caught her full lower lip between her teeth and stared through the sheen of tears. She had worked too many criminal cases not to see this for what it was. The house had been ransacked. The motive could have been robbery, or the destruction could have been the aftermath of something else, something uglier.

"Lucy?" she called again, her heart sinking like a stone at the sure knowledge that she wouldn't get an answer.

Her gaze drifted to the stairway that led up to the loft where the bedrooms were tucked, then cut to the telephone that had been ripped from the kitchen wall and now hung by slender tendons of wire.

Her heart beat faster. A fine mist of sweat slicked her palms.

"Lucy?"

"She's dead."

The words were like a pair of shotgun blasts in the still of the room. Mari wheeled around, a scream wedged in her throat right behind her heart. He stood at the other end of the table, six feet of hewn granite in faded jeans and a chambray work shirt. How anything that big could have sneaked up on her was beyond reasoning. Her perceptions distorted by fear, she thought his shoulders rivaled the mountains for size. He stood there, staring at her from beneath the low-riding brim of a dusty black Stetson, his gaze narrow, measuring, his mouth set in a grim, compressed line. His right hand—big with blunt-tipped fingers—hung at his side just inches from a holstered revolver that looked big enough to bring down a buffalo.

He spoke again, his voice low and rusty, his question jolting her like a cattle prod. "Who are you?"

"Who am *I*?" she blurted out. "Who the fuck are *you*?"

His scowl seemed to tighten at her language, but Mari couldn't find it in her to care about decorum at the moment. From the corner of her eye she caught sight of a foot-long heavy brass candlestick lying on its side on the table. She inched her fingers down from the back of the chair and slid them around the cold, hard brass, her gaze locked on the stranger.

"What have you done with Lucy?"

He tucked his chin back. "Nothing."

"I think you ought to know that I'm not here alone," Mari said with all the bravado she could muster. "My husband . . . Bruno . . . is out looking around the buildings."

"You came alone," he drawled, squinting at her. "Saw you from the ridge."

He'd seen her. He'd been watching. A man with a gun had been watching her. Mari's fingers tightened on the candlestick. His first words came back to her through the tangle in her brain. *She's dead.* Terror gripped her throat like an unseen hand. *Lucy.* He'd killed Lucy.

With a strangled cry she hurled the candlestick at him and bolted for the door, tripping over an uprooted ficus. She heard him grunt and swear as the missile hit. The candlestick sounded as loud as a cathedral bell as it met the pine floor. The scramble of boots sounded like a herd of horses stampeding after her. She kept her focus on the front door, willing it closer, but as in a nightmare, her arms and legs weighed her down like lead. The air around her seemed to take on a heaviness that defied speed. She scrambled, stretched, stumbled, sobs catching in her throat as she gasped for breath.

He caught her from behind, one hand grabbing hold of her vest and T-shirt. He hauled her backward, banding his other arm around her waist and pulling her into the rock wall that was his body.

"Hold still!"

Mari clawed the beefy forearm that was pushing the air from her lungs. Wild, animal sounds of distress mewed in her throat, and she kicked his shins with vicious intent, connecting the heels of her sneakers with bone two swings out of three.

"Dammit, hold still!" he ordered, tightening his arm against her. "I didn't kill her. It was an accident."

"Tell it to a lawyer!" she managed to shout, pushing frantically at the big hand that was pressed up against her diaphragm. She couldn't budge him. She couldn't hurt him. He had her. The panic that thought bred nearly choked her.

"Listen to me," J.D. ordered sharply. Then he gentled his tone as skills from other parts of his life kicked in. He knew better than to fight fear with force. "Easy," he murmured to her in the same low, soothing voice he used with frightened horses. "Listen to me now. Just take it easy. I'm not here to hurt you."

"Yeah? Well, you're doing a pretty damn good imitation of it," she snapped, squirming. "You're pushing my spleen into my lungs."

Immediately he loosened his grip but still held her firmly against him. "Just settle down. Just take it easy."

Mari craned her neck around to get a look at his eyes. Men could say anything, but their eyes seldom lied. She had learned that in the courtroom and in the offices of countless lawyers. She had taken down testimony word for word, lies and truths, but she had learned very early on to read the difference in the witness's eyes. The pair boring down on her were tucked deep beneath an uncompromising ledge of brow. They were the gray of storm clouds, and slightly narrow, as if he were permanently squinting against the glare of the sun. They gave little away of the man, but there was nothing in them that hinted at lies or violence.

She relaxed marginally and he rewarded her by easing her down so that her feet touched the floor. Air rushed back into her lungs and she sucked it in greedily, trying not to lean back into him for support. She was already too aware of his body, the size and strength of it, the heat of it. His left hand encircled her upper arm, the knuckles just brushing the outer swell of her breast. The fingers of his right hand splayed over her belly, thumb and forefinger bracketing the inner and under contours of the same breast. The contact sent electric currents of alarm and awareness zipping through her. A shift of inches and he would be cupping her, filling his hand. Her nipples tightened, an automatic, autonomic response.

He smelled of hard work, leather, and horses. *Concentrate on that, Marilee. He smells like a horse.*

As he murmured to her in his low, soothing voice, his breath drifted like a warm breeze across the shell of her ear and the side of her face. Butter mint. She couldn't think of a single psychopathic killer who had been described as having butter mints on his breath.

"You gonna be still?" J.D. asked softly, his voice swimming through a rising tide of unexpected, unwanted arousal.

Her curvy little body was pressed back into his, reminding him just how soft a woman could be. His line of sight down over her shoulder gave him an unobstructed view of the rise and fall of her breasts as she struggled to slow her breathing. The loose vest she wore had slipped back during the struggle, revealing small, plump globes covered by thin white cotton. The outline of a lacy bra was unmistakable, reminding him just how delicate a woman's underwear could be.

She was soft and warm beneath his touch. All he needed to do was turn his hand a fraction and he could fill his palm with the weight of her breast. His fingers flexed involuntarily against her rib cage, ready and willing. The scent of her rose up to tease his nostrils—a light, powdery perfume that reminded him just how good a woman could smell. The curve of her neck beckoned him to lower his head and sample the taste of her.

His blood pooled, hot and thick in his groin. Her backside brushed against him and he choked off a groan at the base of his throat.

Damn. He'd gone too long without. That was clear enough. He didn't allow himself to indiscriminately want women. He had too many more important things to focus his attention on. He shouldn't have even considered the possibility with this one. A friend of Lucy Mac-Adam's. He didn't have to know any more about her than that to know she was trouble.

Trouble was, he *hadn't* considered. His hormones were reacting all on their own. He was a man who prided himself on his control. He didn't like the idea that after thirty-two years, his body could crack that control in a heartbeat.

He dropped his hand away from her belly abruptly and took a half-step back, distancing himself from temptation.

Mari turned to face him, her sneakers crunching on the kindling that had once been an end table constructed of raw twigs. Still trembling, she planted one hand on her hip and snagged back a tangled mass of hair from her eyes with the other, anchoring it at the back of her neck.

She was shaken by and vaguely ashamed of the lingering sense of sexual awareness that hummed through her. The man had practically attacked her. There was nothing in the act that should have been condoned or responded to sexually. She didn't know him, didn't know that he wasn't responsible for Lucy's . . . absence. She had no business finding him attractive even on a subconscious level. But as he stared at her with those gray eyes, his face a rough-hewn sculpture of masculinity, his massive shoulders set, hands jammed above his lean hips, one muscular leg cocked, the heat of powerful magnetism glowed deep inside her in a place she had heretofore been blissfully unaware existed.

"Who are you?" she demanded, wary.

"J. D. Rafferty." He bent to pick up the hat he'd lost in the scuffle, never taking his eyes off her. "I live up the hill a ways."

"And you're in the habit of just walking into people's homes?"

"No, ma'am."

"But you saw me come in, so you just thought 'Hey, what the hell? I might as well go scare the shit out of her'?"

He narrowed his eyes. "No, ma'am. The lawyer asked

me to look after the stock. I saw you come in, saw the lights. Didn't want anything funny going on while I was down here."

Mari cast a damning glance around the room, stricken anew by the utter destruction. "Looks to me like something already happened, Mr. Rafferty. And I don't happen to think it's particularly funny."

"Kids," he muttered, staring at the broken frame of a bentwood rocker. He detested waste, and that was what vandalism was—waste of time, energy, property. Waste and disrespect. "Town kids get a little tanked up. They go riding around, lookin' for trouble. Don't usually take 'em long to find it. This happened a week ago. I called the sheriff. A deputy came out and wrote it up, for what that's worth."

Putting off the inevitable, Mari went to the ficus that had foiled her escape and righted it carefully, her hands gentle as she stroked the smooth trunk and touched the dying leaves.

"I didn't catch your name while you were kicking my shins black and blue," Rafferty said sardonically.

"Marilee. Marilee Jennings."

"Mary Lee—"

"No. Marilee. It's all one word."

He scowled at that, as if he didn't trust anybody who had such a name. Mari almost smiled. Her mother wouldn't like J. D. Rafferty. He was too rough. Crude, Abigail would say. Abigail Falkner Jennings thrived on pretention. She had given all her daughters pretentious names that only snooty people didn't stumble over—Lisbeth, Annaliese, Marilee.

"She's dead," he declared bluntly.

She would have put the question off a while longer, would have thought of inane things for another moment or two. Her fingers tightened on the trunk of the ficus as if trying to hold something that had already slipped beyond her grasp.

"Happened about ten days ago . . ."

Ten days. Ten days ago she had been crying over a man she didn't love, giving up a career she'd never wanted, breaking ties to the family she had never fit into. Lucy had been dying.

She brought a hand up to press it over her trembling lips. She shook her head in denial, desperation and tears swimming in her eyes. Lucy couldn't be dead—she was too ornery, too cynical, too wise. *Only the good die young, Marilee.* She could still see the sharp gleam of certainty and caustic humor in her friend's eyes as she'd said it. Jesus, Lucy should have lived to be a hundred.

". . . hunting accident . . ."

Rafferty's words penetrated the fog only dimly. He sounded as if he were talking to her from a great distance instead of just a few feet away. She stared at him, her defenses raising shields that deflected the harshness of the subject and focused her attention on unimportant things. His hair—it was sensibly short and the color of sable. He had a little cowlick in front at the edge of his high, broad forehead. His tan—it ended in a line of demarcation from his hatband. Somehow that made him seem less dangerous, more human. The paler skin looked soft and vulnerable. Stupid word for a man with a six-gun strapped to his hips—vulnerable.

"Hunting?" she mumbled as if the word were foreign.

J.D. pressed his lips together, impatience and compassion warring inside him. She looked as fragile as a china doll, as if the slightest bump or pressure would shatter her like the lamps and pots that lay scattered on the floor. Beneath the tangled fringe of flaxen bangs and the soft arcs of dark brows, her deep-set blue eyes were huge and brimming with pain and confusion.

Something in him wanted to offer comfort. He labeled it foolishness and shoved it aside. He didn't want anything to do with her. He hadn't wanted anything to do with Lucy, but she had drawn him into her web like a black widow spider. He wanted this place, that was true enough, but he didn't want *this*. He had plainly and purely hated Lucy MacAdam. Couldn't figure why someone hadn't shot her on purpose years before. The woman before him was her friend, another outsider, which made her tainted by both association and circumstance. The sooner he was rid of her, the better.

He steeled himself against her tears and settled his hat firmly on his head, an insult she would probably never fathom.

"Lucy didn't go hunting," she mumbled stupidly.

"It was an accident. Some damned city idiot shot without looking."

Ten days ago. It seemed impossible to Mari that she could have lived ten days oblivious of the death of a friend. Shot. God, Lucy had been shot! People moved to the country to *avoid* getting shot, to escape city violence. Lucy had come to paradise only to be gunned down. It was ludicrous.

Mari shook her head again, trying to clear the dizziness, only making it worse. "W-where is she?"

"Six feet under, I reckon," he said brutally. "I wouldn't know."

"But you were her friend—"

"No, ma'am."

He moved toward her slowly, deliberately, his expression dark and intense. Mari's pulse kicked up a notch, but she held her ground. The news had stunned her. Beneath the layer of numbness she was very aware of Rafferty—the heat of his big, muscular body, the raw, powerful sexuality that hummed around him, the hard gleam in his eyes—but she seemed incapable of moving away from him.

He came too close. Close enough that she had to tilt her head back to look at him. Close enough to make her skin tingle.

"We had sex," he said bluntly, his voice low and rough and silky at once. "Friendship never entered into it."

Mari's heart fluttered at the base of her throat. Arousal pulsed hard between her legs and shame surged through her in an attempt to burn it out, but the response was instinctive and immune to morality.

Rafferty raised a hand and traced his thumb down her cheek to the corner of her mouth. Holding her gaze, he probed gently, parting her lips, rubbing the lower one slowly, methodically, back and forth. "How about you, Mary Lee?" he whispered. "You want to give a cowboy a ride?"

He was being a bastard. J.D. didn't give a damn. He would either scare her off or get the ache in his balls taken care of. Either way was fine by him.

"How about it, Mary Lee?" he murmured. "I'll let you be on top."

"You son of a bitch!"

Thinking she would choke on her outrage, she kicked him in the shin. He jumped back from her, swearing, his face flushing dark with pain and fury. Belatedly she questioned the wisdom of making him angry. He could take what he wanted. They were in the middle of nowhere. No one knew she had come to Montana. He could rape her and kill her and dump her body in the mountains, never to be found. Christ, for all she knew, he had killed Lucy. But the deed was done. She couldn't cower from him now.

"Get out!" she screamed. "Get the hell out of here!"

J.D. gathered his temper with a ruthless mental fist. He sauntered to the front door and leaned a hand against the jamb, looking back at her from under the brim of his black hat. The door stood open to the night, inviting a swarm of bugs to buzz around the antler chandelier in the foyer. "All you had to do was say no."

He tipped his hat in a gesture that seemed more mocking than polite. Mari followed him out and watched as he mounted a stout sorrel horse that stood waiting in the puddle of amber light that spilled from the house.

"There's a motel on the edge of town," he said, settling into the saddle. "Drive slow on your way down. You hit an elk with that damned Japanese car and there won't be enough left to make a sardine can."

She crossed her arms against the chill of the evening and glared at him. "You could at least say you're sorry," she said bitterly.

"I'm not," he replied, and reined his horse away.

She watched him ride off at an easy lope, away from

the ranch yard, away from the road. The darkness swallowed him up long before the hollow drum of hoofbeats faded.

"Bastard," she muttered, turning back to go inside.

The adrenaline ebbed from her system, leaving the weight of exhaustion in its wake. The last vestiges of shock lingered like novocaine, keeping the first sting of grief at bay. She tried to fix her mind on the mundane tasks of getting back to town and finding a hotel room, tried to forget the residual feel of J. D. Rafferty's hands on her, his big body pressed against her back, his raw-silk voice murmuring indecent proposals. But the sensations lingered disturbingly, adding a vague, grimy film of guilt to the complex layers of emotion. Feeling a need to wash both physically and psychologically, she went in search of a bathroom, finding one on the second floor.

It had fared no better than the rest of the house. The lid from the toilet tank had been smashed. It looked as if someone had taken a jackhammer to the shower stall, then broke up the tile floor into rubble and dust. The faucets still worked, and she filled the sink with cold water, bending over to bathe her face with it. She pulled the bottom of her T-shirt out of her jeans and used it as a towel, then stood, staring for a moment into the cracked, gilt-framed mirror that hung above the vanity.

The woman who stared back was pale and dark-eyed with pain. She looked like the survivor of a hurricane, ravaged by wind and elements that had roared so far beyond her control that she felt as insignificant and powerless as a gnat. She had packed up her life and run to Montana, to a friend who had been dead more than a week. Lucy would have seen a bitter, ironic humor in that.

She thought of her friend, of what Lucy would have had to say about the way things had turned out, and tears swelled over her lashes and slid down her cheeks.

It started out as a bad hair day and went downhill from there.

•   •   •

He watched her through a Simmons Silver 3×9 wide-angle Prohunter scope. Not his favorite, especially not for this time of night, but it was all he had with him. He came here nearly every night, not because he expected to see the blonde, but because he wanted to draw her down off his mountain. She lingered there, a pale apparition among the dark trees, a phantom carried on the wings of owls. She haunted him. Too many things did.

He never slept at night. The dead came to him anyway. There was nothing he could do to stop them, but he stayed awake and watchful, willing them to leave. An exhausting vigil that was never rewarded.

He watched her cross the yard toward a small foreign car, his heart galloping, a dozen hammers pounding against the plate in his head. The fine lines of the sight crossed her chest. His cheek rested against the stock of the Remington 700 rifle. Half a breath settled in his lungs. His heart rate slowed in conditioned response. His fingertip remained still against the trigger.

There was no killing a ghost. He knew that better than anyone. He could only pray for it to leave and not come back to his mountain.

If only there were a God to hear him . . .

CHAPTER 2

"*C*ome on, come on, you big gear-jamming son of a bitch! Oh! Oh! OH!"

Mari focused an exasperated, exhausted glare at the wall beyond her rented bed. There was a starving-artist-quality painting of a moose in a mountainscape hanging above the imitation mahogany Mediterranean-style headboard. The painting bucked against the cheap, paper-thin wallboard in time with the heavy thumping going on in the adjacent room. The clock on the nightstand glowed 1:43 in pee-yellow digits. She had gotten the last room in the place.

"Ride me, Luanne! Eee-hah! Ride me! Ride me! Christ all-fucking mighty!"

The verbal commentary disintegrated into animal grunts and groans and panting that rose in pitch and volume to a vulgar crescendo. Blessed silence followed.

Mari cast a glance heavenward. "Please let them be dead."

Heaving a sigh, she bent her head and pinched the bridge of her nose between a thumb and forefinger. She stood slumped back against the imitation mahogany dresser, half sitting, half leaning, still dressed in her wilted jeans and wrinkled T-shirt and vest. She couldn't bring herself to take her shoes off and walk barefoot on the grungy carpet, let alone undress and crawl between the sheets.

She had turned off the single sixty-watt lamp on the nightstand, but the room was still bright enough for her to see every depressing detail. The relentless white glare of the mercury vapor light in the parking lot burned through the thin drapes that refused to meet in the middle of the window. Adding to the ambience was a dull red glow from the old neon sign that beckoned the road-weary to the Paradise Motel.

There was nothing vaguely resembling paradise here. A ghost of a cynical smile twisted Mari's lips at the thought that Luanne and Bob-Ray and his amazing gearshift of steel would probably say otherwise. It was all a matter of perspective, and Mari's perspective was bleak. She looked around the room with its tacky appointments and ratty shag carpet, a fist tightening in her chest. She hadn't envisioned her first night in Montana being spent in a fuck-stop for truckers.

There would have been humor in the situation if Lucy had been here to share the entertainment and the six-pack of Miller Lite Mari had hauled with her all the way from Sacramento. But Lucy wasn't here.

Mari lifted a can to her lips and sipped, beyond caring that it was flat and warm. She had found half a pack of cigarettes in her glove compartment and had lit them all in a relentless chain that left her throat raw and her mouth tasting like shit. Her eyes burned from the smoke and from the tears she had been holding at bay all night. Her head throbbed from the pressure and from the effects of beer on an empty stomach.

She had been too shocked to cry in front of J. D. Rafferty, which was just as well. She doubted he would have offered her anything in the way of sympathy. He didn't even have the decency to pretend he was sorry for Lucy's death.

"Jeez," she muttered, shaking her head as she pushed away from the dresser to pace slowly along the foot of the bed. "Now I *want* a man to lie to me. There's a first. Bradford, where are you when I need you?"

Back in Sacramento with the woman he had dumped her for, the jerk.

After two years of "serious commitment," as he had labeled it, Bradford Enright had dropped her like a hot rock. He had already moved in with Ms. Junior Partner before he bothered telling Mari about her demotion. Their relationship had suddenly become null and void in the face of more advantageous opportunities. Ms. Junior Partner was more in tune with him, he said. Ms. Junior Partner shared his goals and his philosophies.

Their parting argument played through her mind like a videotape that had been shown and rewound again and again over the course of the past two weeks.

"What philosophy is that, Brad? Screw everybody and bill them for double the hours?"

"Jesus, Marilee, what a bitchy thing to say!"

"Well, ex*cuuu*se me! Getting dumped has that effect, you know. It makes me cranky."

"It wasn't working, Mari, you know that. It hasn't been working for the last six months."

"Coincidentally, about the same amount of time has passed since the iron bun joined your firm."

"Leave Pauline out of this."

"That's kind of hard to do, seeing as how the two of you have been playing merger games after hours for—how long now?"

"It doesn't matter."

"It matters to me."

"I wasn't getting much here, Marilee. You're always too tired or too stressed or—"

"*You! You* have the gall to complain to *me* about our sex life?"

"What are you saying? Are you saying I didn't satisfy you?"

"I'm saying I've had better orgasms by myself!"

"Fine. Reduce the conversation to a gutter level. The bottom line is we don't have a future together, Marilee. We don't want the same things professionally or socially. There's no point in going on with it."

"Bottom line. You want to talk bottom line? Fine. Here's a bottom line for you, Bradford. You owe me about three thousand dollars for services rendered in my professional capacity. Would you care to cough that up before you pack your toothbrush, or should I bill the firm?"

She would never see a dime of it, not that she cared so much about the money. It was the idea that burned her cookies. She felt used. He had taken advantage of their relationship while he had been struggling to get a toehold at the firm. *I have to share a secretary, Marilee. Please, can't you just type this up for me. Just this once (twice, three times, eighty-five times). Don't you want me to look good? Couldn't you just help out a little with those transcripts? It would make such a good impression if I could have this done . . .* He had treated her as if she were his personal, free-of-charge legal secretary. Now that he was moving up in the world, he wouldn't have to save pennies by literally screwing a court reporter out of her fees.

She felt like a fool. How she had ever managed to fall for a lawyer in the first place was beyond her. No. That was a lie. In her heart she knew what she had been doing with the upwardly mobile Bradford Enright, and it was so Freudian, it was depressing. Her family had approved of him. They may have seen her career as a court reporter as being a giant step down from their expectations for her, but Brad had made a nice consolation prize. They could look at him and still hold out some hope that she would settle into the life of pleasant snobbery to which they were all accustomed.

What a hypocrite she was. In her heart she knew she'd never really loved Brad. He was right: they didn't want any of the same things—including each other. She had gone through the motions, pretended passion, lied to him and to herself time and again by saying she was happy, when the truth was a partner at Hawkins and Briggs didn't come close to making the list of things she wanted out of life. The time had come to admit that.

She'd spent too much of her life as a square peg trying to fit into a round hole. She'd spent too much time trying to fit into the lifestyle her family thought of as normal. She wasn't Annaliese or Lisbeth. She was Mari the Misfit. She'd spent too much time trying to atone for that. No more.

She sold her court reporter's equipment, sublet her

apartment for the summer, loaded her suits and her guitar in the back of her Honda, and headed for Montana. She had made no plans beyond summer, beyond basking in the glow of enlightenment. She was free to be herself at last. Born anew at twenty-eight.

Still, all the self-revelation of the past two weeks didn't completely dull the sting of Brad's betrayal. Lucy would have understood that, having won, lost, and dumped an astounding number of men herself. She and Lucy should have been sitting on Lucy's bed right now in their nightgowns, eating junk food and trashing Brad, and then trashing men in general until they ended up laughing themselves into tears.

Dammit, Lucy.

Guilt swept through her, chasing a current of resentment. She wanted Lucy to be there for her. How selfish was that? She had a case of wounded pride and jitters over finally finding the nerve to stand up and be herself. Lucy was dead. Dead was forever.

Feeling disjointed, disembodied, Mari sank down on the edge of the bed and put her pounding head in her hands. She reached out blindly for the guitar she had propped against a chair and pulled it into her arms like a child, hugging it against her. She held it at an angle so she could rest her cheek against its neck. The smell of the wood was familiar, welcome, a constant in a life that had too often seemed alien to her. This old guitar had been a friend for a lot of lonely years. It never found fault in her. It never cast judgment. It never abandoned her. It knew everything that was in her heart.

Her fingers moved over the strings almost of their own volition, callused fingertips of her left hand pressing down above the frets, the fingers of her right hand plucking gently at a tune that came from a private well of pain deep inside her. The emotions that fought and tangled like wrestling bears crystallized simply in the music. In just a handful of notes the feelings were expressed more eloquently than she could ever have spoken them. Sweet, sad notes, as poignant as a mourning dove's call, filled the stale air of the room and pierced her skin like tiny daggers.

The tears came hard, almost grudgingly, as if she didn't want to give them up without proof that her friend wasn't going to come waltzing through the door with a smirk on her face. That would be like Lucy. To Lucy, life was just one big practical joke perpetrated on the human race by bored and cynical gods.

The joke's on you this time, Luce.

A dry, broken sob tore Mari's throat and then she was spent, exhausted, drained as dry as the gas tank of her Honda. She set the guitar aside and fell back across the bed, staring through her tears at the water stains on the ceiling. The silence of the night rang in her ears. The loneliness of it swelled in her chest like a balloon. Above her the moose from the starving-artist painting gazed down on her with melancholy eyes.

She'd never felt so alone.

Her dreams were a jumble of faces and places and sounds, all of it underscored by a low hum of tension and the dark, sinister sensation of falling into a deep black crevasse. J. D. Rafferty's granite countenance loomed over her, shadowed by the brim of his hat. She felt his big, work-roughened hands on her body, touching her breasts, which were exposed because—much to her dismay—she had forgotten to wear anything but an old pair of boxer shorts and hiking boots. She glared at him, detesting him with her brain while her body warmed to the consistency of melted caramel beneath his touch.

Lucy lingered in the shadows, watching with wicked amusement. "Ride him, cowgirl. He'll let you be on top."

Rafferty ignored her. As he massaged Mari's breasts, he murmured to her in a low, coarse voice.

"Man, Luanne, you've got the biggest tits I've ever seen."

She shivered. Her brain stumbled in confusion at the name. He pulled the revolver from the holster on his hip and fired it over his head. *Bang! Bang! Bang! Bang!*

Mari jolted awake in time to see the moose descending on her. She shrieked and brought her arms up to deflect the blow, knocking the painting onto the floor. The banging she had interpreted as gunshots in her dream went on without cease.

Luanne and Bob-Ray were at it again.

She tried to swing her legs over the side of the bed and discovered that in her fitful sleep she had rolled into the Grand Canyon of mattress valleys.

"I think I saw this bed on *The Twilight Zone*," she grumbled, trying to rock herself into a sitting position. "People fell through it into an alternate universe."

Wishing fleetingly she had stuck with one of the dozen aerobics classes she had signed up for in the last three years, she heaved herself out of the chasm and tumbled onto the floor. A shuddering groan vibrated through the room as the air conditioner kicked into high gear, blasting arctic air and the smell of mildew. The control knob was missing and the plug looked like something no certified electrician would touch without first shutting down power to the whole north end of town.

Rubbing her frigid hands up and down her cold, bare arms, she peered out through the separation in the drapes to see the first faint pink tints of dawn streaking behind the snow-capped peaks to the east. At the edge of the parking lot, the Paradise Motel sign buzzed and flickered. Not a creature was stirring . . . except Bob-Ray and Li'l Sizzler, the Amazing Human Breakfast Sausage.

"God*damn*, Luanne! You could suck the white off rice!"

Mari groaned and rubbed her hands over her face.

"I could never get enough of you, Bob-Ray."

"A sad truth that's been made abundantly clear in the last five hours," Mari said through her teeth.

"Well, come on up here, then, darlin.' I'll give you all you can handle."

Luanne squealed like a mare in heat and the banging—audio and physical—began again.

Her temper frayed down to the ragged nub, Mari

grabbed the Gideon Bible from the nightstand and used it as a gavel against the wall.

"Hey, Mr. Piston!" she bellowed. "Give it a rest, will ya!"

There was a moment of taut silence, then the perpetrators burst into giggles and the bed springs started squeaking again.

Giving up on any hope of rest, she headed toward the bathroom.

She hadn't taken in more than a glimpse of the town of New Eden on her way to Lucy's place. Coming back after her encounter with Rafferty, she had gone no farther than the motel on the north edge of town. Now she drove down the wide main street slowly, glancing at the ornate false fronts of brick buildings that had probably witnessed cattle drives and gunfights a century before. They were mixed with clapboard storefronts and the odd, low-slung "modern" building that had gone up in the sixties, when architects had been completely devoid of taste.

New Eden had a rumpled, dusty look. Comfortable. Quiet. A curious mix of shabbiness and pride. Some of the shops were vacant and run-down, their windows staring blankly at the street. Others were being treated to cosmetic face-lifts. Painting scaffolds stood along their sides like giant Tinker Toys. Among the usual small-town businesses Mari counted four art galleries, three shops devoted to selling fly-fishing gear, and half a dozen places that advertised espresso.

In the gray early morning, a trio of dogs trotted down the sidewalk and crossed the street in front of Mari, looking up at her but not seeming at all concerned that she wouldn't slow down for them. She chuckled as she watched them head directly for a place called the Rainbow Cafe. Trusting their judgment, she pulled her little Honda into a slot along a row of hulking, battered pickups and cut the engine.

In keeping with its name, the front of the Rainbow

Cafe had been painted in stripes of five different pastel colors. The wooden sign that swung gently from a rusted iron arm was hand-lettered in a fashion that made Mari think of teenage doodling—free-form, naively artistic. It promised good food and lots of it. Her stomach growled.

A small, dark-haired waitress stood holding the front door open with one hand, letting the smell of breakfast and sound of George Strait on the jukebox drift out. The other hand was propped on a wide hip, a limp dishrag dangling from the fingertips. Her attention was on the trio of dogs that sat on the stoop. They gazed up at her with the kind of pitiful, hopeful look all dogs instinctively know people are suckers for. She frowned at them, her wide ruby mouth pulling down at the corners.

"You all go around to the back," she said irritably. "I won't have you stealing steaks off the customers' plates on your way through to the kitchen."

The leader of the pack, a black and white border collie with one blue eye and one brown eye, tipped his head to one side, ears perked, and hummed a little note that sounded for all the world like a canine version of *please*. The waitress narrowed her eyes at him and stood fast. After a minute, the dog gave in and led his cohorts down the narrow space between the buildings.

"Moocher," the waitress grumbled, her lips twitching into a smile.

Someone should have captured her on film, Mari thought, her artist's eye assessing and memorizing. The woman whose name tag identified her as Nora was pushing forty, and every day of it was etched in fine lines on her face. But that didn't keep her from being beautiful in an earthy, real way. Beneath the dime-store makeup, hers was a face that radiated character, broken hearts, and honest hard work. It was heart-shaped with prominent cheekbones and a slim, straight nose, lean-cheeked and bony, as if the fat beneath the skin had been boiled away in the steamy heat of the diner kitchen. Her mane of dark hair was as frizzy as a Brillo pad, its thickness clamped back with a silver barrette. The pink and white polyester uniform was a holdover from the seventies. It buttoned over nonexistent breasts, nipped in on a slender waist, and hugged a set of hips that looked as if they had been specifically designed for a man to hang on to during sex.

"This must be the best restaurant in town," Mari said, clutching an armload of Montana travel books against the front of her oversize denim jacket.

"You better believe it, honey," the waitress said with a grin. "If there's a line of pickups out front and dogs begging at the door, you know you'll get a good, honest meal. No skimping here, and the coffee's always hot and strong."

"I'm sold."

Nora shot a discreet glance at the brown and white polka-dot dress that swirled around Mari's calves and the paddock boots and baggy crew socks, but there was no flash of disapproval in her eyes. Mari liked her instantly.

"I love your hair," the waitress said. "That your real color?"

Mari grinned. "Yep."

She followed Nora inside and slid into a high-backed booth that gave her a view out the wide front window.

She deposited her books on the Formica table and forgot them as she tried to absorb everything she could about this first experience in the Rainbow. She had read every travel guide and tourist brochure there was anyway. One of her vows to herself when she had decided on a new life was not to let it speed past her while she was too busy trying to fit in. She had spent too much time with her nose to the grindstone, the world and its people hurtling past her in a blur. When she had decided to come to Montana, she had gone to the library and checked out and read every book available about the state. She had immersed herself in tales of cattle barons and copper barons and robber barons, and in descriptions of mountain ranges and meadows and high plains. But the Rainbow was the real thing, and she didn't want to miss a sliver of it.

The air in the restaurant was warm and moist, redolent with the rich, greasy scents of bacon and sausage, and the sweet perfume of pancake syrup. Beneath it all lingered the strong aromas of coffee and men, and above it hung a pall of cigarette smoke. The tables were cheap, the chairs serviceable chrome and red vinyl that had probably been sitting there for three or four decades. Mari wondered if anyone realized the decor would have been considered trendy kitsch in the hip diners of northern California. Somehow, she didn't think anyone at the Rainbow Cafe in New Eden, Montana, would give a good damn. The thought made her smile.

A quick reconnaissance of the customers told her she was the only woman in the place who wasn't wearing a pink uniform. Regardless of shape or size, the men all had the look of men who worked outdoors and made their living with their hands—creased, leathery faces, narrow eyes that gave her hard, direct looks, then slid away almost shyly.

She ordered all the fat and cholesterol on the menu, not in any mood to count calories. She hadn't had a substantial meal in weeks, and she had a long day ahead of her. Better to face it on a full stomach. While she waited for Nora to bring the food, she gazed out at the wedge of town she could see through the front window.

There was an old-fashioned hardware store across the street with a wide front porch and an old green screen door. Shiny new spades and rakes and pitchforks leaned against the weathered white clapboard. A sign in the window advertised a special on wheelbarrows. Next to the hardware store was a drugstore that had been established in 1892 according to the ornate gold lettering on the front window. Next to the drugstore, gaudy spandex in neon colors hung like pieces of indecipherable modern art in the window of Mountain Man Bike and Athletic.

The sight of the bike shop was jarring, but not nearly so jarring as the sight of a money-green Ferrari purring down the street. Incongruities.

"Here to buy land?" Nora asked as she set down a plate heaped with golden pancakes and another loaded with bacon and a Denver omelette.

"No, I'm . . ." It didn't seem right to say she was on

vacation in the wake of Lucy's death. "It's more of a pause at a life crossroads."

The waitress arched a thinly plucked brow and considered, accepting the definition with a nod of approval. "Guess I've seen a few of those myself."

Mari snapped off an inch of bacon and popped it in her mouth. "I came to visit a friend for a while, but that isn't going to work out after all."

Nora hummed wisely. "Man trouble, huh?"

"No. She's—um—she's dead."

"Mercy!" Her dark eyes went wide in a quick flash of surprise. Then she pulled her practicality back down around her like a skirt that had been caught up by a sudden gust of wind. "Well, yeah, that'd put a damper on things, wouldn't it?"

"Yeah." Mari forked up a chunk of omelette and chewed thoughtfully, letting a moment of silence pass in Lucy's honor. "Maybe you knew her," she said at last. "Lucy MacAdam? She'd been living here for about a year."

Several other diners glanced her way at the mention of Lucy's name, but her attention was on the waitress. She already thought of Nora of the Rainbow Cafe as being honest and dependable, a woman who would know the score around whatever town she called home.

"No . . ." Nora narrowed her big brown eyes in concentration and shook her head as if trying to shake loose a memory to connect with the name. "No . . . oh, wait. Was she that one got shot up on Rafferty's Ridge?"

Rafferty. The name gave Mari a jolt that was like an electric shock.

"Oh, sweetie, I'm sorry," Nora cooed in sympathy, giving her a motherly squeeze on the shoulder. "I didn't know her. That crowd she ran with don't come in here much."

"What crowd?"

"That Hollyweird bunch. Bryce and all them. Don't you know them?"

"No. I never met any of Lucy's friends here." She had heard bits and pieces about them, details Lucy dropped extravagantly into her few letters and conversations, like brightly colored gemstones, designed to dazzle and impress. Celebrities. Important people. Movers and shakers who came to New Eden for some trendy communing with nature. The kind of crowd Lucy would be drawn to for the excitement, the novelty, the notoriety. She had always thrived on being at the center of the storm.

"Well, that's a strike in your favor with me," Nora said dryly. "They're big tippers, but I don't go much for their attitudes. I'm not some trick poodle for them to come in here and snicker at. They can just take all their money and go play somewhere else as far as I'm concerned."

"Come on, Nora," a warm male voice sounded from the booth behind Mari. She craned her neck around and looked up as a cowboy rose and slid his arms around the waitress. He was trim and athletic with silky dark hair falling across his forehead and sky-blue eyes brimming with mischief. He grinned a grin that would have put Tom Cruise to shame. "You tellin' me you don't want a part in Clint Eastwood's next big western?"

A grudging blush bloomed on Nora's cheeks even as she set her features into a scowl. "I'm tellin' you to keep your hands to yourself, Will Rafferty."

He ignored her command, rocking her from side to side in time with the crooning of Vince Gill on the jukebox. He laid his lean cheek against hers and his eyes drifted shut dreamily. "He'd go for you, you know. You're five times better looking than Sondra Locke ever was. He'd make you a star, Nora Davis."

"I'll make you *see* stars," Nora snorted. She pulled her order pad from the pocket of her starched apron and smacked him in the forehead with it.

"Ouch!" Will stepped back, making a pained face, rubbing at the spot where the binding had nailed him.

Nora cut him a look. "You're married, Romeo, in case you forgot." She snatched up her coffee urn and walked away, turning back when she was three tables away, a sassy smile canting her wide painted mouth. "And I am *ten* times better looking than Sondra Locke with her stringy hair and runny red nose and no eyelashes."

Will Rafferty threw back his head and laughed, delighted. "Nora, you're a wonder!"

"Don't you forget it, junior," she drawled, sashaying off toward the kitchen, her wide hips swinging.

From under her lashes Mari studied the man standing beside her. *Rafferty.* He had to be a relative. There was a strong family resemblance in the square jaw and chin, the straight browline. He was younger than the man she had met last night—probably around her own age—and slighter of build, not nearly so imposing physically. He had the lithe, athletic look of a dancer. But the biggest difference was that this Rafferty had no trouble smiling.

He turned the power of that bright white grin on her, blue eyes on high beam, a dimple biting into his cheek. The smile was irresistibly incorrigible. Mari half expected to see canary feathers peeking out from between his teeth. It was the kind of smile that made sensible women do foolish things. She felt her knees quiver, but the weakness never made it to her head. She considered herself temporarily immune to charming men. One of the few benefits of getting dumped.

"Will Rafferty." He introduced himself with a flamboyant little half-bow, then held a hand out to her in greeting. "Welcome to the Garden of Eden."

"Marilee Jennings. Are you supposed to be Adam or the snake?" she asked with a wry smile as she shook his hand.

"Cain." He slid into the seat across from her and bobbed his eyebrows. "As in 'raisin' Cain.'"

"A comparison your wife finds amusing?"

The smile tightened and he glanced away. "We're separated."

Mari reserved comment and forked up a spongy cube of pancake.

"So you were a friend of Lucy's, huh?"

"We used to hang out together when she lived in Sacramento. Did you know her?"

"Yes, ma'am." He stole a strip of bacon from her plate

and bit the end off it, his blue eyes, as bright as neon, locked on hers once again. "She was something."

He didn't specify *what*. Mari wondered if J.D. was the only Rafferty who had known Lucy in the biblical sense. Lucy wouldn't have cared that Will Rafferty was married, only that he was cute as sin and filled out his jeans in a way that pleased her roving eye. Lucy said it wasn't up to her to be any man's conscience. Her attitude toward infidelity had always bothered Mari. Come to that, her attitude toward sex in general had been too liberal for Mari's tastes. Lucy had called her a prude. She wasn't; she just didn't like the idea of needing a score card to keep her lovers' names straight.

"Nora said that Lucy was—that the accident happened someplace called Rafferty Ridge," she said. "Are you *that* Rafferty?"

"One of," Will replied, sneaking a triangle of toast out from under the edge of her half-eaten omelette. "Do you always eat this much?"

"Do you always mooch food off strangers' plates?"

He grinned. "Only when I'm hungry." She slapped his hand with her fork as he reached for another piece of bacon. "The Stars and Bars is up the hill a ways from Lucy's place. That's Rafferty land. Most of that ridge is ours. Some's BLM land—that's Bureau of Land Management—some's Forest Service—"

"You have to be related to J. D. Rafferty, then."

"Yep. That's what my mama always told me," he said with a devilish grin. "He's my big brother. I never had any say in the matter. You've met St. John, have you?"

"In a manner of speaking," Mari grumbled.

She tucked a tumble of wild hair behind her ear and polished off her second cup of coffee. Nora swept in and refilled her cup, shooting Will a look. He blew her a kiss and chuckled with good humor when she rolled her eyes.

"He scared the shit out of me, told me point-blank my friend was dead, and went on to make it clear to me that he wasn't the least bit sorry about any of it." She kept the rest of his sins to herself, still ashamed of the way her own body had betrayed her in reacting to him.

"Yep." Will sat back in the booth and stretched his arms out in front of him, working a kink out of his shoulder. "That's J.D. He got all the tact in the family."

Mari sniffed and speared the last piece of bacon just as Will's fingertips brushed over it. "Must have been a defective gene," she said caustically. "No offense, but your brother is about the biggest jerk I've run into."

"None taken," he said, his face glowing with unholy glee. "He can be an abrasive son of a gun."

"He could give lessons to concrete."

The sound of someone rising in the booth behind her sounded to Mari like the ominous roll of thunder. Her heart sank like a rock into the morass of heavy food she'd consumed as J. D. Rafferty stepped into view. He stood beside her table, looming like an oak tree, not so much as sparing her a glance. Slowly he settled a pale gray hat in place and pulled the brim low, his unwavering gaze on his brother.

"You done shooting your mouth off?" he said quietly, his low voice setting off discordant vibrations inside Mari. "We got work to do."

"That's what I love about you, bro," Will said, the finest razor's edge in his tone as he slid from the booth. "You're just a great big bundle of fun."

"Fun?" The corner of J.D.'s mouth curled in derision. "What's that?"

The air between and around the two brothers was suddenly charged with enough electricity to make hair stand on end. Mari watched with guarded fascination as some tense, silent communication passed between their eyes. Will broke contact first, turning for the door without a word.

J.D. turned toward Mari, his gaze heating from gray ice to molten pewter as it lingered on her lower lip. Mari fought the urge to squirm in her seat. It was all she could do to keep from covering her mouth with her hand. Warmth rose inside her. She called it embarrassment and knew she was lying.

Rafferty met her eyes and smiled, the slight curve of his

lips radiating male arrogance. "You don't have to like me, Mary Lee," he murmured.

His meaning was crystal clear. Mari glared at him, wishing they weren't in quite so public a place so she could feel free to rip him up with her opinion of him. Still, she couldn't let him get away unscathed. She gave him a look of utter disgust and mouthed *Fuck you.*

The gray eyes darkened, the smile took on a feral quality. "Anytime, city girl."

"When hell freezes over."

He leaned down close, his eyes never leaving hers. He curled his big hands into the fabric of her old denim jacket and pulled the edges closed. "Better button up, sweetheart. I feel a cold spell coming on."

Mari shoved his hands away. "It's called rejection, slick," she said through her teeth. "Have the local schoolmarm look it up for you."

J.D. stepped back, chuckling at her sass. He tipped his hat ever so slightly, conceding the round but not the war. "Miz Jennings."

Mari said nothing. She felt used and furious. Will Rafferty had set her up and egged her on to get a rise out of his brother. And J.D. . . . She decided the initials stood for Jackass Deluxe.

Nora appeared beside the booth, rag in hand, and leaned across the table to wipe away the crumbs Will had left. "Those Raffertys are enough to give a girl cardiac arrest," she said matter-of-factly. "They don't make men like that anymore."

"No," Mari said, scowling as she watched J. D. Rafferty through the front window. He climbed into a battered blue and gray four-by-four truck with STARS AND BARS emblazoned across the bug guard. "I thought they broke the mold after the Stone Age."

CHAPTER 3

"*It* was a joke. Lighten up, will you?"

J.D. didn't say a word as he climbed into the cab of the battered Ford pickup. He nursed the engine to life carefully. The old truck had 153,000 hard miles on it. It needed to go a few more. There was no extra cash for buying new pickups. What money didn't get eaten up this year by Will's gambling or by the astronomical property taxes they had to pay because of the influx of elitists to the Eden valley would be sunk right back into the operation.

Fortify and strengthen. A siege mentality. Well, by God, if they weren't in a war, he didn't know what else to call it.

And in this war, Miz Marilee Jennings stood squarely on the other side of the DMZ.

"She's a friend of Lucy MacAdam's," he said tightly, pronouncing the name macadam, like the pavement. She had been that hard, that abrasive. Even in bed she had had sharp edges.

He backed the pickup away from the curb and headed north on Main, automatically glancing in the rearview mirror to check the feed sacks. Zip, their black and white border collie, stood with his front paws on a stack of plump bags and surveyed the passing scenery with a big grin on his face. Behind them a maroon Jaguar purred impatiently. J.D. eased off on the gas.

"So she's a friend of Lucy's," Will snapped irritably. "So what?"

The sun cutting through the clouds pierced his eyeballs

and rejuvenated the hangover he had fought off with mass quantities of caffeine and food. He pulled a pair of mirrored sunglasses out of his shirt pocket and slid them on.

"So she's one of them."

"Jesus. She came to visit a friend who turns out to be dead. Give her a break."

"Why? Because she's pretty? Because she's a woman?" Disgust bent J.D.'s mouth into a sneer. "I swear, if it wears a bra, it can lead you around by your dick and you'll just go grinning like a jackass eating sawbriars."

"Oh, Christ, will you lay off?" Will exploded, the volume of his own voice setting hammers swinging inside his temples. He fought off the need to rub the ache, not wanting to exhibit any sign of physical weakness in front of J.D. "You know what your problem is?"

"I'm sure you'll tell me."

"You live like a goddamn monk. Maybe if you went out and got a little every once in a while you wouldn't begrudge the rest of us."

"I get as much as I want. I just don't go around shooting my mouth off about it."

Behind his shades, Will's gaze sharpened. "Or maybe you want her for yourself? Is that it, J.D.?" He hooted, wincing at the needles the laughter stabbed into his brain. "That's it! Ha! She doesn't seem like your type. More like mine. 'Course, damn near every type is my type."

J.D. leveled a deadly stare at him as they idled at the town's one and only stoplight. "You'd do well to keep your eyes in your head and your pants zipped. You're married, ace."

The words were both accusation and reminder. Will wanted neither the censure nor the guilt that rose at the prodding. He knew damn well he was married. The knowledge was like a yoke around his neck. He may not have remembered the ceremony. Even the drive to Reno was hazy—it had been a hell of a party that had led up to the event. But he was very much aware he had come back with a wife. Nearly a year after the fact, the idea still scared the hell out of him. A wife. A commitment. He didn't want it, couldn't handle it, wasn't ready. The excuses piled up at the back of his throat in a sour wad.

In a soft, unguarded corner of his heart he wondered fleetingly how Samantha was faring without him.

"Shit," he snarled half under his breath.

He fell back against the seat, jerked an old University of Montana baseball cap off the gun rack behind him, and pulled it on, settling the brim just above the rims of his sunglasses. As if he were in disguise. As if he thought he could hide his character flaws from his brother with a costume. Will Rafferty incognito as Everyman. Christ, as if J.D. couldn't see through that in two seconds. J.D. could see through bullshit the way Superman could see through steel. He wondered how long it would take before J.D. found out about the sixty-five hundred and the busted flush of last night's poker game in Little Purgatory. He figured he had maybe a day and a half to live.

J.D. studied his brother from the corner of his eye as they headed out into the rolling green velvet countryside. Half brother, really, though he had never been one to use the term. The only child of Tom Rafferty's second marriage, Will was J.D.'s junior by four years. Twenty-eight going on seventeen. The joker, the charmer, this generation's wild Rafferty. He had a natural disdain for responsibility that rubbed hard against J.D.'s grain. But then, Will was his mother's son, and J.D. had never thought much of Sondra either. She had pampered and indulged Will in exchange for the kind of unconditional love and blind forgiveness J.D. had never been willing to give her.

He had seen Sondra for what she was early on—a spoiled city girl who had fallen in love with the idea of loving a cowboy but had quickly fallen *out* of love with the realities of ranch life. She had taken out her unhappiness on her husband, punishing Tom Rafferty for her own failings and miseries, and punishing his eldest son for seeing past her pretty golden façade. Will had been too young to know the difference. J.D. had never been that young.

He shoved the memories away, succeeding in shutting out all but the lingering, bitter aftertaste. That he very easily transferred onto outsiders as the maroon Jag roared past, all shiny new chrome and dark-tinted windows hiding the rich interior and the richer occupants.

There had been Raffertys on the Stars and Bars for more than a century. That heritage was something J.D. had been born proud of and would fight to the death to preserve. As a rancher, he had several enemies—capricious weather, capricious markets, and the bone-headed government. But as far as he was concerned, no threat loomed larger than that of outsiders buying up Montana.

Their pockets were bottomless, their bank accounts filled by obscene salaries for work that seemed a parody of the word. They paid the moon for land they didn't need to make a wage off and drove the property values out of sight, taking the taxes along and leaving production values in the dust. Half the ranches around New Eden had sold out because they couldn't afford not to, sold out to people who wanted their own private paradise and didn't care who they stepped on to get it. People who had no respect for tradition or the honest workingman. Outsiders.

Lucy MacAdam had been one of those outsiders, camped on the very edge of Rafferty land like a vulture. Marilee Jennings was too. It didn't matter that she had the biggest, bluest eyes he'd ever seen or that those eyes were set deep beneath brows three shades darker than her unruly mop of blond hair, which suddenly struck him as being incredibly sexy. It didn't matter that she was soft and curvy and he'd spent half the night dreaming about losing himself in that softness.

The muscles in his jaw clenched at the reminder of his restless night. She was trouble. He had made up his mind to dislike her. Unfortunately, the message hadn't made it to the less discriminating parts of his anatomy. Below his belt buckle all he could remember was the feel of her bottom pushing back against him while his cock strained to set a hard-on-of-the-year record. From his waist down he liked Marilee Jennings just fine.

She thought he was a jerk.

You don't have to like me, Mary Lee.

Lucy had been of the opinion that emotions just got in the way of great sex, an attitude J.D. had been more than happy to share. He would bed Marilee Jennings if he got the chance, but damned if he would like her. She was the last thing he needed in his life. She was an outsider.

"You're not from around here, are you?" Sheriff Dan Quinn tried to sound nonchalant, but he couldn't quite keep from raising his eyebrows a little as he took in the sight of Marilee Jennings. There were too many contradictions—the faded denim jacket two sizes too big, the feminine, silky dress, the shit-kicker boots and baggy socks. Dangling from her earlobes were two triangles of sheet metal dotted with irregular bits of colored glass. Her hair was a wheaten tangle with near-black roots. She scooped back a rope of it and tucked it behind her ear.

"No. I'm from California."

The sheriff hummed a note that all but said *it figures*. He tried to look noncommittal. He had to deal with a lot of outsiders these days. Part of his job was to be diplomatic. With some of these big shots, that seemed harder than saying the right thing to his mother-in-law. As he looked down at Marilee Jennings, he worried a little that she might be someone famous and he was failing to recognize her. She looked as though she could have come off MTV.

"What can I do for you, Miz Jennings?"

"I was a friend of Lucy MacAdam's," Mari said, staring up a considerable distance to his rugged face.

He could have either been a boxer or gotten kicked in the face by a horse. His nose had a violent sideways bend in it, and small puckered scars tugged at his upper lip and the corner of his right eye. Another scar slashed an inch-long red line diagonally across his left cheekbone. He was saved from ugliness by a pair of kind, warm green eyes and a shy, crooked, boyish smile.

He stood in the middle of the squad room with his hands on his hips. Around them, dotting the small sea of serviceable metal desks, several deputies were working, clacking out reports on manual typewriters, talking on the phone. Their eyes drifted occasionally toward their boss and his visitor.

"The shooting," he said, nodding as the name clicked into place. "Did someone get a hold of you? We been trying to call since it happened. Your name and number were in her address book."

They'd been trying to call a phone she had had disconnected as she had hurried to dump her life in Sacramento for something truer. Mari rubbed a hand across her eyes. Her shoulders slumped as a vague sense of guilt weighed her down. "No," she said in a small voice. "I didn't find out about Lucy until I got here."

Quinn made a pained face. "I'm sorry. Must have been a terrible shock."

"Yes."

Two phones began to ring, out of sync with each other. Then a burly, bearded man with a face like a side of beef and lurid tattoos from shoulder to wrist came hurtling through the door. He wore biker basics—jeans riding down off his butt and a black leather vest with no shirt beneath it, a look that showcased a chest and beer gut carpeted with dense, curling dark hair. His hands were cuffed behind his back and he was dragging a red-faced, angry deputy in his wake.

They crashed into a desk, toppling a coffee cup on a stack of reports and sending the deputy at the desk bolting backward. The air turned blue with assorted curses from three different sources. Quinn scowled as he watched the fiasco. He slid a hand around Mari's arm, ready to jerk her out of harm's way. But the biker was finally wrestled into a chair by a pair of deputies and the excitement began to dissipate.

Satisfied that the worst was over, Quinn turned back to Mari. "Let's go in my office."

Keeping his hand on her arm solicitously, he guided her into a cubicle with one windowed wall that looked out on the squad room, and shut the door behind them. Mari sat down on a square black plastic chair that was designed neither for comfort nor aesthetics, her eyes scanning the white block walls, taking in the diplomas and certificates and framed photographs of rodeo events. One was of Quinn wrestling an enormous steer to the ground by its horns. That explained a lot.

The sheriff settled into the upholstered chair behind his desk and adopted the most official mien he could manage, considering he had unruly yellow hair that stood up in defiant tufts in a rogue crew cut.

"We were unable to locate any kin," he said, taking up the threads of their conversation as if they had never been interrupted.

"Lucy didn't have any family. She grew up in foster homes."

He looked unhappy about that, but didn't pursue it. "Well, the case is closed, if that gives you any peace. It was all pretty cut and dried. She went riding up on that mountain, got herself mistaken for an elk, and that was that."

"Forgive me," Mari said. "I don't know a whole lot about it, but I thought most hunting seasons were in the fall. It's June."

Quinn nodded, his attention drifting through the windows to the biker, who was bellowing at Deputy Stack about his civil rights. "The guy was a guest of Evan Bryce. Bryce's spread—most of it, anyway—lies to the north of the Rafferty place, north and east of Miz Mac-Adam's land. Bryce breeds his own herds—elk, buffalo— so they're considered livestock. Limited hunting seasons don't apply. He lets his guests take a few head now and again for sport."

"And this time they took a human life instead," Mari said grimly.

He glanced back at her and shrugged a little, bulging shoulder muscles straining the seams of his khaki uniform shirt. "Happens now and again. 'Spect it'll happen more and more with the increase in tourism and second-home owners coming up here out of big cities. Most of these people don't know beans about handling firearms. They get all dudded up in their L.L. Bean safari jackets, sling a big ol' elephant rifle over their shoulders, and off they go.

"The guy that shot your friend? He didn't have a clue. Didn't know he'd hit her. He didn't even see her. Took two days before the body was found."

"Who was he?" Mari asked numbly, needing a name, a face she could picture and attach guilt to. He hadn't even known. Lucy had died up there all alone, had lain there for days while the jerk who killed her went on with his vacation, oblivious.

"Dr. J. Grafton Sheffield," Quinn said, swiveling his chair toward a black file cabinet that took up the entire width of the room behind the desk. "There's a trust-fund name for you," he mumbled as his thick fingers flipped through the files. He pulled one out and checked the contents. "Plastic surgeon from Beverly Hills. When word got out what had happened, he came in and confessed he'd been up there hunting. He was sick about it. Really was. Cried the whole time in court. Cooperated fully."

"The ballistics matched up, I take it?"

Quinn's brows sketched upward.

"I was a court reporter for six years, Sheriff," Mari explained. "I know the drill."

He rubbed one corner of his mouth with a stubby forefinger as he studied her, considering. Finally he nodded, selected a thin sheaf of typed pages from the file, and handed them across the desk. She scanned the initial report, her eyes catching on familiar words and phrases.

"There wasn't anything left of the bullet that nailed her," Quinn said. "It passed through her body and hit a rock. We couldn't test for a match. The shell casings in the area were consistent with the loads Sheffield had been using—7mm Remington. He confessed he'd been in the area, didn't know he'd wandered off Bryce's land. He pleaded no contest."

"You mean it's over already?" Mari said, stunned. "How can that be?"

Quinn shrugged again. "The wheels of justice move pretty quick here. Our court dockets don't see the same load yours do down in California. It didn't hurt that Sheffield was a buddy of Bryce's. Bryce swings a lot of weight in these parts."

"Sheffield is in jail, then?" Mari said, sounding hopeful and knowing better. Plastic surgeons from Beverly Hills didn't go to jail for accidents they readily owned up to.

"No, ma'am." Quinn's attention went to the squad room again. The biker was standing, the chair shackled to his wrists sticking out behind him like an avant garde bustle. Quinn started to rise slowly. "He pleaded guilty to a misdemeanor count of negligent endangerment. One year suspended sentence and a one-thousand-dollar fine. Excuse me, ma'am."

He was out the door and barreling toward the melee before Mari could react. She stared through the window at the surreal scene for a moment, Quinn and his deputies and the woolly mammoth tussling around the room in what looked like a rugby scrum. She dropped her gaze to the file in her lap. Surreal had been the theme of her vacation so far.

She glanced at the notes made by the deputy who had originally been assigned to the case, then at Quinn's comments. The coroner's report was appallingly brief. *Cause of death: gunshot wound.* There were scanty notes about entrance and exit wounds, contusions and abrasions. A broken nose, lacerations on the face, probably caused by the fall from her mount. It seemed pitiful that the cessation of a life could be boiled down to two words. *Gunshot wound.*

The battle raged on in the squad room, the biker smashing cups, coffeepots, computer screens with the chair attached to his butt. Good thing Quinn had experience wrestling enormous hairy animals to the ground.

Across the desk lay the file folder that held whatever other meager comments on Lucy's death Quinn had not planned to make privy to her. Mari bit her lip and battled briefly with her conscience. What she held in her hands seemed so scant. . . . Her friend was dead. . . .

A roar that sounded like an enraged moose sounded beyond the door. The men went down in a heap of tangled arms and legs. Mari scooted up out of her chair and

slipped around the desk to flip open the manila folder.
Her heart stopped, wedged at the base of her throat just
ahead of the breakfast she was still digesting.

The only things left in the case file were the crime scene
Polaroids. Lucy's body. Lifeless. Grotesque. She had lain
there at the edge of that meadow for two days. Nothing
about the corpse bore any resemblance to the vibrant
woman Mari had known. The brassy blond hair was a
dirty, tangled mat. The fingernails that had been meticulously manicured and lacquered at all times were dirty
and broken. Features were unrecognizable, the body
bloated out of shape like a Macy's parade balloon. The
bullet had hit her square in the back and exited through
her chest, leaving massive destruction.

*Hideous. God, she's hideous. She would have hated to
die this way.*

Alone.

Ripped apart.

Left for the carrion feeders.

Tears spilled over her lashes. Chills raced down her
from head to toe. Trembling, she dropped the reports on
top of the pictures and ran out of the office, choking on
the need to vomit and the necessity to breathe. The biker
was being dragged off to a holding cell. Quinn dusted his
pants off with his hands, glancing up from beneath his
brows as Mari rushed into the squad room. She swept a
fist beneath both eyes, trying in vain to erase the evidence
of her tears. She gulped a deep lungful of air that was
sour with the scent of male sweat and bad gas. Her stomach rolled over like a beached salmon.

"I—I—thank you for your help, Sheriff Quinn," she
said, her voice hitching. "I—I have to go now."

The sympathy in his eyes nearly undid her. "Sorry
about your friend, Miz Jennings."

The images from the Polaroids burned into the backs
of her eyes. Bile rose up in a tide. She managed to nod.
"I—I have to go."

"Stop by and see Miller Daggrepont," he called as she
hurried toward the door.

The name went in one ear and out the other. The only

stop she had on her mind at the moment was the ladies' room down the hall. Saliva pooled in her mouth. *Lucy. Oh, Christ, Lucy.* But she pulled up at the squad room door, the one question she had forgotten to ask stopping her short. Bracing one hand on the jamb to keep herself upright, she looked back at Quinn.

"Who found her body?"

"That'd be Del," he said with a nod. "Del Rafferty."

CHAPTER 4

$\mathcal{T}$he Mystic Moose had been the finest saloon, hotel, and house of ill repute for miles around during the days of the cattle barons. Of course, it wasn't called the Mystic Moose in those days, but the Golden Eagle—both for the majestic birds that hunted in the mountains around New Eden and for the gilded replica sent to the first proprietor of the hotel by Jay Gould in honor of the grand opening.

Madam Belle Beauchamp had built the place with the considerable fortune she had accrued on her back beneath the richest of the robber barons and cattlemen, and on her knees peering through keyholes while those same gentlemen wheeled and dealed both above the tables and under them. Madam Belle had known all the great men of the day and had made a killing in the stock market. Even though she had traveled extensively, she had called New Eden home until her death because she loved the land, the mountains, and the hearty, hardworking, God-fearing, mostly honest people who had taken root there.

No expense had been spared in the building of the hotel. Every room had been gaudy and grand. The chandeliers that hung in the main salon had been shipped west from New York City by train. The twenty-foot gilt-framed mirror behind the bar had reportedly come from a castle in Europe, courtesy of an adoring duke. Montana had never seen anything more extravagant than Madam Belle's Board and Brothel, as it had been called by some.

Sadly, Madam Belle's popularity faded with her beauty, and her fortune trickled away into bad invest-

ments and worse lovers. As spectacular as the Golden
Eagle was, New Eden was too far off the beaten path for
any but the most curious to visit. The hotel fell into disre-
pair. Madam Belle fell to her death from the second floor
gallery, a victim of dry rot in the balustrade. And so
ended the flight of the Golden Eagle.

Mari stood on the veranda of the renovated hotel,
reading the story that was beautifully hand-lettered on
yellowed parchment and displayed tastefully in a glass
case on the wall beside the carved front doors. The details didn't even make a dent on her brain. She wasn't
even sure how she had come to be standing at the doors
to the Mystic Moose.

After leaving the sheriff's office, she had just started
walking, needing to clear those awful scenes from her
memory—Lucy's body from a distance, Lucy's body up
close, entry wound, exit wound. Her head pounded from
the effort to eradicate those horrific images of blood,
death, decay. She had walked the west side of Main
Street clear out to the Paradise Motel, then crossed and
walked back down the east side, oblivious of the sights
and sounds and people around her.

The contradictions of the town penetrated in only the
most abstract of ways—the pickups that looked as
though they had been gone after with tire irons and the
luxury cars that cost more than most people's houses; the
boarded-up, bankrupt stores and the windows displaying
extravagant silver jewelry and custom-made sharkskin
cowboy boots; the ruddy-faced cowboys and ranchers in
town on errands and the faces of people who had graced
the covers of *People* magazine. All of it seemed more
dreamlike than real. In keeping with the theme of the
day.

She walked for hours, heedless of her surroundings,
unaware of the curious and pensive looks she got from
the locals; preoccupied by thoughts of death, fate, justice,
injustice, coincidence, Raffertys. Fragments of thought
hurtled through her mind like shrapnel, sharp-edged and
painful. There were too many bits and pieces. She
couldn't seem to grasp any one of them long enough to

make sense of it. Caffeine and grief and exhaustion pulled at her sanity and shook her nerves like so many ragged threads, until she wanted to grab her hair with both hands and just hang on, screaming.

She needed to sit down somewhere quiet and dark, have a drink to dull hypersensitive senses, smoke a cigarette to give herself something ordinary to focus on.

The double doors of the Moose swung open, and a tall, handsome woman in a long denim jumper and expensive-looking suede boots strode out, her jaw set at a challenging angle, her eyes homing in on Mari from behind a pair of large glasses with blue and violet frames. Her face was a long oval with strong features and a slim, unpainted mouth. A dense, wild mane of red-gold hair bounced around her shoulders.

Mari started to step out of her way, murmuring an apology, but the woman took hold of her shoulders with both beringed hands and looked her square in the face.

"Dear girl," she said dramatically, her expression dead serious. "You have a very fractured aura."

Mari's jaw fell open, but no words came out. A jumble of quartz crystals on sterling chains hung around the woman's neck. Opals the size and shape of sparrow eggs dangled from her elegant earlobes. "I—I'm sorry . . . I guess," she mumbled, feeling more and more like Alice on the other side of the looking-glass.

The woman stepped back, tipped her head, and laid a long hand against her forehead. " 'Weep not for me, nor all the pieces of my shattered heart,' " she said loudly, her voice suddenly dripping the honey of the Deep South. " 'I shall gather them to me and go on, valiant and undaunted.' " She straightened and heaved a cleansing sigh, her features settling back into the same fierce, businesslike expression she had worn a moment before. "From *Lila Rose* by Baxter Brady. It closed after three weeks in the St. James, though through no fault of mine. I assure you, *I* was brilliant."

Mari just blinked.

The woman pulled a small highly polished black stone from the pocket of her jumper and pressed it gently into

Mari's palm, curling her fingers up to hold it in place. "There. That will help."

Without another word she strode away, boots clumping on the wooden steps as she left the veranda for the parking lot on the south side of the building. Mari stared after her, forcing a couple in Rodeo Drive western wear to step around her on their way into the hotel. As the doors swung shut behind them, a puff of air brought out the aromas of fresh bread and simmering herbs. Mari's nose locked on like a bloodhound's. Food. Food always made sense. Rousing herself, she went in search of it.

The Mystic Moose bar was magnificent. Instead of re-creating the fussy opulence of Madam Belle's Golden Eagle, the new owners had opted for rustic chic. Rough white stucco walls and heavy, carved mahogany woodwork. Massive versions of Lucy's antler chandelier hung from the thick exposed beams in the high ceiling. The back wall was dominated by a series of tall multipaned windows and French doors that led onto a broad terrace and gave a magnificent view of the mountains that rose to the east. The centerpiece of the south wall was a huge fieldstone fireplace, over which hung an enormous mounted moose head. The moose looked straight across to a beautiful bar that gleamed in the soft afternoon light with the rich patina of age and loving care. Behind it, Madam Belle's gilt-framed mirror still hung; twenty feet of homage to an illicit affair of a bygone era.

There was a fair number of customers for the middle of the afternoon. A few cast curious looks in Mari's direction as she made her way to a table near the fireplace and settled into a large, comfortable captain's chair. She put her rock on the table and stared at it vacantly.

"If you don't mind my saying, luv, you look positively knackered."

The cultured British tones brought her head up and added another layer of confusion to the fog shrouding her brain. "Excuse me?"

"I say, you look all done in," he said, a gentle smile curving his mouth. He looked fortyish and attractive with wavy auburn hair, a bold nose, and a kind shine in his eyes. An afternoon beard shadowed his lean cheeks, but took nothing away from the overall impression of style and quality he projected in a loose-fitting ivory silk shirt and coffee-brown trousers. He leaned across the table and placed a cocktail napkin beside her stone. "Is something the matter?"

"Well, for starters, I have a fractured aura."

"Ah, you've met M.E." At her blank look he expanded. "M. E. Fralick, maven of the Broadway stage and patron of all things New Age."

The name rang a dim bell, but it didn't cut through the pounding in her temples.

"How about a cappuccino?" he suggested.

"I was thinking more along the lines of a G and T— with a capital G—and a large plate of anything edible."

"A woman after my own heart. By the bye, my name is Andrew Van Dellen. Aside from playing waiter on occasion, I'm one of the lucky owners of the Mystic Moose."

"Marilee Jennings," she said, trying to offer a smile.

He straightened a bit and stared at her for a moment, brows knit. Humming a note, he tapped a forefinger against his pursed lips. "Marilee. Marilee Jennings?" The light bulb went on. "Oh, my God, you're Lucy's friend!"

Across the room, at the bar, Samantha Rafferty scooped up her serving tray, sloshing imported beer and Pellegrino. The bartender shot her a look, and tears instantly burned at the backs of her eyes. Not that she really gave a damn about the drinks. She had bigger things on her mind. This was just a job she was screwing up. How important was that, when her whole life was one big, balled-up mess?

If only she'd had the sense to go straight home last night. But no. Glutton for punishment that she was, she just had to take a few turns past the Hell and Gone, cruising the street in her ancient rusted-out Camero until Will stumbled out the door of the saloon with his arm around a buxom blonde.

The tears pressed harder, glazing across her vision. She

clenched her jaw and held her breath as she set the drinks on the long table, heedless as to who had ordered what. What did any of them have to complain about? They were rich, they were movie stars, they didn't have to drive around in a fifteen-year-old car in the middle of the night, looking for a cheating husband.

Damn you, Will.

Damn me for loving you.

Her vision blurred to a jumble of watery colors. As she bent to set down the last of the drinks, she misjudged the distance to the table and let go of a tall mug of beer too soon. The glass hit the table with a *thunk* and beer spewed out of it like water from a floodgate, drenching the tabletop. Several women at the table gasped. The man whose drink it was bolted backward, shooting up out of his chair as the beer ran off the edge of the table. Samantha gaped in horror at the mess that seemed so symbolic of her whole life, and burst into tears.

"No, no, sweetheart, don't cry!" Evan Bryce laid a fatherly hand on Samantha's shoulder. "It was an accident. No harm done."

Mortified, Samantha mumbled behind the hands she had pressed over her face, "I'm so sorry, Mr. Bryce! I— I'm s-so sorry!"

He slid his arm around her and gave her a comforting squeeze. "Hey," he said with humor in his voice. "I've had beautiful young women do far worse things to me!"

The courtiers who sat around his table all laughed indulgently. Samantha wished the floor would open and swallow her whole. Evan Bryce was the most powerful among New Eden's new power elite. He was some kind of celebrity, a producer or something. Samantha had seen him on *Lifestyles of the Rich and Famous* and *Entertainment Tonight*. He was always on the awards shows or the judging panel at the Miss America pageant. The people who visited him at his ranch outside of town were like a Who's Who of Hollywood and California politics. And she had managed to dump a pint of beer practically in his lap.

"Come on, now," Bryce said, leading her toward the

chair he had so hurriedly vacated. "You've obviously been working too hard, Samantha. Sit down. See that there's no hard feelings."

That he knew her name jolted her for an instant, until she remembered it was pinned to her chest. *Stupid.* The word lashed her like a whip. *Stupid kid.* She'd heard it from her father often enough when she'd been growing up, so that now, even though she had been living away from her family for over a year, it came back to her and crumbled the debris of her self-confidence into even smaller pieces.

"No, I couldn't," she mumbled, backing out of his grasp. She could feel the eyes of the others on her, and imagined she knew what they thought. They thought she was a hick, a stupid, silly half-breed girl who couldn't even manage to keep a drink order straight. "I have work to do."

Bryce pulled a face. "I don't think Drew would begrudge you five minutes as my guest."

"I don't know, Bryce," one of his friends said slyly. "He may get jealous. I think he's had his eye on you."

The rest of them laughed. Samantha took in their faces in a glance—beautiful beyond what was normally human, teeth too white and too straight, eyes gleaming with some kind of sharp emotion she knew nothing about.

"I have to go," she blurted out. Then she wheeled and ran for the service door beside the bar, laughter ringing in her ears, her long black braid slapping her back like a whip as she went.

A long red-carpeted hall was at the rear of the building. Doors off it led into the kitchen, into Mr. Van Dellen's and Mr. Bronson's offices. Samantha went past these and hit the bar of the door that led outside. The stone terrace ran most of the length of the hotel, but the north end was divided from the rest by a tall, weathered lattice screen, giving the employees an area to slip out to for breaks.

Samantha thanked God it was empty at the moment. She had never been one to cry in front of people. Even

Will. Even the night he'd left she had managed to keep the tears at bay until he was out the door.

Damn you, Will.

She couldn't remember a time when she hadn't loved Will Rafferty. Even in junior high she had secretly pined away over him, when she had been a lowly eighth-grader and he one of the coolest boys in the senior class. Will Rafferty with his devil's grin and to-die-for blue eyes. Practically every girl in school had a crush on him. He was a rebel, a rascal, and a small-time rodeo star. And for a while he had been all hers.

The thought that that time was over, maybe for good, made her shake inside. She leaned over the split-wood railing at the edge of the terrace, doubling over in emotional pain, the tears crowding her throat like jagged rocks. It wasn't fair. She loved him. He was the one thing she had ever asked for in her whole miserable life. Why couldn't he love her back in the same way?

She knew he had married her on a whim. He had won a little money in the saddle bronc riding at the Memorial Day rodeo in Gardiner. She had won a little money in the barrel racing. They had ended up at the same celebratory party. Will, full of himself as always, caught up in the thrill of victory, and made uninhibited by innumerable shots of Jack Daniel's, had declared his love for her. Three days later they had driven to Nevada in his new red and white pickup and tied the knot.

In her heart of hearts Samantha had suspected at the time he wasn't truly serious about getting married, but she had grabbed the chance with both hands and hung on tight. Now she was living alone in the little cottage they had rented over on Jackson Street. She had her freedom from her family. She had a ring on her finger. And now she had nothing at all.

The loneliness that gripped her heart squeezed as hard as a fist.

"Can it really be all that bad?"

Samantha started at the sound of the soft voice, but there was no running away this time. She'd already made enough of a fool of herself. Evan Bryce took a position at the rail beside her. When he offered her a monogrammed linen handkerchief, she took it and dabbed her eyes. He didn't watch, looking instead toward the mountains, giving her a kind of privacy, a moment to compose herself. She used it to study him.

She supposed he was about the same age as her father, though all similarities stopped there. Her father was a hulking brute of a man, coarse and dark. Bryce was small. Catlike, she thought; lean, wiry, and graceful. His forehead was very high and broad, and beneath a ledge of brow, his eyes were a pale, startling shade of blue, his mouth a wide, thin line above a small chin. He wore his shoulder-length sun-streaked blond hair swept back, emphasizing his forehead.

She had seen him in the Moose many times. He came to hold court. The people he brought with him treated him like royalty. Sometimes he came in looking like something out of *Gentleman's Quarterly*. Most of the time he was dressed as he was now—in faded jeans that fit him like a glove and a loose, faded chambray shirt, which he wore with the sleeves neatly rolled up and the front open halfway to his belly button, exposing a thick pelt of dark chest hair. It was his version of cowboy dress, she supposed, though anyone who had ever known a cowboy would never mistake him for one with his long hair, fancy silver jewelry, and custom-made, high-heeled boots.

He turned toward her then, catching her looking at him. Samantha thrust his handkerchief out to him and turned toward the mountains. She could feel him staring at her for a long while before he spoke.

"I'm sorry if my friends embarrassed you, Samantha. They didn't mean to."

"It wasn't them."

"What then?" he asked softly. "A young woman as lovely as you should never have to cry so hard."

Samantha sniffed, her full lips twitching upward at one corner. She never thought of herself as lovely. She was tall and slender with almost boyish hips and no breasts to speak of—something that had never bothered her in her tomboy days, something that bothered her a great deal when she thought of Will and the buxom blonde coming out of the Hell and Gone. As far as her face went, she had always found it an odd mix of white and Indian, a jumble of oversize features that didn't quite go together.

"Boyfriend trouble?" Bryce ventured.

Glancing at him out of the corner of her eye, she weighed the wisdom of confiding in this man. She couldn't imagine why he should care what went on in her life. She was just a nobody cocktail waitress. But the kindness and concern she read in his tanned face touched a very tender spot inside.

She didn't have anyone else to turn to. Her parents were no shining example of wedded bliss. When her father wasn't drunk, he wasn't home. Her mother had six kids to raise and no energy or enthusiasm for the job. Samantha didn't have many friends who hadn't been Will's friends first. And she had always been too reticent for a tell-all girlfriend anyway. She might have gone to Will's brother for support, because she trusted him, but she had always felt J.D. didn't approve of the marriage. She had always felt he'd somehow known exactly what was what between her and Will, that he had seen past the façade of newlywed bliss from the first.

But here was this kind man, taking an interest, offering her a chance to unburden herself a little.

"My husband," she said in a small voice, looking down at a cluster of pink bitterroot that grew in a rock garden beyond the fence. "We're having some problems. . . . He moved out."

Bryce made a sound of understanding and slipped an arm companionably around her shoulders. "Then he's a fool, isn't he?"

Will was a lot of things. Samantha couldn't find it in her to voice a single one of them. Her throat closed up with misery, and scalding tears squeezed out of her tightly closed eyes. Needing nothing so badly as a shoulder to cry on, she turned and pressed her face against the one being offered to her.

•   •   •

They drank a toast to Lucy.

Andrew Van Dellen and his partner, Kevin Bronson, joined Mari at her table. Kevin was tall and rangy with an Ivy League look about him. He hadn't seen thirty yet. Tears glazed his eyes when he raised his glass in Lucy's memory.

"It was so senseless," he murmured.

"Death often is," Drew commented impatiently. The look they exchanged said they had already had this conversation at least once. "There's no use contemplating it. People live their lives until fate intervenes, that's all."

Kevin set his handsome jaw. "You can't say it couldn't have been prevented, Drew. Why should Sheffield have been up there with a gun in the first place? Lucy's dead because he had to go tramping through the woods like Rambo and try to prove his manhood by killing some poor dumb animal."

"He wasn't doing anything illegal."

"That doesn't mean it wasn't immoral or that it wasn't preventable. If Bryce—"

Drew cut him off with one gently raised finger and a tip of his head. "Don't speak ill of the customers, dear boy. It's bad form."

Kevin leaned back in his chair and stared up at the moose head above the fireplace, visibly struggling to rein in his temper. Drew shifted toward Mari, who had watched their exchange with avid interest while she ate. She had already devoured half a breast-of-chicken sandwich and most of the accompanying herbed fries. The food was rejuvenating her, sending fuel to a brain that had been running on empty. The drink was taking the edge off her nerves. Kevin and Drew were giving her mind something solid and real to focus on.

"Kev thinks the NRA will destroy civilization as we know it," Drew said with a touch of humor. Kevin's frown only tightened. "The truth is that Bryce is well within his rights to offer those elk for hunting. Hunting is a time-honored sport. And if one wants to get terribly deep, we are, after all, a species of hunters. It's gone on for eons."

"Men used to hit women over the head with mastodon bones and drag them off by the hair. We don't still do that."

"Some do."

"It isn't funny."

Their eyes held for a brittle moment, then Drew cupped a hand over his partner's shoulder. "Don't let's fight about it," he murmured tiredly. "At least not in front of a guest."

Kevin looked across the table. "I'm sorry, Mari. The whole subject just makes me crazy."

"I don't exactly like the thought of my friend getting killed in place of an elk, myself," she said, setting aside the last bite of her sandwich. She tucked a lock of hair behind her ear and fiddled with the bauble that dangled from the lobe.

"What makes me so angry is the hypocrisy," Kevin said, his voice lowered to keep it from traveling to the wrong ears. "Bryce pledges money and land to the Nature Conservancy and then runs around killing everything on the planet."

"It's not at all unusual for hunters to support conservation efforts," Drew argued. "Their purpose is sport, not annihilation."

"I fail to see how anyone can derive pleasure from denying another living creature of its life."

"Oh, bloody hell, here we go again."

"No." Kevin jerked his chair back from the table and rose. "Here *I* go again." Drew rolled his eyes and dropped his head against one hand. Kevin ignored him. "Mari, I'm sorry we couldn't have met under better circumstances."

He shot a look at the blond man approaching the table, his lips thinning, then turned and headed for the lobby.

"Kevin still has his nose out of joint, I see," Bryce commented mildly.

Drew rose from his chair, looking as if the effort were physically taxing. "Do forgive him, Mr. Bryce. It's easier for him to blame someone than to believe life can be so randomly senseless."

"He's forgetting that Lucy was a friend of mine as well as his."

"Yes, well, Kevin is young; he tends to think in absolutes."

Bryce's attention had already moved on from Kevin Bronson to Mari. She met his gaze, finding the Nordic blue of his eyes almost chilling, but his smile was warm as he offered her his hand. She wiped the smear of dill-speckled creme fraiche from her hand onto the bottom of her jacket and accepted the gesture.

"Evan Bryce."

"Marilee Jennings. I was a friend of Lucy's, too, from when she lived in Sacramento. In fact, I came here to spend some time with her at her ranch."

He offered just the right amount of sympathy, the corners of his mouth tugging down, concern tracing a little line up between his eyebrows. "Lucy was too young to die. And so vibrant, so full of life. I miss her as much as anyone. I hope you don't blame me for her death, as some do."

Mari shrugged and shoved up the long sleeves of her jacket to expose her hands again. "I don't know who to blame," she said carefully.

"It was an accident; there is no blame," he said, settling the issue, at least in his own mind.

Mari knew it would be days, weeks, months before she could resign herself that way. It might have been easier if she hadn't come into the play in the middle, if she had been here and lived through the circumstances surrounding Lucy's death.

"Will you be staying long in New Eden?" Bryce asked.

"I don't know. I'm too shell-shocked to think about it yet. I just found out about Lucy's . . . accident . . . last night."

He stroked his small chin and nodded in understanding. "I hope you'll be able to enjoy some of your stay. It's a beautiful place. You're more than welcome to come out to my ranch for a visit. It's not far from Lucy's—have you been there?"

"Last night."

"Xanadu—my place—is just a few miles to the north. Any friend of Lucy's is welcome in my home."

"Thank you. I'll remember that."

He said his good-byes and left them. Mari watched as he returned to his table by the window. The others heralded him like a returning monarch. She recognized two actresses and a supermodel among the beautiful faces. They were the kind of people Lucy would have gravitated toward. Gorgeous, rich, important or self-important depending on point of view. In the chair directly to Bryce's right sat a stunning statuesque blonde with strong, almost masculine features and sharply winged brows. The woman met her gaze evenly, lifted her wineglass in a subtle salute, and tipped her head. Then she turned casually toward her companion and the contact was broken, leaving Mari wondering if she had imagined the whole thing.

"Well, darling," Drew said, drawing her attention back to him. "I hate to rush off, but I've got to see that all's well in the kitchen before the dinner crowd arrives." He lifted her hand from the tabletop and pressed it between both of his, his expression earnestly apologetic. "I'm sorry for all the unpleasantness."

Mari shook it off. "I think I'd feel worse if everyone were pretending nothing had happened. It's all just too 'twilight zone' as it is."

"True."

"Thanks for the drink and the meal."

"Our compliments. And you'll stay, of course."

"Well, I—"

His brows pulled together as the thought hit him. "Where did you stay last night?"

"The Paradise."

"Good Christ!" He screwed his face into a look of such utter distaste that Mari almost had to laugh. "The Parasite! I hope to God you didn't sit on the toilet seat."

"I didn't even lie on the sheets."

"Smart girl. No arguments now. You're staying here as

a guest of Kevin and myself. I'll tell Raoul at the desk on my way out."

"Thanks."

"The Parasite," he muttered, shuddering. "What Philistine sent you there?"

There was a crash from the vicinity of the kitchen and a sudden burst of Spanish that sounded as angry as a blast of machine-gun fire. Drew muttered a heartfelt "Bloody hell," and rushed off.

Popping one last fry in her mouth, Mari pushed her chair back from the table and headed for the front door. She had to go find her car. Then she would check in and crash. The idea of sleep uninterrupted by the X-rated antics of Bob-Ray and Luanne brought a smile to her lips. No more nights in the Parasite Motel. As she left the Moose, though, her thoughts drifted automatically and unbidden to the Philistine who had sent her there.

Rafferty.

A dangerous kind of heat drifted through her. Residual feelings from being pressed against him when she hadn't known whether he was friend or foe, she told herself. It was some kind of weird pseudo-sexual response to the combination of fear and the feel of a magnificently made man, that was all. The rest of the uneasiness was the result of having too many encounters with the name Rafferty in one twenty-four-hour period. Her initial run-in with J.D., the awkward scene with his brother in the Rainbow Cafe, the mention of a Rafferty finding Lucy's body. There was something about it all that struck her as bad karma.

She stuck her hands in the pockets of her jacket. Her fingers found the smooth black stone M. E. Fralick had given her and began rubbing it absently. The image of J.D. lingered in her mind—a big, solid block of blatant male sexuality with eyes the color of thunderheads. Her heart beat a little harder at the memory of his fingertips brushing against her breast.

She hadn't known whether he was friend or foe.

A tremor of realization snaked down her back.

You still don't know, Marilee.

• • •

"Do you think she knows anything?"

"It's difficult to say." Bryce twined the cord of the telephone around his index finger, bored with the conversation.

He lounged on a Victorian chaise upholstered in soft mauve velvet. He detested Victoriana, but the suite he maintained at the lodge had come furnished and he preferred not to bother himself with it. He spent time in it only when he didn't care to drive all the way to Xanadu after an evening's entertainment or when he wanted a break from his entourage.

His attention was on the woman across the room. Sharon Russell, his cousin. She wore sheer white stockings and a virgin-white lace bustier that contrasted dramatically with her tanned skin. She was a sight to stir a man's blood, her body long and angular with large, conical breasts and long nipples that grew out of the centers like little fingers, like small penises. The blatantly female body contrasted almost perversely with the strongly masculine features of her face. The contrast excited him further.

He took a sip of Campari and tuned back into the telephone conversation. "She gave no indication of knowing anything, but they were close friends. She has been to the ranch."

"We'll have to watch her."

"Hmm."

"You're certain you haven't found anything?"

"Of course I'm certain. There's nothing to find. The house was thoroughly searched."

The voice on the other end of the line took on a truculent tone that quivered with fear beneath the surface. "Goddammit, Bryce, I mean it. Don't jerk me around. No more games."

Bryce rolled his eyes at the phone on the table, derision twisting his features as he pictured the man on the other end of the line. Weakling. He had no real power and he knew it. Bryce had only to snap his fingers and he would wet himself. Without much more effort, Bryce could crush him, ruin him. He let the weight of that knowledge hang in the air as silence crackled over the phone line.

"Don't be tedious," Bryce said at last, the edge in his voice as fine as a tungsten blade. He didn't wait for a reply, but cradled the receiver and turned his full attention to his cousin.

Sharon was the only person in his retinue who wasn't at least vaguely frightened of his power, an attitude he rewarded by considering her to be his equal in many ways. They were both ambitious, ruthless, ravenous in their desires, not afraid to take or to experiment. Not afraid of anything at all.

She sauntered toward him, her stiletto heels sinking into the mauve carpet, her eyes glowing with lust. Bryce lay back on the chaise and smiled as she straddled his naked body.

"He's afraid of this Jennings woman?" she asked, lightly raking her fingernails through his chest hair.

"He's afraid of his own shadow."

"Well, I admit, I don't like her showing up here either," Sharon said mildly. "There's no way of knowing what Lucy might have told her or what she might suspect."

Bryce sighed and arched into her touch. "No, there isn't. We'll find out soon enough."

"What's your game with the waitress?" she said. Her voice was nearly as masculine as her features, low and dark and warm. It set his nerve endings humming.

"Just testing the waters," Bryce assured her, reaching up to fill his hands with her breasts. The plan was still too fresh in his head to share; he wanted to savor it a bit first. "Don't concern yourself."

In a swift and practiced move Sharon twisted a length of black silk around his wrists, jerking it tighter than was strictly necessary. She pushed his hands above his head and fastened the tie around a decorative wood scroll on the end of the chaise.

"No," she growled, smiling wickedly as she positioned

herself above his straining erection. "Don't *you* concern yourself. Only with me. Only with this."

"Yes," he whispered on an urgent breath, thinking he might explode soon. Then she impaled herself on him, and he didn't think at all.

CHAPTER 5

$\mathcal{J}$. D. worked the horse around the pen, stepping ahead of her to make her turn, snapping a catch rope at her hindquarters when she slowed down. The rhythm of it was as natural to him as walking. He could read the mare's slightest body language, knew when she would try to turn away from him, knew when she was most in need of a breather. He let her take one now, stepping back slightly. She stopped immediately, her huge brown eyes fixed on him.

She read his body language as well. J.D. knew that ninety percent of a horse's communication was visual. That was one of the few great mysteries to mastering a horse. He had never been able to understand how anyone who had ever dealt with a horse couldn't see that in five minutes. It was stupid simple.

He made a kissing sound as the mare's attention began to drift away from him. Immediately she pricked her ears and faced him. He moved toward her slowly, held a hand out for her to blow on.

"That's a girl," he murmured, rubbing the side of her face. "Good for you. You're all right."

When he turned to walk away from her, she dropped her head and began to follow. J.D. wheeled and chased her off, putting her back on the rail of the round pen at a trot. This was one of the other great mysteries—establishing his place at the top of her pecking order. Dominance had nothing to do with force and everything to do with behaving in a way the horse could understand. He was the boss hoss. She had to move when he wanted, turn when he wanted and how he wanted. She rested when he allowed it. She learned to turn and face him, to keep her attention on him, because if she didn't, he would make her run some more and she was already hot, tired, and breathing hard.

He turned her in an easy figure eight with barely more than a shift of his weight and the motion of a hand. She was a pretty mare. Small, stocky—a quarter horse of the old style, built for cutting cattle. Her coat was a dark gold, made muddy now by sweat and dust. Her mane and tail were platinum—skunky, he called it—a mix of silver, white, and black. Her forelock hung in her eyes and she tossed her dainty head to fling it back. She belonged to the pharmacist in New Eden, who wanted her broke and safe for his twelve-year-old daughter to ride. She was one of four outside horses J.D. had in training at the moment. He enjoyed the work, and it brought in extra cash, something they never had enough of, ranching being what it was.

"Nice mare, good mare," he murmured, letting the palomino rest again.

Mare . . . Mary . . . Marilee. His mind drifted as he rubbed the horse's neck and slicked a gloved hand down her heaving side. Marilee. What the hell kind of a snooty name was that? Some kind of California name. Well, by God, he wouldn't use it.

No reason to think he'd ever get the chance. She had come to see someone who was dead. She'd stay a day or two, until the shock wore off, and then she'd leave.

He tightened his jaw against the feeling that thought inspired. Will was right, much as he hated to admit that. He needed a woman. He'd gone too long without. He was feeling edgy and distracted.

In his mind's eye he could see Lucy standing in the open door of her fancy little log house wearing nothing but a pair of high-cut black panties and a see-through blouse. She leaned against the jamb, completely relaxed, her eyes glittering with amusement, her brassy yellow hair tumbling over one shoulder in a wave of silk.

How about it, cowboy? Want to ride tonight?

He didn't like her, didn't respect her, thought she was a selfish, mean-spirited bitch. She had a similar string of names and sentiments for him as well, but they hadn't let any of that get in the way of what either one of them had wanted. It had all been a game to Lucy. She knew J.D. wanted her land and she had dangled it in front of him, a shiny, empty promise she had no intention of making good on. The bitch. Now she was gone for good. The land still teased him.

A glance at the sun sliding toward the back side of the Gallatin Range told him it was quitting time for the day. He needed to shower and shave and drive back down the mountain.

Damned waste of time, citizens groups. They got together and squawked and bickered worse than a gaggle of geese, and nothing ever came of it. They could make all the noise they wanted, but in the end the money would talk and that would be the end of it. What the common man had to say wouldn't matter. They would all be ground beneath the wheels of some outsider's idea of progress.

Not the Raffertys.

That conviction was what pushed all other cynical thoughts aside. Not the Raffertys, by God. The Stars and Bars wouldn't fall. He wouldn't let it. That was the legacy left him by three prior generations of Rafferty men—protect the land, keep it in the family. He took that duty to heart. It wasn't so much a chore as a calling. It wasn't so much a sense of ownership as a sense of stewardship for the land, for tradition. He had been entrusted with a history, with the life of the ranch and everything and everyone on it. There was nothing in him stronger than his sense of personal accountability to that trust.

Forgetting about the mare, he wandered to the far side of the round pen and laid his arms against the second rail from the top. From there he could see for miles down the slope of the mountain to the broad valley that was carpeted in green, studded with green. Pines stood shoulder to shoulder, ranks of them marching down the hillsides. In the breeze, the pale green leaves of the aspen quivered like sequins. He didn't know if the shades of green here compared with those in the birthplace of his Irish ancestors; J.D. had never been farther than Dallas. But he knew each shade by heart, knew each tree, each blade of grass. The idea that some outsider believed he had a better right to all of it was like a punch in the gut.

The mare had come to stand beside him. She nudged him now, rubbed her head against his shoulder, tried to reach around and twitch her heavy upper lip against his shirt pocket. J.D. scowled at her. "Quit," he growled in warning. She backed off a step, then tossed her head, eyes bright, not intimidated by his show of annoyance. He chuckled, pulled off a glove, and dug into his pocket for a butter mint.

"Can't fool you, can I, little mare?" he mumbled, giving her the treat.

Little mare . . . Mary Lee . . . She reminded him a little of Mary Lee—small and curvy with a tangle of streaked blond hair hanging over wide dark eyes. Of course, the woman smelled a whole lot better. The horse was a lot less trouble.

"Reckon you can get that citizens' commission to eat out of your hand that way?"

J.D. looked across the pen to where Tucker Cahill stood with his foot on a rail and a chaw in his lip. Tucker had a face that was creased like old leather, small eyes full of wisdom and kindness, and a hat that had seen better days. He claimed women told him he was a dead ringer for Ben Johnson, the cowboy actor. Ben Johnson had seen better days too.

He was one of two hands kept on at the Stars and Bars, as much out of loyalty as necessity. The other, Chaske Sage, claimed to be the descendant of Sioux mystics. It might have been true or not. Chaske was a wily old character. He had to be at least as old as Tucker, but had warded off the rheumatism that plagued his cohort. He attributed his stamina to sex and to a mysterious mix of ash, sage, and powdered rattlesnake skin he took daily.

"Nope," J.D. said. "All together they don't have the

sense God gave a horse." He patted the little mare and headed for the gate. She followed him like a dog. "Couple of them sure do resemble the back end of one, though."

Tucker spat a stream of brown juice into the dirt and grinned his tight, shy grin, showing only a glimpse of discolored teeth. "That's a fact, son. A bigger bunch of horse's patoots I never did see." He swung the gate open and stepped past J.D. to snap a lead to the mare's halter. "I'll cool her out. You better get a move on if you're gonna make that meeting. Will already went up to the house."

"Yeah, well, he spends an hour in front of the mirror. If he spent as much time with his wife as he does picking out his clothes—"

"Got that line of fence done up east of the blue rock."

Tucker changed the subject as smoothly as an old cowhorse changing leads. J.D. didn't miss the switch. Tucker had been on the Stars and Bars a lot of years. He'd been a pal of old Tom, had stood by faithfully and worked like a dog during all the years Sondra had made their life a misery. He'd been a surrogate father to J.D. when Tom had been caught up in the agony of heartbreak, and a mentor after Tom had died, leaving the ranch to J.D. and Will when J.D. was only twenty. His role these days as often as not was that of diplomat. He didn't like dissention among the ranks, and did his best to smooth things between the brothers.

"You find Old Dinah?" J.D. asked as they walked across the hard-packed earth of the ranch yard, their battered boots kicking up puffs of dust.

Tucker chuckled. "Yep. In the back of beyond with a big good-looking bull calf at her side. She's got a mind of her own, that old mama cow. Just like every female I ever knew."

The little mare snorted as if in affront, blowing crud down the back of the old man's shirt. He scowled at her, but kept on walking, grumbling, "Jeezo Pete."

"That's why you're single," J.D. joked, turning toward the house.

"Yeah, well, what's your excuse, hotshot?"

"I'm too smart."

"For your own good."

J.D. thought about that as he climbed the broad steps to the old clapboard ranch house with its wide, welcoming front porch. He planned to dodge matrimony for as long as he could. He didn't have time for courtship rituals and all the related nonsense. When he couldn't put it off any longer, he supposed he would go find a sensible woman with a ranching background, a woman who understood that the land and the animals would always come first with him. They would marry out of a mutual desire to raise a family, and the next generation of Raffertys would grow up on the Stars and Bars, learning the duty and the joy of life here.

There was nothing romantic about his plan. Growing up he had seen firsthand the folly of romance. His father had lost his heart twice. First to J.D.'s mother, Ann, who died of cancer. J.D. had been only three at the time. He had no memories of the woman herself, only of sensations—comfort and safety, softness. But he remembered vividly her death and the way it devastated his father. Then along came Sondra Remick. Much too soon. Much too pretty. Much too spoiled. And Tom Rafferty lost his heart again to a woman. Totally. Utterly. Beyond all pride or reason.

In the end, he damn near lost everything. Sondra had eventually left him for a more exciting man. Because of her infidelities, Tom had had a strong case against her as an unfit mother, and might have ended up with full custody of her darling Will. That was the only thing that had stood in her way of suing him for divorce and taking away half of everything he owned, including the Stars and Bars. They fought bitterly over his refusal to release her from her marriage vows, but he was unrelenting. He would not let her go. His obsession for her went too deep. In retrospect, J.D. thought he probably could not have let go even if he had wanted.

They had stood right there on this porch, J.D. and his daddy, looking down across the ranch yard at the sturdy old buildings, the corrals, the horses, the valley and mountains beyond. Lines of strain were etched in Tom Rafferty's face like scars, his eyes were bleak with hopelessness. He looked like a man waiting to die.

"Never love a woman, son," he mumbled as if he were remembering words told to him by someone long ago. "Never love a woman. Love the land."

Citizens for the Eden Valley ordinarily met in the community center—a kind euphemism for a room off the fire station garage filled with rickety folding chairs and mismatched card tables people had donated over the years. That this meeting was being held in the Mystic Moose Lodge was a bad sign as far as J.D. was concerned. The enemy had invited them into its camp. Some saw it as an overture of friendship, an invitation to work cooperatively with the newcomers. J.D. wasn't so optimistic.

The meeting room was bright and clean with ruby carpeting on the floor and rustic beams across the ceiling. It smelled pleasantly of fresh coffee instead of diesel fuel and exhaust fumes like the community center. The tables were draped in hunter-green linen. The chairs were all new. J.D. chose to stand at the back of the room.

There were perhaps a hundred people in attendance, milling around, buzzing premeeting gossip. Most of them were lifelong citizens of New Eden. Businessmen and women from the community. Ranchers who had, like J.D., quit work hours early to clean up and put on freshly pressed western shirts, Sunday trousers, and good boots. Scattered among the common folk were new faces— Hollywood types, artists, environmental activists, Evan Bryce.

J.D.'s hackles went up at the sight of Bryce working the room. He made the rounds, singling out the mayor, the chairman of the citizens' commission, the banker's wife, dazzling them with his smile, undermining any wariness they might have had with a phony show of concern. As if he gave a damn about the people of New Eden.

What Bryce cared about was power. That had seemed glaringly apparent to J.D. the first time they had met—from the way Bryce threw money around to the way he surrounded himself with people who believed he was important. J.D. refused to be impressed by him, an affront that had set the tone for their acquaintance. Bryce wanted to be king of the mountain along the south face of the Absaroka range, but J.D. wouldn't play the game. No Rafferty had ever bowed to a king—real or otherwise. No Rafferty ever would.

As if he sensed J.D.'s eyes on him, Bryce looked up and their gazes caught and held for one burning moment. A slow smile pulled across Bryce's mouth. His pale eyes gleamed with amusement. The look clearly said *I've got the keys to the kingdom within my grasp, Rafferty, and you can't do a damn thing to stop me*. Then he moved on to kiss another cheek and shake another hand.

"Hey, J.D." Red Grusin stuck out a hand and clapped him on the shoulder. "Don't see much of you these days."

As owner of the Hell and Gone, Red had never seen much of him. J.D. had better things to do than sit around a honky-tonk and drink beer. "Will spends enough time with you all for the both of us," he said with a half smile. For all he knew, that was where Will was at that very moment. His brother had yet to make an appearance in the meeting room.

Grusin chuckled. He was a big man with skinny legs and a thick chest and belly that made him look as if he were wearing an umpire's padding beneath his shirt. He had the hair and freckles his name indicated. His cheeks and the end of his bulbous nose were perpetually pink. "That's a fact. Why, just last night he hit the jackpot on the mouse races. 'Course, that didn't hardly make up for what he lost downstairs in the poker game," he said, lowering his voice conspiratorially. His blue eyes twinkled. Just a little joke among friends—Will and his weakness for wagering. "But it'll all come out in the wash, as my mama always said."

"Will was in Little Purgatory last night?" J.D. asked, his voice as dead calm as the air before a storm.

Grusin's jowly face dropped a little, and he swallowed hard as he realized his slip.

"How much did he lose?"

Grusin made a face, his eyes dodging around the room as if he were afraid the sheriff might overhear and suddenly decide to shut down the illegal gambling that had been going on in the basement of the Hell and Gone for the last two decades. "Don't worry about it, J.D. He'll win it back. He's been on a bad streak and he's in the hole a little now, but—"

J.D. stepped a little closer in front of Red and stared at him hard. "How much?" he whispered.

The older man's mouth worked as if he were chewing a mouthful of chalk. "Sixty-five hundred," he mumbled. "Don't worry about it, J.D." His gaze scanned the room frantically for anyone near enough to rescue him, landing on Harry Rex Monroe from the Feed and Read. Relief brightened his face like a man having a vision. "Hey there, Harry Rex!"

J.D. just stood with his hands on his hips, staring at the floor and breathing slowly through his mouth. Sixty-five hundred dollars. Will did not have sixty-five hundred dollars. The bank held the mortgages on everything they owned, practically down to their underwear, and Will was whiling away his nights in Little Purgatory, throwing money down a rat hole after busted poker hands.

"I heard talk of a ski resort on Irish peak . . ."

". . . Some developer wants to put up condos north of town."

"They'll turn the place into another goddamn Aspen with cappuccino bars and prissy Swiss chalets and rents so high, everyone who works here will have to drive in from someplace else. . . ."

Random lines of conversation penetrated the fog. J.D. forced himself to pay attention, forced his brain to function. He had come here for a reason. Will could be dealt with later.

$6,500. He felt ill, but damned if he would show it.

Lyle Watkins, who was his neighbor to the south of the Stars and Bars, stood staring down into his coffee cup. He looked thin and miserable, as if worry had been eating away at him beneath his skin. "Yeah, well," he snapped suddenly, breaking in on the antidevelopment talk of his fellow ranchers. "You can't feed your kids on pride and scenery."

"Can't feed them at all if these damned actors bring in buffalo and elk herds infected with brucellosis and TB," J.D. said calmly.

Lyle dodged his gaze, rubbing his fingertips against his coffee cup as if it were a worry stone. "Ain't nobody proved Bryce's herds are infected."

"I don't want the proof to be my cattle dropping over. Do you, Lyle?"

Watkins tightened his lips and said nothing. The silence curled like a fist of foreboding in J.D.'s chest. He swore softly under his breath. "You're selling out."

The words were barely more than a whisper. Lyle flinched as if they struck him with the force of hammer blows.

"Deal's not done yet," he mumbled. He stared down at the toes of his boots, his head hanging with the weight of his shame. He had been one of the first and the loudest to decry the buyout of ranchers by people who wanted the land for their own private playgrounds, and now he was giving in, giving up, betraying his neighbor.

"I can't afford not to, J.D.," he said miserably. "You know what the market's been like. And I got Debbie and the kids to think of."

"Jesus, Lyle," J.D. said, desperation running through him like a sword. He felt as if he was standing on a narrow ledge and another piece had just crumbled out from under his boots. "How long has your family been on the place? Seventy—eighty years?"

"Long enough."

"Who?"

Watkins shook his head a little and started to move with the rest of the crowd toward the chairs as Jim Ed Wilcox began blowing into the microphone at the podium. J.D. grabbed him roughly by the arm, ignoring the stares the others directed his way.

"Dammit, Lyle, I asked who," he demanded through his teeth.

The fact that Watkins didn't want to answer was answer enough. J.D. felt as if he'd had the wind knocked out of him. He stared hard at this man he had known all his life, the neighbor he had worked with side by side at brandings and roundups, and felt as if a member of his own family had turned on him.

"Bryce." He growled the name in disgust.

Lyle Watkins looked up at him, his tired eyes soft with apology. "I'm sorry, J.D.," he whispered. "He's got more money than God. Me, I don't have two nickels left to rub together." He lowered his voice another decibel, his eyes cutting from side to side to make certain no one else could hear his confession. "I sell the place to him, or it goes to the bank. That's all there is to it."

"The hell it is."

Watkins pulled away and headed for a chair, not looking back. J.D. stared after him, furious, stunned, frustrated. He didn't even hear the opening remarks of the chairman. He just stood there behind the last row of chairs, his mind spinning, his eyes on Evan Bryce, who sat at the table up front with all the local indignitaries, as J.D. called them. If Lyle Watkins sold the Flying K, Bryce would own everything from Irish Peak south to the edge of Yellowstone—everything except the Stars and Bars and the little chunk of property that had belonged to Lucy MacAdam.

Bryce sat up there in his faded denim work shirt with the sleeves rolled up to reveal his tan forearms. Christ, the man had probably never done an honest day's work in his life. Nobody was even sure where all his money had come from. Or where *he* had come from, for that matter. Hollywood was all anyone knew for sure, and God knew big money didn't get made down there by the sweat of any man's brow.

He has more money than God. God was exactly the role Bryce wanted to play here, J.D. thought bitterly.

Bryce fielded questions from the audience with all the aplomb and paternal benevolence of a supreme being, telling them everything would be wonderful, their financial cups would runneth over, and all would be bliss in Eden.

To the credit of the citizens of New Eden, not everyone bought the routine. People rose readily to debate the issues. When one person pointed out that development would bring jobs to the valley, another countered that the jobs would be low-paying service occupations. When one charged that the influx of tourists was a disruption to a way of life, another argued that the town would die without those tourist dollars. Cattlemen spoke out angrily about the political clout wielded by radical left-wing environmentalists who owned second homes here and were fighting to stop everything from grazing on federal land to eating red meat. Environmentalists fought back, slamming the cattle industry for overgrazing and destroying wildlife habitat.

Jim Ed Wilcox, chairman of the committee, cut in as the debate edged toward an exchange of blows. He broke in again when a new argument heated up between a Mormon rancher from over on Bitter Creek and the owner of the New Age rock shop, or whatever the hell it was—a tall, fierce-looking woman named M.E. who was some kind of Broadway actress when she wasn't playing around in Montana. The rancher accused her of practicing witchcraft. She accused him of having a negative energy field and a constipated mind. Wilcox shouted them both down and, when order had been restored, introduced another of the people at the front table.

Colleen Bentsen was a squarely built woman with a cap of soft brown curls and large tortoiseshell glasses. She was dressed in a blue silk tunic and slacks with a wildly patterned scarf swathed around her shoulders and pinned in place with what looked to J.D. like a chunk of welder's solder. She took her place behind the podium as two men carried a draped object in from a side door and set it on the table beside her.

"Good evening, everyone," she said so softly that Jim

Ed got up and bent the neck of the microphone down, making it screech in protest. A blush bloomed on the woman's cheeks. She cleared her throat demurely and started again. "As many of you know, I am a sculptor. I came to New Eden two years ago and made this my permanent home. It troubles me to see so much dissention over the issue of new people coming here. I feel what we all need is a spirit of cooperation. As a symbol of that spirit, I have decided to donate to the town a sculpture that embodies the theme of cooperation and blends harmoniously the rough elements of the ranching community with the influx of sophisticated and artistic qualities from the outside."

She unveiled the model with a flick of the wrist, snapping the white cloth from it. Half the room gasped in awe and wonder. The other half stared in dumbfounded astonishment. J.D. fit squarely into the second group. It didn't look like anything to him but a big hunk of smooth metal and a big hunk of jagged metal twisted together, like something that could be found on the road in the aftermath of a major car wreck.

There was a smattering of enthusiastic applause for the piece, which, Miss Bentsen said, would stand as a focal point in front of the county courthouse. She would begin work on the project immediately, and would create the piece on the site so people could witness the progress.

"I expect that's a nice gesture, Miz Bentsen," J.D. said neutrally, drawing the eyes of everyone in the room. "But I don't see how a big ol' hunk of metal is gonna to help me pay taxes that have been raised to the moon because of inflated land prices. A gesture doesn't keep my neighbors from selling out prime ranch land to people who think food is manufactured in a room out back of the A&P. Bottom line here is, we dig our heels in now and hang on to what's ours, or in five years we'll all be steppin' and fetchin' for rich folk. That's not what my ancestors came west for a hundred-some years ago."

While the sculptress turned scarlet with embarrassment, Bryce rose gracefully from his chair, steepling his bony fingers in front of him in a scholarly pose. His pale eyes locked on J.D. "Mr. Rafferty, are you saying only natives should be allowed to live in Montana? That this land and freedom you so cherish shouldn't be offered to anyone born in another state?"

J.D. narrowed his eyes. He didn't raise his voice above its usual low growl, and yet each word snapped in the air like the crack of a whip. "I'm saying I won't sell my heritage to some slick-ass smart-mouth rich boy so he can impress his witless, feckless friends from Hollywood.

"I can't stop people from coming here, but they can damn well respect my way of life and leave me to it in peace. I won't be bought out. I won't be run off. And I sure as hell won't stand by and smile while speculators turn this place into some kind of snotty elitist playground."

He settled his Stetson on his head, signaling to one and all that the argument was over as far as J.D. Rafferty was concerned. "If I want to live in an amusement park," he said softly, firmly, "I'll move to Disneyland."

Will sat at the bar, one arm on the polished surface, fingers absently stroking a sweating mug of imported beer. He swiveled sideways on his stool to survey the place. It was a little tony for his tastes. A fire crackled in the stone fireplace, chasing off the chill of the spring evening. Soft guitar music drifted out of hidden speakers, calm enough to lull a man to sleep.

Will preferred the Hell and Gone down the street for its noise and truculence and nightly mouse races. The juke there played country as loud as thunder and nobody talked below a shout. The liquor was better in the Moose, but hell, after two or three, what difference did it make?

About half the tables in the Mystic Moose lounge were filled with newcomers and vacationers, pretty people in expensive clothes. One exotic-looking blonde sitting alone at a nearby table caught his eye, returning his stare with open boldness, but Will looked past her. He hadn't come in to get himself picked up by some rich bitch looking for a cowboy to lay. He had come in because his wife moved among the clientele with a serving tray and a smile that was softer than silk and warmer than the sun.

Damn, but she was a pretty thing. Somehow, he hadn't managed to realize just how pretty until after they had split up. He had always thought of Sam as cute—when he thought of her at all. A cute kid, a tomboy with a crush on him. Now he looked at her as she bent to set a glass of wine in front of a customer and her jeans snugged up tight against her bottom, and he wished to hell they'd never gotten married. He would have loved nothing better than to charm his way into her bed tonight, but he couldn't do that, things being what they were.

He shook his head and swilled his beer. He liked his life a whole lot better without complications.

He watched as Sam made her way back to the bar, head bent over her order pad. Her waist-long black hair was in its usual utilitarian braid. Will pictured it loose, falling around her naked shoulders so that her nipples peeked out from between the silken strands. He shifted uncomfortably on his stool and took another pull on his beer to dull the sudden throbbing in his groin.

Samantha felt his eyes on her the instant she set her tray on the bar, and her heart jumped up into her throat. Two weeks had passed since Will had moved back out to the Stars and Bars. She hadn't seen him up close since their last fight.

The memory of the blonde from the Hell and Gone warred with the image of him sitting there on the barstool, looking too handsome for his own good, his eyes too blue and his smile too tempting. The pressure made her heart feel as if it were swelling and cutting off her air.

"Aren't you even gonna say hello, Sam?" he said softly.

She turned her head to look at him squarely, wishing he would see cool indifference in her eyes, knowing he would see pain instead. "What are you doing here?"

Good question. He bit the inside of his lip and tried to think of something clever, something that didn't sound as screwed up as he felt. He was the one who wanted out of the marriage; he couldn't very well tell her he missed her.

"It's a free country," he said at last, all but wincing at how lame that sounded.

Samantha tightened her expression into a glare, hoping the hurt wouldn't show through. In her heart she had wanted him to say that he missed her, that he needed her, that he wanted to try again to make their marriage work. Over and over she had envisioned him coming to her and begging her forgiveness, telling her with tears in his eyes that he wanted her more than anything, that he wanted her to have his baby. That was what *she* wanted. And she kicked herself for it. She wasn't a dreamy young girl anymore; she was a woman with a husband who cheated on her without compunction.

"Well then, you're free to go on down to the Hell and Gone," she said sharply. "I'm sure there's a bimbo or two waiting for you."

Will's protest caught in his throat as she wheeled around and stalked away with a loaded tray in her hands. Heaving a sigh, he leaned both elbows on the bar and hung his head. "Hey, Tony," he muttered to the bartender, "gimme a shot of Jack in the black, will you?"

J.D. intercepted the whiskey. He tossed it back, slammed the glass down on the bar and fixed his brother with a steely glare. "We're leaving."

Will shot him a look. "What's your problem?"

"Besides you?"

"That meeting can't be over yet."

"It is as far as I'm concerned."

"Oh, well, then," Will drawled sarcastically, stretching his arms out in an expansive gesture. "Then we can *all* go home. St. John has spoken."

His declaration met with a thunderous scowl. "Save your lip for someone who wants to hear it. Let's go."

Will shook his head, only mildly incredulous at his brother's high-handedness. "Contrary to what you seem to think, big brother, you are *not* my keeper. I have my own truck, you know."

"Yeah. And some night you might even be sober enough to drive it home."

"I'm driving it home tonight," Will said tightly.

"Before or after you lose another grand or two in Little Purgatory?"

Will squeezed his eyes shut. "Oh, shit."

"Yeah," J.D. said, his gaze cutting around them to make certain no one was within earshot. He signaled the bartender for a refill on the Jack and leaned heavily against the bar. "Jesus, Will," he whispered. "How could you? Sixty-five hundred!"

"I had a straight, J.D.," he said, cupping his hands in front of him as if he could call up a vision of the cards across them. "I had it right there and I kept looking at that pot and thinking, Judas, that's the loan on my truck, that's three payments to Stark Implement, that's a down payment on that hay ground across the valley. . . ."

"It's sixty-five hundred dollars you could just as well have flushed down the toilet."

Will glared at him. "Thanks, J.D. Make me feel worse about it than I already do. I was trying to win."

"But you didn't, Will." He held his tongue as the bartender refilled his glass. He tossed the whiskey back and set the glass down with a dull thunk. "You never do."

Will reached for his beer mug and J.D. slid it beyond his grasp. His temper was simmering. He felt as if everything in his world was slipping beyond his control, sliding through his hands like wet rope. "We got cattle to move in the morning. Remember that. If you're not downstairs by four-thirty, I'll haul your sorry ass out of whatever bed I find it in and tie it on a horse. You hear me?"

"I hear you fine."

J.D. leaned down into his brother's face, his voice a razor-edged whisper. "You might try to remember once in a while that the Stars and Bars is your responsibility too. Responsibility, not a toy, not something you bet on in a goddamn poker game. Responsibility. Look the word up in the dictionary if you have to, college boy."

Tossing some crumpled bills on the bar, Will slid off

his stool. "I'm out of here. I don't need to take this bull-shit from you."

He headed for the front lobby of the lodge, his mind turning to thoughts of the Hell and Gone and drowning his troubles in Coors and the charms of a cowgirl with a tight ass and loose morals.

J.D. stalked across the room to a side door that led out into the parking lot, tipping his hat to Samantha as he went.

Neither of them paid the least bit of attention to the pair of eyes that had taken in every detail of their argument.

Sharon Russell sipped her scotch and smiled to herself. Dissension among the Rafferty ranks. Bryce would be pleased.

Outside, J.D. was able to breathe a little better. The Jack Daniel's seeped into his bloodstream and calmed him a bit. He turned away from the refurbished lodge and focused on a view he had loved since boyhood. The night sky was a sheet of deep blue velvet studded with diamonds. A wedge of moon was scaling the peaks of the Absarokas to the east, spilling its white glow down the forested slopes.

As he stood there, staring up at it, the anger that seemed so much a part of him these days slipped away, the tension ebbed. The madness of life receded for a moment, and he was left with something that was real and enduring. The mountains would always be here. The moon would always rise. Not wanting to think beyond that, he stepped off the veranda and headed toward his truck at the back of the lot.

He didn't want to think about Will and the resentment that always managed to seep into their conversations from both sides. He didn't want to think about the mental slip he'd made in calling Will "college boy." He didn't want to think why he should consider it a slip at all, the showing of a weakness.

It wasn't Will's fault J.D. hadn't been able to finish his

time at Montana State. That was Tom's fault for dying—which was Sondra's fault for breaking him. Nor was it Will's fault he had gotten a full ride to the university in Missoula. That had been Sondra's doing too. She had insisted her baby get a complete education; had seen to it with the money of her lover. Never mind that Will had majored in partying and minored in rodeo and let his grades skid down the shitter.

The memory set J.D.'s teeth on edge. Waste. God almighty, how he hated waste.

The sound of music caught his ear and he pulled up short, glancing at the lodge. Lights glowed through the array of French doors along the back of the bar. From farther down the street came the drift of noise from the Hell and Gone. But this music was softer, warmer, nearer. He walked on, scanning his surroundings with a narrow gaze.

A split rail fence marked the back of the parking lot. Beyond that lay the rumpled hills that formed the feet of the mountains, dotted with trees and rock outcroppings that loomed in the stark contrast of moonglow and shadows. J.D. slipped between the rails of the fence and walked out into meadow, his senses filling with the scent of grass and wildflowers, the sounds of a warm, smoky voice and the sweet, tender notes of a guitar. A woman's voice, low and strong. The song she sang was poignant and reflective, poetic in a way that went far beyond simple rhyme. It was the song of a woman trying to navigate her way through life despite the obstacles and her own stubbornness, despite mistakes and missed opportunities.

The beauty and the truth of it stopped J.D. from walking up on her. He just stood there and listened as she sang of the moon and St. Christopher. And when it was over and her fingers had plucked out the final notes, he almost backed away out of respect. Then it struck him who she was. Mary Lee Jennings.

She sat on a small boulder, the guitar cradled across her middle and a tall bottle by her side. She wasn't alone. Zip, his cattle dog, sat at the base of the rock, staring up at her, his ears perked attentively. It was Zip who noticed him first and bounded toward him with a jubilant yip.

Mari followed the dog with her eyes, her heart slamming into her breastbone when she saw the man standing no more than a dozen feet away. The brim of a pale gray hat shaded his face, but almost instantly she recognized the set of his shoulders and the stance he had taken with his hands jammed at the waist of his jeans. It seemed odd that she should know him by such subtle signs when she had met him only twice, but she dismissed the thought as he took a step toward her.

"You missed your calling, Rafferty," she said, her tone wry. "You would have made a great spy the way you sneak up on people."

J.D. ignored the commentary. He waded a little closer through the lush grass, until he could almost read the label on the bottle that sat beside her. "You always sit and sing to the moon?" he asked, trying to shake the enchantment of her song. He couldn't afford to be enchanted.

"Doesn't everyone?"

"No, ma'am. Not around here."

She raised a shoulder in a careless shrug and tugged a hand back through her tangled hair to anchor it behind one ear. A lazy smile turned the corners of her mouth. "Oh, well. At least I'm not naked."

The joke was almost lost on him as the image filled his head. He could too easily picture her sitting there on that smooth boulder in nothing but pale creamy skin and her moon-silvered mop of hair.

Mari sensed the tension in him. It was telegraphed to her on a wavelength of instinct she didn't understand, nor did she care to understand at the moment. Not at this time and certainly not with this man. Pretending ignorance, she lifted the bottle that sat beside her and held it out to him.

"Champagne? Compliments of the Mystic Moose."

"You're staying here?"

She gave him a look. "While the place you sent me to

had an undeniably unique ambience, I prefer not to listen while the trucker in the next room gets a lube job."

He almost smiled at that. Dangerous thinking, letting her charm him. Not like him either. He didn't have time to waste on feminine wiles. The occasional roll between the sheets was all he ever wanted from a woman. Not charm, not friendship. Those were things women gave away on a whim and snatched back in the blink of an eye. He had no desire to be on the other end of that exchange.

He focused on the bottle she held by the neck. "You always offer drinks to men you consider jerks?"

Mari had the grace to wince, though more for what she was about to do than for anything she'd said before. She needed information from J. D. Rafferty. It seemed only politic not to antagonize him, even if it did make her feel like a hypocrite, even if he deserved to be antagonized.

She slid down off the rock, holding both the champagne bottle and her guitar out away from her. The guitar she propped carefully against the boulder. The champagne she took with her as she moved toward him, holding it out as a peace offering. "Look, we got off to a bad start. Maybe we should just take it from the top, huh?"

J.D. narrowed his eyes, assessing her from head to toe. She wore a pair of old black leggings, a T-shirt from a Cajun bar in New Orleans, and a blue cotton shirt five sizes too big for her. She hardly looked dangerous, but his guard stayed up just the same. "Why? What do you want from me?"

"Civility?" Mari ventured, swallowing back the question she had held inside her most of the afternoon and evening. When he only went on watching her, she forced a laugh and shook her head. "Christ, you're a suspicious son of a gun."

"I've got reason to be. I knew your friend Lucy, remember? She never offered a damn thing that didn't have strings attached. Why should I think you're any different?"

She put her head on one side and hummed a note of consideration, the champagne dulling the edges of her temper. "This is a first. I've never posed a threat to anyone before. Unless you count social embarrassment. My family has always lived in fear of me eating with the wrong fork at dinner parties—to say nothing of eating with my fingers, which I have an uncontrollable urge to do. My mother considered my lack of social grace a birth defect. I'm sure she would have organized a telethon for the cause if the shame hadn't been too much for her."

He just stared at her for several moments until she began to wonder if she hadn't suddenly begun speaking in a language he didn't understand. A blush of embarrassment and champagne fizzies warmed her cheeks, and she anxiously shifted her weight from one sneaker to the other. Finally he said, "You always talk this much?"

"No. I am capable of deep and abiding silences. But not after half a bottle of champagne," she confessed. "I tend to wax poetic and bay at the moon."

"Naked."

"That was a joke. You know, a brief oral narrative with a climactic humorous twist meant to provoke laughter." Mari peered up at him, trying to see past the shadows of his low-riding hat brim. "Is it too much to hope that there might be a sense of humor lurking behind all that granite and testosterone?"

He gave a snort that might have been disgust or a sinus condition, and started to turn away, motioning the dog to follow him.

"Wait!" Mari rushed to catch up, the grass and the lethargy of alcohol pulling at her feet. "I have to ask you something."

He stopped, but didn't turn around, forcing her to step in front of him. His expression was inscrutable, but she could feel tension emanating from him. She wondered where the wariness came from, wondered if Lucy had been the one who jaded him. She thought of chickening out, but forced the words past the knot in her tongue before she could. "Who is Del Rafferty?"

"Why?"

"He found Lucy's body. Is he a relative of yours?"

"You thought you had to ply me with liquor for that?" J.D. sneered, letting his temper run freely through him and heat the blood in his veins. He welcomed it. It made more sense than the odd exchange they had just shared. It made a hell of a lot more sense than notions of enchantment. This was the face of femininity he knew best —deceit.

She wanted something from him. Plain and simple. Like every other leech who had come into his domain from the outside world. They all wanted something—a piece of this, a scrap of that, a chunk, a rock, an acre, a ranch, a pound of flesh. They wormed their way in with smiles and platitudes and stroked with one hand while they stole with the other. They insulted his intelligence and mocked his basic honesty, and suddenly he wanted very badly that someone pay.

"Damned city bitches," he snarled. "You don't know how to ask a straight question, do you? Everything has to be wrapped in some kind of disguise. Why didn't you just ask?"

"I did just ask!" Mari said, feeling at once both wrongly accused and justly convicted.

His lip curled in derision, he took a step toward her, looming over her. " 'Sorry, J.D., we got off on the wrong foot. Can we start again? Do you want some champagne?' "

He snatched the bottle out of her hand and flung it aside, sadistically gratified by the way she jumped back, eyes wide. He wanted her scared of him.

"What else do you want to know, Mary Lee?" he demanded, backing her toward a cottonwood tree that grew at the edge of the parking lot. "What else?"

"N-nothing," she stammered, stumbling back.

"Are you like your friend Lucy? You want to know what it's like to tease a cowboy?"

"No—"

"You want to know what it's like to fuck a cowboy?"

"No! I—"

"I'm more than willing to accommodate you. Or did Lucy already tell you all about it? Huh?"

"No, she never—"

He gave a rough laugh that held no humor. "*Never* was not a word in her vocabulary."

Mari collided with the trunk of the tree, hitting her head hard enough to snap her teeth together. The rough bark bit into her through the fabric of her cotton shirt as she pressed back against it, as J.D. pinned her against it. There was nothing about his body that was softer than the tree. His thighs were like pillars flanking hers. His fingers were like bands of steel as they wrapped around her upper arms. He leaned down close, until she could see the glitter of anger in his eyes. Her pulse fluttered in her throat like a trapped bird.

"You want to find out, Mary Lee?" he whispered, his gaze boring into hers, penetrating in a way that was disturbingly intimate.

His lips were parted slightly, slick and moist. The lower one was fuller than she had first thought, sexier. His breath came in warm, whiskey-scented puffs that seemed to go directly into her mouth. She felt something tingle through her that was the same confusing, unsettling mix of anxiety and arousal she had felt with him the night before. It pooled in her breasts and swirled lower.

She wanted to slap him, but he had hold of her arms. She might have kneed him, but he was too close. And then there was the fact that she didn't feel as if she had an ounce of strength left in her body.

She managed to form the word *no* with her lips. It came out on a gossamer breath.

J.D. heard it as clearly as if she had shouted it. Everything male in him rejected it. She was soft and trembling against him, her eyes as wide and dark as a new moon. As he stared at her, she moistened her upper lip with the tip of her tongue, and raw need bolted through him like a wild horse.

"Liar," he growled.

He didn't assault. He didn't attack. He lowered his mouth to hers slowly, but Mari did nothing to stop him.

She gasped a little at the first touch of flesh to flesh, and he took advantage, easing his tongue into her mouth slowly, deeply. She shuddered at the blatant carnality of it, but did nothing to stop him. She felt caught in the pull of some incredible magnet, unable to draw away, unable to stop her body from responding as he stroked and explored and tasted her.

This is crazy, Marilee. He's a large, angry cowboy. You don't even like him.

The internal monologue fogged out as he slanted his mouth across hers and increased the pressure and the hunger of the kiss. He was heavy and solid against her, and impressively, undeniably male. His erection throbbed against her belly.

Hunger. God, he was hungry for this. Ravenous. Wild for the taste of her. He crushed her against the tree, wanting to sink into her, wanting to pull her down to the ground with him and into oblivion. He slipped a hand between their bodies and found her small, plump breast. His thumb brushed across the nipple that budded hard and tight beneath the soft cotton of her T-shirt. Need thundered through him neck and neck with anger and frustration, led on by the lure of sweetness and champagne.

He wanted her. Badly. Damn near beyond reason. Another woman he didn't trust or respect. Another outsider. Another of the jackals who had come to scavenge at his life.

The taste of desire soured in his mouth.

As he eased away from her marginally, Mari's senses came rushing back like a chill wind. In their short acquaintance, J. D. Rafferty had frightened her, offended her, embarrassed her, and now this. This went beyond assault, beyond humiliation. He had invaded her, robbed her of her sanity, stripped her of her good judgment.

Locating the hands she had wound into his shirtfront, she balled them into fists and hit him in the chest as hard as she could. She may as well have hit an elephant with a tennis ball. All she managed to do was annoy him.

"How dare you!" she demanded, breathless.

He looked down at her with slit-eyed disgust. "Don't pretend you didn't want it, Mary Lee. You didn't exactly try to fight me off."

He was right, but that didn't lessen her outrage. He had no business touching her in the first place. "Those are your rules of dating etiquette? Screw anything that doesn't hit you in the head with a brick first? Where I come from, that's called rape. This is the nineties, Rafferty. In the civilized world men ask permission."

"Then maybe you ought to go back to the *civilized world*," he sneered. "I sure as hell don't want you here. Go back to California. Stay the hell out of my life."

Mari gaped at him as he moved away from her to pick up the hat he had lost in the heat of the moment. She blew out three hard breaths, trying to jump-start her tongue.

"Me—? Your—? Oh, that's rich! Like I asked you to get up close and personal with my tonsils! Who the hell do you think you are—"

"J. D. Rafferty," he growled, jamming his hat down and tipping the brim in a mocking salute. "Del Rafferty is my uncle. He doesn't like strangers, he doesn't like blondes, and he can shoot the balls off a mouse at two hundred yards. Stay away from him too."

"Yeah, he sounds about as charming as you," Mari tossed after him as he strode away with his dog at his heels. "How will I ever control myself?"

He didn't even give her the satisfaction of looking back, but climbed into the cab of his pickup, fired the engine, and drove away. The dog stood in the back of the box, staring after her until they turned onto Main Street. Mari watched them drive away and then she just stood there in the moonlight with a hand across her mouth, her body humming, her heart racing. He made her furious. He made her crazy. He made her want him.

How will I ever control myself. . . .

He crouched among the trees, waiting. The moon glowed down on the meadow. Coyotes crooned mournfully, unseen, their hollow cries drifting down the valleys. The silvery pall of death lingered like a sticky mist above the ground. He watched it, hidden among the trees on the hillside, and waited. From the mist the bodies would materialize—the blonde, the dog-boys, the tigers. They would take shape and dance their gruesome dance beneath the half-light of the moon, tormenting him, luring him.

He sat among the ranks of limber pine and Douglas fir, his hands slick with sweat on the stock of his rifle, and he waited.

CHAPTER 6

" '*I*'ll tell you how the sun rose,' " Mari murmured, the words slipping out of her almost without her awareness.

She sat on the same rock she had chosen the night before to watch the moon rise over the mountains. Now dawn was streaking the sky behind those same peaks in pastel shades that were at once as soft as mist and strong enough to take her breath away. The experience was new, and yet she felt strangely as if she had seen it a hundred times in some other existence. She felt as if she had been waiting forever to see it again. The beauty of it renewed her as six hours of fitful sleep had not. Something essential in her soul drank it in as if it were the elixir of life, and a deep sense of peace flowed in her veins.

" 'I'll tell you how the sun rose,' " she murmured.

" 'A ribbon at a time,' " Drew finished the line from Emily Dickinson, his voice soft so as not to break the spell of the moment.

Mari turned to find him standing beside her rock. He was dressed for a workout in second-skin black spandex bike pants and a sweatshirt heralding the Oxford Cricket Club. A mountain bike leaned against his right hip.

"I used to enjoy sleeping in," he said. "Then I saw this sunrise. I vowed to never miss another."

Mari pulled her denim jacket closer around her to fend off the morning chill and swiveled around to face him. "Do you ever miss England?"

"Now and again," he admitted with a candid smile.

"But I visit often enough. There will always be an England, as the song goes. This is home now. I love it here."

"It's not hard to see why," Mari said, glancing around, soaking it up. She felt it herself, that tickle and tingle of new love. She hadn't known it was possible to feel that kind of rush for a place instead of a person. She tried to imagine Lucy feeling it, but couldn't see her friend falling for something that sounded so corny.

"I always wondered what drew Lucy here," she said, her gaze sweeping the dew-drenched meadow as she swept a strand of hair behind her ear. "I mean, she always liked to be in the eye of the storm. She had to be in on all the hottest trends and first to know the gossip. I couldn't see her moving to the outback and growing vegetables . . . watching the sun rise. When I knew her, if she saw the sun rise, it was because she hadn't gone to bed yet."

"She wasn't so different here." Drew propped his bike on its kickstand and moved to lean against the boulder, his shoulder half a foot from her hiking boots. "Don't let all the natural splendor fool you. New Eden has its secrets and its conflicts. Lucy was always in the thick of it, stirring things up."

"With Evan Bryce's crowd?"

"Hmm. I dare say, that's a set that runs as fast and flashy as any from her days in Sacramento. Evan Bryce is a powerful man. Powerful men have powerful friends. He always has a host of celebrities of one variety or another tagging after him. Actors, directors, models, politicians, lawyers. Many of them have second homes here as well."

"What you're saying is that Lucy didn't leave the world behind; she was actually on the cutting edge moving here?"

"Montana is the trendy place to be. Much to the dismay of the local ranchers."

Automatically, Rafferty came to mind. His anger, his open hostility toward outsiders . . . his kiss. The heat of it had kept her awake half the night. The memory of it set off a restless stirring inside she labeled as annoyance. A small inner voice called her a liar.

"One has to sympathize with their plight," Drew went on. "Escalating land prices, skyrocketing taxes." He sighed, his shoulders sagging as if the weight of the moral dilemma were pressing down on them. "But then, Kevin and I are part of the problem, aren't we? We may feel sorry for the poor buggers, but we're not about to leave."

"Where did Lucy stand?" she asked, J.D.'s taunts coming back to her like the remnants of a bad dream. He was so bitter, so angry. How much of that was Lucy's doing?

The look Drew gave her was knowing and honest, telling her without words she should know full well where Lucy's loyalties would have lain. "For herself."

An ache echoed through her, leaving behind the useless regret that her friend hadn't been a better person.

"You don't seem much like her, luv," Drew said gently.

A sad smile pulled at the corners of her mouth as she slid down off the rock. "No. We didn't have much in common . . . except that we were friends. That doesn't make much sense, does it?"

He slid a brotherly arm around her shoulders and gave her a squeeze. "It makes as much sense as relationships ever do. I can't say that I found Lucy to be of sterling character, but I liked her as well. She had a rare sense of humor and if she found you worthy of friendship, she would fight to the finish for you."

"She was just . . . well, she was just Lucy. And now she's gone."

For several moments, they stayed side by side, leaning against each other as if they had been friends forever instead of a day. The sunlight spilled over the shoulders of the Absarokas like liquid gold, and the valley began to come to life. A meadowlark trilled. Halfway up the side of the mountain an eagle soared above the tops of the Douglas fir and lodgepole pine, wings outstretched to catch the updrafts.

Mari watched in silence, letting the peace seep into her and wash the rest away. She took a deep breath of cool, clean air that was scented with pine and cedar and the soft perfumes of a dozen wildflowers, and let it soothe her as the line from the poem soothed her. *I'll tell you how the sun rose—a ribbon at a time.*

She was eating breakfast when Miller Daggrepont descended on her. She saw him coming across the dining room and knew with a sense of fatalism that he was homing in on her. Everyone in the dining room paused with forks and spoons in midair as he passed, their expressions ranging from horror to amusement.

He was as wide as he was tall, a virtual cube of a man, with a face like a bulldog's and a shock of ratty gray hair that stood straight up from his head in a style reminiscent of fight promoter Don King. A gold and black brocade vest stretched around his rotund frame over a white shirt, and a black string tie lurked beneath the folds of his wattle. A huge silver belt buckle set with nuggets of turquoise perched at the forefront of his belly like a hood ornament on a Mack truck. The legs of his black trousers were tucked into a pair of snakeskin boots that looked ridiculously tiny beneath his enormous bulk.

Mari froze with a slice of cantaloupe halfway to her mouth, the juice running down her fingertips, as he rumbled up to her table and stopped straight across from her. There was a cigar stub jammed into the corner of his mouth. He looked down on her through Coke-bottle lenses, his dark eyes weirdly magnified behind them.

"Little missy," he said, his voice booming in the high-ceilinged room. "You'd be Marilee Jennings?"

Her automatic desire was to say no in the hope that he would go away and embarrass someone else, but her head bobbed in affirmation. *You're too honest for your own good, Marilee.*

He stuck out a hand that resembled an inflated rubber glove, gripping hers before she could wipe the cantaloupe juice off. "Miller Daggrepont, Esquire," he announced in a voice loud enough to wake the ghost of Madam Belle.

"Attorney-at-law and renaissance man. I've got a surprise for you, little lady."

"I'm not sure my heart can stand it," Mari said, only half joking.

"Come on along," he ordered, tugging her up from her seat. "This is important. You can eat anytime."

He appeared to be an expert on that subject. Stomach grumbling a protest, Mari shuffled after him, thinking that wild elephants probably couldn't drag Miller Daggrepont away from a table. He towed her down the lobby of the Moose and outside, rumbling along like a freight train. Hustling down Main Street, he jaywalked across to First Avenue, and continued on, oblivious of the curious looks people cast their way.

The buildings here, as on Main Street, were a jumble of styles and ages. The shops were a mix of practical and pretentious—a dentist's office, a wilderness outfitter's post, the Curl Up and Dye hair salon. Designer fashions hung in the window of the Beartooth Boutique. Next door an old man sat on one of several riding lawn mowers parked out in front of Erikson's Garden Center.

They turned in at a brick building with an ornate front window. EDEN VALLEY ASSAY arched across the glass in gold gay-nineties-style lettering, but the brass plaque on the door itself read MILLER DAGGREPONT, ESQUIRE. ATTORNEY-AT-LAW.

"This is where I keep my collections," he said, thumbing through an enormous ring of keys. "I collect everything. Signs, toys, farm equipment, you name it. Never know when the next big rage will hit. I made a killing on Indian artifacts when all the Hollywood types started moving in. They think they're going native when they hang an old horse blanket on the wall. Damned fools, I say—not because of the collecting. Nothing wrong with collecting. They're just damned fools in general."

He swung the door open and went in, pulling Mari along behind him like a recalcitrant child. Shelves lined the walls from floor to ceiling. A row of low display cases ran down the center of the floor from the front of the room to the back. Old advertising signs and license plates hung by wires from the ceiling. The floor was littered with a jumble of junk. Toward the back of the main room two of the tall cases had been tipped over, dumping a mountain of toys, glassware, tin canisters, wooden boxes, and God-knew-what onto the floor.

"Watch your step," Miller ordered, grunting his disapproval at the mess. "Some damned drunk broke in the back door last night and turned the place upside down. You know we're just catercorner from the Hell and Gone. Cowboys come into town and they go crazy. It's like bringing a wild pony into the house."

Mari picked her way along behind him, stepping over the prone form of a cigar store Indian and a woman's straw hat decorated with faded silk cabbage roses. "Mr. Daggrepont, I've worked with lawyers for six years, and I have to say I've never come across an office quite like this one."

His booming laugh rattled the tin signs overhead. "Well, little missy, I'm not your run of the mill attorney. Like I said before, I'm a renaissance man."

He led her down a hall and into a smaller room that was an even worse mess than the front had been. An old desk sat in the middle of it all. Somewhere on the desk, beneath a drift of fishing tackle and assorted debris, a telephone rang. Daggrepont ignored it. He let go of Mari to work on the combination lock of an old vault set into the back wall.

"This was the assay office back in the 1860s," he explained. "Gold was discovered up in the Absarokas. The place went bonkers with gold fever. The town boomed. Didn't last long though. The lode wasn't rich enough and it was too damned hard to get to. Those mountains are rugged sons a'guns."

Mari had read all about it in her guide books, but she didn't comment on it as she picked her way across the office. He heaved the vault open and she raised up on tiptoe in an attempt to peer over his shoulder. "Uh, Mr. Daggrepont, would it be too much to ask what this is all about?"

He shot her a look of annoyance, his eyeballs swimming behind his thick glasses. "Lucy MacAdam," he said, cigar stub bobbing above his chins. "I was her attorney. You're her heir."

The news knocked her in the head like a mallet. Mari swayed a little on her feet and stumbled back. "I'm her heir? That can't be. I mean, why— what—?"

Daggrepont ignored her stammering, searching for the proper file among the boxes on the shelves that lined the vault. "Thank heaven for this vault," he grumbled. "There'd be hell to pay if some drunk dumped these files. Inez would be sorting paper from now till kingdom come. Ah! Here it is. Lucy MacAdam."

He pulled the file and herded Mari back out into the office, where he swept off a chair and ordered her to sit. He leaned his bulk back against the desk and told her the gist of Lucy's last bequests.

"She didn't have any living relatives. Left everything to you. Her place, her bank account, this letter—" He held out a sealed envelope to her. Mari took it with limp fingers and held it in her lap. "All subject to inheritance taxes, funeral expenses, and, um, my fees, of course."

"Of course."

"But it's all yours as soon as it clears probate. Oh, and there's one other thing. Damn near forgot."

He trundled back into the vault and came out with a foot-tall old tin replica of Mr. Peanut, which he thrust into Mari's hands. She stared at the smirking peanut, then up at Daggrepont and back again.

"What is it?" she asked at last.

"Why, it's Lucy. She had herself cremated."

She drove out to the ranch with Mr. Peanut strapped into the passenger seat beside her. Daggrepont had immediately tried to persuade her to sell the ranch. Inheritance taxes would be astronomical, considering how property values had gone up. What would she want with a ranch anyway? She had a life back in California, didn't she?

No, she didn't, but she didn't tell that to Daggrepont or to his weasley real estate buddy who had just happened to drop by. The same way a vulture just happens to drop by road kill. She shuddered at the thought of the pair of them—Shamu in cowboy boots and the Earl Scheib of Montana real estate. *I can sell that property for you, little lady. I can sell anything, anytime, anyplace.* On the verge of giddiness, she had nearly asked him if he could paint her car any color for $99.95.

"Lucy," she said, cutting a look at the tin peanut. "You always did have a bizarre sense of humor, but this is really too much."

The peanut just smirked at her.

She had to get away, to think, to try to sort through it all in her mind. The ranch seemed the best place to do it. Somehow she thought an answer might come to her there. But another part of her knew there would only be more questions, and her stomach churned at the prospect.

By daylight the place Lucy had called home for the last year was as picturesque as anything Mari had ever imagined. The log house was set on high ground overlooking a broad valley with a wide, glittering stream running through it. The hills above were covered with pine and aspen. The valley beyond the stream was dotted with grazing horses. She fell in love with it the minute she stepped out of the car. It radiated a sense of peace, a sense of constancy. Nothing about it struck her as being Lucy's style at all.

She climbed the steps onto the porch and followed it around the side of the house to a broad deck that overlooked the stream. The bent willow furniture and Adirondack chairs had escaped the vandals' zeal. Setting the tin on the glass-topped table, she sank down onto the cushions of a high-backed chair and stared out at the panorama.

It was hers. The idea wouldn't penetrate. It made no sense. She had never even been here to visit Lucy. She had never thought of their friendship as being something that went so deep as this. They had shared laughs and gripes over a few beers. They had been drinking buddies, comrades in arms against the vicious lawyer hordes who never wanted to pay them and always wanted to get them into bed. The thought that their relationship had meant something more to Lucy left her feeling confused and vaguely guilty, the way she had felt in high school when one of the nerd boys had revealed that he had a crush on her.

Hoping for an answer or at least a clue, she pulled the envelope Daggrepont had given her out of her jacket pocket and opened it with a nail file from her purse. Inside was a strip of green paper folded in half, torn on both ends. Stenographer's notes, a set of hieroglyphics no one but another court reporter would have been able to decipher. How like Lucy to be dramatic even from beyond the grave.

Mari leaned over the letter with her elbows braced on her knees and read the phonograms.

Dear Mari,

If you're reading this, it means I've gone on to my just reward. Do you think I might get a lawyer to plea-bargain a better hereafter for me? Probably not. The bastards always want the best for themselves and the rest of us can go to hell. Oh, well, God knows I was a very naughty girl. I'm sure He does. But that's between me and the Big Guy.

This is about you. You need a life, pal. I'll give you mine. You have to promise to dump that schmuck Bradford. And you have to promise to devote yourself fully to aggravating your family. We all have our calling in life, that's yours. Mine was being a thorn in wealthy paws. I was a champion. It got me where you are today. Or did it get me where I am?

No matter, my peach. Take the bulls by the horns and ride them into the ground. You won't get into Martindale-Hubbell, but my name will live on in infamy and you'll have some fun for once.

Shed a tear or two for me. No one else will. Raise a glass in my name. Know that you're the only real friend I ever had. And when you bed your first cow-

boy, think of me fondly before you mount up, then ride 'im, cowgirl.

Live it up, sweetheart. Life's too short to play by someone else's rules. Take it from someone who knows.

Yours in a peanut tin,
Lucy

She read it twice. It didn't make any more sense the second time. All she managed to do was increase the ache of loss and the feelings of abandonment and guilt.

She slipped the letter under the feet of Mr. Peanut and curled up in the chair, her gaze fixed, unfocused on the beauty that lay before her. And she thought of Lucy, so brassy, so tough, surrounded by important people . . . alone in the world with just a drinking buddy for a friend. Full of secrets and hidden pain. Dying alone. Left on a mountainside, forgotten.

Foul was a kind word for the mood J.D. was in. As days went, this one had started out bad and gone downhill from there. In the morning Will had shown up just as J.D., Tucker, and Chaske were getting ready to ride out. It had been clear that if he'd spent any time in a bed the night before, he had not been sleeping. His eyes were as red as tomatoes, his pallor a shade of gray generally reserved for corpses. He was in no shape to get on a horse. So, naturally, J.D. had badgered him onto one and then made him ride drag all morning, eating the dust of a hundred fifty cows and their bawling calves.

Will hadn't uttered a word of protest. Tucker had done enough complaining on his behalf. Cut the boy some slack. Give the kid a break. He's going through a rough patch. Have a heart, J.D.

Will didn't need any slack as far as J.D. could see. What he needed was for someone to knock some sense into him. He needed a good kick in the pants. He had needed that his whole life, but their daddy hadn't cared enough to do it. He had conceded Will to Sondra. And

Sondra didn't let anyone lay a finger on her baby. Of course, Sondra's say-so had never meant spit to J.D.

"You can't hit me, J.D.," Will challenged, his lower lip jutting out, trembling just a little despite the fierce gleam in his eyes. He offered up the only real threat an eight-year-old boy could use to ward off his big brother. "I'll tell Mama."

J.D. circled around him, his shoulders hunched, his hands curling into fists. Anger was like a red-hot poker inside him, burning, turning his blood to steam in his veins. He was sick of his little brother's threats. He was sick of his little brother, period. Always slacking, always screwing up and never taking the blame. "I'll hit you if I want, you little snot-nosed mama's boy. And if you tell, I'll whup you all over again. You left that gate open and I had to spend the whole goddamn day chasing horses."

"You swore! You'll go to hell!"

"You'll be there first, brat."

Will started to dart away, quickness being his best defense. But J.D. was quicker, grabbing him by the scruff of the neck and wrestling him to the ground. They tussled in the dirt like a pair of tomcats, howling, arms and legs in a tangle, punching and kicking. Will fought with all the wild fury of someone who knew the odds were stacked well against him, jabbing at his brother with fists and boots and elbows.

J.D., who, at twelve, was in the first growth spurt of early adolescence, was taller by a foot and heavier by half. He was too aware of the disparity as he twisted his little brother over in the dirt and rolled on top of him. He loomed over Will, knees on either side of his heaving rib cage, and wished to God the little snot was bigger. He wanted nothing more than the chance to let out all the pent-up anger and pain that had been storing up inside him practically since the day Will was born, but he couldn't hit something that was so much smaller than him. Picking on little guys was for bullies and cowards, and Tucker had told him no Rafferty had ever stooped so low.

Reining back the tangle of feelings inside, he spit in the dirt beside his brother's head and got up off him. Will scrambled to his feet, glaring, tears streaking mud down his face. J.D. curled his lip in his best sneer. "Go run and tell Mama, you little jerk."

"You're a jerk first!" Will shouted, running after him as J.D. turned and headed for the corral.

"Yeah, I'm everything first," J.D. grumbled. "First to do the chores, first to clean up all your messes, first to ride after the stock you let out."

First and forgotten. That was what he was. Will was the little prince, the apple of his mama's eye. And J.D. was slave labor, doing all the jobs Daddy neglected. The afterthought of a marriage Tom Rafferty had mourned deeply, then forgotten.

He stopped at the gate and unwrapped the chain with angry movements, bruising a knuckle in the process. His eyes burned, and he sucked on the joint and fought off a pain that had little to do with his injury.

Will looked at him sideways, his anger melting into contrition. "I didn't mean to leave the gate open, J.D.," he admitted in a small voice. "I don't want you mad at me all the time."

"Why do you care what I think, worm boy?"

" 'Cause you're the only brother I got."

J.D.'s hands stilled on the bars of the gate. They were family. That was what mattered more than anything between them. They were Raffertys. Raffertys stuck together and took care of their own. That was important, especially now. He had heard the late-night conversations between his parents. Sondra telling Daddy how unhappy she was on the Stars and Bars, how she wanted out. She wanted to break them up, to leave and take Will with her. But Daddy said they were family and family had to stick together. No one could take a Rafferty off the Stars and Bars. Nothing mattered more than family—except the land.

He looked down at Will, a suspicious emotion knotting like a fist in his chest. "Yeah," he muttered. "I guess that works both ways."

He shook the memory off, disgusted with himself. God knew, he had more important things to do than reminisce about childhood. The day was sliding away and he had spent half of it beating his head against a brick wall. He shifted in his saddle now and urged his gelding into a canter, eating up the distance to the gate of the holding pasture.

Will rode out to meet him. If his color was better than it had been in the morning, it was impossible to tell for all the dirt on his face. Both he and the gray horse he straddled looked as if they had been ridden long and hard and were equally grateful to drop down into a walk.

"I just brought in the last of them," he said as he turned his gelding around and fell in step with J.D.'s mount. "Tucker went up to the house to start supper. Chaske's seeing to the horses. Anything more for today, boss?"

Will fielded the narrow look J.D. tossed him with a weary version of his infamous grin. He'd been in the saddle for the better part of ten hours, chasing animals that were too ornery and too stupid to live. He felt as if each and every one of them had trampled over his body on their way to the holding pen. He was beat and dirty. Razzing J.D. was going to be the only high point of his day.

On paper, they were equal partners in the ranch. In reality, J.D. was, always had been, and always would be boss of the Stars and Bars. Even when their father had been alive, Will had felt that the real power had lain in J.D., dormant, but strong, far stronger than Tom Rafferty had ever been. All their father's energy had gone into the useless effort of trying to keep Sondra chained to a life she hated. The ranch, for all he had been bound to it by tradition, had never come first with him. But it was J.D.'s mistress, his first love, his only love outside the horses he nurtured and trained.

Will had never felt anything close to his brother's love of the land. To him it was an anchor, something he had been shackled to by an accident of birth. He had never challenged J.D. for control, had always felt more like a cowboy than a rancher. He did his job and gladly left the worry and the responsibility to fall on J.D.'s shoulders.

That weight seemed to be sitting heavy on his brother now. There was a tightness around his mouth, a grim, angry cast to his eyes.

"You talk with Lyle?" Will asked.

"Yeah. For all the good it did. He said he'd hold off for a time, but his mind is made up. He's selling. It's just a matter of who. I told him I'd try to put something together."

"You can't outbid Bryce."

"I shouldn't have to."

"You can't expect Lyle to give you a bargain when Bryce is offering to make him rich. Loyalty goes only so far."

"Is that so?" He shot a hard glance at his brother, then turned to survey his cattle, not wanting to think about how far Will's loyalty would go.

They sat at the pasture gate, their horses content to stand side by side with their heads hanging, nipping at each other in idle play. In the pasture beyond, the cattle that had been herded in during the course of the long day were grazing quietly. Calves slept, curled into lumps on the ground near their mothers, or played in groups, chasing each other, bucking and running.

For a moment J.D. allowed himself to appreciate the quality of those animals. He had worked hard to establish a breeding program that would improve the size and grade of the Stars and Bars cattle. The cows were black angus, good mothers who were hardy and gave ample milk. Their calves, which ranged in color from near white to near black, were the result of crossbreeding with topnotch Charolais bulls, a cross that produced big, blocky animals that matured early and finished out well in the feedlots. But beyond their value, J.D. enjoyed just looking at them, knowing they had been bred here, knowing he was responsible for them, knowing that all the hard work had produced something good and worthwhile.

He thought of Lyle Watkins and wondered what he was thinking on this spring afternoon as he looked over his cattle. If he sold out—*when* he sold out—everything his family had worked for on the Flying K would simply cease to exist.

"It doesn't mean that much to everybody, you know," Will said, his voice low, as if he were blaspheming in church.

J.D.'s jaw tightened. He straightened in his saddle, the old leather creaking a protest. "It's got to mean that much," he said. "Or what the hell are we doing here?"

With nothing more than the pressure of his legs and a shift of his weight, he turned his horse around and rode away.

CHAPTER 7

$\mathcal{J}$. D. saw the fire from a good distance up the hill. Swearing, he nudged Sarge into a gallop. Lucy MacAdam was proving to be as much of a nuisance in death as she had been in life. He cursed himself briefly for taking on the task of looking after her place, but if Miller Daggrepont hadn't come to him, he would have gone to Bryce, and J.D. didn't want Bryce getting any kind of a foot in the door. He intended to have first crack at buying the property. If that meant he had to put up with the headache of looking after the animals and calling the sheriff after vandals trashed the place, then that was a small enough price to pay.

The sight of orange flames through the curtain of the trees put everything else out of his mind. Panic sparked instantly. If a fire weren't contained immediately, there was every chance that it would sweep across acres of forest and grassland, charring everything in its path. He braced himself back in the saddle as the big gelding skidded down the steep trail. Berry bushes and saplings slapped at him and snatched at his clothes. Then they broke onto clear, flat ground and the horse exploded beneath him, hurtling toward the MacAdam place with his ears pinned and his neck stretched, his powerful body rolling beneath J.D.

He lost sight of the flames as the ground dipped and the trail bent around a thick copse of tamarack. His brain raced, leaving the business of staying astride to reflexes developed almost from infancy. He had to formulate a strategy to fight the blaze, wondered how he would summon help, wondered if Bryce would still want the place if it burned to the ground.

Mari stood in the corral, watching the flames lick high into the air. She felt a certain solemnity for the ceremony and a tickle of giddy excitement that stemmed from exhaustion and cognac. She had used the liquor to help start the blaze, then stood back and took a swig in honor of Lucy's last wishes. It went down like liquid gold, burned in her belly, and spread its own fire through her, numbing the raw feelings and lending a certain romantic glow to the proceedings. She tossed the bottle into the blaze and saluted, then jumped back with a shriek as the glass popped and the remaining alcohol went up in a hot burst.

Sheepishly she glanced at the Mr. Peanut tin, which stood on a gatepost and oversaw the bonfire from a safe distance, top hat tilted to a jaunty angle. Through the wavy haze of heat it appeared to be moving, wiggling like a hula dancer, dancing in celebration.

Lucy would have approved of the festivities wholeheartedly. In fact, Mari had planned on her friend standing beside her for the ceremonial burning of the business suits. The bonfire signaled her change of direction as she stood at this crossroads of her life. In one direction lay the life her family had herded her down, a straight and narrow path paved in concrete and stripped of scenery, a toll road that took something essential out of her at each gate. In the other direction lay the great unknown, all the mysteries of life, all the possibilities her soul had yearned for. It was bumpy and hilly and wound through uncharted territory that may be a little scary but promised never to be dull. On the road less traveled there were no expectations, no standards to fall short of, no boundaries, no burdens—except her own hesitancy.

She imagined her faintheartedness vaporizing in the flames. The funeral pyre of the pinstripes and peplums was a symbol of her decision. No one wore panty hose on the road less traveled.

Mr. Peanut seemed to wink at her from the other side of the heat waves.

Suddenly, a horse burst from the wooded slope beyond the gate, huge and red, ears pinned, eyes rolling, mouth opening wide as it abruptly changed gears from a dead run to a sliding stop. The head came up and the powerful haunches angled beneath him, scraping the dirt of the ranch yard, stirring an enormous, billowing cloud of dust. Mari watched, mouth agape, as the rider stepped down while the horse was still in motion. He hit the ground running, his hat flying back off his head.

Rafferty.

He barreled toward her, his face set in furious lines. Barely slowing down, he grabbed up a bucket, dunked it in the water trough outside the gate, and kept on running in a beeline for her pyre.

"No!" Mari launched into motion, lunging toward him, arms outstretched to try to push the bucket aside. They collided ten feet from the fire, Mari bouncing off J.D. like a rag doll that had been hurled at the side of a moving bus. Crying out, she stumbled and went down on her hands and knees in the dirt, only able to watch in horror as he attacked her tribute.

The water splashed into the center of the blaze, dousing the magnificent flames like a blanket. Rafferty kicked the edges of it, scooping the powdery dirt of the corral into it with his boots and with his hands, suffocating the peripheral flames and sending up mushroom clouds of black smoke tinged with dust.

Mari's heart sank with the dying flames. She sat back on her heels, tears pooling in her eyes as he ran to the water tank and returned with another sloshing bucket. The fire hissed its last agonized breath as he doused it. Her fire. The symbol of the death of her old life. Her tribute and sendoff to her old friend. Ruined. Snuffed out, the way her old life had tried to snuff out the fire inside her; snuffed out as Lucy had been snuffed out. The anger and the frustration and the cognac swirled inside her, rose up like a tide, and Mari rose with it.

"You stupid son of a bitch!" she hollered, hurtling herself at him as he backed away from the detritus of her grand gesture. "You stupid shit-for-brains! That was mine!"

She hit him hard in the back, knocking him off balance, pummeling him with her small fists. J.D. dropped the bucket and twisted around, catching a knuckle in the mouth. Swearing, he stumbled sideways, trying to fend off her blows with his hands and forearms. She came at him like a wildcat, teeth bared, eyes narrowed, all hiss and claw, her tangled hair tumbling into her face.

"Knock it off!" he bellowed, staggering back.

Mari lunged at him again, half jumping on him, arms swinging wildly as all rational thought burned away in the face of her temper. She caught him leaning back, and they both tumbled into the dirt, coughing and swearing at the dust that gagged and choked and blinded.

"That was mine!" she shouted again. *"Mine!"* Her first real act of liberation, her homage to her friend, and he had ruined it. She lashed out in retaliation in every way she could—hitting, kicking—

"Ouch! You bit me!" J.D. shouted, outraged, overwhelmed by the sheer force of her fury.

His own anger kicked in as her knee came perilously close to ramming his balls up to his tonsils. Grunting, he twisted and rolled, tumbling her beneath him, pinning her with his weight. Gritting his teeth, he tried to catch her fists as she rained blows on his head and shoulders, grabbing one and then the other and pinning them to the ground beside her head.

"Dammit, I said, quit!"

His voice boomed in her ears. Mari strained and struggled in one final burst, but to no avail. J. D. Rafferty outweighed her by eighty pounds at least, every ounce of it muscle, and all of it pressed down on her, stilling her against her will. They were nose to nose. His arms pressed hers into the dust. An expanse of steel plate disguised as his chest moved heavily against her breasts with every breath he sucked in. His belly pressed against the most feminine part of her, the contact unbearably intimate even through their clothes. His thighs, as heavy as fallen logs, trapped hers and held her there.

Mari glared up at him, too aware that she was powerless against him. Powerless *beneath* him. The heat of his big body seared her through her clothes in a way the fire hadn't managed. His breath came in ragged pants, gusting against hers, his mouth no more than inches from hers. Even through the static of her fury, the memory of his kiss came back—carnal, possessive . . . insulting, insolent.

J.D. met the blue fire in her eyes and it triggered something primal in him. Or maybe it was the way she felt beneath him. Or the memory of the way she tasted in the moonlight. It didn't matter; his body responded automatically, tightening, hardening. She shifted a little beneath him and the feel of her sex against his belly damn near sent him over the edge.

Damnation, he had gone too long without.

"You have a real way about you, Rafferty," she snarled. "Where'd you go to charm school—the World Wrestling Federation?"

A growl was the only reply he gave her as he shoved himself to his feet. Mari scrambled up, trying to shake the dirt out of her clothes. It had gone up her blouse and down the back of her jeans, working its way into private cracks and crevices. It was in her hair and in her teeth. And she had Rafferty to thank. Overgrown, macho bonehead.

"What the hell did you think you were doing?" J.D. demanded, swinging an arm in the direction of the charred remains of her fire.

"None of your damn business."

She stalked past him, feeling the need to put herself between him and the mess. The ceremony had been personal. She hadn't planned on witnesses or conscientious objectors. The idea of Rafferty probing into it made her feel exposed, vulnerable. Vulnerable didn't seem a very smart thing to be around a man like him. He was too tough, too forceful to show much in the way of understanding or compassion. She had seen that firsthand.

Of course, it was impossible to hide the evidence. It spread out behind her, a black, smoldering, oozing stain in the middle of the corral. She couldn't hope to keep him from it. He walked around to the other side, scowling down into the ashes.

"What the hell—?"

With the toe of his boot he dragged a magenta gabardine sleeve from the cinders. He picked it up gingerly by the unburned end and dangled it down, grimacing as if there were still an arm inside it.

"It was a suit, okay?" Mari snapped, snatching it from him and tossing it back into the embers.

"*You* were burning clothes?" His gaze traveled down her with undisguised skepticism, taking in her old jeans and the baggy purple oxford button-down she wore open over an old Stanford T-shirt.

Mari ground her teeth. "I was cremating my past. It was symbolic."

He stared at her as if she had just claimed to be from the moon.

"Men. You wouldn't know symbolism if you sat in it. I'm at a life crossroads. I needed to make a grand gesture."

"Yeah, well," he drawled, "burning half of Montana to the ground would have been a gesture."

"I didn't burn anything that wasn't mine."

"What if the barn had caught fire? Or the house? Or—"

"What's it to you?" Mari challenged, sticking her chin out as she glared up at him. "They're mine too, so—"

"They're what?" J.D. felt as if he'd just run blind into a brick wall. He actually fell back a step from the force of the mental blow.

A relapse of guilt deflated Mari's truculence. She felt . . . unworthy, undeserving. She couldn't remember the last time she had called Lucy just to shoot the bull. She seemed to shrink as the fight went out of her on a sigh. Raking back a handful of hair, she looked away from Rafferty toward the beautiful log house.

"It's mine," she said quietly. "Lucy left it to me."

J.D. watched her carefully as he tried to digest the information. He wasn't sure how to react. He wanted this land for himself, for the Stars and Bars, as an added buffer against the encroachment of outsiders—of Bryce in particular. He had hoped it would be offered for sale by Daggrepont to settle the estate, though that scenario held no guarantees the land wouldn't go to Bryce. Still, Daggrepont was a local. Mary Lee Jennings was a wild card. There was no telling what she would do with it. The only thing he knew for certain was that she thought he was a jerk. And she was right. He'd been nothing but a bastard to her from the word go.

"Swell," he muttered.

Mari wheeled on him, eyes flashing. "Thank you for your kind condolences. It means so much to know people care."

"I won't pretend I liked her," he growled.

"Fine. Then I won't pretend I like you either."

She started to walk away from him, but his hand snaked out and caught hold of her upper arm. Furious, she twisted around and glared at him. "Get your hand off me, Rafferty. I'm sick of being manhandled by you. And I'm sick of your snide remarks about Lucy. I don't give a shit what she did to you. She was my friend. I didn't always like her. I didn't always agree with her. But she was my friend, and I'll be damned if I'll put up with your smart-ass remarks. If you can't manage to master any of the greater social graces, you can at least show a little respect."

J.D. let her go, watching pensively as she stalked to the gatepost and took down a big tin Mr. Peanut. She stood with her back to him, holding the thing against her. Guilt gnawed on his conscience. She was right. He should have had better manners than to speak his mind about Lucy. Especially with the woman who had just inherited her property.

The addendum sat about as well as a gallstone in his gut. His personal code didn't allow for ulterior motives. A man conducted himself accordingly, regardless of circumstance; it was a matter of honor. Well, he thought, chagrined, Lucy had always managed to bring out the worst in him. Seemed she was still doing it, manipulating him from the next dimension.

He blew out a heavy breath and jammed his hands at the waist of his jeans. Women. They were more trouble than they were worth, that was for damn sure. His mouth twisted as he stared at the back of Mary Lee Jennings. She was crying. He could tell by the jerky movements of her shoulders. She was trying valiantly not to. He could tell by the halting breaths she snatched. A sliver of panic shot through him. He didn't know what to do with a crying woman. The only things he knew to do with women were avoid them or have sex with them. Neither option applied.

Feeling awkward and oversize, he walked up behind her and debated the issue of touching her. An apology lodged in his throat like a chicken bone, and he wished fervently that the world would just leave him alone to tend his ranch and train his horses. And people like Mary Lee Jennings and Lucy MacAdam and Evan Bryce would just stay down in California where they belonged.

"I—a—um—I'm—a—sorry."

He practically spat the word out of his mouth. Mari would have laughed if she hadn't felt so miserable. She suspected words didn't come easily to a man like Rafferty. He didn't need an emotional vocabulary to deal with horses and cattle.

Clutching the peanut tin to her chest, she sniffed and tried to swallow her tears, embarrassed to shed them in front of a man who was embarrassed to see them. But they pushed back hard, slamming up against the backs of her eyes, swimming up over the rim of her lashes. *Lucy's dead. Lucy's dead. Lucy's dead.* The line chanted over and over in her mind, and echoing back were words that made her feel selfish and frightened. *I'm all alone. I'm all alone. I'm all alone.*

The shoulder she would have cried on had been reduced to ashes. She felt bombarded—by the decisions she had made about her own life in the past week and by the shocks that had been delivered since her arrival in Montana. All mental circuits overloaded and blew up.

Sobbing, she turned and fell against Rafferty. Any port in a storm. It didn't matter that he was a jerk. He was something big and solid and warm to lean against. And he owed her, dammit. After all his insults, the least he could do was hold her while she cried.

She buried her face against his shoulder and pinned the peanut tin between them, heedless of the thing's edges. For a moment, J.D. was motionless and dumbfounded, panic bolting through him. Then, almost of their own volition, his hands came up and settled on her shaking shoulders.

She was small and fragile. *Fragile.* The word reverberated as he listened to her cry. Her tears seemed to soak through his shirt and into his heart. He couldn't imagine Lucy crying over anything; she had been too tough, too cynical. But little Mary Lee cried as if the world were coming to an end. Because he'd hurt her feelings. Because she'd lost a friend.

"Hush," he whispered, his fingers stealing upward into the baby-fine hair at the nape of her neck. The soft, fresh scent of her hooked his nose and lured his head down. "Shh. I'm sorry, honey. Don't cry. Please don't cry."

The peanut tin was poking him in the stomach. J.D. ignored it. Dormant instincts stirred to life inside him, feelings that were basic and male—the desire to protect, the need to comfort. They slipped through the wall of his defenses in a spot made soft by this woman's tears. She cried as though she had lost everything in the world. He told himself a man had to be made out of stone not to feel sympathy.

She turned her face and shuddered out a breath, and his head dropped another fraction. His cheek pressed against hers.

"Shhh. Hush," he whispered, his lips moving against her skin. Soft as a peach. Warm. Damp and salty with tears. His fingers slid deeper into her tangled mane, cupping her head, tipping it. "Hush now," he murmured.

His gaze locked on her mouth. Her lips were plump and ripe, slightly parted, shiny, tempting.

Mari stared up at him, her heart thundering. His eyes were the warm gray of old pewter, the pupils dilated and locked on her mouth. He seemed to be breathing hard. They both were. His lips were slightly parted. She remembered the feel of them, the taste of him. A weird magnetism pulled on her, pulled her toward him. He wanted to kiss her now. The message vibrated in the air between them. She wanted to kiss him back.

Would he blame her for it afterward?

She stepped back as J.D. started to lower his mouth toward hers. He didn't like her. She ripped herself up one side and down the other for wanting to kiss a man who had treated her so badly. She may have done a great many stupid things in her life, but falling for Neanderthals was not among her faults.

"I need to blow my nose," she said, doing a wonderful job of killing the sexual tension. "Have you got a tissue?"

J.D. fished a clean handkerchief out of his hip pocket and handed it to her, telling himself he was glad that the madness had passed. He was going to have to go and see about getting this need taken care of soon. As soon as the branding and vaccinating was done . . . and the cattle had been moved to the summer pasture . . . and the yearling colts had been gelded . . .

Mari blew her nose and tried to ignore the adolescent surge of embarrassment at her body functions. "I never mastered the art of crying delicately," she said, folding the handkerchief and stuffing it into her pocket. "My sisters can do it. I'm pretty sure they don't have any sinuses."

She wiped away the last tears from her eyes with the sleeve of her shirt and shot a sheepish glance at Rafferty. "Thanks for letting me cry all over you."

He shrugged, feeling awkward and hating it. Annoyance pulled his brows down. "You didn't give me much choice."

"God, you're so gracious."

The big sorrel horse he had charged in on and then abandoned stepped toward her, his big liquid eyes soft with what looked for all the world like concern mixed with curiosity. He was a handsome animal, his coat a dark, glossy copper, a big white star between his eyes. He inched toward her, his reins dragging the ground. Slowly, he stretched his head out and blew on her gently, then stepped a little closer and bussed her cheek with his muzzle. The gesture struck Mari as being sweet and comforting, and a fresh hot wave of tears rose inside her along with a weak laugh.

"Your horse has better manners than you do."

"I reckon that's true enough," J.D. said softly. Sarge caught his subtle hand signal and stepped back from Mari, nodding his head enthusiastically. She laughed, and J.D. ignored the fact that the husky sound pleased him. He hadn't done the trick to impress her, just to stop her from crying again, that was all.

"What's his name?"

"Sarge."

He gave her the information almost grudgingly, as if he thought admitting he had given the animal a name showed some kind of hidden weakness. Mari bit down on a smile. "He's beautiful," she said. One arm still clutching her peanut tin, she reached up and stroked the gelding's face, indulging his begging for an ear-scratching. He closed his eyes and groaned in appreciation.

"He's a good horse."

The words betrayed no overt sentiment, but Mari caught the carefully even tone and her gaze sharpened on the seemingly mindless pat on the shoulder he gave the horse as he caught his reins and hooked one loosely around a rail in the corral fence. The gelding wasn't fooled either. He gave his master a hooded look and nipped at the flap on his shirt pocket. Grumbling, Rafferty fished a butter mint out and handed it over.

Some tough guy. Mari tried to steel herself against the insidious warmth curling around her heart. Just because the horse liked him didn't mean he wasn't a jerk.

"So what are you doing here anyway, Rafferty? Besides spoiling my fun."

"I came to look after the stock," he said, shooting her a sideways glance as he loosened the cinch on his saddle. "Nobody told me not to."

Stock. She'd forgotten there were animals here, hadn't given a thought to the fact that she owned them now too. In fact, she had yet to see them. She hadn't gotten any farther than the corral in her exploration of the place. The burning of the business suits had demanded all her attention. She couldn't have considered accepting Lucy's bequest until she had officially broken that symbolic tie to her past. Now she thought of livestock and panicked.

"Stock?" she said, falling into step beside Rafferty as he headed toward the old barn. "What kind of stock? I'm not sure I'm ready to handle anything that could be considered 'stock.' "

J.D. shot her a look. She couldn't have been much more than five feet five. What there was of her was swallowed up by a huge purple shirt. The tails hung nearly to the ripped-out knees of her tight faded jeans. Her hair was a mess, and there was a smudge of dirt on her upturned nose. She looked up at him with those huge, clear, deep-set eyes, her dark brows knit together in uncertainty.

"Come to think of it," she went on, suddenly pensive, "I can't see Lucy handling 'stock' either. Christ, she never even wanted to open her own beer cans for fear she'd chip a nail." But then, there were a great many things about Lucy that suddenly made no sense. Mari bit her lip and cast a worried look down at the peanut tin in her arms.

"What is that thing?"

Mari blushed a little. She had almost gotten used to the idea of Mr. Peanut, but when she thought about it, it seemed too bizarre to share. "You don't want to know. Trust me."

J.D. let it go as unimportant. "You know how to ride?"

He led the way into the dim interior of the barn. The

thin scent of dust and the sweet aroma of hay filled her head. Beneath it lay the earthy undertone of animals and their droppings, not exactly perfume, but real and natural. J.D. lifted a lid on a grain bin and scooped mixed feed into a coffee can. Mari dug a hand into the grain and sifted it through her fingers, fascinated by the strange shapes and textures. She could identify the kernels of corn and the slivers of oats, but the rest were a mystery.

"Yes, I can ride," she answered absently. "My mother thought it sounded impressive to tell people I was taking riding lessons. Until I expressed an interest in learning to ride circus horses standing up on their backs. Really, I mainly wanted to wear a glittery leotard, but she wouldn't go for that either."

"Gee, you poor kid," J.D. drawled sarcastically.

Mari gave him a sharp look. "Dreams don't have to be practical. It still hurts when they get broken."

Brushing the grain from her palm, she took the coffee can as he handed it to her. He moved to the next bin, lifted the lid, and started dumping brown pellets into several mismatched buckets that stood on the concrete floor. When the buckets were full, he scooped them up and led the way out a side door.

"Here's your ride, if you're of a mind to," J.D. said, feeling small for sneering at her childhood fantasy. "Get yourself a sparkle suit and knock yourself out."

Mari stopped dead and stared at the creature in the grassy paddock. "A *mule?*"

She wouldn't have been surprised at a sleek Thoroughbred or a handsome quarter horse. Lucy loved anything beautiful and expensive. But a *mule?* The animal pricked his long ears and ambled out of the shade of a lean-to as Rafferty took the grain can and dumped it in a big black rubber tub. Sturdy and slick with a glossy seal-brown coat, he was handsome enough as mules went, she supposed. But the big head and long ears were a lot to get past aesthetically.

"Some actress up Livingston-way bought one last summer. Now they're all the rage," J.D. said dryly, rolling his eyes. He had been raised to see animals as useful and necessary, not trendy. He looked the mule over quickly and expertly, automatically checking for any signs of illness or injury. "Tack is in the barn."

Mari slipped between the bars of the fence and circled the mule slowly. The creature kept his nose buried in his grain, but followed her with his eyes. When she squatted down beside his dish, he raised his head a few inches and stopped chewing, giving her a vaguely peeved look out of the corner of his eye.

"Hey there, Clyde. How you doing?"

The mule gave a little snort, chewed some more, watched her. Mari smiled and held a hand out for him to sniff. Clyde reached over and pretended to nip at her, then stuck his nose back in his feed.

"Clyde?" J.D. said skeptically. "Why Clyde?"

"Why not? He strikes me as a Clyde. How does he strike you?"

"As a mule."

"What an imagination you have. Must be a real struggle to keep it from running away with you."

They left Clyde to his grain and continued on through the small pasture to another gate. Gathered in the feeding area were about twenty llamas. The colors of their shaggy coats ranged from black to white, solid to spotted. They stood expectantly around the feed tubs, their magnificent, long-lashed brown eyes fixed on J.D. and Mari.

"Here's your stock," J.D. said with no small amount of sarcasm.

"Llamas! Cool!" She stood still and watched as a fuzzy white baby came to nibble at her shirttail, her eyes wide with wonder. "Lucy never said anything about llamas!"

"Yeah, well," J.D. grumbled. "She was just full of surprises, wasn't she?"

He watched her as she got acquainted with the peculiar creatures, trying not to be swayed by her obvious delight in them. It would have been better for him if she had run screaming in fright. He never liked a person who didn't like animals. They almost always proved untrustworthy.

He didn't want to like Mary Lee. He couldn't associate anyone from Lucy's world with trust.

Mari ignored him, her attention absorbed by the curious animals that came to inspect her. They craned their long necks, sniffed and nibbled and hummed softly. Their gazes were sometimes direct, sometimes shy, always with a quality of secret wisdom in their limpid brown depths.

She had never met a llama up close before. Now she wanted to know everything about them at once—how soft their woolly coats were, what they were saying when they hummed at one another, what they ate, what they thought about. The peanut tin curled protectively in one arm, she touched them and stroked them and let one rub his soft upper lip against her palm. She chatted with them as if they were people, introducing herself, explaining her connection to Lucy.

One poked at the peanut tin with its small nose, and she laughed and backed away, a little apprehensive as they followed her en masse.

"Bring me up to speed, here, Rafferty," she said, making a face as a black one tried to lick her cheek. The smell of them filled her nose like the scent of damp wool sweaters left on a radiator to dry. "What exactly do llamas do? I mean, they're not dangerous or anything, are they?"

J.D. snorted. They were next to worthless by his scale, a curiosity. Not that that was their fault, he admitted as he absently scratched the back of a black and white male. "If they don't like you, they spit on you."

"Ah. Big, hairy, smelly things that spit. It's like junior high revisited," Mari said dryly, narrowing her gaze on the one that had gotten a firm hold on her shirt cuff. "In fact, this one looks exactly like the guy who sat behind me in science class. I'd recognize those ears anywhere."

She leaned toward the llama as she gently extricated her sleeve from its teeth. "You didn't happen to be called Butt Breath in a past life, did you?"

The llama drew its head back and regarded her with what looked like offense. Mari arched a brow.

"What did Lucy do with them?" she asked as she

watched J.D. pour their feed pellets into various tubs. The llamas abandoned her for their supper. They took dainty mouthfuls and chewed delicately, following her and J.D. with their eyes.

"Made money, I expect," J.D. said, his mouth twisting as if at a sour taste. "I can grow a steer that'll feed a family of four for a year and get next to nothing for it. Grow a llama—which is good for exactly nothing—and the whole damn world beats a path to your door."

Mari gave him a look as they slipped back out the gate. "Not everything has to be edible to be worthwhile."

He just grunted and headed back toward the barn, his long, powerful legs absorbing the distance so that she had to almost jog to keep up to him.

"This is all a little overwhelming," she said, scooping her hair back behind her ear. "I just can't picture the Lucy I knew toting feed and shoveling shit."

"She didn't. She had a hired hand."

That news stopped Mari in her tracks. The ranch, the llamas, a hired hand, the *Lifestyles of the Rich and Famous* friends. Christ, just how much had Lucy inherited in the windfall that let her move here? This all had to have cost a fortune. *Check the bank balance, heiress.*

"Who? Where is he now?"

Rafferty's broad shoulders rose and fell. "Just some hand. They drift around, pick up work here and there. I imagine he took off after the accident. Guess he figured a dead woman wouldn't pay him."

The news he delivered so matter-of-factly rested uneasily on Mari. Lucy had been shot. Her hired hand took off immediately afterward. She caught hold of J.D.'s arm as he reached for the barn door. "Did the sheriff ever question this guy?"

"There wasn't any call for it. The dentist or whatever the hell he was 'fessed up."

"But he claimed he never saw Lucy."

"Idiot shoots a woman instead of an elk. Doesn't surprise me he claims he didn't see her."

He opened the door for her and closed it behind him.

The feed buckets rattled as he set them down next to the bins.

"What about your uncle?" Mari asked, following him as he dumped dry cat food into half a dozen dishes and felines of all descriptions came running from every nook and cranny of the barn. "The one who found her body? Did he see anything?"

He turned around abruptly, suddenly much too close and much too large. He loomed over her, his features set in angry, uncompromising lines that were exaggerated by the shadows of the gloomy barn. "I told you last night to steer clear of him," he said, his voice a low growl. He poked her sharply in the sternum with a forefinger, making her blink. "I meant it."

"Why?" Mari asked, amazed she'd found the nerve. "What has he got to hide? If he didn't do it—"

"He didn't do it," J.D. snarled through his teeth. "Leave him alone. He's been through enough."

Mari swallowed hard as he stepped around her and stalked out of the barn. She rubbed at the sore spot on her breastbone, dimly aware that her heart was knocking hard behind it. A dozen questions rushed through her mind about the mysterious Del Rafferty, about the hired man who had conveniently slipped away. She bit them all back. Rafferty's temper was at the end of its leash, straining for an excuse to rip into her. She really didn't feel up to giving him one.

The sun was disappearing behind the mountains to the west, casting the ranch yard into long shadows and tall silhouettes. J.D. stood beside his horse, snugging up the cinch, preparing to leave. Thoughts of drifters and faceless men with guns slid into Mari's mind like dark, oily serpents. The eerie sense of abandonment the place had given her that first night began creeping in with the shadows.

"Rafferty, wait!" she called, trotting away from the barn.

He swung into the saddle and settled himself, resting his hands on the saddle horn, waiting.

"Look," she said, laying her free hand against the sor-

rel's warm neck. "I don't know anything about llamas—
except that they seem very . . . spiritual. I don't know
what I'm going to do with this place or with them. This
has all happened so fast, I'm not so sure it's even real."

He didn't say a word, just sat up there, staring down at
her from beneath the brim of his hat.

"What I'm saying is, I need some help."

What she wasn't saying was that she wanted him to
answer her questions. She needed answers. She needed to
achieve some kind of closure concerning Lucy's sudden
departure from the present tense. What she wasn't saying
even to herself was that the idea of seeing him again held
a certain attraction. Ornery, obstinate jerk that he was,
he wasn't hard to look at. And those small chinks in his
armor intrigued her—his affection for animals and his
reluctance to let her see it, the gentle way he had held her
while she cried. Besides that, he was a link to Lucy, she
reminded herself.

"If you wouldn't mind," she stumbled on, uncertain of
the local etiquette, wishing he would simply pick up the
ragged threads of the conversation and finish the thought
himself, as anyone in her past life would have done. "It's
just for a week or two. I'll pay you—"

"I don't want your money," he said sharply, offended.
"I don't take money from neighbors."

A part of him was sorely tempted to turn her down all
the way around. He didn't like the feelings she shook
loose inside him. He didn't like where she came from or
who her friends were. But she owned this land now, land
that he wanted. If he didn't help her, she would turn
elsewhere.

She looked up at him, her dark brows tugging together
in consternation. "But—"

"I'll see to the stock," he said, pulling down the brim
of his hat. He lifted his reins and Sarge instantly brought
his head up, ready for the next command. "I just won't
take money for it."

Mari shrugged, at a loss, feeling once again like a visitor in a foreign land. "Suit yourself."

"Yes, ma'am," he murmured, nodding. "I usually do."

She watched him ride away, frustration and weariness rubbing at her temper. Something else thrummed beneath it all, something she didn't have the patience to deal with. She didn't have the patience to handle attraction to a man who made her want to scream and tear her hair out. Men like that, attractions like that, were good for only one thing—wild, hot, mind-numbing sex. She hadn't come to Montana for wild, hot, mind-numbing sex. She had come for friendship and a fresh start.

But as she walked toward the house with the Mr. Peanut tin tucked in the crook of her arm, her mind drifted to a line from Lucy's letter and a warm blush washed through her from head to toe. *Ride 'im, cowgirl . . .*

She climbed the porch steps and sat down on a bench with her back against the log wall and her eyes on the hillside where Rafferty had disappeared among the trees. She had more important things to think about, such as what she was going to do with this ranch and the llamas, and what she was going to do about the uneasiness that tightened like knots inside her when she thought of Lucy's death.

The sun slipped farther behind the mountains. Shadows crept in from all sides. The knots twisted in her belly.

A killer who never saw his victim. A drifter who vanished. A man J. D. Rafferty didn't want her near. A lifestyle that cost the moon. A last letter that made no sense.

"You've got a lot to answer for, Luce," she muttered, her arm around the peanut tin, her eyes on the hillside that suddenly felt as though it were staring back.

He watched the woman through a Burris Signature 6-24X bench rest/varmint scope, clicking the iris adjustment to get the lighting just right. A Ruger M77 Mark II held tight into his shoulder, he rested against the trunk of a fir, silent, still, so still he blended in with his surroundings as if he were a rock or a tree. It was that quality of stillness that had made it possible for him to live as long as he had.

Not that that was such a good thing.

Automatically, his mind calculated range and bullet drop. He had learned the ballistics tables not long after he had learned the multiplication tables, and he knew them better. He wouldn't use the figures now. It was just good to work the mind, that was all. Keep the wheels oiled and moving.

He had told himself to stay away from this place, to stay away from the blonde. But she had haunted him badly the last two nights and he had finally decided he needed to see if she had come back to the house.

This wasn't the woman he had expected. She was blonde, like the other one had been, but different. Much different. He could tell not only by the way she dressed, but by the way she moved, the way she sat. Relief flooded through him, weakening his limbs. The Ruger bobbed in his hands, suddenly weighing a thousand pounds. She wasn't the one.

The woman laughed, a husky, healthy sound that floated up the mountainside and brushed across his ears like sweet music. Not like the other one. Her laugh had held an edge to it, a bitter sharpness. The echo of that laugh brought flashes of memory, like a strobe light in his head. Darkness. Dogs. The crack of a rifle. The sight of blood. The smell of death.

He dropped the Ruger down and pressed the heels of his hands against his eye sockets, as if the pressure might blot out the scenes. Panic rose inside him, clogging his throat, stiffening his lungs, making him shake. The images in his head tumbled into a confusing mix of the distant past, the recent past, the present. Sounds of war, sounds of laughter, screams of the wounded and the dying, orders, shots, explosions, the stench of death and decay and swamp. His heart pounded like an angry fist against his sternum. Sweat soaked his clothing, robbing his body of heat as the cool evening air closed around him.

Sucking in as much air as his aching lungs would allow, he held the breath and concentrated on pushing every thought from his mind. As the mental screen went blessedly blank, he exhaled slowly, counting the seconds, concentrating on slowing his heart rate.

Every moment of his life was like taking a shot—he had to stay centered, in control, tight within himself. Focus, aim, take a breath, exhale half, caress the trigger, start again. That was how he made it. One shot at a time. No distractions.

No pretty blondes with husky voices.

Taking up the rifle, he rose from his crouch and started up the mountain, letting the darkness swallow him up like a phantom.

CHAPTER 8

*S*amantha finished work at four for the first time in a week. The evening was hers. The thought made her stomach cramp with dread. She hated the idea of spending time alone in the small house she had shared with Will. It was so empty without him. The quiet pressed in on her until she could stand it no longer.

She couldn't go into the tiny kitchen without seeing him standing there with messy dishes and pots and pans stacked around him, his grin exuberant as he cooked spaghetti. He always made enough for an army. The freezer compartment of the old refrigerator was virtually an icy wall of frozen spaghetti in Ziploc bags. She couldn't go into the bedroom without seeing him sprawled across the mattress, naked, frowning in his sleep, or with those devilish blue eyes locked on her, one hand reaching out to her, inviting her to come make love with him.

Longing as strong, as desperate as the need to breathe, dug into her heart and tore it open all over again. The pain flowed through her like fresh, hot blood.

What went wrong, Will? Did I need you too much? Did you need more?

She thought of the way she had jumped at his offer of marriage. In her memory it was the most casual of questions. He had asked her with no more concern than if he had asked her to go off on a wild ride with him. And in her memory she all but pounced on him, grabbing on to him with greedy hands that threatened to choke the life out of him.

No matter how she looked at it, the blame always

131

came back to her. She had been too demanding, too clinging, too needy. She wasn't pretty enough or woman enough or experienced enough in bed. As angry as she was with him for walking out, as hurt as she was by his cheating, she always blamed herself.

That truth made her think of her mother, slinking around her father like a whipped dog, her eyes downcast, always apologizing for imagined sins. She hated to think that she compared with her mother in any way, had always hated to think that she was even related to any of those people in that shabby house with the weedy yard and the dirty-faced children. The guilt that thought brought was no more welcome than the truth that the Neills were her family.

She looked around the bar as she untied her apron, folded it, and tucked it into a cubbyhole. People were drifting in for happy hour. Smiling, beautiful, wealthy people. Couples. Her focus homed in on the women, who all seemed to hold some secret wisdom in their eyes that she couldn't even guess at. They had it all. They had their husbands and their fancy cars and lavish homes and beautiful clothes. She imagined that when they looked at her they knew that she had nothing, was no one. All she had waiting for her at home was Rascal, the puppy Will had given her for her birthday two weeks before he left her.

"Are you all right, Samantha luv?"

Mr. Van Dellen leaned close to her, brows knit in question. She fought down the lump in her throat and murmured an answer she hoped would satisfy him.

"You're sure?" he asked. "Because if you need to talk to someone or—"

"No, really, Mr. Van Dellen. I'm fine. I'm just tired, that's all."

He pressed his lips together in way that made her think he was holding back a challenge to her statement. She tried to smile, shrugging off his concern. He didn't look convinced, but he didn't call her on it either.

"All right," he said on a sigh, and moved off to answer a call from one of his customers.

Samantha felt the tension seep out of her like air from a balloon. She couldn't talk about her troubles with him. He was nice and all, but everybody knew he and Mr. Bronson were . . . well . . . queer.

She didn't like the way the word sounded even in her own mind. It seemed harsh and mean, when Mr. Van Dellen and Mr. Bronson were both very kind to her. But she couldn't get past her upbringing either. The thought of two men . . . together . . . She gave a little shiver of revulsion. No, she couldn't talk with Mr. Van Dellen about Will. He couldn't possibly understand.

The problem was, she didn't know a soul who *would* understand. Not for the first time in her life she wished for a real friend and for the courage it took to be a part of that kind of friendship.

With a heart that felt as heavy as the purse she slung over her shoulder, she started for the side exit and stepped directly into the path of Evan Bryce.

"Samantha!"

The smile that stretched across his face was one for old friends, and it threw her off balance more than their near collision had. "I'm sorry, Mr. Bryce," she mumbled. "I wasn't looking where I was going."

"Don't apologize," he ordered with a mock frown as he settled a hand on her shoulder. "And you call me Bryce. All my friends do." She started to object, but he gave her shoulder a little squeeze, his pale eyes shining. "Come on. We *are* friends, aren't we?" he said with a big square grin. "I don't loan my handkerchiefs out to just anyone, you know."

Samantha ducked her head, blushing at the memory of crying on his shoulder. God, he was Evan Bryce and she was just Sam Neill from the wrong side of town, just a little nobody. She couldn't be a part of Bryce's crowd any more than a mutt dog could run with greyhounds.

Bryce studied her reaction from under his lashes. "Come join us," he said, steering her toward his table.

"No, I can't."

"Why not? You're off duty. There's no reason you shouldn't join us for a drink, is there?"

There was every reason. She didn't belong. She wouldn't fit in. She was married. She needed to get home — To what? The thoughts tumbled through her head, clearly visible in her dark eyes.

"You deserve a treat, I think," he said softly, their shared secret warm and kind in his gaze as he tilted her chin up with a forefinger. "Don't you?"

Samantha stared at him for a moment, feeling herself needing his attention like a parched plant needed water. Her loneliness swelled inside her. The thought of going to her empty home had tears pressing against the backs of her eyes.

"Come make some new friends," he murmured.

She looked at the people sitting at his usual table along the back wall. Smiling, beautiful, wealthy people. Laughing. Happy. She could be a part of that for a little while. She thought of Will, feeling that she was somehow betraying him. Then she thought of Will with the blonde from the Hell and Gone . . . and she thought of her empty house, and her empty life. She deserved something more, didn't she? A drink, a friend, a little time away from the aching loneliness.

"Yeah," she said, nodding to herself. "Yes, I'd like that."

"Good girl," Bryce said, flashing his Robert Redford grin again as he herded her toward his table.

Mari walked toward the Mystic Moose, hands jammed in the pockets of her denim jacket. She hadn't been able to manage the idea of dinner in the elegan dining room at the lodge. Even after a shower to wash the smoke and dust off, she felt something of the ranch lingering on her, something that made her long for simpler surroundings and country music on a jukebox. Supper at the Rainbov Cafe had seemed the perfect thing. Chicken-fried steak and white gravy. Lyle Lovett and his Large Band on the side. Nora Davis in her pink uniform and her air of world wisdom.

Replete, she strolled down the sidewalk, letting the

town fill her senses, letting the tensions of the day drift away. Main Street was fairly busy. There was a line of big old pickups out in front of the Hell and Gone, lined up like horses at a hitching rail. Even from more than a block away she could hear Garth Brooks advising folks to go against the grain, the sharp clack of billiard balls breaking over his cowboy voice.

She wondered if J.D. hung out there. She told herself it didn't matter.

The stores that serviced the common folk stood dark and silent, but the trendy shops were still lit up, their doors held open with crocks of geraniums. There wasn't a soul going in or out of those boutiques that didn't look like an outsider.

It seemed odd to her that she should be able to spot them. She was, after all, an outsider herself. But something within her protested the label. She felt as comfortable strolling these streets as if she had been raised here. More so. The upscale haunts of her mother and sisters back in Sacramento had never felt anything but foreign to Mari.

She stopped now in front of the post office and studied her shadowed reflection in the dark glass of the front window. Her hair was a mess. She had let it dry on its own after her shower and it made a wild cloud of waves and tangles around her head, thick strands tumbling into her face. She snatched them back behind her ears, her small hands darting out the ends of her too-long jacket sleeves and disappearing again as she dropped her arms.

She didn't think she looked like an outsider. Certainly, she didn't bear any resemblance to the people drifting in and out of the Latigo Boutique. Even the ones in jeans had an expensive look about them, a sleek quality. *Sleek* was not a word anyone had ever used to describe her.

"Marilee." Her mother ground her name out between her beautifully capped teeth. She flapped her manicured hands at the sides of her Mark Eisen suit in a gesture of futility. "Can't you even try to make an effort to look good? Your hair is impossible and you dress as if you shop at Goodwill."

"*I do shop at Goodwill. It's the best place to get jeans.*"

Abigail Falkner Jennings heaved a sigh of supreme motherly disgust and shook her head. Her perfect champagne-blond tresses swung just enough for effect and settled perfectly into place. "*I don't understand you, Marilee. Why can't you be more like your sisters?*"

Because I'm me, Mom, she thought to herself, her heart sinking. *Mari the Misfit.*

For twenty-eight years she had struggled to be a good Jennings girl like Lisbeth and Annaliese were good Jennings girls. Instead, Marilee had always been known as *that* Jennings girl. The one who stuck out like a bunioned big toe through a fine silk stocking.

She had felt like an outsider her whole life, but she didn't feel that here, standing in front of the New Eden, Montana, post office.

Rafferty thought she was an outsider.

"*Damned city bitches . . . Are you like your friend Lucy? You want to know what it's like to tease a cowboy?*"

"No," she whispered, not wanting to remember the sensation of his body against hers or the taste of his kiss. Not wanting to wonder what Lucy had done to him or with him.

She walked on down the street and turned on impulse into a New Age shop called Selah, just for the distraction of people and lights. The store was tiny, a rough cedar cubbyhole crowded with bookshelves and displays of crystals and candles and baskets of polished stones. The spicy scent of incense filled the air like a thick perfume. From the speakers of a tape deck came the sounds of birds, running water, the wind in the trees—nature in a box. Mari's lips quirked at the idea. Who would come to this land of paradise and settle for its sounds on so many inches of flimsy tape?

"How's the obsidian working?"

She turned away from a display of birch twigs in a bark vase and jerked her gaze up to meet M. E. Fralick's intense visage. She was in another of her jumpers, this one deep blue over a salmon silk T-shirt. A cameo on a strip of blue velvet circled her graceful throat.

"Excuse me?"

Behind the big lenses of her glasses, M.E. rolled her eyes with a drama that befitted her profession, propping one long hand on her hip and gesturing with the other to the heavens, invoking the attention of who knew what gods. "She's not centered," she said with impatient disgust. Turning her attention back to Mari, she explained as if she were speaking to the most backward of children. "The stone I gave you yesterday. Obsidian. Obsidian works wonders for blocking disturbing vibrations."

"Oh, well . . ." Mari shrugged apologetically. She dug the small stone out of her jacket pocket and held it up to the light. "I probably need something more the size of a basketball. But I appreciate the thought. Thanks."

The actress shook her head, frowning gravely. "You *must* get centered. Talk to Damien, darling," she said, nodding to the enormous bald man behind the counter. "He's a Zen master."

Mari eyed him dubiously. He looked like a hairless version of Chef Paul Prudhomme. His bulk took up the entire space behind the counter. She couldn't help thinking that if he got himself truly centered, small moons would go into orbit around him.

A fresh group of customers streamed into the shop, snagging M.E.'s attention, and Mari managed to escape the actress and the store without the pleasure of meeting the Zen master.

She returned to the Moose as the moon was beginning to rise over the Absarokas and went up to her room to get her guitar. Rafferty notwithstanding, she had enjoyed her time out back of the lodge the night before. Just the moon and the mountains and her music. The prospect was more soothing than a wheelbarrow of obsidian.

Kevin Bronson was standing in the hall when she stepped off the elevator. He looked up at her from the stack of reports in his hands and grinned engagingly.

"Hey, Lucy told us you played," he said, gesturing at her old guitar with the papers.

"She did?"

"Yeah, she said you were great. She said you were wasting yourself in lawyers' offices, that you should have been in L.A. or Nashville or someplace, doing justice to your talent."

"Lucy said that?"

It seemed inconceivable to her. Lucy had listened to her play on a few occasions during jam sessions in local bars. Sometimes during their B&B sessions in Mari's apartment when the conversation had run out she would pick up her guitar and just toy with it, sing a few bars of something that had been taking shape in her head, absently, casually; and Lucy would listen and sip her beer and make a wry comment when she was done. *You oughta be a star, Marilee.* Idle talk. Just something to fill the silence after the last note.

Kevin seemed a little baffled by her surprise, but he was too well bred to comment. He stood there in navy pleated chinos and a white polo shirt. A Yale boy from his *GQ* haircut to the tips of his Top-Siders.

"I was just on my way into the bar to join Drew for coffee. Will you come with us?" He smiled again, even white teeth flashing in his lean face. "Maybe we'll be able to persuade you to play something for us."

She laughed and fell in step beside him. "Don't worry about twisting my arm; I'm shameless."

They sat at a table near the fire and talked over French roast spiked with Irish cream. Mari told them about her adventure with Miller Daggrepont, and they both shook their heads and chuckled over Lucy's choice of resting places.

"That's positively macabre," Drew said, sipping his coffee. "How very Lucy."

"I can't believe she left everything to me," Mari blurted out into the silence, needing to say it again even though she felt as if she were confessing to a crime.

Drew and Kevin exchanged a glance, but there were no exclamations of shock or denial. Drew curled his fingers over the head of the guitar she had propped against the table and rocked it gently. "Will you stay?"

"I don't know. I don't know what to think," she said, but she thought of the view off the deck of the log house, the sense of peace she absorbed from the mountains, the sense of fitting in she had longed for in futility her whole life. She thought of Rafferty rolling her beneath him in the dust of the corral, holding her awkwardly while she cried, and a warmth rose inside her that had little to do with the low-burning flames on the fieldstone hearth.

She forced herself to think of Lucy, and the questions came to the surface of her mind like oil on water.

"So what was the deal with this hired man she had working for her?" she asked. "I heard he just vanished after the accident."

"Kendall Morton?" Kevin made a face. "Sleazy. I always thought he looked like Pigpen grown up and gone bad. Tattoos, bad teeth, B.O."

Drew took a sip of his coffee and nodded. "Odd fellow. Never had much to say. Always skulking about in the background."

"The guy is that weird and nobody thought to question him after Lucy's death?" Mari said, gaping in disbelief.

"There was no reason to," Drew explained. "Sheffield came forward and that was the end of it. Besides, Morton had no reason to kill her."

"Since when do people need a reason?"

"Motive," he said with an elegant shrug. "Rules of evidence. You ought to be familiar with the procedure. Morton lacked motive—"

"But not opportunity, probably not means, certainly not suspicious behavior. Do you have any idea where he went?"

His brows came together in a look that seemed more confused than curious. "Why are you trying to make more of this than what it was? It was an accident; they happen." She felt his gaze on her for several moments, probing while she stared down into her coffee. She thought she could feel questions in it, in him, but all he said when he spoke again was "It was an accident, luv. Let it go.

"Play something for us, will you?" he said, tilting her guitar toward her so that she had to take it or let it fall. "Lucy told us you have an extraordinary voice."

Relieved to let the topic go, Mari slid her chair back and took up the old guitar, testing strings, fiddling with the tuning pegs. "I was supposed to be a cellist," she said. "My sister Lisbeth plays the violin; Annaliese, the flute. Mother thought it would impress her friends if we could play as a trio for charity functions."

"What happened?" Kevin asked.

Her mouth twisted at the memory in a soft combination of a smile and a frown. "My instructor said my bow work was reminiscent of a hacksaw on a chain-link fence. I started skipping the lessons in favor of hanging out with an aging hippie who ran a health food store down the block. He used to jam with the Grateful Dead." She arched a dark brow as she settled her fingers on the strings. "Mother was unimpressed when she found out, but . . . so it goes . . ."

She strummed a chord, appreciating as always the perfect resonance of the old guitar; then she began picking out a gentle, familiar rhythm and joined in with the melody in her low, rich voice. The song was about the rain and the end of a relationship, a woman contemplating what she's lost and moving on with her life; a song about the rhythm of the blues. She never gave a thought to how strongly it reflected her own life. It simply came out as honest as the truth. The emotions and impressions twined together inside her and rolled out in a voice as dark and sweet as the coffee they had drunk.

When she finished she sat there for a moment, lost, unaware of the silence that had descended all around the room. A ripple of applause snapped her back. She rolled her eyes a little, feeling sheepish, and raised her hand in acknowledgment, trying to wave the bar patrons back to their conversations.

Kevin looked astonished, enormously pleased with her, which Mari wrote off as his natural state. He had that excited-puppy air about him, a sense of youthful naivete that had nothing to do with age. Drew's scrutiny was more weighty; she tried to shrug it off, reaching for her coffee cup, wishing for a cigarette.

"Lucy was right," Kevin declared. "You were wasting yourself on lawyers."

"Yeah, well, you don't know the half of that," she said dryly, taking a sip.

"You deserve an audience," Drew said. "We'd love to have you play here as long as you're staying. We have a trio that plays on weekends. Do say you'll join them."

Mari made a face. "I don't horn in on other musicians. Maybe I'll talk with them."

"You already have," he said, green eyes shining. "I'm the piano man."

They shared a laugh, and Mari marveled at how good it felt, how good *she* felt, sharing this time with these new friends. Sacramento and Brad Enright and her family suddenly seemed years in the past, half a world behind her.

"I hope that won't be the last we hear from you, Marilee."

Evan Bryce smiled down on her like a long-lost friend. Mari bent her mouth into a polite social smile and murmured something appropriately humble. She had taken an instant dislike to him, in part because of his connection to Lucy's death. The rest was intangible. She didn't question it. Her instincts regarding human nature had been sharpened to a fine point in her years of legal work. She seldom wasted time questioning those instincts. Something about his I'm-your-best-friend act just didn't ring true.

He looked much as he had the first time she had met him—the same high-heeled boots, the same skin-tight jeans that advertised his gender in no uncertain terms, the same expensive-looking belt that was constructed of hand-tooled leather and bone ferrules that looked as if they had been "salvaged" from the breastplate of a Cheyenne warrior. He had traded his denim work shirt for a fine linen poet's shirt with billowing sleeves. Half the buttons were left undone in a look that was calculatedly careless. She got the impression that the bare chest and tight pants were overcompensation for something—probably his height or lack thereof.

"I hear you've suddenly become a property owner in our little paradise," he said, hooking a thumb in the pocket of his jeans. A chuckle tumbled out of him at her surprise. "The curse of the small town, I'm afraid. News travels at an alarming rate. Of course, I've kept an ear to the ground, so to speak. Lucy's property borders mine."

"Yes, I know." *That's why she's dead.* She bit the words back, too well schooled in social niceties to be so blunt. Besides, in all fairness, he hadn't been the idiot with the rifle.

"Does this mean you'll be joining our community?" he asked, looking too hopeful to be believed. "Or will you sell?"

"It's too soon to say."

"Of course," he murmured, tipping his head in concession. "Well, if you would like a tour of the property or the area, don't hesitate to ask. I'd be more than happy to squire you."

"Thanks."

"It's a lovely property. Lucy was very comfortably ensconced there. Did she ever happen to tell you how she came to own it?"

There was an odd sharpness in his gaze. Mari wasn't sure whether he was asking an idle question or waiting to see if she passed some secret test. She answered the only way she could.

"She told me she saw it while she was vacationing here. Then she came into some money and decided to buy it."

If there were more to the story—and Mari was certain there was—she didn't know it. She wondered if Bryce did.

He gave nothing away with his expression. The light from the fire glowed against his high forehead. He dropped his lashes to half mast. "Lucy was very lucky . . . and very clever."

"We all know how clever Lucy was," Drew said, drawing Bryce's scrutiny.

"Yes," he said, pulling the word into extra syllables. "Too clever for her own good at times."

A strange tension held the moment in its grip. Then Bryce turned back to Mari with the grin firmly in place. "I hope we'll get a chance to hear you sing again, Mari. You're very talented."

"Thanks."

He said his good-byes and went back to the entourage at his own table. Kevin glared down into his coffee cup, his jaw set. Drew rubbed a finger along his lower lip, his eyes hooded. He glanced up at her, looking almost sinister in the flickering shadows of the firelight.

"He'd dearly love to have that land," he said softly. "So would J. D. Rafferty, for that matter. Not that a hundred-odd acres will make much of an impression on Bryce's holdings. Rumor has it he's up to eighty thousand acres."

"God."

"Yes." He cut a glance across the room. Bryce was laughing as one of his guests raised a glass in a toast. Samantha Rafferty sat to his right in the chair usually occupied by Bryce's cousin, Sharon Russell. Samantha laughed as well, though her head was ducked down, as if she didn't want anyone to see that she hadn't gotten the joke. Drew frowned. "He collects land like some people collect stamps." He had his own suspicion that land wasn't all Evan Bryce collected, but he kept that to himself and made a mental note to have a private chat with Samantha the next time she came in to work.

"Interesting man," Mari murmured.

Kevin shoved his chair back from the table, his head down. "Excuse me," he mumbled. "I have work to do." With clumsy hands he gathered the papers he had brought in with him and left.

Drew sighed and rubbed his left temple.

Mari felt suddenly as if she were intruding on something very private. She slid the guitar from her lap and rose. "Thanks for the coffee. I think I'll turn in. I want to get up early. Wouldn't want to miss that sunrise."

Drew forced a smile, but it vanished when he caught

hold of her wrist. "Watch yourself with Bryce, luv," he murmured. "Lucy enjoyed playing with snakes, but then, she had fangs of her own. I wouldn't want to see you hurt."

"Hurt how? Literally?"

"Just be careful."

He rose then too, and left by the same back door Kevin had taken, leaving Mari standing by the fire, her eyes on Evan Bryce as he effortlessly charmed the young woman beside him, her thoughts on the serpent in the Garden of Eden.

"You had a good time tonight, Samantha?"

Samantha smiled shyly at the man strolling beside her up the cracked sidewalk to her empty house. Bryce had insisted on following her home to make certain she was all right. His beautiful cousin waited for him in the Mercedes convertible parked at the curb behind Samantha's old junker of a Camero.

"Yeah," she said, shrugging as if to discount the pleasure. "It was a lot of fun."

"Everyone enjoyed having you there. You're a breath of fresh air, so . . . untainted by the world."

"Naive, you mean."

"Not in a way meant to insult you. You're young and beautiful and full of promise, with so much ahead of you."

Like another night spent in an empty bed. Like a future full of days waiting tables at the Moose. The thoughts weighed her down like stones as she climbed the sagging steps to her front porch.

Bryce took her hands and turned her to face him when she would have reached for the door handle. His expression was earnest and fatherly—or what she had always imagined fatherly should be. Certainly her father had never shown this kind of interest in her. He'd never shown an interest in any of his children, had treated them as if they were nothing more than half a dozen stray dogs that seemed constantly underfoot.

"Don't let this broken heart close you off, honey," Bryce advised. "Your husband is a fool. If he fell off the earth tomorrow, the world would go on turning, you would still have a life, and, I dare say, it would be a better one. You have so much within yourself you have yet to discover and explore, so much potential. Don't snuff it out."

Tears sprang to Samantha's eyes. Why couldn't Will be the one telling her how wonderful she was? Because he obviously didn't see in her what Bryce saw. If he had, he wouldn't have gone looking for that elusive something in other women.

"Hey, no tears, now," Bryce murmured, reaching up to brush one from her cheek. "You've cried enough. When is your next day off?"

"The day after tomorrow."

"Perfect," he said, smiling. "You'll come out to the ranch and spend the day. Go swimming, go riding, be with people who appreciate you."

She started to protest, but he didn't listen. He squeezed her hands and leaned forward to brush a paternal kiss against her cheek.

"I'll pick you up myself. Be ready by nine. We'll go riding. Have a picnic. It'll be great."

Then he was gone, gliding down off her shabby porch and striding gracefully toward the sleek Mercedes.

Samantha let herself into the darkened house, not bothering to turn on a light. The light from the street-lamp on the corner shone in through the windows well enough for her to see. As always, she had harbored the secret hope that Will would be waiting for her. It was a hope she never acknowledged until the disappointment struck her.

He wasn't there. He was probably down at the Hell and Gone, laughing and drinking, his arm around some girl with tight jeans and big boobs. He probably wasn't thinking about her, didn't wonder if she was lonely, didn't know she had spent the evening with people who drove sports cars and drank champagne. Would he care?

The question slipped into her heart like a knife. Now

that there was no one to see them, no one to talk her out of them, the tears fell. She sank down onto the scarred wooden floor of the living room, bending over, curling into a ball. Her long braid fell over her shoulder and lay like a length of rope on the floor.

Rascal scampered in from the kitchen, all feet and ears and wagging tail. He was part golden retriever and part who-knew-what, big and clumsy and brimming with love. He barked at her for a moment, growls and whines mixing in his throat as he tried to decide what to do about her. Finally, Samantha sat up and reached for him, and he clambered into her lap, all too happy to give her something to hug and to lick the tears from her cheeks.

And she wrapped her arms around the puppy and sobbed as hard as her heart could stand, crushed by the thought that the dog he had given her cared more about her than Will.

"What do you think? Does the Jennings woman know what Lucy was into?"

Bryce turned and admired his cousin. She was quite stunning by moonlight. "I don't know yet. She hasn't given any indication of it."

Sharon reached back with one hand and freed her blond mane from its neat twist, tossing her head. "I can't imagine Lucy leaving everything to her without including all her dirty little secrets in the bargain."

"It won't matter," he said, thinking of other complications. "Nothing to worry over."

He really wasn't concerned at all. It was a game to him. A game he couldn't lose. The stakes were huge for some, but he held nearly all the cards. That was the beauty of power and a brilliant mind.

Lucy had understood. She might eventually have been a worthy rival for him, or a worthy partner. He had certainly enjoyed her charms in bed and out enough to consider the possibilities.

Pity she was dead.

CHAPTER 9

$\mathcal{M}$ari's first order of business the next morning—after watching the sunrise—was a trip to Our Own Hardware to purchase cleaning supplies. She loaded up on sponges and cleansers, bought a bucket and a mop and a broom, not willing to count on Lucy to have owned this sort of thing. She shot the breeze with Marcia, who worked the counter, starting with a friendly debate over Formula 409 versus Fantastik, and going from there into a light discussion of local politics and the pros and cons of home permanents.

From the hardware she jaywalked to the Rainbow and had a cup of coffee and a slice of lemon meringue pie with Nora. Nora directed her to the Carnegie Library, and she went in search of books about llamas, finding one in the small children's section of the cramped old building. There was nothing on the care and understanding of mules, but since mules were so closely related to horses, she hunted up a couple of texts on horsemanship for a refresher course.

She struck up a conversation with old Hal Linderman, who had taught math in the New Eden high school for forty years before retiring to become the town librarian. An hour later she had a temporary library card and an invitation to join the Presbyterian church.

Pleased, she headed back toward her Honda. She would pick up a supply of junk food at the Gas N' Go and head out to the ranch for a day of cleaning, reading, and contemplating. Cutting across the square, she paused to watch the sculptor at work out in front of the court-

147

house. Marcia at the hardware store had been dubious about the project. She couldn't see what good it would do, but Mari stood outside the roped-off area and studied the model, finding it interesting.

"It symbolizes the conflict of old ways and new ways coming together to bond into something strong and beautiful," Colleen Bentsen said. She was dressed for welding from the mask tilted back on her head to the torch in her gloved hand. She had her coveralls unzipped partway, revealing a T-shirt from Hamline University. Hal Ketchum sang out of the speakers of a boom box on the other side of her cluttered pen. There was a long table lined with tools and piles of what looked like scrap metal.

"Sounds good to me," Mari said. She tilted her head and scrutinized the lines of the model. "I like the elements—the rough and the smooth twining into a single arm that will be stronger than its individual components."

The artist beamed. "Exactly."

That kind of partnership between the old and the new factions of New Eden seemed unlikely, but Mari was the last person to shoot down idealism. Dreams were important. To her way of thinking, even unattainable goals were worth striving for.

She thought of her own goals as she drove out of town. There had been a time when she had dreamed of making it big as a singer and songwriter, but her parents had pressed hard for college and a career in law. She had fought them and fought within herself, the independent young woman in her warring with the insecure child. The factions compromised. Her dreams lost. No one lived happily ever after.

What's wrong with being a court reporter? You wanted me to go into law. That's a job in law.

We wanted you to be a lawyer, Marilee. You're so bright. You have so much potential. You could be anything you want.

Fine. I want to be a court reporter.

It wasn't that she wanted to be a court reporter. She

didn't want to be a lawyer. Court reporting seemed like a fair compromise. She could still see her parents wagging their heads sadly, wondering where they went wrong, wondering why the rogue gene of the Jennings clan had surfaced in their progeny. She could still feel their disappointment weighing down her heart like a stone. She still mourned sometimes for the dreams she had given up in her futile attempt to please them.

"The slate's clean now, Marilee," she said over the twang of Bruce Hornsby's piano. She sped toward the ranch with the windows down, the wind whipping her hair into a frenzy. "Dream new. Dream large."

But there were too many loose ends in the present to focus on the future, and the only large thing that came to mind was J. D. Rafferty.

She spent the rest of the day cleaning. Her housekeeping habits had always leaned toward a binge and purge cycle. She would let clutter accumulate, oblivious of it for weeks, then suddenly she would see it, as if she had just come out of a trance, and she would throw herself into the task of cleaning with dedication and enthusiasm until the place sparkled. The mess in Lucy's house couldn't be ignored. Nor could Mari's need to get rid of it. The destruction by the vandals was too much of an insult to the memory of her friend and too reminiscent of random violence. The pall of that hung in the air, and she opened all the windows in the place in the attempt to dispel it.

She started in the kitchen, scraping the mess off the floor, scrubbing the Mexican tile, washing out the refrigerator. By the end of the day she had worked her way through the great room. The dead ficus had been dragged out, the prints on the walls straightened, the Berber rug vacuumed. There was nothing she could do about the split in the seat of the red leather sofa except hide it with a multicolored serape she had found in a heap next to the woodbox. She salvaged what throw pillows she could and discarded the others. The kindling that had been a rocking chair and an end table were hauled outside.

Mr. Peanut watched the proceedings from his perch on the thick wood mantel of the fieldstone fireplace. Mari imagined Lucy's spirit lurking behind the painted eyes, snickering as she worked herself toward exhaustion. Lucy's knack for avoiding physical work—for roping other people into doing it for her—had been phenomenal.

I should have been born into your family instead of you, Marilee.

God knew she would have fit the Jennings clan like a glove in many respects. Their family motto was "Live well, dress well, and hire help." Mari had always consoled Lucy with the fact that her mother wouldn't have tolerated Lucy's promiscuity. In view of Lucy's taste for life in the fast lane, it was better that she didn't have a mother looking over her shoulder.

Mari found herself regretting the words now when she thought of Lucy dying alone. *Shed a tear or two for me. No one else will.*

With the great room finished, Mari looked through what was left of a glass-paneled door into a cozy study and groaned in agony at the sight of it. There were books and papers everywhere. Smashed statuary and more mutilated plants. A bronze sculpture of an eagle with outstretched wings had been used like a bludgeon on the sleek walnut desk, splintering the top. Mari couldn't even begin to think about tackling it. Instead, she pulled the last two cans of a six-pack of Miller Lite out of the fridge by their plastic collar and went outside.

The sun had begun its downward slide behind the mountains to the west, casting the valley in a warm bath of amber and shadow. She stood on the deck for a long while, staring down at the stream, realizing that the animals she had seen grazing along its banks weren't horses at all, but the llamas.

The thought of their gentle eyes and regal bearing made her smile. She wanted to just go and be with them and listen to their pleasant humming. She would sit on the fence and let them rub their noses over her. She would talk to them and try to absorb their air of wisdom.

They would want their supper and she would tell them to wait until Rafferty came.

She wasn't sure he would come today. The book she had read over her lunch break had been short on details about llama diets. They had an inexhaustible supply of grass and water. Perhaps they got the feed pellets only as a supplement once or twice a week. At any rate, Rafferty probably had better things to do with his time than troop down for a chore any ten-year-old ranch kid could have mastered. God knew, he didn't even like her. He had kissed her in anger, had pinned her down beneath him because she had attacked him.

And he held you while you cried because why, Marilee?

Because I didn't give him a choice.

She scowled at the reminder. Still, he had agreed to help her with the animals. Because she was his neighbor.

That was part of the code of the West, she suspected. Part of Rafferty's personal code. That touched her heart in a spot she hadn't even known was vulnerable. She had spent too many years working in a world where it was every man for himself.

Feeling restless, she walked around to the front of the house and wandered across the yard toward the outbuildings, going in search of llamas. The lawn needed mowing in a big way. Add that to the list for tomorrow: find a lawn mower or bring a llama into the yard. She tried to think what Lucy must have done. Nothing, of course. She had gotten someone else to do it for her. Kendall Morton, hired hand from the Outer Limits.

She wanted to ask Sheriff Quinn a question or two about Morton. If they were in California, she could have called any one of half a dozen friends in law enforcement and had the guy checked out for wants and warrants or a prior record. But this was not California.

A hired hand, she mused. A ranch in a place where land was worth its weight in gold. A herd of exotic animals. A new Range Rover in the garage sitting beside Lucy's red Miata. Where the hell had all the money come from?

A windfall, Lucy had told her. An inheritance from some remote relative. But who would have left her that kind of money when no one had cared enough about her to rescue her from the endless string of foster homes she had endured growing up?

The questions raised an uneasiness in her that itched beneath her skin. *Stupid, Marilee, it doesn't matter anymore. Lucy's gone. Her killer's been punished.*

Punished. She sniffed in disgust. A suspended sentence and thousand-dollar fine. Life came cheap when you were a plastic surgeon from Beverly Hills and had influential friends. She tried to picture the man, tried to imagine him crying all through the brief court proceedings that were mere stage dressing for a guilty plea. He hadn't meant to shoot Lucy. He hadn't known Lucy was there. He had walked away and left her to rot.

No matter how Mari replayed it, she couldn't muster much compassion for Sheffield. It always came down to the same conclusion. He had behaved irresponsibly, cost a human life, and the consequences of his actions hadn't even put a dent in his wallet. She knew damn well if the shooter had been some out-of-work cowboy, he'd be whiling away his days at the expense of the state for a year or better. Lady Justice may have been blind, but she could smell money a mile off, and her scales tipped accordingly.

But what if Sheffield hadn't shot her after all?

Stopping at the corral, Mari hooked a sneaker over the bottom rail and lay her arms on one higher up, the beer cans dangling down. She wished fervently for a cigarette, but denied herself the pleasure. Earlier in the day she had actually stooped to searching beneath her car seats for strays, coming up with three. Two remained in the breast pocket of her jacket.

She had vowed to start a new life. No more dead-end career. No more living in the shadow of her parents' expectations. No more meaningless relationships. Throwing out her cigarettes had been symbolic. She had taken up smoking in the first place to appease the tension and tedium of her job. She had chucked the job, so she had chucked the cigarettes. New Eden had sounded like the perfect place to start that new life. A sabbatical in paradise. No smoking, no stress allowed.

But her head was pounding and her mood was low. Her nerves were jangling like a wind chime in a cyclone. She fingered the flap of the jacket pocket. Just one . . .

Rafferty chose that moment to make his appearance, riding down out of the wooded cover of the hillside on his big sorrel horse. The brim of his black hat shaded his eyes, but his mouth was set in a grim line and he held himself in a way that suggested he hurt all over but would never display the weakness of slouching. Something about that touched Mari, and she did her best to shake it off. She had never had time for bone-headed males who set their pride ahead of their common sense. There shouldn't have been anything appealing about this one.

"Fixing to set the place on fire again?" J.D. drawled, nodding toward the pile of dead plants and splintered furniture that crowned the charred remains of her business suits in the center of the corral.

Mari gave him a look. "Yeah, I wanted the chance to have you tackle me again. I've got three or four ribs you somehow neglected to crack yesterday."

He swung off his horse, swallowing the groan that threatened. He'd been in one saddle or another since dawn. There had been a time when his body hadn't protested that kind of abuse, but that time had passed a couple of birthdays back. He narrowed his eyes at the woman before him. "Way I recall, *you* jumped *me.*"

"Yeah, well, I hate to disappoint you, but don't expect it to happen again tonight," she grumbled, rolling a shoulder. "I'm beat."

She looked more tousled than usual, her wild hair escaping the bonds of a ponytail in rippling waves. She had a smudge of dirt on her chin and her eyes seemed deeper and larger, dominating a face that had a delicate and strained quality to it. Her jacket swallowed her up, making her seem tiny and fragile, in need of a man's strength.

J.D.'s libido nominated him for the job, but he turned it down for the moment, scowling.

"Yeah, I hear those vacations can be hell on a person," he said dryly.

"I stopped calling it a vacation when I found out my friend was dead," Mari said sharply. "And for your information, I've been working all day, trying to set the house to rights. I'm sure that doesn't compare to punching out cows or whatever it is you do with your time, but it's hard work to me."

He growled at her a little and started toward the barn. Instantly, Mari wanted him back. Not that she wanted *him* personally, she assured herself. She just wanted the company. She wasn't used to so much solitude. Even a conversation with Rafferty seemed preferable to the tangle of thoughts and feelings that had been tumbling around inside her all day.

"Hey, wait," she ordered, skipping to catch up with him. "You want a beer?"

"Why?" he asked, turning back toward her. "Trying to ply me with liquor again, Mary Lee?"

He smiled that slow, sardonic smile, a predatory-male gleam in his eye. Mari's pulse rate rose in automatic response, picking up another beat as he cupped her chin in his hand and brushed his thumb across her lower lip.

"I already told you that wasn't necessary," he said, his low voice abrading her nerve endings like sandpaper. "Just say the word. I could stand to ride something softer than a horse tonight."

He marveled a little at the truth of that. Coming down the mountain, he hadn't been able to think of anything better than falling into bed and easing into a coma. The sight of Mary Lee—mussed hair, dirt on her chin, and all —had him thinking more along the lines of falling into bed and easing into *her*. It didn't make sense, but then, it was sex; it didn't have to make sense.

She took a half-step back and tried to look annoyed. "In your dreams, Rafferty. I offered you a beer, not my body."

J.D. chuckled wickedly. He reached out and settled a

hand at the juncture of her neck and shoulder, his thumb dipping into the shallow V above her collarbone. "Your pulse is racing, Mary Lee," he murmured. "You always get this worked up over a can of Miller?"

"Only when I'm contemplating bashing it over the head of an obnoxious man. Do you want the beer or not?"

His throat felt like a gravel pit, his mouth tasted of dust and horses. "Yeah, I guess I'd better disarm you."

Mari rolled her eyes and headed for an old wooden buggy seat that had been converted into a bench and sat along the end of the barn. She plunked herself down, tossed him his beer, and popped the top on her own.

Rafferty eyed the spot beside her but chose to stand, propping himself up against the weathered siding of the barn. He looked exhausted. His shirt was sweat-stained and dirty, his jeans limp and creased. He had obviously splashed water on his face before riding down; she could see the line on his neck where clean left off and the dirt began. The shadow on his lean cheeks told her it had been a while since he'd taken the time to shave.

"Truce, okay?" she offered, raising her can in salute. "I don't think either of us could survive a sparring match tonight."

He tipped his head a little in concession, popped the top on his beer, and drank half of it in one long swallow. Mari's gaze caught on the way the muscles of his throat worked. A shower of sparks shot through her.

"Hard day at the office?" she asked, more to distract herself than anything.

He shrugged. "The usual."

"What's 'the usual'?"

"Finished rounding up the breeding herd for branding and vaccinations. Colts needed riding. Bulls had to be moved."

Mari had a feeling the jobs entailed a great deal more than the few spare words he boiled them down to. He had a talent for understatement, Rafferty did. He compressed his conversation to the bare skin and bones of thought, leaving out all words that didn't seem absolutely necessary. The trait was at once endearing and infuriating. She was used to the enlightened professional men of the nineties who, once they had learned it was okay to open up, never shut up. Brad had always been a virtual font of information about himself, *his* feelings, *his* interests, *his* career.

"Branding like in the cowboy movies? Rope 'em, throw 'em, stick a hot iron on their sides?"

He straightened almost imperceptibly, his jaw hardening. "It's done for a reason," he said tightly, offended by the suggestion that he would unnecessarily harm an animal. "You a vegetarian or something?"

"No. Just curious. Believe me, I seldom discriminate against anything edible—except liver. I don't like liver. And I won't eat anything people claim 'tastes just like chicken.' That almost always means its some kind of animal you wouldn't eat if you knew what it was."

"Rattlesnake," J.D. said, one side of his mouth tugging into a reluctant smile. "Tastes just like chicken."

She made a face and held her hands up to ward off the idea, shuddering visibly inside her gigantic jacket. "No thanks. I learned all about the food groups in the fourth grade. Mrs. Kaplan never said a word about a daily requirement of reptiles."

He laughed, a sound that was rusty from disuse. Mari rewarded him with a smile. He eyed the empty place on the bench beside her, fighting with himself. He didn't want to be amused by her or charmed by her. He wanted to bed her. He wanted to buy her land. Those things were simple, straightforward, safe. The other edged into dangerous territory. He pushed himself away from the barn, telling himself to back off, but his feet were rooted to the spot. "There's chores need doing."

"They'll still need doing in ten minutes. Cut yourself some slack, Rafferty."

"Slackers don't last long in these parts." His gaze strayed to the log house as he eased himself down onto the far side of the bench. Weary disillusionment crept into his eyes. His broad shoulders sagged a little in defeat. "Least they never used to."

"How long has your family been here?" Mari asked quietly, mesmerized by the emotions playing in his gray eyes. She would have bet a dollar he would never give them voice, certainly not to her. All he ever wanted to show her was sexual aggression or orneriness—traits that made him easy to dislike . . . or should have. The idea of that macho attitude being a shield covering something more complex, even vulnerable, struck her as being as dangerous to her as the man himself, and yet she couldn't keep herself from trying to peek around it.

"Four generations," he said, his pride an unmistakable undercurrent in his low, soft voice. He still stared off toward the house, though she had a feeling he wasn't seeing it. His profile was rugged and handsome in the last umber light of day, the face of a man who lived a hard life and was stronger for it. "Since the war," he added.

He said it as if there had been only one in the last hundred fifty years, as if this corner of Montana had somehow existed out of time with the rest of the modern world. Sitting there in the ranch yard, the wild country all around them and no sign of civilization in sight, Mari was almost tempted to believe that could be true.

"The Civil War," she clarified.

"Yes, ma'am."

"And the Raffertys were Southerners?"

"Yes, ma'am. From Georgia."

His answer made her think of his manners. When he chose to display any, they were quaintly formal, the courtly manners of the old Deep South, polished Southern chivalry that had grown a little rough around the edges out in the wilderness. The thought that those customs had survived at all over four generations suggested they had been very carefully handed down, like cherished heirlooms, like his pride in his land and his fierce distrust of outsiders.

She turned sideways on the buggy seat and leaned a shoulder against the rough wall of the barn. "You're very lucky," she murmured, "to have that kind of sense of who you are and where you belong. I come from a place where almost no one is a native, where tradition is something we get out of Emily Post."

"It'll be that way around here soon enough."

"Only if all the natives leave."

"Plenty already have. Most can't afford not to."

"Because of people like Lucy buying land?"

"Nothing's sacred to people with money."

"You say that like they're evil. Maybe they love it here as much as you do. Take it from me," she said dryly, "belonging doesn't necessarily have anything to do with birthright."

J.D. said nothing. His feelings were too strong for words. No one could love this land more than he did. It was as much a part of him as his heart, his hands. He couldn't imagine an outsider feeling that. He didn't want to.

He cut a sideways glance at Mari. She seemed lost in thought, pensive, her plump lower lip caught between her teeth while she fiddled with the frayed ends of a tear in the leg of her jeans. Stray strands of blond hair fell against her cheek. He had to admit, she didn't look much like any of her fellow newcomers. She didn't dress to impress in designer western wear. She didn't even wear makeup—not that she needed any. She certainly didn't bear much resemblance to Lucy with her expensive clothes and long, lacquered fingernails. There was no choking cloud of perfume hanging around her. He pulled in a deep breath and shifted positions, detecting a hint of lemon oil.

"You worked on the house all day?" he said, trying his best to sound nonchalant.

"Mmm . . ."

"Why?"

"Why? Because it needed to be done."

"You fixing to move in, Mary Lee?"

"No. I—"

She heaved a sigh and looked across the yard to the house and the valley that lay beyond. It was hers. She still couldn't get that into her head. This place was hers and she couldn't accept it, yet she had pulled the plug on the life she'd led before coming here. Where did that leave her?

In limbo. What a curious place to be. A fog, where contact to the past had been severed and the future lay beyond the thick white mist. What else was there to do but float along in it, let it take her wherever? That was what her vacation to Montana was supposed to be about anyway—to shut down for a time, to live in the moment.

"I don't know. I didn't come here with the intention of staying. I only wanted some time to decompress. I just dumped my career, and then there was this guy—" She cut herself off, sending Rafferty a rueful look. "Well, that's another story. Anyway, I actually got some poor unsuspecting innocent to buy all my stenographer's equipment. I was coming here to celebrate. Lucy would have loved it—the ultimate nose-thumbing of convention and all that . . . I sure as hell didn't bargain for any of this."

A shiver ran through her, and she pulled her old jacket a little closer around her, the appalling state of her finger-nails catching her attention. The ones she hadn't bitten off had broken off during her cleaning marathon. Her fingers were chapped and raw from countless cycles of wet and dry. Lucy would have hustled her off for an emergency manicure.

"Should have worn gloves," J.D. murmured. He turned her hand over and studied her palm and the cal-lused tips of her fingers. Rubbing those pads of hard flesh, he could still remember the sound of her guitar and her low, husky voice, the sweetness, the poignancy of the music made by these fine-boned hands.

Mari's breath went thin in her lungs as he examined and explored her hand. Currents of something warm and intoxicating traveled up her arm and spread through her body in waves. She stared at him, wondering exactly what it was, wondering if he felt it too. His hand was warm and rough and huge, swallowing hers up as if she were a child. The latent strength in it set off a fluttering in the base of her throat.

"You'll end up with rancher's hands," he said.

Instantly, she thought of *his* rancher's hands—touching her, dark skin against light, calluses caressing the softest parts of her—and a flash fire swept through her. *This is weird, Marilee.* Chemistry—that was the explanation. Too bad she didn't understand chemistry any better now than she had in high school.

J.D. raised his eyes to meet hers and felt as if he had been lulled into some kind of trance. He wasn't the kind of man to lose control, to act the fool over some pretty blonde. That had been his father's role in life. And Will's. But not even that bitter reminder could make him pull his hand away from Mari's or make him look away from her. She stared up at him, her deep, dark, clear blue eyes awash in wonder, her lips parted slightly in surprise. The taste of those lips lingered in his memory, teasing him, tempting him.

It's just sex, he assured himself. Nothing more complicated than a rush of hormones.

He leaned down and settled his mouth over hers. She opened to him readily, a symbolic gesture that shot molten heat through the pit of his belly. He slid his tongue into her mouth, completing the symbol, taking them to the threshold of the next level in the age-old game.

He kissed her deeply, possessively, sliding his free hand into the tangle of her hair to cup the back of her head and hold her at the angle he liked best. His other hand was still twined with hers between them. As desire pooled and throbbed in his groin, he drew her hand to him, bent her small fingers around his erection, and groaned at the heady combination of pleasure and pain.

"That's how much I want you, Mary Lee," he whispered roughly, dragging his mouth from her lips to her jaw to the shell of her ear. He pulled the lobe between his teeth, biting gently, then sucking.

"That's saying a lot." Mari's voice was as thin as gauze. Her brain felt wrapped in gauze, logic trapped between the layers of mindless need, overwhelmed by Rafferty's masculinity and sexuality.

"Let me give it to you, Mary Lee," he breathed urgently. "I want to be inside you. I want to feel you around me. Hot. Wet." He wedged a hand between her legs and rubbed her through her jeans. "Are you hot for me, Mary Lee?"

A moan was the only response she could manage. The heat was incredible. She felt as if she were melting, her whole being liquefying and flowing into Rafferty's hand. She stroked her palm down the length of him and imagined too easily how he would feel entering her, filling her, stretching her.

He kissed her again, roughly, wildly, thrusting his tongue deep into her mouth. His fingers fumbled for the tab of her zipper.

"Let me," he growled, his breath rasping, his lungs working like bellows. He nipped the side of her neck, then kissed where he'd bitten. "Let me fuck you, Mary Lee."

His blunt language shot a jolt of excitement through her. At the same time, it struck a tender nerve. This would mean nothing to him but slaking a need. He had been very plain about that from the start. He didn't have to love her. He didn't even have to like her.

She wasn't a prude. She had gone to bed with men she didn't love. But there had always been a mutual respect and friendship, if nothing else. Here there was nothing else.

And still she wanted him.

The conflicting emotions swirled through her head, making her dizzy, making her feel as if she were falling.

Then her backside hit the ground so hard, her teeth snapped together and her eyes popped open. She had managed to fall off the bench.

"Wow." She struggled to her feet, knees wobbling, and dusted off the seat of her jeans. "I've heard of kisses knocking a girl on her butt," she joked weakly, "but I never took it literally."

Embarrassment burned in her cheeks, and she turned slightly away from him, rubbing the sensation with her fingertips as if she could erase any telltale sign of it. Her hands were trembling. God, her whole body was shaking. Amazing. When was the last time a man had made her tremble with the power of his kiss? Never. And when was the last time a man had made her want so badly, her brain shut down and primal instincts took over? Never.

You're in big trouble here, Marilee.

J.D. took her by the arm and turned her toward him. "Let's go up to the house and finish this in a bed."

Mari stepped away from him, shaking her head. Her hair tumbled down around her face, partially hiding her. "No."

"No?" he said, incredulous. Anger and sexual frustration pounded inside him. "I didn't hear you saying no when you had your hand wrapped around my dick."

"I'm sorry," she whispered, nearly choking on the tension within her. "I can't do this."

"The hell you can't, Mary Lee," J.D. growled. "You drop your panties, spread your legs, and I make us both happy. It's as simple as that."

"Not for me, it isn't. I don't have sex with a man just because I happen to be handy when he needs it."

"Lucy did," he said cruelly.

Mari lifted her chin and stared at him through a thin sheen of tears as hurt coursed through her. "I'm not Lucy."

Her pride kicked him square and hard in the chest. She wasn't being coy. She wasn't playing games. She was standing up to him. Again. And damned if she wasn't pretty, standing there with those big, jewel-blue eyes glaring at him through her tears and her tangled blond hair.

The hard throb of need ebbed a bit. J.D. reached into his hip pocket and pulled out a handkerchief. Scowling, he swiped the tears that had spilled over her lashes, leaving them spiky and dark. He gave her the handkerchief and ordered her to blow her nose. Then he combed her hair back with his fingers and tilted her face up.

"This isn't finished, Mary Lee," he said, his voice quiet, his expression stern. "Not by a long way. It might not happen tonight or tomorrow, but it's damn well gonna happen. That's a promise."

It sounded more like a threat, but Mari said nothing as he turned and went into the barn.

Twilight was fading fast. Night crept down the mountainside in long, cool, black fingers that carried the scent of pine and damp earth. Somewhere along the valley a bull elk called to his harem, a high-pitched, whistling squeal that looped into a trumpet blast. Eerie and beautiful.

Rafferty's horse stood waiting patiently, tied to a rail of the corral, one hind leg cocked, his eyes half closed, his lower lip drooping. A pair of chipmunks had scampered into the corral to inspect the new pile of debris. They ran over it and through it, chattering a mile a minute.

Mari just stood there, trembling, Rafferty's promise ringing in her ears. They would end up in bed together.

Live for the moment, Marilee.

And if the moment included Rafferty?

Where would it lead them? Scary thing about the road less traveled: you couldn't always see around the bend.

The hinges of the barn door creaked a protest. Mari jerked around and blinked against the thickening darkness, wondering how long she had been standing there, mulling over the possibility of having an affair with a man she barely knew.

He came toward her slowly, deliberately, his gaze holding hers. And he stepped too close, as he always did. A shiver of awareness skittered over her.

"What's it gonna be, Mary Lee?" he asked quietly. His eyes were the gray of velvet in the waning light. "Is tonight the night?"

She held herself rigid, afraid if she moved at all, it would be to nod her head. "I'm not ready."

He bent his head and kissed her, slowly, deeply, intimately. Their lips clung as he pulled back.

"Get ready," he growled.

He went to his horse, tightened his cinch, and swung up into the saddle, pointing the big gelding toward the trail to the Stars and Bars.

"Hey, Rafferty," Mari called, uprooting her feet and

moving to stand alongside him. "Mind if I come up to-morrow and see what branding is all about?"

Impulse pushed the question out of her. She bit her lip and waited for his answer, her hands jammed deep in the pockets of her jacket, as if she were bracing herself against a stiff wind.

He stared down at her, his face little more than a sil-houette in the fading light. "Suit yourself."

She gave him a lazy, lopsided grin. "I usually do."

She watched him ride away at a slow jog, feeling a little giddy, a little foolish, a little too pleased that he might allow her to take a peek at his world.

"What the hay, Marilee," she said, turning back toward the house, moving toward it on shaky legs. "Live for the moment."

Midnight. The dead of night. The time of ghosts and hunters.

He couldn't always tell the difference. The images ran together and through each other. The hounds, the corpses, the dog-boys and tigers. They crashed through the woods, making a racket only he could hear. It was as loud as the blasting of an M-16 inside his head, echoing and amplifying off the metal plate. The spotlight ex-ploded before his eyes and behind them.

The blonde was there. He was sure of it. He could hear her laughter and her screams. His head swam and pounded with the sounds and the images. He squeezed his eyes shut and still they came in—through his ears and his fingertips. He felt the tiger ripping open his chest. The blood flowed inward instead of out, and the visions rushed in on the tide and up his throat, choking him.

He cowered behind the contorted body of a whitebark pine, clutching his rifle and weeping like a woman. He couldn't move, couldn't breathe, couldn't think, couldn't escape in any way. He was crying too hard to take a shot. Sobbing soundlessly, his mouth torn open as if to scream, but no sound coming out. It all remained within him. The rage, the fear, the madness. And he gripped the rifle and held on. His only anchor to the real world. His only friend in the night.

The blonde laughed. The tiger screamed. The dog-boys did their dirty deeds.

He clutched his rifle and prayed to an empty sky. *Please, please, fade to black. Fade to black . . .*

CHAPTER 10

*T*he mule eyed her, openly dubious.

"You don't think I can do this, do you?" Mari said, hefting the western saddle in her arms. It weighed a ton. When her mother had sent her to riding lessons at Baywind Stables, it had been in breeches and boots with a little velvet hunt helmet under her arm. The saddle she strapped on her rented mount was small and light. The mount she strapped it on was petite with a dainty head and kind eyes.

Clyde sized her up and all but laughed at her. His eyes were keen and clear, showing a sharp, cynical intelligence that boded ill. He flicked one long ear back and tossed his big, homely head, rattling the snaps on the cross ties.

Mari adjusted her hold on the saddle and pulled together her nerve. "Think again, rabbit ears. If Lucy could do this, I can damn well do it too."

It occurred to her that perhaps Lucy *hadn't* done this. She may have had her hired hand saddle the animal for her. No matter now. The only hands Mari had were the two on the ends of her arms.

Standing on an old crate, she swung the saddle into place on the mule's back and adjusted the saddle blanket, tugging it up at his withers. She wrestled with the long latigo strap and fumbled at the unfamiliar task of dealing with the western girth, trying to remember what Rafferty had done the few times she had seen him loosen and tighten his saddle on his big sorrel horse. She nearly gave up once, ready to jump on bareback, but the thought of the uphill trail to the Stars and Bars and the fact that it had been a decade since she had ridden made her renew her efforts to get the saddle tightened down.

Once she had accomplished her task and managed to get the bridle on, she led her noble steed out into the early morning sunshine and mounted with some difficulty and little grace. She took a moment to settle herself, trying to recall without much success how it had felt to be comfortable on the back of a moving animal. Then she pointed the mule toward the trail and they set off at a walk.

Nerves were forgotten almost instantly as they climbed the trail on the wooded hillside. Mari's surroundings captured her attention almost to the exclusion of the mule. Impressions bombarded her senses—the smell of earth and pine, the delicate shape and movement of aspen leaves, the colors of wildflowers, the songs of birds, the patches of blue that shone through the canopy of branches like bits of stained glass. She breathed it in, soaked it in, taking mental notes and processing them automatically through the creative side of her brain. Fragments of song lyrics floated through her head on phantom melodies.

Clyde plodded onward, oblivious of the creative process but well aware of his rider's distracted state. He took advantage of Mari's inattentiveness, nibbling on the leaves of berry bushes as he ambled along. When they reached a clearing, he stopped altogether and dropped his nose down into the fresh clover. Mari started to pull his head up, but the view from the ridge wiped everything else from her mind.

It was spectacular. Simply, utterly spectacular. The ranch lay below them, and below that lay the valley, lush and green like a rumpled velvet coverlet. The stream cut through it, a band of glittering embroidery, shining silver beneath the spring sun. And far beyond the valley the Gallatin range rose up, paragons of strength, huge, silent, their peaks bright with snow.

From a treetop somewhere above her, an eagle took wing, its piercing cry cutting across the fabric of the morning like a razor. The bird glided toward the valley, a dark chevron against the blue sky.

Mari's breath held fast in her lungs. She had grown up in a city, had traveled to some of the more beautiful sites civilization had to offer, but no place had ever captured her as surely as this place. She sat there, a fine trembling running through her, to the core of her, feeling like an instrument on which someone had struck a perfect note. It vibrated in the heart of her, touched the very center of her, and tears rose in her eyes because she knew just how rare a moment like this was. She felt as if she had been waiting for it her entire life. Waiting to feel that sense of belonging, that sense of finally sliding into place after so many years of not fitting in.

It frightened her a little to feel it now. She had no way of knowing how long it would last, didn't know if she should grab on to it with both hands and hang on or let it pass. She thought of Rafferty and his aversion to outsiders. She wasn't from here, had come only on hiatus from the rest of her life. Just passing through. Just passing time. But time stood absolutely still as she looked out over the valley and to the mountains beyond.

She could have stayed forever right in that spot, suspended in that moment.

But somewhere ahead on the trail cattle were being branded, work was being done. Somewhere ahead on the trail was J. D. Rafferty. Mari tugged Clyde's head up out of the clover and urged him toward the Stars and Bars.

She heard the commotion before she saw it. The bawling of cows and calves filled the air, a frantic cacophony that sang of the confusion and energy of the event. The mule pricked his long ears forward and picked up the pace of his walk, the excitement reaching him even a quarter mile down the road from the ranch. Mari fixed her gaze on the cloud of dust hovering over the corrals in the distance and nudged her mount into a trot, posting in the saddle because it was the way she had been taught. She supposed she looked ridiculous, bouncing up and down on the back of a mule as if he were a prize-winning hunter, but she'd never given a fig for appearances anyway, and this was hardly the time to start.

As she neared the pens she tried to take in everything about the sight at once—the maze of weathered board fences, the movement of the groups of cattle, the men who perched above the chutes, tending to a job she could only guess at. The air was filled with the scents of dust and smoke, fresh manure and burning hide. The scene was something straight out of a John Wayne movie, Technicolor bright, Surround-Sound loud.

"Better click those teeth together, ma'am, or you're liable to catch a taste of somethin' you'd rather not."

Mari pulled herself away from the spectacle and looked down on another walking, talking piece of western lore. The old cowboy who stood beside her was as weathered as, an applehead doll, his skin burned brown and age-freckled from years in the sun. He had the stance of a man who had put in too many miles in the saddle, a little bent, a little twisted. His legs were bowed and spindly even though a fair amount of belly spilled over the top of his belt buckle. He squinted up at her from beneath the brim of a disreputable-looking gray hat, his blue eyes merry and a smile tugging shyly at one corner of his mouth.

"Tucker Cahill at your service, ma'am," he announced. Tipping his head away demurely, he shot a stream of tobacco juice into the dirt, then glanced back up at her. "You lost or somethin'?"

"Not if this is the Stars and Bars."

"It surely is."

"I'm Marilee Jennings. J.D. told me I could come watch the branding if I wanted."

Tucker damn near swallowed his chaw. His eyebrows climbed his forehead until they nearly disappeared beneath his hat. "Did he? Well, I'll be pan-fried and ate by turkeys," he muttered.

"Excuse me?"

He shook himself like a dog, trying to shake loose the shock of her statement. He could hardly remember the last time J.D. had invited a woman to the ranch—leastways a woman who wasn't a veterinarian or a cattle broker or some such. It was a cinch this little mop-headed blonde wasn't anything of the sort.

He grinned his tight little grin, tickled at the prospect of J.D. showing something other than contempt for a female. "Well, why don't you climb on down off that lop-eared creature and I'll get you a ringside seat, Miz Jennings."

"I'd like that."

Mari swung her leg over the mule's back and dropped to her feet, wincing as pain shot up from her toes to the roots of her hair. As pleasant as the ride had been, she was damn glad to have the chance to try to put her knees side by side again—not that it seemed even remotely possible. She felt as bowlegged as Tucker Cahill looked.

Putting off taking those first few steps, she stuck a hand out to the old cowboy. He gripped her fingers with a gloved hand as strong as a vise and gave her a shake. "You can call me Mari," she said with a grin. "Anybody ever tell you you look like Ben Johnson, the actor?"

Tucker cackled with glee. "From time to time. You just climb up that rail over yonder, Mari, and you'll see what branding is all about. I'll see to your mule here."

"You don't have to do that."

"Oh, yes, ma'am. You're a guest at the Stars and Bars. We don't get many, but we treat 'em right."

Mari thanked him as he walked away, Clyde in tow, going off toward a long, weathered gray barn. Gritting her teeth as she forced her aching legs to move, feeling as ungainly as if she were trying to negotiate stilts, she made her way to the corral and climbed up to sit on the top rail. The organized chaos going on below was mesmerizing to watch. After a few minutes, Tucker climbed up beside her, standing on one of the lower rails and laying his arms across the top one.

"I had no idea ranchers still branded cattle," she said, fairly shouting to be heard above the din. "I would have guessed that went out with bustles and steam engines."

"Old ways are sometimes best. No one's come up with

a better way to work cows than from the back of a good ol' quarter horse. No one's come up with a better system for marking cattle than a brand. Lotta open territory in these parts. Cattle wander off, mix in with other herds."

He pointed out J.D. moving through the herd in the far holding pen on a pale gray horse, telling her with no small amount of pride that there wasn't a man for a hundred miles around who knew more about how to get the most out of a horse than J.D. "Knows the cattle business inside and out too. He's up on all the latest—electronic sales networks, computer tracking herd progress, stuff an old duffer like me don't know from diddly. Had two years of college before his daddy died. Yes, ma'am," he said, nodding, "J.D.'s a fine rancher and a fine hand and a good man right down to the ground. You won't find a soul around here to tell you different."

His ringing endorsement sounded suspiciously like a sales pitch. Mari found it sweet and did her best to tame her amusement.

"He's run this place since he was a kid," Tucker said, fixing his gaze on the man J.D. had become in the years since. "And I mean that. Tom—J.D.'s daddy—God rest him, never had his heart in the job. He gave his to women and it'd liked to killed him. Did kill him in the end, after Will's mama left."

Mari studied the old man's weathered profile, a million questions rushing through her mind. A part of her—the part that would have protected her—resented them. She was probably better off not knowing about Rafferty's past. If she didn't know what made him so difficult, so distrustful, so damned hard to deal with, then her soft heart couldn't feel sympathy or goad her into trying to heal his past hurts, or any of the dozen other foolhardy things she would likely do. But she couldn't stop herself from being curious, or overly sentimental, or stupidly romantic. *You'll never change, Marilee. . . .*

And so the question tumbled out. "What about J.D.'s mother?"

"Died when he was just a little tyke. Cancer, God rest her. She was a fine woman. Poor Tom was just lost without her—at least until Will's mama breezed onto the scene. Then he was just plain lost."

And J.D. was lost in the shuffle. Tucker Cahill didn't say that, but Mari pieced together the fragments he had given her and came up with the picture: J.D., just a boy, taking on responsibilities far beyond his years while his father wandered around in a romantic fog. If it was an accurate picture, it explained a great deal. She felt her heart slipping a little further out of her control, and her protective instincts growled at her in warning. To fall for a man like Rafferty would be asking for trouble, begging for heartbreak, she told herself. She had a terrible suspicion her heart wasn't listening.

In what was probably a futile attempt at self-preservation, she derailed Tucker onto an explanation of the process of sorting the cattle through the pens and chutes.

The men perched above the chutes controlled the gates that determined which pen an animal would be directed to depending on age and sex. In the branding corral, calves were being run one at a time into a squeeze chute, which tipped onto one side, forming a table. Will Rafferty and an old man with a long gray braid worked at the squeeze chute, vaccinating, notching ears, castrating bull calves, and marking all with the Rafter T brand of the Stars and Bars. The whole process took little more than a minute per animal.

She watched them do half a dozen before Will looked over and caught sight of her. A big grin split his dirty face, and he abandoned his post without a backward glance.

"Hey, Mary Lee!" he called, striding across the corral with the grace of Gene Kelly, arms spread wide in welcome. "How's it shaking?"

"It about shook loose on the ride up here," she said dryly.

He laughed, swinging up onto the fence and turning his red baseball cap frontward on his head, seemingly all in one motion. He settled himself a little too close beside her, close enough that Mari could smell sweat and the scent of animals on him, close enough that she could see his blue eyes were shot through with the telltale threads of a hangover. She frowned at him, unable to sidle away because of Tucker on her left.

The old cowboy leaned ahead and shot a hard look at Will. "J.D. catches you slacking, boy, he'll chew your tail like old rawhide."

Behind the layers of sweat and grime, Will's mouth tightened. "Yeah, well, J.D. can just go to hell. I been working hard as he has since sunup. I'm taking five. It's not every day we get a pretty lady for company up here in the back of beyond."

"No, they're scarce as hen's teeth," Tucker admitted, clambering over the rail and lowering himself into the corral. He jammed his hands at the low-riding waist of his jeans and gave the younger man a significant look. "Especially the ones your brother invites."

Will pulled a comic face of exaggerated shock, eyes wide in his lean face as he stared at Mari. "J.D. *invited* you? *My* brother J.D. *invited* you?"

"Not exactly," Mari grumbled, scowling as she watched Tucker hobble away toward the squeeze chute to take up Will's place. "I invited myself. He didn't tell me no."

"Well, that's something too, let me tell you. J.D. runs this place like a damn monastery. He doesn't want some evil woman turning our heads from our work."

Lucy came immediately to mind, but Mari bit her tongue. "What about your wife?"

"What about her?"

"Does she fall under the 'evil woman' heading?"

"Sam? Hell no. She's a good kid." *Sweet, trusting, in need of someone to love her.* The description ran through his mind, through his heart like an arrow as he watched the monotonous routine in the branding corral. Every time he thought of Sam, he felt as if he'd been kicked in the head—a little ill, a little dizzy. He'd been doing his damnedest *not* to think about her since the night he had seen her in the Moose.

"Kid? What is she, a child bride?"

"Naw, she's twenty-three." He picked absently at the

rusty fungus that clung to the top of the rail. "I've known her forever, that's all. It's hard not to think of her like a kid sister."

Which might explain why he wasn't living with his wife, Mari thought. If she had a husband who treated her like a kid sister, and chased anything in a skirt besides, she figured she'd dump him too.

"So," Will said, slapping a hand on her thigh, "whatcha doing here, Mary Lee? Looking for trouble?" He bobbed his eyebrows and grinned. "That's my middle name."

"I guessed as much." She pried his fingers off her leg and scooted away a foot, fixing him with a look. "I came to see how a ranch works."

"I'll tell you how a ranch works." Bitterness crept in around the edges of his voice. "Day and night, week after week, month after month, year after year, until death or foreclosure."

"If you don't like it, why don't you quit?"

He laughed and looked away, not sure whether it was her suggestion or his answer he found so funny. A part of him had wanted nothing more than to be rid of the Stars and Bars ever since he was a boy. But that part of him was forever tangled with the boy who looked up to his big brother. And the part of him that didn't want to be a screwup was forever tripping over the part that longed to tell J.D. to go to hell. The cycle just tumbled on, like a rock down an endless mountainside.

"You don't quit the Stars and Bars, gorgeous," he muttered, staring off across the chutes to the back pen, where J.D. was sorting cattle. "Not if your name is Rafferty."

J.D. worked the herd from the back of a washed-out gray mare. This was only her second year working cattle, but her talent was bred bone-deep. She kept her head low and her ears pinned as she danced gracefully from side to side, cutting calves away from their mothers and sending them into the chutes, sorting out young heifers and sending them into another holding pen to wait. The mare ducked and dodged, adjusting her speed as necessary. Her reins hung loose, her movements guided by intuition and the subtle touches of J.D.'s spurs against her sides.

J.D. sat easily in the saddle, one gloved hand on the pommel, shoulders canted back, bracing himself against the sudden moves of the horse beneath him. His mind was working on three levels at once—studying the cattle, assessing the performance of the horse, and wondering if Mary Lee would really show up.

He cursed himself up one side and down the other for letting a woman take his thoughts away from his business. He didn't need the distraction of thinking about her or the distraction of seeing her standing outside the fence. If he wanted a distraction, he could wonder what the hell he would do a year from now, when Lyle Watkins and his boys would no longer be around to help work the chutes. Tucker and Chaske would be another year older, too old for a full day of this kind of work. God only knew where Will would be. His only other neighbor would be Bryce.

Bryce wouldn't offer to trade work. J.D. doubted Bryce knew what real work was. He wouldn't know or care about the code that had always existed between neighbors here. Like the rest of his kind, Bryce had brought his own set of values and priorities with him to Montana, all of them foreign to J.D.

The little mare pulled herself up and blew out a heavy breath, drawing J.D. back to the matter at hand. The group of cattle he had been working was sorted. They would brand and vaccinate this lot, break for dinner, then start all over again.

He would hand the mare over to Tucker to cool her out and to give the old man a break. Tucker didn't like to admit his age, but J.D. saw it creeping up on him a little more every day, bending his back a little more, stiffening joints that had already taken too many years of abuse. In another job, Tucker Cahill would have been forced to retire by now, but there was no such thing as retirement for a cowboy. Cowboy was *who* a man was as much as *what.* Tucker Cahill wouldn't retire any more than he would quit having blue eyes and a crooked pecker.

Besides, the Stars and Bars was Tucker's home as much as if he were a Rafferty, J.D. thought. He had spent the best years of his life and then some working this ranch for damn little pay, and he would stay here until the pallbearers carried him off feetfirst. It was up to J.D. to make that possible. It was his responsibility to take care of the old man, to see to it that he had a roof over his head and food in his belly and a purpose in his life, just as it had been Tucker's role to play surrogate father when Tom Rafferty had been too lost in his obsession to do the job.

The weight of that and every other responsibility pressed down on his aching shoulders for a minute. Just a minute. He didn't allow any longer, couldn't afford the time. Brooding didn't get a job done.

He turned the mare toward the out gate and was struck by the sight of Mary Lee sitting up on the far rail of the branding corral, laughing at something Will said to her. He couldn't hear her over the bawling of cattle, but the husky sound tumbled through his memory, striking chords inside he would rather have left untouched. Even through the coating of grit in his mouth he could remember the taste of her kiss.

Will made a wild gesture with his arms, his wide, handsome grin lighting up his face as he entertained his audience of one. Jealousy stormed through J.D. like a charging bull. He would never have called it that out loud, but a spade was a spade. From the day Sondra and Tom had brought him home from the hospital, Will had been the center of attention, a magnet for any spotlight. He basked in even the smallest glow, and everyone laughed at him and was charmed by him. No one seemed to care that he aspired to nothing or that he gambled away two months' worth of bank payments at a crack or that he was about as trustworthy and reliable as a stray tomcat.

Letting himself out the gate without dismounting from the mare, J.D. jogged the horse around the outside of the pens and pulled up when he reached the pair perched on the top rail. He shot Mary Lee a narrow look, withering her smile on the vine, then dismissed her without a word and turned to Will.

"You sit here hanging your butt over the fence while a man pushing seventy does your job for you? What the hell are you thinking about?"

Will's face set in hard, tight lines to mirror his brother's look. "I was thinking I hadn't had two minutes' rest since I landed on my feet this morning. I was thinking it might be polite to say hello to our guest—"

"Yeah, right," J.D. sneered. "Like a fox just wants to say hello to a quail—"

"Well, hell, J.D., if you're jealous, maybe you ought to do some—"

With a jab of a spur J.D. jumped his horse ahead and sideways, pinning his leg against the fence. Ignoring the pain, he cuffed Will across the kidneys with the back of his arm, knocking him from his perch into the corral.

"I'm mad as hell, that's what I am," he snapped. "Get off your lazy ass for once and do your job instead of letting an old man take up the slack for you."

Will glared at him over the bars of the fence. His cap had come off in the fall and his dark hair spilled across his forehead. His face was almost as red as the T-shirt he wore, embarrassment and rage pumping his blood pressure up.

"Fuck you, J.D.!" he spat out. "I work like a goddamn dog around here—"

"When you're not out playing rodeo or down in Little Purgatory."

"—not that I ever see anything for it—"

"No shit, you lose it all playing poker—"

"You're not my boss and you're not my keeper, and if I want to take five stinking minutes to talk to somebody, I'll do it!"

Mari watched the exchange from the uncomfortable position of outsider. She had the distinct feeling their fury had its roots in something deeper than her ability to distract Will from his work. She knew all about sibling rivalries and resentments. Growing up the odd one out among the Jennings girls, she had felt her share of ill feelings toward Lisbeth and Annaliese. The Rafferty brothers undoubtedly had their own version of the same story. Will, the gregarious, charming rascal, and J.D., so stern, so rigid—it wasn't hard to imagine them clashing. She just didn't particularly want to be an eyewitness while it happened, or the spark that touched it off.

"Hey, guys, look," she said, straddling the fence, raising her hands in a peacemaking gesture, "I didn't come here to make trouble—"

J.D. shot her a glare. "Well, you damn well managed to do it anyway, didn't you?"

"Don't blame Mary Lee," Will snapped. "It isn't her fault you're an ornery son of a bitch."

"No, and it isn't her fault you think with what's between your legs instead of what's between your ears."

"If my being here is a problem," Mari said, "I'll just go."

"Your being in Montana is a problem," J.D. snarled half under his breath.

The remark cut. Mari held herself rigid against the urge to wince; she wouldn't give him the satisfaction. She raised her chin a notch, looking down her nose at him. "Yeah, well, when somebody dies and makes you king, you can have me and all my kind exiled."

J.D. set his jaw and turned away from her, not liking the fact that he felt even a little chastened by her words. A whole host of uncomfortable and unfamiliar feelings crawled like ants inside his skin. He shouldn't have jumped on Will in front of the whole crew. Work in the branding pen had come to a standstill while everyone watched them and waited for the outcome.

This was what happened when a woman came prancing around; men lost their heads.

"Now, boys," Tucker said diplomatically, ambling away from the empty squeeze chute. He clamped a hand on Will's shoulder, turned his head, and spat a stream of tobacco juice. "Maybe what we all need is a good hot meal and a chance to sit on something that ain't movin.' I got a big ol' pan of my famous lasagna in the oven.

Ought to be ready about now. Why don't we all go on up to the house?"

J.D. had no appetite for food or for company. He started to tell the others to go on, when his mare raised her head and stared off toward the northwest, ears up. She whinnied loudly, a call that was immediately answered by several different equine voices.

From the cover of pine and fir trees emerged a group of riders. There were six in all and a pack mule bringing up the rear. Even from a distance J.D. could make out Bryce at the front of the entourage. The sun gleamed off his long pale hair and wide white smile. He rode a handsome chestnut that danced beneath him, impatient with the leisurely pace of the rest of the group.

It took them several minutes to close the distance, but no one at the ranch said a word while they waited. At least not until the riders were close enough for all their faces to be made out.

Will's breath caught hard in his lungs as he recognized Sam riding among the pack on a leggy Appaloosa. Her eyes locked on his for a second, then she glanced away, pulling her horse back to hide behind a dark-haired man on a bay.

Sam, *his* Sam, with Evan Bryce's crowd? It seemed inconceivable in every way. She wasn't one of them. She was a cocktail waitress, for Christ's sake! She was a tomboy poor girl from the wrong side of town. She was his wife.

"Hello, neighbor!" Bryce called as he rode up, his grin brimming with bonhomie.

"Bryce," J.D. acknowledged, not even bothering to tip his hat to the ladies in the company, though he ran his gaze across each face.

The strong-featured blonde who was often with Bryce rode beside him now, her gaze bold and amused as she met J.D.'s eyes. Behind her was a skinny, giggling redhead in a man's white dress shirt that she hadn't bothered to button at all, just tied in a knot at her midriff. She leaned over in her saddle and whispered something to a dark-haired man who had "city" written all over him in spite of his western-cut shirt. Bringing up the rear with the pack mule loaded down with picnic baskets was Orvis Slokum, who had worked on the Stars and Bars for a time before he had tried his hand at robbing convenience stores. Bryce had hired him right out of prison and got his name in the paper for being a great humanitarian.

Beside Orvis, obviously trying to make herself invisible, was Samantha. She ducked her head, staring down as if the cap of her saddle horn had suddenly become the most fascinating thing in the world. But there was no mistaking the way she sat a horse or the long curtain of black hair that fell over her shoulder to obscure one side of her face.

J.D. cut a glance out the corner of his eyes at Will, who had turned chalk white beneath the morning's layer of dirt.

"What's going on here?" Bryce asked, looking amused by the quaintness of it all. "A big roundup or something?"

"Work," J.D. growled, curling his fingers over the pommel of his saddle. "You may have heard of it once or twice."

Bryce laughed, unoffended. "Mr. Rafferty, I concede you know more about ranching than I do. But then, I know more about getting rich than you, don't I? My friends and I are out enjoying the fruits of my past labors as it were, taking a little tour of my land."

A muscle ticked in J.D.'s jaw. "You got a might lost."

The smile that curled the corners of the man's mouth was almost feral. "Not at all." He let the remark hang for a second, but went on before J.D. could call him on it. "We're only passing through on our way to the Flying K."

J.D. could hear Lyle Watkins clear his throat in embarrassment. He wanted to look to his old neighbor with accusation. *See what you're letting in here?* But he wouldn't look away from Bryce.

"We just thought we would do the neighborly thing and stop by to let you know," Bryce said.

J.D.'s fingers curled a little tighter on the swell of his

saddle. He wanted to yell at the man to get the hell off his land. He could feel the shout building in the back of his throat, but he swallowed it down. Control. He'd lost his cool once already today. He wouldn't lose it now, not with this man.

"You don't own the Flying K," he pointed out calmly. "Yet."

"Well," J.D. drawled on a long sigh, affecting a boredom he didn't feel. "We could sit around here all day and talk about nothing, but I'd rather eat pig shit than spend time with your kind, so if you'll excuse us, we've got work to do."

He waited just long enough to see the color rise behind Bryce's tan before he started to rein his horse away.

"Am I to take it, then, that you wouldn't be interested in coming to my little party tonight, Mr. Rafferty?"

"Yep."

"Too bad," Bryce said tightly, his smile looking like plastic. He jerked his gaze to Mari as Rafferty rode past him toward the back of his band. "I hope Mr. Rafferty's opinion doesn't extend to you, Mari. We'd love to have you join us. Bring your guitar if you like. There'll be some music people there. Could be an opportunity for you."

Mari felt she was straddling the fence metaphorically as well as physically, caught between two very different factions of acquaintances. She could feel a dozen pair of eyes on her like spotlights. The one pair she didn't feel was J.D.'s, and the absence was somehow weightier than all the other stares combined.

"Thank you for the invitation," she mumbled, her voice little more than a whisper. "I'd love to."

She ignored the feeling that she was betraying Rafferty. She didn't owe him any allegiance. She owed Lucy. And the dark-haired man sitting on a bay horse had once known Lucy MacAdam very well indeed. Ben Lucas, king turd on the Sacramento shit pile of trial attorneys. Mari knew him by sight, and she knew him by reputation. What she didn't know was what the hell he was doing with Evan Bryce.

"We'll look forward to seeing you tonight, then." Bryce started to rein his horse around, pulling up as his gaze fell on Will. "Mmm, my, this is a little awkward," he said, feigning embarrassment. "You would be welcome too, of course, Mr. Rafferty, but as your ex-wife will be there, I think this could be uncomfortable for Samantha. You understand."

Will said nothing, his gaze fixed on Sam, willing her to look at him. She turned the other way. *Ex*-wife. *Ex*-wife. The word flashed in his head like a red neon light. They weren't divorced . . . yet. Was that how Sam thought of him? As her *ex*-husband?

J.D. sat like a sentinel at the back of Bryce's cadre, showing them the figurative door. He watched impassively as Bryce led the way, saying nothing until Samantha started past him. He tipped his head and spoke her name. She ducked behind the cover of her curtain of hair, avoiding his eyes. He tightened his jaw and turned to Orvis Slokum, who was fumbling with the lead of the pack mule, getting himself hopelessly tangled.

Orvis had been born a loser and gone downhill from there. He was scrawny and grubby with a ferret's face, thin hair, and bad teeth, and no matter if he meant well, he always managed to do the wrong thing. He had been a screwup as a ranch hand and piss-poor robber. Still, J.D. wished he had had more dignity than to take up with the likes of Bryce.

"Sad to see you come to this, Orvis," he sighed, as if even prison were preferable.

Orvis fumbled some more with the lead rope, his horse getting nervous as the rest of its stablemates headed back for the trail. Not liking the horse bumping against him, the pack mule pinned its long ears and tried to bite the brown gelding, narrowly missing Orvis's skinny leg. Orvis split his attention between the contrary mule and his former employer, not quite sure which one scared him more. "Sorry you feel that way, Mr. Rafferty," he mumbled. "Mr. Bryce, he pays real good."

The mule pinned its ears and raised up a little on its hind legs. The horse hopped up and down. Orvis turned gray, eyes bugging out of his head. The lead rope seemed like a live tentacle wrapping itself around him. "Whoa, mule! Whoa!"

Rolling his eyes, J.D. leaned over and jerked the rope away, untangling it with a flick of his wrist. "There's more important things in this world than money, Orvis."

As he tossed the rope back to Orvis, the mule bolted and ran after its pals. Orvis wheeled his horse around, nearly falling off, and galloped away in hot pursuit, one hand clamped on top of his head to keep his bedraggled hat from flying off.

J.D. shook his head and turned back to his own people. Lyle and his two boys and Chaske were halfway to the house. Tucker hung back, looking uncertain. J.D.'s concern was with the two who remained rooted to their spots.

Will roused himself and climbed through the bars of the fence. He turned toward the house, but his gaze was fixed on his shiny red and white pickup. He wanted to get out, away, go anywhere his wife wasn't and his brother wasn't and people didn't look at him with pity or contempt. The Hell and Gone came to mind.

He would go to the Hell and Gone and in a little while he wouldn't be wondering why the sight of his wife riding around with Evan Bryce and company made him feel as if he'd been dropped on his head from ten stories up. He wanted out of the marriage. He should have been glad to see her out living it up. What he needed was a drink or two to numb the shock and then he would be able to think straight again. Maybe he'd go downstairs to Little Purgatory and play a hand of stud while his mind stewed on what to do about this latest turn of events.

J.D. cut off his escape route to the truck. "We got a big problem here, little brother," he said in a soft, dangerous voice.

"Drop it, J.D." In his own head he sounded twelve all over again, a shaky layer of false bravado over a mess of anger and fear. He didn't look up. He didn't blink. His eyes were burning. He clenched his fists at his sides and caught himself wishing, as he had wished back then, that

he were able to beat the tar out of J.D., just for the sake
of doing it. But J.D. had always been bigger, stronger,
better, smarter.

"Will—"

"Just drop it. Please." It nearly crushed him to add
that last weight to his humiliation, but he did it. He
ground his teeth and waited, not breathing again until
J.D. backed his horse away and let him pass.

J.D. watched him climb into the pickup and tear out of
the yard, then turned his attention to Mari. She still sat
atop the fence, looking like a waif in her faded jeans and
too-big denim shirt, the wind inciting her wild hair to
riot. Her big blue eyes were locked on his face, and he
steeled himself against their effect.

"Bryce a friend of yours?" he asked carefully.

"I wouldn't call him that, no. We've met."

"And you'll go drink his champagne and rub elbows
with his famous friends?"

"For my own reasons."

His gray eyes narrowed. She thought he was probably
trying to look tough, blank, uncaring, but she thought
she could feel his disappointment, and it meant more to
her than it should have.

He shook his head. "You need to hang out with a better class of losers, Mary Lee."

He picked his reins up and rode off toward the barn,
leaving Mari sitting on the proverbial fence. She watched
him go, cussing herself for caring what he thought. Behind her, the cattle bawled incessantly, the noise making
it impossible for her to think straight. At least that was
the excuse she chose as she climbed down off the rail and
headed to the barn.

J.D. left the mare in the cross ties and walked out the end
of the barn. From there he could see nothing but wilderness. Mountains, trees, sky, grass laced with wildflowers.
It was a view that usually soothed him. He looked at it
now and felt as if he were seeing it for the last time.
Something like fear snaked through him, a feeling so un-

familiar, so unwelcome, he refused to recognize it for what it was. But he couldn't do anything to stop its catalysts from hurling through his mind. Bryce's smiling face was branded into the backs of his eyes as surely as the Rafter T was burned into the hides of his cattle. Bryce, grinning like the goddamn Cheshire cat, as if he had a fifth ace. And, by Christ, he did, didn't he? He had Samantha.

He blinked like a man in deep physical pain, rubbed his hands over his face, and swore a litany of curses under his breath. What the hell could he do? He couldn't stop Lyle from selling his land. He couldn't stop Samantha from seeing who she wanted. He couldn't stop Will from running off half-cocked to do who knew what fool thing next. He couldn't do a damn thing. The wolves were closing in and he couldn't do a goddamn thing to stop them. The knowledge shook him right to the core.

Mari stood in the shadows just inside the barn, holding her breath, caught between stepping out and sliding away. She had little doubt J.D. would not appreciate her intrusion on the moment. He stood there with his hands braced on a section of split rail fence, looking out over an open meadow. The naked vulnerability in his face struck her like a physical blow. It was like seeing the Lone Ranger unmasked and realizing he was just a regular man. She wanted to reach out to him, to offer him a touch, some comfort. She knew instinctively he wouldn't want it, and that knowledge made her heart ache.

Oh, Marilee, what are you getting yourself into here? Trouble with a capital J.D.

She moved backward down the aisle on tiptoe, then coughed loudly and came ahead, scuffing her feet on the cement as she went. When she reached the end of the barn again, J.D. was trying to settle his iron-man mask back in place. He cleared his throat and shot her a scowl.

"Thought you were leaving."

"Can't go anywhere without Clyde," she said, catching herself dropping her pronouns as if she had lived there her whole life.

"Who—? Oh, the mule." He made no move toward

the barn, just stood there leaning against the fence, pretending nothing at all was the matter.

"I'm not much for parties as a rule," Mari said, stepping up beside him. She tried to mirror his stance and found herself staring at a fence rail. Undaunted, she climbed up onto the lowest bar and hooked her arms over the top, a position that put her eye level with Rafferty. "I don't like much of anything I have to shave my legs for."

"So don't go."

"I'm just curious about a couple of things, that's all. I had sort of lost touch with Lucy since she moved here. I'm curious about the crowd she ran with."

"So go see them," J.D. growled. "Do what you like."

"It's not a matter of what I like. Lucy left me everything she had in the world. I feel a certain obligation."

J.D. sniffed, dry amusement kicking up one corner of his mouth. He knew all about obligation. He clung to his while the world came apart around him.

"Has Bryce asked you about selling yet?" he said.

"Not really."

"He will." He turned and studied her, his eyes narrowed. "Will you sell it?"

"I don't know."

"He's a ruthless, obnoxious little son of a bitch who doesn't give a damn about anything but getting what he wants."

Mari arched a brow. "I could say the same thing about you—except the little part."

He didn't bat an eye. At that moment it was difficult to reconcile the image before her with the one she'd seen from the shadows. This man didn't look as if he had ever been afraid in his life. He looked like bullets would bounce off his chest.

"Will you sell it to me?" he asked bluntly.

"I told you, I haven't decided to sell it at all."

He stepped over and very deliberately planted a hand on either side of her on the rail. Mari twisted around to face him, her heart beating a little harder as he leaned close. His gaze held hers like a deer in headlights.

"Don't play games with me, Mary Lee," he warned.

"I'm not interested in games," she whispered, her heart pounding harder behind her breastbone.

For a moment J.D. looked into those big deep blue eyes, looking for lies, looking for reasons not to trust. Then he felt as if he were drowning in them, and lies and Bryce and everything else went right out of his head. Losing himself seemed a welcome option at the moment. He pressed his lips over hers and submerged himself into a blissful oblivion.

Mari kissed him back, bracing her hands on his shoulders. They were like rock beneath the damp cotton of his shirt. Her fingers kneaded the muscle, moving up the back of his thick neck and down again. All the while their tongues slid against each other, their lips clung, their breath mingled with the taste of strong coffee and dust.

J.D. pressed her back into the rails, sliding a hand between them to undo the buttons of her shirt. She made no move to stop him. And she made no move to stop him when he lowered his head, tugged the lacy cup of her bra aside, and took her nipple into his mouth. Desire exploded through her like a nuclear blast. His mouth was hot. The insistent tugging seemed to reach down into the core of her and pull at something vital. She slicked her hands over his head, brushing her fingers back through his dark hair, pulling him closer.

She wanted him. She wanted to comfort him and offer him something soft and gentle. . . .

Then somewhere in the last bastion of sanity she thought of what kind of games he might be playing. He wanted her land and he wanted her body, and she was damn sure he would want nothing else she had to offer. She was an outsider. She didn't belong.

As if he sensed her sudden shift of mood, J.D. raised his head and looked at her, his eyes the color and intensity of hot charcoal. She couldn't find her voice anywhere, and simply shook her head. His face tightened. He stepped back, pulling the two halves of her shirt together, and she stepped down from the fence, not at all certain that her knees wouldn't give out.

"I don't play games," she said again. But as she walked away from him into the dim interior of the barn, she had the terrible feeling she was already caught up in a game with rules she didn't understand and stakes that were far too high.

CHAPTER 11

"*I* wish you hadn't done that with Will," Samantha said quietly. She stood just outside the door to Bryce's stable. The rest of his entourage was halfway to the house. She hung back, feeling more at home near the barn than near the mansion. In the dimly lit aisle of the stable, a dirty, tattooed ranch hand unsaddled the Appaloosa she had ridden. The man watched her over the gelding's back for a moment, the gleam in his eyes making her skin crawl. She frowned at him and his mouth twisted in amusement, revealing a glimpse of discolored teeth.

Bryce rubbed his fingertips along his jaw, idly contemplating shaving before the party. He studied Samantha at the same time. He stood behind her and to the side, out of her line of vision, very coolly, very calculatingly assessing her emotional state. She looked more like a stable hand than his usual sort of guest. The jeans she wore were old, the blouse cheap cotton. She had pulled her hair back into its serviceable braid again and secured it at the end with a pink rubber band.

"He needed shocking, sweetheart," he said with just the perfect touch of consolation and paternal wisdom. "Now maybe he'll wake up and see what a fool he's been for neglecting you. If he doesn't, he doesn't deserve you." He picked up the end of her braid, slipped the band from it, and began to sift the strands free with his fingers. "Personally, I'm quite certain he doesn't deserve you," he murmured. "Any sensible man would cherish you, pamper you, encourage you to come into full bloom instead of leaving you to wither on the vine."

He lifted her hair, spread it out across her shoulders. When he turned her to face him, his expression was one of fatherly concern, gently chastising. "Your hair is gorgeous, Samantha. You should wear it loose, show it off. Don't hide your beauty, sweetheart. Glory in it."

Uncomfortable with his flattery, Samantha tried to glance away from him, but his pale eyes had a way of mesmerizing her, and she kept glancing back at him like a nervous horse. He had to think she was a stupid, naive kid. She had never been anywhere or done anything. She didn't have a clue how to act around his kind of people. And yet he was still taking the time to be nice to her. She may not have liked his methods, but he was trying to help her with Will, even though he didn't think much of her choice of husbands.

"I've never really thought of myself as beautiful," she admitted shyly, feeling as if she at least owed him her honesty and her confidence. He was only trying to be a friend to her, and God knew she didn't have many of those.

Her confession actually surprised Bryce. A rare shock showed on his face. She had the bone structure of a model, and an exotic quality that had the potential to be stunning. How could she not know that? He didn't know a woman who wasn't fully aware of every weapon in her arsenal. But Samantha was not being coy or fishing for compliments. He could easily read the uncertainty in her eyes, and it touched him as very few things could.

Gently he hooked a finger beneath her chin and tilted her face up. "Honey, you could set the world on its ear," he said sincerely. "All you need is someone to point you in the right direction and encourage you. Didn't your parents encourage you?"

The bitter laugh was automatic, though it mortified Samantha and she immediately wished she could have sucked it back into her lungs and held it there. She couldn't talk about her family with Bryce. They were poor and dirty. Trash. That was what everyone around town said. That was what she had grown up hearing sneered behind her back. The Neills were nothing but half-breed trash. The shame of that clung to her still, like a film of grime she could never wash off no matter how hard she scrubbed.

"I should go home," she mumbled, glancing at the cheap oversize watch she wore strapped to her wrist, the band wrapped twice around. It was Will's. She wondered if he missed it any more than he missed her. "I have to feed my dog."

"I'll send Morton to take care of it," Bryce said. He didn't want her slipping away now, when she was in this melancholy mood. She would likely talk herself out of returning for the party, and he couldn't have that.

"You don't have to. I'll need to change clothes anyway," Samantha said, doing a bleak mental inventory of her wardrobe. She had nothing good enough to wear to a party the likes of this one. Because she didn't belong here, she reminded herself. She wasn't Cinderella. She had no fairy godmother. Her Prince Charming had dumped her for chance to ride off into the sunset with honky-tonk heroines night after night.

Bryce waited, letting the moment ripen, stepping forward just as the first glitter of tears glazed across her eyes. Taking hold of her hand, he granted her a subdued version of the Redford smile. "Wait here just a minute. I have a little surprise for you."

He went into the stable and gave instructions to the hired hand brushing down the Appaloosa to drive into town and see to Samantha's dog. When he came back out, he took her by the elbow and led her up the path to his house. Samantha thought it was nearly as large as the Moose, all gray wood and fieldstone, sparkling windows and soaring roof lines. Passing by a living room, she caught a glimpse of sparkling windowpanes that rose to a peak in the center of the wall, making her think of a cathedral, as did the beamed, vaulted ceiling. Seemed like a lot of wasted space, but it was beautiful. The view was incredible. It was like standing in heaven and looking down on paradise. She could have fit her whole house into this one room.

Bryce led her up a curving open staircase to the second floor and down the quiet, elegant hall of the guest wing. Five of the ten guest rooms were occupied, though there was no sign of the guests. Everyone had retired to get ready for the party.

The suite of rooms Bryce took Samantha to far outstripped anything she had ever encountered in terms of luxury. Thick beige carpet, antique furnishings, real paintings on the walls, a huge bouquet of fresh flowers in a Chinese vase on a table in the small sitting room. In the bedroom a pine wardrobe stood open near the bed with an array of jeweltone clothing hanging inside.

"Take your pick," Bryce said, brushing a hand across the dangling sleeves and setting the garments swinging. "I had Sharon stop in at Latigo Boutique and pick up a few things in your size. The colors are perfect for you. You'll find whatever else you might need in the bureau."

"I can't accept this," Samantha whispered, too stunned to speak louder—or too afraid that he might agree with her. One blouse from Latigo was enough to swallow her whole paycheck. There were half a dozen in the wardrobe.

"Of course you can," he insisted, grinning. "We're friends."

"Yeah, but—"

"But nothing. I'm a generous man. I enjoy giving things to my friends, especially those in need of a little something special in their lives." He softened his expression and brushed the knuckles of one hand down her cheek. "This is my gift to you, sweetheart. Enjoy it. Enjoy the rooms. Enjoy the clothing. Enjoy the party tonight. My payment is getting to see you smile and have a good time."

Samantha backed away from him, a grin tugging at her mouth. Laughter bubbled up inside her as the pendulum of her emotions swung upward again and the shift of momentum threatened her equilibrium. She turned around, taking in the room, the clothes. Through the partially open door to the bath she caught a glimpse of marble and gold fixtures. "It seems too good to be true."

"Not at all," Bryce murmured, curling his fingers around the doorknob. "This is opportunity, Samantha. The doors to the whole world are open to you. You have only to choose to go through them."

He left her on that note, pleased with his flair for drama, certain Samantha would soak it in like a dry sponge. Poor kid. He knew what it was to be stuck in a life devoid of quality; financially, culturally, socially bankrupt. That was the life to which Will Rafferty would anchor her. She had to be allowed to glimpse the world she could have if she would cut the anchor free.

He glanced at the watch he'd had crafted by a silversmith in Missoula—a platinum Rolex set in a wide cuff of sterling that was shaped and engraved into the likeness of an eagle with its wings spread to encircle his wrist. Two hours to prepare. Ample time. Everything was under control.

Except J. D. Rafferty. Bryce scowled at the reminder. Damned cowboy. So pious, so smug, wearing his air of entitlement like a king's robe when it was nothing more than a shabby rag handed down by another dirty cowboy. He thought his humble Montana birth somehow elevated him morally. The idea made Bryce want to choke.

"I'll bring you to your knees, Rafferty," he snarled beneath his breath. "I'll have your damn ranch."

The knowledge that he already had the key brightened his mood and the anger rolled away like storm clouds that had threatened, then moved on. He was smiling by the time he reached his suite. The smile turned carnal as he walked into the bedroom and found Sharon lounging back against a mountain of suede pillows, naked except for one of his narrow, silver-tipped western belts and a pair of tall snakeskin cowboy boots.

"How's our little pigeon?" she asked as he came to a halt at the end of the bed and began to undress.

"Roosting. She likes your taste in clothes."

"I should hope so," she said with a wry smile. "You spent a small fortune on her."

"Investment." He slipped his shirt off and tossed it onto the seat of a caramel-colored leather chair. "You have to spend money to make money. Samantha won't cost me a fraction of what I'll gain."

"Rafferty's land."

"Mmmm . . ." His mind drifted a bit, down the hall, to the beauty who couldn't see past her own sense of inadequacy.

"Have you touched her?" Sharon asked, trying to keep her voice neutral. She rose on her knees on the bed and moved toward him, the long tail of the belt hanging down across her patch of carefully trimmed dark pubic hair.

"Of course not."

Laughing, she closed the distance between them. Her hand shot forward and she grabbed him by the balls through his jeans, squeezing. Her wide painted mouth twisted up at the corners and her eyes sparkled with mischief. "Swear it," she demanded, teasing him, taunting him.

Bryce groaned, letting the pain throb through him. He snatched a handful of her blond hair and jerked her head back, his eyes locked on the almost masculine features of her face, and lust burned through him. "I swear. Why would I want a girl when I can have you?"

She smiled darkly and released him, her fingers turning to the task of unfastening his belt and unzipping his fly. "Why wouldn't you? She's beautiful. Innocent. I know I would enjoy her."

"I'm sure you would," Bryce whispered, stroking her head as she took his swelling penis into her mouth. "But you can't have her, cuz. Not until I get what I want."

Mari climbed out of her Honda, making one final check of her appearance. She wouldn't knock anybody off their feet with her fashion statement, but then, she hadn't come here to attract attention to herself. Out of the limited clothes she had left, she had selected a purple silk blouse with a square-cut bottom that she let fall over a short slim black skirt. Having thrown out all her heels before leaving Sacramento, she wore simple black flats. Having burned all her panty hose, she had made a quick stop at the Gas N' Go for a pair of L'eggs that some diabolical man had designed so that one leg was perpetually twisted. She scowled now as she glanced around for witnesses and tried to adjust the stupid thing with a discreet tug.

The paved parking area of Bryce's little homestead was lined with an incongruous assortment of European imports and American four-wheel muscle. A bass rhythm thumped on the early evening air, carrying out from somewhere behind the enormous lodge-style log house.

"God, he must have felled half of Oregon to build that," she whispered, staring in awe at the sheer mass of the place. It looked big enough to house Congress. A turret rose on one end like a rocket pointing to the big Montana sky. The roof was slate, the foundation massive fieldstones. The overall impression was of one thing: power.

A shiver skittered down Mari's back. She called it a chill and strode around the side of the house in search of the source of the music and in search of some answers.

Bryce met her at the edge of the terrace as if he had been waiting especially for her. Dressed in loose-fitting navy raw silk trousers and a billowing white silk shirt worn open down the front, he was the picture of elegant hip. His hair was swept back into a neat queue, emphasizing his towering forehead. He beamed a smile at her that was almost iridescent in his tanned face.

"Marilee, I'm so glad you've come," he said, taking both her hands in his. "I was afraid your friend Mr. Rafferty might have talked you out of it."

"Rafferty doesn't tell me what to do," she replied, dodging the kiss he tried to brush across her cheek. She ducked around him, making a show of taking in the terrace and pool area that was cluttered with major and minor celebrities. "Quite a spread you've got here, Mr. Bryce."

"Well, it's home," he said, chuckling with false modesty. A waiter appeared beside him, and Bryce took two slim flutes of champagne from the tray, handing one to Mari. "Call me Bryce. All my friends do."

"Did Lucy?" she asked baldly, glancing at him from beneath her lashes as she raised the glass to her lips.

"Of course. Lucy was a regular here." He made a mournful face, shaking his head, clucking his tongue. "Such a spirit. God, it's a pity we had to lose her so young."

"Yes. I'm beginning to feel I hardly knew her."

He sipped his champagne and watched her, his pale eyes keen. "You weren't close? She spoke of you. I'm surprised she didn't tell you everything about her life here."

"We shared a profession once. We were friends. But we weren't very good about staying in touch after she moved here. As I said, I almost feel as if I didn't know her at all anymore."

Her gaze drifted across the small sea of faces, the thirty or so chosen elite who mingled on the flagstone terrace, talking, drinking, looking gorgeous. She recognized the redhead who had been in Bryce's company at the Stars and Bars—Uma Kimball, Hollywood's latest find who had been described as a cross between Tinker Bell and Madonna. She stood along the low stone wall that edged the terrace, wearing what looked to be a burlap sack with a belt of twine. A fortune in diamonds hung from her earlobes. She was stuffing her skinny face with canapes while a male model bimbob with a flowing golden mane tried to impress her with the size of his naked pecs.

Near the pool, the Rhine maiden stood in a stark black knit tank dress that hugged her body and dispelled any thoughts that she may actually have been a guy. Her eyes locked on Mari like a pair of lasers, beaming cool amusement.

"For instance," Mari said, turning back to Bryce, "the sheriff told me Lucy was off riding by herself when she was—when she had her accident. I never knew Lucy to be the solitary type. I honestly can't picture her communing with nature."

"Yes, well, Lucy was full of surprises. Let me introduce you to some people," Bryce offered, steering her by the elbow straight for the towering blonde at poolside. Even in his high-heeled boots, the woman was able to look down her nose at Bryce, something that brought a nasty gleam of satisfaction to her eyes. "Marilee, this is my cousin, Sharon Russell. Sharon, this is Lucy's friend, Marilee Jennings."

Sharon's gaze raked down Mari from her unruly mane to the tips of her cheap flat shoes and back again. "Oh, yes," she said, her wide mouth twisting sardonically, "the little singer."

A razor-sharp smile cut across Mari's face. "How nice to meet you," she said sweetly. "You're Bryce's cousin? My, the two of look so much alike, I thought you were brothers—I mean, brother and sister."

The look Sharon Russell gave her could have melted granite.

"You didn't bring your guitar?" Bryce said, his mouth curving in disappointment.

"Were you going to make me sing for my supper?"

"Not at all. There are some people here from Columbia Records. I thought this might be an opportunity for you. You have a rare talent, Marilee."

Which he had heard exactly once across a crowded room. Mari met his cool blue gaze for a moment, trying to figure out his game. Was he really so benevolent? Or was it a matter of playing God, manipulating people, bestowing blessings, then basking in the afterglow of their gratitude?

"Some other time, maybe," she said as a glimpse of dark hair and handsome features flashed in her peripheral vision. Ben Lucas. "I'm still too shaken over everything that's happened with Lucy and all to even think about my future. I just came to mingle, you know, meet some new people, eat some free food."

"By all means." Bryce flashed his teeth and gestured to the crowd around him. "Enjoy yourself."

She nodded to him, ignored Sharon, and strolled away, snagging a stuffed mushroom off the tray of a passing waiter as she went.

Lucas was busy charming the black-haired girl from the riding party. They stood at the end of the pool, the underwater lights shimmering up on them in rippling waves. He was a good-looking man, a fact that had not escaped his own notice. Like most of the high-powered trial lawyers Mari had known, he was vain and arrogant to the point of megalomania. He had chosen his audience tonight unerringly. The young woman was hanging on his every word. She looked all of twenty, too fresh-scrubbed and innocent to be running with this crowd. Fresh meat. And Lucas was sniffing after her like a hungry wolf.

". . . The press had Lana Broderick tried, convicted, and executed," Lucas announced. "They were stunned by the acquittal."

"But was she really innocent?"

He gave the girl a finely honed look of combined wisdom and compassion that had swayed many a juror, letting it soak in just right before dropping the dramatic finish line. "She should have been."

Mari rolled her eyes and tried to keep from gagging on her mushroom. "I'm sure the unfortunate late Mrs. Dale Robards wished your client had been innocent," she said dryly as she made a trio of their little duo. "If Lana Broderick had stuck with the baton-twirling squad instead of opting for extracurricular activities with Mr. Robards, Mrs. Robards might be alive today."

The muscles in Lucas's jaw tightened and his eyes narrowed slightly, but he took her counter and parried smoothly, expertly. "My point exactly. If Dale Robards hadn't seduced an innocent sixteen-year-old girl, the entire tragedy could have been avoided. Robards should have been the one on trial for crimes of moral corruption."

Mari polished off her mushroom and flashed him a smile, enjoying the sparring match, enjoying the idea that she could mouth off to an attorney and no longer have to worry about him ruining her career for it. "Dale's moral corruption didn't pull the trigger. Sweet little Lana did that all by herself."

"I guess I should be glad you weren't on the jury, Miss—?"

"Jennings. Marilee Jennings. We've met, actually. A couple years ago. I used to be a court reporter in Sacramento. I did some work for one of your partners once. State of California versus Armand Uscavaro. He claimed voices from hell compelled him to murder his parents in their sleep, then make it look like a robbery so he could inherit two million dollars. Poor kid. Turned out they wouldn't let him listen to heavy metal. I suppose they deserved to die."

Lucas ignored the bite of her words. Her sarcasm slid off him like oil on Teflon. "Small world." He flashed her a bright smile. "I'm ashamed to say I don't remember our meeting. I like to think I never forget a pretty face."

"You probably remember my friend better. She used to do quite a bit of work with your firm. Lucy MacAdam?"

He blinked at the mention of Lucy's name, as if some invisible hand had slapped his face. Mari catalogued the reaction and turned to the young woman with an apologetic smile. "In the midst of all that weirdness and macho stuff going on this afternoon, I didn't get your name."

Samantha looked down on the little blonde with the husky voice and curvy body and felt like a giant wooden totem, oversize with exaggerated features, big and clumsy. The beautiful teal silk blouse and slacks she had chosen from the wardrobe suddenly felt garish and huge on her, the makeup she had so carefully applied, clownish. She wished fervently she could become invisible or wake up and discover this had all been a dream, that she was really in bed beside her husband and not standing at a posh party chatting with one of his mistresses. But she didn't become invisible and she didn't wake up, and Marilee Jennings and Ben Lucas were staring at her, waiting.

"Samantha," she mumbled, clutching the stem of her wineglass as if she expected it to snap and fall with a crash to the blue tile that edged the pool. "Samantha Rafferty."

It was Mari's turn to blink in shock. "Rafferty? Are you Will Rafferty's wife?"

"Yes."

The answer came complete with a stony look Mari didn't immediately interpret. She was too busy putting together the pieces of the afternoon's little drama. Suddenly Will's reaction made some kind of sense. J.D.'s remark to his brother played over in her mind—*We got a big problem here, little brother.* Will's estranged wife in the company of Evan Bryce, the man who would be king of the Eden Valley. *Oh, boy.*

She cut a glance across the pool at Bryce. He was laughing, pinching the bimbob's pecs as Uma Kimball shoveled another cheese puff into her mouth. In her mind's eye she imagined him suddenly levitating above the crowd, shooting lightning bolts down from the tips of his fingers. He had that air about him, that he was a warlock who had taken human form just for sport. Was it really all a game to him—playing with people's lives? Was that why he had brought his little retinue to the Stars and Bars—to watch the drama of human life unfold before his eyes? The thought gave her a chill.

The feeling of Samantha's petulant gaze on her brought Mari's attention back to the matter at hand. The source of that look booted her mentally. Jealousy. God, the poor kid probably thought she was one of Will's many conquests. She called him half a dozen slanderous names in her head. He'd gotten her into enough trouble already, the jerk.

"J.D. invited me to watch the branding," she lied. "He's been helping me out with Lucy's animals. My animals, now, I guess. I can't quite get used to that idea." She turned back to Ben Lucas, who seemed as well composed as a Mozart quintet. "I suppose you heard about Lucy's accident?"

"Yes. It was a terrible tragedy for all concerned. Graf —Dr. Sheffield—was beside himself with grief."

"Too bad he wasn't beside himself while he was out

hunting. One of him might have seen it was a woman he was shooting at." The words came out as sharp as knives, as sharp as her resentment. Mari knew she should have tempered them, but the feelings weren't dulling with time. Just the opposite. The shock was burning off like fog in the face of a strong morning sun. Every day the irony and the stupidity came a little clearer into focus, a little brighter, a little more painful.

Lucas was frowning at her.

"You know Dr. Sharpshooter?" She took a swallow of champagne, hoping in vain to cool her hot tongue a little. She wished fervently for a cigarette.

"I'm his attorney."

Oh, God, what have you stuck your foot in this time, Marilee?

All around her she could hear the noise of the party like the distant sound of bees swarming. The music boomed out of hidden speakers, all thumping and discordant static. The light from the pool flickered and rippled across Ben Lucas's handsome features in bars of bright and dark like moonglow through a venetian blind. His mouth was moving. Mari could barely hear him above the pounding in her temples. Something about having a second home across the valley and belonging to the Montana bar.

"How convenient," she said tightly. *Lucy had worked for Lucas. Lucas had been her lover at one time. Lucas worked for Sheffield. All of them knew Bryce, the puppet master. Wasn't that nice and cozy?* All the bits and fragments of information swirled around inside her head like colored glass in a kaleidoscope. "You must be proud of yourself, pleading the value of a human life down to a misdemeanor and pocket change."

His dark eyes took on a flat quality. Like a shark's, she thought. How apropos. "It was an accident, Ms. Jennings."

"Yeah, I know the drill," she said bitterly. "No malice, no premeditation. If he wasn't innocent, he should have been."

She glared up at him, hating him, hating his kind. He

was the breed of lawyer who made a mockery of the system. He played the courts like an elaborate game of *Let's Make a Deal*. The only thing that mattered was his record of acquittals. Not the law. Not justice. Not innocence or guilt.

"Pardon me, but I've had it up to here with lawyers," she said, slashing a hand across her throat.

She flung her glass into the pool and strode for the house, ignoring the curious looks that turned her way.

A pair of French doors stood open, leading into a huge room in the center section of the house. Mari waded across a sea of champagne-colored carpet, taking in only peripherally the white leather sofas and earthtone pillows, the Georgia O'Keeffe prints on the walls, the Native American artifacts displayed in tall lighted glass cases.

Stepping up into a foyer area of glazed Mexican tile, she took a left and headed down a wide hall, looking for a bathroom. She needed a few minutes alone and she had the most overwhelming need to wash after her conversation with Lucas. Beneath the male-model looks, inside the $1,500 suit and the Cole-Haan loafers, he was an eel, a slimy, ugly, beady-eyed eel. He was the kind of man who billed his clients $300 an hour for thirty-hour days and refused to pay his court reporter until the final gavel had fallen on a litigation that had taken eighteen months to complete.

A door swung open in front of her, nearly smacking her in the face, and Uma Kimball staggered out, giggling and glassy-eyed, a demented pixie in sackcloth. Her skin had a translucent quality, as if it were stretched very thin and very tight over her small, fine bones. Her red hair was short and ragged, looking as if rodents had chewed it off while she slept. She wiped her collagen-plumped mouth on the back of her hand, smearing her lipstick.

"Hi!" she gushed, as excited as a cheerleader at a pep fest. "Hey, great party, huh? Have you met Fabian yet? God, he's got like the biggest tits I've ever seen and they're *really his*! Isn't that wild!"

"Is this the bathroom?"

Uma giggled, setting the cascades of diamonds swinging on her earlobes. "It better be. I just hurled about a pound of hors d'oeuvres. Eat till you puke—that's my motto." She nearly fell over laughing, grabbing on to Mari's shoulder to keep herself upright. Her breath reeked of Binaca.

"Oh, yeah, that's catchy," Mari said, her sarcasm lost on the actress, who had suddenly become fixated on Mari's hair.

"This is so radical!" She reached up to rub a strand between her fingers. "Where did you *get* this color? José?"

"DNA."

"Where's *that*?"

"In my genes. It's the real thing. I was born with it."

Uma looked confused for a few seconds, then amused again. "People still *do* that?"

"Call me old-fashioned," Mari said on a sigh. Her temples were throbbing like a pair of hammer-struck thumbs. "You wouldn't happen to have a cigarette, would you?"

"God, no." Uma's overinflated lips bent into a huge sad-clown frown. "Smoking's like *bad* for you. But ask Brycie if you really need one. Brycie can get you anything you want."

"Yeah, I'll bet he can."

"No shit. Like he's got the best blow I've ever had. Want some?"

Mari started to tell her newfound friend she preferred to stay on planet earth, but she bit her tongue at the last second. She wanted to know more about Bryce. She wanted to know more about the crowd Lucy had run with before she died. Somewhere along the line, the answers were going to start making some kind of sense instead of leading her deeper and deeper down the rabbit hole.

"Come on!" Uma grabbed her arm and led her down the hall, her pale, thin face polished by excitement and the burnoff of cocaine. They turned a corner and came to a set of tall carved double doors. She gave Mari a look brimming with conspiracy. "You have to know the secret knock."

She pounded out a beat that sounded vaguely like "The Rain in Spain," and fell against the door in a fit of giggles. Mari watched her, thinking that if Uma got any more wired than she already was, something was going to short-circuit. She didn't wait for anyone to answer her secret code, but turned the knob and stumbled into the room with the swing of the door.

"Trick or treat! Got any nose candy?"

Uma righted herself and made a beeline for a huge billiard table with carved mahogany legs. The only light in the room came from the hanging brass fixture above the table. The light shone down in three perfect cones on a long mirror that had been situated on top of the slate, illuminating a dozen neat white lines of cocaine just waiting for some itchy noses.

Mari came to a dead halt three feet into the room as she recognized the man bent over the table with a rolled hundred-dollar bill poised under one nostril. Her heart slammed into her breastbone and bounced back and forth between her ribs.

MacDonald Townsend. U.S. District Court judge MacDonald Townsend.

He glanced up and their gazes collided with all the force of a pair of trains.

"I just came looking for cigarettes," Mari mumbled, turning away from the puddle of light around the table. Someone handed her a pack of French Gauloises. Instead of shaking one out, she took the whole thing, stumbled over a thanks, and ducked out the door into the dimly lit hallway.

MacDonald Townsend was one of the most highly respected men on the bench in northern California. Rumors already had him placed on a seat in superior court. He had the governor's ear, a wealthy wife, and, apparently, an appetite for Colombian snow.

And for one long, hot summer, MacDonald Townsend had been Lucy's lover.

The questions loomed larger, boomed louder with every beat of her pulse in her temples. She hurried down a maze of halls, finding an exterior door just when she was sure she was hopelessly lost. Desperate for fresh air, she let herself out and stood a moment to get her bearings. She was downhill from the parking area, nearer to the stables than the cars. Still trembling a little, her heart still pounding, she walked down a paved, landscaped path toward the dark barnyard. The smell of horse manure and pine trees seemed a big improvement over the stench of greed and power that hovered like smog around Bryce's crowd.

She wandered down along the end of the long building where a big sliding door had been left rolled back. She leaned a shoulder against it and stared in at the row of box stalls. Music from the party drifted down the hill, diluted enough to be pleasant. More comforting were the sounds of the horses eating and stamping flies, but not even that could loosen the tension in her nerves.

Christ, what a party. Lawyers trolling like sharks in a swimming pool. A pillar of the bench snorting coke. She felt like Alice down the rabbit hole on LSD. The sinister quality of it all crept over her flesh like a thousand worms. It grew and pressed in on her until it felt as if it had taken a solid form and stood staring out at her from the shadows of the stable.

Mari straightened away from the building, unable and unwilling to stop herself from overreacting. All she wanted was away from this place. Wonderland had offered her all the revelations she could stand for one night.

She hurried up the path for the parking area, headed for her Honda, never thinking the feel of eyes on her back was real.

Judge Townsend paced the elegant confines of Bryce's private lair. He was fifty-two and favored Charlton Heston. Many said he was a man with a brilliant future ahead of him. At the moment, that future was going up in flames in his imagination. His nerves were strung tighter than piano wire.

"Dammit, Bryce, how could you invite her here? She could be another Lucy—or worse." He stopped his pacing at the window that overlooked the valley and stared out into the darkness for a moment. His thin mouth quivered. He brought a hand up and pressed it against his forehead as if he were feeling for a fever. "Jesus, I don't believe this is happening to me."

Bryce watched him from a casual perch on the edge of his desk. He held his expression calm and vaguely amused, but inwardly he sneered at Townsend. *Spineless.* The man didn't have the nerve to play in the big leagues. He was weak—weak of mind, weak of spirit. He constantly succumbed to temptation—women, cocaine, money. He *succumbed,* he did not *indulge.* The difference was huge. Bryce might have admired Townsend if he had plunged himself into his vices with joy and verve. But MacDonald Townsend was like a tightrope walker afraid of heights. Every time he slipped from his lofty position, he screamed and sweated and soiled himself. Bryce despised him and enjoyed pushing him, shaking the wire, luring him over the edge.

"We don't know what Lucy might have told her," Townsend said. "We don't know what evidence she might have left."

"We searched the house," Bryce said calmly. "There was no videotape. Lucy was playing games with you, taking your money and laughing at you behind your back."

"That bitch." His whole body was trembling now. He squeezed his hands into fists at his sides. "I never should have touched her."

"No," Bryce commented mildly. He slid off the desk and sauntered to the window with his hands steepled before him like a priest. Ignoring the view, he turned toward Townsend, his pale eyes glowing with contempt. "No, my friend, you should never have touched Lucy. You didn't have the nerve to play her kind of games. You are, however, very fortunate to have me to look out for your well-being."

"You'll take care of the Jennings woman?"

"I'm keeping an eye on her. I'll take care of everything. I always do."

Bryce started for the door, eager to rejoin the party. Townsend was tedious. He wanted to turn his attention over to Samantha. Her innocence was genuine, her beauty fresh. He wanted to stand beside her and watch the wonder in her eyes as she took in the experience of meeting famous people and living the good life for the first time.

The judge's voice bit into him as he reached the door. "Bryce, do you know who killed Lucy?"

Bryce gave him a hooded look. "Of course. Sheffield. It was an accident. Wasn't it?"

Mari sat on the deck, curled up in an Adirondack chair, covered with the serape from the sofa. Staring down at the moon-silvered creek, she let her mind tumble and race. She smoked the expensive French cigarettes one after another, not tasting them, just grateful for the nicotine. She *would* quit—just not tonight. She *would* have that fresh start—if her old life would ever give up and let go.

God, Townsend snorting coke, Lucas representing the man who shot Lucy. All of them slithering around in Bryce's den of vipers. *Watch yourself with Bryce, luv. . . . Lucy enjoyed playing with snakes, but then, she had fangs of her own. . . .*

Snakes in the Garden of Eden. The image sent shivers crawling down her spine.

"What the hell were you into, Lucy?" she whispered, staring through tears at the Mr. Peanut tin she had brought out and set on the table.

In one hand she clutched the letter her friend had left behind. She didn't try to read it. She only held it, as if it were a talisman, as if merely touching it might give her the power to see into its author's past. But all that came was a sense of dread and a sense of confusion, and she didn't know if she wanted to try to reach past either of them.

What she wanted was someone to confide in, a shoulder to lean on. She felt so alone. She had cut herself free of her family, free of everyone she had known. Somehow it only made her feel worse to think that no one from that life would have understood or helped her anyway. She could hear her mother's voice ringing with disapproval. *Well, Marilee, what do you expect? The people you run with. Honestly, it isn't any wonder one of them was shot dead. If you'd listened to your father and me and gone to law school . . . if you'd married that nice Enright boy . . . if you were more like your sisters . . .*

In the private theater of her mind she could see Lisbeth and Annaliese sitting primly, their legs crossed, arms folded, smug spite shining in their eyes. It was a cinch no one Lisbeth or Annaliese knew had ever been shot or had an affair with a married district court judge or screwed a top trial attorney on his desk while his client waited in the anteroom. They wouldn't understand or offer support. She thought of Brad and knew his biggest concern would have been the possibility of her getting him an introduction to Ben Lucas.

She thought of the people she knew here. Drew would listen to her, but what would she say? All she had were fragments and hunches and bad feelings. Then there was the ugly possibility that he would tell her something she didn't want to hear. What she wanted most was a pair of arms around her, reassurance, and the awareness of strength. Someone well-grounded in sanity. Someone there to catch her. Someone to hang on to.

J. D. Rafferty came to mind. She didn't want him to, but he came anyway, which was just like him. What a joke that she would want to turn to him, she thought, trying in vain to muster up a sense of humor. He didn't even want her in the state.

He wanted her only in his bed.

J.D. stood at the rail of the corral and watched the horses by moonlight. They ignored him now that his supply of butter mints had run out. The little palomino mare turned and looked at him every once in a while, curious about him, but the others all stood with their hind legs cocked and their ears back, dozing. For the horses that had worked, the day had been long and hard. They weren't interested in losing any sleep over J.D.'s presence.

J.D. knew how they felt. Physically, he was beat, his body aching, muscles protesting even necessary movement. Mentally, he felt as though someone had taken a lead pipe after his brain. Spiritually, he had a big old stone tied around his neck, and he was going under in deep, deep water.

The sight of Will's wife with Bryce's crowd had scared the hell out of him. He had been able to fool himself up to then, believing he could thumb his nose at Evan Bryce, play his game, and beat him. But Bryce had just been toying with him, amusing himself. Now he was upping the ante and J.D. was playing with a busted hand.

If Samantha divorced Will—and God knew she had grounds for it—she could drag him to court and sue him for his part of the Stars and Bars. If she won, Bryce would be standing right there beside her, ready to stick his foot in the door. And once Bryce got a toehold, that would be the end. Four generations of Rafferty stewardship would be over, and J.D. would be the one who let it happen. The burden of guilt, the shame, would be his to bear. Beyond that, if he didn't have the Stars and Bars, he had nothing at all.

He looked out over the horses to the hills and trees beyond, and felt as bleak as a sun-parched bone.

He would have nothing.

He had no one.

He thought of Mary Lee and couldn't quite steel his heart against the insidious desire to pull her close and just hold her.

Fool.

"You were mighty hard on the boy today."

J.D. glanced over as Tucker hobbled up to the fence and hooked a boot over the bottom rail. The old man met his glare, unblinking, then turned and spat a stream of Red Man into the dirt.

"He's not a boy. He's a man," J.D. said. "It's time he acted like one."

"He's going through hard times, J.D."

"Aren't we all? It's a hard life."

"You don't make it any easier—on yourself or anyone else."

"I don't want to hear it, Tuck," J.D. said wearily. Hanging his head, he looked down at the hands he dangled between the bars of the fence. Workingman's hands, thick, tough, callused. "I'm hanging on by the skin of my fingertips. Like those idiot rock climbers who come out here on the weekends."

Tucker was silent, working his chaw, thinking. The pharmacist's palomino mare wandered over and sniffed at him, rubbing her nose against his beard stubble. He pushed her away with a gentle hand. "You're not the only one hanging on, son. We're right there with you— me, Chaske, Will."

"What if he just lets go, Tuck?" J.D. said, for the first time giving voice to a fear that went deep and well beyond thoughts of the Stars and Bars. The thread that bound them as brothers had always been strained as their parents had pulled them in opposite directions. What if it broke? What would he feel? Relief?

"He won't," Tucker said with more conviction than he felt. He stepped back from the fence, spat, and wiped his chin on the sleeve of his shirt. "He won't. He's a Rafferty.

"You oughta get some sleep, son," he ordered.

He moved off toward the house, his gait the pained shuffle of an old cowboy. J.D. stayed at the fence, knowing he would feel more peace with the horses than he would in his bed. In his bed his thoughts would drift toward Mary Lee and dangerous longings for things he could never have.

He turned toward Bryce's place, imagining that he could catch snatches of music on the wind. She was there tonight, drinking Bryce's champagne and laughing at his jokes. She was one of them, which quite simply meant she could never be anything more to him than temptation.

Too bad. On nights like this one it would have been nice to have someone to rub his shoulders and share his concerns, warm his bed and ease his needs. And the taste of Mary Lee Jennings lingered in his mouth, and the feel of her lingered against him. On nights like this one, when dawn seemed a long way off, temptation was damn hard to resist.

Will sat on the back steps of the little house he had once shared with his wife. *Ex*-wife. *Ex*-wife. The word still pulsed in his brain. The moon was up, shining down on the fenced backyard. Rascal had been busy excavating. The place looked like the site of a treasure hunt. The pup lay on the steps beside him with his big head on his big clumsy paws, twitching as he dreamed puppy dreams.

The house behind them was dark and empty. Sam had abandoned it. Will wondered if she would ever come back once she'd gotten a taste of life on Mount Olympus.

"What's she got to come back to, Willie-boy?" he asked, Jack Daniel's turning his speech to a molasses drawl. The bottle stood between his booted feet, empty. He wasn't drunk. He couldn't seem to get drunk tonight. The liquor couldn't penetrate the fear, it only slowed down time, an ugly trick. He didn't want more time to think. His thoughts ran around and around, like a pup chasing its tail.

He didn't want a wife. Marriage was a prison sentence. He'd seen that growing up. His father had sentenced his mother to a life she'd grown tired of, then held on to her anyway. Marriage was stupid. He'd thought so all along. People should be free to move in and out of relationships as the tides of attraction dictated. No ties, no guilt, no hard feelings.

So why did you marry Sam in the first place, Willie-boy?

And why did that word stab at his chest like a dagger? *Ex*-wife. *Ex*-wife. *Ex*-wife.

And why did he sit there feeling so damn scared and so damn lonely when the moon was bright and the night was fragrant with the perfume of other women?

Because you love her, stupid.

"You screwed up again, Willie-boy," he whispered as two tears swam over his lashes and streaked down his face.

CHAPTER 12

$\mathcal{M}$ ari woke in the Adirondack chair as the first hint of morning turned the sky a pearly gray. Every part of her hurt from sleeping out in the cool damp night in an unnatural position. She struggled up out of the chair and slumped around the deck like Quasimodo, trying to work the kinks out, snagging the feet of her convenience store nylons on the wood planks of the deck. Her head was pounding from the French cigarettes and from the dreams that had wrecked what little sleep she'd gotten. The images had slammed around inside her head, screaming to get out, never finding the door, never lining up neatly the way she wanted them to so that she could make sense of all the dark clues and sinister feelings.

She leaned against the back of the chair and groaned, bringing a fist up to rub her eyes and push her hair back. Still clutched in her fist was the letter Lucy had left behind for her. Unable to face it before coffee, she tucked it under the base of the dew-covered peanut tin and went inside.

While she heated water on the stove for instant caffeine, she went into the powder room off the kitchen and went through an abbreviated version of her usual morning routine, trying not to look at herself in the mirror. But like driving by a car wreck, morbid curiosity got the better of her and she chanced a glance, gasping in horror at the reflection. Her eyes were shot through with jagged bolts of red and underlined with raccoon rings of mascara. Rummaging through the small medicine cabinet, she found a bottle of Murine and a jar of petroleum jelly and did her best to repair the damage.

In Lucy's bedroom, where the aftermath of the vandals had yet to be cleared away, Mari dug through the rubble for something fresh to wear. The mattress had been torn off the bed and slit open. A table lamp had apparently been hurled into the large beveled glass mirror that hung above the dresser. Clothing spewed out of open dresser drawers and trailed across the floor from the closet, blouses and dresses lying on the carpet with sleeves bent at strange angles, looking like inanimate casualties. The only piece of glass intact in the room was a goldfish bowl on the nightstand that was half full of condom packets.

Mari pretended there was no mess. She ignored the condoms and the statement they made about Lucy's life-style and went in search of something to wear, digging up clean underwear, jeans, a T-shirt from Mazatlan, and a neon-orange sweatshirt with an enormous, raised hot pink outline of a woman's lips slanting across the front.

Coffee in hand, she went back out to the deck and lit the last of the Gauloises. As sweet smoke curled up from the end of it, she picked up the letter and studied it again.

We all have our calling in life. . . . Mine was being a thorn in wealthy paws. . . . It got me where you are today. Or did it get me where I am?

The lines had made no sense at all when she had first read the letter. Now her attention homed in on two sentences: *It got me where you are today. Or did it get me where I am?*

Where you are today—the ranch. *Or did it get me where I am*—dead.

Mari bit her lip as she sifted through the possibilities, each one uglier than the last. Her heart picked up a beat and then another. Caffeine, she told herself. Nicotine. Or the chance that Lucy had foreseen her own murder.

Murder. She couldn't think of the word without seeing blood, without seeing the photos from Sheriff Quinn's file. Lucy's lifeless body lying in the grass, a hole blown through her.

Lucy knew things she shouldn't have about people

with power, people with money. The summer she had been sleeping with Judge Townsend, he had brought her to Montana for a weekend. She told Mari that was how she found her little ranch. Her hideout.

Outlaws had hideouts. Outlaws got shot.

Dr. Sheffield claimed he hadn't seen her. What if he had? What if Lucy had known something she shouldn't have about him? What if the tears he'd spilled at the hearing hadn't been from abject grief, but abject guilt?

She stared down at the peanut tin, acutely aware of the expensive log house behind her and the priceless land that stretched out before her, of the llamas and the Range Rover, the pricey clothes strewn across the floor of the bedroom, and the lavish lifestyle.

Lucy knew things she shouldn't have known about people with money and power. Lucy was dead.

Mari folded the note and tapped it against her pursed lips. She had to see where the shooting had happened, to see for herself if it could have been an accident. And she had to talk to the man who had found the body—Del Rafferty—J.D. or no J.D.

By noon Mari and Clyde were headed up the mountain, map in hand, for all the good it would do her. Sheriff Quinn had drawn it on the back of an old Burger King wrapper, scrawling instructions such as "bear left at the blue rock" and "head north at the dead cow." Mari figured she would be lucky if she didn't end up in Canada.

The sheriff's words regarding Del Rafferty had been less than encouraging. "You won't find him unless he wants you to, which he won't. He don't take to strangers."

Mari tried not to dwell on J.D.'s claim that his uncle could shoot the balls off a mouse at two hundred yards.

The higher they climbed up the side of the mountain, the more nervous she became. The terrain was rugged, the trail obscure. The scenery might have taken her breath away if she hadn't been too preoccupied to notice it. Fragrant, shaded pine forests gave way to beautiful green meadows, which gave way to more forest. All of it pitching up and up, hurling itself at the huge Montana sky. All Mari could think was that the Lucy she had known would never have taken the time to bruise her butt in this godforsaken saddle, riding a mule halfway up the side of a mountain. Never—unless there was something major in it for her.

Maybe she had come to rendezvous with Sheffield for a liaison. But why here, when there were a million easier private places to get to?

"Too bad you can't talk, Clyde," she said to the mule, stroking his slick warm neck. "You could tell me exactly what happened. Maybe we should get M. E. Fralick to help us. She could probably hang some crystals on you and commune with you on a psychic plane."

Clyde glanced back at her, a cynical look in his eyes, long ears wiggling as a deer fly buzzed around them.

They stood at the edge of a clearing, resting. Mari had let the mule take a drink from the stream they had pretty much followed up the mountain. Now she let him bury his nose in the clover for a moment, the reins sliding through her fingers. She longed to climb down and stretch her legs, but she was already stiff and sore from her ride to the Stars and Bars the day before, and she was afraid if she got off, she may not be able to get back on.

Overhead, gray clouds were rumbling across the sky like bloated sponges, filling up the blue bowl, shutting out the sun. Great. They were a zillion miles from home, and now it was going to rain. Consulting the map, she tried to discern where they were while ignoring her stomach's growls at the aroma of cheeseburger that clung to the paper.

She was fairly confident about having passed the blue rock, but the dead cow was another matter. They had come across a scattered pile of bleached bones, but she wasn't exactly an expert on the skeletal remains of farm animals.

"It might have been a cow," she muttered. "Or we might be *way* lost."

Clyde's head came up suddenly and the mule jumped

forward, gathering his muscular body beneath him, ready to bolt and run. The map flew out of Mari's hands as she scrambled to keep her seat and haul in the reins, and the rattling paper further served to frighten the mule, who leapt ahead another ten feet. Across the clearing, a pair of whitetail deer bolted in unison and glided away into the cover of the forest.

Mari pulled the mule around in a galloping circle, her heart in her throat, every muscle tensed. *Stay on, stay on, stay on!* The words chanted through her mind a hundred miles an hour as she fought for control of her mount. If she fell and Clyde took off, it was a hell of a long walk back. Of course, if she fell and broke her neck, she wouldn't have to worry about walking.

The mule came in hand and stopped, his head still high, his body quivering like a race car idling at the starting line. He pinned his long ears back and blew loudly through flared nostrils.

"Good mule, nice mule," Mari gasped, stroking his neck with a trembling hand. "Chill out, will you, Clyde?"

The adrenaline rush subsided, leaving her feeling wobbly and light-headed. The cool, meadow-scented air surged in and out of her lungs in ragged gusts. But as Clyde made no further attempt to bolt, she began to relax. Belatedly, she wondered what had spooked him. The deer, probably. Or another of Bryce's hunting buddies?

"Hey, anybody out there with a gun!" she called breathlessly. The mule shuddered beneath her. "I'm not an elk!"

Silence. The breeze stirred. Thunder grumbled over the next mountain range to the west. A chipmunk chattered at her from its perch on a fallen tree trunk. Her call was not returned. The mule was still quaking beneath her.

She didn't hear the crack of the rifle until a split second before the bullet smashed into the dead stump behind her. Then everything happened so quickly, her brain couldn't keep the order straight. She was falling backward. Clyde was a rear view of bulging hindquarters and flying hooves. She wondered dimly if she had been shot. Then she hit the ground and everything went black.

When the world began coming back into focus, she didn't know if she was dead or alive. Alive, she suspected, wincing. Dead shouldn't hurt. Awareness of her body came back pain by pain, and she opened her eyes and gasped at the face staring down at her. It wasn't the face of anyone she had been told she would see in heaven, and she fully expected to go there even though she wasn't a regular at church. No, the face that stared down at her was the face of a cowboy, and something in his eyes told her he may not have come from hell, but he had very likely seen it.

Beneath the brim of his gray cowboy hat, beneath the heavy rim of his brows, his narrow eyes were a stormy mix of gray and blue, swirling with what looked to Mari like madness. Anger, fear, a brittle tension that threatened to snap. He was probably fifty. His face was lean and weathered, brown and carved with lines like a tooled belt. Some mishap had left him with a puckered round scar the size of a penny on his left jaw. It pulled the corner of his mouth into a grotesque, perpetual frown. In his big, raw hands he held a very large, very deadly looking rifle.

"Don't kill me," Mari whispered, wondering wildly what she might do to prevent him, wondering if death might not be the most pleasant alternative she had. She was suddenly all too aware of just how remote this area was. Fragments of lines from her guidebooks flashed through her head—nearly a million acres of wilderness, ninety percent of it roadless. He could take her anywhere, do anything to her, and there would be no witnesses except the wildlife. Her heart shuddered like a dying bird.

"If I had meant to kill you, ma'am," he said in a low, hoarse voice, "then you'd be dead."

The voice. She blinked hard, as if that might somehow clear her head. The voice was J.D.'s voice, but lower, rustier. The face was a harder, abused version of J.D.'s face. Slowly, she pushed herself into a sitting position, her gaze darting from the face to the rifle and back.

"Del Rafferty?" she ventured weakly.

He narrowed his eyes to slits. "Yes, ma'am."

"And Quinn said I'd never find you."

Del walked ahead of his horse, his mood as sour as the acid churning in his stomach. He hadn't meant to saddle himself with the blond woman. He had meant to scare her off. The last thing he wanted was a woman at his place, especially *this* woman.

His mind tried to scramble things around, as it often did, tried to make him think she had followed him up here, had been stalking him because she had sensed his presence, because she *knew*. It tried to tell him she was the other one in disguise, come to haunt him. But he brought the boot heel of reality down on those wild rantings and squashed them like June bugs. She wasn't the other one. She was the new one and she was just here, that was all. He didn't have to like it. All he had to do was deal with it. Tolerate her, then get rid of her.

Her mule was probably halfway home by now. Damn shame she couldn't have managed to keep her fanny on its back.

"So, you live up here?" she asked.

Del glanced at her over his shoulder and said nothing. She sat in his saddle on his grullo gelding, her hair a wild mop of streaky blond, a bruise darkening on her right cheekbone. He supposed she was pretty, but he had long ago given up thinking about women in a sexual way. He tried never to think of them at all, same as he tried never to think about the 'Nam or the period after he had come home, which he referred to as his black hole period, when everything had been sucked into the dark void of his mind. He lived his life a second at a time, focusing totally on the moment, just to get him from one to the next.

"My friend was killed somewhere around here a couple of weeks ago. Shot in a hunting accident. The sheriff told me you're the one who found her body."

Del just walked on, trying not to hear her. He concentrated on his breathing, on putting one foot in front of the other as he led the horse up the steep trail to the summer cow camp. If he ignored her, she might become invisible to him—or he to her. That idea held great appeal. If he were invisible, she might stop talking.

"I was hoping you could answer some questions for me. If you don't mind, I'd like to get some details. You know, fill in the gaps in the story."

On the other hand, there was always the grim possibility that she *never* stopped talking. She had been talking to the mule when he had first brought her up in the cross hairs of the Leupold 10X scope.

"Quinn told me you didn't come across the body until two days after the fact, but I was wondering if you might have heard anything or seen anything that day she was shot?"

The images flashed before his eyes—darkness, moonlight, the woman running. Suddenly blind to his surroundings, he stumbled on the trail and jerked himself back to the present, cursing himself mentally and cursing the woman. He could hear her ragged breathing, roaring in his ears as if it were coming over loudspeakers. He could hear the dogs. His heart pumped hard in his chest.

". . . Anything might be helpful. I just need to know—"

"I don't know!" he screamed, wheeling around so fast he frightened the horse. The gelding spooked and, wide-eyed, jerked back against the reins. Del ignored him. His gaze was hard on the blond woman, a corpse sitting in his saddle with a ragged, gory hole blown through her chest so that he could see straight through her, halfway to the Spanish Peaks. "I don't wanna know what happened to you! I don't wanna know about the tigers! Leave me alone! Leave me alone or I'll leave you for the dog-boys, damn you!"

In a blink, the corpse was gone and the new woman

was staring at him as moon-eyed as the horse, her face chalk white.

"L-Lucy," she stammered weakly. "*Her* name was Lucy. I'm Mari."

Del jerked around, ashamed and embarrassed, and kept on walking. This was why he stayed at the summer camp. He couldn't be around people. They broke his concentration, snapped it like a thin rubber band, and then everything in his head came apart, the jagged fragments exploded outward, bright and dark and bloody. Beneath the metal plate, his brain began to throb.

The sky rumbled overhead and rain began to fall.

Mari didn't say another word on the ride to his cabin. Del Rafferty had told her to begin with that he would radio for someone to come and get her. After his little break from reality, she could only hope it wouldn't take that somebody too long to get up here. His mind obviously wasn't firing on all cylinders. It would have been nice if someone had seen fit to tell her that right from the start. Of course, Quinn hadn't believed she would find the man, and J.D. had warned her off—twice—which would have been enough in his mind. He probably couldn't conceive of anyone going against his high-handed dictates.

The camp finally came into sight through the branches of the pine trees. A small cabin, complete with outhouse, a three-sided shed, and a corral with four horses in it. A trio of dogs raced out to meet them, barking, baying, yipping with excitement as they dashed around the horse and their master. Rafferty ignored them. He tied the horse to a hitching rail and went into the cabin without so much as glancing at Mari.

The rain came a little harder. Mari slid down off the gelding and darted for the shelter of the cabin before the man could lock her out. As she reached for the doorknob, she turned her head casually to the left and came face-to-face with a rattlesnake.

A scream ripped from her throat and she threw herself back, clutching at her heart. The snake sat coiled and poised to strike inside a box constructed of a wood frame covered with two layers of chicken wire. The cage was one foot square and nailed to the wall of the cabin at head height half a foot away from the door. The snake looked big enough to wrap itself around its prison several times over. It was as thick as her wrist, tan and brown and black with elliptical eyes as bright and shiny as jet beads. It flicked its tongue at her, its tail quivering.

What kind of lunatic kept something like that nailed to the side of his house?

The door swung open and Del Rafferty glared at her. "Leave my snake alone. Get in here where I can see you."

He grabbed ahold of her wrist and pulled her into the cabin, jerking her past the snake so quickly that she had no time to worry about the thing striking her.

The cabin consisted of just one large room. There was a kitchen area with a one-burner wood stove, a tiny refrigerator, a crude table with two chairs. Open shelves were stocked with necessities. Canned foods, condiments, canisters of sugar and flour, cans of Dr Pepper. There was a sink with a pump-action faucet. The rest of the cabin was taken up by an old couch, a narrow, neatly made iron bed, and a dozen or more rifles, cleaned and polished and lined up in racks along the end wall.

Mari stared at the arsenal, jaw slack. The guns were all huge and deadly looking, some with scopes of exotic size and shape. Del Rafferty slipped the one he'd shot at her with off his shoulder and went about the business of unloading it and wiping it down, completely ignoring her as he did so. She thought of the way he'd fired at her, never offering so much as a word of apology afterward. She thought of Lucy riding into that same clearing.

Sheffield claimed he hadn't seen her. Had Del Rafferty?

She backed away from him, her gaze locked on the scar that disfigured his jaw. The backs of her knees hit the edge of a kitchen chair, and she sat down abruptly, her hand landing on the tabletop, sending a hunting knife skittering.

Her stomach rolled over like a dead dog as she turned and, for the first time, took in the knives neatly lined up beside a sharpening stone and a can of 3-In-One oil. Del walked straight up to her, picked up the buck knife with its wide, vicious blade, and set it out of her reach, as if he thought she might somehow spoil its edge just by touching it. Her heart slid down from her tonsils to the base of her throat.

He called the Stars and Bars on a radio tucked among the condiments on the small kitchen counter. His only words on making contact were "Get up here. There's a woman. I want her gone." Then he went out to tend to his horse, leaving Mari alone with her imagination.

It took J.D. an hour to reach the camp. An hour in the cab of his truck, lurching up the side of the mountain on the old logging trail, a torrential downpour obscuring his vision to a watery blur and turning the trail into a quagmire. The old truck slid and skidded, bounced and jolted, rattling J.D.'s temper with every bump. By the time he climbed out of the mud-splattered 4X4, he was fit to wring somebody's neck. Del hadn't named names, but there was little doubt in J.D.'s mind that the woman plaguing his uncle's solitary existence was Mary Lee.

Del's hounds came running through the puddles, baying. Zip jumped out of the truck bed with a bark of welcome for his pals. The four dogs trotted around the pickup, sniffing and peeing on the tires. The rain had moved on to the other side of the Absarokas, on toward the Beartooth range, leaving everything dripping, glistening, fragrant. A million bugs filled the air, and the birds sang sweet spring songs.

All J.D. noticed was the mud that sucked at his boots as he stomped across the yard toward the cabin. When he got back home, they would be inoculating steers and heifers up to their asses in muck. On the up side, he could put off changing the irrigation dams to the hay ground for another day or two. He would give that job to Tucker and let Chaske get a start on trimming and shoeing the cow horses while he drove into New Eden to meet with the banker about the Flying K deal. The plans and schemes and worries zoomed around in his head like the swallows swooping through the air to feast on the post-rain insect swarms.

Del appeared out of the shadows of the woodshed looking pale and angry. His forehead was banded with lines of tension. The scar on his jaw jerked his mouth down at the corner.

"I don't want her here," he said tightly.

"That makes two of us," J.D. grumbled.

"She never stops talking."

"She claims to be capable of silence. I haven't witnessed it yet myself."

Del grabbed his arm in a viselike grip. His eyes were glassy. "Sometimes she's the other one," he blurted out desperately. "I don't want the other one coming back. I don't want anyone here. This is my place."

"I know." J.D. gentled his tone, reining back his own temper as he turned and faced his uncle.

His heart sank like a stone. Del was on one of his mental ledges. There had been a time when J.D. had fully expected him to hurl himself off into the great abyss—literally—but he had thought those times were past. The old soldier had been passing fair for a long time. He did well up here by himself—as well as could be expected, considering the war had fractured his mind beyond repair. He tended the cattle when they came up to summer pasture. The rest of the time he spent with his rifles and his dogs.

City people would have called that crazy, but for Del it was a reasonably sane existence, better than what he'd had in the V.A. hospital, better than what he had found in countless bottles of Jack Daniel's after he had come back from the war. He had found a balance. Now that balance was slipping—thanks to Mary Lee Jennings.

"I'll take her away," J.D. said. "She'll never come back. That's a promise."

A shudder jolted through Del. He stared at his nephew and wanted to cry like a child. He was a disgrace: weak, crazy, a burden on his family. The shame of that twined inside him with the threads of old memories, old fears, things from the past, from the 'Nam. All of it coiled together in his brain like snakes, writhing and biting one another, impossible to separate. He had tried to calm himself, to push all the bad stuff out of his head, but he was beyond calming. He had reached the point where the mental fist of self-protection had closed tightly over that small part of his mind that was sanity while the snakes battled and twisted and his heart pumped frantically.

"What about the other one? I don't want the other one coming back."

J.D. sighed heavily. "She won't come back, Del. She's dead."

Del shook his head and turned away, rubbing the disk of smooth, hard flesh on his jaw, his fingers coming away wet with saliva. The North Vietnamese bullet that had shattered his face and blown a hole through his skull had severed nerves en route. Now he drooled like an idiot. He wiped the trail of spit with his shirt-sleeve. J.D. didn't know the dead came back to him on a regular basis. J.D. didn't know he often saw them in the trees at night, moving among the dark trunks—the corpses of men he had served with, the rotted bodies of men he had shot. The blonde. People said the dead were dead and gone. They didn't know anything.

"You want me to send Tucker up?" J.D. asked, trying to hide the resignation and sadness in his voice with a businesslike tone. "Make sure everything's ready for when we move the cattle up?"

"No, no," Del mumbled, rubbing his scar, then its companion hidden beneath his graying dark hair. Sometimes he dreamed the knot of mended flesh was a screw he could remove and the whole top half of his head would come off and the serpents would crawl out and wither and die in the light of day. "No. I just want to be left alone. Leave me alone."

J.D. watched him stagger away, his gait burdened by the leaden weight of the nightmares and torments that never left him. His heart ached at the sight. His uncle had been a good man once, honorable, strong. He had joined the marines and volunteered for combat duty because he was a patriot and his convictions ran deep. He had given himself in service to his country and his country had sent him back bent and broken, disfigured physically and mentally, a twisted shell that held little of the fine young man he had once been. He had gone away a hero and come back another responsibility to add to J.D.'s never-ending list.

When he turned toward the cabin, J.D. caught a glimpse of Mary Lee darting away from the front door, which stood ajar. His anger surging back full-force, he strode to the door and jerked it open. She stood ten feet from him, eyes wide, small hands clasped beneath an enormous pink mouth on her neon-orange sweatshirt. She looked young and frightened and unaccountably sexy. Something hot stirred beneath his temper. Desire. It only made him angrier, and the anger only magnified the need.

He started to reach for her, then jerked his hand back and swung it in the direction of the door instead. "Get in the truck and don't say a word," he ordered through his teeth.

Mari obeyed without complaint. She wanted to get away from Del Rafferty. There would be plenty of time to fight with J.D. once the cabin was behind them. She darted through the door and past the snake, then stopped to roll up the legs of her jeans and slopped through the mud to the truck. Standing on the running board, she toed her gooey sneakers off and tossed them to the back. With a curt hand signal, J.D. ordered Zip to the back also and climbed in on the driver's side. He didn't speak until they were pointed down the mountain and the woods had swallowed up the camp behind them.

"I told you to leave him alone."

"You're not my father," Mari said tightly. "You can't tell me what to do. Come to think of it, neither could he."

He looked at her as if just the idea of her disobedience were incomprehensible. "I *told* you to leave him alone. I meant it. Did you think I said it just because I like the sound of my own voice?"

"I'm sure I don't know why you said it. You never bothered to explain. It apparently never occurred to you to say, 'oh, by the way, Mary Lee, steer clear of my uncle because he's certifiably bizarre.'"

J.D.'s grip tightened on the steering wheel as the pickup bucked down the logging trail. He clenched his jaw and blinked hard, as if his fury were impeding his vision. "You don't have any idea what you've done."

"What *I've* done! Excuse me, but *I* was the one he tried to shoot."

"He didn't try to shoot you. If Del had wanted to shoot you, you'd be dead now."

"Like Lucy?" The words were out of her mouth before her brain had a chance to snatch them back.

J.D. shot her a narrow glare. "What the hell is that supposed to mean?"

"What do you think it means?" she snapped. "Your uncle is a psychotic with enough guns to invade Cuba single-handed—"

"He's not psychotic."

"He shot at me. He mistook me for a talking corpse—"

"He's got problems," J.D. admitted grudgingly while wrestling for control of the steering wheel. The pickup roared a protest when he shifted gears, pumping the brakes as they angled down a steep grade. "I told you to leave him alone. If you'd listened—"

"If you'd bothered to explain—"

"I don't have to explain anything to you!" he roared, the anger and frustration tearing through him. He hated having outsiders messing with his life, his land, his family. He especially hated this one because a part of him he seemed to have no control over wanted her so badly. "I don't owe you nothing, lady, you got that? You don't belong here—"

"Oh, give me a break with that King of the Mountain crap," Mari sneered, bracing a hand against the dash as the truck pitched violently from side to side. "It's a free country, your highness. I'm here and I don't give a rat's ass whether you like it or not. My friend is dead and I'm going to find out why. I don't care what you—"

"It was an accident! Christ, why can't you just leave it at that? It was an accident. It happened. It's over. Justice was served."

"Not by a long way. I don't call a fine and a slap on the wrist justice. And frankly, there's something about this whole accident scenario that smells like an open sewer under a hot sun at high noon."

J.D. stared at her through slitted eyes, his foot easing off the gas. "What do you mean?"

Mari opened her mouth to answer him and had it shut for her as the front end of the truck flung itself downward and they came to a jarring halt. She slammed sideways into the dashboard and fell to her knees on the floor. J.D. banged his head on the windshield and pulled himself back, swearing loudly. He shifted the truck into reverse and tried to rock it up out of the hole, spewing mud in all directions as the tires spun. The pickup stayed rooted to the spot.

"Great," he snapped, clambering down out of the cab and slamming the door.

Mari swung her door open and tumbled out, forgetting she was barefoot, annoyed at the interruption of their fight. She staggered and stumbled around the nose of the truck, struggling to keep herself upright on the steep hillside. Mud and dead leaves oozed up between her toes. Zip leapt out of the back of the truck and dashed off into the woods after adventure, a big grin on his face.

"Great job of driving, Rafferty," Mari jeered.

He lifted a finger in warning. "Don't start with me, Mary Lee. I'm mad as hell the way it is."

"*You're* mad? I've been shot at, kidnapped, had the pee scared out of me, and spent the last hour wondering if anyone would show up to save me before Rambo decided to skin me with one of his many knives and fashion lampshades out of my hide. If anyone has a right to be angry here, it's me."

J.D. leaned over her, towering above her more than usual with the added advantage of standing uphill. "You don't have any rights," he bellowed. "You don't belong here. I told you to stay away!"

"And I told you to quit bossing me around!" Mari shouted. She planted both hands against his chest and shoved him as hard as she could.

He shoved back automatically, knocking her off balance. Mari let out a little shriek and caught him around the knees as she slipped. Off guard and off balance, J.D. dropped like a felled sequoia, and they went down the hillside in a tangle of arms and legs and bodies, grunting, swearing, tumbling over each other.

They came to rest in a spot where the ground flattened out just before a huge moss-covered boulder. Mari was on the bottom. J.D. rose up over her, the heels of his hands digging into the soft ground on either side of her head.

She stared up at him, her deep clear blue eyes unfocused until she blinked hard to clear away the fog. There were twigs and leaves stuck in her hair and a bruise darkening on her cheek. Her lips were parted, her breath puffing in and out. Her legs were tangled with his, and her feminine mound arched invitingly against his swelling manhood. The need that had gripped J.D. in its talons for days now tightened its hold ruthlessly.

Instantly the air around them seemed suddenly hotter, thicker, redolent with the ripe, fertile scents of the forest. Their gazes locked and held. J.D. moved slightly, experimentally, against her. Her breath caught. Her eyes widened. She made no move to protest.

He wanted her. *Damn*, but he wanted her! He was hard and throbbing with it. Aching with it. Burning with it.

"You make me so damn mad, Mary Lee," he whispered. Mad with need of her. Every other emotion he had felt toward her—the anger, the frustration, the kinder feelings he wouldn't name—channeled themselves into the desire, making it burn hotter, brighter. It didn't matter that she was wrong for him. Nothing mattered except the need. "You make me want you," he growled.

Mari started to deny the charge but stopped herself.

She could feel his erection against her and didn't bother to tell herself she didn't want him. She did. She wanted him with every fiber of her being. The need burst through her, radiating out from the hard fist of desire in the core of her, astonishing her. She wasn't the sort to live by her hormones. She didn't tumble into bed with just any man. And this man made her as angry as he made her hot. He was stubborn, arrogant, high-handed, hard-headed. She remembered thinking that the attraction that flared between the two of them was good for nothing but wild, hot, mind-numbing sex.

At the moment she could not for the life of her see what was so bad about that.

"I don't want you here," he murmured, lowering himself onto her. He leaned on one elbow and with his other hand stroked the tangled strands of hair back from her face. His breath came harder at the feel of her breasts against his chest. "I don't want you here, but I want you so bad I can't stand it. I want you now. Right now. You gonna try to stop me this time, Mary Lee?"

It wasn't a challenge, it was her last chance. The moment shimmered between them, quivered with tension. J.D. stared down into her eyes, waiting. She was too aware of his arousal, too aware of her own. The sensitive flesh between her legs was pounding with need, aching for the feel of him, and he was more than ready to comply. Would she try to stop him? The implication was that she may not be able to. Did she want to?

Slowly she shook her head.

He lowered his mouth to hers, sealing their fate. The instant their lips touched, the second his tongue slid against hers, all sanity was lost, vaporized by the heat that flared between them. He kissed her roughly, wildly, possessively. She locked her hands around the back of his head and kissed him back with equal abandon.

They tore at their clothes. The snaps of his work shirt pulled apart and her small, cool hands were on his chest, combing through the thicket of dark hair. Her fingers ran down over the taut muscles of his belly and back. He pulled her sweatshirt and T-shirt off in one tangle, barely breaking the kiss, and blindly flung the knotted mess aside into a huckleberry bush. Then her breasts were naked against him, and whatever scrap of reason he might have had left was incinerated.

Mari gasped at the touch of his body against hers. He was fever hot. Her every nerve ending was vibrating, quivering at the slightest contact. She was aware of each chest hair that brushed across her nipples. She wanted to scream at the sensations and beg for more in the same breath. They kissed and groped, rolling around on their little plateau of ground, oblivious of the mud, the leaves, the twigs; blind to everything but passion.

They came up on their knees and J.D. bent her back over his arm and fastened his mouth on her breast, flicking his tongue against her nipple, then sucking hard, wringing wild cries from her. Mari's fingers tangled with his at the waist of her jeans, fumbling with the button, wrestling the zipper down.

Pants and panties were shoved out of the way. Her legs parted and his big hand found her most tender flesh. Hot. Wet. Aching for his touch. He parted the delicate folds with his callused fingertips and she arched against him, inviting him, begging him. He dipped into the warm honey of her woman's body, rubbed and stroked and teased. As he plunged his tongue deep into her mouth again and again, he tormented her with feather-light touches at the mouth of her femininity.

Mari twisted and bucked against him, mindless with need, desperate for the feel of him inside her. She worked a hand between their bodies and held him, pulling on him, rubbing him through the soft fabric of his old jeans, wringing a deep moan up from the depths of his chest.

Dragging his mouth down to her breasts again, he kissed her and nipped her as he tore his belt loose and struggled to free himself. Mari pushed him back, sinking to her knees in the soft ground, kissing his chest. Eager to please and torture him as he had her, she found the brown button of his flat male nipple and captured it lightly between her teeth, rubbing the tip of her tongue back and forth across it. She shoved his hands aside and fought with the fly of his jeans, wrenching the zipper down, setting his bulging erection free. His white cotton briefs were tugged down quickly, and he was in her hands, as hard and smooth as a steel rod, hot and heavy and throbbing with life.

J.D.'s control broke at the feel of her fingers closing around him. He shoved her back down and mounted her, driving fully into her in one powerful thrust. She called his name and came immediately, powerfully. J.D. gritted his teeth and hung on as her woman's body tightened rhythmically, exquisitely around him. Her fingertips dug into his back. Her wild cries called him to join her in ecstasy. Beyond holding back, he began to move, pumping in and out of her, reaching deep with every stroke.

"Wrap your legs around me, Mary Lee," he commanded, then groaned as she did so, pulling him deeper still.

Mari locked her thighs around his hips, her arms around his heaving ribs, then she tucked her head against his shoulder and hung on for the ride. She was past identifying individual sensations. There were no words for the place he was taking her. Paradise had been found in that first moment of joining, but he was taking her beyond paradise into uncharted territory at a pace that stole her breath. The heat was engulfing them. She was on fire with bliss. Every thrust touched a place inside her no other man had ever managed to find.

The second explosion was even more enormous than the first. Behind her eyelids everything went white. She heard J.D. groan as he buried himself deep one last time and came in a hot rush. Then time and space ceased to exist.

Awareness returned layer by gossamer layer. She was breathing, a chore that consumed her concentration for several moments. When she thought she had it mastered, she worked at opening her eyes. Her eyelids seemed to weigh ten pounds each and required incredible mental stamina to raise. When the feat was accomplished, she was staring into J.D.'s ear. He lay heavily on top of her, motionless.

"Are we still alive?" she asked in awe.

He raised himself up slowly. His chest was heaving. There were bits of dead leaf caught in his chest hair. Mari reached up and gently brushed it away, focusing on the task, putting off the inevitable.

J.D. studied her carefully, taking in her fading blush and hooded eyes. There was a bruise on her cheek. He couldn't remember whether she had it before. Her wild mane was snarled and tangled with twigs and crumbs of earth.

Christ almighty. They were in the middle of the woods, lying naked on a carpet of wet dead leaves. Around them life on the mountain went on as usual. A jay called *thief!* from somewhere in the canopy of branches above them. A yellow warbler sang merrily—*wee-see-wee-see-wiss-wiss-u.* A red squirrel darted past them and Zip bounded from between a pair of aspen saplings and gave chase, gracefully leaping over his master's prone form.

Embarrassment washed through J.D. He never lost control with a woman. Never. Even as a teenager he had managed his lust with an iron fist. It was a point of honor, part of the pledge he had taken all those years ago. It rattled him to think he could forget those hard lessons in the time it took to unzip his jeans.

Mary Lee was looking up at him now, watching him carefully. Mary Lee, the outsider. Mary Lee, heir to the throne of Lucy MacAdam.

Jesus, Rafferty, what were you thinking?

He moved away from her, jerking his pants up and fumbling with the zipper. Mari watched him, a cold, hard lump of dread settling in her stomach. It occurred to her belatedly that *this* was what was wrong with wild, hot, mind-numbing sex. Afterward, when the novocaine of arousal faded, you were left with whatever pains and problems were there to begin with. Rafferty didn't want her on his precious mountain. He couldn't look at her without seeing Lucy and Bryce and everyone else who was trying to take his homeland away from him.

She sighed and reached for the multicolored ball of fabric that was her shirt. Untangling the sleeves, she pulled T-shirt and sweatshirt over her head together, then shook her hair and tried to comb her fingers through it to dislodge the debris.

"Well, it was fun while it lasted," she said dryly.

J.D. shot her a look as he shrugged into his shirt. She was trying to be tough. She was trying to be as nonchalant about this as Lucy would have been. But she didn't look tough or unconcerned. She looked fragile. As if she needed holding. God knew he wasn't the man to offer comfort or reassurance. He shouldn't have wanted anything more between them than animosity. That was safest. That was best.

Their gazes caught. Her eyes were clear and huge, like blue glass jewels set deep beneath her dark brows. Her mouth was a soft, vulnerable bow, her lips swollen from his kisses. Possessiveness surged through him. He couldn't seem to stop it. He reached for her, pulled her into his embrace, his gaze locked on hers.

"If you think this is over, you'd better think again, Mary Lee."

Mari blinked at him, breathless at the prospects his words opened up. "We're not finished?"

"Not by a long shot." He bent his head and nuzzled her cheek, nipped her throat, her earlobe. He stroked a hand down her back to her bare bottom. His fingers cupped and kneaded the ripe swell of one buttock. He pulled her snug against him and growled low in his throat as arousal tightened again in his groin. "Hell, we just barely took the edge off."

CHAPTER 13

$\mathcal{T}$he truck was dealt with. Upon arriving back at Lucy's ranch, Clyde, the traitorous mule, was dealt with. In the bathtub of the guest room the mud was dealt with. Then they dealt with each other.

Mari felt strangely shy with him, considering. The time that had elapsed had given the reservations a chance to take root. What would this mean? Where would it lead them? She didn't allow herself to answer. She wanted to live in the moment. She wanted to put the tangle of questions and doubts and fears on hold and exist just on instinct for a while.

J.D. seemed content with that idea as they stood in the tub. He focused his attention on her body, exploring with his hands and his mouth, experimenting with touch and pressure as the water rained down on them from the shower head. He seemed unhindered by qualms of any kind as he washed her back and chased the soap suds down with his hands, hands that then found their way around her rib cage and up to her breasts. He rubbed her nipples with his thumbs, enticing them to peek out through the lather. She closed her eyes and whimpered softly as he slid the bar of soap between her legs and teased her until she was breathless.

Dripping water all over, they found their way into the guest room. Too impatient to make it all the way to the bed, J.D. pressed her up against the wall just inside the door. He bent to take her breast into his mouth as he swept a hand down over her belly to the thatch of dark curls at the juncture of her thighs. He trailed his kisses back up her throat to her lips, easing his tongue into her mouth as he slid a finger deep between her legs. Mari groped blindly for him, wanting to curl her fingers around his shaft and draw him to her, into her. But he twisted out of her reach, chuckling darkly.

"Not yet, honey." He murmured the words in her ear, his voice low and rough as he stroked her. "I want you ready for me this time."

"I *am* ready, J.D., *please.*"

She slid her arms around his neck and leaned into him, raising up on tiptoe, rubbing the tips of her breasts against his chest. J.D. groaned and pulled her up against him in a crushing embrace, kissing her deeply and wildly. Without breaking the kiss or the hold, he carried her to the bed.

They fell across it, oblivious of the tears in the mattress and sheets, oblivious of everything but each other. The afternoon was cloaked in gray, the room cloaked in shadows that softened the chaos the vandals had left behind. Outside, another thundershower had rolled across the valley from the Gallatin side and the rain fell steadily, drumming on the roof and the skylight above the bed.

Mari felt wilder than the weather, out of control of herself, as if her body had taken on a will of its own, making up for all the time she had spent bending to the expectations of others. The sensations were thrilling and frightening, overwhelming all thought. She gave herself over to them, gave herself over to J.D., arching her back when he caught her nipple between his lips, arching her hips as he found the bud of her desire with his thumb.

He kissed his way down her body, lingering on the curve of her waist, the point of her hip, the sensitive spot just above the delta of curls on her groin. Mari moaned with a mix of pleasure and frustration and tried to urge him lower, but J.D. had other ideas. He slid his body up along hers in one long, exquisite caress and buried his face against the curve of her neck, murmuring hot, dark words in her ear.

Burning with need, Mari took the initiative, setting off on an exploration of his body. He was powerfully built.

His was the body of a man who had done hard physical work his whole life. Beautiful was too feminine a word; handsome too civilized. Male. Utterly male. Shoulders broad enough to carry the weight of his world. A chest thick and deep and rough with dark hair. A belly ridged with muscle. A horseman's powerful thighs and calves.

He was tough, muscular, scarred in spots. Mari kissed those spots, wanting to offer him softness and comfort, knowing he would take only what he wanted—her body.

She stroked his shaft, brushed her cheek against the velvet-soft head, breathing deep the musky scent of his arousal. She kissed him lightly, her tongue rubbing across the drop of fluid that had pearled at his tip.

J.D.'s control snapped abruptly. He hauled Mari up into his arms, twisting her beneath him in an aggressive move. The need astonished him. He was a man with a healthy sexual appetite, but with Mary Lee he was ravenous. The need to take her, to possess her, to make her his in nature's most fundamental way was urgent. Blinding.

Just sex, he told himself, *it's just sex.* The disclaimer chanted through his mind over and over. The assurance didn't make the need any less or the urgency any tamer. It didn't even begin to loosen the tension at the core of him.

He dug in the drawer of the nightstand for a condom, resenting the need to use it. Resentment not from a comfort standpoint, but from somewhere deeper, some basic, instinctive place inside him. He had always taken precautions with women. He was too wary of getting trapped in a relationship he didn't want. But he didn't want anything coming between himself and Mary Lee. He already knew how good it felt to be buried inside her tight, silky heat. He had already experienced the primitive pleasure of spilling his seed inside her. The desire to do so again damn near outweighed his common sense.

Mari took the decision away from him, taking the condom from his fingers and rolling it down over him. Then there were no decisions left. No thought. Nothing but the need and the woman.

He slid into her, groaning at the warmth, the tightness

of her body. He slid his arms around her, groaning at the feel of her breasts, the silk of her skin, amazed at the sense of rightness, of belonging inside her. Somewhere in his wary heart he thought dimly that he shouldn't allow himself to feel this way. But then all thought was swamped by sensation, absorbed by instinct. He eased nearly out of her and thrust back into her core slowly, powerfully, filling her.

He whispered something softly. "Good."

Her breath caught and eased. "Yes."

Their gazes held. They moved together.

Thunder rumbled overhead. The rain washed across the skylight. None of it mattered. Only this ritual as old as time. Only having her take the essence of what made him male deep within the most feminine part of her.

He rode her gently, strongly, thrusting deep with each slow stroke. She moved with him in perfect rhythm, accepted him in a way that was as simple, as complex as life. The pleasure was acute, the need for release potent.

"Come for me, Mary Lee," Rafferty growled against the side of her neck. "Come on, honey, come for me."

His voice was low and rough and dark, as dark as the gray of his eyes as he stared into hers. Mari whispered his name between gasps, between strokes. He filled her completely, lifted her hips from the mattress with each thrust. The intensity of the pleasure was almost too much, riding the fine line on the edge of pain. It built inside her—a powerful hybrid of tension, passion, need. She felt as if they were being pulled up the side of a mountain, then teetering at its crest.

J.D. slipped a hand between their bodies, parting the delicate petals of her femininity, tapping gently against the aching bud of her desire. "Come for me, Mary Lee. Come on. Come on, sweetheart . . ."

She whimpered and strained against him, closer, closer to the edge. He slipped a finger lower, pressing at the entrance to her body where he already filled her, where his thick, pulsing shaft pumped in and out, in and out.

"*Come on . . . come on . . .*"

"*J.D. . . . J.D.!*"

Over the edge. Into a free fall. Sensation rushed through her like the wind, wild, pounding, exquisite. J.D. fell with her. She wrapped her arms around him and held tight as consciousness dimmed and she became nothing but a pounding heart and humming nerve endings and burning, throbbing muscles.

And then there was stillness, within and all around. Stillness and self-revelation. That she had never known anything quite like this with another man. That she was in over her head. That what had begun in the heat of the moment on the side of the mountain might be more than she wanted to handle. That Rafferty might be more than she wanted to handle.

Mari opened her eyes slowly. She lay tucked beside J.D., her cheek pressed to the hollow of his shoulder, one leg tangled with his. His arm was around her, holding her loosely. The light in the room had faded to the dark grainy texture of an underexposed black and white photograph. Rain still fell beyond the log walls. It ran in sheets over the skylight. It was the only sound. Soothing. Melancholy.

Day was slipping into night. She had no idea what time it was, how much time had passed. She didn't know whether Rafferty was awake. His breathing was deep and regular. He didn't say a word. Mari flexed the fingers of her left hand, tangling them in the coarse dark hair that grew across the hard planes of his chest. His heartbeat was slow and even.

What was he thinking? What was he feeling? What did this mean to him?

She wouldn't ask for fear he would answer her. She didn't want to hear him say it in that same callous tone he had used the night they met. *We had sex. Friendship didn't enter into it.*

Was that all it meant to him? A release. Scratching an itch.

Did she want it to mean more?

That was the sixty-four-thousand-dollar question. She was supposed to be living for the moment, not looking for a future with a man she barely knew. They weren't exactly a match made in heaven. He was stubborn and ornery and bound and determined that she didn't belong here.

Pain seeped through her like a wash of salt across old wounds that never healed. All she had ever wanted was someplace to belong. All she had ever looked for was somewhere to fit in. J.D. said she didn't belong here. He wouldn't let her fit into his life, not beyond this. He would leave her on the outside looking in. He would come and go from her life at will, but he didn't want her in his.

She had told herself she would live in the moment, float on in that odd state of limbo, but she wasn't made that way. In her heart of hearts she wanted more, had wanted more all along.

The joke's on you, Marilee.

The loneliness that enveloped her was a chill that went soul deep.

"You cold?" His voice was deep and soft as rumpled velvet.

Mari bit her lip and nodded, feeling close to tears. Ridiculous. She had no business crying. She swallowed hard against the lump in her throat as J.D. pulled the tattered coverlet around her.

"You're quiet," he murmured. "Too quiet."

He crooked a knuckle under her chin and tilted her face up. She sat and turned away from him, but not before he caught a glimpse of those huge, deep eyes, luminous with tears. The sight kicked him in the gut with all the power of a horse.

"Mary Lee? What's wrong? Was I too rough? Did I hurt you?"

"No." *Not yet.* She stood as he reached for her, his fingertips grazing her bare back.

This room had seen its share of action from the vandals. Clothes that had hung in the closet were strewn across the floor. Mari spied a terry-cloth robe near the foot of the bed, picked it up, and shrugged it on. It swallowed her whole, the sleeves falling well past her fingertips. Fine. She wanted to cocoon herself, insulate herself.

Tucking her hair back behind her ear, she wandered to the dormer window and stared out at the rain-drenched mountainside and the gathering darkness. J.D. watched her from the bed. She could feel his gaze on her, steady, powerful, willing her to turn around. When she didn't, he got up and came to her, completely unconcerned with his naked state.

"I was thinking about Lucy," she said, feeling bleak and raw inside. "Wondering if you ever . . . were together in this room."

"Lucy doesn't have anything to do with us."

"My mistake." She tried for sarcasm in her laugh and winced at the hollowness of it. "I forgot. It wasn't anything personal. Just sex."

"I told you once, I won't pretend I liked her."

"What about me, J.D.?" She looked up at him, too proud, too hurt, leading with her chin. "Will you pretend you like me?"

He swore under his breath. "What's this about, Mary Lee? You want a promise from me? You want pretty words? You got the wrong cowboy."

She shook her head and looked back out the window. She didn't have the right to ask for anything more than what he'd given. She was a big girl. She'd known from the start what J.D. wanted; he'd been very plain about it. It wasn't his fault her moment of self-revelation had come too late.

"Give me a break here, Rafferty. It's been a tough week, you know," she said softly.

J.D. stepped up behind her and slid his arms around her, fitting her against his body, enveloping her in his strength. "Tired?" he asked, pressing his lips to her temple.

The tears burned hot behind her eyes. He couldn't know how tired she was—tired of being the odd one out, tired of being confused. She had come to Montana to rest, to rejuvenate, to pass some time with a friend. Instead, she was being put through tests of endurance and strength. Her nerve endings felt raw, exposed. Her friend was dead and she wasn't sure why. She wasn't sure she wanted to know.

But the questions wouldn't go away. There was no one else to find the answers. No one else cared.

"These vacations are hell on a person, you know." The words were little more than a rasp through the knot of tears in her throat.

"Come here," J.D. whispered, turning her around in his arms. He cradled her head against his chest, fingers tangled in the hopeless wilderness of her hair. He rubbed her back and murmured to her, and his heart squeezed at the sound of her grudging tears. He didn't question the tenderness that ached through him like a virus; he ignored it. It didn't mean anything. It was just a moment in time.

A moment he wouldn't have given Lucy MacAdam or any woman who had come before her. A moment some nameless, lonely part of him wanted to go on forever.

"You caught me fresh out of handkerchiefs," he said.

Mari sniffed and laughed, amazed that he would come up with a sense of humor when she needed it most. "That's okay," she said, wiping her nose on her sleeve. "It's not my robe."

He caught hold of the end of a sleeve and gently dried the tears from her cheeks. "I suppose you burned yours in a symbolic gesture against terry cloth."

"Another joke! Careful, Rafferty, you'll strain yourself." She shot him a wry look. "You're being awfully nice. What's your angle?"

"I reckon I owe you," he answered, dancing around the truth. "My uncle took a shot at you. You didn't have any business going up on that ridge after I told you not to, but I don't guess you deserved to get the bejesus scared out of you either."

"Your compassion is overwhelming."

He didn't smile at her sarcasm. He studied her face, lifting a hand to touch the bruise on her cheekbone. "You got this when you fell off the mule?"

"That one and a few others. I suppose I should be glad I didn't break my neck."

You should be glad Del didn't want you dead. The words scrolled through his brain, but J.D. kept them to himself, them and the sense of dread that rose inside him.

"He just wants to be left alone," he said. "The war tore him up inside, ruined his mind."

"Shouldn't he be in a hospital?"

"He was for a few years. It nearly killed him being locked up like that. The doctors didn't help him. No one gave a damn. Finally I just brought him home. He's family. He belongs on the Stars and Bars."

"Just like that? A lot of people wouldn't want him around. A lot of people wouldn't want the responsibility."

"Yeah, well, that's what's wrong with this country. People have no integrity anymore, no sense of accountability."

Except J. D. Rafferty. The thought brought a pang of tenderness to Mari's heart. J. D. Rafferty, the last cowboy hero, the last honest man. He had a code of honor and a way of life that had died out everywhere but in Clint Eastwood movies. He was a hard man; it wouldn't be wise to romanticize that. But then she thought of him going to take his uncle out of some bleak V.A. hospital. He couldn't have been more than a teenager at the time, and yet he had taken that responsibility. As he had taken responsibility for the ranch. She thought of what Tucker had told her about him, thought of the child he had never been, thought of the man he had become and the vulnerability he showed no one. Dangerous thoughts. As dangerous to her heart as Del Rafferty had been to her health and well-being.

"He scared me, J.D. Not just when he shot at me. What if he killed Lucy?" she said softly.

"He didn't."

"Can you really be that sure?"

No, he couldn't, but he'd die before he said so. A part of him died just thinking it. Del was family. The Raffertys stuck together, come hell or high water. Lucy was gone; nothing would change that. "Let it go. It was an accident, Mary Lee."

But as they stood there, staring out at the rain, each lost in private thoughts, neither one of them really believed it.

J.D. left at eight to go to a Montana Stockgrowers meeting in town. He would miss the bulk of the meeting, but he needed to talk with a couple of people about putting a deal together for the Flying K.

Still wrapped in the terry robe, Mari stood on the porch and watched him drive away into the gloom of the rainy night. A thick fog hugged the ground, soft gray, eerily buoyant. It crept around the tree trunks like smoke and drifted down across the ranch yard. Mari pulled the oversize robe tighter around her and shivered. It might have seemed romantic while J.D. was here. Alone it was just plain creepy.

Her thoughts kept drifting to Del Rafferty, living alone on the side of the mountain. Del and his guns. Del and his visions. He didn't like blondes. He didn't like strangers. Staring up at the wooded hillside, she thought she could feel his tormented gaze on her. She could imagine him bringing her into focus behind the cross hairs of a rifle scope. Had he seen Lucy the same way?

Stomach churning—from anxiety *and* starvation—she went back into the house. She needed to borrow some more clothes and go back to town. As peaceful as she found this place during the day, she didn't relish the idea of being there alone at night when her mind was filled with thoughts of madmen. She preferred her room at the lodge, not only for safety purposes but because she had yet to accept that this place belonged to her. She couldn't quite bring herself to take the gift. She couldn't see why she deserved it. She couldn't see what strings Lucy might have left attached to it.

She found a pair of jeans a size too small, a T-shirt from Cal-Davis three sizes too big, and a pair of Keds that fit just right. Not high fashion, but no one at the Burger King drive-thru was liable to complain. She jogged down the stairs and started for the front door

with visions of bacon cheeseburgers dancing in her head.
But as she turned at the foot of the stairs, her attention
caught on the broken door to the study, and another
jumble of questions tumbled through her mind. Questions with names attached. MacDonald Townsend. Ben
Lucas. Evan Bryce.

Stepping over broken glass, she went in and flicked on
a brass desk lamp that hadn't been smashed during the
vandal's spree. The desk itself was ruined, the bronze eagle sculpture imbedded in the center of its splintered top.
Another ficus had died a lingering death, uprooted from
its pot. The stenotype machine Lucy had apparently kept
for old time's sake sat undisturbed on an oak pedestal
near the picture window. A monument to her past life.
The floor was littered with papers that had been torn
from a filing cabinet. Meaningless stuff—warranties,
ownership papers, llama journals, tax files.

Books had been hurled from the shelves built in along
the back wall and lay scattered across the pine floor.
Mari's gaze scanned the titles and authors' names absently. Lucy's tastes had run from courtroom thrillers to
potboiler glitz novels to *The Prince of Tides*. There were
law books and books devoted to enhancing sexual performance. One thick volume of the Martindale-Hubbell
law directory lay on the floor beside a copy of *Shared
Intimacies*.

Martindale-Hubbell.

*You won't get into Martindale-Hubbell, but my name
will live on in infamy. . . .*

The line from Lucy's letter played through her head.
She picked up the book from the floor and fanned
through the pages. Volume three, listing California attorneys P–Z. Another volume rested on the bookshelf–volume nine, which included listings for six states–Montana
and five that began with the letter N. There was nothing
out of the ordinary about either book. They were the
standard tomes, bound in mustard-gold cloth with titles
in tasteful, discreet gold-foil type. Between the covers
was the usual listing of practice profiles, professional biographies, services, and supplies.

A complete set would have been composed of fifteen volumes, plus indexes, but Lucy would have had no use for all of them. Mari wasn't even sure why she would have had the book for Montana when she had left the profession before moving here. She would have expected to find only the two fat volumes embracing the names of the zillion lawyers that infested California.

Two volumes.

"So where is A to O?" she whispered.

She looked under the furniture, in the cold ashes of the stone fireplace, beneath the desk drawers that had been pulled out and dumped. There was no sign of Martindale-Hubbell volume two, California A–O.

Mari looked around the room at the utter destruction, a chill radiating outward from the pit of her stomach. What if this hadn't been vandalism? What if it wasn't a drunk from the Hell and Gone who had broken into Miller Daggrepont's office? Daggrepont was Lucy's attorney. Lucy, who had known secrets about powerful people.

We all have our calling in life. Mine was being a thorn in wealthy paws. . . .

She thought of the ranch, the llamas, the cars in the garage, the fortune in clothes strewn across the bedroom floor. Money. Where had she gotten all the money?

Only one answer made any sense at all. A terrible logic that allowed jagged puzzle pieces to fall into place.

Blackmail.

In her mind's eye she could see Lucy grinning her secretive, cynical grin, eyes glittering with sardonic amusement.

"Oh, God, Lucy," she whispered, trembling. "What have you done?"

CHAPTER 14

$\mathcal{M}$iller Daggrepont was a man who knew how and when to seize opportunity. He knew the value of patience and the advantages of remorselessness. He was a man of many talents and schemes, none of them large. The talents were just enough to navigate him through the small labyrinths of the schemes. The profits weren't huge, but they were growing.

He had been helping himself to trust funds and estates for years. No one questioned him. He didn't take much from any one place. In his own larcenous heart he considered the ill-gotten gains "gratuities." A street lawyer in a place like New Eden, Montana, didn't get a whole lot more. Most of his clients were ranchers whose wealth was tied up in land, livestock, and equipment. The new wealth in the Eden valley had come equipped with their own lawyers. Miller made out on divorces and the odd wrongful-death settlement. And his "gratuities." And his schemes.

He eyed the woman on the other side of his cluttered desk and smiled benignly. She had already put a fair amount into his piggy bank without having a clue. His avaricious brain buzzed with thoughts of what more she might give him.

"Hey, there, little missy!" he boomed, slapping his fat hands against what little desktop showed through the mess of fishing flies and reels and documents that needed filing. "What brings you out on a night like this? It's a real toad strangler out there, hey? You decide to sell that land?"

Mari forced a smile. Daggrepont's eyes were swimming behind the Coke-bottle lenses of his glasses. Not even that nauseating special effect could hide the gleam of greed. "No, not yet."

"Well, now, you just say the word and I'll take care of the whole ball of beeswax for you."

"Thank you. You're very"—*opportunistic, exploitative, vulturelike*—"industrious."

Daggrepont took it as a compliment.

"I'm still in shock, to tell you the truth," she said. "I can't think about the land yet. There are just so many unanswered questions. I was driving by and saw your lights on. Thought I'd just drop in and see if you might be able to answer any of them for me."

His brow furrowed into burls of flesh. He rubbed his sausage fingers over his third chin. "What sort of questions? Financial questions?"

"Sort of." She cast about for a place to sit, finally settling a minimal portion of her fanny on a chair taken up by a towering stack of old *Life* magazines and a shoebox half full of old military medals. She set the shoebox on the floor and leaned back against the magazines. "I thought you might know something about the inheritance Lucy came into before she moved here."

Daggrepont heaved out a gust of pent-up breath. " 'Fraid I can't help you there, little lady. I wasn't privy. She had me draw up her will, named me executor, that's all."

"Did she say why? I mean, she was young, healthy, not the kind of person given to planning that way."

"She owned property and livestock. Had money in the bank. It's just sound thinking!" he shouted up at the ceiling. His eyes narrowed and swam in Mari's direction. "You ought to think about having one yourself. I'd be more than happy to take care of that for you. I've got the forms right here—"

"Not just now," Mari said, halting his search of the desktop. "Thanks anyway."

He stared at her hard, his fat hands dripping fishing

tackle, his mind calculating what he might have made in additional fees. "Well, if you're sure . . ."

"Maybe later on."

She sighed and glanced around the room. This had been a shot in the dark, but now that nothing had come of it, she realized she had actually hoped Daggrepont might prove to be something other than chronically weird. Her gaze scanned the bookshelves that were crammed with legal tomes, collector's price guides, and mail-order catalogues.

"Did you know anything about her finances at all?" *God, what's he supposed to say, Marilee? You mean, was Lucy a blackmailer? By golly, little missy, she sure was!*

Daggrepont looked at her sideways. "How do you mean?"

"I mean, she seemed a lot more well off than when I knew her. I was just wondering how that came to be."

The grin that split the lawyer's face made him look like a cowboy-kitsch Buddha. Buddha with a string tie and Don King hair. The image didn't faze Mari, which told her just how far gone she was.

"You're the first client I ever had who worried about getting *too much* money!" He let loose a belly laugh that shook the cobwebs in the corners of the ceiling.

"No. I was just curious, that's all. Lucy and I kind of lost touch over the last year."

"That's a shame."

"Yeah, well . . ." His collection of the Martindale-Hubbell directories caught her eye as she stood. He appeared to have volume nine dating back to the time of Moses. Also the volumes that included Idaho and Wyoming. No California A–O. "Mr. Daggrepont, Lucy didn't leave anything else for me that you may have forgotten about, did she? She mentioned a book in her letter. I haven't been able to find it."

Daggrepont frowned like a bulldog as he rocked himself to his feet. The springs of his desk chair shrieked in relief. "No, ma'am, there was no book. If she'd left a book, I surely would have passed it along to you. I'm not the sort of unscrupulous shyster who keeps things he isn't entitled to."

He graciously offered her the use of a thirty-year-old umbrella to get out to her car. Mari was wrestling to get the thing closed, when an old pink Cadillac pulled up alongside her Honda on First Avenue. Nora Davis buzzed down the window on the passenger side and shouted to be heard above the rain.

"Hey, there, Mary Lee, let's go honky-tonkin'!"

The umbrella turned itself inside out. It seemed like a sign.

The Hell and Gone was an oasis of life in a night canceled due to weather. Amber lights and Coors signs glowed a welcome out the windows and swinging front doors. Sweethearts of the Rodeo harmonized above the dull roar of pool games and high spirits.

Nora squeezed her boat in between a pair of ranch trucks a dozen feet from the side entrance of the bar.

"Aren't you worried about getting your doors bashed in?" Mari asked. She had to hold her breath to get out of the car.

Nora laughed as they dashed up onto the boardwalk and out of the rain. "Honey, you won't find a cowboy on this earth willing to get pink paint on his pickup. That's a bonus to having that old car—the Mary Kay-mobile I call it. My mama won that ugly thing selling miracle night cream to homely old ladies in Bozeman. It sucks gas by the gallon and uses a quart of oil every thousand miles, but there's not a red-blooded man in Montana who'd steal it or put a dent in it."

"You're a wonder, Nora," Mari drawled.

The waitress tossed her frizzy dark hair and grinned. "Don't you forget it, girlfriend."

Laughing, each slung an arm around the shoulders of her new friend and they headed inside.

The rain had driven the cowboys into town early. Most of them were well on their way to hangovers. All of them were glad to see unescorted females. Shouts went up as Nora and Mari walked in. They all knew Nora. She basked in the glow, waving to friends, shouting hellos and smart remarks as she led the way through the throng to a booth. She had traded her waitress uniform for a tight T-shirt with Garth Brooks's likeness plastered across her flat chest and tighter jeans that hugged her wide hips and disappeared into the tops of red, high-heeled, looking-for-trouble cowboy boots.

They ordered beers. Mari ordered a Hell and Gone Bull Burger with the works and double onion rings.

Nora raised her thinly plucked brows. "You eating for two, honey?"

"I haven't had anything since breakfast. I worked up an appetite."

"Like a ranch hand. What you been doing all day—riding wild horses?"

"Something like that." Mari glanced away, hoping the warmth of the bar would explain her blush.

She'd been in her share of working-class bars, not for the liquor or the horny tough guys, but for the music. A lot of great music got played in places like the Hell and Gone. A poster on the wall advertised a band called Cheyenne coming in on the weekend. She wondered if she might persuade J.D. to come listen with her, then almost laughed at herself. A date. God, what would he do if a woman asked him out? Was that done in Montana? The cowboy code would probably require him to perform ritual suicide.

Nora launched into a narrative of who's who, pointing out this cowboy and that cowboy and the mechanic from the John Deere place and the best hairdresser at the Curl Up and Dye. Mari memorized their faces, their grins, their laughter. She took in everything about them and stored the images in her mind to be called upon later. She drank in the rowdy atmosphere of the bar, the smell of beer and cigarettes, and warm male bodies and strong perfume.

The Braves were playing baseball on the TV that was crammed up on a shelf above the bar. People booed them enthusiastically. Ted Turner was not a popular man hereabouts. He had bought up most of the next valley and promptly declared the land off limits to local hunters, then sold off his cattle and replaced them with buffalo, angering all the area ranchers who feared his buffalo herd might spread diseases to their cattle.

Over the speakers Alan Jackson shouted out above the hoopla—"Don't Rock the Jukebox." Half a dozen couples zoomed around the small dance floor, twisting and twirling, trying to impress one another in a courtship ritual as old as time.

A crowd gathered around an old Ping-Pong table on the far side of the room, where pinball machines blinked and billiard balls cracked together.

"They're fixin' to start the mouse races!" Nora called, her face bright with excitement. "Let's go!"

They were across the bar in a flash, Mari squeezing her way between cowboys for a better view. The betting was lively as the entries were held up above the crowd for introduction. A mouse named Pink Floyd was a narrow favorite. She put a dollar on Mouse O'War and screamed at the top of her lungs with the rest of the fans as the doors were pulled up on the tiny starting gate and the racers started their mad dash down their lanes for a reward of peanut butter and stale cheese.

Mouse O'War nosed out Godzilla for the win. Pink Floyd jumped the rail and made a mad dash for freedom, miraculously dodging the heavy boots of his disgruntled followers and disappearing under a video poker machine along the wall.

Mari collected her winnings and made her way back to the table just as her supper was being delivered. Nora intercepted a cowboy en route and herded him onto the dance floor as Hal Ketchum came roaring over the speakers—"Hearts Are Gonna Roll."

The burger was heaven. Mari sank her teeth in, closed her eyes, and groaned in heartfelt appreciation. Half a pound of prime Montana beef on a spongy white bun. She could barely get her hands around it. Melted cheese oozed out the sides and over her fingers.

"I never saw a woman eat the way you do, Mary Lee. How do you keep that sweet figure?"

Will slid into the booth across from her and plunked a long-necked bottle of Coors on the table. By the looks of him, it wasn't his first. His blue eyes had a blurry sheen to them. The incorrigible grin was lopsided. His dark hair tumbled across his forehead. He hooked a giant onion ring off her plate and bit into it, flashing handsome white teeth.

"I work it off."

"J.D. work it off for you?" he said archly.

Mari didn't blink. "A gentleman wouldn't ask a question like that."

Will squinted and craned his neck, looking all around the bar. "Not a gentleman in the place. Not a gentleman for miles. No one here but us shit-kicking losers looking to get lucky or pass out."

He was feeling sorry for himself. He'd been feeling sorry for himself since—hell, forever. At least two days. Wasn't it two days since he'd seen Samantha? His *ex*-wife, *ex*-wife, *ex*-wife. It seemed like two days that he'd been working on alternately tormenting himself and trying to wash her out of his memory.

"I met your wife last night," Mari said, baptizing her burger in a puddle of ketchup.

She kept an eye on Will while she chewed, trying to read his reaction, wondering what was at the heart of his trouble—his drinking? his wife? J.D.? Maybe he was just a jerk, but she didn't want to believe it. There was a sweetness to Will's charm, a genuine sense of innocence to his clowning, even though she imagined he was guilty of many things. He cheated on his wife, which should have made him despicable, but Mari couldn't get past thinking there was some deeper reason than a testosterone imbalance.

Lucy would have laughed at her.

His grin tightened and soured. He put the onion ring back on the plate. "Oh, yeah? Was she having a high old time dancing with the rich boys?"

He could picture it too easily now that he'd had a

chance to torture himself with the possibilities. Sam with her hair down, all that long black silk swinging around her shoulders. He saw her in high heels and a skimpy dress with a glass of champagne in her hand, laughing, smiling, dazzling the city boys.

"Actually, she didn't look very comfortable there," Mari said. "She seems too sweet to be hanging out with that crowd."

"Yeah, well, you don't see her hanging out with me."

"That might have something to do with the fact that you're too busy coming on to anything with two X chromosomes. I'll give you a clue here, Will: infidelity is not a trait most women find desirable in a husband."

Will tried to find a snappy comeback, but his brain stalled out. He started picking at the label on his empty beer bottle instead. He was a jerk. He was a heel. He was a loser, a screwup. He had told himself he wanted out of his marriage, and he'd even managed to fuck that up. He felt as though he had thrown himself into a pond and now his feet were caught up in the weeds and he was getting sucked under, drowning in confusion. He didn't know how to get out.

He had pushed Sam away; now she was getting drawn into the swift current of the good life. How could he even hope to get her back? Why would she want to come back? What was there to come back to? Hell, he would have taken the diamond life in a flash and never thought twice about what he was leaving behind.

What does that say about you, Willie-boy?

He peeled a strip down the center of the label, lifting an O out of Coors.

"Look," Mari said. "It's none of my business. God knows I've got enough to think about without butting into your life. She just seems like a nice girl, that's all."

"She is," he murmured. Looking up, he flashed her a grin that was as phony as a three-dollar bill. "So why do you suppose she got hooked up with a jerk like me?"

"Maybe you should ask her that."

"Maybe she thought she could redeem me, huh?" He held up the beer bottle beside his face as if he were posing for a commercial. "Sorry, ladies, not redeemable. No deposit, no return."

A waitress came by with a tray of drinks for another table. Will snatched a bottle of Coors and set his empty in its place, flashing the woman a wink and a devilish smile when she would have chewed him out.

Mari shook her head in amazement. He gave the impression that life was just a game of three-card monte and he was the wheeler-dealer with all the charm and all the luck, but she had the distinct feeling he wasn't at all sure which card was the queen. The smile was a front. The charm was a smoke screen to hide the secret fear. She couldn't find it in her to dislike him.

"Mary Lee," he said, waxing philosophical. "Did you ever feel like a pair of left-handed scissors in a world of northpaws?"

"Yeah," she murmured, "I have."

Nora returned from the dance floor, flushed and euphoric. Will tugged on her frizzy ponytail and teased her about her choice of dance partners, trying to goad her into going back out on the floor with him. When she refused on account of exhaustion, he turned to Mari.

"Come on," he coaxed. "Work off that burger, chow hound."

"I don't think you're sober enough to stand up."

"Hell no, but I can dance. It's sorta like people who stutter being able to sing. I am the Mel Tillis of the Texas two-step."

She went with him against her better judgment. He proved to be a better dancer drunk than any man she knew sober. He was athletic, graceful, with a natural feel for the rhythm of a song. They danced until her calves felt as though they might explode, and then they danced some more. Mari reasoned that if he was dancing, he wasn't drinking—though he still managed to empty a couple more bottles—and if he was dancing with her he was dancing with someone who wasn't about to invite him to bed after the bar closed down.

At midnight Nora declared the evening over. She had to get her beauty sleep before the breakfast shift. Will followed them out the side door, trying to cajole them into staying another hour.

"Come on, Mary Lee," he begged. He caught hold of her hand and tried to reel her in. "One more dance."

"No dice, cowboy. I've had enough, and so have you." Mari pulled her hand from his, pulling Will off balance. He staggered sideways a step. "Maybe you'd better find someone to drive you home."

He tucked his chin back, offended. "I can drive."

"Yeah, right into a tree."

"Mary Lee's right," Nora said, holding out a hand palm-up. "Hand over the keys, Romeo."

Will shuffled back a step. "Jeez, what is this? *Thelma and Louise?* I don't need a couple of women bossing me around."

"You need a goddamn keeper, that's what you need."

Will's heart started pumping at his brother's words. "Oh, shit, it's the voice of doom!" he pronounced, cringing dramatically. He shot J.D. a look. "What you gonna do, J.D., ground me?"

J.D. ignored him, turning instead toward the women. "You slumming tonight, Mary Lee?"

"I'm a social egalitarian," she declared, refusing to be baited. "What's your excuse?"

"Thirst."

"Why don't you go on over to the Moose?" Will said irritably. "You can run into Bryce and chew his ass instead of mine for a change."

"Yeah," J.D. sneered, taking a step toward his little brother, "the taste of yours is getting pretty old."

"So why don't you back off?"

"So why don't you straighten up?"

Mari put a hand on his arm, trying to draw his attention away from Will. He shot her a ferocious look. "Ease up, J.D.," she said softly. "He's had a little too much to drink."

"Will's always just had a little too much to drink. It's the one thing he does really well. That and fucking up. You're just a regular wonder at that, aren't you, Willie-boy?"

"Shut up." Inside his head Will felt ten years old, sick of looking up at his big brother and always falling short of J.D.'s standards. His temper swelled and he reached out and shoved J.D.'s shoulder. "Shut up, John Dickhead. I'm sick of you."

"Then you finally know how I feel," J.D. growled. He was tired and his temper was run ragged. The stockgrower's meeting had netted him nothing but sympathy and a headache. He needed a fight with Will like he needed dysentery, and the absolutely last thing he needed was Mary Lee sticking her pretty little nose into the fray. That was too reminiscent of Sondra coming between them as boys, always taking Will's side, protecting him no matter what he'd done.

"You been down in Little Purgatory again?" he said to Will, his gut knotting at the possibility. "What'd you lose tonight, hotshot? The shirt off my back?"

Mari tugged on his arm, trying to pull him back a step. "J.D., maybe you should just—"

"Maybe you should just butt out, Mary Lee!" he roared, wheeling on her. "You don't know a damn thing about this."

Mari backed away with her hands raised in surrender. "Fine," she said tightly. "Knock each other out. Nora, I think we missed our cue to leave."

Nora gave J.D. a look that had reduced lesser men to squirming pulp. "Yeah, I get enough senseless violence on TV. Let's go, honey."

It was nearly one when Mari stepped out of the elevator on the seventh floor of the lodge. She felt beaten, exhausted, hurt. Being hurt was pointless. If she had an ounce of sense, she wouldn't let J. D. Rafferty hurt her. Trouble was, she wasn't sure she had an ounce of sense left. She was running on empty in too many respects.

"Tomorrow is another day, Marilee," she muttered, digging her key out of her purse. "Isn't that a pleasant prospect?"

She flipped the switch for the entry light and got nothing. Swell. Sighing heavily, she toed off her sneakers and left them in the doorway to keep the door open and let a sliver of light into the gloom so she could navigate her way to a lamp.

She sensed trouble a second before she saw it. The hair on the back of her neck went electric. She turned instinctively toward the bed and started to scream.

The large, dark shape hurtled into her with all the force of a linebacker, driving her back against a side table, knocking the telephone off onto the floor with a clatter. Her heart racing out of control, Mari grappled with her assailant, struggling to stay on her feet, fighting to draw in a breath. Their arms and legs tangled and they tumbled sideways. She landed on her back, the last of the air from her lungs whooshing out. Colors burst and swirled before her eyes as she wheezed and gasped.

Fight! Fight!

Her brain screamed the message. She thought her arms and legs were flailing madly, trying to fend off the attack, but the fall seemed to have severed her mind's connection to sensation. She wondered wildly if she would feel anything while she was being raped and killed.

Suddenly her lungs reinflated and adrenaline surged through her in a powerful rush. The smell of sweat and fear burned her nostrils. She swatted the attacker with one hand and groped for a weapon with the other, her fingers stumbling over the body of the telephone. Grasping it frantically, she swung it as hard as she could. The bell jingled as the phone smashed against the man's shoulder and he grunted in pain.

Fight! Fight!

Her feet working frantically to gain purchase on the carpet, she tried to scoot out from under the attacker as she hit him again and again with the telephone. He blocked the blows with his arms, leaning back, taking his weight off her. Sensing a chance at escape, Mari twisted onto her belly and shoved herself toward the door.

Stand up! Run!

The light from the hall beckoned like a beam from

heaven and she headed for it, trying to crawl, to run, to escape.

Run! Run!

Something large and hard connected violently with the side of her head, and everything went black.

The intruder ran into the hall and to freedom.

Mari lay on the carpet, motionless, the telephone a foot out of reach, her mind floating in a void.

A voice came over the receiver sounding pleasantly concerned. "Front desk. How may we help you?"

CHAPTER 15

$\mathcal{D}$rew was despondent over the attack. He paced back and forth along one end of the room in a black Reebok warm-up suit. His shoes were untied. His hair stood up in tufts that he continuously ran his hands back over as if to soothe himself. "This is terrible," he said for the fourth time. "We've never had anything like this happen."

Mari tried not to watch him pace. Moving her eyeballs intensified the pain drumming relentlessly in her head. Sheriff Quinn had been rousted out of his bed for the event—on Drew's insistence. He leaned against the dresser, looking glum, while a deputy poked around the room. Raoul the night manager hovered outside the open door, trying not to appear superfluous.

"God, I feel so guilty," Kevin said. He reached for Mari's hand and gave it a squeeze. He sat beside her on the disheveled bed, looking like an ad for Calvin Klein nightwear. A navy blue silk robe was loosely belted at his slim waist, the V opening revealing a smooth, tightly muscled chest. Baggy beach shorts stopped just short of his knees. He was barefoot. "We've been talking about replacing these old locks with card keys for months. Maybe if we'd done it, this wouldn't have happened."

"It's not your fault, Kev," Mari murmured, tightening her fingers around his, offering him more comfort than he was giving her.

"You didn't get a look at the fella at all?" Quinn said on a yawn.

She started to shake her head but caught herself. "It

was dark. I hit the first switch when I came in, but the light bulb was burned out. At least, that's what I assumed. Then everything happened too fast. He had on dark clothes and a ski mask. That's all I can say for certain."

"Was he tall, short, big, small?"

"Taller than me. Stronger than me." At the moment she figured anyone not on a life support system was probably stronger than she was. Nausea swirled through her head and stomach. Her skull felt like a cracked egg. She gingerly touched the sore spot just behind her right temple. Her fingers came away sticky with congealing blood.

Kevin turned a little gray at the sight. "I'll go get you an ice bag," he offered, and left the room, nearly bowling Raoul over on his way out.

"Can you tell if anything was taken?" Quinn asked, rubbing the bridge of his crooked nose. He looked as if he had been sleeping in his uniform shirt. His hair was a field of wheat stubble that had been ravaged by cyclone winds.

Mari's first instinctive fear had been for her guitar, but it sat unharmed in a corner. The rest of the room was strewn with clothes and upended furniture. She didn't have anything worth taking. No expensive jewelry, no stashes of cash or traveler's checks. The thief had struck out picking her room—if it had been a thief at all.

Her head boomed and echoed with the possibilities.

"Nothing was taken as far as I could tell," she said. She looked sideways at the big sheriff, wondering if he would be receptive to hearing her theories concerning Lucy. Not, she decided. Dan Quinn struck her as a simple man. Steak and potatoes. The missionary position. Lee Harvey Oswald acted alone.

He glanced at Drew. "Anybody else report hearing anything, seeing anything unusual?"

"Not at all. It was a normal night until this." Drew dropped down on one knee in front of Mari and gazed up at her, tortured with guilt. "I'm so very sorry, luv."

"It wasn't your fault."

"I'll have Raoul move your things to a suite while we're gone to the emergency room." At the door, the night manager brightened like a terrier at the prospect of importance. Drew's expression toughened as Mari opened her mouth to protest. "You're having that bump checked, and that's the end of it. I'll drive you myself."

"We'll dust the room for prints," Quinn said, fighting another yawn. "And we'll question the rest of the guests on this floor in the morning. See if they might have noticed anything. I've got the deputies on patrol looking out for anyone suspicious. Reckon he's either long gone or gone to ground by now, but we'll keep our eyes peeled."

He looked as if he needed his peeled with a paring knife. The man was ready to fall asleep on his feet. Mari bit back her own questions. They could wait until morning, at least until the sheriff had gotten some sleep.

As promised, Drew delivered her to the New Eden Community Hospital himself. Kevin, admittedly woozy at the prospect of needles and blood, stayed behind to supervise while the deputy dusted the room for fingerprints and Raoul began the moving process. They took Drew's black Porsche to the small hospital. Mari leaned back in the reclining leather seat and tried to concentrate on something other than the need to throw up.

"It's such a shock," Drew said. "One simply doesn't expect crime in a place like New Eden. That's part of the lure, isn't it? Clean air, idyllic setting, utopian values."

He was talking to himself. Trying to reason away the shock. Mari listened, understanding perfectly. Paradise wasn't supposed to have a dark side. She felt as if that were the only side she was seeing—the parallel universe, where everything was cast in sinister shadows. Like cutting open a perfect apple and finding it full of rot and worms.

Her stomach rolled at the analogy.

"Drew," she said weakly as sweat misted across her skin. "Do you have any idea what Lucy might have been into?"

"Into?" He wheeled the Porsche under the portico at the emergency room entrance. The white glow of fluorescent lighting spilled out of the hospital doors like artificial moonlight. "How do you mean?" he asked carefully.

"You said she liked to be in the thick of things, stirring up trouble. What if she poked at the wrong hornet's nest? Did you ever think about that?"

He frowned, looking handsome and rumpled, his lean cheeks shadowed with stubble, his brows slashing down above his green eyes. "I think you took a nasty smack on the noggin. We ought to concentrate on that for the moment. Don't let's worry about Lucy. There's nothing we can do to help her now."

He started to turn for the door, but Mari caught his arm. Just that much movement unbalanced her enough to send dinner sluicing up the back of her throat. Her brain felt disconnected from her body, as if her psyche were trying to escape.

"Drew?" she asked, wanting desperately to slide into unconsciousness again. "Do you think Lucy could have been blackmailing someone?"

"I think you're on the verge of delirium," he said brusquely. "Let's get you inside."

She spent what was left of the night in the hospital. Dr. Larimer—who also had to be called in from the comfort of his bed—checked her eyes and reflexes, put three stitches in the cut on her head, and pronounced her fit.

"Fit for what?" Drew demanded, incensed at the man's lack of concern.

The doctor, a squat man with unflattering horn-rimmed glasses and a retreating dark hairline, gave Drew an impatient look. "For whatever. It's just a mild concussion."

Nothing he didn't see every day in the course of treating ranch hands and rodeo cowboys. This was tough country full of hardy folk. The look he leveled at Drew clearly set him outside that realm.

"We'll keep you overnight for observation," Larimer

pronounced to Mari, obviously sensing the potential for trouble from these outsiders.

Mari sent Drew back to the Moose. All she wanted was a bed and a handful of painkillers, something to shut out the pounding and the suspicions for a few hours. What she got was a room across the hall from a crying baby. She lay in bed, the smell of bleach from the pillowcase burning her nose, thoughts of Lucy chasing each other through her head, the sound of crying rubbing her nerve endings raw.

She longed for comfort and thought of J.D. Had it been only hours earlier that she had lain in bed with him, listening to the rain? The memory was real enough for her to recall the warmth of his body, the strength of his arm around her, the pleasant scent of man and lovemaking. And yet it seemed surreal enough to make her wonder if she hadn't imagined the whole encounter. She didn't fall in lust with alpha males. She hadn't come to Montana looking to bed a cowboy.

Even so, she closed her eyes and pretended he was there now, that she was tucked back to front against his big, muscular body. She pretended they belonged together, she pretended that he cared. The alternative was to feel alone. And on a night when thoughts of Lucy haunted her, thoughts of a death in the wilderness and a life with no one to love, alone was the last thing she wanted to feel.

Quinn looked better with a shave and a fresh shirt. His mood hadn't improved with the light of a new day, however. He sat behind his desk, longing to sink his teeth into the fudge-caramel brownies his wife had sent to work with him for his coffee break, but he had the sinking feeling his coffee break wasn't going to happen any time soon.

Marilee Jennings sat across from him, pale, dark-eyed with an ugly bruise on her cheek and an earnest expression that boded ill. It was almost enough to distract him from the fact that she was wearing another of her incongruous outfits—a filmy flowered skirt, paddock boots, a man-size denim jacket over a Save-the-Planet T-shirt.

Quinn didn't like to think of anyone getting attacked in his territory. He especially didn't like to think of any *outsider* getting attacked. They tended to squeal like stuck pigs at the least provocation—not that getting clubbed wasn't just cause for outrage—and they tended to drag lawyers around with them like Dobermans on leashes. A simple case could suddenly be blown into the crime of the century with packs of roving media people sniffing around town for dirt and the lawyers preaching on the street corners like demented evangelists. The prospects set his stomach to churning. He frowned at the pyramid of brownies and the coffee growing cold in his Super Dad mug.

Life here had been a whole hell of a lot simpler B.C.—before celebrities.

"How are you doing this morning, Miz Jennings?" he asked politely. Leaning his elbows on the desktop, he discreetly pushed the plate of brownies out of his range of vision.

She gave him a crooked smile that held more humor than he would have expected. "I have a new sympathy for soccer balls—which is exactly what my head feels like. I'm told I'll be fine in a day or two."

"You didn't really need to come in this morning, ma'am. It could have waited."

"I take it there's no sign of the man who attacked me?"

He shook his head, waiting for the diatribe on the incompetency of small-town police to begin. Marilee Jennings just looked sad, a little haunted maybe.

"I wouldn't worry about him bothering you again," he said. "He's likely moved on to another town. Thieves tend to get skittish when they've come close to being caught."

"If he was just a thief."

Quinn tipped his head. "What do you mean?"

Mari took a deep breath, tightening her fingers into a knot in her lap. "I'm not sure he was there to rob me. I think he may have been looking for something in particular."

"Such as?"

"I'm not sure." He looked impatient and she rushed on before her courage could run out. "You know Lucy Mac-Adam's house was broken into a few days after her death—"

"Vandals," he said, moving his huge shoulders. "Sure I know about it. J. D. Rafferty called me out to have a look."

"But what if it wasn't vandals? Miller Daggrepont's office was broken into not long after. Daggrepont was Lucy's attorney. Don't you find that strange?"

"Not especially." He cut a glance at his brownies, unconsciously flicked his tongue across his lower lip, and looked back at Mari. He seemed to get larger and more intimidating the thinner his patience became. "It's not unusual for a ranch house to get broken into when kids think there's no one around to care or to catch them. I'm not saying it's a common thing, but it happens. As for Daggrepont's office, it's just across the alley from the Hell and Gone. Gets broken into a couple times a year. I keep telling Miller to put a better lock on the door, but I guess he'd rather collect the insurance on that junk he claims is antique."

"But now my hotel room has been broken into," Mari pointed out, struggling to hold on to her own small scrap of patience. She was exhausted and her head was pounding. She wanted to take a couple of the painkillers Dr. Larimer had prescribed, climb into bed, and sleep for a week, but she had thought—hoped—she could arouse Quinn's cop instincts first. If he saw anything in her suspicions, he might assign someone to check out the coincidences, and he might approach the case of her attack from a different angle.

He wasn't looking aroused.

"Doesn't that seem a little too coincidental?" she pressed on. "I was a friend of Lucy's. She left all her stuff to me. What if she left me something someone wanted badly enough to commit a crime to get?"

"Did she?"

She closed her eyes against the frustration and the pain. He probably already thought she was a lunatic. Another "I don't know" would seal her fate with him. "She left a letter for me in the event of her death—which in itself was strange. In the letter she mentioned a book—Martindale-Hubbell, it's a directory of attorneys. There's a set in her study, but one is missing."

"If it's missing and you think it's what the thief was after, then why would he break into Miller's office or into your room? He could have gotten it out of Miz MacAdam's study when he broke in there."

"Lucy might have hidden it. He might have thought she gave it to Daggrepont for safekeeping or that I had somehow managed to get ahold of it."

"And why would she hide a directory of attorneys?"

"Maybe there's something in it."

"Such as?"

I don't know. Three words guaranteed to jerk a cop's chain. They were linear thinkers, cops. They liked evidence and logic and simple explanations. She could give Quinn none of those things. All she had was a matrix of ugly possibilities and hunches with Lucy at the center. If she told him she saw Judge MacDonald Townsend snorting cocaine at a party, he would likely ask her what *she* was on at the time.

Townsend was above reproach. She probably wouldn't have believed it herself if she hadn't seen it with her own two eyes, and if she hadn't known about the judge and Lucy. Nor was Quinn liable to see anything strange about Ben Lucas representing Sheffield in the matter of Lucy's death. Lucas was a prominent attorney with a license to practice in Montana. He ran in the same circles as Sheffield. So what if he had known Lucy back in Sacramento?

"I don't mean to sound like a crackpot. But there are just some things about Lucy's death that have bothered me from the first. Now this happens."

"It was an open and shut case, Miz Jennings," Quinn said tightly. "We got the man responsible."

"Sheffield claimed he never saw Lucy."

"I imagine he was lying about that. He shot a woman by mistake. When he realized what he'd done, he panicked."

"Or someone else might have shot her."

The sheriff blew out a gust of air. His brows plowed a deep V above the bridge of his crooked nose. The scar on his cheek was a vivid slash of red. "I suppose you have some idea who? I suppose you figure it was this mystery man who wants this mystery book you don't really know anything about."

"I'm only saying there are other possibilities. What about this hired hand of Lucy's who disappeared after she was killed? Kendall Morton. By all accounts, he was a shady character."

"That isn't against the law in Montana, miss."

"But did you check him out?" Mari badgered. "Did you at least check his criminal record?"

"I can't divulge that kind of information," Quinn said, color creeping up his thick neck into his face. "We did all that was necessary—"

"Necessary?" Mari scoffed, her hold on her temper slipping. "You hung a misdemeanor on a socialite and sent him back to Beverly Hills to liposuction the fat out of rich women's butts. Did you even consider any other suspects? What about Del Rafferty? He took a shot at me yesterday!"

Quinn didn't bat an eye. He went on as if people getting shot at was as ordinary as grass growing. "But he didn't kill you, did he? If Del wanted you dead, we wouldn't be having this conversation."

"Maybe he wanted Lucy dead."

"Because *he* wanted this directory of attorneys so he could hunt them all down and kill them too?"

"Don't patronize me, Sheriff," Mari snapped, leaning ahead in her chair. "Del Rafferty's elevator stops well short of the top floor. He shot at me for coming into his territory. He might have thought he had reason to get rid of Lucy altogether."

She felt like a traitor for saying it. Automatically she

thought of J.D., of the way he protected and defended his uncle. She thought of Del. He had scared the hell out of her, but the look in his eyes kept coming back to her, tearing at her heart. Hell was his state of mind.

Quinn fixed her with a look of cold anger. "Listen, Miz Jennings: Del isn't quite right in the head. Everybody knows that. But he don't go around killing people. And if he somehow accidentally shot that woman—which is next to impossible—he would have 'fessed up. No Rafferty I ever knew would let an innocent man take the blame for something he did."

Defeated, Mari held up a hand in surrender. Quinn would settle for nothing less than a smoking gun. He wasn't about to make his life any harder by opening a case for which he already had a conviction. *You should have known better, Marilee. Must have been that knock in the head.* "Okay, I give up. I can see this is pointless."

"Yes, ma'am," Quinn said, rising to his full height, jaw set in affront. "I believe it is. I'm sorry your friend was killed. I'm sorry you were attacked. Believe me when I say I wish to God it hadn't happened. I especially wish it hadn't happened here."

Which was his not-so-subtle way of saying he wished she and Lucy and all of their kind had never come to New Eden.

Mari stood slowly and looked Quinn square in the eye. "I wish that too, Sheriff. With all my heart."

"What are you doin' with that colt?" J.D. demanded.

Will, who was turning twelve that very day, was already in the saddle. The Appaloosa gelding was just two and wild as a cob. He'd run loose his whole life, had never felt the hand of man until Chaske ran him down from the hills three weeks before. J.D. had taken a shine to him instantly. The young horse had a fine way of carrying himself and a smart look in his eyes. He was a copper chestnut with white legs and blanket of snow white over his hindquarters. J.D. had been working him in the round pen with Chaske's help, trying to get the colt used to people, then to a saddle. He hadn't been ridden more than twice.

As Will took a short hold on the reins, the colt danced, his head sky high. He rolled his white-ringed eyes back, trying to see the unfamiliar person on his back.

Will shot J.D. a smug grin. "I'm gonna ride him."

The feeling that burst through J.D. was jealousy, pure and simple. The colt was his. He had a natural talent with horses, and that was one thing his snot-nosed little brother couldn't horn in on. Except now he was. Nothing was sacred.

"You're gonna get dumped on your bony little butt, shithead. Get off him."

Will took a tighter hold on the reins. The colt danced around in a circle, blowing through flared nostrils. The color was gone from Will's face, but he showed no other sign of losing his nerve. "I can ride him if I want, John Dopeface. You don't own him."

"I own him more than you do," J.D. shot back. He jumped up on a rail on the corral fence and reached for the colt's bridle. The horse shied sideways, beyond trusting anyone. "Get off before you ruin him!"

Will ignored him, his attention snagged by the sound of Sondra's voice as she and some of her town friends came down across the yard toward the corral. She was laughing and talking, her voice like the sound of water tumbling down a mountain stream. She dressed like a town lady, which J.D. hated, but then, he hated most everything about Sondra and Sondra's snotty friends. He was too busy glaring at them to notice that Will was taking the colt out through the gate.

Everything seemed to happen at once then. Will said something to catch his mother's attention. She turned toward him, smiling brightly, and raised a hand to wave. The colt went off like a rocket. He shot straight up in the air, all four legs coming off the ground. Will's eyes went as round as silver dollars, then squeezed shut as the horse came down, driving his head down between his knees and jerking him halfway over the animal's neck in the process.

There was nothing to do but watch the wreck happen. J.D. stayed on the rail, his fingers digging into the rough wood. Sondra was screaming. Her lover went running to find help, but there was no helping Will. He would be the victim of his own stupidity. So would the colt.

J.D. watched, sick at heart, as the colt pitched and squealed, wild with fright. Will somersaulted off and hit the dirt with a sickening thud. The colt wheeled and ran away from the crowd and straight into the corral fence. He hurled himself up against it, trying desperately to clear the high rail, tangling his forelegs between the bars in the process.

As the townspeople crowded around the groaning Will, J.D. went to the aid of the horse, talking to him softly, trying to calm him, praying the animal wouldn't break a leg in his scramble to free himself from his predicament. The colt's copper coat was nearly black with sweat and flecked with lather. Blood ran down the white stockings on his forelegs, where he had scraped the skin away against the bars of the fence.

Chaske came and took the horse, frowning darkly at the damage that had been done to the animal—physically and mentally. Every bit of work they had done was ruined that quickly, that carelessly. J.D. started to follow him toward the barn, but the old man shook his head and shot a meaningful glance at the crowd gathered around Will.

"See to your brother first."

J.D. started to protest, but bit the words back as Chaske stared at him long and hard.

Will was alive and moaning, soaking up the sympathies of the townspeople like an obnoxious little sponge. J.D. was more worried about the colt. Getting dumped was a common enough occurrence; people seldom died of it and it was generally their own fault anyway. The colt, on the other hand, might never lose his mistrust of people now. And that was *all* Will's fault.

He took up a stance where he could scowl down at Will. Sondra glared up at him through her tears. She kneeled in the dirt beside her baby, cradling his head in her lap, stroking his cheek as he cried softly and held one arm against his middle. "How could you do this!"

J.D. all but jumped back at the attack. "It wasn't my fault! I told him he'd break his stupid neck!"

"You should have stopped him. My God, J.D., you're sixteen. Will's just a little boy! Don't you have any sense of responsibility at all?"

She couldn't have hit him any harder with an ax handle. Responsibility? What would she know about responsibility? She was the one who had left her family for her own selfish reasons. She didn't know spit about responsibility. And she'd bred a son in her own selfish image. J.D. knew without question that Will would turn the story around so that none of the blame would rest on his own head. It would all be J.D.'s responsibility—like the chores and the house and every job Dad ignored because he was too busy pining away for a wife who was as faithless as a bitch in heat. And J.D. would take it and bear up and never say a word to anyone, because he was a Rafferty, and *that* was his biggest responsibility.

J.D. brought himself back to the present, shaking his head at the fog that had shrouded his brain. It wasn't like him to look back. What was done was done. It didn't matter anymore.

But as he looked across the pen at Will, he knew that wasn't true. It *did* matter. It mattered a lot. The stakes had only gotten higher and higher with the passage of time, until now everything hung in the balance. The ranch sat on the pinnacle, teetering precariously. Will was the weight that could tip it either way.

They hadn't spoken a word since the scene outside the Hell and Gone. J.D. hadn't trusted himself. He knew his temper only made things worse, but he could hardly look at Will these days without seeing red. From the beginning he had been the one who loved the ranch, worked the ranch, fought tooth and nail for the ranch, yet Will had the power to lose it for him. Between his gambling and his womanizing, he seemed hell-bent on doing just that.

The idea of not being in control of his own destiny made J.D. furious and terrified in a way nothing else could. All their futures—his, Del's, Tucker's, Chaske's— were sliding into the hands of a man who had never taken responsibility for anything in his life.

Will leaned against the side of the barn, bent over at the waist, drinking from the hose. He had shown up in time for breakfast, refused everything but black coffee, which he drank in silence, leaning back against the kitchen counter. Mirrored aviator sunglasses shaded eyes that were most probably bloodshot. He took them off now and sprayed himself in the face with the water.

They had spent the day finishing inoculations and all the other miscellaneous checks on the steers and heifers. As predicted, the corral was a sea of mud, churned deep by the hooves of thousand-pound animals. J.D. was covered with muck to his waist. He could feel flecks of it drying on his face and the back of his neck. Pushing himself away from the rail, he made his way toward the hose.

Will handed it to him, then stood back, settled his sunglasses into place, and slicked his dark hair back with his hands, turning his profile to the setting sun. He looked like a movie star bathed in golden light. Tom Cruise come to play cowboy for a day in Hollywood's newest fun spot. The analogy only fueled J.D.'s temper. He used the hose to douse it, letting the cold well water pour over the back of his head and down the sides of his face.

Tucker had already gone to the house to see about supper. Chaske was doing the chores. The day was winding down, the sun sliding toward the far side of the Gallatin range. Down the hill from the pens, the cattle dogs were hunting mice, bounding through the bluebells and needlegrass, setting the tall stalks of beargrass bending to and fro like the stems of metronomes. Somewhere in the woods beyond, a wild tom turkey gobbled, advertising for a date.

J.D. turned the water off and straightened slowly, taking in all of those things, feeling a sharp pang of longing in his chest, as if they were already lost.

"We need to talk," he said quietly.

Will regarded him from behind the one-way glass of his aviator lenses. There was no infamous grin, no joke, no dimples cutting into his cheeks. "Translate that for me, J.D. You want to talk *with* me or *at* me?"

"We need to talk about Samantha."

He shook his head, turned, and looked out at the meadow where the dogs were chasing each other. "I don't want to have this conversation."

"Neither do I."

The grin cut across his face then, as sharp as a scimitar. "Then let's skip it."

"And pretend nothing's wrong? You don't want to deal with it, so we should ignore it?" J.D. shook his head, struggling to hold his temper when what he wanted to do was wrap his hands around his brother's throat and choke him until his eyes bugged out. "Do you have any idea how serious this could be—her falling in with Bryce's crowd? Do you even have a *clue*, Will?"

"Yeah, I've got a *clue*," Will sneered. "She's my wife. How do you think *I* feel?"

"I can't imagine. You act like you don't give a damn what she does. You're off to the Hell and Gone every night, trying to nail anything in a skirt. Am I supposed to think you're heartbroken?"

"You don't understand anything," Will said bitterly, and started across the yard for his truck.

J.D. grabbed his arm and hauled him back around. "Don't pull that act with me," he growled, jabbing an accusatory finger in Will's face. "You're not the innocent victim here; you're guilty as hell! You married that girl, then you dumped her. Now she's in a position to cut all our throats, and all you do about it is get drunk and go dancing!"

"What am I supposed to do?"

"Get her back. Face up to your responsibilities. Act like a man for once."

"Why should I?" Will taunted, his own temper simmering in an oily mix of pain and inadequacy. "Why should I, when you're man enough for the whole fucking state of Montana? I could never measure up in your eyes no matter what I did, so why should I bother?"

"Jesus. Is that all this is about for you? Who's got the biggest dick? Some shithead case of sibling rivalry? I'm talking about our lives here, Will!"

"That *is* our life," he spat back. "Haven't you been paying attention for the last twenty-eight years?"

J.D. stepped back with his hands raised as if to ward off the entire conversation. "This is unbelievable," he muttered more to himself than to Will. "We could lose the ranch and all you want to do is sulk over a whiskey because you were born second! Christ almighty, don't you have any pride at all? Don't you have an ounce of self-respect?"

Will stared at him long and hard from behind his disguise, sure that J.D. could see right through it, as he always did, always had. He stood there, feeling stripped bare. The eternal screwup, fooling everyone with a wink and a grin. Except J.D. Never once had he fooled J.D. Now the act was wearing thin all the way around. The curtain wasn't just coming down, it was coming unraveled, and he was scared as hell that when it was over, there would be nothing left to hide behind and nothing left to hide.

"No," he said quietly, stunned by the truth of it. "I don't."

This time when he started for his truck J.D. let him go. He stood there by the side of the barn, completely still, drained of everything but fear. Around him was the only life he had ever wanted. The ranch. The mountains. The horses and cattle. The coolness and the quiet that crept out from under the trees as the sunlight drained away. The squealing call of a bull elk. The eerie whirring sound of a nighthawk diving through the twilight for its prey.

This was all he had ever allowed himself to want, all he had ever loved. It hung now by a thread, swinging in the breeze.

CHAPTER 16

$\mathcal{M}$ari sat on the glass-topped table, staring down at the valley bathed in the soft velvet tones of twilight. She sat there as the sun went down, staring, thinking, her fingers moving almost absently over the strings of her old guitar.

Quinn didn't believe her. Did it matter? Lucy was dead. Dead was forever. Nothing could bring her back. If someone had killed her because she had been blackmailing that person, wouldn't the story end there? No more Lucy, no more blackmail. End of plot. Mari didn't know anything about Lucy's schemes. She didn't want to know.

But what if Kendall Morton had killed Lucy? He was still at large.

And if Del killed Lucy? He had motive, means, opportunity. God knew, he had the temperament for killing. The government had trained him to kill.

Oh, Del.

Oh, J.D. . . .

He loved his uncle. He protected his family. A rough-edged knight on a big sorrel horse. The defender of his kingdom. The last man of honor. So tough, so impenetrable. So vulnerable.

Not smart, Marilee. He's a lot harder than he is soft.

She didn't know why she was even thinking about him. He didn't want her around; he wanted her only in bed. She liked to think she was more liberated than to go for a man like that. She liked to think she would have become a nun before she went for a man like that.

What a shock *that* would have been to her mother, seeing as how the Jennings clan were devout followers of the show-up-Sunday-in-a-killer-outfit-no-one's-ever-seen Episcopalian church.

She tucked a strand of hair behind her ear, started a new song, a new train of thought.

Old train of thought.

Quinn didn't believe her. The odd pieces of truth and suspicion she had collected over the last week didn't add up to anything when he looked at them. Mari felt as if she were looking at an abstract painting and only she could see the zebra represented by the incongruous slashes of color. It stood out to her more and more, the lines of it becoming bolder, stronger, while everyone else saw only a jumble of unrelated brush marks. More bits of information floated up from the depths of her memory, adding detail and definition to the zebra.

Contusions, abrasions, broken bones. The notes from the brief coroner's report flashed through her mind for the hundredth time that day. She had blocked it all out after reading it that first day, but now the details came back to her again and again. Cuts, bruises, a broken nose. Injuries that may have been incurred in the fall from Clyde, but Mari had taken that same fall and come away with nothing more than a few bruises.

She closed her eyes and visualized the grisly scene as it must have happened—the bullet striking Lucy in the back, pitching her forward, the mule bolting out from under her, Lucy falling headlong. Into a deep cushion of meadow grass. Where had the cuts come from? How had she broken her nose? She might have landed on a rock, but that still didn't explain the cuts or the dirty, broken fingernails.

After a brief nap plagued by disturbing dark images, Mari had spent much of the afternoon tracking down the county coroner to see if he could answer any of her questions. As it turned out, he was a veterinarian who had never wanted to take the job of coroner. No one in the county wanted the job. It was traditionally passed down as a booby prize to the newest person in the county with medical training—which was, he had pointed out defensively, better than in some counties, where the coroner ran a filling station or feed store. The job didn't require a diploma of any kind. It was an elected position no one ever wanted to run for. His job was to view corpses and fill out forms. He did not perform autopsies. If one seemed necessary, the unfortunate victim was shipped off to the medical examiner in Bozeman. He hadn't found it necessary in Lucy's case. A half-wit could have seen what killed her.

Could he explain the contusions, abrasions, broken bones? Incurred in the fall from her mount. Period. Had she been sexually assaulted? Didn't know, had no call to look, and what kind of dumb-ass question was that anyway? The woman was killed in a hunting accident. End of story. End of conversation.

He had been more interested in his job of castrating yearling horses than in discussing post-mortem exams. He offered no support or sympathy.

Mari drove away from the interview feeling defeated and nauseated, the smell of blood in her nostrils and the image of a German shepherd trotting across the ranch yard with discarded horse testicles held like a prize in his mouth burned indelibly into her brain. She shuddered now as it came back to her. That wasn't something the average court reporter got to see every day. Thank God. Turning her mind back to Lucy was almost a relief.

What was she doing up on that mountainside in the first place? Whom had she gone to meet?

J.D.?

The thought brought a sick, hollow feeling to her stomach. Lucy died on Rafferty Ridge. She'd been sleeping with J. D. Rafferty. Del Rafferty saw ghosts and could shoot the balls off a mouse at two hundred yards.

Del might have seen Lucy as a threat. She was an outsider who had bought a piece of Montana at the foot of the Stars and Bars, just one of many who would try to encroach on his sanctuary.

What if Del had killed her? What good could come of proving that? To lock him up would be a sentence worse than death. It wouldn't bring Lucy back. It would destroy whatever fragile thread there was between her and J.D.

And just what do you think will come of that thread anyway, Marilee?

Nothing. It wasn't strong enough to bind them. She wasn't looking for that anyway. God knew, he wasn't.

And where does that leave you, Marilee?

Alone. The odd one out. Drifting in limbo in a dark paradise.

Staring out over the valley, listening as an elk called, she plucked out the poignant opening bars of a Mary-Chapin Carpenter song. "Not Too Much to Ask." It was just a song. Something to sing, to occupy her mind and her fingers. She told herself it didn't come from her own heart, the words of longing and jaded hope. She didn't need to be anything to J. D. Rafferty. She didn't want to know about the past that had toughened the armor around his heart. She played it only because playing had always calmed her mind and soothed her.

Her voice carried out on the cool evening air, strong and warm and honest. Too true to everything she was feeling.

A silver mist floated above the stream, as soft and smoky as her voice. Far up the valley the elk called again. A coyote answered in a faint voice. The evening star winked on above the mountains to the west.

J.D. hesitated in the deep shadows along the side of the house. He stood there, transfixed, mesmerized by her voice—the aching tenderness, the world-weariness, the complex shades of emotion and experience.

With a handful of keenly chosen notes on the guitar, she segued from a love song to a portrait of a place. A place of mountains and water. A land of sky. Simple strengths and dying traditions. Horses in high grass. Elk beside a stream. Sagging porches and an old church in need of paint. A feeling of innocence and wisdom and stillness. Of desperately clinging to a time that was already gone, and mourning for its passing.

With just a few simple sentences she unerringly painted this place. *His* land, *his* feelings, *his* fears. The words touched him in a way no woman ever had. They reached inside and cradled a part of him he never let anyone near —his heart. For a few moments he leaned against the rough logs of the house and allowed himself to exist in her words. Allowed himself to hurt. Allowed himself to need something he couldn't even name. And when the song was over and the guitar ran out of notes, he just stood there and ached at the sense of loss.

Slowly he stepped from the shadows. Mari turned and looked at him, her eyes wide and dark.

"Taking a night off from the social whirl, Mary Lee?" he asked, but he sounded more weary than wry, the edge of his mood dulled by feelings too heavy to ignore.

"Yeah," she said, her voice husky with cynical humor, her pretty mouth kicking up on one corner. "I usually try to sit one out when I've got a concussion. People with head injuries tend to drag a party down."

J.D.'s gaze sharpened as he tried to discern whether or not she was joking. In the faint light that came from inside the house he could see the lines of strain in her face. She looked gaunt, fragile, her skin as pale and translucent as a lily's petal.

"I don't suppose it'll make the papers until Thursday —seeing how that's the only day the paper is printed," she said, looking vaguely embarrassed as she set her guitar aside and climbed down off the table. A filmy skirt swirled around her calves. The sleeves of her denim jacket fell to her fingertips. "I got beat up last night."

"You what!"

He charged forward a step, looking as if he thought he ought to pick her up or sit her down or do something, but the emotions that compelled him were obviously too foreign to decipher and so he did nothing but stare at her. Mari found his reaction sweet, but she didn't let herself dwell on it.

"Someone thought it would be cute to hide in my hotel

room and smack me in the head with the telephone when I came in." She said it simply, as if she hadn't been terrified. Inside, the residual fear quivered like a tuning fork. "I wasn't amused."

"Jesus Christ, Mary Lee!"

He took the last step to close the distance between them and brought his hands up to cradle her face and turn it to the light. She winced as his fingertips slid back into her hair and grazed the tender spot.

The feelings that tore through him were unfamiliar, unwelcome, but too strong to hold back. He couldn't stand the idea of anyone physically hurting her. She was little, delicate . . . *his*. Dammit, she was his. Maybe not forever, but for as long as she stayed here. The protective instincts he reserved for his family and his land surged past all barriers to include Mary Lee. He would have cheerfully wrapped his hands around the throat of the man who had done this and torn his head off.

"Who was it?" he demanded.

She gave a little shrug. "Sorry. I hate to sound like a bigot, but all those guys in ski masks look alike to me."

"Are you all right?"

The rough concern in his voice touched Mari in a place more sensitive than her injury. The vulnerability, the loneliness, the longing for something beyond her reach, rose like a tide.

"No," she whispered. She tried for a smile. It trembled and fled. "I could stand to be held for a while."

He slid his arms around her and gathered her into him, wrapped her carefully in his strength. Mari burrowed her face into his shoulder and breathed deep. Ivory soap underscored by a subtle male musk. He had showered before coming down. His shirt was soft and smelled of sunshine. Above all, he was warm and strong and she fit against him perfectly. As if she belonged there.

She slipped her hands around to the small of his back, absorbing the feel of washed cotton and hard muscle through her fingertips. "This is nice," she whispered.

"Did they steal anything?"

"I don't have anything worth stealing." *Except my heart.* She felt it slipping away.

"He didn't hurt you . . . otherwise?" Christ, if some bastard had raped her—

"No. No," she whispered, hugging him. "I don't think it was me he was after, but I'd rather not talk about that just now."

Mari tilted her head back. The light that spilled out from the house was just bright enough to highlight the chiseled planes and hard ridges of J.D.'s face. No sculptor could have better captured the essence of the West. Everything about it—and about him—was etched into his face—his pride, his arrogance, his integrity, his toughness. A pair of lines slashed across his broad forehead like taut stretches of barbed wire. His nose was a bold, straight blade, nothing fancy, a no-nonsense kind of nose. Above the rock that was his jaw his mouth was habitually a tight, compressed line.

"You didn't come here to talk, did you, Rafferty?"

"No." A hint of a smile played at one corner of his mouth. "I came here to get laid." The smile vanished like a ghost, and he touched her cheek just below the bruise Clyde had given her. "But it won't kill me to do without. I don't reckon you feel up to it."

"Oh, I don't know," she murmured wistfully. "It might be nice to feel wanted. Why don't you kiss me and find out?"

"You sure?" he asked, the concern in his voice and in his eyes almost more than she could stand.

"Kiss me," she ordered.

He complied with the lightest, sweetest of kisses, as if he thought her lips were made of spun glass. His care brought tears to her eyes. He was so big, so tough, and yet he handled her so gently, showing her something he would never tell her—that he cared . . . at least a little. Her heart pounded at the idea. The tears burned her eyes. She felt too vulnerable, too fragile. What she wanted suddenly was passion hot enough to temper steel, hot enough to burn away the sense of defenselessness and hopelessness.

Rising up on her toes, she cupped the back of J.D.'s head with one hand and pulled him into the kiss, into her mouth. She kissed him deeply, hungrily, wildly. The sparks struck and flared instantly. J.D. pulled her against him, bending her back over his arm. He answered her aggression with aggression, opening her mouth wider with the pressure of his, thrusting his tongue deeper. His hand slipped between them, inside the open front of her jacket, and found her breast. Kneading, squeezing, fondling her through the soft fabric of the old chambray shirt she wore. Then his fingers hooked in the placket and the buttons gave way, dropping to the deck like discarded pearls, skittering and rolling.

Mari groaned as he captured her breast again. His hand was big, broad, callused, and rough. His fingertips rubbed across the aching point of her nipple, pinched it gently, drew on it. The fire of need burned hotter within her. She felt strong, wild, giddy as she broke free of the shroud of powerlessness. She had power, here, with him, within herself, within these moments of mutual need.

Her hands wound into the fabric of his shirt, tugging it free of his jeans, tugging it open snap by snap so she could touch him. She loved touching him. The heat of his skin. The crisp silk of his chest hair. The hard ridges of muscle and ribs. She felt drunk on it, on desire. Dizzy. Floating. Then she realized dimly that he had lifted her up.

He settled her on the glass-topped table. Laying her down, he opened her jacket and shirt, baring her to the starlight. She stared up at him, dreamy, drugged, her deep-set eyes glowing. J.D. forgot everything—what she had been through, who she was, the terrible weariness that had pressed down on him. There was only this. Need. Uncomplicated. Simple. Sweet, hot desire. No games. No subterfuge. Just need. His need. Hers. She was not ashamed to want him. She reached a hand up toward him, inviting him.

He bent over her and kissed her breasts, one and then the other. She arched into the contact, encouraged him to taste her, to take the tender bud of her nipple between his lips and suck her. J.D. granted her wishes as his own turned greedy. This was what he needed tonight. The solace of her body. The comfort of having her take him inside her. He felt so raw, so tired from the war he seemed to be waging on his own. He needed these moments of wild abandon. He needed to be lost.

He crushed the fragile fabric of her skirt in his fists and pulled it up into a drift across her waist. Too impatient to be civilized, he dealt with her panties by tearing them free, shredding the lace with his bare hands. Spurred on by the need, he parted her legs roughly and buried his face against the hot moist flesh of her woman's body, ravenous for the taste of her.

Mari gasped his name, wound her fingers into his hair, and lifted her hips to give him better access. He opened her with his fingers and kissed her deeply, devouring her. When the pleasure crested in a heavy wave, stars swam before her eyes, and she couldn't tell if they were inside her head or in the big Montana sky that stretched above them like a black velvet sea.

J.D. straightened away from her, panting, chest heaving. Mari sat up and reached for him, drew him to her. She kissed him slowly, softly, deeply, savoring the taste of loving.

"I want you," he growled, kissing her lips, her cheek, the side of her neck.

"I want you too," she answered back, her voice as faint as a dream. She felt like a dream—her mind floating, her body throbbing, senses magnified a thousand times. "I want you inside me."

"Then take what you want, Mary Lee," he murmured darkly, his hands skimming down her sides.

Her fingers fumbled with his belt buckle, dealt with the button and zipper of his jeans. They kissed again as she freed him. Frantically, desperately. J.D. backed away from the table, drawing her with him. He dropped down into one of the armless deck chairs, pulling Mari onto his lap, straddling him. Mouths locked, teeth clashed, tongues dueled. Her hair tumbled forward across her cheeks and his, shrouding their faces like a curtain of rumpled silk.

J.D. closed his big hands on her hips, lifted her, and pulled her down on him, impaling her on his shaft. Mari's fingers dug into the steely muscles of his shoulders. She held herself stiff for several exquisite moments while the line between pleasure and pain blurred. Then slowly she began to move on him, riding him, caressing him with her body, filling herself with him. The tempo gained speed with every stroke, until they were both gasping, groping, exploding. As the climax came in a white-hot rush for both of them, J.D. crushed her in his embrace and she held on, riding out the storm of sensation.

Afterward, she sank down against him, her arms looped around his neck. She felt utterly spent, physically and mentally drained of all energy. Her head was throbbing. Her skin was tingling. She had never felt so wanton or so helpless in the aftermath. J.D. held her. His heart beat strongly against her breast. She felt safe in the circle of his arms. She wished the sensation would last forever, but she knew it wouldn't. That knowledge lay like a rock in her heart.

"You all right?" His voice was a low purr.

"At the risk of sounding immodest," Mari said, trying to stretch humor over the vulnerability, "I thought I was better than all right."

"Mmm . . ." he growled, nuzzling the side of her throat. "Fishing for compliments, Mary Lee?"

"If you don't want to use up your daily quota of adjectives, I'll settle for a butter mint."

He chuckled and fished one out of his shirt pocket. Their eyes locked as he slipped it into her mouth. Mari caught hold of his wrist and kissed his fingertip, then drew it between her lips and sucked gently. J.D.'s nostrils flared. He was still buried deep inside her. As their gazes heated and sparked, her body tightened around him.

Mari shivered, not at the night air, but at the desperate need to keep him with her—not just for a few moments of bliss, but much longer. A time she wouldn't set a limit on even in the deepest corner of her heart. She felt safe with him in a way that wasn't smart. She felt complete in a way that she prayed was false. But tonight, when she was feeling so beaten and so lost, she couldn't find the strength to let it go.

"Stay the night," she whispered, terrified at the way the need made her voice tremble.

J.D. stared at her, knowing this moment was more than he would have allowed himself on any other night. She wanted more than he could give. He needed her more than he would ever admit.

Just tonight, he promised himself. *It's just sex.*

He didn't give the lie a chance to ring in his ears. He pushed past it with a hundred excuses.

"Stay the night," she whispered.

J.D. lowered his mouth toward hers, his heart beating a little harder. "Try to make me leave."

Del watched the lights go out in the downstairs of the house and come on in the bedroom that faced the yard. There was no shade at the window. He could see them clearly through the 6 × 44 sniper scope on the Remington 700. No night vision green haze. Amber light spilled out from the dormer into the ranch yard, falling just short of J.D.'s pickup. J.D. and the blond woman taking each other's clothes off. Kissing. Touching.

J.D. and the blond woman. Like before, but different, Del knew. A different blond woman; the talker, not the dead one. Still, he didn't like it. Not a bit. Things were getting too confusing. The blondes were running together in his mind, their features melding until they were almost interchangeable. Their images multiplied until he felt as if he had a swarm of fireflies in his head, swirling around, blinking on and off, distracting him from the business of maintaining his sanity. He needed to concentrate, but he couldn't. He needed to stay within himself, but he couldn't hold his mind steady enough. It kept exploding outward in a dozen directions at once. In his mind's eye he saw that happening as if his head were a pumpkin exploding upon the impact of a 168-grain .308 hollowpoint load. Boom! Pumpkin pudding. That was his mind.

He was breathing hard as he lowered the nose of the Remington. His vision blurred. He pressed his lips together as best he could. Still, spittle drooled down over the button of puckered flesh on his jaw and dripped onto his shirt. There was something he ought to do. He knew there was. The blondes were haunting him day and night. They were after J.D. J.D. said they were after the ranch.

There had to be something he could do. He'd been nothing but a burden since the 'Nam. During those glory days he would have known what to do. During that time his mind had been as sharp as a blade, his instincts honed to perfection. He'd been a hero, a machine, a human rifle with a hair trigger and a true shot. Now he couldn't hold his train of thought long enough to form all the right questions, let alone find the answers. The tracks ran together in his mind in an indecipherable tangle, like the rails at the big stockyards in Billings.

This blonde, that blonde, dead blondes. Tigers in the night. The dog-boys stealing through the trees to do their dirty business. How could he tell J.D. any of that when he didn't have the slightest clue what was real and what wasn't? It was all real to Del, but he knew his nephew didn't see dead girls in the night, or tigers on the mountain.

The shame of that trembled inside him like a fist that had been tightened and tightened until the knuckles turned white. If only he could do something to stop it all. If only he could make the blondes go away forever. If only he could be strong again, his mind whole for just a little while. He didn't ask for much from this life. If he could just have this one thing for just a little while.

He would have asked, but there was no God to hear him or He would have answered years ago.

CHAPTER 17

$\mathcal{T}$he crowd in the Moose lounge was edgy and electric. Talk of the break-in rippled through the room. Being questioned by the sheriff's department had put an unexpected spark of excitement into a number of vacations. Strangers swapped interview stories and traded theories about the vanishing bandit. He was a local lunatic who had been lying in wait to attack the woman. He was a local lowlife who saw the well-heeled patrons of the Mystic Moose as easy targets. He was an infamous jewel thief who had followed his prey up from Hollywood. He was an infamous jewel thief by night who was a famous actor by day. He was Robin Hood, Jesse James, and Hannibal Lecter rolled into one, and it was all the more exciting that he hadn't been caught. Lodge management had assured there would be no repeat performance, and extra security people prowled the halls, only adding to the frontier atmosphere people had come here for in the first place.

Samantha listened to the stories and speculation as she worked the tables, a little worried about spending the night alone. She didn't sleep well by herself on the best of nights. She had grown up in a small house bursting at the seams with people. Nights had been filled with the sleep sounds of her brothers and sisters—bedsprings creaking, covers rustling, her sister Rae talking in her dreams, her father snoring, bare feet padding to the bathroom in the middle of the night. All those years she thought she would have given anything to sleep alone, in her own bed, in her own house. Now she dreaded the idea. The bed was too empty. The house was too quiet. Most nights she lay awake, staring in the dark at the space beside her, where Will should have been. Tonight she would lay awake and stare at Will's spot and wonder if the mystery bandit might break in and attack her. And if he did, would Will even care when he heard about it?

She had spent the night of the party in the guest room at Bryce's. Her mind filled with the bright afterglow of excitement, sleep had been a long time coming. She may have felt out of place during the evening, but in the aftermath she relived every scene with enthusiasm, remembering the people she had met and the conversations she had been a part of. It was like a dream, like stepping into a whole other world—the celebrities, the beautiful clothes she had worn, the music, the champagne, the pool glowing as darkness crept down the mountainside.

A wry smile touched her mouth as she served a Falstaff and a Chivas to a couple from Beverly Hills. A fairy tale. Sam Rafferty as Cinderella with Evan Bryce as the fairy godfather. But the clock had struck, the enchantment was over, and she was back hustling for tips at the Moose, working the late shift until she could go home to her dumpy little empty house to sleep alone.

The black mood swooped down on her like a vulture and dug its claws into her stomach. Tears gathered behind her eyes and she blinked them back as she made change for a fifty and gave service with a smile. Half an hour to go, then she could cry all she wanted and there would be no one to see her except Rascal.

When she turned to go back to the bar, Bryce caught her eye. He was at his usual table, drinking Pellegrino with lime. The crowd around him was small. Just Sharon, Ben Lucas, and another man she had seen briefly at the party, a tall, stiff-looking man who might have been a television news anchor or a leading man from the era of Kirk Douglas. Of the foursome, only Bryce appeared to be having a good time. He flashed her a grin and motioned for her.

"Hey there, beautiful, what time do you get off?"

Samantha gave him a crooked smile, not quite sure

how she was supposed to react. If she hadn't been stuck in New Eden, Montana, her whole life, she might have come back with a witty remark, but she felt awkward trying to pretend sophistication she didn't possess.

"They've kept you hopping tonight," he said. "I guess everyone is charged up over that break-in we heard about."

"Yeah," she said, pulling her empty tray up in front of her, warming to him. He went out of his way to include her, to make her feel more important than she knew she was. She greedily soaked up his generosity and tried not to worry about what the rest of his friends probably thought about her. "Did you hear whose room it was?" she asked, excited at the prospect of sharing what little gossip she knew. "Marilee Jennings. She was at your party."

Ben Lucas raised his eyebrows and glanced across the table at the older man—Townsend.

Bryce frowned and rubbed his chin. "Really? That's terrible. Was she hurt?"

"He hit her in the head. I heard she had a concussion, but she's not in the hospital or anything. She was lucky."

He had a faraway look in his eyes, as if he were doing math in his head. "Yes, I guess she was," he murmured.

"It's creepy," Samantha said, shivering a little, the fear showing through. "That kind of thing doesn't happen here. People getting attacked and robbed and stuff like that."

Bryce sharpened, his blue eyes narrowing. Concern creased his high forehead as his brows pulled together. "You're home alone. Will you be all right?"

"Sure," she said without much enthusiasm.

"No, no, no." He wagged his head. "I don't like that idea at all. Come and stay at the ranch."

Samantha blinked at the offer and the temptation that hit hard on its heels. A vision of the guest room played through her head like a commercial for a luxury hotel. "No, I couldn't," she said automatically.

"Of course you could. We'd be glad to have you, wouldn't we, Sharon?"

Samantha flicked a glance at the statuesque blonde. Sharon didn't look glad to her. The smile that twisted the woman's thin lips was the kind that usually comes as a reaction to sucking on something unexpectedly bitter.

"No, thanks, really," Samantha said as her self-esteem sank. She imagined she could hear the words behind Sharon Russell's flat gaze—*stupid little hick waitress.* "I'll be okay. I'm used to staying alone. Besides, I don't have anything a thief would want."

"Maybe he wasn't a thief," Sharon pointed out calmly, running a finger around the rim of her margarita glass.

Samantha's eyes widened. Bryce shot his cousin a glower. "Way to go, cuz, scare the poor girl to death."

Sharon licked the salt off her finger and shrugged, unrepentant. "Better safe than sorry. A woman has to consider all the possibilities and act accordingly. If you don't feel safe, Sam, by all means, come out to Xanadu. You'll be safe with us."

Three tables over, a man cleared his throat noisily and raised an empty glass when Samantha glanced his way. She held up a hand to acknowledge him and turned back to Bryce. "I've got to go. Thanks for the offer, but I'll be okay."

He reached up and gave her hand a squeeze, made eye contact, and gave her a dose of sincere and fatherly. "Think about it. We won't be leaving for a while yet."

He watched her walk away, her thick braid twitching across her slim back as she went. Then he brought Drew Van Dellen's frown into focus at the bar beyond.

"Bryce, we need to talk," MacDonald Townsend said in a harsh, low voice.

A dull throb started in behind Bryce's eyes. Townsend had been chanting that phrase all evening. Bryce kept putting him off just to be perverse. He was in no mood to listen to the judge's whining.

"In a minute, Townsend," he said irritably, his gaze never leaving Van Dellen. Gracefully he pushed himself to his feet and sauntered away from the table, smiling to himself as Townsend complained bitterly to Sharon and Ben Lucas behind his back.

Drew set his pencil down atop the liquor inventory sheet as Bryce approached the bar. He didn't bother with a smile. "Mr. Bryce."

"Drew." Bryce flashed the Redford grin and dropped his elbows on the bar. "I hear you had a little trouble last night."

"Nothing that will happen again if we can help it."

"How is Marilee?"

"Well enough, all things considered. She had a nasty scare."

"No sign of the culprit?"

"None."

"Hmm . . . Well, I imagine it was just a random burglary. Or someone got wind of her inheritance and thought maybe she'd gotten something valuable from our friend Lucy."

"Not the case," Drew said neutrally. "Not something small enough to keep in her room, at any rate."

Bryce nodded as if he were conceding a point in a subtle debate. "One could never tell with Lucy. She was full of surprises."

"People are. Not all of them pleasant." He cut a meaningful glance to Bryce's table. "Take, for example, your friend the judge. In person he doesn't seem quite the genial fellow the press would paint him."

"Yes, well, Townsend is under some personal strain these days," Bryce said, smiling like a shark.

Drew arched a brow and looked supremely bored. Bryce studied him intently for several moments, trying to read, trying to gauge and calculate angles.

Drew went on, unperturbed by the scrutiny. "I wanted to have a word with you about Samantha."

"Did you?"

The idea seemed to amuse him. Drew had all he could do to keep his expression bland. "Yes. She's very young, you know. Not terribly sophisticated when it comes to the ways of the world outside Montana."

"And?" Bryce spread his hands and raised his eyebrows, feigning ignorance. "Are you warning me off, Drew?" he asked with a chuckle.

"Merely pointing out that she's inexperienced. And married."

"You couldn't tell it by the way her husband treats her."

"They're having their problems—"

"She deserves better," Bryce declared flatly. "She's a bright, lovely girl. I'm just letting her have a taste, giving her a little fun, a little attention."

And hoping to profit by it. Drew kept the opinion to himself. It would do no good to get into a figurative shoving match. Bryce swung enough weight to put a sizable dent in their business if he so chose, and nothing would be accomplished other than boosting the man's ego another notch toward the ionosphere.

"I just don't want to see her hurt, is all," he said diplomatically, his gaze drifting to Samantha as she delivered a round to a table of tourists from Florida. She smiled at them and listened thoughtfully as they asked her a question about the history of the lodge. Pretty girl, sweet girl, as unspoiled as the wilderness. Pity she had such poor luck with men. Pity men had to be such bastards. The thought of her being caught in a tug-of-war between Bryce and the Raffertys made his heart ache. The knowledge that she wouldn't confide in him because of his own orientation only added to the sadness and the sense of helplessness.

Bryce's eyes strayed to Samantha as well. Beautiful, exotic, innocent, fresh, ripe to taste what the world could offer her. She was youth and opportunity. With guidance and tutelage, her potential would have no bounds. The thought was as seductive to him as it should have been to her.

"I don't have any intention of hurting her," he murmured as plans shifted and realigned in his head. "Get me a whiskey, will you, Drew?"

He took the drink back to the table, where Lucas was playing at seduction games with Sharon, and Townsend sat stewing. Lucas was out of his depth and didn't know it. Sharon's eyes gleamed with secret amusement. Townsend finished off a Stolichnaya, his stare petulant as Bryce eased back down into his chair at the head of the table.

"How much longer are you going to put me off?"

Bryce narrowed his eyes and made a pained face. "I'd say until you became too annoying to stomach, but that moment is already a distant memory."

Townsend ignored the insult. "Did you get the videotape?"

"No."

A fine sheen of sweat misted across the judge's face. Even in the glow of firelight he looked abnormally pale, his skin stretched tight against the bones of his face. His eyes had taken on a haunted, paranoid quality. Bryce rubbed his chin and wondered just how much coke his honor was doing these days. Too much, the fool. If the man had ever possessed any nerve, it was gone now, burned away by excesses his spineless conscience couldn't handle.

"Goddamn you, Bryce," he snarled. His hand was trembling as he curled it tightly around his empty glass. "You never should have made it in the first place!"

Bryce laid his elbows on the table and leaned forward, nonchalantly scanning the room for curious onlookers. Everyone was either engrossed in retelling a personal brush with crime or in making a last trip to the bar. Satisfied, he tilted his head in Townsend's direction, his lips thinning, pale eyes going cold.

"It's part of the game, Your Honor," he said softly. "You know what they say. If you can't stand the heat— Or what's the version in cop vernacular? If you can't do the time, don't do the crime."

Townsend's whole body began to quake visibly. The rims of his eyes went red. Bryce half expected an alien creature to burst from the man's chest. "If that tape falls into the wrong hands, my life is over!" His voice was a raw whisper, as if unseen hands were choking him.

Bryce studied his fingernails, unconcerned. Nothing on the tape could be linked to him. He always made certain of that. That was part of his edge, one of the keys to his power. In his own mind, Townsend was already written off as a loss. The man was killing himself a thousand times over a phantom. He was a coward. Cowards could be used only so many times before there was nothing left of them.

"You should have thought of that, my friend," he said, glancing up to meet Townsend's eyes, "*before* you pulled the trigger."

"You're sure you won't come out to the ranch?"

"I'll be fine," Samantha said.

Bryce sat behind the wheel of her old Camero, looking just as comfortable as he did in his Mercedes, which trailed behind them with Sharon driving. He shifted into neutral and left his hand on the knob as they idled at New Eden's stoplight. His hands were bony and roped with veins. An onyx ring with a gold crest rose up like a small mountain at the base of his middle finger and gleamed richly in the dashboard lights.

Rich. The word tasted like chocolate and made her think about the feel of silk against her skin. She hefted her purse off her lap and set it on the floor, mentally counting her tips. If she set some of her tip money aside every day, she might be able to go into Latigo and buy herself something nice—in a month or three.

"You'll be fine," he said, giving her a wry look. "What about me? I'll be awake all night worrying about you."

She smiled at him softly, sincerely, her heart suddenly brimming. "That means a lot to me. It's nice to know someone cares."

It would have been nicer if that someone had been Will. Her gaze strayed to the glow of lights at the Hell and Gone.

"Of course I care, Samantha." He put the car in gear and eased his foot off the clutch as the light turned green. "I consider you a friend. How many times do I have to tell you that before you start believing me?"

"I don't know," she admitted guilelessly. "It's hard for me to imagine someone like you being friends with someone like me."

"Why wouldn't I want to be friends with a bright, beautiful young woman?"

"I'm a cocktail waitress."

"That's what you do, not who you are. Never confuse the two, Samantha. That kind of thinking only limits you."

They turned onto Jackson Street and he pulled the Camero up to the curb in front of her house. The car's engine grumbled on for a moment after he turned the ignition off, like a stomach with indigestion. Bryce ignored it and turned sideways on the vinyl bucket seat to face her. In the pale glow of the streetlight his expression seemed earnest. He reached out with one hand and brushed the tips of his fingers against her cheek, pushing a stray strand of black hair back behind her ear.

"You should have no limits but the sky, Samantha," he said softly. "Don't let anything in your life hold you back."

The Mercedes pulled in behind them and the glare of the headlights gave Samantha an excuse to look away. He didn't understand her life. He didn't know where she had come from or what kinds of obstacles that life had built into it. He was rich and powerful. He was like a being from another world, a world she had no access to, a world she could only look at and wish for in the most frivolous of her fantasies.

"I once had a job cleaning grease, dirt, and dead cockroaches out of a diner in Hell's Kitchen," he said. "I owned one pair of shoes and washed my underwear in the sink of the communal bathroom in a rooming house I shared with drug addicts and transients.

"We aren't always born to it, Samantha. Sometimes we have to have the courage to take a leap into the life we want."

He handed her the keys and climbed out, coming around to open her door for her. Samantha unfolded herself from the low-slung Camero. She kept her head down, pretending to be concerned about which purse compartment her keys went into. Bryce's words rolled around in her head like marbles, tumbling through a wash of con-

flicting feelings that had been building inside her for days
—loneliness and dissatisfaction and longing and hunger
for something more than she had. What *did* she have? A
junker car. A rented house that looked forlorn even by
moonlight. A puppy. A husband who ignored her. She
thought of the party. The air of excitement. The important people who had spoken with her. The sense of, if not
belonging, being included in something special.

Bryce went into the house ahead of her to check for
intruders. It took him all of three minutes to see every
shabby room and look in every closet. Embarrassment
burned Samantha's cheeks. She left most of the lights off,
hoping he wouldn't notice her blush or the fact that everything she owned was second-hand.

"Are there locks on these doors?" he asked as they
stepped back out onto the front porch.

She nodded, crossing her arms against the cool breeze
and the onslaught of loneliness. Rascal rubbed up against
her legs like an overgrown cat, then dropped at her feet
and began gnawing on her shoestrings.

"Good. Use them. If only to give me an hour's sleep."

"I will. Thanks for seeing me home."

He gave her a look. "I'm glad to do it. Someone should
be looking out for you."

That the someone should be Will didn't need to be
spoken. The censure was there in Bryce's voice. Samantha felt guilt on Will's behalf, then wondered if Will ever
felt a shred of it himself. If she were attacked, as Marilee
Jennings had been, would he feel the least bit responsible
for abandoning her?

"Call me if you need anything," Bryce said. "Even if
you just get tired of playing it brave."

"Thanks," she whispered, fighting the threat of tears.
"You're a good friend."

He nodded and hummed a note of agreement, but his
mind was elsewhere. He had a look about him as though
he were considering whether or not to tell her something
important. In the end he just sighed, leaned forward, and
kissed her cheek. His hand lingered on her shoulder, and
he squeezed gently as he stepped back.

"Good night, sweetheart. Think about what I said."

Rascal dove off the porch and gave chase halfway across the yard as Bryce headed for the Mercedes. Samantha called the dog back, patting a hand against her thigh. The puppy wheeled around, charged back up the steps and flung himself against his mistress as she lowered herself to sit on the edge of the porch. Samantha cradled the wiggling dog against her and stroked his head absently, avoiding his eager tongue by tipping her head back to look up at the stars.

You should have no limits but the sky. It was a million miles away. She could see it but never touch it. She tried to imagine what it might be like to cut loose all the bonds that held her to this spot on earth and soar up there among the stars. How free she would feel. How special. The only times she had ever felt special in her life had been with Will, when she believed that he loved her, when she believed they could have a life and a family together. Small dreams. Sweet dreams. Dreams that now seemed as distant as the diamond points of light in the sky. Broken dreams that tied her to a life of emptiness.

Will sat in the cab of his pickup half a block down Third Avenue from the corner of Jackson. He had a clear view of his house. There was enough light from the streetlamp to see Sam sitting on the edge of the porch with Rascal in her arms.

He'd been sitting there a long while. Long enough to put away the better half of a pint of Jack and chase it down with half a dozen cans of Coors. The cans lay discarded at his feet, rattling merrily every time he shifted position. The sound reminded him of the cowbells on the bucking bulls at the rodeo. Appropriate. He had asked Sam to marry him at the rodeo in Gardiner . . . or was it Big Sky? The detail was lost in the murky slop that clouded his mind like pond water.

Crystal clear was the memory of Sam looking up at him after he'd asked her. That memory was sharp as a Polaroid. Painfully bright. She looked like a princess, radiant in the firelight. Dark, exotic eyes widening, those soft, full lips parting slightly in surprise. Hair hanging over one shoulder in a thick plait of black silk. He remembered clearly what was in her eyes. Hope. Deliverance. Love. Excitement. She had looked at him like a poor child finding Santa Claus. Like he was a hero. He'd never felt so important in his life.

What a fraud you are, Willie-boy. That was all he had ever been, an impostor, a con man. Prince Will, pretender to the throne of Rafferty. Nobody's hero. Nobody's husband. He didn't do commitment. He specialized in meaningless charm. The man with no substance. Style, guile, and a pretty smile.

He had fooled her into loving him. Married her without a hint of conscience. Hurt her with selfish intent, dealt heartache with a lavish hand. Why would she ever take him back? Any woman in her right mind would sooner cut his black heart out with a rusty knife and feed it to the coyotes.

Seeing Bryce kiss her had nearly spared her the trouble. He had been as faithless as a tomcat, remorseless and smug. But seeing that one kiss had turned it all right around on him and plunged the blade straight into his chest.

What did you expect, Willie-boy?

Had he thought she would wait forever? Had he expected her to pine away for him the way his father had done over his mother's betrayal? What had he thought?

That the trouble of his marriage would just go away so he wouldn't have to deal with it or take the blame or face the consequences.

What a bright, shining boy you are, Willie.

Teflon Man, shirking liability with a wink and a grin. *How you gonna get out of this one, smart boy?*

What would J.D. do?

J.D. the hero. Man's man. Man of principles. Do the right thing. Do the hard thing.

What would J.D. do if he caught Evan Bryce kissing his woman? He'd kick Evan Bryce's ass all over Montana. That was his right, his obligation according to the code of the West. You didn't steal another man's horse, you didn't kick another man's dog, you didn't touch another man's woman.

If Evan Bryce was going to live in Montana, he had a few lessons to learn.

It felt good to transfer the anger. That was one thing Will knew he did with the proficiency of a great magician. He slipped out from under the weight of blame and dumped the load on Bryce's head. It was all Bryce's fault. Bryce was trying to steal his wife. Bryce was trying to steal his land. Never mind that Will had claimed to want neither. All he wanted now was a target for his anger that wasn't pinned to his own chest.

As Samantha got up and went into the house, he turned the key in the ignition and flipped the headlights on. The truck roared to life. Three-quarters of a ton of power and metal rumbled beneath him. His temper growled in the core of him, fueled by Coors and the Jack.

He kept to the side streets on the edge of town, avoiding the main drag and the deputies that patrolled it. Turning out onto the ridge road at the Paradise Motel, he hit the gas and let the truck fly. Seventy came and went in a roar. He ran the windows down and cranked the radio up. Travis Tritt spelled out T-R-O-U-B-L-E at the top of his lungs. Will howled and whooped, working up adrenaline, letting it run through his mind like madness.

The road ran straight for a long way. A blessing for a man whose equilibrium was saturated with booze. He concentrated on keeping the truck between the white lines that marked the edges of the tarmac and looked out ahead for the taillights of a Mercedes ragtop. The night was a black tunnel around him. The truck was a rocket, cutting through the void, jumping up and ducking down with the flow of the flight path until he felt disembodied. He was a pair of hands on a steering wheel, a brain with eyes attached, bobbing in midair; he was a pair of boots on the floor amid the empties, pushing the pedal past the point of sanity.

He came up on the Mercedes so fast, he zoomed past it and hit the brakes. The wheels locked up and the back end of the pickup started fishtailing. Will wrestled for control, his brain unable to take in all the facts, formulate a plan, and execute it in smooth order. The information came in too quickly. The messages departed brain-central too slowly. The Mercedes sped around him, horn blaring.

"Fuck!" Will screamed. "You fucking stole my wife, you son of a bitch!"

The taillights of the Mercedes winked mockingly in the distance.

"I'm gonna kick your ass all the way back to Hollywood, shithead!"

Bellowing a rebel yell out the window, he punched the gas and gave chase with a squeal of burning rubber. The truck ate up the ground and closed on the car as the road began to climb and snake its way up the ridge. The truck swayed from side to side on the winding road. The empty beer cans rolled back and forth across the floor.

Will felt as though he were riding a bronc that had too much buck for him. In over his head. Hanging on for dear life. He tried to stay focused on the car, on the idea of ramming Bryce off the road. But the Mercedes kicked in the afterburners and was gone, and Will was left riding a rank one with no hope for anything but a wreck.

He went into a sharp switchback with too much speed, jerked the wheel too hard, then overcompensated. Then everything was tumbling, like socks in a clothes drier, end over end over end over end. And the beer cans rattled in the midst of it all like alarm bells ringing too late to save anyone.

"Are you worried about Townsend?" Sharon poured herself a scotch from the decanter on the antique Mexican sideboard and wandered barefoot across the thick sea of carpet. Bryce stood by the windows, staring out, hands steepled before him as if in prayer. The only light in the room came from the spots that glowed in the display cases of Native American artifacts and from the light bars on the paintings.

He made a moue of dismissal. "He's nothing. He's finished."

"He might try to drag us down with him."

"With what? Even if the videotape surfaces, there's nothing that links it to us except the charges of a desperate man whose career will be going down in flames." He shook his head. "No. I'm not worried about him."

"What about the Jennings woman?"

"If she plans on making trouble, she's taking her time doing anything about it. I think she would have made a move by now." He took Sharon's glass and sipped absently at the scotch, pressing his lips together as it slid like molted gold down his throat. He still faced the wall of windows, but his gaze turned inward, visualizing all the puzzle pieces but he couldn't make them fit together. "She's nothing like Lucy."

"Disappointed?" Sharon asked, her voice sharp with irony.

Bryce swiveled a measuring look at her, a smile playing at the corners of his lips. "Still jealous? Lucy's dead, darling."

"Hurray." She snatched her glass back from him and lifted it in a toast. The scotch was gone in single gulp.

"You're such a poor sport," Bryce complained. "Do I complain when you're fucking other men?"

"Only if your view becomes obstructed."

Bryce walked away from her, not in the mood to spar. His mind was working, calculating, zooming down a new trail. The excitement was intoxicating. A bubble of euphoria grew in his chest, making it difficult to breathe.

"I keep thinking about Samantha," he admitted, smiling the Redford smile, though there was no one there to be impressed by it. "Drew tried to warn me away from her tonight."

Sharon glared at him. "How quaint."

She stalked back to the sideboard for a refill, but she just stood there with one hand around the neck of the decanter and the other twisting the stopper around and around like a screw.

"She has so much potential and she doesn't see any of

it," he said, amazed at that kind of innocence. Enchanted by it. "I could open doors for her that would lead her to the top of the world."

The hand on the decanter tightened until Sharon could feel the cut of the crystal imprinting her flesh. "She's a means to an end," she reminded him, not liking the tone of his voice.

He sounded beguiled, on the brink of obsession. The idea made her nervous. Bryce obsessed was Bryce unpredictable. And frankly, she was tired of his bouts of obsession with other women. She was the one who stood by him through everything. She was his partner. They had fought their way up from poverty together. It stung to have her loyalty and her sacrifices overshadowed by the bright glow of infatuation. Bryce turned his attention away from her and she suddenly found herself demoted to chauffeur, gofer, fifth wheel.

She would have to distract him from the fixation before it went too far, as it had with Lucy.

Bryce waved a hand impatiently. "Yes, that's all she was at first, but don't you see the possibilities? My God, her face could be on every magazine in the country. I could get her a movie deal—"

"I'm sure she'll jump at the chance to let you run her career after you've ruined her husband's life."

"He's ruining his own life. Once I've convinced Samantha to step back away from him and take a good look at what he is and what he has to offer versus the life she could have with me—"

Sharon swung around and flung the scotch decanter at him. The missile went wide and exploded against the window frame, spitting liquor and bullets of crystal across the glass and onto the rug. As an attempt to get his attention, the action worked brilliantly. Bryce stared straight at her as she crossed the room with angry, purposeful strides. She narrowed her eyes to razor slits.

"She's a stupid child. She's nothing," she snapped, her voice hoarse and masculine. She stopped within a foot of him, her whole body rigid with fury, hands knotted into fists held ready at her sides. Her upper lip twitched in contempt. "You're such a fool. There's so much more at stake here than your chance to play Professor Higgins. The girl is a means to an end. You want her husband's land; you can get it through her. That is the plan," she said, speaking very clearly and deliberately, because she knew he tended to hear what he wanted to hear when he was falling into one of his preoccupations. "You don't need her for anything else. *I* can give you everything you need."

"You can't give me the joy of rediscovering the world. You can't give me innocence," he said cruelly. "You never had any."

That quiet jab punctured her anger and deflated it. She seemed to shrink a little before his eyes, drawing inward on herself. "You bastard," she hissed, tears rising, mouth trembling. "You rotten bastard. Can't you see I'm only trying to protect you?"

"From Samantha?" He laughed.

"From yourself."

"Don't worry, cuz," he said softly, reaching out to touch her cheek. He ignored her concern. His priorities were shifting. Nothing mattered but the new goal. "I never had any innocence either," he murmured absently. "We're two of a kind."

Sharon was crying now, her sobs a low keening sound stripping up the back of her throat. The glazed, preoccupied look in Bryce's eyes frightened her. Still angry with him, she turned her face into the palm of his hand and bit him hard, then kissed the impressions her teeth had made, licking the dents with the tip of her tongue.

"I'd do anything for you," she whispered. "I'm worth a hundred stupid, naive girls. You need me."

Bryce smiled distractedly and took her hand, interlacing their fingers. "We're partners."

She could see his mind was elsewhere. On the girl, no doubt. And so the obsession had begun. Again. And there was nothing she could do about it but wait. Despair knotted in her chest. She stepped closer and kissed him, a blatantly carnal kiss that was unmistakable in its message. She was still here, available, willing. She would take what he would give her.

"Partners forever," she murmured, stepping back. She lifted her chin and cloaked her hurt with pride and a wry look. "Amuse yourself with your little Indian princess. Sleep with her if you have to. But fall in love with her and I'll cut your heart out."

Bryce chuckled. "I love it when you talk mean."

"You love it when I *am* mean." An irony she enjoyed. She could take out her frustrations on him and actually have him enjoy it. There were advantages to loving a man with a twisted mind. She sent him a feral smile as she took his hand and led him toward the stairs. "Tonight's your lucky night, cousin."

CHAPTER 18

J. D. woke at four out of habit. Mary Lee was tucked up against him like a little woodland creature seeking warmth. Her nose was burrowed into the hollow of his shoulder. He had his arm curved around her in a way that seemed entirely natural and comfortable. If he canted his head an inch, he could kiss her hair. He already knew that it felt like raw silk and smelled vaguely of coconut and jasmine—just as he knew how every other inch of her felt and smelled and tasted. Every part of her was imprinted on his brain. She was his.

His. He had never thought of any woman as his. Had never wanted to. Had always guarded himself diligently against the risk. How this one had slipped under his guard, he wasn't sure. He should have been immune to her if for no other reason than her association with Lucy. But he couldn't look at her without wanting her, couldn't have her without wanting more.

That truth scared him deep. The fear was a cold rock in his gut. They couldn't have anything together but what they shared in the heat of passion. He couldn't allow it. All his energy, all his attention, had to go to the ranch now. He had to protect the land. He had to preserve the Stars and Bars and the way of life that had been entrusted to him. He couldn't afford a distraction like Mary Lee. He sure as hell couldn't afford a distraction whose best friend may have been killed by his uncle.

J.D. stared hard at the ceiling, trying to will that thought away. In the cold light of day, when reason was easy to come by, he could tell himself Del's only role in the drama had been finding the body, that the city boy Sheffield had killed her accidentally. By night, when the world was all dark and shadow, he couldn't stop thinking about the crazy things his uncle said.

Del was his responsibility. The Stars and Bars was his responsibility. Stopping Bryce from buying up the whole of the Absaroka range was his responsibility. His whole damn life was nothing but responsibility. The weight of it pressed down on his chest.

A dull pain stabbed behind his eyes. He brought his arm up around Mary Lee's shoulders and checked his watch by the light of the bedside lamp they had never bothered to shut off. Time to go. Past time. He had never spent the night with Lucy, had never wanted to. But then, Mary Lee wasn't Lucy. She was sweet and earnest, honest and quirky and loyal. He could still hear the sound of her voice, smoky and low, singing about this land, painting a picture that was startlingly sharp, taking a handful of words and touching an emotion inside him that was deep and nameless.

He stared down at the top of her head, at the small hand that lay curled against his chest, and a fine tremor shuddered through him like the precursor to an earthquake.

Her lashes fluttered upward and she looked at him with those big, deep eyes.

"Is something wrong?" she asked in a voice that was half whisper, half rasp.

"I have to go."

"It's the middle of the night."

"It's after four." He moved away from her and sat up, swinging his legs over the edge of the bed, reaching for his shorts. "If I don't get a move on soon, I'll be burning daylight. There's work to be done."

Mari sat up and stretched, then pulled the coverlet around her. Her head hurt. Having him leave hurt more. *That's bad news, Marilee.* She combed her hair back behind her ear and frowned.

"You want a cup of coffee before you go?"

J.D. hiked his jeans up and did the button and zipper. "Go back to sleep. You didn't get much to speak of last night."

"Neither did you."

She climbed out of the bed and began a search for clothes. Her brain throbbed like a beating heart as she bent to pick up the green robe she had worn before, and she briefly reconsidered the option of remaining in a prone position for another eight or nine hours. Her stubbornness won out. If Rafferty was getting up, she would damn well get up too.

She shot him a look as he shrugged into his shirt. "What do you take me for—some kind of city girl?"

"Yeah."

"Yeah, well," she drawled, swaggering toward him with her fists on her hips. "I can ride a mule, I've been to a honky-tonk, and I haven't missed a sunrise in a week. So what does that make me?"

"City girl on vacation in Montana."

"Jeez," she grumbled, reaching up to do the snaps on his denim shirt. "They'll whisk you away to be on *Letterman* yet."

Rafferty wasn't amused. "You are what you are, Mary Lee."

Her hands stilled on his shirtfront and she stared hard at a white pearl snap. *You are what you are.* She was a misfit. She'd been a misfit all her life, a social nomad looking for a place where she could blend in without compromising her soul. She thought this might be the place, but J.D. was telling her she would always be an outsider in Montana. Or was he talking about his heart? *Either way, you lose, Marilee.*

"You don't know me, Rafferty," she murmured. "You're too busy slapping labels on me to see who I am."

A muscle tightened in his jaw. He said nothing.

"I'll go make that coffee," she said softly, tightly, turning away so he couldn't see her eyes. "It's instant. I hope you're not fussy."

"As long as it's black and hot," he said, following her downstairs, guilt riding him every step of the way. He tried to shrug it off, resenting the intrusion, resenting the implication that his judgment wasn't infallible. Just another reason to get the hell out, he thought. But he followed her into the kitchen instead of turning for the door.

"My specialty: hot, black sludge. Other court reporters used to call me up and order pots of it when they were pulling all-nighters on transcripts."

"That's a good job, isn't it—court reporter?"

"Sure, if you're an independently wealthy perfectionistic masochist."

She put water on the stove and got two mugs down from the cupboard. One was blue with white line drawings of cartoon rabbits having sex, the other was brown with cartoon dogs in the same line of pursuit. That Lucy, such a classy broad.

"That wasn't fair," she said, sighing as guilt nudged her with an elbow. "It's a great job for the right person. I wasn't the right person. Surprise!" She flashed a big, phony, prom-queen smile.

J.D. leaned against the counter and watched her with narrowed eyes. "What will you do now that you've given it up?"

"Well, my mother speculates I'll get a job in a seedy bar, fall into the drug culture, and end up on the streets selling my body for pocket change. I'm slightly more optimistic."

He didn't chuckle. He didn't so much as clear his throat. He just waited for a straight answer. Mari rolled her eyes as she filled the mugs and stirred in Folgers crystals. "So I guess you were absent the day they passed out the senses of humor."

The corners of his mouth flicked up. "Working."

"I should have known." She handed him his mug and blew on her own before hazarding a sip. It tasted like crank-case drippings that had been boiled and strained through dirty sweat socks. Heavenly. All she needed was a cigarette, an impossible deadline, and a lawyer in dire need of mouthwash breathing down her neck and she'd be right at home. She shuddered at the thought.

"I don't know what I'm going to do next," she confessed, leaning back against the counter. "That was one of the things I was supposed to ruminate on during my fun-filled summer vacation in the Garden of Eden."

She sighed, sipped, stared at Rafferty's belt buckle—a tarnished silver oval with a bronze rope edge and a figure of a calf roper in the center. The words FRONTIER DAYS CHAMPION 1978 were engraved on a ribbon of bronze that arched above the roper. He would have been sixteen or seventeen at the time. She wondered what he had been like as a teenager, as a child. She couldn't imagine him any way but serious and hard as nails. The idea of those somber gray eyes and unsmiling mouth on a little boy made her heart ache. She thought of him losing his mother to cancer, losing his father to grief and then to another woman. She wanted to put her arms around him and just hold him. She called herself a fool.

"I don't have to make up my mind tomorrow," she said, more to distract herself than to make conversation. "I have enough to live on for a while from the sale of my equipment. God, once Lucy's estate is settled, I'll have enough to live on until my teeth fall out," she said, struck anew by the shock. "I suppose most people would be overjoyed by that prospect. I feel . . . I don't know . . . sleazy."

J.D. arched a brow. "You feel sleazy because she left you money and property?" Lucy wouldn't have felt guilty. Lucy would have grabbed what she could get her claws into and run away laughing.

"We were pals, not relatives. What'd I ever do to deserve all this?" she asked, waving a hand to encompass the house, the ranch. Her dark brows tugged together above her eyes as she bit her lip and shot him a troubled glance. "Maybe what bothers me most is wondering what *Lucy* did to deserve it."

He shrugged and gulped another shot of battery acid. "You'd know more than I would. She was your friend."

"You don't have any idea what she was into?"

"Trouble, I expect. She was the kind who liked to poke sticks at rattlesnakes just for fun."

Mari frowned. "Yeah, well, I'm afraid one of them might have killed her."

J.D. set his cup down on the counter with a sharp *clack*. "Jesus, Mary Lee, will you give it up? It was an accident. Accidents happen."

"And it was just a coincidence that this house was broken into, then Miller Daggrepont's office was broken into, then my hotel room was broken into?" She shook her head, then impatiently snagged a rope of wild hair and tucked it behind her ear. "I don't buy it. I think there's something going on, and if I could find a couple more pieces to the puzzle, I might know what it is. I don't believe Lucy just went riding up on that ridge for the hell of it. I think she was up there for a reason, and I think someone killed her for a reason."

"What difference does it make now?" he said roughly. "Dead is dead."

Mari gaped at him. "I can't believe you said that! Mr. Code of Honor. Mr. Integrity. What difference does it make?" she sneered, gesturing sharply with her small hands. The too-long sleeves of her robe swayed from side to side. "There's a big fucking difference between misdemeanor negligent endangerment and felony murder. How can you condone letting someone skate with a fine when a woman's life has intentionally been ended?"

J.D. tightened his jaw and looked past her, coffee and shame churning in his stomach. He couldn't condone murder. He just wished like hell he could forget Lucy MacAdam had ever existed, let alone had her existence taken from her. He wished she had never come here, that she had never bought this land on the edge of his world, that her friends hadn't come here—Mary Lee included. Christ, *especially* Mary Lee. She distracted him and poked at his conscience and tied him in knots. What the hell did he need with any of that?

"I've got work to do," he growled, and started for the door.

Mari stuck out an arm to block his escape from the kitchen. She stared up at him, feeling sick inside—angry and frightened for her heart and ashamed of herself because of that fear.

"Did she really mean so little to you that you don't even care if her killer is punished?" she asked softly, her voice a strained rasp. *And if Lucy meant so little to him, then what do you think you mean to him, Marilee?*

J.D. thought of Del, he spoke of Sheffield. His eyes stayed on the Mr. Peanut tin that stood on the mantelpiece across the great room, smirking at him. "He's been punished, Mary Lee. Leave it alone and get on with your life."

"Yeah. Yeah, right," she whispered bitterly. "What's one dead sex partner when another will come along and take her place?"

He looked down at her, something wrenching in his chest as he took in the fierce anger and fiercer pride. Tears shimmered in her eyes, magnifying them, making them look like huge liquid jewels. She stuck her chin out defiantly, asking for it.

He didn't need her. Didn't want her here. He didn't need the feelings that were spooking him, making him feel like a trapped wild horse.

"You said it," he growled, "not me."

Mari stood in the kitchen, not moving. Dimly, she heard the front door slam, heard his truck come to life and rumble out of the yard and start up the mountain. She wondered vaguely why she hadn't heard him drive in last night. Too lost in her music, she supposed. Too bad. She might have steeled herself against him if she'd had fair warning. But probably not.

At any rate, all thoughts were peripheral to her pain. Her focus was inward, on the smoldering knot of emotions that crowded her chest. Tangled and painful, a ball of raw nerve endings; she wanted no part of it. She wanted no part of Lucy's violent death. She wanted no land, no windfall that chained her to that death. She didn't want trouble. She didn't want pain. Most especially, she didn't want to be falling in love with a man as hard, as uncompromising as J. D. Rafferty.

Falling in love. It seemed impossible, a bad joke, a bizarre dream. He was arrogant, bad-tempered, hard to the point of cruelty. What was to love?

The vulnerability in those world-weary gray eyes when he looked out across the land that had been his family's home for a hundred years, land that was being taken away piece by piece. The gentleness of his big, rough hands when he touched an animal. The gentleness of those hands when he touched her. The fierce tenderness of his lovemaking. The loyalty to an uncle most people would have shipped out of sight and out of mind. His determination to carry the weight of the world on his broad shoulders and never utter a word of complaint.

He was a complex man, not some cardboard cowboy. He was all sharp angles and hard edges protecting an inner core most people would never try to reach. He wasn't just pride and bravado. He was a man whose way of life was being threatened. He was a man used to controlling his own destiny, and now that control was being wrested from him by strangers. He was a man who had been raised to show no weakness, but she knew he was afraid—for his home, for his livelihood.

For his heart?

It was dangerous to hope so. Dangerous and foolhardy. She hadn't come here looking for love, just acceptance. She didn't want to love a man who made it a chore and a challenge. Every step would be a fight and she was so weary of fighting. Fighting her parents, fighting her own nature, fighting to fit in where she didn't belong. She just didn't want to fight anymore. She wanted life to be simple and sunny.

But life was neither of those things. Life was as complex as Rafferty, full of hard edges and shadows, and she couldn't sit back and let it pass. She had come to Montana as a first step of being true to herself. Part of that truth was Rafferty. Part of that truth was loyalty to her friends. She had a friend who was dead, and if she didn't find out why, no one else would. No one else cared.

Anger shimmered through her all over again as she thought of J.D.'s attitude. He'd never made his feelings for Lucy a secret, but she hadn't expected him to be so callous. He wanted to pretend a woman he had been intimate with had never existed, to bury her memory and ignore the circumstances of her death.

Because he was that cold, that unfeeling? Or because he didn't want anyone to know what had really happened?

Del. Was J.D. protecting his uncle? Could Del have shot Lucy in cold blood? Would he even have known what he was doing? His world was peopled by ghosts. His days were nightmares and he clung to the ragged edge of sanity by callused fingertips.

Head pounding, Mari wandered to the doors of the deck. She pulled them open and leaned a shoulder against the frame and looked out over the valley as the first light of dawn pinked the sky. Fog blanketed the low ground in thin, gauzy strips and ribboned among the dark trunks of the trees. The scene was like a photograph, sepia-toned and faded, like a memory. The coolness kissed her face with the scent of pine and cedar and damp grass. Down along the creek an elk raised its head from the water and its high, eerie call carried up the hillside.

Tears leaked from the corners of Mari's eyes and trickled down her face. She loved it here so much. Why couldn't it simply be the haven she wanted?

"Why does it have to be so hard?" she whispered aloud, the words laced and strained with pain, with confusion.

No one answered her. Not God. Not inner wisdom. The valley was silent. The elk moved on. She was alone.

Her guitar stood next to the door, tucked into the small corner where the wall met the kitchen cabinets. She reached for it like a child reaching for a security blanket. She pulled it into her arms and hugged it tight as she wandered out onto the deck.

"It's just you and me, old pal," she whispered, lovingly caressing the strings.

She climbed up onto the table and sat with her legs crossed, oblivious of the dew that had gathered thick on the glass, the oversize green robe tucked around her like a blanket. Closing her eyes, she lay her head down close to the body of the guitar and began to play. The piece was poignantly sweet, achingly tender, full of longing, brimming with need. It asked no questions, voiced no opinions. It was feeling, pure and simple, raw and painful. Everything her heart felt. Every bruise upon her soul. And when it was over, she just sat there in the quiet and hurt.

"That was damn pretty, Mary Lee."

Bolting from her meditation, she jerked around, eyes wide. Will stood leaning against the corner of the house. *Propped up* by it was more like it. His shirt was torn, his face was bloody, his right eye was ringed with purple swollen flesh, and there was a gash in his forehead. He tried to give her a crooked smile, but winced halfway into it.

"Oh, my God!" Mari gasped, scrambling down from the table. "What happened?"

"Had a little accident," Will said, grimacing as he straightened away from the wall.

He didn't add that he was lucky to be alive. At the moment he didn't feel lucky. He felt as if the entire batting rotation of a major league baseball team had gone after him, swinging for homers. His head hurt, his ribs hurt, he had a wrenched knee, and had popped his old bum shoulder out of joint. A good hard slam up against a tree trunk had remedied the latter problem, but it still hurt like holy hell.

"A little accident?" Mari cried, anxiously looking him up and down. "You look like you took on a Mack truck!"

"It was a Ford," he said, rubbing his tongue over the edges of the three teeth he had chipped. "It looks worse than I do. Lucky for me I've got nine lives."

"I'd say you just used one of them up, tomcat. What are you doing here? You should be in a hospital!"

"Well . . ." He started to sigh, but his lungs stiffened up at the pain. "Do you think I could sit down while I explain this? I just walked the better part of a mile to get here."

"Jesus! You can sit in my car while I take you to the hospital."

"No. No hospital. I'm suffering enough. Trust me, Mary Lee, if I didn't die during the night, I'm not going to. No hospital. All I want is a ride home, if you'd be so kind."

She rolled her eyes and muttered something wholly unflattering about cowboys as she took him into the house and seated him at the pine harvest table in the great room. Will watched through a haze of pain as she ran off in search of first-aid supplies. She came back with a towel and washcloth, a bowl of warm soapy water, a bottle of alcohol, and a box of Band-Aids. She scowled at him as she set about cleaning the gore from his face.

"Spill it, Rafferty." She wrinkled her little nose. "God, I guess maybe you already did. You smell like a brewery."

"Beer tends to slosh a bit when the truck is rolling."

"If someone lit a match, we could use you for a torch. What the hell is the matter with you, driving drunk? Do you have a death wish, or were you just out to kill and maim some innocent victims?"

"I don't need a lecture, Mary Lee," he growled. "Ouch! Damn, that hurts!"

"Sit still and stop whining. If you weren't already so beat up, I'd beat you up myself."

"Don't bother. J.D. is gonna kick my ass good." He spread his hands and bared his teeth in a parody of his infamous grin. "See the Amazing Will Rafferty fuck up again! He dazzles! He mystifies! He takes a lickin' and keeps on tickin'!"

Mari gave him a look. "I fail to see the humor in nearly getting yourself killed."

"It's subtle. More like irony, really. Pull your robe together, Mary Lee. I'm getting a free show here. Not that I mind, but I'm in no condition at the moment."

She stepped back, fuming, and tightened the belt around her small waist. "If you're not in imminent danger of death, I guess I can go get dressed. Make yourself a cup of coffee if you can stand up. I'll be right back."

"You got any aspirin?" he called as she started up the stairs.

"In my purse."

He dragged the handbag across the table and rummaged through it, fumbling through a mind-boggling array of junk until he came up with a little travel tin of Bayer aspirin and a brown prescription bottle of Tylenol with codeine. He tossed the aspirin back in and went for the good stuff, washing the pills down with half a can of Pepsi from the fridge. On his way back to the table he caught a glimpse of himself in a cracked mirror with a willow twig frame.

"Whoa, you look like the butt end of ugly, son," he grumbled, frowning at the discoloration around his eye and the angry-looking cut on his forehead.

Of course, he could have looked like the dead side of alive. That was what his truck looked like. All that pretty, shiny metal, crunched and ruined. It broke his heart. He remembered crying over it some as he had lain half conscious among the wreckage. Mostly he remembered thinking about Sam and how this wreck was symbolic. He remembered wondering if she would ever know he had died while trying to smash into the man who was taking her away from him. Now he wondered how long it would be before she found out their insurance rates were taking another jump toward the moon.

She wouldn't have to help pay for it after she divorced him.

Ex-wife. *Ex*-wife. *Ex*-wife.

Groaning, he sank back down on his chair and sat with his elbows on his thighs and his hands hanging down between his knees.

Mary Lee came trotting down the steps in tight jeans and an oversize lavender sweatshirt with the Mystic Moose logo across the front in tasteful white print. If she had run a comb through her hair, it didn't show.

"Look, Will," she said, caught somewhere between contrition and resignation. "I'm sorry I jumped all over you. I'm sure you feel bad enough as it is. It's just that I like you and I hate to see people I like doing things that can get them killed. I just lost one friend. I don't want to lose another."

"That's okay." He watched as she went into the kitchen and dug through a grocery bag on the counter. She came up with a box of doughnuts and a packet of paper napkins. "Nobody knows more than I do how stupid this was. 'Course, J.D. will claim he knows more and he will proceed to tell me all about it until I wish the truck had blown up with me inside it."

He sounded so glum, Mari couldn't help but feel a pang of sympathy for him. And empathy. She may not have been as self-destructive as Will, but she certainly knew what it was to incur the disapproval of her family. She opened a Pepsi for herself and joined him at the table, setting the doughnut box between them.

He lifted a cinnamon doughnut and saluted her with his soda can. "Breakfast of champions."

"Meets all the daily requirements for chemical additives and preservatives." She chose powdered sugar for herself and nibbled at it, shaking down a miniature blizzard on her napkin. "You really ought to see a doctor."

Will made a face. "I've been hurt worse falling out of bed."

"You must be a fun date."

"Wanna find out?" He tried to waggle his brows as the codeine kicked in. The pain was suddenly bearable, the numbness pleasant. He laughed a little at the look Mary Lee gave him. "Oh, yeah, that's right. You're dancing with the boss hoss. So is this serious? Do I get to call you Sis?"

"Not."

She seemed to take an inordinate interest in picking up doughnut crumbs from her napkin with the tip of her finger. Something about the tension around her mouth struck a warning bell. Her eyes had been red when she had first turned around and looked at him out there on the deck, as if she had been crying. Way to go, J.D., so smooth with the ladies. About as smooth as the business end of a porcupine. Poor Mary Lee.

"You drew a tough one, sweetheart," he said softly,

never thinking that she may not understand rodeo jargon, the dialect of the cowboy. "He's married to the job, you know, to the land. I guess he figured that would be safest. Didn't think the land could duck out on him. 'Course, we have since found out that the land is just a pretty whore that goes to the highest bidder. Ain't that a kick in the butt?"

"Do you care?"

"Not the way he does. The ranch is a lot of things to J.D.—mother, lover, duty. For me it was the thing that tied my mama to a marriage she didn't want. I never had much of a taste for duty."

"But you stay anyway. Why?"

Why? That was a question he asked himself on a regular basis. Why not just leave? Why not just cut the ties and run free? He never came up with an answer. He never wanted to dig deep enough to find it. Too afraid of what he might unearth. *What a coward you are, Willie-boy.*

He didn't answer. Mari didn't press. She of all people respected the confusion that tangled around the human heart. Why had she gone to school instead of to seek her fortune as a songwriter? Why had she stayed on the job when she hated it? Why had she tried to sell herself on Brad Enright when she didn't really love him?

Why couldn't life be sunny and simple?

She sighed and dusted the powdered sugar off her hands. "You need stitches for that cut. Come on, cowboy," she said, pushing to her feet. "I'm driving you in to see Dr. Charm."

CHAPTER 19

$\mathcal{M}$acDonald Townsend paced back and forth along the length of the picture window in his study. The view out that window, a panorama of wild Montana beauty that included a spectacular slice of snow-capped Irish Peak, had cost him a considerable chunk of money. He didn't so much as glance at it that morning. He was beyond admiring scenery. He was beyond enjoying much of anything about his getaway "cabin," two thousand square feet of pine logs and thermal-pane windows and fieldstone fireplaces. On the other side of his study door Bruno, his German shorthair, whined and scratched at the woodwork. Townsend didn't hear it.

His life was going to hell. It was as simple as that. He paused beside the heavy antique oak desk to light a cigarette, but his hands were shaking too badly to accomplish the task and he gave it up, too wired to try again. He knew what he needed, what his nerves were screaming for. There was a stash in the upper right-hand drawer of the desk, but he fought the need, desperate to break free of it. Sweat filmed his face. His nose was running. He pulled a damp, wadded-up handkerchief out of his hip pocket and wiped it across his upper lip, resuming his pacing.

His heart was racing like a rabbit's, something that seemed to be happening more and more often. He didn't know if it was the cocaine or the stress or both. They seemed to feed off each other, chasing around and around in a vicious circle that was taking him closer and closer to the point of no return.

He stopped and stared out the window, seeing nothing. How had he ever come to this? He'd had the world at his fingertips. His career had been poised perfectly on the ladder that would eventually take him to the Supreme Court. He was respected and admired. He had a wife who was respected and admired. There hadn't been so much as a speck of lint on his record.

Then he met Lucy MacAdam. He dated the start of his decline into this hell in which he was living to the night they met, as if her appearance had been a portent sent from the netherworld. As if she had been a familiar of the devil sent to destroy him by leading him down the paths of degradation.

He still remembered that first meeting as if it had happened last night. He had seen her across the room at a party in the elegant home of Ben Lucas. Her gaze hit him like a laser beam. Then that patented smile canted the corners of her mouth, wry and knowing, as if she were fully aware of her evil power over men and delighted in it. His skin had tightened from the scalp down, tingling with raw sexual awareness. At the time her hair had been nearly platinum blond, cut in a jaw-length bob that perpetually looked as if a lover had just run his hands through it. She wore a simple gold metallic knit dress that began in a snug collar around her throat and hugged her figure like a glove, ending high on her slender thighs. She wore nothing beneath it. He had discovered that fact later in the evening, when she had led him by the necktie into a little-used guest bathroom.

At the time he had been, if not a happily married man, a contented one. Irene, his wife of thirty years, had lost interest in sex. All her time and energy was taken up with her causes. He remembered thinking it was a relief. One less obligation to distract him from his career plans. He had been sliding comfortably along on the track that would take him to the superior court bench and onward.

Everything changed in a heartbeat. He was astonished, looking back on it, that he could have been so easily tempted, that temptation would take him so deep, that it all could happen so quickly.

Madness, that was what it was. It had infected him and swept through him like a cancer. First it was Lucy, then the cocaine, the parties, the forays into the world of Evan Bryce and the people who sought him out. He had been so smug at first, flattered and full of himself. He had believed he could handle it, that he could keep his new-found vices separate from his public image. But the task had grown increasingly difficult, until he felt as if he were being asked to juggle bowling balls while balancing on one foot on the head of a pin. His control had slipped bit by bit, and now his life was spiraling downward like a plane with all engines smoking. He could almost hear the wind roaring in his ears.

His need for cocaine was out of control. Between the drugs and the blackmail, his finances were eroding at an alarming rate. Irene was leaving him. God only knew what would happen when her attorney started demanding money and property that had long since gone to fund his secret life. Bryce had him under his thumb and there was a very incriminating videotape floating around that would end his career at the very least if it fell into the wrong hands.

"I have to get that tape," he muttered.

He could scarcely hear above the thundering of his pulse in his ears. The trembling that had been contained to his hands quaked up his arms and down through his body. He felt as if he might explode. Panic choked him. On the brink of tears, he flung himself into the leather-upholstered desk chair and reached for the handle of the drawer. His fingers curled around it and tightened and tightened until his knuckles were the color of bone.

He had to stop. He had to, or the madness would never end. During the night he had promised himself he would quit. He would extend his vacation into a six-month leave of absence from the bench and clean up his act. He would go to another state, where no one would know him, and check himself into a clinic. There was a place in Minnesota he'd heard about. Top-notch, discreet. He would go there, and when he came back he would be a new man, his old self, back on the straight and narrow.

The plan brought with it a kind of euphoria, a high not unlike that he got from the drugs. For a moment he saw the future through a watery white light, like something inside a free-floating soap bubble. He would quit the drugs, get the stress under control, distance himself from the people who had dragged him down into this muck. Then the phone to his left shrilled a high, birdlike call and the bubble burst.

He grabbed the receiver, his heart rate spiking upward again, expecting to hear Bryce on the other end. "Townsend."

"Judge Townsend." The voice was unfamiliar, male, ringing with a quality of false joviality. "I was a friend of a friend of yours. Lucy MacAdam."

Townsend said nothing. The silence vibrated against his ears. A hundred thoughts raced through his mind, none of them pleasant.

"Are you there?"

He tried to swallow the bile that rose up the back of his throat. His mouth was dry as chalk dust. "Y-yes. I'm here."

"I happen to know you and Lucy had a little thing going. Thought maybe we could discuss it."

The tape. Jesus, he had the tape! He thought of denying the charge, but what was the point? His nerves couldn't take a cat-and-mouse game. Better to get it over with. "What do you want?"

"Not over the phone. I prefer to do business in person."

"Where, then?"

"Do you like to fish, Judge?"

"What? What the hell—"

"Of course you do. You're a rugged outdoors type, or you wouldn't have come here. There's a great spot I just discovered over on Little Snake. Meet me at the Mine Road turnoff on old county nine in an hour and I'll lead the way. Know where that is?"

"I'll be there."

"Good. Oh, and, Judge? Better bring your wallet."

He fumbled to re-cradle the receiver, his attention on the pressure that was building inside his head. Maybe he would just have an aneurism and die and that would be the end of all his troubles. The pressure pounded behind his eyes like a pair of fists.

Would this nightmare never end?

If he could get the tape back, he thought desperately. He'd pay whatever he had to. He'd sell this place to raise the money as long as he could be assured of never being bothered again. That would be best anyway. Get rid of this place. That would be part of the process of turning himself around. The situation wasn't beyond damage control yet. He would sell this place, get himself straightened out, get Irene back before the divorce proceedings revealed his ravaged finances.

Having a plan calmed him somewhat, but he was still trembling. He pulled his handkerchief out and wiped his nose again. He had to give the appearance of being in control when he met this new blackmailer. It wouldn't be wise to show fear.

His fingers curled into the handle of the drawer again and pulled it open. Just one more time . . .

Mari went into the emergency room with Will to make sure he actually got himself on the list of patients to be seen, then left him there with a promise to come back in an hour. As she drove through town, she made a pass around the square to take in the progress on the sculpture.

Colleen Bentsen was going at it with torch in hand and an iron mask over her face. The sculpture was still little more than scrap metal. A knot of New Eden housewives with babies in strollers stood frowning at the model, turning their heads sideways and back in an attempt to get a perspective that made sense. M. E. Fralick stood beside the pedestal, swinging her long arms in exaggerated gestures as she tried to explain the scope of the project.

At the Moose, tourists were trooping through the main lobby in their pseudo-western wear, heading for breakfast before a day in the great outdoors. Mari went up to her rooms and pried herself out of Lucy's jeans. After a quick shower, she dressed in a pair of old black leggings, crew socks, and hiking boots. She pulled a T-shirt over her head with the words BO KNOWS YOUR SISTER stamped across the front in black, and completed the ensemble with a man-size denim shirt with the sleeves rolled up half a dozen times. She tried to clamp her hair back with a big silver barrette, but the mane was too much for it. The clasp gave way and launched the barrette across the room like a missile.

She went down to the dining room, scanning the faces for Drew. Kevin sat alone at a table near the kitchen door, going over paperwork while he sipped coffee. Mari wound her way to the table and pulled out the chair across from him.

"Didn't your mother ever tell you not to do homework at the breakfast table? You'll ruin your posture."

He glanced up at her and grinned. Automatically, he came halfway to his feet, even though she had already seated herself. "No, I never heard that one. The big one around my house was 'Don't run with a pencil in your hand—'"

"You'll put your eye out," they finished in unison.

Mari laughed. "I think my mother's real fear was the social stigma of a daughter with an eye patch. There are so few designers who consider it an acceptable fashion accessory."

Kevin snagged a passing waiter for coffee. "Breakfast?"

"No, thanks," she said halfheartedly, eyeing the plump golden blueberry muffin he had yet to touch. "I had a doughnut."

"Have some fruit at least." He nudged a chilled bowl heaped with melon slices and fresh berries in her direction.

Mari picked out a chunk of cantaloupe with a fork and nipped off a corner.

"How are you feeling?" Kevin asked, concern tugging his brows into that worried-puppy look he wore so well.

"I'm fine."

"We still feel terrible, you know."

She gave him a wry smile. "I could share my painkillers with you."

"Seriously. This place is our home. The idea of someone breaking in and hurting a guest is just appalling. It's a violation."

"Have you heard anything from Quinn about catching the guy?"

He shook his head. "Doesn't look likely. It would be a different story if he had stolen something he could be caught in possession of or trying to pawn or sell."

"My family would be gratified to hear I'm finally suffering for my lack of material greed." She snagged a blueberry on a fork tine and popped it in her mouth. "I'd just like to know if he *expected* to find something. Lucy mentioned a book in her final letter to me. I haven't been able to find it."

"What kind of book would be worth attacking someone for?"

She shrugged, not wanting to go into the whole mess with Kevin. Something told her he hadn't been privy to Lucy's schemes; he was too inherently sweet. On the other hand, she was willing to bet his partner knew more than he was saying.

"Is Drew around?"

"No," Kevin said shortly, dropping his gaze as he cracked open his muffin. Steam billowed up from its interior in a fragrant cloud. By contrast, the air temperature around him seemed to drop by ten degrees. His smile was nowhere in sight. "He's off communing with nature. Fishing or something. I haven't seen him this morning at all."

"Oh." Mari nibbled her lower lip, her attention split between the muffin and Kevin's sudden change of mood. "Is anything wrong?"

He sighed, staring blankly down at his plate. "No. Nothing. Why did you want to see him?"

"Nothing major. We were just talking about Lucy the other night. I thought maybe we could finish the discussion over coffee."

"Oh, well, he'll be back eventually. Five at the latest. The trio starts playing in the lounge at seven." He brightened hopefully as he looked up at her. "Will you be joining them?"

"Oh, I don't know—"

"Come on," he cajoled. "You're not stage shy. It'd be great to hear you sing again."

"Maybe. We'll see."

She checked her watch and stood, leaning over to pinch a bite of muffin. "Gotta go," she said, popping the morsel into her mouth. She wiggled her fingers at him and backed away as he laughed.

Most of the morning was spent chauffeuring Will around town. From the hospital they went to Chuck's Auto Body to procure the services of a tow truck. From Chuck's they went to Big Sky Insurance to report the bad news. After being told his coverage would probably be canceled because of his driving record, he had Mari drive out to Cheyenne Used Car Corral on the outskirts of town, where he proceeded to try to weasel a loaner out of his good friend Big Ed Twofeathers. Big Ed told him to take a hike.

At the Gas N' Go Will bought a pair of cheap sunglasses to replace the ones he'd lost in the wreck. They both bought greasy pizza slices and Barq's root beer and ate lunch at a picnic table with a view of the diesel pumps, then climbed back in the Honda and headed for the ranch.

Depressed and drowsy from the painkillers, Will nodded off on the drive out to the Stars and Bars. Mari stuck Shawn Colvin in the tape deck and let her mind wander with the flow of the music, turning the facts and clues and questions over like playing cards in a mental game of solitaire. Her chain of thought was momentarily disrupted as they passed the site of Will's wreck.

The truck had gone off the road in the middle of a tricky curve. Luckily, the embankment wasn't steep, or he would almost certainly have been killed. Mari thought it was a wonder he wasn't killed as it was. The pickup looked like a toy that had been stomped on by an irate giant. It lay on its side, crumpled and twisted.

Will woke as they rolled in through the gate at the ranch. From behind the dark lenses of his new mirror sunglasses, he did a quick scan for any sign of J.D. The longer he could put off a confrontation, the better. Zip trotted down from the house porch to bark at them. He could see Chaske at the end of the barn, trimming the hooves of a blocky bay gelding. J.D. was nowhere to be seen.

"Thanks for the lift, Mary Lee," he said, popping open his door. He gave her a pained, weary smile. "You're a pal."

"Yeah." She slid her sunglasses down on her nose and looked at him over the rims. "Remember that the next time you climb behind the wheel with a buzz on."

He didn't promise he wouldn't do it again. He'd made enough promises he couldn't keep.

As he climbed out of the Honda, the front door of the house swung open and Tucker and J.D. came out onto the porch. Tucker's eyes bugged out at the sight of him. He had thrown his tattered, bloody shirt in the hospital trash and sweet-talked a nurse into giving him the top half of a set of green surgical scrubs. But even with the sunglasses there was no disguising the fact that he was beat up. A row of neat stitches marched across his forehead. His lower lip was puffed up like a porn queen's. A bruise darkened his left cheekbone to the color of a rotting peach.

"Boy, you look like you stuck your head in a cotton sack full of wildcats!" the old man declared, hobbling down the porch steps. "Judas!" He turned his head and shot a stream of tobacco juice into the dirt. "Your mama wouldn't know you from red meat! What the hell happened?"

Will squirmed, feeling like a bug under a microscope. Tucker was up close, scrutinizing his face, but far more piercing was J.D.'s gaze, which came all the way down from the porch. The shit was about to hit the fan. He could feel it the same as a radical shift in air pressure before a storm.

"Finally wrapped that truck around a tree, didn't you?" J.D. said tightly, slowly descending the steps.

Will forced a sour grin. "Close, but no stogie. Rolled it sideways down a hill." He spread his arms. "As you can see, I survived, but thanks so much for expressing your concern, brother."

J.D. shook his head, angry with Will, but angrier with himself for the belated fear that came on his brother's behalf. After all the bad blood that had passed between them, they still shared the same father. Will was a Rafferty and he had nearly gotten himself killed. J.D. wished he didn't have to care. It hurt too much to care. Not for the first time, he wished he were an only child.

"Jesus. I ought to finish the job," he snarled. "Of all the stupid, shit-for-brains—"

"I don't need a lecture, J.D."

"No? What *do* you need, Will? You need some pretty young thing to hold your hand and give you sympathy? You might try your wife." That galled him almost as bad as caring about Will—caring that Will was with Mary Lee. The jealousy was like a live wire inside him, like a coiled snake, and he resented it mightily.

Mari climbed out of the Honda and leaned on the roof. "Lighten up, J.D. I just gave him a ride home from the hospital."

"Well, that's right neighborly of you, Mary Lee," he drawled sarcastically.

"Jesus Christ, J.D.," Will snapped. "Leave her out of this. It's me you're pissed at."

"You're damn right I'm pissed. We've got cattle to move up the mountain tomorrow and you're in no shape to get on a horse. How the hell am I supposed to pay for an extra hand when every nickel you haven't gambled away is tied up in trying to keep this place? And what about the doctor bills and the towing bill and the repair bill? Did any of those thoughts once cross your pickled mind while you were weaving down the road on a full tank of Jack Daniel's?"

"No, J.D., they didn't," Will said bitterly. He curled his hands into fists at his sides and leaned toward his brother. "Maybe I've got other things on my mind besides this goddamn ranch. Did you ever think of that? Maybe I'm sick of being tied to it. Maybe I don't give a flying fuck what happens to it!"

Tucker shifted nervously from foot to foot. His weathered old face screwed up into a look of sick apprehension. "Now, boys, maybe this ain't the time—"

"Maybe the time's passed," J.D. said, his voice a deadly whisper.

Will felt as though his mirror glasses offered him no protection at all from J.D.'s penetrating gaze. As always, his brother could see right through them, right into his own weak soul. He didn't measure up. Never had. Never would. No point in trying. No point in staying.

He met J.D.'s hard, cold gaze unflinching, and his childhood and youth passed before his mind's eye—him tagging after J.D., the fights, the uneasy truces, the rare moments of camaraderie. They were brothers, but J.D. had never forgiven him for being born and he never would. *Half* brothers. The tag made him feel like half a man. Half as good. He felt something inside him shrivel and die. Hope. What a sad, sorry feeling.

"I'll go pack a bag," he said softly.

Tucker swore under his breath and tried to catch up as Will started for the house. Will raised a hand to ward him off and the old man faltered to a stop, looking helpless and angry. He wheeled on J.D., sputtering.

"Damnation, if you don't have a head harder than a new brick wall!"

"Save your breath, old man."

J.D. turned and walked away from him, toward the corrals. He willed himself not to look at Mary Lee, but he couldn't hold himself to it. He cut a glance at her as she stood beside her car. Her eyes were stormy, her stare direct. Displeasure curved her ripe little mouth. Guilt snapped at him. He kicked it away. To hell with Mary Lee Jennings. To hell with Will. He didn't need either one of them.

Mari told herself to get in the car and drive away. She had enough problems of her own without adding the burden of someone else's sibling rivalry to the load. But she couldn't seem to make herself leave. Will, for all his flaws, was a friend. J.D., in spite of many things, was her lover. She couldn't just stand back and watch them tear their brotherhood apart. She knew only too well how irreparable damage like that could be.

Swearing at herself under her breath, she trotted after him. "J.D.—"

"Stay out of it, Mary Lee." He kept on walking, his long strides forcing her to jog beside him. "It's none of your goddamn business."

"He could have been killed in that accident."

"It would have served him right."

"Damn you, Rafferty, stop it!" she snapped, slugging him in the arm as hard as she could, succeeding in making him turn and face her. "Stop pretending nothing and no one matters to you except this ranch."

"Nothing does," he growled.

"That's a lie and you know it! If you were such a bastard, you wouldn't keep on hundred-year-old ranch hands and an uncle whose mind went around the bend twenty years ago."

"That's duty."

"That's caring. It's the same thing. And you care about Will too."

"What the hell do you know about what I feel or don't feel?" he demanded, furious that she had managed to strike a raw nerve. "You think going to bed with me makes you an expert? Jesus, if I'd known you were gonna be this much trouble, I'd've kept my pants zipped."

Scowling blackly, he started once again for the corrals, where half a dozen horses stared over the fence with their ears pricked in interest. Mari went after him, calling herself seven kinds of a fool.

"I could say the same thing, you know," she pointed out. "You're never going to win any prizes for charm, and I sure as hell didn't come to Montana to get stuck in the middle of a family feud."

"Then butt the hell out."

"It's too late to pretend we don't know each other." She wanted to say it was too late to pretend they didn't care, but she knew that would be asking for a kick in the teeth. She'd had enough pain to last her. "All I'm saying is, Will is the only brother you've got, J.D. Yes, he's screwed up, but he's not a lost cause. He needs help. You could drop the tough-guy act for ten minutes and show a little compassion."

"You want compassion?" he sneered. "Go see a priest. It's not an act, Mary Lee. I'm exactly what I appear to be." He spread his arms wide. "Nothing up my sleeves. No trick mirrors. You think I'm a hardcase and you don't like it? Tough shit. Go find yourself another cowboy to screw. There's plenty around for the time being. Shit, you like my brother so well, maybe you'd rather be fucking him too."

Mari blinked hard and jerked back as if he'd slapped her. He may as well have. Tears flooded her eyes. She refused to let them fall. "Jesus, you can be the most obnoxious son of a bitch!"

"If you don't like it, leave. Nobody's gonna stop you, city girl."

"Fine," she whispered, her voice trembling too badly to manage anything more. With a violently shaking hand she swept an errant chunk of hair behind her ear. "I'm out of here. And don't bother coming down to Lucy's place again. I don't need you either."

"Good. I've got better things to do. Call me when you decide to sell the place."

Fighting the tears, she started for her car, a blurry white blob across the yard, but she pulled up and turned to face him again, shaking her head. "You're so busy protecting what you own, you don't even see that you're losing everything that's really important. I feel sorry for you, Rafferty. You'll end up with this land and nothing else."

"That's all that matters," J.D. said, but Mary Lee had already turned away from him and was stalking back to her car, her hiking boots scuffing on the dirt and rock as she went.

He stood there and watched her drive away, stubbornly ignoring the ache in his chest. She couldn't matter to him. He couldn't let her. She wouldn't stay in his life. In another week or two she would tire of the rustic life and head back to California, and he would still be here, working the ranch and fighting to preserve his way of life from extinction. He couldn't let anything intrude on that.

As he turned back toward the corral, the word *martyr* rang in his head and left a bitter, metallic taste in his mouth. He spat in the dirt and climbed through the bars of the fence to catch a horse.

How she got down from the Stars and Bars without crashing into a tree was beyond her. A miracle. As if such things existed. Angry and hurt beyond all reason, Mari jumped out of the Honda and headed for the barn. Urgency pushed her to a jog, then she was sprinting into the dark interior and out the side door. Clyde raised his head from dozing and brayed at her. She kept on going to the llama pen and over the gate. She ran into the pasture until her knees threatened to give out and her lungs were on fire, then she fell down into the deep grass and lay there, sobbing.

She wasn't even sure why she was crying. Because Rafferty had hurt her feelings? He could have made a living at that, the bone-headed clod. Because she hurt for Will, for what the two brothers were losing? Because her friend was dead? Because she wanted a cigarette so badly, she would have gotten down on her hands and knees in the gutter to scrounge for butts? All of those reasons and more.

She lay in the grass and cried until she couldn't cry

anymore, then she just lay there. The sun shone down, as warm and yellow as melted butter amid popcorn clouds. A breeze fanned the grass and brought the scents of earth and wildflowers. Opening her eyes, Mari watched them bow to the breeze—delicate violets, bluebells just starting to open, windflowers with their thick, hairy stems and showy blooms. Their beauty calmed her, their simplicity soothed her. A bumblebee buzzed lazily from blossom to blossom, oblivious of the human world and all its self-made agonies.

Maybe J.D. was right in giving his heart to this land. She could have given hers too. She felt a part of it, nourished by its beauty and its strength. Turning onto her back, she gazed up at the sky. It really was bigger here. A huge sheet of electric blue, stretching on forever. There were moments like this one, when she felt more at home here than she ever had anywhere. That sense of belonging had nothing to do with birthright. It had to do with things deeper than circumstance, with matters of the soul.

A llama nose descended on her, small and furry, twitching inquisitively as it bussed her cheek. Smiling, Mari sat up and reached out to stroke the baby's neck. This one was brown from the shoulders back with a white front half and splotches of brown on his face, as if God had been forced to abandon the paint job to go on to more pressing matters.

"I'll call you Parfait," she announced, startled at the hoarseness of her voice.

The llama's long ears moved from angle to angle like semaphore flags. A brown spot on her muzzle made her look as if she were smiling crookedly. Half a dozen of her older relatives stood a few feet away, studying Mari with their luxurious sloe eyes. They hummed softly to one another.

Mari curled her legs beneath her and stood slowly, worried that she might frighten them away. They just looked at her, chewing their grass and violets, their expressions gentle and wise. They were beyond the petty cruelty humans inflicted on one another. It didn't matter to them that she'd fallen in love with a man who was both hero and villain. The scope of their simple world was so much greater. They held the secret to inner peace and looked on her with gentle pity for her ignorance. They offered solace in the form of company, understanding in their quiet manner.

She spent the afternoon with them, resolutely ignoring the various messes in which her life had become entangled. She mingled with the llamas, petting them and scratching them, talking with them about the greater meaning of life. For a few hours nothing else was important. She pretended she had stepped through a portal into a place of calm and reason. She let the llamas take the tension away, let the sun recharge her soul. Then, as the sun began its descent toward the mountains to the west, she stepped back into the real world of people and trouble and the mysteries of llama feed.

CHAPTER 20

J. D. rode the pharmacist's yellow mare down across the wash above Little Snake Creek. The mare picked her way along uncertainly, awkward with the unaccustomed weight of a man on her back. Her small ears flicked forward and back. She leaned on the bit. Automatically, J.D. dickered with the reins, moving his hands gently, just enough to get her to soften her mouth and bring her nose back an inch.

His mind wasn't on the job. He hadn't gone on this ride for the benefit of the mare. He'd saddled her only because his work ethic wouldn't allow him to do much of anything that wasn't productive in some way.

What about Mary Lee?

Time spent with her might have been productive had she shown any sign of offering him the chance to buy Lucy's land. But then, the idea of prostituting himself went against his ethical grain. It was a no-win deal. If he went to bed with her for the purpose of gain, he was nothing but a gigolo. If he went to bed with her for any other reason, he was asking for trouble he swore he didn't want.

The point was moot. He wouldn't be going to bed with her again.

He made a sour face and shifted his weight back in the saddle as the mare negotiated her way down the last slope to the creek bottom. Life in general was turning out to be a no-win deal. He'd gotten nowhere in his attempt to put together an offer for the Flying K. A call to set up an appointment with Ron Weiss, vice president of the

First Bank of Montana, had netted him condolences on Will's unprecedented losing streak at Little Purgatory. Bryce was probably sitting back laughing at his futile attempts to keep the property out of Bryce's hands, biding his time and counting his money. With Samantha in his camp, he had to be thinking ownership of the Stars and Bars wasn't that far off.

And now Will was leaving—had in fact already left. J.D. had watched him drive out of the yard in Tucker's old International Harvester pickup. He had always expected him to relinquish his claim to the family land and move on to greener pastures. Now that the day had come, J.D. felt neither relief nor triumph, but a sick hollowness in the pit of his stomach. Old guilt revisited. Remorse for losing something he thought he had never wanted in the first place.

They were family, and there was a strong obligation there. But he had taken that sense of duty as a license to badger and bully and preach. He treated Will more like a screwup ranch hand than a brother. Only he couldn't fire Will for his drinking or for not showing up to work or for gambling away ranch money or for playing them into the hands of their biggest enemy or for totaling his pickup, which brought him back full-circle to the drinking.

Mary Lee thought Will needed help, that his drinking was out of control. J.D. had viewed it as a nuisance. This was rugged country with rugged people. Drinking was part of a cowboy's life. Too big a part in too many cases. Alcoholism was a problem in the ranching culture. The stress, the loneliness, the code of manhood, all contributed. He'd seen Will drunk more times than he could count, and all he had ever done was ride the kid about wrecking his truck or being late to work.

The guilt dug its teeth a little deeper and gave him a shake. The truth pulled on him. The lead weight of accountability. He had come out here to escape the burden of his responsibilities, not put them under a microscope. He had come out here to lose himself in his first love— the land.

This stretch along the Little Snake was a favorite spot —when there weren't half a dozen city idiots in their Orvis vests and waders fly fishing. Luck was with him for once. He could see a red Bronco parked some distance downstream, but no sign of its owner. Probably someone hiking in the woods, looking for morels. He might stop and pick a few himself on the way home. Tucker could fry them up a feast of fresh trout and wild mushrooms for supper.

This little valley and the slopes on either side belonged to the Bureau of Land Management. Once upon a time the McKeevers of the Boxed Circle spread had owned the grazing lease, but the McKeevers had sold out in 'ninety-one to a network news anchor who didn't raise anything but a few head of horses a year, and the lease had gone back to the BLM. J.D. had considered trying for it, but an environmental group had taken up the "Preserve the Little Snake" banner for fly fishermen and weekend hikers from Bozeman and Livingston, and the small amount of grass hadn't been worth the trouble of a fight.

He still liked to ride over here when he got a chance. It was secluded, unspoiled for the moment. The Little Snake, which was actually a small river, wound between columns of cottonwood and aspen. Fed by mountain runoff, it ran fast this time of year, and was cold and clear and studded with boulders. Along the banks the grass grew in a lush strip dotted with wildflowers. Wooded slopes rose sharply beyond. It wasn't uncommon to see mule deer drinking from the creek, their black-tipped tails flicking nervously. He'd seen bears here more than once. The Absarokas were thick with grizzlies and black bear. The encroachment of man pushed them deeper into the wilderness areas every year, but conflicts with ranch stock and tourists still happened from time to time.

He rode the yellow mare to the edge of the water at a shallow spot and urged her to step in. She arched her neck and blew through her nostrils at the water rushing past. J.D. spoke to her and coaxed her, urging her forward with his legs. She lifted a foreleg and pawed at the water, splashing herself, then moved tentatively forward, her attitude telling J.D. she wasn't too sure about this idea, but she trusted him not to get her into trouble.

When she was standing knee-deep in the water and had relaxed enough to bob her head around, checking out the scenery, he reached into the tubular boot he had strapped to his saddle and extracted the components of his fishing rod. The mare looked back at him with curiosity, but stood quietly as he assembled the rod.

He had ridden her only half a dozen times, but she was naturally sensible and bright. She would make the pharmacist's daughter a good, safe mount. She brought her head up the first time he cast, and danced a little as he reeled it in, her muscular body tense beneath him. But when she saw that this process was not so different from having a rope thrown from her back, she relaxed again. The true test would come when he hooked a trout.

J.D. relaxed as well. He cleared his mind as he found his rhythm with the rod. The sun shone down, warm on his back. The water chuckled and hissed as it rushed on its way to the Yellowstone River. The air was sweet with the scent of the grass, sharp with the vaguely metallic undertone of the water. The cottonwood and aspen leaves quivered and chattered. The reel whined as he cast, clucked when he cranked the line back in to try again. A kestrel hovered over the far bank, beating its blue wings furiously as it waited for the perfect second to drop on its prey in the grass below.

Nothing was biting. J.D. reeled in and waded the mare across to the opposite bank. She climbed out and they moved downstream sixty yards. This time when he asked her to step down into the stream, she didn't hesitate. He patted her and talked to her, then took up his rod and started fishing again. An hour passed this way. When he couldn't get a nibble in one spot, they would move down to another, crossing from bank to bank, sometimes walking downstream in the shallows. He had no desire to run into the owner of the Bronco, but the best spots happened to be downstream. J.D. figured he would try his luck until someone came along, then they would start back for home. The ranch was an hour's ride and the afternoon shadows were already growing long.

As they moved closer, he recognized the truck. Miller Daggrepont's name and the titles he had bestowed on himself were emblazoned across the driver's side door in three lines of gold gay-nineties-style lettering: MILLER DAGGREPONT, ESQ., ATTORNEY AT LAW, DEALER IN ANTIQUITIES. Miller wouldn't hike up a mountain to hunt for mushrooms unless they were lined with gold. He was a fisherman, but there was no sign of him along the banks of the Little Snake.

J.D. frowned, more at Miller's imposition on his thoughts than out of any concern for the lawyer's whereabouts. Thoughts of Daggrepont brought thoughts of the land Mary Lee had inherited, and, therefore, brought thoughts of Mary Lee, and he flat-out didn't want to think about her. They were through. He should never have gotten tangled up with her in the first place.

He cast his line, flicking it at the edge of a brackish spot in a bend of the creek. Here the bank had eroded away over the years, creating a marshy pool that filled with water every spring and during hard rains. Rushes and cattails grew in profusion. More than one lunker had been caught browsing at the border between the pool and the stream.

J.D. snapped his wrist and swore as his fly went sailing into the tangle of growth. Thoughts of Mary Lee had broken his concentration. She was a distraction—a *pretty* distraction, but a distraction nonetheless. He had too much trouble brewing in his life as it was; he didn't need to add a woman to the mess. He snarled to himself as the image of those big, deep eyes glittering with pain rose up to haunt his memory. He had hurt her and it bothered him more than he ought to have let it. She was nothing but trouble, butting her little upturned nose between him and Will, toying with the likes of Evan Bryce, snooping around Del, looking for clues to a mystery that had already been solved as far as the court was concerned.

He jerked back on the line, hoping it would come free without a lot of trouble. It didn't. He tried reeling it in slowly, but succeeded only in tightening the line against whatever the fly had snagged. He waded the mare across to the other bank, let her climb ashore, and stepped down off her. Reins in one hand, rod in the other, he moved toward the marshy spot, wishing the mare were far enough along in her training to ground-tie reliably.

He decided to take his chances as he reached the stand of cattails without freeing the damned line. If he had to wade out into the muck, he didn't want her with him. The bottom was soft and muddy, and she would likely become frightened as her footing sank beneath her. Fear could spoil a young horse as quickly as mistreatment. He dropped his reins and backed away from her, scowling at her as she started to follow. He took an aggressive step toward her. She stopped and tossed her head, ears pricked as she watched him turn back toward the bank.

Reeling in more line, he stepped off into water thigh-deep, flushing a blue-winged teal out of its cover. The duck flew up with an angry squawk, wings pummeling the air like a fighter shadow-boxing. Glancing back over his shoulder, J.D. checked to see that the mare hadn't spooked. She watched him with interest, and he maintained eye contact for just a second to let her know he hadn't forgotten her. As he waded forward, his left knee connected unexpectedly with something solid, and he lost his balance. His right foot slipped in the mud and he went down . . . landing squarely across the body of Miller Daggrepont.

"Jesus, I've hauled dead cattle out of rivers easier than this." Deputy Doug Bardwell sloshed through the reeds, waist-deep in water, trying to get a better hold on the body. "Hey, J.D., you wanna throw a rope around him and drag him out with that yellow mare?"

Quinn brought his head up from examining the footprints in the soft ground of the bank and glowered at his deputy. "Peters, get in there with him and haul the body out the other side of the slough. I don't want any more tracks on this bank than we already got. Look at this mess," he grumbled, turning back to his task. "God knows how many people been out here since it rained, tramping up and down."

J.D. was hunkered down beside him, frowning at the ground. "I reckon there's been a few, but see here in this area? Looks to me more like two people maybe scuffling around. Don't see these kind of tracks anywhere else along the bank."

"Still don't mean nothing," Quinn said, tipping his hat back to scratch through his wheat-colored hair. "Could have been two people milling around, digging through their tackle boxes, for all we know. Besides," he said, standing and stretching out his bad knee, "looks to me like ol' Miller had himself a heart attack and fell in. You see the way he was clutching his chest?"

They walked around to the far side of the pool, where Bardwell and Peters were struggling with Daggrepont's lifeless body. Rigor mortis had yet to set in, and the lawyer's massive weight and rotund shape made their task as much fun as moving a stranded whale.

"Jesus, Bardwell!" Quinn barked. "Don't be pulling on his arm that way! Get your legs under him and push!"

Groaning with the effort, the deputies hauled the dead man onto the bank.

"Man." Bardwell heaved a sigh and sat himself down half a foot from the body. "My daddy always said the only good lawyer was a dead lawyer. Guess he never had to move one."

"See here?" Quinn said, crouching down by Daggrepont. He pointed to the right hand that was frozen in a death grip over the dead man's sternum, clutching a wad of his brown madras plaid western shirt and the ends of his bolo tie. "That's called a cadaveric spasm. Means he was hanging on that way when he died. Had a bum ticker, you know, Miller did."

"Ain't no wonder," Peters commented. He had his face behind a 35mm camera and was clicking off photos of the corpse. "You ever see that man eat? I've had feeder cattle couldn't pack it away the way Miller could."

"He'd'a ate them too if he had a chance," Bardwell

said as he pulled his boots off and dumped the water out of them.

J.D. let their banter roll off him. He knelt beside the body, studying every detail. A dark uneasiness had settled over him as he waited for Quinn to arrive after calling from Daggrepont's car phone. Daggrepont had been Lucy's lawyer. Mary Lee had it in her head that there was something fishy about Lucy's death. His own take on that scenario had been to let dead dogs lie. Bryce's pal had taken the blame, which was a hell of a lot better than Del taking the blame. But now Daggrepont was dead, and J.D.'s gut told him there was more to it than a bum ticker.

He glanced up at the wooded slopes beyond the valley. Del knew those hills like the back of his hand.

"Look here," he said, pushing the half-formed questions from his mind. He pointed to splotches of discoloration that marred the folds of Daggrepont's fat neck. "Looks to me like somebody had him by the throat."

"I can think of only twenty or thirty people woulda liked to choke Miller," Bardwell said. "You think of more than that, Pete?"

"You countin' old ladies or just the men?"

Quinn frowned as he turned the lawyer's head to the side. "Rigor's just starting to set in in the jaw," he mumbled. "He hasn't been in here long."

He fingered the dead man's jowls, noting the way the discoloration remained when he applied pressure, indicating bruising rather than any strange kind of lividity. He hummed a little to himself, as if he were trying to come up with a list of viable suspects when he was really just wishing the whole damned mess away. Lucy MacAdam's lawyer was dead under suspicious circumstances. He'd have Marilee Jennings camped out on his doorstep, trying to sell him her conspiracy theory. Blasted outsiders. Nothing could ever be simple with them.

"Well," he said, rising and wiping his hands off on his pants, "we'll ship him up to Bozeman and have them take a look."

"Slice 'em and dice 'em," Bardwell commented.

Quinn scowled at him. "Bardwell, shut up and get the body bag." He turned back to J.D. "Guess I'll have to go break the news to Inez that she's out a boss. He didn't have any family that I know of. Can you think of anyone else ought to know right away?"

"Yeah," J.D. said on a sigh. He started for his horse with anticipation and dread pushing against each other in his chest. "I'll tell her myself."

He didn't like the idea of her being caught in the middle of this mess. He liked her propensity for sticking her nose in where it didn't belong even less. The prospect of seeing her again, despite any arguments he would have made to the contrary, he liked a little too well.

CHAPTER 21

$\mathcal{D}$rew's trio played from seven till one in the lounge at the Moose. Mari joined them, alternating two songs for every two played by the group. They offered the affluent crowd an eclectic mix of jazz, folk, country, and crossover rock. She drew heavily on her soft and bluesy repertoire, as always, her music reflecting her mood. She called on old favorites from Jackson Browne and Bonnie Raitt, and newer tunes from Rosanne Cash and Shawn Colvin, throwing in some of her own creations when the mood struck her. When the band members knew the song, they joined in and backed her up. It was one of those fine, rare instances where musicians' styles and instincts meshed immediately, resulting in magic.

The audience, who had come into the lounge to socialize with friends, abandoned their conversations or toned them down to whispers as the music captivated them. The small dance floor was never empty. The applause was always enthusiastic.

At the start of the first break, Mari slid onto the piano bench beside Drew. The other two members of the band waded out into the crowd in search of drinks and friends. The noise level of the conversations rose to compensate for the lack of music.

"This is great," she murmured, giving Drew a soft smile. "Thanks for inviting me."

"The pleasure is ours, luv. You've a rare talent." He picked up his tonic and lime and took a slow sip, wincing a little as he reached to set the glass aside.

"You okay?"

"Fine," he said absently, rolling his right shoulder back. "Strained a muscle, that's all. Clumsy of me.

"You seem a bit subdued tonight," he said. His gaze was speculative above freshly sun-kissed cheeks.

Mari cringed. "God, do you think I'm depressing people?"

"Not at all," he said with a chuckle. "They're enraptured with you. It's just there's something awfully sad in those lovely blue eyes. Anything I can do to help?"

She shook her head, making a rueful comic face. "Got myself into something I shouldn't have. Never fear. I'm a big girl; I can take it on the chin with the best of them."

He frowned and reached up to tuck a rumpled strand of silver-blond hair behind her ear. "What do you mean, something you shouldn't have gotten into? Does this have to do with Lucy?"

"No, why? Do you know something I should know?"

He glanced away, across the sea of faces in the crowd, wishing he hadn't said anything at all. "I know if there was trouble to be had, Lucy would sniff it out, that's all."

"The kind of trouble that might have gotten her killed?"

"I didn't say that."

Mari leaned into him and tugged sharply on the full sleeve of his emerald silk shirt. "Dammit, Drew," she whispered harshly. "If you know something, tell me. I don't think Lucy's death was an accident, but I haven't been able to find a soul who gives a damn."

Scowling, he turned his attention to the sheet music stacked against the piano's scrolled music desk, thumbing through the titles impatiently. "I resent the implication, thank you very much. I know that Lucy was involved with MacDonald Townsend in a way he wasn't entirely happy about, that's all."

"Was she blackmailing him?"

"Perhaps," he said evasively. "Certainly he was footing part of the bill for her lifestyle, but he couldn't have killed her."

"Couldn't he?"

He dropped his hands to the keyboard and stared at her. "My God, Mari, the man's a judge!" he exclaimed under his breath. "Judges don't go about shooting women."

"And plastic surgeons do?"

"It was an accident. Sheffield had no reason to want Lucy dead."

"Which makes him a very convenient fall guy, don't you think?" Mari pressed on doggedly. "No motive, no murder indictment. He pleads guilty to making a boo-boo with a high-powered rifle and gets a slap on the hand. Ben Lucas is Sheffield's lawyer. Lucas and Townsend are old pals. They all hang out together at Bryce's little hacienda. . . ."

Drew shook his head, exasperated. "You're grasping at straws."

Mari spread her hands and shrugged. "Maybe, maybe not. You think Townsend is above reproach? District court judges aren't supposed to snort coke either, but I saw him nosing up to a line in Bryce's billiard room. Makes me wonder what other nasty habits he has."

"I'd rather you didn't find out."

He turned back to the music. Mari didn't think he was even looking at the titles as he pretended to sort through them. He was merely using it as an excuse not to meet her eyes. She sat there for a while, trying to probe his brain like a psychic, trying to deduce by Holmesian logic what secrets he knew. Her efforts met nothing but a stony expression and a mind closed like a steel strongbox.

"What else do you know, Drew?" she asked at last.

"I can't shed any light on Lucy's death," he said, his voice low and impatient. "I don't know that I would if I could. Sometimes it's best to let sleeping dogs lie."

He wasn't the first to express that point of view; still, it made Mari furious. She was well aware Lucy hadn't been a model citizen in life, but did that mean she didn't deserve justice in death? Did her flaws make her life any less valuable? Did no one but Mari remember that she had possessed good qualities alongside the bad?

"Do these dogs have names?" she asked tightly.

He hissed a long sigh out through his teeth and squeezed his eyes shut. "Marilee . . ."

"Fabulous music!"

Bryce's voice snapped the tension and took it to a different level. Mari swiveled around on the piano bench to face him, manufacturing a polite smile. "Thanks."

He stood with a bottle of Pellegrino dangling from his bony hand, a thousand-watt smile cutting across his tan face. Mari wondered uncharitably if the look was really just a grimace of pain with the corners tucked up: his jeans looked tight enough to raise his blood pressure into the danger zone. His arm was draped casually across the shoulders of Samantha Rafferty.

The girl looked uncomfortable with the situation, her dark eyes darting toward Drew and away, as if she were contemplating bolting from the room. Disapproval rolled off Drew in waves. Mari wondered if Samantha had heard about Will's accident. The question was on the tip of her tongue, but she bit it back. Hadn't she taken enough lumps for butting into Rafferty business as it was?

"It's really too bad you didn't bring your guitar to the party the other night," Bryce said, tilting his head and giving her a look of censure. "Rob Gold from Columbia would have loved you. Now he's gone back to L.A."

Mari shrugged, her excitement at the prospect of meeting a record exec tempered by the source of the information. "Some other time, maybe."

"Maybe, nothing," Bryce declared. "You ought to hop a plane and go to him. I can make a couple of phone calls if you like—"

And get me out of Montana. "Thanks anyway, but I don't think this is the right time for me to jump into anything."

"Opportunities don't happen along every day."

"No, well, I don't have friends killed every day either. I'd like a little time to recover."

He gave her his patronizing fatherly look, tipping his small chin down almost to the puff of chest hair billowing out the open placket of his white oxford shirt. "You're loyal to a fault, sweetheart. Lucy's probably looking down at you, snickering. She would have pounced on a plum like this. Lucy was never one to miss a chance to get ahead—was she, Drew?"

Their gazes locked for an instant. Mari watched them, a fist of tension clenching in her chest. Drew rose gracefully from the piano bench and took Samantha by the arm.

"Samantha luv, may I have a word?"

Samantha's eyes went wide. "I'm off tonight, Mr. Van Dellen."

"Yes, darling, I'm well aware," he countered smoothly, drawing her away from Bryce and toward the side exit to the veranda.

Bryce let her go without a hint of objection. He dropped down on the bench in the spot Drew had vacated and took a long pull on his Pellegrino. His Adam's apple bobbed like a cork in his throat. Pressing his lips together and blotting the residual moisture with the heel of his hand, he adjusted his position a quarter turn toward Mari and pretended to be gravely concerned.

"How are you doing, Marilee? We heard you had a run-in with a burglar the other night."

"Yeah, or something." She shrugged it off. "Lucky for me he hit me in the head. My head is generally considered hard to the point of being impenetrable."

"Not a laughing matter, angel," he said with a frown. "You could have been killed."

"Could I?"

"It happens." It was his turn to shrug, as if to say violent death was just one of those things, an unforseen inconvenience on any tourist's itinerary. "So when are you going to come out and spend a day at Xanadu? With all that's happened, you could probably use an afternoon by the pool with nothing to worry about."

With nothing to worry about except which of the

snakes in Bryce's pit might be a murderer. What a relaxing scene—stretched out in a chaise with a daiquiri in one hand, scanning the suspects through the dark lenses of a pair of Wayfarers. Bryce and his court of vipers: the coke-snorting Judge Townsend, the shark lawyer Lucas. Maybe Bryce could fly in the sharpshooting Dr. Sheffield just to make things really interesting. Then Del Rafferty could climb up in the turret of Bryce's rustic palace and pick them all off one by one with an assault rifle. What a swell day that would be.

"I'll let you know," she said, brushing the wrinkles out of her jeans as she stood. "Break's over. Time to entertain the troops."

"Knock 'em dead, sweetheart."

He beamed a smile at her. Ever the benevolent monarch. He made his way toward his regular table, the high heels of his cowboy boots tilting his slim hips to an angle that encouraged swaggering. Waiting for him were Lucas, the actress Uma Kimball clinging to him like a limpet. There was no sign of Townsend. At the far end of the table, the bimbob was amusing himself by working his pecs behind a blue muscle shirt that looked like body paint. Sharon Russell was in her right-hand-man seat, wearing a black leather halter top with a neckline that plunged below table level and a scowl that would have done Joan Crawford proud.

Mari grimaced as she shrugged her guitar strap over her shoulder. "Careful, Shar baby," she muttered. "Didn't your mother ever tell you your face could stay that way? Guess not."

Samantha came in the side exit looking on the verge of tears. Bryce intercepted her and steered her back out the door. Drew stalked past the piano, through the crowd, and out the door that led to his office.

Stepping up to the microphone, Mari strummed a chord and sang the opening line of a Mary-Chapin Carpenter tune, thinking that life around New Eden was getting curiouser and curiouser.

•   •   •

J.D. heard her voice before he set foot in the lounge. It grabbed his heart like a fist and squeezed. Smoky and low, strong with emotion—pain, confusion, longing for something beyond her reach. He edged inside the door and stood in the shadows.

She sat on a stool in front of a small band, a soft spotlight gilding her silver-blond hair in an aura of gold. Propped on her knee was the old guitar that seemed almost a part of her when she played it. Her fingers moved over the strings, plucking out a slow, melancholy tune. She sang of a relationship growing cold, a man slipping away behind a wall of silence and indifference; painful words left unspoken and hanging in the air, their invisible weight oppressive. A woman helpless to stop an inevitable loss. Regret for what might have been, but never would be.

He thought he might have heard the song before, but he'd never heard it like this—with the ache of loss an almost palpable thing. He tried to shut out the words, tried to detach himself from the dull throb of guilt that reverberated in his chest with each low note on the guitar. He tried to tell himself he had no reason to feel guilty. He hadn't taken more than she had offered. Hell, he hadn't taken that much. With that thought came not vindication, but regret, and he shoved that aside as quickly and ruthlessly as the rest.

Between verses he moved up along the wall and slid into a vacant chair at the far side of the stage area. Like warm blue magnets, her eyes found his unerringly in the gloom. He thought her voice thickened a bit, but her fingers never faltered on the strings. As she plucked out the final notes, she dropped her head down near the body of the old guitar, her unruly mane tumbling forward to hide her face. She sat motionless while the crowd applauded, then set the guitar aside, walked off the stage, and out the side door.

The trio struck up a jazz number. J.D. rose and cut in front of them to exit through the door Mary Lee had taken.

"What's with you, Rafferty?" she asked as he stepped out onto the veranda.

She stood with her butt against the railing, arms crossed in front of her. A slice of amber light from the last of the sunset cut across her, turning her half-gold, half-shadow. She wore tight faded jeans with a rip in the knee, a white T-shirt, and a dark pinstripe vest. Not glamorous by any means, but appealing in a way he couldn't quite understand. He thought of what she had said about him not really seeing her and some dubious feeling shifted in his chest.

She narrowed her eyes at him. "You ruined my morning. You ruined my afternoon. You won't be happy until you ruin my evening too?"

"I tried to catch you at the ranch, but you'd gone already."

"So now you can ruin my evening in front of a hundred witnesses. That should make your day."

J.D. took the verbal jabs without complaint. He supposed he deserved them. It was better this way, anyhow, that she stay mad at him, that she would rather strike out at him than get close. He would rather be a bastard now than broken later by some emotion that served no useful purpose. Or so he told himself.

"I don't have to take it, you know," she said, her voice hoarse, the muscles of her face tightening. Blinking furiously, she shoved herself away from the railing and started past him.

J.D. caught her by the arm and pulled her in alongside him. "I never set out to hurt you, Mary Lee. In fact, I came here to see that you don't get hurt."

Mari glared up at him and jerked her arm from his grasp. "That boat sailed a while ago, skipper." She started away from him again, not sure of where she was going, knowing only that she didn't want to see Rafferty when she got there. But his next words stopped her cold.

"Miller Daggrepont is dead."

Shock struck like a fist to the solar plexus, forcing half the air out of her lungs. She turned back to face him, a little unsteady on her feet. "What? What did you say?"

"Miller Daggrepont is dead. I found him out on Little Snake Creek this afternoon. Quinn thinks he had a heart attack."

"And what do you think?"

"Looks to me like someone choked him."

Automatically, Mari's hand went to the base of her throat. She walked past J.D. to the spot along the rail she had vacated and leaned against it, staring out into the gathering gloom of twilight. But she didn't see the mountains turning purple or the orange of the sky or the parade of ranch trucks heading to the Hell and Gone. She saw Lucy's lawyer, his weird eyes rolling behind the slabs of glass in his spectacles as some faceless killer strangled the life from him. The image made her shudder.

J.D. stepped in behind her, cupped a big hand on her shoulder, and ran it down her arm. No more than an inch of air separated their bodies. All she had to do was lean back a little and she would be enveloped by his warmth, his strength. He took the decision away from her, closing the distance, resting his cheek against her hair.

The action was both foreign to him and automatic, natural. He wasn't the kind of man who offered comfort easily. But she looked so small, so lost. And despite every warning he had given himself, despite every rotten thing he had said to her, the sense of possession was still there, primal, basic, answering some invisible call from her. She was vulnerable; he wanted to be her strength. She was frightened; he wanted to be her courage.

It was foolish. It was dangerous. He thought. She thought.

Mari had no doubt that in the end he would push her away for getting too close. But in the meantime . . . In the meantime, she could close her eyes for a moment and imagine . . . pretend . . . wish . . . hope . . . all those futile, naive practices. She could imagine he loved her, pretend he cared, wish that he were not so distant or so hard, hope that her love could change him.

God, you're such a fool, Marilee . . . stayed with a man you don't love, love a man you can never have . . .

He had made it clear where she stood with him. Any tenderness he showed her now was only token or worse, a means to an end. She was so tired of feeling used and abused. And yet she still wanted . . . and wished . . . and hoped . . .

She curled her fingers tight around the railing and held on.

"Quinn's sending the body up to Bozeman to be posted," he said.

"Why are you telling me?"

"He was Lucy's lawyer."

"So? You think Lucy's death was an accident—not that you'd give a damn either way."

"That's not true."

She laughed and twisted her head around to look at him. "Yes, it is. You don't care about anyone, remember, J.D.? You're the lone wolf protecting his territory. The land—that's all you care about."

A denial was as bad as an admission that he felt something special for her. Something that quivered and shimmered in his chest like mercury, slippery and dangerous. The kind of thing that had killed his father because it could never be trusted. She had him neatly trapped. Just like a woman, he thought, his jaw working against the frustration.

"There are probably a dozen people who would have liked to see Miller dead," he said, simply ignoring the subject of feelings as deftly as he ignored the feelings themselves. "He had his fingers in a lot of shady land deals. But if this has anything to do with Lucy, then it might have something to do with you. I don't want to see you dead, Mary Lee."

"Well, I suppose that's a comfort," she said sarcastically. Turning to face him, she crossed her arms again and tipped her chin up to a challenging angle. "But then, if I were dead, you'd have a hard time trying to screw me out of Lucy's land, wouldn't you?"

She meant to hurt him, as he had hurt her, and she struck unerringly at his integrity and pride. But it didn't make her feel any better to see his eyes narrow or his jaw harden. It only made her feel more alone.

He leaned over her, big and tough and menacing, and braced his hands on the rail on either side of her. "I admit I want the land," he said, his voice a rumble as low and throaty as a cougar's growl. "But the screwing part was strictly for fun. You gonna try to tell me you didn't enjoy it, Mary Lee?"

"You bastard," she snarled through her teeth. He had her pinned against the railing. As she bent back over it, her hips lifted into contact with his and a liquid warmth ignited in instant response.

His eyes were as hard and dark as raw granite. The slow smile that curved his lips did not reach them. "That's not what you called me when I was inside you, Mary Lee," he murmured. "Tell me you didn't want it." He brought one hand up to touch the side of her face and lowered his mouth toward hers. His breath was as warm as his fingertips on her skin. "You can't. You didn't give a damn what I was after as long as I gave you a good ride."

"I think you have me confused with someone else," she said, glaring at him. "Too bad for you she happens to be dead. I'm beginning to think you were made for each other."

J.D. stepped back an inch and looked away, planting his hands at his waist. He didn't like the role he was trying to play. He hated himself for playing at all. Games had been Lucy's forte, not his. He'd been raised to deal fair and square. That was part of the code. God help him that he'd let himself be reduced to this.

Mary Lee looked up at him, her big eyes shining with tears and condemnation. He could feel the weight of her stare, could see her in his peripheral vision. Standing up to him again. Fighting for herself. That nameless thing swelled in his chest.

"I cared what you were after, J.D.," she said tightly. "My mistake was in thinking you had something in you worth putting up with all your macho bullshit. Something good. Something tender. Stupid of me to think you might let me find it. Stupid of me to think it was ever there."

She held herself as if she were cold as she paced a short distance down the walk, her paddock boots thumping dully on the wood. When she turned around, a hunk of rumpled blond hair tumbled across her face and she tossed it back. Tears leaked in a steady stream from her eyes and glistened over the translucent blue irises like crystal. The end of her nose had gone red. And still it struck him hard how pretty she was, and how fragile for all her strength.

"You keep confusing me with Lucy," she said. "Well, let me set you straight on a few things, cowboy. I'm not Lucy. I don't like being used. I don't like being hurt. I don't play games. When I care about someone, it's real— not always smart or what's best, but it's real. If you don't want that, fine. It's your loss. But don't come around telling me what to do or who to trust or where I belong or don't belong. You can't have it both ways, Rafferty. You can't just take what you want and leave the rest."

J.D. lowered his head and sighed. The pressure in his chest was as heavy and spiny as a mace. He didn't want it. He told himself he had never wanted it, had never lain awake in the night craving it. It would be far easier to keep himself intact without it. He had battles to fight, a ranch to run. He couldn't afford to expend energy needlessly.

Mari watched him, breath held, waiting. The foolish part of her heart was waiting for him to beg her forgiveness and confess his feelings. Capital F on foolish. He wasn't that kind of man. The tenderness she had glimpsed in him had been an aberration. He'd been bred tough enough to spit tacks and wrestle bears; a man made for the life he had inherited. But that kind of toughness didn't come without a price and it didn't magically stop short of his heart. She couldn't change his past or alter the rules he lived by. What they had together was not what she needed. There was no point trying to hang on. Better to cut her losses early and just walk away.

The side door to the lounge opened and Drew leaned

out, his eyes flicking from J.D. to her. "Is everything all right, luv?"

Mari held that breath just a little bit longer, just another few seconds of pointless hope, her stare hard on Rafferty's bowed head. He didn't say a word.

"No," she murmured hoarsely. "But I'll get over it."

She slipped in the door past Drew and headed for the ladies' room.

At one-thirty only the hired help were left in the Mystic Moose lounge. Tony the bartender wiped down bottles and arranged them to his satisfaction beneath Madam Belle's gilt-framed mirror. A custodian who bore a striking resemblance to Mickey Rooney put the chairs atop the tables and vacuumed the floor. Gary and Mitch, Drew's trio partners, said their good-byes and left together, talking music. Kevin stood at the cash register behind the bar, checking the receipts and laughing at Tony's cowboy jokes. Mari settled her guitar in its case and flipped the latches.

"Would you care to talk about it?" Drew asked softly.

He stood in the curve of the baby grand's side, no more than two feet from her. Mari shook her head a little, embarrassed at how easily the tears rose. It didn't make sense to hurt this badly. She'd hardly known Rafferty a week, and he'd been ornery most of that time. Forcing a smile, she rose and pulled the guitar case up into her arms and held it like a dance partner.

"There's not much to tell. I led with my heart. That's never a very intelligent thing to do."

Drew frowned a little. His warm green eyes were brimming with sympathy. "Perhaps not, but think what a grand place the world would be if we all dared do it."

He slipped his arms around her and the guitar and hugged her tight. "If you decide you need an ear to bend or a shoulder to cry on, you know who to come to."

"Thanks."

"Get some sleep tonight, luv," he said, stepping back. "You look all done in."

"Yeah, well . . ." Mari shrugged. "It started out as a bad hair day and went downhill from there."

He smiled gently then grew serious. "And as for the other . . ." He reached out and brushed back an errant strand of her hair. "Let it go, darling. No good can come of it now. I shouldn't want to see you hurt trying to change something that can't be changed."

She watched him as he glided between the tables to the bar, another line of Lucy's coming back to her—*All the good ones are married or gay*. She was sure Drew knew something more about Lucy's life here than he was telling her, but he claimed he couldn't shed any light on her death and she had to accept that as truth. He was just too good a friend to hide something so ugly.

Saying good night to Tony, she let herself out the side door and wandered down the boardwalk along the side of the lodge. Echoes of her fight with J.D. rang in her hollow footfalls. She ignored them as best she could. Even though she'd gotten little sleep the past two nights, she was too wired to go straight to her room. She couldn't imagine finding much solace in sleep. She had too much stewing in her subconscious to allow her to rest.

She thought fleetingly of going out to the ranch, dragging blankets out to the field to sleep beneath the stars among the llamas, but visions of grizzly bears and wandering madmen chased the fantasy away. Miller Daggrepont had been found dead in the middle of nowhere. And Lucy. There would be no sleeping in the guest bed at the ranch either. Aside from spooking her, the mere thought of spending the night way out there alone filled her head with Rafferty's warm male scent. Damned mule-headed cowboy.

He thought he had to take on the whole world with one hand tied behind his back and no one standing on his sidelines. He was Alan Ladd in *Shane,* only bigger and ornerier. John Wayne without the knee-knocking walk. Hercules on a horse. Superman in a Stetson. Chivalrous and cruel. As hard as granite. As vulnerable as a broken heart. He didn't want to admit caring about anyone who could possibly care about him—not Tucker or Will, certainly not Mary Lee the outsider.

Romanticizing again, Marilee? How like you.

Rafferty was no silver-screen cowboy hero. He was hard as nails and he didn't want her for anything other than to relieve his testosterone imbalance and increase his property holdings. Nothing terribly romantic about that.

Even as she tried to convince herself of his villainy, she saw him in her mind's eye, standing at the end of his barn where he thought no one could see him, looking out at the land he loved, his face a bleak mask of desperation.

Half resigned and half disgusted, she waded through the dew-damp meadow grass to her rock and climbed up to sit and stare back at New Eden. Oblongs of golden light marked windows of individual rooms in the Moose, where other people were having trouble winding down. She wondered which of the lights belonged to Drew and Kevin. She wondered how much Drew kept from his partner. She wondered if they ever had the kind of fights where one of them walked away feeling as if his heart had been kicked black and blue.

Things were still going strong at the Hell and Gone. The place lit up the night like a house afire. Noise pounded out through the walls and doors and windows, losing definition with distance so that all Mari could make out was the distorted thump of a bass guitar and the high crash of cymbals like glass shattering. She wondered if Will was inside, drinking himself blind again.

Her heart ached for him. Will, the screwup, the Rafferty black sheep. Funny he wasn't the one she had fallen for; they had the most in common. But then, he had a wife.

She started to think about Samantha and shook her head. What a mess. She'd come to Montana for a break from reality and had fallen splat in the middle of a soap opera—good versus evil, greedy land baron versus the small family rancher, intrigue, infidelity, and God only knew what else. The road less traveled was turning out to be pretty damned crowded and rougher than a son of a bitch.

There was a part of her that wanted nothing more than to walk away. But it was a small part, a remnant of the old Marilee. She pushed it away like a dry husk and felt a little stronger. She didn't want to leave Montana. She wanted to belong here—not just live here, *belong* here. She wanted to be as much a part of the place as Rafferty and the mountains and the big, big sky. And if she was to be worthy of the place, then she would have to adopt its codes—to do the right thing, to prize integrity and courage and accountability. And her first mission on this quest would be to find out the truth about Lucy's death.

No small task with no easy answers. And no one to help her.

Tipping her head back, she looked up at the millions of stars that were scattered across the night sky and found the North Star shining bright above the peaks. *Star light, star bright.* She stared up at the blue-white diamond points and wished for just one thing, knowing in her heart of hearts it wouldn't be coming tonight.

Will lay in the bed of Tucker's old H truck, staring up at the stars through a sheen that might have been tears or the blur of too much booze. He was beyond knowing. Too bad he wasn't beyond remembering. Images rolled across the back of his mind like a silent movie: sleeping out in the pickup bed when he was a kid, J.D. slipping into the cab and taking the truck out of gear to roll down through the yard, scaring the piss out of him. The two of them staying out all night then down in the high grass beyond the pens, where you couldn't make out the yard light because of the barn, and you could pretend you were anywhere.

Then suddenly he was fifteen, sleeping off a bender in the back of Tucker's H, staring up at the spinning sky and cursing God for giving him a stubborn son of a bitch for a father and a brother who made Tom Rafferty look soft by comparison. Wishing he could be free and at the same time wishing he could be more like J.D. He wanted to be everything to everybody. Instead, he was nothing. Not good enough to be a Rafferty. Not tough enough to run the Stars and Bars. His mother's son—a crime that made him suspect in the eyes of every rancher in the valley, a title that made him a prince among the crowd his mother ran with. Prince of the do-nothings.

Then a few more years spun past and he was lying in the back of his own truck with Sam tucked in beside him. A silly grin on his face. A big warm feeling in the middle of his chest. Feeling edgy and wild. On the brink of something new, something he couldn't name.

And then he was alone, parked on Third Avenue in front of the house the Jerry Masons had vacated in the dead of night six months before on account of a little discrepancy with Jerry's creditors. Alone and drunk, listening to the airy purr of a Mercedes engine as it idled in front of the house he used to share with his *ex*-wife, *ex*-wife, *ex*-wife . . .

You're gonna be free now, Willie-boy.

Free of the ranch. Free of J.D. Free of Sam.

Free to be me.

The fear of that started in his belly and swallowed him whole. And the stars blurred together as tears ran down his face.

Sharon turned her face up to a heaven as black as pitch and studded with pinpoints of light. She tried to imagine the heat of all the stars flowing into her and feeding her, recharging her, but their light was cold and white, and she felt nothing but emptiness.

She lay on a chaise on the balcony outside the bedroom, naked and alone, her long, angular body stretched out, silicone-enlarged breasts thrusting toward the sky like pyramids. She knew she was fully visible to the ranch hands who lived in an apartment above the horses in the stable. She knew one was watching her now, but she didn't care. On another night she might have performed for him. On another night she might have invited him to join her as she had on other occasions because he shared her taste for the rough stuff and because the idea of that kind of sex with a man who was dirty and ugly seemed only fitting to her. But tonight she had other things on her mind.

Bryce had yet to come up to bed. He had sequestered himself in the inner sanctum of his study to think.

Not an uncommon occurrence. Bryce's mind was like a Swiss watch—precision cogs and wheels running perfectly, ideas spinning through the workings. His mind and an absence of conscience had made him a wealthy man. She respected that. But Sharon suspected tonight he wasn't thinking of business, he was thinking of Samantha Rafferty, and the idea pierced her like a skewer.

The obsession was deepening, as it had with Lucy MacAdam. With Lucy the attraction had been her style and cunning and her self-professed power over men. Theirs had been a clash of wills, a mating of cobras. Samantha Rafferty's appeal was opposite in every way— guileless, clueless, unsure.

Sharon closed her eyes, blocking out the sky, filling her head with the vision of Bryce and the girl together. Tormenting herself with the vision. Fear slithered through her, twining around her heart, squeezing like a python. Arousal curled through it like a barbed vine. The images tilted and shifted. The partners changed. Other faces came into view, other bodies—her own among the tangle of arms and legs, light skin and dark. Memories of degradations past, the things she would do for Bryce, to Bryce, to herself. All of it for him.

The girl would never be a strong enough partner for Bryce. Her innocence would bore him eventually. His tastes would repulse her. Sharon tried to soothe herself with that promise. She closed her eyes and thought of Bryce, and satisfied herself with her own touch as she visualized him. She loved him. He was the only person in the world she loved—herself included. When the end came and she was thinking of him, there were stars behind her eyelids and heat rushing from within.

But when she opened her eyes she was alone. The stars were a million miles away.

J.D. sat on the porch with his legs hanging over the edge and his narrowed gaze on the night sky. Clear sky. Good weather. They would have a good day to move the cattle tomorrow—only they wouldn't be moving the cattle tomorrow. They were short a hand.

He should have been glad Will was gone. No more screwups. No more questions of loyalty or duty. No more wondering when he would pick up and leave to go rodeo, or when he would gamble away two months' worth of bank payments. No more reminder of the long, sad history of the Rafferty boys. He should have been glad. Instead, there was a yawning emptiness inside him.

He could have attributed it to a lot of things—the supper he had missed while tramping along the banks of the Little Snake with Dan Quinn and his deputies, the specter of an uncertain future that loomed over the ranch, the dead ends he'd run down in his attempts to stop Bryce from buying out the Flying K. But those answers were untrue and he'd never been a liar. He prided himself on that and other things that no one seemed to care about in the world beyond his own. Integrity. Accountability. Courage to do the right things, the hard things.

What did it matter if it mattered only to him?

What was any of it worth if he was the last of his kind?

I feel sorry for you, Rafferty. You'll end up with this land and nothing else.

Christ, he hated irony, and he hated being wrong. He had never wanted Will to be a part of him or a part of this place. Now Will was gone. The relationship they had bent and twisted and abused was finally broken. And he cared. A lot.

He had never wanted a woman to matter to him. Then along came Mary Lee from a world he distrusted and despised, as wrong for him as she could be. And she mattered. Finding Miller Daggrepont's body had sent a jolt of fear through him. Fear for Mary Lee.

Can't be afraid for somebody you don't care anything about, can you, J.D.?

Never been a liar. What a lie that was.

He tried to tell himself he hadn't been affected by her tears or her words outside the lounge at the Mystic Moose. That it didn't matter that he'd hurt her or that he'd been the biggest son of a bitch this side of Evan Bryce. They weren't suited. He didn't need the kind of woman she was. And what would she need with a man like him? She was a bright, modern woman on the brink of a rich new life. He was an antique. His life was obsolete. He was tied to a tradition that was dragging him under like an anchor in high water. Skilled in ways that didn't matter. A self-trained isolationist who had honed loneliness to perfection and called it inner peace.

Never been a liar.

The hell you say, J.D.

"A fine night."

Chaske appeared from nowhere and lowered his lean old body to sit down the porch from J.D. By starlight he looked like a Native American version of Willie Nelson— the long braids, the headband, faded jeans, and a Waylon Jennings T-shirt. J.D. glanced at him sideways.

"You gonna tell me I'm a jackass too?" he challenged. "Tucker beat you to it."

Chaske shrugged as if to say, You win some, you lose some, and dug the makings of a cigarette out of his hip pocket. The thin paper glowed blue-white against the dark.

"I don't need to hear it," J.D. said.

"Mmmm."

"Will is who he is. I am who I am. This day was bound to come."

"Mmmm." The old man opened a cotton pouch and stretched a line of tobacco down the crease in the paper. He tightened the pouch string, using his teeth, then rolled the paper and licked the edge in a movement that had been perfected over a great many years.

"Will's gone," J.D. said, essentially talking to himself. "We'll just have to deal with that. I'll get on the phone tomorrow and find us a hand. We can still have the cattle up the mountain by Wednesday."

Chaske struck a match against the porch boards and cupped his hands around his smoke, creating a glowing ball of warm light. He took his time, concentrating on the moment, savoring that first lungful of smoke. When he finally exhaled he said, "The cattle can wait. The grass will be better in a week or two. Now that we got rain."

J.D. studied the weathered old face, an impassive face that gave nothing away and at the same time hinted at many deeper truths than those on the surface of his words.

"He won't be coming back, Chaske. Not this time."

Chaske grunted a little, still staring out at the night. Pinching his little cigarette between his thumb and forefinger, he took another long drag and held it deep. When he exhaled, the smell of burning hemp sweetened the air.

"The cattle can wait. You got a lotta cattle. You got one brother." He took another toke, inhaling until it looked as if he were pinching nothing more than a red-hot spark. He ground the butt out on the porch floor and dropped it over the edge into the dirt. Slowly and gracefully, he rose, stretching like a cat. "Gotta go. Got a date."

J.D. raised his brows. "It's after one in the morning."

"She's a night owl. A man has to appreciate each woman for her own qualities. This one's got some pretty good qualities," he said nodding. Willie Nelson as Chief Dan George. Wisdom in a Waylon Jennings T-shirt. "That little blonde—bet she's got some good qualities too. She's got a look about her. Maybe you oughta find out."

J.D. worked his jaw a little, chewing back the desire to tell Chaske to mind his own business. The usual rules had never applied to Chaske. He claimed his ties to the ancient mystics let him live on a different plane. That or what he put in those little cigarettes.

"She's just passing through, Chaske. Anyway, I got no time. Someone's gotta keep this place hanging together. Near as I can figure out, that's the only reason I was born," he said, wincing a little at the bitterness that crept in around the edges of his voice. "To keep the Rafferty name on the deed."

"Kinda hard to do if there's no Raffertys after you," he pointed out. He turned his profile to J.D. once again and stared off across the ranch yard and beyond, his gaze seeming to encompass the whole of Montana.

J.D.'s thoughts drifted to the hazy image of a dark-haired baby nursing at his mother's plump breast. A son he had yet to sire and a woman he claimed was all wrong for him. Somehow, she looked pretty damn right in that picture.

"Man can't own the land, you know," Chaske announced. "Man comes and goes; the land will always be here. White men never figure that out. All we own are our lives."

Everything he left unsaid pressed down on J.D.'s shoulders, forcing a sigh out of him. He was too tired to argue philosophy, too exhausted to defend the principles of tradition or try to impress Chaske with a white man's code of honor and responsibility. There was no impressing Chaske; he was above it all on his plane with the mystics.

"Damn pretty night," the old man said, pointing at the sky with a thrust of his chin. "Look at all those stars." He glanced at J.D., his small, dark eyes glowing with amusement. "Good night for night owls."

Then he was gone and J.D. was left with the night and the stars all to himself. Alone. The way he was meant to be, he told himself. Tough guy. Didn't need anyone. Never had.

You lying dog.

Townsend sat at his desk, oblivious of the swath of galaxy that stretched across his windows like a sequined band of black velvet. He was shaking. He was sick. His tongue felt like a bloated eel in his mouth. He could barely breathe around it without gagging and choking. His nose ran in a continuous stream of thin, salty mucus.

Tears leaked from his eyes, burning the lids raw. A drift of cocaine glowed against the dark wood of the desk. He had lost track of how much he had used and how much he had wasted, sweeping it into the leather wastebasket as he sobbed. Amid the fine white powder lay a revolver.

It was a Colt Python .357. A six-shooter with a huge barrel. Pathetically phallic, but then he was a pathetic man. Fifty-two years old, a straight arrow trying to swing with the hip crowd, falling in lust with a woman young enough to be his daughter. He had bought the gun to impress Lucy. Lucy, his obsession, his demon. Everything had happened because of her. She had led him down the yellow brick road to Oz and on to hell.

Just that morning he had thought he might climb out of the pit. He thought he might be able to salvage something of his life. Get free of the slime, cleanse himself, start fresh. But no. Another of the leeches had tried to hook on to him. He could never be free of it. Not now. Especially not now.

The fat lawyer—Daggrepont—was dead. He hadn't meant to kill him. They had stood on the riverbank, talking, birds singing above the rushing sound of the water. The sun shone down. The mountains thrust up around them as they stood in the emerald velvet valley. All that beauty . . . and Daggrepont, ugliness personified, a fat, grotesque pouch of greed, avarice shining in his magnified eyes . . .

. . . Knew a little something about Lucy and him . . . ought to be worth a dollar or two . . . not greedy, just wants his due for holding his tongue . . .

One minute he was just standing there, listening to the music of Montana while that toad spewed poison and called it a "business arrangement," "an understanding between gentlemen." The next minute he'd had his hands buried in the wattle of fat around Daggrepont's throat. He had watched as if from outside his body, as if the hands choking the man belonged to some anonymous third party.

Choking, choking, choking. Daggrepont's eyes rolling behind the thick lenses of his glasses, his tongue thrusting out of his mouth as his grotesque face flushed purple. Townsend heard shouting, a long, loud roar that might have come tearing from his own throat or been inside his own mind. He didn't know, couldn't tell.

Some small shard of sanity pierced his brain, and his hands let go. He thrust himself away from the lawyer, hurtled backward as if he were being jet-propelled down a tunnel. But Daggrepont went on choking, eyes rolling, tongue lolling. His face was the color of an eggplant. Foam frothed out of his mouth and he fell onto the bank, his arms and legs jerking wildly. Townsend stood watching, hallucinating that his arms had stretched to nine feet long and his thumbs were still pressing against the fat man's windpipe.

Daggrepont tried to stand. Couldn't control his body. Fell into the water among a stand of cattails and rushes.

Run. His first thought had been to run. But as he sped in his Cherokee toward his cabin, other thoughts shot across his mind in bright, hot arcs. Evidence. There would be evidence. Tire tracks. There would be tire tracks. And footprints. Marks on the dead man's throat. Evidence hidden somewhere tying Lucy to Townsend to Daggrepont. There would be no simple explanation to hide the truth this time. Even in this wilderness a coroner would know the marks of strangulation.

It was over. There would be no redemption. No rebirth. The grime of this life he had fallen into would never come off. It was like ink, like grease, and every move he made, every thought he had, smeared it over more of his soul. He was ruined, thanks to Evan Bryce and Lucy—the devil and his familiar.

There was no turning back. The truth enveloped him like a cold black shroud, like the big black night sky of Montana. A sky with no heaven above it. As black as death. As black as Evan Bryce's heart.

With one trembling hand he lifted the receiver off the phone and punched the button to speed dial Bryce's number. With the other he reached for the Python.

•   •   •

The stars were like promises in the sky. Bright and distant. Well out of his reach. Too far off to chase away the darkness. Around him the night was matte black, electrically charged. The hair on the back of his neck and on his arms rose up like metal filings dancing beneath the magnetism of the moon.

. . . Dancing beneath the moon. As the blonde danced down the slope. She swayed from side to side, hair spilling in her wake. A wave of silk. Moonlight silvering her skin, glowing in her eyes, glowing through her wounds. Del rolled back behind the tree and squeezed his eyes shut so hard that color burst behind his lids, red and gold like the flash of rockets over the rice paddies. He could feel the concussion of the blasts against his skin. The smell of napalm and the putrid-sweet stench of burning, rotting flesh seared his nostrils.

Then he opened his eyes and the 'Nam was gone. The breeze cooled the sweat on his skin, filled his head with the scents of pine and damp earth. The war was gone. He held his rifle against him like a lover and brushed his lips against the oiled barrel. An absent kiss, a superstitious reflex, as if the gun had chased away his ghosts.

A high, keening wail skated across his eardrums, like fingernails on a chalkboard. The old ghosts were gone. New ones took their place. The blonde danced through his nights like a siren beckoning him to crash on the jagged rocks of madness. Panic rose up in his throat and numbed the side of his face like a wash of novocaine. She was there to steal his mind, to steal his land, to steal his family. She ran with the tigers. She died and rose again. A mythic creature.

He thought it might be his destiny, his quest, to kill her. To kill her might redeem his honor, banish his shame, give him back his place in the order of things. Right all the wrongs.

Rolling back around against the bark of the tree, he brought the gun up into place. Found the woman through the scope. Traced the cross hairs over her chest like a benediction. Raised the barrel slightly to account for drop. His finger kissed the trigger.

Kill her.
Kill her!
Save yourself!
Or chase yourself into madness.

What if the test was of control, of reason, of patience? What if he failed?

The possibilities tumbled through his head like rocks in an avalanche. He saw himself tumbling with them. Riding shotgun down the avalanche. Being crushed by the brutal weight of it. He didn't know what to do.

Kill her.

The blonde danced on. Taunting him. Inviting him. Oblivious of him. Whirling like a dervish. The dance of the dead. An apparition in the night.

Kill her.
Kill yourself.

She turned to a blur in the glass. A kaleidoscope image shifting as he watched. The battle within him wrung his heart like a wet rag, wrenching out tears, squeezing out pain. Trembling, he let go of the trigger and pointed the rifle to the sky, the stars jumping down at him through the barrel of the scope. The bright lights of hope. Still out of reach. Always out of reach.

CHAPTER 22

Judges don't go about shooting women. . . .

Mari played the line through her head like a magic chant to ward off danger as she wheeled her Honda in beside a mud-splattered black Jeep Cherokee. Townsend was the one who had brought Lucy to Montana. They had been lovers. Drew thought he had been giving Lucy money—or that Lucy had been extorting money from him. That made him a key to the truth about Lucy's death. Or a suspect in her murder. She tried not to dwell on the latter as she climbed the steps to the front porch of the judge's "cabin."

It was a log house on the same lines as Lucy's, only larger and with a more expensive view. The back side faced Irish Peak, which was sparkling as the sun poured down on the mountain's cone of snow. An extravagant getaway from the pressures of the bench. Justice apparently had its rewards. Or the Townsends past and present had been loaded from other pursuits.

MacDonald Townsend was highly regarded in legal and political circles. Mari had met him once, had seen him from afar on numerous occasions. If they ever made a movie about his life, they would cast Charlton Heston in the lead role and tell him to play it as stiff as an over-starched collar. It was difficult to reconcile that public image with the image of him bending over a billiard table to help himself to a little toot of classic coke. Of course, it was just as difficult to envision the squeaky-clean, all-American public man whose wife was the head of half the charities in Sacramento as the kind of man who would climb into bed with Lucy and set the sheets on fire either. But he was.

The question was, what else might he be?

She rang the bell and waited, trying to formulate a conversational strategy. *Did you kill my friend* seemed a tad blunt and more than a little foolish. After all, what was to stop him from just popping her one and dumping her body down a ravine someplace? What she was really after was hints, feelings, expressions to read. Something more to add to the theory Sheriff Quinn didn't want to hear.

Inside the house a dog was barking. Mari stepped up to one of the side lights that flanked the door, cupped her hands around her eyes, and pressed her nose to the glass. A sleek-looking German shorthair was pouncing and bowing at an interior door beyond the foyer and to the right of the living room. The dog barked and scratched the door, seeming frantic to get inside the room.

Perhaps the door led to a bedroom and Townsend was auditioning replacements for Lucy. Perhaps it was a study and Townsend was meeting with a co-conspirator. Paying off the hit man Sheffield had taken the rap for. A picture of Del Rafferty flashed through her mind, and she shook it away. Del may have been many unfortunate things, but no Rafferty would ever be a hired gun.

"You're starting to sound like a native, Marilee," she mumbled, amused and a little dismayed by her automatic defense of the clan. Keeping her eyes on the dog and the door, she reached down and jabbed the doorbell again, holding it an annoyingly long time.

There was always Lucy's hired hand to consider for the hit man lineup. Kendall Morton, shady drifter. She knew little about him, but by his description he sounded as if he just might be the kind of man willing to waste someone for spending money and then disappear. She wondered if she could get his criminal record if she called the sheriff's department and claimed to be a business owner checking Morton out before hiring him. Quinn wouldn't give it to her any other way.

She heaved a sigh and hit the doorbell yet again. The interior door remained closed, but the dog was diverted. It bounded toward her, loping through the house with big, loose-limbed strides, ears up, pale eyes boring into hers. It jumped up and put its paws on the side light, toenails clicking against the glass, and stared Mari in the face. He was very clearly male and, as he slurped his long, pink tongue against the glass, he was very clearly not a killer watchdog. He jumped down from the window, galloped around in a tight circle, barking, made a dash toward the closed interior door, then dashed back toward Mari, whining.

Mari tried the front door. Maybe the old geezer had keeled over while auditioning paramours and was lying on the bedroom floor, praying his trustworthy dog would fetch help. Or maybe the hit man had wasted him.

The door was unlocked. She slipped into the foyer, feeling like a thief. The dog danced around her, his thunderous barks resounding off the adobe-look walls.

"Judge Townsend? Anybody home?"

After the third call, the dog tried again to get her to follow him to the closed door beyond the living room. He had scratched deep gouges into the door, leaving raw open wounds in the pine. Not far from the door, beside a potted fig tree that sat along a bank of windows, he had left a big pile of doggie business that was fresh enough to make Mari wrinkle her nose.

Standing close beside the door, she listened for voices. Silence.

"Judge Townsend?" She drummed her knuckles against the center panel, inciting another booming bark from the dog, then silence again. The dog shoved his wet nose into her hand, as if he thought he could physically compel her to reach for the doorknob. Scowling, Mari wiped the dog snot off her palm onto the leg of her jeans and reached for the knob of her own accord.

The door swung open to reveal a spectacular study. Dark wood and big windows, a forest of leather-upholstered wing chairs, and a fieldstone fireplace. The heads of a number of unfortunate creatures were mounted on the wall above the fireplace. A mule deer, an elk, a mountain goat, several antelopelike creatures she had never seen outside the pages of *National Geographic*. There was a zebra hide tacked up on the far wall with an enormous tiger skin beside it. The disparity in size would have made zebras glad they didn't live in tiger country. A grizzly bear stood in the far corner, petrified for all eternity on his hind legs with his lips curled back in an ugly snarl.

Centered along the windowed wall was Townsend's desk, a massive polished walnut piece with brass accents. Slumped over, facedown on the desk, was Townsend. By the look of things, he had stuck a gun in his mouth and blown the top of his head off.

For a long while Mari stood frozen, staring. Every detail of the scene soaked into her memory like indelible ink. She wanted to look away, but couldn't. The shock had shorted out the brain synapses that had to do with motor functions. She was trapped there, staring at the carnage, a detached corner of her brain studying the play of the sunlight through the blood and brain matter splattered on the window glass behind the desk. *Blood*stained glass. The air in the sun-warmed room was rank with the thick, gagging stench of violent death.

Her gaze drifted to Townsend again. The body was a dead husk, crumpled and discarded. The essence of the person had gone on to places unknown. His right hand was still wrapped around the handle of the pistol that had shattered the crown of his head like the shell of a soft-boiled egg.

In a heartbeat Mari's brain kicked back into action and she jolted into motion. Her whole body jerked backward.

"Oh, my God!" she whispered, as if she were afraid of waking him. "Oh, my God!"

The gasp jammed in her throat as her breakfast rushed up from her stomach. Clamping a hand over her mouth, she stumbled back through the maze of wing chairs and out of the room. There wasn't time to hunt for a bathroom. The kitchen was a straight shot through the living room on the other end of the house. She managed to make it to the sink before the sight of the judge and the smell of dog shit made her gag.

When there was nothing left of her Rainbow Cafe buttermilk pancakes, she turned the faucet on and stuck her face under it, as if she could wash away what her eyes had seen. Trembling violently, she reached for a dish towel and pressed it against her cheeks.

Townsend was dead. Lucy was dead, then Miller Daggrepont, now Townsend had killed himself. She could still see the look of surprise in his eyes, as if he had seen something unexpected in that final split second between life and death. She could still see the blood that had run out of his mouth to puddle on the desktop, and the hand that still gripped the butt of the gun.

She used the kitchen phone to call the sheriff's department, shaking so badly she had difficulty punching out 911. The dispatcher assured her a car would be sent out right away—as soon as they could determine where exactly Judge Townsend lived.

Too shaken to sit still, Mari wandered through the house. She found a bottle of Glenfiddich on the sideboard in the dining room and drank a little to soothe her jangling nerves and calm the chaos swirling like a cyclone through her head. Townsend's grisly last portrait remained in her brain, but she was now able to concentrate on other aspects of the picture—a clean slice of sky in the window; the scales of justice sitting front and center on the desk, one side weighed down by a handful of change and a roll of stamps; the telephone, black and high-tech, its receiver nowhere in sight, a red light burning on the console.

No receiver. She stared out the window at the front yard, waiting for the distant cloud of dust that would signify the imminent arrival of a deputy. She took another sip of scotch and held the cool, heavy tumbler against her cheek. No receiver. Had he taken the receiver off the hook so as not to be interrupted by some telemarketing flunky as he carried out his final verdict on himself? Or had he been calling someone?

If his suicide had anything to do with Lucy's death
. . . if he had been talking to someone shortly before his
own death . . . might that person have some connection
to Lucy?

The dog came into the dining room, whining, and
bumped against Mari's legs, gazing up at her with worried eyes. She stroked his head absently and set her glass
aside. Quinn was fed up to his eyeteeth with her theories.
He wouldn't want to hear this one either. He certainly
wouldn't allow her to nose around the crime scene. She
would be summarily removed from the vicinity and es-
corted back to the station to make her statement with no
embellishments or queries allowed.

With the German shorthair trailing despondently after
her, she went back into the living room and stared at the
open study door while her heart did a slow drumbeat
against her sternum and the scotch simmered in her
stomach. She ordered the dog to stay and walked on into
the study as purposefully as her quaking knees would
allow. Keeping her eyes trained away from the judge, she
skirted around the front side of the desk to the end where
the telephone sat with its red light glowing like an evil
eye.

The redial button was just to the left of Townsend's
ravaged head. Concentrating on the button, she reached
out with the eraser end of a pencil and punched it. The
electronic music of modern technology played over the
receiver, which lay on the floor. Mari watched the number appear in the LCD display above the answering machine cassette compartment, listened to the phone ringing
on the other end of the line. On the third ring a woman
with a heavy eastern-European accent answered.

"Mr. Bryce's residence. 'Ello?"

Samantha stretched out in the lounge chair, her eyes
shaded from the glare of the sun on the pool by a pair of
sunglasses that cost more than she made in a week. Bryce
had loaned them to her. Actually, he had given them to

her, but she felt more comfortable considering it a loan than a gift.

She had called in sick to work. After their discussion the night before, she had no desire to run into Mr. Van Dellen today. Bryce told her not to worry about it. Drew was meddling where he didn't belong without knowing all the facts, he said. Drew didn't understand their friendship, he said. He didn't understand what she was going through with Will. He was feeling protective of her—like a brother for a sister—but wasn't that ironic, since Bryce felt the same way? No need for a conflict when their goals were essentially the same.

Bryce's words had soothed her last night. Just the sound of his voice soothed her, warm and rich as it was. He smiled at her with that movie-star smile, his eyes kind and wise, and for a moment her life didn't seem quite so screwed up. But when she woke up alone in her bed with the morning sun glaring like a spotlight on her shabby room, Bryce's comfort had faded away and Mr. Van Dellen's disapproval had shone through.

Think what you're doing, Samantha! You're not like them. Can't you see that?

Yes, she could see it. Apparently, everybody could see it—that she was just a dumb, gawky half-breed kid trying to be something she wasn't. Everybody saw it except Bryce. He treated her as if she were just as good as, just as important as any of his rich and famous friends. He treated her like a beautiful woman instead of a kid sister. That was what she could see: that she had a husband who didn't care and a man—a *friend*—who treated her better than her own father ever had, even in her dreams. Bryce saw possibilities for her; he gave her encouragement when all she had ever gotten from anyone else was pity or ridicule or nothing at all. Nobody else seemed to understand that.

So she had sought refuge today with her friend. She could spend the day on his mountain, beside his pool, hiding away from the reality of her life. She could leave Sam the tomboy barmaid behind on the dusty side streets of New Eden and become Samantha of the hip crowd for a day. She could lie by the pool with Uma Kimball in the next chair and a famous trial lawyer bringing her drinks and staring at her cleavage.

Actually, the last part made her uncomfortable, so she turned onto her stomach on the chaise and pulled her long hair over her shoulders for a curtain.

"Thanks," she murmured, setting the margarita aside on a low glass-topped table.

Ben Lucas grinned at her as if she had just said something truly witty. He stood between her and the pool, a tan, health-club body in orange Speedo trunks.

"You'll get a better tan without the shirt," he said.

Samantha stared up at him, seeing her reflection in the mirror lenses of his sunglasses. From the selection of swimwear in the guest room, she had chosen a simple, modest turquoise tank suit, which she had felt compelled to cover up with the white oxford shirt she'd taken out of Will's end of the closet at home that morning. In the chair to her right, Uma Kimball lay soaking up the rays, wearing nothing but the bottom portion of a yellow thong bikini, a scrap of fabric too small to clean her sunglasses with. Uma's chest was as flat as a Cub Scout's, her nipples tiny pebbles in coins of brown flesh.

"I have a built-in tan," Samantha said, feeling conspicuously overdressed and far too conscious of her long-limbed body. A direct contrast to the people around her, who never seemed self-conscious about anything.

Sharon sauntered up to Lucas and made a production of running an ice cube along her lower lip, then dropping it in the glass he held. She was slightly taller than he in her gold eelskin slings. Her bathing suit looked like one long piece of black silk gauze that criss-crossed her chest, wrapped down between her long, perfect legs, and disappeared between the firmly rounded cheeks of her buttocks.

"Sam is modest," she said, her amusement as cool as the cube she'd presented Lucas with. "Isn't that sweet, Ben?"

Uma rolled over onto her side, her glassy eyes bright

with amazement as she fixed them on Samantha. "So are you *really* like an Indian, or what?"

"Part," Samantha murmured.

"The kind from *A Passage to India* or the kind from *Dances with Wolves*?"

"The kind from Montana. My mother is Cheyenne."

"The singer? How *cool*!"

Sharon breathed an impatient sigh. "Jesus, Uma, are you ever *not* on something?"

The actress slid a pair of sunglasses down from the top of her head to the tip of her pixie nose. She sent Sharon a look over the frames and smiled slyly. "Are you ever *not* a bitch?"

Something like embarrassment crawled over Samantha's skin as raw dislike charged the air between the two women. She ducked her head down, hiding behind her curtain of dark hair. Mr. Van Dellen's words rang in her ears—*You're not one of them.* . . .

"Reisa is setting out a light snack," Bryce announced, walking blithely into the thick of things. He was unaffected by the tensions in the air, looking chic and relaxed in a pair of full-cut white gauze pants and an open jungle-print shirt. His sun-bleached hair was swept back into its usual queue. He smiled a pleasant, even smile, a flash of ivory in his lean, tanned face as he regarded Sharon through the lenses of his sunglasses. "Why don't you go sink your teeth into something that won't bleed, cuz?"

"Join me," Sharon countered, holding his gaze. "We have business to discuss."

"In a minute." Bryce dismissed her and started to turn back toward Samantha.

Sharon touched his arm, wanting to drag him away. Business always came first with him—unless he was smitten. "Bryce—"

"I said later," he said sharply.

Sharon bared her teeth at him and glided away with no outward sign of the hurt or the uneasiness that churned inside her. Lucas followed with Uma tagging after him, a finger hooked in the back of his swim trunks and a towel slung over her shoulders to cover her token breasts.

"Have you worked up an appetite yet?" Bryce grinned.

Samantha's lips twisted in a wry little smile as she swung her endless legs over the side of the chaise and sat up. Mona Lisa in Montana, Bryce thought. If she ever realized the power she could wield over men with those secret, amused smiles, she could be formidable. An irresistible challenge. Of course, she was that already; she just didn't know it. The irony only made her more desirable.

"This isn't considered work where I'm from," she said, swinging her hair back over her shoulder.

Bryce eased himself down on the chaise to sit beside her. He nodded toward Fabian. Oversize pecs glistening with baby oil, the blond male model appeared in deepest concentration as he tilted his sun reflector to direct the maximum rays to the underside of his lantern jaw. "Don't tell him that. He'll make a million doing a calendar if he keeps his tan even."

Uncertain whether or not he was teasing, Samantha gave him a look that managed to combine skepticism and puzzlement. Bryce reached up and stroked the back of his hand down her cheek, then tipped her chin up. "You could make a million too, if you wanted."

She laughed. "Me? I don't think so."

He frowned a little. "You could do anything, sweetheart. No limits—"

"—But the sky," she finished. "There's a lot of sky in Montana."

"And plenty of opportunities elsewhere. You're a beautiful young woman, Samantha. You could be the toast of L.A. or New York. All you have to do is believe in yourself."

"I can't go to L.A. I have a husband."

"Not in evidence," Bryce said, not bothering to disguise the disapproval in his voice. She flinched, almost imperceptibly. He pressed harder on the nerve he'd struck, without remorse or pity. "He treats you like a second-class citizen. No, it's worse than that. He doesn't treat you like anything at all."

Samantha bit her lip and looked away from him, fixing her gaze on the glazed lapis tile that bordered the pool so he couldn't see the tears fill her eyes. Bryce slipped an arm around her shoulders and gave her a compassionate squeeze, pressing a phantom kiss to her hair.

"I'm sorry, sweetheart," he murmured. "I didn't mean to upset you. It's just that it makes me angry to see the way he ignores you."

It amazed him a little that he felt so strongly about the girl, when she had been nothing more than a chess piece a week before. He sat there beside her with his arm around her and wanted good things for her. He couldn't remember the last time that had happened. Years. Never. His focus had always been ruthlessly on himself. Now he broadened the scope a little to include Samantha. He could have everything he wanted—the power, the land, Samantha—and give her things too—opportunities, fame —and watch her blossom and know that he was responsible. Heady stuff, playing the part of a magnanimous god. He thought he just might grow to like it.

"You can have so much more than he's giving you," he murmured, pushing a little harder, reminding her that Will Rafferty was giving her nothing but heartache.

Samantha looked away to the shaded patio tables on the other side of the pool. Uma was devouring a small mountain of fresh fruit. Across the table from her, Ben Lucas dunked a strawberry in a glass of champagne, popped it in his mouth, and flashed a smile. Sharon sat at a separate table, ignoring the others, ignoring the food, paging idly through *Cosmopolitan*.

"I don't think your cousin likes me very much," Samantha said softly.

"Sharon?" Bryce shrugged, tightening his arm around Samantha. "Sharon doesn't like anyone. She's very . . . territorial. And that's one of her better qualities."

"Sounds like you don't like her very much."

He thought about that for a moment and sighed, stroking his hand absently up and down her arm. "I'm tired of her theatrics, I suppose. But we have a long history, Sharon and I. And she is, after all, family."

Loyalty would appeal to Samantha, he thought, make him look kind and good when he was generally neither of those things. And it was easier to explain than the truth. The truth would shock her, repulse her. She was too naive, had led far too sheltered a life up here in the mountains, where people still believed in quaint concepts like morality.

The French doors to the house swung open and Reisa, his housekeeper, trundled out. The woman had the body of an oil drum and a face with the shape and expression of a frying pan, but she could cook and she spoke little English, two essential requirements for the job. Marilee Jennings trailed in her broad wake. Bryce felt his interest shift and heighten, like a bird dog going on point.

"Marilee!" he called, rising from the chaise and drawing Samantha up with him. He herded the girl around the end of the pool to meet his newest guest.

Mari tried to muster a smile, a monumental task after spending two hours in the company of Sheriff Quinn and his deputies. The sheriff had been none too pleased to find her in the company of a corpse.

Bryce showed no outward signs of having received a distress call from a buddy. If he knew anything about the judge's demise, then he was as cold-blooded as the lizards that had given up their hides for his belt. He graced her with his brilliant smile. The sun shone down like a benediction on his high forehead.

"I'm glad you decided to join us after all," he said. "Have a seat. I'll have Reisa get you something to drink."

"This isn't exactly a social call," Mari said, her gaze skating across the faces of the assembled personalities and coming back to rest on Bryce. "I thought you should know—since you were a friend of his—MacDonald Townsend is dead. He killed himself sometime last night."

Bryce's features folded into an appropriate expression

of grim disbelief. He jammed his hands at his waist. "Jesus, you're joking."

"My sense of humor doesn't run that black. He's dead."

Ben Lucas shoved his chair back, legs scratching against the flagstone, and rose to come stand beside Bryce. Shoving his sunglasses on top of his head, he scowled at Mari as if she had been the one to pull the trigger. "Townsend is dead? Christ, what happened?"

Mari shrugged. Her hands found the pockets of her baggy jeans and slipped in, fingers knotting into tight fists. A gentle breeze swept across the terrace, blowing a chunk of hair across her face. She tossed it back with a jerk of her head. "I couldn't say. I don't think he left a note. I stopped by his place this morning because, well, he knew Lucy and I thought we could just talk, you know. I found him in his study."

"That must have been terrible for you," Bryce murmured. He closed the distance between them and hooked an arm around her shoulders, steering her toward a seat at the table where Sharon sat stonefaced, her eyes narrowed.

"Sit down." He looked over his shoulder at the housekeeper hovering near the French doors. "Reisa, will you bring Ms. Jennings a cognac?"

"No, thanks," Mari said. The scotch she'd consumed at Townsend's had long since burned off. Her mind was achingly clear, and she intended to keep it that way as long as she was in this snake pit. "Just a Coke would be fine."

Bryce frowned a little, but nodded to the woman.

"I wonder if the police have called Irene," Lucas said to Bryce. He cut a glance at Mari, his mouth set in a tight line. "Mrs. Townsend," he explained. Before she could acknowledge that in any way, he focused on Bryce again. "I'll call her. It's better if this kind of news comes from a friend."

"Yes, of course. Use the phone in my office," Bryce said, rubbing his chin. "In fact, I'll come with you. I'd like to offer any help I might be able to give."

The two disappeared into the house. Mari curbed the urge to follow them. She wasn't sure what she had hoped to gain by breaking the news. Bryce didn't strike her as the sort of man who would break down under the weight of an overloaded conscience, and confess. Nor was she about to confront him with any of her nebulous suspicions. That would be a good way to get dead if he turned out to be an evil overlord, a good way to make herself a powerful enemy, in any event.

A strained silence descended on the pool-party crowd. Samantha Rafferty slid down into the seat Lucas had vacated and pulled the oversize man's shirt she wore close around her. Her dark eyes were wide with uncertainty now that Bryce had left her side. Sharon sat stiffly in the chair across from Mari, an ice sculpture in St. Tropez swimwear. Across the way, the bimbob rolled over on his chaise and flexed his buttocks.

"MacDonald Townsend," Uma said as she picked up half a dozen slices of star fruit off her plate and crammed them all into her mouth at once. Her face pinched into a knot as she chewed, an expression that might have been concentration or a commentary on the tartness of the fruit. She wiped the juice from her overinflated lower lip with the back of her hand. "Did he used to be on *Days of Our Lives*?"

Sharon rolled her eyes. The bimbob made no comment.

"Do you think she knows about the phone call?"

Bryce swiveled his chair behind his massive teak desk, elbows on the armrests. "It doesn't make any difference. The call will be a matter of record. All anyone has to do is check Townsend's phone bill to see that call was made. On the other hand, no one can prove I ever received the message."

He plucked up a microcassette from the desktop and tossed it to Lucas. "Damned answering machines. Always on the blink."

Lucas walked the cassette between his fingers. "No one

would expect you to answer a call in the middle of the night. There's no staff on at that hour to take it for you."

"Just that damned machine," Bryce said, practicing his frown. "I've been meaning to get a new one. Maybe if I had . . . well, I suppose I would have been too late in any case."

"Nice." Lucas nodded. "A small show of conscience and regret. Very believable."

"I could have been an actor," Bryce conceded, "but it wouldn't have been nearly so exciting."

There was no question he would have been too late to save Townsend even if he had made the effort. He had listened to the tape first thing that morning. After a tearful, rambling monologue of confession and accusation had come the sound of a small explosion. Townsend had left his suicide note on the answering machine and recorded his own death. Self-destruction in the age of technology.

"He never had any nerve," Bryce said without compassion. "I detest a man with no nerve. It's just as well he's dead. I couldn't have stood watching him grovel and whine much longer."

Lucas tossed the cassette up and caught it with the same hand. "As long as he didn't leave behind anything that might be incriminating to the rest of us."

"He didn't have anything on anyone. He wanted to be a player, but he had no leverage in the game."

"He might have left behind a signed affidavit for all we know," Lucas said, a small line of worry digging in between his brows. It was the same look he used in court to put doubt in the minds of jurors. He tossed the tape up again.

Bryce rose from his chair and snagged the cassette in one fluid move. He gave the attorney a steady look. "He didn't."

With a flick of the wrist he pulled the tape out of the cassette, set it ablaze with a twenty-four-carat-gold lighter, and dropped it into the Baccarat ashtray on his desk.

CHAPTER 23

*B*ryce persuaded Mari to stay. He was the only one who made any effort to do so. She declined the offer of a swimsuit. It didn't seem wise to get half naked with this crowd. For one thing, she didn't consider herself to be in the bikini league, bodywise. Her self-esteem was already reeling from Rafferty's rejection. She really didn't need to compare belly buttons with the likes of Uma Kimball or Sharon Russell. Especially Sharon, whose figure belonged in a Frederick's of Hollywood window display.

Besides, with the possible exception of Samantha, she trusted none of them. Lucas tracked her every move with his shark eyes. Sharon's gaze was clinically cool, like that of a scientist watching a mouse in a maze. The bimbob was on another planet and Uma was *from* another planet. Mari felt as if she'd fallen into an alternate reality, one that was littered with corpses and shadowed with menace.

Bryce played host with a subdued air. He chose to sit with her in the shade, Samantha to his right side and an untouched glass of scotch in front of him.

"He was distraught over Lucy's accident," he said, tracing patterns in the condensation on the glass. "I suppose that was part of it."

"They were that close?" Mari asked, her eyes on his bony hands as he fondled the tumbler. The action seemed borne of impatience rather than a need to soothe some inner restlessness.

Bryce's eyes cut to her sharply, though he didn't move

a muscle. His voice was perfectly calm. "He gave Lucy the money to buy the ranch. She didn't tell you?"

"I suppose I didn't really want to know. I'm not a big advocate of illicit affairs."

Samantha shifted uncomfortably in her chair, ducking her head as if she wanted to make herself very small and disappear. She had gone in and dressed with obvious attention to detail, like a little girl playing dress-up in her mother's closet. It somehow made her seem just as vulnerable as she had looked in the bathing suit. Mari thought of Will and bit her tongue for punishment.

"That's the irony, you know," Bryce said on a sigh as he rattled the ice in his scotch. "Townsend wasn't either. He was obsessed with Lucy, but he carried around a lot of guilt because of it. He wouldn't leave his wife for her, even though he and Irene haven't had much of a marriage in recent years." He took a sip of the drink, just enough to taste the smoky quality of the liquor, and stared off across the pool. "Foolish, hanging on to something meaningless when he could have started fresh."

Again, Samantha's chair rattled against the flagstones as she shifted positions. "Maybe he still loved his wife," she said quietly. "Maybe he just couldn't help himself."

Bryce gave her a long, level look. "We can always help ourselves, sweetheart."

The girl's eyes filled. Mari wanted to hug her and tell her Will still loved her, that he was worth hanging on to, worth fighting for, but she didn't know that. Not really. It was just a feeling, and feelings had already gotten her in trouble with the Rafferty brothers. Still, she couldn't just sit there and watch Bryce try to lure an innocent into his fold. It would have been like standing by with her hands in her pockets while satanists made off with the village virgin. She was here and she was accountable. In her heart she had made her commitment to this land, a commitment that had nothing to do with ownership and everything to do with personal integrity.

"If people could always help themselves," she said, "then Betty Ford wouldn't have a clinic. There's a lot more to people's problems than weakness."

Bryce's small mouth tightened. Mari ignored him and met Samantha's pain-filled gaze, trying her best to communicate the personal applications of her statement through mental telepathy.

"That's a very romantic notion: to think that everyone is redeemable—or worth redeeming," Lucas said. Apparently feeling near nudity was an affront to the memory of the dead, he had changed out of his Speedos into a pair of loose black lounging pants and a wood-block print shirt worn open à la Bryce. "Rates of recidivism in our prisons dispel your theory, Marilee."

"We're not talking about hardened criminals. We're talking about a good man who made some bad choices."

Ostensibly Townsend, though Bryce knew the conversation had passed beyond the judge. He couldn't call her on it without making another strong attack on Will Rafferty, and clearly Samantha was not ready to hear it. He sighed and tipped his head, conceding the point to Marilee, and reevaluating her status as a threat.

"You have a very naive view of humanity," Sharon said, raising a margarita to her lips. She sat between the two men, still in her bathing suit with a sheer black cover-up falling back off her angular shoulders, not covering much of anything.

"I prefer to think of it as optimistic," Mari countered with a brittle smile.

"Stupid," she pronounced bluntly. Her attention had shifted to Bryce, who was captivated by Samantha, who was staring down through the glass-topped table at her toenails. "Everyone is out for their own selfish interest. The smart ones climb over anyone they need to to get what they want. The ruthless ones wear cleats. The fools are trampled and left for dead. It's every man for himself."

Mari raised her brows. "Well, you'd know more about that than me," she said pleasantly. "I've led a very sheltered life," she added as Bryce's cousin began to redden around the gills.

"Stick around," Sharon said, rising. "You'll learn fast enough."

"Fun girl," Mari murmured, rolling her eyes as the statuesque blonde dropped her cover up on the tile apron and dove into the pool. Her long body sliced into the water like a knife. "I'll bet the film-noir crowd thinks she's a million laughs."

"Sharon learned the hard way that life can be exceedingly cruel," Bryce said. "She's had to develop a survivalist's perspective."

"Hmm." Mari pictured Bryce's cousin in eye black, a chic camouflage jump suit with an M-16 in her hands. It really didn't seem much of a stretch.

From the front side of the mansion came the sound of a truck engine with no muffler, a loud roaring that even managed to rouse Fabian from his concentrated sunbathing. Everyone looked toward the side gate expectantly.

"Delivery truck," Bryce grumbled, rising. "For what they charge to come out here, they should be able to afford gold-plated exhaust systems."

He let himself out the gate and came flying backward through it a moment later. The tall, weathered wood gate slapped against the stone wall with a resounding *crack,* and Bryce landed on his ass on the terrace. Everyone at the table came to attention as one, like a herd of wildebeest ready to bolt and run.

"Will!" Samantha shouted, vaulting to her feet.

Will came through the open gate, fists doubled before him, and went straight for Bryce. "You sonofabitch! Leave my wife alone, you goddamn sonofabitch!"

His words were slurred and he swayed a little on his feet, but he zeroed in on Bryce, who was scrambling to get up on the wet tile at the pool's edge. Will took a big roundhouse swing with his left, landing a glancing blow on Bryce's small knob of a chin. Bryce went down, spitting blood, and rolled out of range.

"Will, stop it!" Samantha cried, running at him. A part of her was mortified at his behavior, shocked at his appearance—he had stitches in his forehead and a black eye. Another part of her was elated that he cared enough to come here and make a scene. A million things flashed through her head: he loved her, he'd come to take her home, they would live happily ever after, Bryce would hate her, her opportunities for better things would vanish.

His brain down-shifting slowly and awkwardly, Will turned toward his wife. The young woman he saw was a stranger to him. Her hair hung loose in a shimmering curtain of black silk. She wore makeup and jewelry. The faded jeans and T-shirt had been traded for something chic and silk in a copper shade that enhanced her natural coloring. She looked like a model, like some snooty bitch from the pages of fucking *Vogue*. Not *his* Sam. Too good for him. Slipping out of his reach. Wanting more than he could give her. His *ex*-wife . . . *ex*-wife . . . *ex*-wife . . .

"What's the matter, Sam?" he asked, dredging up anger to mask the fear. "You don't want me busting your lover's face?"

"He's not my—"

"Save your breath. I know what he's after." He turned around in an unsteady circle, raising his arms to gesture to all visible trappings of Bryce's wealth, a bitter smirk twisting his lips. "Mr. Rich Sonofabitch. He gets you, he gets a chunk of the Stars and Bars and a nice young piece of ass all in one." He leaned into her face and gave her a blast of Jack Daniel's fumes. "Helluva deal, huh, Sam?"

Samantha felt as if he had physically knocked her off balance. She felt as if she were tipping backward, her whole world rolling off its axis, and she threw herself at Will to save herself and to strike out at him all in one move. Her fists slammed against his chest.

"You bastard! How dare you say that to me! After all you've done, after all the women!" She choked on the rage and the hurt. Tears brimmed up and spilled down her cheeks in a torrent, smearing her freshly applied mascara. "After all you've done to hurt me!"

"Hurt you?" Will managed a caustic laugh as he tried to rub the sting out of his cheek. "Yeah, you look like you're hurting, baby. Dressed up like a goddamn fifty-dollar whore, sitting around drinkin' champagne with all your famous friends—"

"That's enough, Rafferty," Bryce said, circling around to stand behind Samantha. Blood leaked from a cut inside his lower lip. He fingered a tooth and winced; the cap had come loose.

Will sneered at him. "What you gonna do, rich boy? Tell Sam here to kick my butt for you? You sure as hell can't do it. You just fuck people over with your money."

"Will—"

Mary Lee moved into his field of vision. She was frowning at him. He hadn't expected to see her here. He really didn't know what he had expected as he'd roared up the mountain in Tucker's old truck. The haze from the Jack Daniel's had obscured everything but impulse. Most of the day was a vague memory shimmering like a mirage in his brain: Sam gone when he'd stumbled into the house to see her, to try to tell her—what? That he loved her? That he was scared of loving her? Didn't matter, she wasn't there, wasn't at the Moose . . . Bryce, that bastard, giving her things, making her want things . . . Pure damn wonder he made it up the mountain . . . Should have crashed . . . wished he had crashed . . .

"Will—" Mari stepped closer and put a hand on his arm. He jerked away, snarling, feinting toward Bryce and laughing when Bryce dragged Samantha back two steps with him in retreat.

"You want my wife? Take my wife!" he shouted, desperation twisting inside him like a whirlpool. "Take my wife, *pul-leeeeeeze*! Hell, I never wanted one in the first place!"

Samantha gasped as if he'd reached out and cut her. Sobbing, she broke away from Bryce's hold and ran into the house. Bryce shook his head in disgust.

"You're pathetic, Rafferty."

Will held his hands up and pretended to be afraid. "Oooooh! You nailed me that time! Have mercy!"

Bryce glared at him. Beyond reckless, Will jumped at him, coming within inches of Bryce's nose with a jab.

"Come on, jerk," Will taunted, jabbing again. "Give me the satisfaction. Fight back, city boy. Let's see what you got besides money."

Mari watched him weave a little as he shuffled. He seemed to be having trouble focusing, as if he might be seeing multiple Bryces. She took another half step toward him and raised a hand. "Come on, Will. You've done enough damage."

Yeah, Willie-boy, you're the screwup. Fuck up again. It's what you do best. Anger and frustration and fear rushed through him like a fire, and he launched himself at Bryce with a wild cry.

Bryce caught him in the nose with a right cross. The bone gave way with a sharp *snap* and blood gushed down like water from a fire hose. Will staggered sideways, stunned and surprised. Bryce gave him no time to regain what faculties he had. With Samantha out of sight, he grabbed a chair from poolside and swung it like a baseball bat, catching his adversary in the ribs with one blow and in the side of the knee with a second.

At first contact with the chair Will doubled over as a pair of ribs cracked. The second strike forced his knee to buckle inward sharply and he felt something tear. He went down on the flagstone in a bloody, groaning heap. Bryce kicked him once in the belly for a final touch, the toe of his boot driving deep, driving up a good measure of whiskey and the indistinguishable remains of his lunch.

"Get off my property, Rafferty," Bryce said coldly. Then he turned and walked away.

Shaken by the violence of Bryce's attack, Mari dropped down on her knees beside Will and laid a shaking hand on his shoulder. "Can you get up?"

"Maybe." He looked up at her—all three of her—and tried to grin through the blood and the vomit. "But you got lousy timin', Mary Lee."

Mary Lee frowned at him. "Come on, hotshot. I'll give you a ride—to the hospital."

The housekeeper rushed out onto the terrace, followed

by a pair of ranch hands. Bryce nodded from the hands to Will.

"Get him out of here. Morton, drive that piece of junk he calls a truck into town. I don't want it cluttering up my driveway."

Mari's head came up sharply. *Morton.* She pushed herself to her feet and stepped back on wobbly legs. *Kendall Morton.* Pigpen grown up and gone bad. He wore a dirty plaid shirt with the tails hanging out and the sleeves cut off to reveal an array of tattoos on his sinewy arms. His round face twisted in an ugly grimace as he hauled Will, flashing teeth that were varying shades of yellow and brown.

Kendall Morton hadn't vanished at all. He was working for Evan Bryce. *Oh, Christ, what next?*

"You gonna give me a lecture, Mary Lee?" Will mumbled through the wad of blood-soaked tissues he held beneath his broken nose. He sat in the passenger seat, doubled over and listing heavily to the left in a vain attempt to relieve the pain in his ribs.

Mari pulled her gaze off the rearview mirror and shot him a look. "Why should I waste my breath? You're too drunk to listen. I doubt you'd listen anyway. You seem to have a handicap in the area of listening. Maybe you should have the doctor check the connection between your ears and your brain."

He started to chuckle weakly, but groaned instead as one of the Honda's wheels dipped into a pothole. Mari winced in sympathy and eased off the gas. But the sympathy took a backseat to her anger and to her fear. Those two fermented inside her like sour mash with a good dose of frustration compounding the process.

She was beginning to understand why J.D. was so hard on Will. Will's insistence on being a repeat offender in the drunk, disorderly, and stupid category was enough to make her want to shake him. And she had known him only a matter of days; J.D. had put up with a lifetime of Will's shit.

She'd had the nerve to preach to J.D. about compassion and tolerance. Maybe Will didn't deserve compassion. Maybe what he really needed was a kick in the butt. Maybe she should have been dragging him behind her car instead of letting him bleed all over the upholstery.

Her head began to pound as she chanced another glance in the mirror. Kendall Morton followed her in the truck Will had been driving. Another hand brought up the rear of their little motorcade in one of Bryce's ranch trucks.

What the hell was Morton doing working for Bryce? Or had he really been working for Bryce all along? Her brain buzzed with the possibilities.

In the emergency room Dr. Larimer looked from Will to Mari and back again with an expression of extreme displeasure. He apparently preferred to see a variety of patients instead of the same cracked noggins and busted faces day in and day out. When Mari asked if they got a discount for being frequent casualties, his only reply was a grunt.

"Bet he cracks 'em up in the doctor's lounge," Will said, trying to grin despite the novocaine Larimer had injected around his smashed nose.

The doctor had been called into the next examination room to deal with a more urgent case. Mari sat on a straight chair and looked up at Will, humor beyond her where Will was concerned. His eyes were clearer than they had been. He might have been close to sober; it was difficult to tell.

"You know, I can't begin to guess what you were thinking, coming up to Bryce's place that way—"

"Thinking? What's that?"

"—But it was so unbelievably stupid I can't even find words to describe it."

He scowled at her, his eyes tearing from the novocaine.

"Will," Mari said, pressing her hands on her knees and leaning toward him. "Bryce doesn't screw around. He plays for keeps. You piss him off, there's no telling what he might do. The guy's got more money than God, and I really don't think he was hanging around when they passed out consciences. He has the power to ruin the Stars and Bars."

"Yeah, well, that's J.D.'s problem now, not mine."

She ground her teeth and stood up. "I'd hate to guess which one of you has the hardest head," she grumbled, dragging a hand back through her hair. "Okay, forget Bryce. What about Samantha? Where the hell do you get off raking her over the coals?"

"It's none of your business, Mary Lee," he mumbled, staring down as he rubbed a bloodstain on his jeans with his thumb. "Just drop it. You don't know anything about me and Sam."

"I know that if I were your wife, my running around with another man would be the least of your worries, because I would have taken a club to you by now."

He raised his head an inch, petulance shining in his watering eyes and turning down the corners of his mouth. "Back off, Mary Lee. I got problems enough. I don't need you chewing my tail. I don't need it."

"No," she said, shaking her head. She hauled her purse up off the floor and looped the strap over her shoulder, then started for the door, fed up to the back teeth with Rafferty men. With one hand on the knob she turned back and gave him a hard look. "What you need is to grow up."

J.D. leaned ahead in the saddle a little as his horse surged to the top of the knoll at the blue rock. He reined the gelding in and sat for a moment with a hand braced against the pommel, listening, watching, waiting. Sarge turned his head from side to side in a lazy arc, ears flicking at the sounds of birds.

Del considered the blue rock the lower boundary of his territory. He maintained a diligent vigil over his space, patrolling the perimeter all hours of the day and night. He would have been ashamed of having J.D. know that. The thought weighed heavy in J.D.'s heart. Del didn't want to be a burden on the family. He saw himself as an embarrassment, less than a whole man because of the fractured state of his mind. He lived up here year-round in part to hide himself—the ugly skeleton in the family closet. He worked the summer cow camp to redeem himself.

What else might he do for redemption?

Memories of bits of conversations swirled and bobbed in J.D.'s belly like backed-up sewage. Del's crazy talk about his guns, the things he let slip about what he thought he saw up there at night, the way he had mistaken Mary Lee for Lucy. And he kicked himself mercilessly for the things he had said himself over the course of the last year. He had sounded off to Del about the outsiders pressing in on Rafferty land. He had vented his spleen about Lucy more than once. He had used his uncle as a sounding board, as if Del were too far gone to form his own opinions, never once thinking there might be a danger in it.

Christ, if Del had taken all that talk to heart, he might have seen killing Lucy as a noble cause. One act of violence could have pulled him off that narrow, crumbling ledge into the void.

J.D. didn't want it to be true. Even considering the possibility seemed a betrayal. But he couldn't keep the questions from forming or the possible answers from taking shape. Nor could he simply insulate the Stars and Bars from the outside world, as badly as he wanted to. There was no escaping society or its ambitions. They would have to fight and adapt to survive. He was responsible for the ranch and everyone on it, for their well-being and for their actions.

Responsible.

Will's battered, angry face came to mind and threatened to pull him down another rough road, but the sharp *crack* of a rifle farther up the mountain shattered the image. Heart sinking lower, J.D. nudged his horse back into motion and continued on up the trail.

There was no sign of Del at the camp. No dogs ran out to greet him. The buckskin mare was gone out of the string in the corral. J.D. tied his horse to a rail and loosened his cinch, his gaze scanning the area the whole time for signs that Del had gone off the deep end. There were none. The place was immaculate as always. The snake curled in its cage nailed to the side of the cabin. That was hardly normal, but it was vintage Del, not out of what was ordinary for him. One of the first things his uncle had done when he moved up here was nail that cage to the cabin and stick a rattler in it.

Some unworthy part of his brain urged J.D. to go into the cabin and look around, but he flatly refused. Del's cabin was sacrosanct; no one went in without his invitation. J.D. had always respected his uncle's privacy. He wouldn't step over that line now.

He sat himself down on a bench in the shade alongside the equipment shed to wait. If Will hadn't gone, they would have been moving the herd that day. There wouldn't have been time or energy to ponder questions of accountability and loyalty. But Will had gone. *You gave him the boot, J.D. Your own brother.* And now he sat waiting to question his uncle about the possibility of his involvement in two deaths. What kind of loyalty was that? Which of his obligations held the upper hand—to do what was legally right? morally right? right in his own mind? If he pledged allegiance to the family, then how could he turn his back on Will or his suspicions on Del? If the land came first, then was he really no better than Bryce?

He dropped his head in his hands and blew a breath out, wishing he could just snap his fingers and make it all disappear. A wish from his childhood, from the days when Tom had first taken up with Sondra, and the days when he had been blamed for Will's mistakes or punished for some minor crime against the brother he had never wanted.

Damn foolish waste of time, wishing for things. Time, like most other factors, was not on his side. A man had to play the hand life dealt him. That was that. No whining, no slacking, no wishing for better cards.

From somewhere down the dark corridor of wooded

trail that led to the north, a hound sent up an excited howl. Then Del's black-and-tan coon dog came bounding into the yard, long ears fluttering behind him like banners. J.D. stayed where he was, looking idly down the trail. Seconds later Del burst from the thick growth east of the path. His buckskin horse exploded out of the woods like a demon erupting from another dimension, her ears pinned flat, nostrils flaring bright pink in her dark muzzle. They came into the yard at a gallop, Del standing in the stirrups, a rifle butt pressed back into his shoulder and J.D. in his sights.

"Jesus, Del!" J.D. shouted, vaulting up off the bench.

Recognition struck an awful spark behind Del's eyes, beneath the metal plate that was heavy on his brain and charged with an evil current of electricity. He dropped the rifle out of position and reined the mare hard left. God damn, he'd nearly shot J.D.! He had nearly let the monsters inside him push him into pulling the trigger.

His legs were as rubbery as sapling trees as he stepped down off his horse. He gripped his rifle by the fore end of the stock to keep his hand from shaking.

"What the hell—" J.D. bit back the worst of what he wanted to say. *Are you crazy? Have you lost your mind?* He could see the shame in his uncle's downcast eyes as he turned away to tie his horse to the corral railing.

His heart was running at a hard clip. The adrenaline that had burst through him ebbed now and his body shuddered as it receded. "You got the drop on me, pard. Guess I should have radioed ahead I was coming."

Del didn't comment. He flipped a rein around one of the rails. The mare had her head up and was still dancing a little from the excitement. The rest of the string abandoned J.D.'s sorrel and trotted over to their companion with their tails raised and eyes bright. Del focused on the Ruger 77, ejecting the brass-cased loads into his hand like peas from a pod.

"I heard a shot when I was down at the blue rock. That you?"

"Could be."

"What'd you get?"

"Nothin.' "

J.D. narrowed his eyes. "Not like you to waste a shot, Del."

Del turned away from him and slid the rifle into the scabbard on his saddle. "Too far out," he mumbled. "Didn't have a clear line."

"What was it?"

Del swallowed hard and rubbed his scar with his fingertips. He couldn't say he'd thought he'd seen a tiger. Tigers didn't come out in the daylight. He shook his head and winced at the ache of his brain sloshing against the sides of his skull. No, dammit, J.D. didn't know about the tigers. He couldn't talk about the tigers—same way he couldn't talk about the blondes dancing in the moonlight.

"Del?"

"Cat," he said. "Don't want cougars around with the cattle coming up."

"Mmm. Well, we'll be a little late bringing the herd," J.D. said, falling into step beside his uncle. Del's three dogs stood, hopeful of an invitation, in front of the cabin door. Their master growled at them and swung a hand, sending the trio scrambling away with their tails between their legs. "A week, maybe."

Del didn't ask why. He was glad though. He didn't want the cattle up here now. He wanted the blondes gone first. The women and their familiars. He wished he could decide what to do about them. He wished he had the courage to do *something*, the sense to know what was right.

The rattlesnake raised its head and hissed at them. Del didn't spare it a glance. He went into the cabin, to a shelf in the kitchen, and pulled out two cans of Dr Pepper. J.D. eased down on one of the chairs at the table and sipped on his while Del paced the room like a caged animal, rubbing his scar. The cabin was neat as a pin, as clean as every single rifle on the gun racks. The smell of Shooter's Choice bore solvent served as an air freshener.

"You didn't happen to be down on the Little Snake

over by the Boxed Circle yesterday, did you?" J.D. asked casually.

Del jumped as if he'd been hit with a switch. "No . . . no . . ." he mumbled, his eyes on his rifles at the end of the room. "No." He stopped suddenly and stared hard at J.D., the gray of his eyes seeming to glow like polished pewter in the filtered light that came through muslin at the windows. "You didn't bring that blond woman, did you?"

J.D. bit back a sigh. "No."

"I don't want her here. She's trouble." He shook a finger at his nephew. "You mind my words, J.D."

J.D. wasn't sure whether Del meant Lucy or Mary Lee. He wasn't sure Del knew the difference. He told himself he should have listened sooner in either case. "Never mind about her, Del. You leave her be, you hear? I can handle her. There's no need for you to concern yourself."

"Don't you trust her," Del growled. "I don't trust none of them blondes. They're all trouble."

"Well, that's a fact," J.D. mumbled to himself. He took another sip of Dr Pepper and braced himself for the rest of the conversation. "I found Miller Daggrepont dead in the Little Snake yesterday. Guess he had a heart attack. Thought you might have seen him out there fishing."

He sipped on the warm Dr Pepper absently, his gaze trained on his uncle's face, looking for any sign of recognition . . . or guilt. His own guilt ate away at him, bubbling in with the warm pop to gnaw at his stomach lining.

"Did you see anything, Del?"

I saw a tiger on the mountain. I saw the corpses dance in the moonlight. Crazy things. Del felt his throat trying to close up, like one of the ghosts had hold of his windpipe. He tried to gulp a swig of Dr Pepper. Half of it ran out the dead side of his mouth and spilled onto his shirt.

"I—I saw a cat, that's all," he mumbled, wiping the stain with his handkerchief. "Don't want cats up here with the cattle coming."

He thought he might have already said that, but he

couldn't be sure. Beneath the plate his brain was buzzing like a swarm of mosquitoes. He couldn't remember the last time he'd slept more than two hours. He couldn't remember sleeping without the dark dreams. It was important for him to stay awake now, he told himself. He had to help guard the ranch. He had to make sure the blondes didn't steal it, or the city idiots, or the men who ruled the dog-boys.

J.D. drew a long breath in through his teeth. "Del, I have to ask you if you saw anything back when that woman was shot." He searched painfully for the most diplomatic words he could find. Del had his problems, but he had his pride too. "Is there anything about that deal you might want to tell me?"

Del stared hard at his guns, his broken mouth opening and closing like a fish's. His eyes gleamed with unshed tears and the dark light of a thousand nightmares. J.D. felt as if something inside his chest were being crushed. Loyalties and obligations pressed against one another and pushed and pushed. The pressure weighed on him like lead as he stood and crossed the room.

"Del? Do you have something to say about that?"

"No," he murmured, staring at the rifles and shotguns with their oiled barrels and polished stocks. "You don't want cats on the mountain when the cattle come up."

J.D. rubbed his eyes. He knew he should have pressed. He knew he should have asked Del outright if he'd had anything to do with Lucy's death. But, God help him, he couldn't bring himself to do it. He got burned either way. Quinn took his word that Del hadn't done more than find the body. If he lied to the sheriff, his integrity suffered. If he turned Del over, he didn't think he'd ever be able to live with himself.

And if your uncle is a killer?

No win. The answer slipped through the loop. Hang up your rope and call it a day, cowboy. Catch one tomorrow.

"Where'd you see that cat?" he asked softly. "Maybe I'll have a look-see on my way home."

CHAPTER 24

*H*umiliated and hurt, Samantha spent the remainder of the day in the guest room Bryce had allocated her. He checked on her within moments of the scene on the terrace, but she refused to let him in the room. He talked to her through the bedroom door, telling her everything would be all right, that she shouldn't shut him out. But she kept her face buried in the pillow and eventually he went away.

She cried until she thought she would be sick from it, then, exhausted, she fell into a deep, dreamless sleep. When she woke up, the sun had slipped behind the mountains and the room was dim with shadows.

Disoriented and groggy, she sat up and looked at her surroundings. For a moment she thought she was dreaming, that she had only to shake herself and she would be on her own lumpy mattress in the little house she shared with Will.

Will.

She closed her eyes as it all came rushing back. Every bit of it. Her crumbling marriage. Will stumbling drunk on Bryce's terrace. The way he had punched Bryce. The ugly things he'd said to her and about her.

Take my wife . . . Hell, I never wanted one in the first place!

Samantha's eyes burned and her throat closed, but no tears came. She had cried them all. More miserable than she'd ever been in her life, she leaned back against the headboard of the elegant bed and looked down at herself. The elegant copper silk outfit she had put on before

Will's arrival was a roadmap of wrinkles and creases. It looked terrible and she felt that somehow the fabric had undergone some kind of chemical reaction from contact with her skin, as if something so fine had been designed to sort the worthy from the worthless.

Poor, stupid kid. Thought you could pretend different, didn't you? Stupid dreamer. Grow up, Samantha. Grow up and see what you really are.

Trembling at the self-castigation, she got up from the bed and went to look at herself in the huge beveled mirror above the bleached pine bureau. The reflection wasn't pretty. Not even the dim lighting could hide the effects of her earlier crying jag. The makeup she had applied so carefully had run and streaked on her puffy face. Her hair hung limp and disheveled. She'd lost an earring somewhere, and then there was the outfit.

She looked pathetic. She felt pathetic.

No wonder Will didn't want her. She wasn't worth wanting. She was naive and foolish. Bryce's friends were probably downstairs laughing at her. Poor little dimwitted tomboy barmaid, pretending she could fit in with the rich and beautiful people.

Her breath coming in broken, disjointed spasms, she turned away from the mirror. She felt hollow inside, aching and hollow, as if everything in her had been yanked out and discarded. Her shoulders pulled forward and she curled in on herself as she moved, walking like an old woman. She felt as ugly and freakish as a giant praying mantis, and as fragile; as if someone could grab her and snap her in two, just crunch up her long bones and toss them aside.

She moved to stand by the window that looked down on the pool and pressed her forehead against the glass. The underwater lights had been turned on, but there was no sign of any of Bryce's guests. She wondered if they were gathered downstairs, wondered if she could somehow slip past them and leave the house without being seen.

She didn't belong here. She didn't feel as if she belonged anywhere, but she *knew* she didn't belong here.

Bryce wouldn't want her here anyway, not after what Will had done. And she couldn't bear the thought of facing the rest of them—Ben Lucas and Uma Kimball and Sharon. Especially Sharon. Just the thought of Sharon's possible comments regarding the afternoon were enough to make her feel ill.

No. Cinderella's time at the ball was up.

Dry sobs croaked in her throat as she took off the clothes Bryce had bought for her and hung them in the wardrobe. She removed the remaining earring and the necklace and bracelets, then went into the bathroom and scrubbed off the makeup and the lingering traces of perfume. She plaited her hair in its serviceable braid and secured the end with a rubber band from her purse. She pulled on her old jeans, but stopped short of putting on the white oxford shirt.

It belonged to Will. She rubbed the soft, worn collar between her fingertips, bunched the fabric in her hands, and brought it up to her face. She imagined she could still smell his scent on it, could still feel the warmth of his body in the fibers. But she knew she couldn't. Will was gone from her life. The shirt may have belonged to him, but *she* didn't belong to him anymore. He didn't want her. Had never wanted her.

Her heart breaking, she folded the shirt and put it in a dresser drawer, trading it for a white silk T-shirt—the plainest thing she could take.

She straightened the bed covers and tidied the bath, wanting to leave as few traces of her existence as possible. She would just slip out of the house and out of the lives of the people in the house and go back to what was left of her own life. A shabby house and a rusty car and a puppy.

She would have to borrow a car. Or maybe she could hitch a ride with one of the hands—

"Samantha?" Bryce's voice sounded outside the door to the sitting area of the suite.

She froze in her tracks on her way to the door, her heart bumping up against the base of her throat. She didn't want to see him, didn't think she could face him. Maybe if she didn't answer him again—

"Samantha, I know you're awake. I heard you moving around. Open the door, sweetheart. I've brought you some dinner. We'll talk."

"I—I don't know what to say," she mumbled.

"You don't have to say anything," he said gently. "You can just eat and I'll talk for both of us. How's that?"

Too kind, she thought, biting her lip.

"Samantha?"

"All right."

Dreading the moment, she opened the door. Bryce stood with a tray in his hands. He looked elegant and exotic, "western chic" she'd heard it called, in a faded denim shirt and jeans, his hair swept back off his high forehead. The only visible signs of his fight with Will were a bruise and cut on his chin and raw spots on the knuckles of his right hand. His lower lip was split and puffy. He took in her attire in one long, speculative look and hummed a little.

"I thought I would just go," she admitted, turning the lamp on the dresser to low. Just enough light so Bryce could see what he was doing, not enough to spotlight her raw eyes and puffy face.

He set the tray down on the small round table near the window and busied his hands, uncovering the plate and pouring two glasses from a bottle of chardonnay. He had anticipated this reaction. The humiliation would be far too heavy for Samantha's fragile ego to bear. Rafferty would have to pay for this. Long and painfully. The bastard didn't deserve anything better. He had held a perfect wild rose in his grasp and crushed her with his carelessness. He didn't deserve mercy; he deserved to be ruined.

"Why do you think you should do that, honey?" he asked gently.

Samantha stared at him with a weird feeling of having just awakened from a dream. His tone of voice was calm and unaffected, as if nothing at all had happened. "Well . . . with what happened this afternoon and all . . . I just thought . . ."

He turned to her and gave her his warmest, most understanding smile. Fatherly, he thought. Kind. "That wasn't your fault."

"Will is my husband—"

"Will is a fool. He didn't have any right to come here. He didn't have any right to say those things to you."

Samantha swallowed the knot of guilt in her throat. "I'm his wife."

"He doesn't deserve you." He tilted his head as he came toward her, reading the emotions in her clear, dark eyes as easily as he would a grade-school primer. Gently he tugged her fingers out of the pockets of her jeans and curled his bony hands around them. "He doesn't own you."

He doesn't want you.

That truth ached like a laceration in her heart. It rang in her ears. She couldn't be a wife to a man who refused to be a husband. She wasn't a wife. She didn't have anyone. She didn't have anything.

A fresh wave of tears filled her eyes, and her mouth began to tremble.

Bryce smiled to himself as he drew her against him and wrapped his arms around her. "He doesn't deserve your tears, Samantha. He had a diamond and he threw it away. That's his loss, not yours."

She pressed her face down on his shoulder and sobbed as if the world were going to end. He supposed her world was ending, shattering like a cheap Christmas ornament. Like an egg breaking to allow her to emerge into a newer, larger, better world. His world. He liked the analogy. She was a beautiful baby bird in the lush paradise that was his world. And he would guide her and flaunt her. She would be more, have more, than she had ever dreamed. And she would be his.

"I—I'm s-sorry," Samantha stammered, trying to draw back from him. She had been raised not to cry in front of people. This was just another humiliation—crying on Evan Bryce for the second time in the scant few days she'd known him. "I n-never d-do this," she said by way of apology. "I—I n-never cry on p-people."

Bryce let her move back just enough so he could reach up between them and brush the tears from her cheek with the pad of his thumb. The gentle smile curved his wide mouth again and he held her eyes with his. "I'm honored, then," he murmured. "You feel comfortable with me. You trust me. That means a lot to me—to be your friend. I want only the best for you, Samantha."

She looked into his bright eyes, eyes shining with kind lights, and felt something like desperation claw inside her. She was nothing, she had nothing. He wanted the best for her. He liked her. He thought of her as his friend.

"I need a friend," she whispered.

"I'm here." He drew her slowly into his arms again and held her close, stroking a hand over her hair. His other hand rubbed up and down her back in a hypnotic rhythm. "I'm here," he whispered, his lips brushing her ear. "I'll be anything you need."

She slipped her arms around him and he rocked her in a lazy, languid slow dance, pressing her closer still. Outside, the world had faded away to black. Time took on a dreamlike quality, surreal and dim. Samantha let herself float on it. She anchored herself to her only friend and let her mind drift in the mist.

She didn't have anyone, anything in the world, except this kind man who held her.

His lips pressed against her temple, grazed her ear.

I'll be anything you need, Samantha. . . .

I'll give you anything. . . .

I love you. . . .

She soaked in the whispered words like a dry sponge. She wondered if he'd even said them or if she had only wanted so badly to hear them from someone, anyone at all. She might have been dreaming. She'd thought so before.

"I love you," he whispered, and kissed her cheek and the corner of her mouth. His erection poked against her belly, and she felt her body quicken and twitch in response.

"We can't," she whispered, but she made no move to pull away. Drifting, drifting still on the fog, in the dream.

"Yes," he murmured. "I love you, Samantha. Let me show you what that's like."

"But I—"

"Shhh . . . Let me love the pain away."

She thought she should stop him, but his hands were inside her blouse and tracing mesmerizing patterns on her back and sides, and it felt so good. Then he was cupping her breast and the air in her lungs thinned.

It had been so long. She had been so lonely.

This is just a dream. . . .

He lowered her to the bed and followed her down. The spread was cool against her bare skin. He had loosened her hair and it spilled like silk around her. His mouth fastened on her nipple and need tore through her. The need to be loved, to be touched.

His fingers slid into the tangle of dark curls between her legs and she opened to him, melted in his hand like warm honey. He was kind and gentle. He wanted her. Will didn't. She looked up into his strange light eyes as he poised over her.

"Do you really love me?" she murmured.

Bryce held himself motionless. Energy pulsed down through his body. He felt supercharged, electrified, on the brink of a new greatness. New power.

"Yes," he answered, knowing it was as true as it ever had been in his life. Then he plunged himself into pure, sweet bliss.

"You fucked her, didn't you?" Sharon spat out the accusation, deliberately choosing the harshest, ugliest word she could to describe what she knew had happened.

Bryce didn't dignify her charge with a response. He stood before the big windows in the elegant living room, looking out at the night. In fact, he was barely paying attention to his cousin. He felt huge, as if power had enlarged his entire body in order to contain the humming energy that coursed through him. His brain was racing with ideas and plans. In the all-important center of his thoughts, Sharon had already been dismissed.

She didn't take to the idea with grace. She moved across the dark room like a stalking tigress. She wore her hair slicked straight back from her face, secured in a chignon, a style that only emphasized the harshness of her features. In the tarnished light from the display cases, her eyes glowed with anger.

"She's so sweet," Bryce murmured to the world at large, marveling in the concept of sweetness. "I can't believe how sweet she was, how needy."

His wonder struck Sharon like a hail of jagged gravel, pelting her ego, biting into her heart. She couldn't be sweet. She had never held any sweetness inside her. Need she knew too well. What she needed now was to distract Bryce from his preoccupation. If he became too fixated on the girl, he would shut her out altogether. The idea terrified her, but she would never show him that fear. Never.

"We're all needy," she breathed, brushing up against him.

She let him feel her full breasts through the sheer fabric of the black lounging pajamas she wore. Rubbing against him like a cat, she started to cup him through his jeans. He turned and moved away from her without a hint of interest.

Panic balled like a fist in the back of Sharon's throat, and she had to fight to keep it out of her voice. "If she was so wonderful, what are you doing down here?"

Bryce paused by the sideboard, considered the idea of a small drink, then discarded it. He didn't want anything interfering with the high. He didn't want anything slowing his thought processes. He envisioned himself as a diamond—brilliant, hard, powerful.

"She's fragile," he said. "She'll need finessing. She'll probably have second thoughts. If I smother her with possession, she'll bolt." He rubbed his chin for a moment, staring off into the middle distance, his face aglow with his pleasure in his own brilliance. "Finesse." He smiled the Redford smile. "That's the ticket."

"How about finessing me?" Sharon said, forcing a smile as she closed in on him again. A subtle tremor of desperation thrummed in her low voice. She hoped he didn't notice it. Something like a spring coiled tighter and tighter in her chest.

"Not tonight," Bryce said impatiently.

He walked away from her for a second time. Without looking at her. Without touching her or promising tomorrow. The spring wound tighter.

"Not tonight," she snapped, her voice low and vibrating with anger. She stalked around a white leather sofa and cut off his path to the window. "You have to save yourself for your precious virgin princess. Is that it?"

Bryce gave her a flat, hooded look. "Spare me the jealous-woman act. You stood right here and told me to sleep with her."

"For *us*," she clarified. "Not for *you*. For us, for the plan, to get what *we* want, not so you can wander around in a fog, dazzled by innocence."

He huffed out a breath. "Take a Valium and go to bed. You're getting on my nerves."

"How dare you dismiss me like some bothersome servant."

"That's exactly how you're behaving."

"You bastard!" she spat out, her voice a feral, animal sound low in her throat as the anger burned away her control. "After all I've been to you! After all I've *done* for you!"

When he tried to turn away again, she grabbed his arm and dug her fingernails in to hold him while she tore her top open with her other hand, baring her breasts. "Look at me!" she snarled. "Look at me, damn you!"

He looked. Without desire. Without emotion. He stared at her, repulsed by what he saw—desperation, degradation, dissipation; a jaded, aging harlot whose depravity knew few bounds. Never once did it occur to him that he was looking in a mirror. He was above and beyond. Bound for new glory. Reborn in the eyes of an innocent.

He brought his eyes to his cousin's and said without inflection, "You're losing control."

Sharon fell back, clutching the ruined front of her top

together. Ashamed, beaten, stunned at what he had reduced her to. Numb with the shock of it.

"I'm not the one who's losing control," she whispered. "Look at yourself. Your brain is infected with this girl. She's all you think about. A week ago you wouldn't have given her a second glance."

"That was a week ago. Now I know her. Now I see the possibilities. That's one of your many faults, Sharon, you lack foresight."

"No. I can see perfectly," she said bitterly. "You're obsessed with her. The way you were obsessed with Lucy—"

He shook his head and grinned that damned Redford grin, having the gall to be amused at her. "No. You're so wrong. It's not that at all."

She stared at him, forcing herself to read the expression in his eyes, the strange euphoria. "You think you've fallen in love with her, don't you?" she whispered, barely able to stand the sound of the words. She could feel her world crumbling around her. Her mind raced for some way to stop the damage. She had leverage. Bryce couldn't drop her altogether; she had enough on him to make her an invaluable ally or a formidable enemy. She could destroy him if she had to.

But she couldn't make him love her. She hadn't thought him capable of romantic love. He was a man capable of many things, but love was not among them.

He didn't turn back as he walked to the doorway and killed the lights in the display cases. "I don't think, I know I love her."

"She'll leave you, you know," she said, struggling for calm, clinging to some small scrap of pride and cynicism. "She'll find out what you really are and she'll hate you, and she'll leave you."

"No," he murmured, feeling omnipotent. "I won't allow that."

The dream was of death. Filled with a cast of people who were either in fact dead or metaphorically dead to her.

Lucy with a clean round hole through her body. Townsend with no skull above his eyebrows. Miller Daggrepont wearing a jaunty purple ascot around his fat throat. Del Rafferty with the lower part of his face gone. Then there was Brad Enright, a stick-on label on the pocket of his Egyptian cotton shirt that read HELLO, MY NAME IS: ASSHOLE. And Will wearing a goofy cap that had been outfitted to hold a beer can on either side of his head. Clear plastic straws looped down in a circuitous route to his mouth.

The guests milled around at a cocktail party held in Del Rafferty's cabin. Her family stood off to the side, near the guns, refusing to mingle. Kendall Morton leered at them from the corner, where he stood in a cloud of self-generated dust.

Mari walked in wearing a cowboy hat, boots, and a vest and nothing else, and realized immediately that she was severely underdressed. Her mother and sisters shook their heads.

"Marilee, you're just not one of us," her mother said.

"She's sure as hell not one of us," Will said.

They circled around her and started moving in closer and closer, their faces grim with disapproval. Except Lucy's. Lucy was smiling her wry half-smile. J.D. stood beside her.

"Here, peach," she said, holding out the Mr. Peanut tin. "Something to take with you on your trip."

"What trip?"

"The trip to find yourself."

Then the floor opened up and she was falling straight down into a black hole, staring up at the ring of faces and half faces.

Lucy waved. "Be sure to send a postcard!"

She jerked awake and her heart sprinted into high gear as she tried without success to get her bearings. Darkness. Cool, damp. She was sitting up . . . on the deck outside Lucy's house.

Drawing in a deep breath of night air, she pressed a hand over her breastbone and assured herself that she was real and alive. Her eyes adjusted to the lack of light, and familiar shapes came into focus—the rail of the deck, the towering pine trees, indistinct outlines of the llamas in the pasture near the creek.

She had come out from town to feed them, had meant to sit in the Adirondack chair on the deck only a moment or two as the sun set. She had certainly never meant to fall asleep. Now the sense of being alone in the wilderness seeped into her like cold dew.

Three people had died violently in this dark paradise. Each of those deaths had touched her in some way. She could feel them touching her now, like bony fingers reaching up from the afterlife, clawing at her, pulling at her, trying to draw her deeper into the evil.

And she was going with them. Willingly. Not exactly the kind of trip she'd had in mind when she piled her business suits in the back of her Honda and left Sacramento a lifetime ago.

She had come here for fun. She wasn't having any. She had come here to find herself and was instead trying to find a killer. She had come here for companionship. She was alone.

Somewhere down the valley, coyotes began to sing. In contrast to their high, thin voices, the air on the deck seemed to thicken with an electricity that raised the hair on the backs of Mari's arms. She was alone, but suddenly she didn't feel alone. She felt the intensity of a gaze on her, eyes that could have been anywhere in the darkness.

Kendall Morton's round, ugly face floated through her imagination. She had called a friend who worked the night shift in the California Highway Patrol computer room and called in six years' worth of markers for favors. Could he contact the Montana computer banks— providing Montana had computer banks—and get a rap sheet on Kendall Morton? He had sighed heavily, made noises about losing his job, then promised to have something for her by morning.

Kendall drifted away and a vision of Del Rafferty took his place. An apparition. A ghost. Another of the walking dead from her dream. One of the suspects. She wanted to pity him, but she couldn't discount him. He had been a paid killer in the service, and the war had never ended for him. Or maybe he had traded one war for another; service to his country for service to the Rafferty land.

She didn't want to find out the hard way.

She eased herself forward in the chair, trying to breathe slowly, straining to hear above the drumbeat of her pulse in her ears.

"You sleep like a city girl."

J.D. eased out of the shadows at the corner of the house, hands in the pockets of his jeans, big shoulders hunched. Mari glared at him over her shoulder as she rose from the chair.

"What are you doing here?"

"Some big mountain lion could have had you for supper."

"Not likely," she retorted, calling up her guide-book facts. "There's never been a report of a mountain lion attacking anyone in this area."

He raised a brow. "Maybe the poor son of bitch wasn't around afterward to tell the tale."

Refusing to play games, Mari ignored his line of questioning and stuck with her own. "I asked you what you were doing here, Rafferty. You weren't invited."

"I saw a light in the upstairs window," he said, leaning back casually against the railing. He didn't feel casual. He felt like a clenched fist. He felt pressure from all sides compressing him into something hard and dangerous. And she looked soft and sleep-rumpled. If he pulled her against him now, he imagined her body would be warm, her nose cold, and her hair would smell like dew and pine. But her eyes were wary beneath the slash of dark brows, and he knew she wouldn't willingly come to him now. He had seen to that. He had pushed her away. Because it was for the best. Because he didn't want the distraction or the danger of a woman in his life.

Never been a liar, J.D.?

"You've been relieved of your duties as caretaker," Mari said. "You're not responsible for this place."

His concern hadn't been for the place, but he wouldn't admit that. It wasn't the time. The time had passed.

"Habit," he said.

"Break it."

"Del says he saw a big cat up along Five-Mile Creek," he said, looking off to the south, as if he half expected to see something prowling among the dark stand of trees.

"Yeah, I'll bet Del sees a lot of things," Mari said, more sharply than she had intended. She would have skinned snakes with her teeth for a cigarette. Her fingers flexed and clenched, nervous for something to do.

"Don't, Mary Lee," J.D. warned, his voice tight and weary. "This day's been too damn long already. I don't want to talk about Del." *Or think about Del, or deal with Del, or believe what Del might have become while living under the protective banner of the Stars and Bars.*

"Tell me about it. I started out the morning by finding a dead body. That just set the tone right off, you know what I mean?"

J.D. pushed himself away from the railing and stared at her. "You what!"

She gave a look that said she had been the butt of a tasteless practical joke. "Found a dead body. Yesterday was your lucky day; today was mine."

His gaze had the intensity of lasers. The tension that suddenly held his whole body rigid hummed in the air around him. "Who?"

"MacDonald Townsend. Esteemed judge. Philanderer. Cokehead. *That* MacDonald Townsend. You'll like this; it's very macho: he blew the top of his head off with a .357 Colt Python."

"Judas," he said, the word blowing out of him on an exhaled breath. He narrowed his eyes and focused hard on Mary Lee's face. She looked as pale as cream in the dark. "Are you all right?"

She jammed her hands in the pockets of her denim jacket and tipped her chin up, as if he had affronted her pride. "I don't think I'll eat grits again anytime soon."

"Judas," he muttered again.

He had to give her credit for not falling apart just in retelling the tale. He thought most women would have. But then, as Mary Lee liked to remind him, she was not most women. She was seldom what he expected her to be —or wanted her to be, for that matter. He would rather she sobbed and threw a fit of histrionics. He would have been less inclined to pull her into his arms and hold her. But she just stood there beside him with her chin up, daring him. Tough little cookie.

He raised a hand and cupped her face, the tips of his fingers brushing the baby-fine hair at her temple. Her cheek was soft and white against his work-roughened skin. Her lips parted slightly as she stared at him. An invitation. He wanted to accept. It didn't matter that it was foolish. It didn't matter that he had been the one to push her away. His heart beat harder now in anticipation. The need to protect, to shelter, to comfort ached through him. And then there was the need to shut out the madness of the world around them. He wanted to pull her into his arms and transport them both to some new Eden, an untouched paradise where there was only the two of them and endless time and no intrusions, no obligations, no battle lines, no bodies.

Slowly he lowered his mouth to hers and touched her lips with his. Mari shuddered at the contact, at the need. God, the need terrified her. She could have melted into him, lost herself forever in his embrace, in his kiss. But *forever* wasn't a word that applied to her and Rafferty. She couldn't afford to lose herself. Her breath hitched in her throat as she forced herself to turn her head and she closed her eyes tight against the pressure of tears as the moment slipped away.

"Where did you find him?" J.D. asked in a thick voice, stepping back as she stepped away.

Mari cleared her throat and tucked her hair behind one ear, staring hard at the boards of the deck. "In his study. I went to talk to him about Lucy. I thought he might know something. They were involved, you know. I think Lucy might have been blackmailing him."

She cut a glance at J.D. for his reaction. He didn't so much as blink at the suggestion. As if he expected as much from Lucy or thought that blackmail was perhaps a common hobby among the kind of people Lucy had associated with.

"Townsend," he said, his brows drawing together in concentration, a deep line of concern digging into his forehead. "He a friend of Bryce's?"

"Was. Past tense. Why?"

J.D. didn't answer. He just stood there, stroking his thumb back and forth across his lower lip as his mind worked. He had ridden back up along Five-Mile Creek after leaving Del, as much to clear his head as to look for signs of Del's phantom cougar. The creek ran through a narrow strip of Forest Service land that acted as a buffer of sorts between Rafferty land and Bryce's land. Heavily wooded, it had seemed like twilight in the middle of the day—a sensation that might have been peaceful if it hadn't been oddly disturbing.

He hadn't expected to find much of anything worth looking at. Some tracks maybe, nothing more. The area was isolated, with no easy access. Not the sort of place the tourists and hikers sought out. The Absaroka—Beartooth wilderness offered miles of trails for them, although he had seen backpackers and signs of backpackers on Rafferty land more and more as the legitimate park areas became more crowded. What he found on Five-Mile Creek he couldn't attribute to weekend foot traffic.

Signs of horses—a number of horses—and dogs. The carcass of what had been a big, strong hunting dog a week or so ago lay half in the creek, its body torn and rotting, fouling the water. He pulled it out and left it on the bank for nature to dispose of. The state of decay made it difficult to determine how the dog had met his end. He thought of Del's claim of a big cat, and wondered. A cougar would turn and fight if it had to.

Horses, dogs, cigarette butts, and shell casings on the ground. Signs of a hunt. But there was nothing in season. Cougars were protected, at any rate—not that some didn't meet untimely ends every year. There were guides who would promise big cats to hunters for a price.

Poaching was one of the most common—and most profitable—crimes in the state of Montana.

Horses, dogs, signs of a hunt. And just north of Five-Mile Creek lay Evan Bryce's private paradise. Bryce the sportsman. Bryce the high roller. Bryce, who was a friend of the dead judge who was the lover of the dead Lucy, who was the client of the dead lawyer, Daggrepont.

"I broke the news to Bryce myself," Mari said. "He was devastated." She rolled her eyes and made a face. *"Not."*

J.D. looked at her sharply. "What'd he do?"

"He made the appropriate noises, but his heart wasn't in it. Actually, I think he couldn't have cared less. I didn't see any genuine emotion out of him until Will crashed the party. Talk about uncomfortable moments. I don't think Emily Post ever covered what to do when a drunken cowboy assaults the host and accuses him of playing the ol' bump and grind with his wife."

"Oh, Jesus," J.D. swore, driving a hand back over his forehead and through his short dark hair. He cocked a leg and huffed out a sigh as he tried in vain to massage the knots from his neck. "What happened?"

"Will took a couple swings at Bryce, said some mean things to Samantha. Samantha ran into the house in tears, then Bryce broke a chair on Will's ribs. He's got an ugly temper. I wouldn't want to get on the wrong side of it."

"I'd rather you didn't get on any side of him."

"Yeah, like you have anything to say about it."

She started to turn from him, as if she meant to walk away. J.D. snagged her by the arm and took a subtly aggressive step toward her. "I mean it, Mary Lee. I don't like the feel of any of this."

"And I don't like you telling me what to do," she said, scowling at him. She felt as if she hadn't slept in days and the insulation on her temper was being stripped away layer by layer, exposing a tangle of raw nerve endings, which Rafferty poked at every time he came around. "You're not a player here, cowboy, as far as I can see. You made that very clear last night. And before that, and before that. All you ever wanted from Lucy or me was sex and this land. You're not getting either now, so that puts your nose out of joint. Tough.

"You don't want me nosing around Lucy's death. You don't want me checking out your loony uncle. You don't want me hanging around Bryce. Well, guess what, Rafferty? I don't care what you don't want. You don't want me on mutually acceptable terms, so get the hell out of my life."

She pulled her arm free of his grasp and started toward the house, feeling old and battle-scarred. Fleetingly she wondered what the folks back home would say if they could see her now. Little Marilee, who had almost compromised her life away in a failed attempt to please everybody else. If someone asked her to compromise now, she thought she would probably just haul off and punch that person in the mouth.

"You know," she said, turning back toward J.D., "you're nothing but a hypocrite, Rafferty. You sit up on your big horse on your precious mountain and pontificate about integrity and personal accountability. Look in a mirror. I'd say you're about a quart low on both."

J.D. said nothing. He stood on the deck and watched her go in. A few minutes later, her Honda started up on the other side of the house and gravel crunched and popped beneath the tires as she drove out of the yard.

He told himself it didn't matter. He shouldn't care. It was all for the best. He had more important things to worry about. He didn't need a woman in his life, wouldn't let this one in his heart.

An empty ache throbbed in his chest.

Never been a liar, J.D.?
You lying dog.

CHAPTER 25

Samantha lay in the center of the king-size bed, staring up at the ceiling, listening for night sounds. There weren't any. Not like there was in her house in town. No dogs barking. No late traffic from the patrons of the Hell and Gone on their way home. No grinding groan from her dinosaur of a refrigerator as it edged its way toward extinction. No ringing in her ears from straining to hear Will come in when she knew in her heart that he would not.

Oh, Will. What happens now?

The decision had already been made, she supposed. Will had made his feelings clear, and she had taken her first step away from him. A giant step. Onto shaky ground. Her heart beat at the base of her throat while she waited to take a long fall.

Bryce had made love to her. It seemed like a dream, but she knew it wasn't. Her body hummed with the after-effects.

He had told her he loved her.

She should have felt . . . something. Happy. Relieved. Excited. Vindicated. But she mostly felt numb. She was a naive stranger in uncharted territory. She didn't know what was expected of her or what to expect of anyone else.

Bryce had slipped from the bed as she slept. She wondered now where he was, wondered what he might be thinking. Probably that she was an inexperienced girl and not very good in bed. If she had been good in bed, Will would never have left her.

Sighing, her heart weighing heavy in her chest, she sat up and propped herself against the headboard. There was a stem of purple snapdragons on the empty pillow where Bryce's head should have been. Beneath the flower he had tucked a note. She opened it and read it by the soft light of the lamp on the nightstand.

Samantha,
*   I knew you would want some time to think. Please don't feel guilty. We followed our hearts; they are seldom wrong.*

*   Bryce*

Her heart had steered her wrong more than once. Into Will's arms. To the altar with a man who had no business being married. She no longer trusted it. She held her breath now and tried to listen to what it might tell her, but all she heard was the low buzz of the clock-radio on the nightstand.

Too tense to be still, she slipped out of bed and into the jeans and T-shirt that had been discarded. Barefoot, she padded across the thick carpet and stood staring out the window. The pool lights had been switched off. A thin sliver of moon turned the water to liquid pewter.

A memory surfaced, sweet and painful. Will grinning at her with a wicked gleam in his eyes. A pool behind a house in Reno. They were on their honeymoon—two whole days of unbridled lust. They had blown all their cash but three dollars and ninety-seven cents playing slots and keno. Will had finagled a room for their wedding night in the Biggest Little Honeymoon Motel as a part of the package deal with the Biggest Little Wedding Chapel, but they had no money for a second night and Will's MasterCard privileges had been revoked.

Knowing they would be spending the night on the air mattress in the back of Will's pickup, they had gone driving in search of a scenic, private parking spot. The night was hot. Samantha had longingly wished for a dip in a swimming pool. Then there was the pool—shaped like a peanut, shimmering under the moonlight behind a dark, low-built brick house.

"We'll get caught," she whispered, barely able to contain her excitement. The high of becoming Mrs. Will Rafferty made her dizzy. The prospect of doing something forbidden compounded the sensation.

Giggling and shushing each other under their breath, they stripped their clothes off in the shadows along the garage and slipped carefully into the cool water. After their swim they lay in the back of the truck and named the stars and made slow, sweet love.

Tears slipped over Samantha's lashes and rolled down her cheeks as she brought herself back to the present. Loss clenched inside her like a fist. At that moment she would have given anything to have him back. Why did it have to be so hard? Why couldn't she be what he needed? Why couldn't he love her as much as she loved him?

She still loved him. The knowledge didn't make her feel anything but despair. She loved a man who didn't want her, and had given herself to a man she didn't love. There was a word for that, but she couldn't think what it was. Bryce would know, she thought, moving away from the window, but she couldn't ask him.

Her thoughts chased each other around in her brain until she wanted to shake them all out. What should she do, what should she say to Bryce? Did she go on as a hopeless, stupid kid, waiting for Will to come back to her, or did she take that step into a new world as an adult and start working on a new life?

The room seemed to press in on her. The questions and recriminations swirled faster inside her head. Careful not to make any noise, she slipped out into the hall and crept downstairs and out the French doors to the terrace. She avoided looking at the pool, going instead to the low stone wall that edged the area, where she climbed up and swung her legs over.

Below her, the ground fell away in a steep, rock-strewn, tree-studded slope, down and down to the valley, where fog crept off the creek and seeped outward. The air was cool and thick with damp, and Samantha shivered and wrapped her arms around herself, glad for the distraction. Far to the west she could make out the dark ridge of the next range, the snow on the peaks like a strip of white lace in the thin moonlight.

She sat there for a long time. Not thinking. Not deciding. Just sitting and absorbing the still of the wilderness. The sensation of being watched crept up on her from behind slowly, touching like fingertips between her shoulder blades. Then the fingers trailed lightly up her spine to the base of her neck, and she twisted around on the wall so quickly that she nearly slipped off.

There was no one on the terrace. The chairs were empty. The lounges where Uma and Fabian had sunned themselves had been stripped of their beach towels and lined neatly three feet back from the pool. A soft breeze toyed with the umbrellas tilted above the tables, but nothing else moved. No eyes glowed in the night. She looked up at the house, expecting to see someone staring out at her from one of the windows. But the windows were vacant.

Must have imagined it. Probably wanted it to be Will. Stupid kid. He's never coming back to you. You shouldn't want him to.

She slipped off the wall and let herself out through a side gate, thinking she would walk down to the stables, but the sensation followed her, hovered around her shoulders like a swarm of gnats. Up in the towering pines that grew thick around the edge of the grounds, a barred owl let out a series of low, rhythmic hoots—*who cooks for you . . . who cooks for you . . .*

The sound skimmed over her flesh like a clammy hand. Superstitions from childhood floated up from the depths of her mind. Owls were bad luck, bringers of omens, the familiars of evil spirits. Her Cheyenne grandfather, whom she remembered only as a stooped, gnarled man with a face like tree bark and the sour stink of liquor on his breath, had told her and her brother Mike that owls brought news of death.

Silly. Why should she think of death? But the night

seemed suddenly too still around her, and the air seemed suddenly too thick to breathe. The stables loomed dark too far down the path and the trees closed in all around. Fear rose like a scream up the back of her throat. For a moment she hesitated, hovered between logic and instinct. Then everything seemed to happen at once and in super-slow motion.

A dark figure stepped out of the shadows as Samantha wheeled back toward the house. A figure without features, without gender, clad in black with a mask and gloves. The sight drove terror into her chest like the blade of a knife. Samantha opened her mouth to scream, but the sound was caught and snuffed out as a black bag descended over her face and was pulled tight by a drawstring around her throat. She lashed out wildly with her fists, with her feet, but the sudden and total darkness robbed her of her equilibrium and she staggered and fell.

Crushed rock bit into her palms and elbows and knees as she hit the ground. She scrambled to stand, but her assailant beat her back down with something that felt like a baseball bat. The blows landed over and over on her back, on her sides, on her arms. She tried frantically to crawl out of the path of the club, but the ground sloped sharply down and she fell and skidded face first, the rocks tearing at her cheek and chin through the rough fabric of the hood.

Questions pulsed like a strobe light through her brain as she lay there. *Who? Why? What would become of her? Would anybody care?* Tears pressed like fists behind her eyes and leaked out to soak into the hood. She wanted to sob, to wail out the pain and the terror that was choking her, but the hood was suffocating her and it was all she could do to draw in enough air to breathe.

The drawstring tightened around her throat, pulling her head up, hanging her. Driven by self-preservation, Samantha clawed at the hood. She got her feet back under her and surged upward, tearing at the string with one hand, lashing out at her attacker with the other. The heel of her hand connected with bone and she heard a grunt of pain and surprise.

Then she was trying to run and pull the hood off all at once, and the world, the night, tilted crazily around her, everything a blur of black and white. Her legs pumped, her arms swung wildly, but she seemed to go nowhere. As in a nightmare, the house looked farther and farther away. Her heart beat wildly, drowning out everything but the scrape of boots on gravel behind her.

She glanced back over her shoulder just as the bat swung forward. The pain was a brilliant orange and red explosion inside her head. Then everything went black, as if the plug had been pulled, and the world ceased to exist as the barred owl called.

CHAPTER 26

$\mathcal{M}$ari walked the streets of New Eden in the predawn gray. Fog shrouded the buildings and houses, casting everything in an indistinct haze, like a half-forgotten memory. Somehow the old buildings looked older, the old businesses obsolete. Quaint traditions hanging on as progress overtook them. Sweet and sad. Lockhart's Ladies' Shop with its window display of polyester pant suits next door to the trendy Latigo Boutique. The shabby old Rexall drugstore with its original soda fountain and special on Geritol standing shoulder to shoulder with Mountain Man Bike and Athletic. Monroe Feed and Read combination feed store/bookstore, its shelves stocked with teat dip and fly spray and dehorning paste, its racks full of old Louis L'Amour titles and hunting magazines and cheap cookbooks printed on Xerox paper by the ladies auxiliary of the Lutheran church, just down the street from M. E. Fralick's New Age bookstore with its Zen master clerk and thousand-dollar quartz crystals.

Sadness seeped into her muscles and bones, and she curled her hands into fists in the pockets of her old denim jacket. She jaywalked across the street to the square and settled on a bench in front of the Carnegie Library. Across the park, Colleen Bentsen's sculpture, which Mari had first appreciated as a symbol of cooperation, was taking shape in its pen in front of the courthouse. The courthouse had been built of red brick in the 1890s. A pair of Doric columns held up the portico at the top of the stone stairs. The paint was flaking off them like dandruff, but it was a venerable old building. Not very big, not very fancy, but proud of its heritage. Out in front of it the sculpture looked like a chunk of wreckage from a collapsed suspension bridge. Out of time, out of place, an unintentional insult on the place it was meant to honor.

Restless, and disgusted with herself for her melancholy mood, she left the park and started back toward the Moose. She wouldn't stay there much longer. A week or so. The suite Drew and Kevin had given her was beautiful, but it wasn't a home. The ranch was a home. Hers. It was time to accept it, to stop questioning Lucy's motives in leaving it to her. She might never know exactly what had compelled Lucy. She might never find the evidence that would explain so many things. That wouldn't change the fact that the ranch was hers now. As soon as she felt comfortable being out there at night alone, she would move into the house for good. Work on her music. Hang with the llamas. Maybe start a garden.

And up the mountain Rafferty would prowl the boundaries of his kingdom and look down on her. She wanted to believe he would feel regret at the chance he had missed with her. She wanted to lie in her bed at night and imagine remorse squeezing his heart like a fist. She didn't want to think that she had loved him and lost him in a scant week's time. Better to think she'd never loved him at all. Better to dust herself off and move on with her life.

Even as she told herself that she thought back to the night and wondered what might have happened if she had let him kiss her.

The pickups were gathering in front of the Rainbow. Ranch dogs patrolled the open truck beds with ears up and eyes eager for the sights of town. No blue and gray Ford with a Stars and Bars bug guard. No sign of Zip. Mari contemplated a cup of coffee and a plate of steak and eggs with crisp hash browns on the side, but her heart wasn't in it. She wasn't in the mood for camaraderie. Maybe she'd stop by for a late supper and she and Nora could go honky-tonkin' after her shift was over.

But the chance of running into Will dampened the prospective fun and she discarded that idea too.

She cut through the lobby of the Moose, not expecting to see anyone but Raoul at that hour, but Kevin stood behind the desk, scowling down at a computer printout. He glanced up at her with tired eyes and a face drawn from lack of sleep. He looked like a man sorely in need of a shave and a cup of coffee.

"Hey, Kev, what's up?" Mari asked, propping herself against the counter. "You pull the graveyard shift?"

The boyish smile made a halfhearted appearance, flickering and fading in the blink of an eye. "Not exactly. I knew I wasn't going to get any sleep, so I gave Raoul the night off."

"Insomnia?"

"Fight with Drew."

"Oh." She winced in empathy. "Ouch. I'm sorry."

"Me too," he mumbled, flipping a page of green-lined paper without even looking at it.

"Bad one, huh?"

"Bad enough." He shook his head, staring across the lobby and into the bar, his gaze fixed on the moose head that hung above the fireplace. "You think you know someone and then suddenly you look at them and you don't know them at all. . . ." His thoughts trailed off into a sigh of frustration and confusion. He snapped his mouth shut and shook his head again, his brown eyes bleak.

"Is he around?" Mari asked. She didn't want to meddle in their personal lives, but Kevin looked so forlorn, and then there was the matter of Townsend. She wanted to bounce the news off Drew in hope of getting something more from him. No harm in killing two birds with one stone.

"I don't know where he is," Kevin mumbled, glaring down at the computer paper. "He blew out of here last night. I haven't seen him since."

Mari's eyebrows scaled her forehead. It had to have been some fight. She wondered if there was any possibility it had to do with what Drew knew of Lucy's life and times, then she chided herself for being a mercenary. Poor Kevin looked like a lost puppy. It was not her place to grill him for information. He was a friend, as Drew was a friend. What he needed from her was support and understanding.

"You'll work it out," she said softly, touching his sleeve.

He didn't meet her eyes. His face tightened and he flipped another page on the printout. "Yeah. Sure. Umm —a—will you excuse me, Mari? I think I hear the phone in my office."

He turned away and was gone through a door marked AUTHORIZED PERSONNEL ONLY before Mari could so much as nod.

She went into the empty lounge and slipped behind the ornate bar. A multiline telephone sat beside the cash register. She hit an open line and punched the number for the CHP computer room in Sacramento.

"California Highway Patrol."

"This is Marilee Jennings. Can I speak with Paul Kael, please?"

"Hang on."

She jammed the phone between her shoulder and her ear and passed the time picking at her ragged cuticles. When she had begun to think the connection had been cut, Paul came on the line, out of breath.

"You owe me, Blue Eyes," he said without preamble.

"Not hardly," she scoffed. "Did I or did I not introduce you to the lovely Mrs. Kael?"

"Irrelevant. She is outranked on the list of women who strike terror into my heart by one Beverly Tarbon, my supervisor, who damn near caught me violating about a million rules."

"Close only counts in horseshoes," Mari said without sympathy. "Did you find anything?"

"Yeah. You're not dating this guy, are you?"

"Don't make me gag. He's a major sleaze."

"You don't have to tell me; I got a peek at his report card. He flunks social skills in a big way. The guy's had half a dozen charges filed and dropped. Two stuck and he went away to the state resort for a while."

"For what?"

"Criminal sexual conduct and assault. You sure know how to pick 'em, Marilee."

Mari's heart dropped into her stomach. "It's a talent."

She let herself out the side door of the bar and walked in a daze to the parking lot, fishing in her purse for the keys to her Honda. The llamas needed feeding. There were still rooms in the house that hadn't been put to rights.

Kendall Morton was a sex offender.

She shuddered at the thought and the implications. Lucy's hired man had been a rapist. Was there any way she could have known that? More important, did it have anything to do with her death? Mari recalled the coroner's distinct lack of enthusiasm when she had asked him whether Lucy had been sexually assaulted. He hadn't bothered to check.

She stopped at the Gas N' Go on her way out of town, bought a jumbo coffee to go, a bear claw, and a chocolate doughnut, hoping to pique her appetite. She drove out the ridge road listening to Vince Gill's thin sweet tenor voice lament the pains of love.

The fog dissipated bit by bit as she climbed up out of the floor of the valley, tearing apart like wisps of cotton candy and disintegrating. But the sun refused to shine. The big sky hung like a leaden blanket, threatening rain but not making good on it. Beneath the gray the shades of green on the hills and in the valley looked deeper, richer. The wildflowers hid in the grass, their heads bowed demurely in deference to the wind. The mountains looked black in the distance, their snowcaps hidden by the bellies of low-hanging clouds.

The day suited Mari's mood. She sat at the table on the deck and had her breakfast, trying to clear her mind of the clutter of suspects and motives for a few minutes, trying halfheartedly to identify the birdsong that went on continually in the trees around her. A magpie landed on the railing and squawked at her indignantly, fanning out his metallic-green tail and bobbing down and up, looking like a tuxedoed dandy in his black-and-white plumage. She left him the last bites of the bear claw and headed out to feed the llamas.

The barn was as dim as a cave inside. Mari flipped on the light and wished there were a dozen more. She felt as if all her nerve endings were reaching up out of her skin, humming with electric anticipation. Her imagination conjured Kendall Morton lurking in every corner.

She pulled out the feed buckets and leaned down into the bin to scoop out Clyde's grain first. The llama pellets were nearly gone and she practically had to dive head-first into the bin to reach the last of them. She would have to make a trip to the Feed and Read. Order more pellets, maybe pick up a copy of *People*. She dug into the feed with the scoop and pried up the end of something heavy.

"What the—?"

A strange apprehension started in the pit of her stomach and traveled outward as she straightened. The buried treasure had been upended. One corner stuck up through the drift of feed pellets. A book sealed inside a plastic bag. She knew without unearthing it what the title would be and a part of her wanted nothing more than to turn and walk away, pretend it wasn't there. Even though she had searched for the book, certain it would shed some light on the puzzle Lucy had left behind, a part of her had never really wanted to find it. She knew she wouldn't like the answers it gave her, wouldn't like the truths it told about her friend.

If she filled the bin with fresh llama feed, how long would it take before she would be confronted by the evidence again? A month? Two? Even as her brain pondered the question, though, she was bending over into the bin again. She was all through avoiding truths about herself or anyone else. She would confront this one head-on and deal with it and get on with her life.

She pinched the end of the clear plastic bag and tugged. The brown pellets rolled aside. She came up out of the bin with Martindale-Hubbell volume 2, California attorneys A–O, and a videotape labeled simply "Town-send."

Samantha drifted up toward consciousness like a diver drifting up toward the surface from the depths of the ocean. Out of the blackness toward rippling, shimmering light. But as soon as she broke the surface, she wanted to go back down. The light stabbed into her eyes. Pain hit the back of her head and exploded in bolts down through her back and arms and legs, tumbling her stomach over en route.

Moaning, she tried to curl into a ball and turn on her side, but she couldn't bring her knees up because her ankles were tied to the foot of the bed on which she lay. Her wrists were bound as well, each to a post in the iron headboard. It rattled as she tried to pull her arms down, the sound hitting her raw brain like a bundle of steel fence posts.

Panic and nausea swirled inside her, rolling up the back of her throat, choking her as it hit the gag that was stuffed in her mouth. She swallowed convulsively, choking as tears blurred her vision. Memories of the night hovered in the back of her pounding head. The darkness. The stillness. The call of the owl.

It came back in a rush. Fear. Fighting for her life. The hood suffocating her. A tall figure clad in black. A mask. The club hitting her blow after blow after blow.

She had no idea what had happened in the time since she had lost consciousness. She had no idea where she was. She had no idea who had attacked her or why, or what their plans might be for her. Panic went through her like a thousand volts of electricity, jerking her body against its tethers, arching her back up off the bed. Pain went through her in spasms and she sobbed, but she couldn't seem to stop fighting. She kicked and thrashed until the adrenaline ran out, then she lay there aching, crying softly, feeling the blood drip off her wrists.

Slowly, her surroundings began to penetrate the small sphere that had been her world since coming to. Rough cabin walls. A small window filled with gray light. She could hear the birds singing outside and the snort of a horse. In the cabin there was no sound at all. As far as she could tell, she was alone.

"Where the hell is she?" Bryce demanded, slamming the cordless phone down on the glass-topped table. The juice glasses shuddered and sloshed. No one had answered the phone at Samantha's house. She wasn't at the hotel. Most important, she wasn't in the bed in his guest room. She was gone. That hadn't been a variable in his plan.

Sharon calmly rescued her croissant from a dousing and dabbed the puddle on the table delicately with her napkin. "She probably caught a ride into town with one of the hands. You said she would have second thoughts."

"I didn't think she would leave!"

He paced beside the table like a tiger, his hands on his narrow hips. He had prepared himself meticulously for breakfast, dressing down in jeans and old boots and a hunter-green oxford shirt, an ancient tooled belt around his waist with six inches of excess leather hanging limply down alongside his fly. He had planned to take a breakfast tray up to Samantha's rooms, make love to her again, then invite her to go riding—just the two of them. Time alone for them to bond. Time for him to impress upon her what a fine life she could have with him.

Sharon sent him a look as she tore her croissant in two and baptized one end in currant jam. "I knew she would leave," she muttered. "I just didn't think it would be so soon. Apparently she has a low threshold for sin."

Bryce wheeled on her, his eyes bright with fury. "I'm tired of your little asides, Sharon," he snapped. "I tolerate too much from you, but I have limits, and you've just about reached them."

She rose from her chair like a queen, an icy exterior draped in white silk and a core of hurt that glowed in her eyes. Her hair was slicked back into a knot, the look emphasizing the heavy bone structure of her face. She stared hard at Bryce—*down* at Bryce, because she had chosen to wear a pair of gold mules with heels, needing to feel superior to him in some way, any way.

"Don't you threaten me," she warned, her voice trembling with emotion. "Your little whores will come and go. I will *always* be here. I know you too well. I know too much. I can make your life hell—and don't think I won't." She narrowed her eyes and smiled, cobralike. "Don't think for a minute I won't, you ungrateful son of a bitch."

Reisa came out onto the terrace with a coffee urn and a vacant look in her eyes. Sharon stalked past her and into the house, trailing a fluttering train of white silk and a cloud of perfume.

"Coffee, Mr. Bryce?"

"Get out of my way," Bryce snapped. Stepping around the housekeeper, he headed for the side gate and his Mercedes.

Mari expected the tape to be pornographic, the result of a little game of "Candid Camera" in Lucy's bedroom. A video chronicle of Townsend's escapades in Lucy's bed or some other bed or with donkeys or children. Since Lucy was involved, she expected sex to be involved. But as she sat amid the ruins of her friend's study, her eyes trained on the television that had somehow escaped destruction, sex was not what she got.

The opening shot was taken from horseback. On the trail ahead of the cameraman were Townsend and a small, thin man with a face like a carp and dark hair that looked like thread that had been stitched into his scalp. The two were dressed in safari khaki and camouflage hunting gear. Ahead of them was a rough-looking character with a drooping crumb-duster mustache and a crunched old water-stained cowboy hat pulled low over his eyes. There was talk of rifles and scopes and other hunts. Townsend sounded excited. There was a flush on his cheekbones. Someone off-camera said the name "Graf" and the little man swiveled around in his saddle.

Graf. J. Grafton Sheffield. Mari had heard Ben Lucas

call him Graf. He didn't look like the kind of man who could pick up a rifle and kill anything, let alone a human being.

They rode up a trail, thick woods all around. A lot of thrashing sounds and horses snorting. Somewhere in the distance, hounds bayed relentlessly. Townsend talked about trophies, about shooting a grizzly from a helicopter in Alaska. Then the party broke into a clearing and Sheffield's horse spooked.

The hounds yapped without cease. The camera caught a glimpse of them and their scruffy-looking handlers as it panned the clearing en route to a battered four-by-four with a small flatbed trailer behind it. On the trailer was a stainless steel cage perhaps three feet high and seven or eight feet long. Inside the cage was a full-grown tiger. A magnificent, beautiful creature.

The riding party dismounted and the horses were led away. The cowboy and Townsend busied themselves preparing rifles. The camera slowly circled the tiger's cage. The animal was breathing heavily through its mouth, saliva dripping off its chin. Its eyes looked glassy and unfocused. One of the dogs was set loose and sprinted for the cage, snapping at the tiger's long tail that protruded between the bars. The cat let out a startled roar and tried to jump to its feet, but the cage wasn't tall enough for him to do anything but crouch, his muscles quivering. The dog barked furiously, lunging at the cage, then wheeling away, inciting his cohorts to riot.

Townsend and the cowboy walked off across the clearing, rifles on their shoulders. Yet another scruffy minion climbed atop the tiger cage and pulled the door open. He drove the cat from the cage with a cattle prod. It stumbled down off the trailer and stood swaying on its feet, looking confused. Then the dogs were set loose.

They charged the tiger as a pack, howling madly, teeth bared. Terrified, the cat bolted and tried to run under the four-by-four, but was headed off by a pair of dogs. He shied away and a third dog hit him broadside and sank its teeth into the tiger's flank, drawing blood. Screaming, the tiger twisted around and knocked the dog ten feet with a single swipe of its paw, then it dashed across the open ground as best it could, heading toward the woods with the rest of the pack in hot pursuit. Once he stumbled drunkenly and went down, the dogs diving at him, tearing at him. But he managed to regain his feet and run on.

Twenty yards from the edge of the woods Townsend took aim and fired twice. The tiger went down in a boneless heap. The dogs were on him instantly, then the flunkies ran out and knocked the dogs back with clubs.

Mari sat on the small couch with tears streaming down her cheeks, her stomach turning over. She watched the cowboy and Sheffield congratulate Townsend. Townsend posed, holding the head of the dead cat up by the ears, a big grin on his face, as if he were genuinely proud of what he had just done. The memory of Townsend's office played through the back of her mind—the mounted heads, the skins on the wall, the bear rearing and snarling ferociously in the corner. The son of a bitch had shot it from a chopper. He hadn't confronted the beast face-to-face, as the pose suggested. He had never seen the poor animal do anything but run for its life. And the tiger skin was not the result of some death-defying battle in India. It was the result of slaughter, plain and simple. Not sport, not challenge, no test of manhood.

The tape turned to static. She hit the stop button on the remote and immediately a rerun of "Murphy Brown" filled the screen, the laugh track sounding obscenely inappropriate. Killing the volume to a dull mumble, she tossed the remote aside and stood up on wobbly legs.

Everything on that tape with the exception of the horseback riding was illegal, to say nothing of unethical and immoral. One whiff of this in the press and Townsend's career would have been over. Ample ammunition for a blackmailer. And ample motive for the murder of a blackmailer.

Her first impulse was to take the tape to Quinn, but what did it really show? No one on the tape spoke of where they were. The face behind the camera was never identified. Townsend was dead; what did it matter now that he had shot an endangered animal in a canned hunt? Quinn might recognize the dirtballs who ran the hunt. He would recognize Sheffield, but there was nothing much to charge him with. Christ, the man had walked on what should have been at the very least a manslaughter charge. She would have to be the queen of naive to think they would haul his bony ass back to Montana for simply being present at Townsend's illegal hunt.

She was still clutching the volume of Martindale-Hubbell in her arms. She had yet to open it because she knew without looking she wouldn't like what was inside. But the ball was rolling now and there was no stopping it. She would see this through to the end because that was what she had to do. Taking a deep breath, she turned back the front cover.

The first hundred pages of the book had been cut out to make room for a stack of court reporter's notes. Lengths of familiar green paper with reporter's phonograms in rows of red ink. Mari leaned back against the desk and paged through them, frowning, her heart sinking lower and lower as she read Lucy's notes about the people she was blackmailing.

Townsend, whom she disdained as an egotistical old fool. *He doesn't have the guts to run with the big dogs, but here he is anyway. He'll be eaten alive. It serves him right.* . . . Kyle Collins, an actor whose boy-next-door qualities were crucial to his image. *If his fans only knew what he's capable of after a few lines of Bryce's cocaine . . . I've told him I'll let him use the pictures I took for his next publicity campaign. Won't his public be surprised to see him in those leather undies?* A state senator from Texas who apparently had a blood lust hunting mentality and had taken a number of trophy animals illegally while visiting Bryce's chunk of paradise. *Matthew's motto is: If it moves, shoot it. Christ, the NRA must be so proud. Expensive hobby, though, Senator. Let's see, that leopard cost you $8,000 outright. My cooperation should be worth that much.* . . .

She explained in detail how Bryce's little hunt club worked, how Bryce arranged for the purchase of exotic animals through a black market network. The cost to the hunter depended on the animal and on the circumstances. Sometimes Bryce offered the hunt at no charge if his "friend" was reluctant. Bryce's game was to videotape the event and then hold the tape as security to ensure future favors from businessmen, politicians, Hollywood players. He didn't blackmail them outright; he simply kept the tape. He didn't need their money. Lucy doubted he needed their loyalty. What he really wanted, what he really cherished, was the power.

I enjoy the game with Bryce. He's a player. He knows the rules. He appreciates another player of equal talent and I really don't think he minds me making money off his friends. He believes in survival of the fittest. The careless have to pay for their mistakes. It truly is a game with us. The game of life. All this and great sex too—not as good as with the cowboy, but certainly more . . . adventuresome . . . Cousin Creepella doesn't like sharing him with me. I'd say fuck her, but she would probably take me up on it. . . .

There were more details. Lucy told without a hint of conscience how she had managed to get a copy of Townsend's hunt tape and how she had tormented him with threats of mailing it to CNN. She told of her escapades at Bryce's parties, the things she had seen and heard and profited by, the weaknesses she had preyed upon, the money she had made.

Mari closed the book with shaking hands and set it aside. Her friend, her drinking buddy, had been a blackmailer. A despicable, parasitic blackmailer. Thousands of dollars. Tens of thousands of dollars. Maybe more. Extorted from the rich and the famous and the powerful. They had paid handsomely for the tenuous promise that their dirty secrets would be kept. According to the notes, there were half a dozen men—and several women—who would gladly have seen Lucy dead.

"Oh, God, Lucy," Mari muttered, rubbing her hands over her face. She felt dirty and sickened. Through a haze of tears she looked around the room of this pretty log house she had inherited and saw nothing but filth. It was

tainted, all of it—the house, the land, the cars—bought
with dirty money. She wanted to run away from it, burn
it to the ground, take a long, hot shower.

You need a life, pal. I'll give you mine. . . . The line
from Lucy's final letter came back to her, and everything
inside her rejected the implication that she could take up
where Lucy had left off. How could Lucy have thought
that? Had the decadence of her life here warped her so
badly that she saw everyone as corrupt, or was corruption so commonplace in her world it had become the
norm?

Mari shook her head and cried a little, mourned for
the lost soul of her dead friend, a soul lost long before
she had died. She tried to reconcile the Lucy who had
been comrade and comforter with the Lucy who had
been blackmailer and seductress. The images wouldn't
mesh, and she knew she would forever think of them as
two separate people, one she had known and liked and
one she would rather never have met, even posthu-
mously.

On the TV in the background, Eldon the painter made
a pithy remark and the audience laughed like hyenas
while Candice Bergen looked disgusted. Then June Al-
lyson came on to extol the virtues of disposable underwear for women with bladder control problems.

Just another day in paradise. Sitcoms and stupid com-
mercials. Blackmailers and libertines. Beauty and beasts.
Incompatible worlds inhabiting the same time and space.
Surrealism in motion.

"And you're caught smack in the middle of it, Marilee," she muttered.

Her brain whirled with all the information, the possibilities, the questions. She now had proof of many
things, but no proof of who had actually murdered Lucy.
She thought she might have enough to get the case re-
opened, but she wasn't so sure Quinn would agree. Lucy
was dead, Sheffield had been punished in the eyes of the
court. If Townsend had killed her, what did it matter—he
was dead too. But there were other suspects.

Everything tied to Bryce. According to Lucy's notes, he

arranged the hunts. He made the tapes. He held the strings of a dozen powerful people. The puppet master. He seduced his friends into the hunt, deftly turning the tables so they became the ones in the cross hairs. Not because he needed their money or the favors they could grant him, but because he loved the game.

Bryce stood to lose the most by Lucy's enterprise. Maybe the stakes had outstripped the enjoyment he took from playing with her. Maybe she had overstepped a boundary line. Maybe Bryce was the man for whom Sheffield taken the fall. Or maybe her death had nothing to do with Bryce. Maybe Kendall Morton had acted alone. Or maybe all the theories were bullshit and Sheffield *had* accidentally shot her.

Mari didn't know what to do. What she needed was someone to corroborate the evidence, at the very least someone who would be willing to listen to her as she tried to sort it all out. Drew came immediately to mind. Uncertainty came immediately after. Was this what he knew and wouldn't talk about—Bryce's little hunt club? If he knew, why hadn't he done something about it? Because he was guilty too? Like a faded dream, she could just barely remember the argument Drew and Kevin had fallen into that first day she had stopped into the Moose. They had fought about the ethics of hunting, and it was obvious that was not the first time the subject had been the source of contention for them. For all she knew, this could have been the fight that had sent Drew storming away from the lodge the previous night.

You think you know someone and then suddenly you look at them and you don't know them at all.

"Ain't that the truth," she muttered.

Almost against her will other fragments of thoughts came to mind. The night she surprised the intruder in her hotel room. A man in black. Drew standing in the room later, looking harried, wearing black.

"God, you're going conspiracy cuckoo, Marilee." She pushed herself away from the desk to pace again and to run her hands into her hair. "Drew isn't involved. Don't be crazy."

Crazy.

Del Rafferty was crazy.

I don't wanna know what happened to you! I don't wanna know about the tigers! Leave me alone! Leave me alone or I'll leave you for the dog-boys, damn you!

Not *didn't know*, didn't *want* to know.

She had discounted the whole idea of Del helping on the basis of the tiger remark. It sounded crazy. He had mistaken her for a corpse and thought he'd seen a tiger. There were no tigers in Montana. And what the hell were dog-boys? The guy was so far gone around the bend, he would never get back without a guide. Or so she had thought.

But what if Del wasn't completely crazy? What if he had seen one of Bryce's hunts? He might have thought himself that it was insane. But Mari had seen the tiger now too. She could assure him what he had seen was real. That would give them something in common, and if she could establish common ground, maybe he would tell her what—if anything—he knew about Lucy's death.

I don't wanna know what happened to you!

Which implied that he did know.

The sheriff wouldn't like Del as a witness, and J.D. wouldn't like her going up into his uncle's territory at all. But she needed to find the truth and close the door on this ugly chapter of her friend's life. Now more than ever she wanted it over and done with, dead and buried. Mentally she told Quinn and Rafferty to go take a flying leap, and went out to the barn to saddle her mule.

CHAPTER 27

$\mathcal{H}$e watched her through the Leupold 10x scope, the Remington 700 resting comfortably against his shoulder. She looked a foot away. He could see all the strange, subtle shades in her hair, the frown of determination curving her little mouth as she talked incessantly to the mule. Beside him one of the hounds whined. He gave the dog a hard squint and it lay down with its head on its paws and a woeful look in its eyes.

He had tracked her up from the blue rock. She came boldly, brazenly, riding that mule as if she already owned the mountain. The blondes would try to take it away. He knew that. That was why they came at night—to taunt him, to drive him away. And now she was coming back in the daylight again. Bold as brass.

He could pick her off now. The air settled in his lungs. His finger came back and took a little slack out of the trigger, but he didn't shoot. He wasn't certain this wasn't part of the test. And he could see that this was the little blonde. The talker, not the dead blonde, not the blonde who danced under the light of the moon. J.D. would be disgusted with him if he shot this one. He had said to leave her be.

Del let the trigger out, but remained as still as if he were a rock or a tree. Maybe J.D. didn't know that the blondes would take control. He was under their spell, wasn't he? Maybe that was their master plan and it was left to Del to stop them from taking the Stars and Bars. He would be a hero if he stopped them. His family could be proud of him again instead of secretly ashamed. He could be proud of himself, and that was something he hadn't been in a very long time. Since before he could remember. Since before the 'Nam.

As silent as nothingness, he rose and started up the hill. The blonde was heading for his cabin. She couldn't be allowed inside. He would be there before her.

Mari's boots scuffed in the dirt of the yard as she paced. She switched her hands from the hip pockets of her jeans to the front pockets and marched on, trudging slowly around the corral. The horses watched her with idle curiosity. Tied to a post, Clyde closed his big brown eyes and went to sleep.

Waiting had not been part of the plan. Somehow, it had never occurred to her that Del Rafferty would not be here when she arrived. In fact, she had fully expected him to take a shot at her long before his cabin came into view. Her legs ached from gripping Clyde's sides in anticipation of the mule bolting at the sound of the rifle shot. But no shot came.

Not too keen on coming eye to eye with Del's reptilian doorman, she hadn't gone up to the door of the cabin to knock. She walked around the side and knocked on a window, but she couldn't see in because he had covered the glass with muslin from the inside. She called his name and tapped on the glass. The only answer she got was the ominous sound of the snake's rattle as the noise roused it from its nap.

She checked her watch and sighed. Once Del showed, there was no telling how long it might take to get him to talk—if indeed he would talk to her at all. The sky remained heavy and lead-colored, threatening rain, threatening an early nightfall. She didn't want to be caught riding down the mountain after dark. It was dark enough in the woods during the day. She wasn't familiar with the trail or with the mule. And there was always the threat of a close encounter of the wildlife kind. Hadn't she read that grizzly bears were nocturnal?

She leaned against the corral rail and made kissing

sounds to entice a buckskin mare her way from the water trough. Her own throat was parched. It hadn't occurred to her to bring a canteen or a Thermos. She had been in too big a hurry to get to the truth. Stroking her fingers over the mare's nose, she stared back at the cabin. There was a water pump in the cabin and cans of Dr Pepper on the kitchen shelf. There was no lock on the cabin door. There was the rattlesnake.

Of course, she knew the snake wasn't a real threat. It was in a cage. Obviously, it was too large to crawl through the double layers of chicken wire, or it would have done so. It couldn't actually bite her. Unless the force of its striking body ripped the flimsy wire, in which case it would probably land on her shoulder and bite her in the neck.

She swallowed hard and grimaced at the taste and grit of dust.

"Del Rafferty goes through that door every day and doesn't worry about getting bit," she mumbled. "Of course, Del Rafferty is insane."

Her tongue stuck to the roof of her mouth. A roan gelding stuck his muzzle in the water trough and splashed himself and Clyde on the other side of the fence. Clyde cracked an eye open and gave the horse a dirty look.

Mari checked her watch again and tried to sigh, but her throat closed up and stuck to itself like a wad of plastic wrap.

Mustering her nerve, she set off across the yard toward the cabin at a brisk, no-nonsense pace. The rattlesnake lay in its cage like a coiled length of hose. Its head came up when she was twenty feet away. Its tongue flicked the air experimentally. Fifteen feet away and its early warning system came on, the sound of the rattle skating over her skin like skeletal fingers. Ten feet away from the cage, she dropped down on her hands and knees, praying she was out of sight of the watch-snake and praying the door wouldn't be locked.

She scrambled across the packed dirt, her heart sounding like the snake's rattle. Then her hand was turning the knob.

The shot came as she pushed the door in, and she lunged instinctively for the shelter of the cabin just as the bullet struck the snake box and smashed into the side of the building. Its latch sheered off, the door of the snake box flopped down and the rattler dropped to the ground six inches behind Mari's right foot.

Mari screamed and hurled herself forward into the main room of the cabin, scuttling to get her feet under her. The snake collected itself and followed her in, winding its way across the floor. Mari stared at it, her eyes burning from not blinking. Sweat beaded on her forehead, ran into her eyebrows, and dripped down. She could stay in a crackerbox cabin with a venomous snake or run outside and be shot by a madman. Wonderful options.

"You couldn't just become a tax attorney, could you, Marilee?" she muttered, backing toward the kitchen as the snake slithered its way across the pine floor, displaying a body that had to be in excess of four feet in length and as thick around as her forearm. "You've never seen any tax attorneys scrambling to get away from rattlesnakes, have you?

"Stupid question, Marilee. All the attorneys you know *are* snakes."

She saw too late that she had backed herself into a corner. There was no escape from the small galley area without going over the snake that was snuggling up to a pair of cowboy boots on a mat beside the stove. Mari pulled out a kitchen chair and stood on the seat, trying to recall if any of her Montana studies had mentioned rattler's abilities to scale chrome chair legs. Her legs were shaking visibly. As she stared down at the snake, she could see her heart fluttering beneath her lavender T-shirt. Her tongue felt like a dead gerbil in her mouth.

This wasn't going at all the way she had envisioned. She had expected to approach Del Rafferty cautiously, beaming good intentions and trustworthiness. She would open with an overture of friendship and segue into an apology for intruding on his privacy. He would sense her innate goodness and tell her everything.

But the man who stepped into the doorway of the cabin didn't look ready to confide in anyone. He held an ugly black rifle at the ready and wore a black baseball cap backward on his head, presumably so the bill wouldn't interfere with the scope when he was taking aim. His eyes were slits beneath his heavy brow. His mouth pulled down at the corners—severely down on the side with the scar. Saliva leaked across his lower lip and ran in a thin trail to the knot of flesh and down his jaw.

Mari tried to put together a coherent sentence as she raised her hands in surrender. They were shaking like a palsy victim's. "P-please don't shoot."

"I don't want you here," Del growled. He squared his shoulders to her and brought the rifle up. "You maybe fooled J.D. You don't fool me. You're one of them blondes."

What was she supposed to say to that? She couldn't deny being blonde. "Y-yes, but I'm the *good* blonde," she improvised. "Remember? I'm not Lucy. I'm not the dead blonde."

He squinted at her until his eyes looked like pencil lines across his face. "I know that," he grumbled defensively. "I don't want you in my place. Nobody walks into my place."

"I'm sorry. My mother tried to raise me right, but I missed out on the gene for etiquette. It probably skipped a generation with me. My children will undoubtedly have impeccable manners—provided I live to bear them," she added under her breath.

On the mat beside the stove, the rattlesnake had coiled itself and reared up, drawing a bead on Del. Its tail buzzed ominously. Its mouth flashed pink as it hissed at him. Del flicked a glance at it, backed across the small room to the hearth, and came back with the rifle cradled in his right arm and a fire tongs in his left hand. He moved close enough to entice the snake to strike, then stepped gingerly on its head and took hold of it by the neck with the tongs. All this as if it were the most ordinary of household chores.

Mari shuddered as he lifted the writhing creature off

the floor and carried it to the door, where he dropped it into the woodbox outside and flipped the lid down with the nose of the rifle barrel. She climbed down off the chair, but kept her arms up.

Del swung the rifle toward her as he stepped back inside. "What do you want? What did you come here for?" To taunt him, he thought. To seduce him, maybe, the way she had seduced J.D. Then he would be under the spell too, and the ranch would be lost. He would have to stay alert if he was to redeem himself. His fingers flexed on the stock of the rifle.

Mari's gaze darted from the business end of the rifle to his face. The suspicion in his eyes boded ill. He wouldn't talk if he didn't trust her. Trust did not appear imminent. "I need to talk with you, Del," she said as calmly as she could. "I need to talk to you about the tigers."

He jolted as if he had been hit with a cattle prod. The tigers. She knew about the tigers. "Is this a trick?"

"No."

"Do you dance with the dog-boys?"

"No," she whispered, tears crowding her throat. "Did Lucy? The dead blonde—did she?"

Del didn't answer. His brain was cooking beneath the metal plate, bubbling and throbbing. Throbbing so hard he thought it might pop his eyeballs right out of his head. He stared at the little blonde. Her eyes were deep-set and clear as colored glass. She looked right at him. Most people didn't. Most people looked at the deformed part of his face or looked past him as if he didn't have a head at all.

"It's important, Del," she said softly. "I know you saw the tigers. I know they're real."

Del just stared at her.

It's a trick. She'll put you under the spell too.

He didn't know what to do. He backed away a step, then turned to pace the width of the cabin, the 700 pointed at the floor. He paced hard, making military turns, as if the precise, purposeful motion would somehow direct his thoughts into some kind of order. He couldn't trust her. She was an outsider. She was a blonde.

She had come into his home uninvited. Come to take what was left of his mind, no doubt. She would lure him with talk of the tigers and pull him over the edge.

He couldn't allow that. He had to stop the blondes and make the dog-boys go away. There couldn't be tigers on the mountain. It was up to him. He could be a hero.

He mumbled some of this out loud, not aware that he was speaking, never thinking that the woman could hear him.

"I saw the tiger too," she said. "I know they shot it— Bryce's people. I think one of them might have shot Lucy too."

His eyes cut hard to her. He did not slow his pacing. "She's the dead one. You're not the dead one; you're the talker. Stop talking."

"But, Del, we need to talk. You need to tell me—"

"Stop talking!" he roared. He wheeled on her, bringing the rifle up, and charged her, screaming at the top of his lungs. "Stop talking! Stop! I told you to stop!"

Mari stumbled backward and crashed into the counter. The back of her head smacked against a shelf, and three cans of Dr Pepper tumbled off, bouncing onto the floor. There was nowhere to go. She was leaning back as far as she could, the thin edge of the countertop biting into her back. The muzzle of Del Rafferty's ugly black rifle bit into her right cheek in the hollow just below the bone. At the other end of the gun, Del was trembling as if he were standing on the epicenter of an earthquake. His eyes were wild, the irises swirling like liquid pewter, the pupils expanding outward like ink dropped into the mix. The muscles of his face pulled taut against the bone. His mouth tore open as if the mutilated side had been caught with an invisible fishhook.

The face of death. Somehow she had expected death to be calm and sane, as if there were some logic to the scheme. She wondered if she would feel the bullet. She wondered if she would see that same revelation that had stricken MacDonald Townsend in the instant of his death. She didn't want to find out. The will to live pumped inside her. Her mind spun like the wheels of a Swiss watch, scanning for a plan, a way out.

Jesus, Marilee, if you survive this, J.D. will kill you.

"Don't do it, Del," she said softly. The charged air seemed to magnify the sound a hundred times. He made an animallike growl in his throat and the muscles of his forearm contracted as he prepared to pull the trigger. Mari fought the urge to close her eyes. Her lips barely moved. The words were a breath between them. "A hero wouldn't."

Hero. The word pierced his pounding brain like a lance. He could be a hero. Make the family proud. Redeem himself. If he pulled the trigger? If he didn't? The questions wrestled inside him, slamming against his ribs, jostling his aching mind. His hands were shaking on the gun, the palms sweating. He could end it. He could kill her. But that wouldn't be the end. The dead didn't go away. He knew. She would haunt him, and he would have to pretend she didn't, or J.D. would be ashamed of him.

Mari watched the battle wage within him, watched his brow tighten and furrow, watched the moisture come up in his eyes and his mouth quiver. It broke her heart. Even with his gun in her face, it broke her heart. His mind was fractured. He wanted so badly to do the right thing, but he didn't seem to know what the right thing was.

"You can be a hero, Del," she murmured, fighting her own tears. "Help me, Del. J.D. will be so proud of you."

She was offering everything he wanted. Small things to most men, but small things were all he dared ask for. To do the right thing. To make J.D. proud. He didn't ask to be made whole. He didn't ask for the kind of life other men had. Just to be a help and not a burden. To be a hero to his family, not the world. It didn't seem too much to ask, but all the prayers had gone unanswered.

"Do the right thing, Del," she whispered. "Put the gun down."

She met his eyes, not blinking, not condemning, not ridiculing. She wasn't like the other one. He knew that. She wanted him to help. She wanted him to be a hero too. The blue of her eyes was like a lake under an autumn sky, calm and deep. An angel's eyes. Something in them reached out and touched him in a place no one had tried to enter in such a long time. . . .

"If this is a trick, ma'am," he said softly, stepping back, lowering the rifle, "I'll kill you later."

CHAPTER 28

$\mathcal{T}$he sound of dogs pulled Samantha up from the depths of unconsciousness, up through layers of dream and memory. There were always dogs at her grandfather's place. Skinny mongrels. The old man told stories about eating dogs. When they had supper, he would whisper in her ear that they were having puppy stew and laugh at her when she didn't eat anything but bread. She thought of Rascal and wondered if he was worried about her. She felt guilty that she'd been neglecting him. The guilt made her feel tired, and she drifted back toward the black void.

A sharp howl that ended in a sharper yelp flipped a switch inside her, and her eyes flew open. She was still in the cabin, tied to the bed. It was still daytime—or it was daytime again. She had no idea how long she had been out. All the same pains were throbbing in her body and in the base of her skull. Her hands, lashed to the headboard, had gone numb. The smell of urine and the dampness of the sheets beneath her told her her bladder had given up while she had been unconscious.

She could hear indistinct voices outside and she tried to call out, but the gag was like a cork in her mouth and there was no way to dislodge it. Hope surged like a geyser inside her. Maybe the voices belonged to hikers and they would come in and rescue her. Or hunters—with the dogs. But it wasn't hunting season.

Hope receded with the thought that the voice might belong to her captor.

A door opened somewhere behind her. She couldn't

crane her neck around far enough to see. No one spoke. The minutes stretched on, stretching her nerves into brittle, hair-thin strands. Her head pounded. She wondered dimly if she had hallucinated the door opening, the sound of boots on the wood floor. How could she hear anything at all with this pounding in her brain? How could any of this be real? Who would want to kidnap her? She wasn't worth anything.

The boots sounded again against the wood floor. Closer. Closer. Right behind her. She struggled to twist her head around, but couldn't see the owner of the boots, and the pain from the movement was excruciating.

Then she felt a warm breath on the top of her head, and a pair of gloved hands slid between the bars of the headboard, one on either side of her, and she jolted hard against her bonds out of fright. The hands cupped her face, thumbs caressing her cheekbones and along the corners of her mouth, down over her jaw to her throat. The black leather was cool and fragrant, the touch bold and strangely sensual.

"How's my little Indian princess?" The low voice was almost masculine, sharp with sarcasm and secret amusement.

Sharon.

A shudder went through Samantha. A nameless fear that sank deep into her bones. She had no idea what this woman was capable of doing. Naive as she was, she had sensed from the first that Sharon had seen things, experienced things Samantha had never even imagined. Dark things. Squinting at the pain, she tipped her head back, wanting to see her tormentor. Sharon pressed her face against the thin iron rods of the headboard and smiled.

"It's just us girls, princess. No men to fight over." She settled her thumbs in the hollow at the base of Samantha's throat and pressed experimentally, choking her briefly, then sliding her hands down over her breasts. "Just us girls," she muttered.

Slowly she rose and came around the side of the bed, her boots thumping dully against the worn wood floor. She wore a skintight black catsuit with a dark brown hunting jacket over it. Her hair was slicked back against her head as tight as the body suit, her thin, wide mouth was a slash of bloodred lipstick. From a deep pocket on the coat she extracted a slim, deadly looking knife. A dagger that gleamed as she turned it from side to side and admired the blade.

Samantha's eyes went wide and sweat filmed her body in a fine mist.

Sharon's mouth curved in amusement. "Oh, yes, little princess, this is for you." She seated herself on the edge of the bed and rolled the handle of the knife between her palms, twisting the blade around and around. "I can't have you turning Bryce's head. I was willing to share, but I won't let you take him away from me. I wouldn't let Lucy have him. I won't let you have him. He has *always* been mine. I won't let his obsession with you change that."

With one hand she grabbed the bottom of the T-shirt Samantha wore and with the other brought the knife down swiftly. She laughed as Samantha strained against her bonds and tried to scream behind the gag.

"Not yet." She let the tip of the blade nip into the silk and sliced the fabric open from the neck down. Her eyes locked on Samantha's, as cold and elliptical as a snake's. "I haven't had my fun yet," she whispered as she peeled back the halves of the shirt to reveal Samantha's breasts. They were small and pretty. Soft-looking with dusky brown centers. A young girl's breasts. Natural and unembellished. She thought about slicing them off.

"I wanted Bryce to share you, but he wouldn't. He thought you were too pure. Untainted," she sneered, her mouth twisting in disgust. "His little virgin. You won't be untainted when I finish with you. You won't die untainted."

Setting the knife aside, she rose from the bed and undressed.

Tears leaked from Samantha's eyes as Bryce's cousin fondled her. She tried not to cry, because the gag choked her and because it only made her head pound harder, but she couldn't seem to stop herself. She was caught in a nightmare that was her own fault. If she hadn't fallen in with Bryce's crowd . . . if she had remembered her place . . . *Think what you're doing, Samantha! You're not like them. . . .*

She had thought she could pretend for a while, be a part of the good life, live as if she were somebody special. But she wasn't Cinderella and life wasn't a fairy tale. She didn't even want a fairy tale, she thought, her heart breaking at the realization. All she had ever wanted was Will and a home and a family. She cried as much for those small lost dreams as she did for the degradation Sharon Russell put her through. The violation of her body seemed incidental to the breaking of her spirit, the shattering of hope.

She would never have Will. She would never have a family. She would die out here at the hands of a madwoman in payment for the sin of her own stupidity. Those were the things she cried for, not the hands that touched her or the mouth that plundered or any of the vile acts Bryce's cousin committed with twisted hedonistic joy.

"You're tainted now, little virgin," Sharon said, straddling Samantha's hips. Her shoulders were as wide and angular as a man's. Her breasts thrust out from her chest, twin cones of plastic encased in flesh. There was no fat beneath her skin, only muscle and sinew. She reached for the knife on the stand beside the bed. "You're tainted, and you'll be ugly too."

She brought the dagger up and pressed the tip of it just beneath Samantha's right eye, pressing, pressing ever so slightly. Samantha bit down hard on the gag and tried in vain to stop her body from shaking. She could see Sharon's hand on the hilt of the knife. She could see most of the blade as she angled it up and down, playing, toying with her. The point bit into the tender flesh, and Samantha strained to push herself down into the mattress. Terror clawed through her, raw and primal. Sweat streamed down the sides of her face. She could smell her own fear, sour and strong above the ammonia stink of urine and the sickeningly sweet scent of arousal that radiated from Sharon.

Her tormentor laughed deep in her throat. "You'd be ugly if I cut your eyes out, wouldn't you? Bryce wouldn't want you then. He wants only beautiful things. Beautiful, like you, with your long, silky black hair."

Abruptly, she lifted the knife and grabbed hold of Samantha's braid. Her face twisting into a grotesque masque of hatred, she pulled the braid up hard, winding it around her fist. Samantha squeezed her eyes shut against the pain of having her head jerked to the side. It felt as if Sharon would pull her hair off her head, scalp and all, but she hacked at it with the knife instead, sheering it off raggedly at the base of her skull.

It was a relief when the last strand gave way against the blade and pressure went with it. She tried not to think of how her hair had been one of her few sources of pride, or how Will used to love to play with it when they were in bed, rubbing it between his fingers, stroking it over her skin and his skin. She tried not to think of Will at all. She tried not to think. Maybe if she could stop thinking, she could simply cease to be. She could become invisible, and Bryce's cousin with the insane gleam in her eye would lose interest and go away.

She prayed desperately for that to happen. She prayed for deliverance from the nightmare. She prayed for a miracle.

No one answered.

Sharon leaned down and whispered in her ear. "No more pretty hair, little princess. No more pretty face," she whispered as she laid the blade of the knife against Samantha's right cheekbone.

Orvis Slokum sat in the cab of his ramshackle '79 Chevy pickup, enduring what was for him a rare experience: a crisis of conscience.

Most everything that had ever happened in his life he could blame on somebody else. He flunked out of high school because the teachers had it in for him on account of he was a Slokum and his brother Clete had gone ahead of him, laying a trail of trouble. He had never been able to hang on to a decent job because every last boss he'd ever had was a son of a bitch who expected too much and paid too little and had no understanding of a man's need for latitude. So he was late to work once in a while. That wasn't his fault. It was the fault of his alarm clock, his mother, a woman, his truck, the weather, the clerk at the Gas N' Go. Nor was it his fault he had landed in prison. That was the fault of his partner, the cops, the public defender, the judge, the prosecutor—all of whom had no respect for him on account of he was a Slokum—which wasn't his fault either.

He regretted many things—not the least of which was being born a Slokum—but one of the few regrets he had regarding jobs he had landed and lost was that things had not worked out for him on the Stars and Bars. The Raffertys were good people. Will knew how to have a good time and was always friendly—had never looked down on him 'cause he was a Slokum. J.D. was a tough bastard, but he was fair and he was the kind of man other men could admire. He'd been three grades ahead of Orvis in school, and Orvis had watched him with a kind of awe. J.D. had always had an aura about him, as if he were stronger and wiser and more clear-minded than the average man. He always seemed to just know what was right, which was a true mystery to Orvis, who always seemed to do what was wrong regardless of his intentions.

Yes, sir, he regretted that J.D. had worked him too hard and then fired him for screwing up the irrigation dams—which was not his fault. He hadn't cared so much about losing that job when Mr. Bryce had hired him fresh out of the penitentiary. Mr. Bryce paid real good and there wasn't that much work to be done on his place, which allowed a man that all-important latitude. Orvis had thought himself pretty smart at the time. Just out of the can and getting hired on at the biggest spread for miles around to do hardly anything for twice what he would have earned elsewhere. That had to make him pretty darn smart, didn't it?

But things were turning sour on him. Bryce's people treated him like he was dog shit on a stick. The ranchers and hands around New Eden all hated Evan Bryce and extended that dislike freely to the people who worked for him. And there were jobs here he didn't much like doing. Jobs that made him feel a little sick at his stomach sometimes.

The hunting dogs were part of his job—feeding them, keeping them fit, seeing to them on the hunt. Seemed simple enough, but he'd found out quick that Bryce and his snooty friends weren't sportsmen and the animals they hunted were never in season in Montana. Lions and leopards and all kinds of exotic creatures he'd never seen anywhere but on "Wild Kingdom."

Bryce bought them from some shady middleman who bought them as excess zoo stock. They were trucked in onto Bryce's land by back roads in the dead of night and were sometimes kept for days in cages not much bigger than they were. The animals were never given much of a chance in the hunt. Often times they were drugged and could barely make it out of the cage before the dogs were on them or one of Bryce's guests shot them in order to have them stuffed and stuck in their dens, where they could lie to their friends about the dangerous safari they went on and how they risked their lives and all in order to kill this tiger or panther or whatever.

Orvis told himself it didn't matter, that the animals were no different from livestock and a man had the right to do as he pleased with his livestock. But he couldn't seem to make that excuse sit very well in his belly when he watched those people laugh and smile after they'd shot some poor drugged animal or when they made him do the dressing out.

More and more he caught himself thinking about what J.D. had said to him that day at the Stars and Bars. *There's more important things in this world than money, Orvis.*

Sad to see you come to this, Orvis. He was feeling a little sad himself.

He didn't like Bryce's people. He especially didn't like Mr. Bryce's cousin, who looked like a female impersonator. Because he occasionally liked to steal a peek through windows, he'd seen her do some things that just plain turned his stomach. Sex with other women. Sex with two or three men at once. Unnatural things. It had made him ashamed to see it.

She had done some twisted things with Kendall Morton too. He knew, 'cause Morton had told him, snickering the whole time. Orvis couldn't imagine any woman with Morton. The smell alone should have drove them off. But he didn't doubt that it was true. Miz Russell had come asking for Morton to do this job, but he had gone to the Hell and Gone last night and had yet to return. And so Miz Russell had told Orvis to truck a pair of dogs up to a hunting shack northwest of the Five-Mile creek and leave them, and she'd paid him a hundred dollars cash money to keep his mouth shut about it. He was supposed to get lost and come back in the morning and never say boo to anybody—especially Bryce. She'd see he was fired if he screwed up, and if he didn't have a job, he'd lose his parole. She told him she had arranged a little hunt for herself and she didn't want anybody horning in.

Orvis had followed orders. What was it to him if Sharon Russell wanted to go hunting on her own? If they were all lucky, maybe she would be eaten by a grizzly. But he had a feeling she wasn't alone. Just to remind himself why he didn't like her, he parked the truck out of sight on the old logging trail and looped back around through the trees to take a quick gander in the back window of the cabin.

The dogs, a pair of big African something-or-others, barked at him, but they were chained to a tree and they never quit barking anyway, so it was hardly an alarm. Orvis was unconcerned with getting caught as he sidled up to the window.

Sure enough, she was with a woman. He had a bad

angle on the bed, and the window was so dirty, it was like looking through a glass of milk, but he could tell a few things without any trouble—they were both stark naked and the other one was tied to the bed. Damned queer. Sick stuff, really, he thought, somehow managing to detach his conscience from his body as arousal stirred his pecker like a swizzle stick in his Wranglers. He could make out black hair and dark skin on the woman Sharon was doing things to. He couldn't see her face, but the only woman around Bryce's crowd lately who fit that description was Sam Rafferty, Will's wife.

Now Orvis sat in his pickup, wondering what to do. He had a pretty good idea Will didn't know his wife had gone lesbo on him. But then, he couldn't quite accept that image himself. Sam was a nice girl. Orvis knew all the Neill kids, and aside from Ryder, who was mean and drunk much of the time, they were all real nice. He couldn't figure out what Sam was doing hanging around with Bryce's people to begin with. He sure couldn't picture her taking up with the dragon lady.

The ropes bothered him, though he knew there were folks who went for that kind of thing. He rubbed his scrubby little chin and sucked on his crooked teeth. His ferret's face screwed up into a look of supreme concentration, and he bounced on the seat of the truck as though he had to pee. He didn't want to do the wrong thing. He didn't want to go to Will Rafferty and tell him his wife was getting naked with another woman and get himself punched in the mouth for no reason. On the other hand, if there was something kinky going on here . . .

Sad to see you come to this, Orvis . . .

The dilemma wrestled around inside him like a pair of wildcats in a cotton sack. He started the truck and put it in gear and let it start rolling down the grade.

Sure wished he automatically knew the right thing to do, like J.D. always did.

Damned sorry he usually did the wrong thing . . . not that it was his fault.

CHAPTER 29

"
. . . *A*nd so I said to Harry Rex, why would I want her? She's got so many wrinkles, she's gotta screw her hat on to go to church." Tucker shook his head in disgust, leaned to the left in his saddle, and spit a stream of tobacco juice that sent a marmot scuttling for cover. "Well, Harry Rex, he just laughs like the big old jackass he is. I swear, he's about as useless as a dog barking at a knothole. If brains were ink, he couldn't dot an I."

J.D. let the old man ramble on, tuning himself out of the conversation. Tucker and Harry Rex Monroe of Monroe's Feed and Read had been buddies since God was a child. They bickered and goaded each other like a pair of old hens. He could remember when he was a kid, Tucker and Harry Rex and their ongoing competitions of thumb wrestling, wrist wrestling, arm wrestling, tobacco spitting, watermelon-seed spitting, cherry-pit spitting. They went from one challenge to the next, neither willing to let the other have the final victory or the final word. The prattle was familiar and unimportant. J.D.'s thoughts were elsewhere.

Down the hill, to be precise. On Mary Lee. She had certainly told him what-for. Twice. At least. He felt like a bull that had to get knocked on the head over and over before he took the hint to quit pushing on the fence. For so long now his focus had been on the ranch. The ranch was everything. The ranch *took* everything—his energy, his money, his heart, his soul, his integrity. He didn't like thinking about what he had become in the guise of knighthood to the Stars and Bars. A martyr. A hypocrite. A mercenary. A liar. He had spent years creating the image of the noble rancher only to find out there was nothing behind it but fear. Fear of losing the ranch. Fear of letting anyone too close. Fear of losing himself. The irony was that there wasn't that much to lose; he'd given it all away . . . to the ranch.

Christ, he hated irony.

He rode alongside Tucker, amazed that the old man could ramble on about nothing at all, as if he didn't have a clue that the world was coming unglued around him. He was amazed that there weren't visible signs—the sky ripping open like a blue silk sheet, the earth cracking and separating as the various factions warring over it tore it apart. It all looked perfectly ordinary. The grass was green. The air smelled sweet with the promise of rain. The ranch buildings in the distance looked as they had always looked, aging but neat, one or two in need of paint. In the pasture they rode through, calves bucked and chased each other. Most of the cows were lying down—another sign of the coming rain. Normal sights.

He thought of what Chaske had said to him about owning the land, and knew that if the Raffertys ceased to exist tomorrow, the land would still be here. Ownership wasn't the important thing. Stewardship was. Tradition was. He had pared down his life to the point that tradition was just about all he had, and it could be lost in a heartbeat, in the time it took a banker to sign a note.

His heart felt like a lead ball in his chest.

". . . J.D.?" Tucker leaned ahead in his saddle, stretching his back, frowning at J.D. The chaw of tobacco looked like he had a golf ball in his cheek. "You use them things on the side of your head for anything but hanging your sunglasses on?"

J.D. shook himself out his ponderings and scowled to cover his embarrassment. "What?"

"I asked, had you figured out the water yet. If we're moving the herd next week, who's gonna change the water?"

The way of ranching. In the spring and summer everything needed doing at once. During the long, cold winter there was hardly anything to do at all. It was time to start irrigating the hay ground. The system on the Stars and Bars was an old one of ditches and dams that cost nothing but required almost constant manpower as someone had to periodically move the dams to make certain all the land would be irrigated. With Will gone, they had postponed driving the herd up to the high pastures, and now the move would conflict with the irrigation. With the two jobs happening simultaneously, they were essentially short two hands on a ranch that ran with a skeleton crew as it was.

"I'll see if I can get Lyle's boys to help move the cattle. You'll have to see to the water. I can't trust some kid to that job." Which was true enough. The job, while boring as hell, required experience. It was also far less physically taxing than driving a herd of cattle up the side of a mountain.

Tucker digested this with a nod. He spat and kept his gaze forward, trying too hard to be nonchalant. " 'Course, if Will comes back—"

"I don't see that happening, Tuck."

"Well, I dunno. If that ain't my old truck parked up in the yard, then I'll be giving some poor fool my condolences for having one just like it."

J.D.'s gaze sharpened. The truck was unmistakable, a hulking, inelegant block of rusted metal. Someone sat on the tailgate, throwing a Frisbee for Zip. The dog blasted off the ground, did a graceful half-turn in midair, and came down with the brilliant yellow disk in his mouth.

Normal sights. As if nothing were wrong. As if his brother weren't an alcoholic who went around picking fights with billionaire land barons. As if the rift between the two of them weren't as wide as the Royal Gorge.

"Now, go easy on the boy, J.D.," Tucker began.

J.D. nudged his horse into a lope and left the old man behind.

Zip played keep-away with the Frisbee, trotting toward Will, then ducking away when he reached for the toy. There was a certain sadistic gleam in the dog's blue eye that made Will think he knew perfectly well the pain it caused him to bend over and reach. His ribs ached as though he had been crushed between a pair of runaway trains, and when he bent over, his broken nose throbbed like a beating heart.

Each pain was brilliantly clear and separate from the next, dulled by neither drugs nor drink. The colossal stupidity of what he'd done at Bryce's had struck full-force sometime after Mary Lee had left him and Doc Larimer had yanked his nose straight and wound twenty yards of tape around his ribs tight enough to keep his lungs from expanding. He had limped out of the emergency room to find Tucker's truck waiting for him in the parking lot. Sent down by Bryce, no doubt. He wouldn't have wanted the brute cluttering up his driveway and ruining the presentation of Mercedes and Jaguars. It was a wonder he hadn't just run it off a cliff.

His temper still simmering, Will climbed behind the wheel with every intention of going straight to the Hell and Gone to throw a little fuel on the fire. But as he drove through town, he caught himself turning down Jackson and parking in front of that empty little sorry-looking house he had once shared with his wife.

Ex-wife. *Ex*-wife. *Ex*-wife.

It squatted there on the corner of a yard that was weedy in patches and bare in others, where the dog had done his business. The place looked forlorn and abandoned. Mrs. Atkinson next door came out onto her porch with her hands on her bony hips and stared at him as he made his way up the walk. He gave her a wave. She scowled at him and went back into her house.

You've sunk pretty low when the folks in this neighborhood turn their nose up at you, Willie-boy.

He let himself in and wandered aimlessly around the living room and kitchen, then into the bedroom he hadn't seen in weeks. The bed was made, the cheap blue chenille spread tucked neatly beneath the pillows. Sam was a good housekeeper, even though she'd never had much of a house to keep. Nor had she ever asked for one. He knew she dreamed of a nicer place, a place with shrubs and flowers in the yard and a kitchen big enough that you didn't have to go into the next room to change your mind. But she had never asked him for that. She had never asked him for fine clothes or expensive jewelry or a fancy car.

She had never asked him for anything but that he love her.

One thing to do and you managed to screw that up, didn't you, Willie-boy?

He stood in front of her dresser and ran his fingertips over the collection of dime-store necklaces and drugstore cosmetics and recalled the look on her face when he said he'd never wanted a wife.

You sorry son of a bitch, Willie-boy. Stood right there and broke her heart in front of God and all the millionaires. Way to go, slick.

He looked up at the reflection in the old mirror that needed resilvering and saw a pretty poor excuse for a man. Excommunicated by his family. A lost cause to his friends. Just a beat-up, boozed-up cowboy who had thrown away the one good thing in his life.

You wanted your freedom. You got it now, Willie-boy.

But it didn't feel like freedom. It felt like exile. And he ached from the loss of those things he had never wanted. The ranch. The wife.

He sat on the bed and cried like a baby, his head booming, his face feeling as if someone had stuck it full of thumbtacks, his cracked ribs stabbing like a rack of knives with every ragged breath. The sun set and the moon rose and he sat there, alone, listening to the distant sounds of traffic and screen doors slamming and Rascal whining at the back door. Samantha did not come home. No one came to rescue, redeem, or reconcile. Mary Lee's parting shot was like a sliver beneath his skin: *grow up.*

He straightened now, ignoring Zip as he pranced by with the Frisbee in his mouth. J.D.'s big sorrel had dropped down into a jog. His brother's face was inscrutable beneath the brim of his hat, but he stepped down off the horse as he drew near the truck and Will took that as a good sign. A gesture, a courtesy. Better than a kick in the teeth.

J.D. looked at Will's battered face and pained stance and choked back the automatic diatribe. Too many bitter words had already been spoken between them. This was no time for accusations. He was as guilty as Will, just for a different set of sins.

"You look a little worse for wear," he said, pulling off his hat and wiping the sweat from his forehead with the sleeve of his shirt.

Will cocked his head and tried to grin, but it held little of the usual mischief and a lot of pain. "Got my clock cleaned by a city boy. It was a sorry sight to see."

"I should think so." He sat himself down on the tailgate of Tucker's old H, his reins dangling down between his knees. Sarge leaned down and rubbed his nose against a foreleg, then promptly fell into a light doze. "Looks like you'll live to fight again."

"I'll live," Will said, sitting down gingerly on the other end of the tailgate. Zip came with the Frisbee and presented it with much ceremony, placing it in the dirt and looking up with contrition and hopefulness that went unrewarded. "Don't guess I'll fight that fight again. I pretty well blew it."

"Samantha?"

"If she comes back to me, it'll only be to serve me with papers or to stick a knife in my chest. Can't say that I'd blame her either way."

J.D. made no comment. He looked up at the house where they had been boys together and tried to imagine strangers living in it. The idea cut as sharp as glass.

"What about you and Mary Lee?" Will asked.

He moved his big shoulders, trying to shrug off the question and his brother's scrutiny. "That's not gonna work out."

"Because you're a stubborn son of a bitch?"

"Partly."

Will sighed and picked at a scab of rust on the tailgate. "That's a poor excuse for losing something good. I oughta know."

J.D. said nothing. He thought Will was hardly the man to give advice on the subject, but he wouldn't say so. He didn't kick a man while he was down. Besides, if he cared to look, there was probably too much truth in his brother's words, and it was just better to let this thing between him and Mary Lee die a natural death. In a week or two she would be back in California. Life would go on.

"I figured I could sign over my share of the ranch to you," Will said. "Keep it out of divorce court. I'll sell it to you outright if you want to make it permanent. We'll have to get a lawyer, I suppose. Man can't take a crap in this country without needing to have a lawyer look at it."

J.D. said nothing. This was what he had always wanted, wasn't it? To have the ranch to himself. He was the one who lived for it. He was the one who loved it. Sitting beside a brother he claimed he'd never wanted, that sounded pretty damn sick. He braced his hands on his knees as if to balance himself against the shifting of his world beneath him.

"What are you gonna do? Rodeo?" He heard himself ask the question and almost looked around to see if someone else had joined the conversation. From the corner of his eye he could see Tucker, fifty yards away, climbing down off his chestnut by the end of the barn.

"Naw. There's not much of a living in it unless you're a star. I'm not good enough to be a star," Will said flatly and without self-pity. "It's time to quit playing around." He looked at J.D. sideways and flashed the grin, weary and worn around the edges. "Never thought you'd hear me say that, did you?"

He sighed and marveled at the crispness of the pain that skated along the nerve endings in his back and shoulders. "I thought I'd go up to Kalispell and get a job. Got a buddy up there gettin' rich selling powerboats to movie stars on Flathead Lake. I figure if I kiss enough celebrity ass, I could make back that sixty-five hundred I owe at Little Purgatory in no time."

J.D. gave him a wry look. "You don't know spit about powerboats."

He grinned again, flashing his dimple. "Since when have I let my general ignorance stop me from doing anything? Besides, I could sell cow pies at a bake sale and have 'em coming back for more."

J.D.'s smile cracked into a chuckle, and he shook his head. "Pretty sure of yourself."

All the guile went out of Will's face, leaving him looking naked and vulnerable and young. "No. Not at all. But it's time to grow up. It's past time."

They sat in silence for moment, neither of them able to put feelings into words. J.D. felt the weight of regret on his shoulders like a pair of hands pressing down, compressing the emotions into hard knots inside him. Regrets for a brotherhood that had been tainted even before Will's birth. Regrets for the wedge their parents drove between them for their own selfish reasons. Regrets for not seeing the worth of what they might have had before it was too late. He thought of his priorities and he knew this might be the last chance he had to change one. Kalispell was a long way from the Stars and Bars.

He looked across the way at the mountains, black and big-shouldered beneath the clouds. A red-tailed hawk held its position high in the air, as if it were pinned against the slate-gray sky. He thought of the song Mary Lee had sung while he stood in the shadows of her porch, about pride and tradition and clinging to old ways, desperation and loss and unfulfilled dreams. And he could hear the faint echo of boys' laughter, could almost see the ghosts of their boyhood running through the high grass and scarlet Indian paintbrush. Not all the memories were bad ones.

"You've got a place here if you want," he said quietly. "Some things would have to change, but our being brothers isn't one of them."

Will nodded slowly. He studied the backs of his skinned knuckles with uncommon interest. "Maybe after a while," he said, his voice a little thick, a little rusty. "I think it's best if I leave here for a time. You know, stand on my own two feet. See who I am without you to lean on or knuckle under."

The silence descended again and they sat there, absorbing it and feeling the paths of their lives branching off, knowing that this moment was significant, a turning point, a crossroads, but having neither the words or the desire to call attention to it. It wasn't their way.

"If you can wait a day or two, I'll help move the herd up," Will offered.

"That'd be fine," J.D. murmured, his eyes on the beat-up Chevy pickup that had just broken through the trees and was rumbling up the drive, engine pinging, gears grinding, Orvis Slokum at the wheel.

CHAPTER 30

She could hear the dogs baying in the distance. Thunder rumbled farther back, just clearing the mountains to the west and rolling over the Eden valley, a warning that was coming too late.

Samantha thought she should have seen a sign, a clue, some foreshadowing of this, even though a more logical part of her brain knew no normal person could have imagined the kind of madness that infected Sharon Russell. She still blamed herself for being naive and stupid. But that was pointless and she had no time to waste.

She ran through the woods, pain shooting through her with each jarring step. Her ribs and back ached from the beating she had taken the night before. Cramps knotted her shoulder muscles from the unnatural position she had been tied in, and her hands throbbed mercilessly now that the circulation had been restored. They were swollen and discolored, and fears of amputation flashed through her mind when she looked at them, but then, that was stupid, because she was probably going to die.

None of it would matter—her hands, her ragged hair, the cut that extended in a bloody throbbing red line from her right cheekbone diagonally across her face to her jaw. It wouldn't matter what she looked like when she was dead. It wouldn't matter if the dogs fell on her and tore her to shreds. She would have ceased to exist.

She wondered who would mourn her passing.

The notion was stunning, impossible to grasp. She had too much life ahead of her to die now. That thought compelled her to keep her feet moving and her heart pumping and her lungs working. Instinct and adrenaline spurred her to run, and she ran with no thought to pacing herself as she hurled her body between trees and through brush. Thorny brambles ripped the bare skin of her legs, lashed them with a hundred tiny cuts, and snagged the remnant of the white silk T-shirt that hung in tatters around her neck. With no shoes, her toes caught on exposed roots, and thistles and twigs bit into the soles of her feet, but she kept running. Her head felt as if it would explode, and her lungs burned until they felt like sacks of blood in her chest, but she kept running.

South. She didn't know where she was, but she assumed they were still on Bryce's property. If she ran east, she would only take herself deeper into the Absaroka wilderness. North would take her back to Sharon. South. Toward Rafferty land. She had no idea how far that might be. She had no idea how far Sharon would allow her to run. She didn't let herself think about it. She made her mind go blank and focused only on putting one foot ahead of the other. She broke into a wide clearing and sprinted across it, thinking too late that she should stick to the cover of the trees. But what would it really matter? The dogs had her scent. Better to take the quickest route than one that afforded cover. Wasn't it?

She could hear the hounds baying, their voices carrying on thin, wavering currents through the trees. The air was heavy and still, dense with anticipation of the storm. Sound bounced through it, traveling and echoing until she couldn't tell where it originated. Were they behind her still? Or had Sharon taken another approach, circling around to cut off her escape? She pulled up to listen and get her bearings, falling heavily against the rough trunk of a lodgepole pine.

Darkness was creeping up from the forest floor and pressing down from above, creating a nightmarish twilight. Samantha looked around her, trying to establish a heading. She was weak with exhaustion and fear and hunger; dizziness swirled around and around her brain, making it difficult to determine direction or decipher the simplest of thoughts. The sweat chilled on her skin and she shuddered and strained against being sick, against panic that was like a ball in her throat. Tears blurred her vision and rained down her cheeks, through the dirt and the blood. She tried to wipe them away with the back of her hand and cried out at the pain in her fingers and in her cut cheek.

You'll die out here, Samantha. Naked, beaten, shot in the head by a madwoman. Stupid kid. Stupid dreamer. The dream is over now.

Stupid girl. Stupid, silly virgin.

Sharon watched her quarry through a night vision scope attached to a Browning rifle. *I could kill you now, little slut.* But she wasn't ready to end the hunt just yet. She had given the little bitch a fifteen-minute head start before riding out after her. The hounds had caught her scent immediately. The scent of blood and fear. A perfume of which Sharon found herself growing fond. Lucy MacAdam had been her first human kill. She thought the rush might be addictive. The idea excited her.

Her victim was perhaps four hundred yards away, leaning against a tree, barely in the cover of the woods. She could have given the dogs the command to take her down as she crossed the clearing, but it wasn't time yet. She wanted to chase, to hunt. She wanted the girl's fear to be so thick, she could taste it on the air.

She would be no challenge to kill. The fun was in the game of cat and mouse, and in the knowledge that she had the power to strike terror like a lightning bolt into the soul of her prey. For too much of her life that power had belonged to others. Now it was hers, and she relished it more than money, more than sex, more than any drug. Power. Control. The power to play God. A dark god. A dark avenger, taking back what was hers and punishing those who dared get in her way.

This was her private game. No one would ever know. She had made a mistake in leaving Lucy's body, assuming no one would come across it. She would not make that mistake with Samantha Rafferty. The girl would vanish from the face of the earth. She would be gone without a trace. Life would go on.

Sharon wondered how Bryce would react to the girl's disappearance. Had he been in love with her long enough to grieve? Would he ever wonder, ever suspect?

Will he look into my eyes and know? And what if he does? What will he do?

I killed for you, you bastard. Twice.

She had saved him from his obsessions. She had preserved her own spot at his right hand. She knew too much, was too valuable to him to be pushed aside by an object of simple lust.

What would Bryce do if he knew she had killed for him? Would he recoil from her or would that knowledge be an aphrodisiac? Would he want to watch the next time she went on a hunt and make love with her afterward, when the blood was still fresh on her hands? The image sent heat sluicing through her.

The dogs howled, eager to be off. The bigger one started to bolt down the trail across the clearing. Sharon ordered him back, pointed a remote control in his direction, and hit the button that delivered a jolt of electricity to the animal through a device in its collar. The dog let out a yelp of pain and wheeled around as if he had been yanked back on a leash.

She raised the rifle once more and smiled as she looked through the scope. Bryce's little Indian princess was moving again. Running toward safety she would never find.

Slinging the rifle across her back, she gathered her reins and spurred her horse into a tightly controlled canter moving to the south and west.

Clyde picked his way down the trail as if he had some knowledge of where he was going. Mari suspected he was faking it. She was pretty certain they had zigged when they should have zagged, but darkness was sweeping down the mountain beneath the trees, making it difficult for her to recognize the vague landmarks that had guided her up here. All in all, this did not strike her as the ideal time to get lost in the woods. There were dangers on this mountain that made bears look dull by comparison.

She had not been able to persuade Del to come down the mountain with her. The idea of actually going into New Eden to speak with the sheriff had upset him to the point of stuttering. Nor would he go with her to her place. Agitated by everything that had been going on and by simply telling her about what he had seen, he had insisted he stay put. He had to keep watch. He had to guard the ranch.

Mari hadn't argued with him. He was in a fragile state of mind, a man teetering on an unstable ledge. She didn't want to be responsible for pushing him off. J.D. would never forgive her.

"J.D. As if he's still part of the big picture, Marilee," she mumbled. "You just don't know when to quit, do you?"

As big a jerk as he had been, he should have been the furthest man from her mind. But she couldn't stop thinking about him with his back up against the wall, trying to protect what was his—his land, his uncle, his heart. She blamed him for her missing her turn on this damned trail.

God knew, she had more pressing matters to consider. She had to take the videotape and Lucy's notes to Quinn and relate to him everything Del had told her. She worried a little about him believing Del, but then, Del was a Rafferty and that would weigh in his favor, and the tape corroborated his stories of the hunts.

It had been difficult to listen to him try to sort fact from fiction in his tale of the tigers and the dog-boys, but it had torn her heart out to hear him struggle through the recounting of Lucy's demise. He told the story in fragments, with many pieces missing and some borrowed from other nightmares, but Mari was convinced he had seen Lucy running for her life, that he had heard the hounds that pursued her and seen the murderer take the killing shot.

The other blonde. The blonde that danced with the dog-boys.

Sharon Russell.

Mari could only guess at motive. Perhaps Lucy had tried to squeeze blood out of the wrong stone. Maybe she had had something on Sharon that would have threatened her position with Bryce. Or maybe Bryce and Sharon had decided jointly that they were tired of Lucy scavenging off their pigeons. Whatever the reason, Sharon Russell had hunted Lucy down like an animal in the dead of night, killed her, and left her body for the carrion feeders, then blithely went on with her life as if nothing had happened.

The thought made Mari's stomach turn.

She pulled Clyde up and looked around for anything that was even vaguely familiar. Trees. One looked pretty much like the next. *City girl.* The mule shifted restlessly beneath her. Thunder grumbled in the sky like an empty belly. Swell. The storm would bring an early end to what daylight there had been. And she was lost on the side of a mountain where millionaires killed endangered species for sport.

"You'll be the endangered species if they catch you up here, Marilee."

She could just see the horrified look on her mother's face when the cops came to tell her her rebel daughter had been gunned down while riding a mule in the wilds of Montana.

Somewhere far off to her right she thought she heard dogs barking and she tensed in the saddle. Clyde shook his head angrily in an attempt to snatch the reins from her control and danced from foot to foot. Lightning cracked like a whip above the canopy of trees, and the mule sat back on his haunches.

Mari's heart sprinted into overdrive. Her hands tightened on the reins. Dogs. Scenes from the videotape flashed through her memory. The rough-looking guide with his shark eyes. The dirty dog-boys. The muscular hounds, straining at their leashes, with their teeth bared and lips curled in feral snarls.

Thunder boomed and the mule leapt forward, his muscles bunching and quivering with nervous energy. Defying the pressure exerted on the bars of his mouth, he leaned against the bit and lunged forward, skidding down the grade with his hind legs tucked beneath him. Gritting her teeth, bracing herself back in the saddle, Mari wrestled for control, trying to turn him to the right. His big ugly mule head came around until she could nearly look him in the eye and still he pushed his stout body forward and down the hill.

Lightning lashed across the sky, flashing surreal white light into the gloom of the woods. Thunder shook the air. The world was tilted at a crazy angle and Clyde was hell-bent on hurling them down it headlong. Then the thicket of growth to their right ripped open, and a woman burst through, naked and bleeding, her eyes huge and her mouth open in terror. Her scream was swallowed up by another crack of lightning. Hands outstretched in desperation, she flung herself at the mule.

As in a dream, everything seemed to go to slow motion. The woman lunging at them. Clyde bolting sideways with such power that Mari felt herself coming out of the saddle. She pulled back on the reins, realizing a split second too late that she had hold of only the right one and that in hauling it back she sealed her own fate.

Jerked off balance, Clyde went down heavily, flipping ass over teakettle down the grade. Already half out of the saddle, Mari was flung clear of the tangle of hooves and thrashing legs. She hit the ground hard and tumbled like a rag doll, end over end. The dead stump of a broken pine tree brought her to an abrupt halt. Dazed, she lay there among the dead leaves and pine needles, her ears ringing, her eyes crossed, pain telegraphing along her entire network of nerve endings.

The woman ran toward her, a trio of ragged, bloody images.

"Help me! God, please help me! Please!" Hysterical, she flung herself down on her knees and began pulling at Mari's arms.

Mari shoved herself up into a sitting position, thrusting an arm out to fend off the woman's frantic pawing. "Stop it!" she ordered, scrambling to get her feet under her despite the dizziness. Terror gripped her by the throat and shook her hard. She couldn't think beyond the moment, couldn't see beyond the woman with her ragged black hair and wild dark eyes and slashed face, and her hands, grotesquely swollen and purple, grabbing at her clothes. She wanted to push her away and run. Then recognition hit as the lightning snapped across the sky.

"Jesus," she muttered, stunned. "Samantha? Oh, my God! Samantha?" She managed to get hold of the girl by the upper arms and she shook her hard, as if she might shake the panic out of her. "What happened? Who did this to you?"

Samantha tried to control her terror, but a wild keening sound strained up out of her throat and tears came scalding out of her eyes and down her cheeks. "Run! We have to run! She'll kill us!"

"Who!"

"Sharon! She'll kill us!" She doubled over from the pain and the fear, sobbing. "She killed that other woman. She'll kill us too!"

Sharon.

"Oh, shit," Mari mumbled as a chill poured down her back and arms and legs, raising goose bumps in its wake. She stared at Samantha in shock and disbelief. The beautiful long hair had been chopped off savagely. Her face was filthy and tear-streaked, the cut that bisected it open and raw. She was naked except for the dirty rag that had once been a T-shirt, and her arms and legs were lashed with tiny cuts and dirt and bits of bark and dead leaf.

"Sharon did this to you?" she said, shrugging out of her denim jacket. She tried to give it to the girl, but Samantha either couldn't grasp it with her purple hands or was too consumed by her terror to think of what to do with it. Mari took hold of one of her arms and awkwardly worked it into the sleeve.

"She's crazy!" Samantha cried. "We have to run!"

She tried to grab Mari by the arm to drag her down the trail where the mule had disappeared. Her fingers fumbled on the ends of her hands like sausage links, numb and useless. The baying of the hounds in the distance triggered a need to scream, but she stifled it to a pitiful mewing that seeped out between her teeth with bubbles of spittle.

"Hurry!" she begged.

Mari looked around them, not able to see anything but the dark trunks of the trees. She thought the sound of the dogs had come from down the hill. She had no clue as to where they were on the mountain. A good long way from home, she was willing to bet. The only thing she knew for certain was that up the mountain Del Rafferty had a cabin and an arsenal of weapons large enough to fend off an army.

"This way," she ordered. She grabbed Samantha by a coat sleeve and started up the way she had come down.

"Up the mountain! Are you crazy! She'll be on us in no time!"

"We go up, she has to go up too," Mari said as she climbed.

"She's on a horse!"

"Christ." She cast a hopeless look down the hill. Clyde was long gone. All they had was themselves. And snarling dogs on their tails. And a murderous psychotic after them.

She turned to Samantha. "Look, Sam, we don't have any options here. Del Rafferty's cabin is this way. If we can get to Del, we'll be safe." She started up the trail again, adding under her breath, "Provided he doesn't shoot us."

They climbed the steady grade as fat raindrops plummeted down through the cover of the trees. Mari prayed for a downpour. No one listened. The clouds hung over the mountain, snarling and snapping, but holding their water. Between thunderclaps the baying of the dogs grew steadily closer.

This was what it had been like for Lucy. Tracked down by dogs, run down like a rabbit and shot for sport. Mari could feel Sharon Russell behind them, could sense her presence as ominous as the storm clouds above, and terror clogged her throat and shot through her mind in bright, hot arcs. She had to fight to keep her thoughts focused. She had to think. Their brains were the only weapons they had.

Sharon was on a horse. She had dogs. She could have been on them by now if she wanted. This was some kind of sick game to her. In a corner of her brain Mari wondered if insanity had pushed Sharon to this or if the decadence of her life-style had lured her further and further out into the waters of depravity until the depths were bottomless—the way it had pulled Lucy deeper and deeper, until blackmail seemed like an acceptable profession. At least Lucy had posed a threat. Samantha was just a kid who knew nothing of Bryce's world. What could she possibly have done to deserve this?

What could they possibly do to escape?

They were too far from Del's cabin. She knew that, but she kept on putting one foot in front of the other and pushing herself up the trail.

Samantha ran behind her, beyond exhaustion, choking on her fear, broken sobs catching in her throat. Her legs were rubber beneath her. She wanted nothing more than to lie down in a ball and have the nightmare be over, but it went on and on. She wanted to be held and comforted. She wanted Will. Stupid to think of him now. Stupid to want him when he didn't want her.

They broke out of the woods onto the edge of a meadow. Mari stopped and stood bent over with her hands on her knees, her lungs working like a pair of bellows. The wind had come up and the tall grass rippled and waved, the shades of green altering with every movement the way velvet looks when a hand draws across it. The rain came a little harder. She recognized the place with a sense of doom. This was where Lucy had met her end. Karma. The skin at the base of her neck tingled.

They were both as good as dead. Sharon was after Samantha for reasons known only to her own insane mind, but Mari knew she would not discriminate when it came to doling out the bullets. She wouldn't leave a witness.

Sam sank down into the grass, pressing the heels of her purple hands against her eyes, crying soundlessly. Mari's heart broke looking at her. The poor kid. Bryce had sucked her into his world for his own purposes and she had gone, no doubt overwhelmed by the fine things and the excitement and the celebrities. And Bryce's people had taken her in and used her and abused her without a thought to her innocence.

Goddamn him. Goddamn the lot of them. How dare they come here and poison this paradise. The anger that burned through her was proprietary, territorial. Mari didn't question it. There wasn't time.

The sound of the dogs breaking through the brush some distance back in the woods pushed her upright.

"Come on, kiddo, let's haul ass."

"I can't," Samantha sobbed, facedown on the ground. She already looked like a corpse, bloody and dirty, her limbs bent at odd angles.

Mari wanted to lie down beside her and offer comfort, but comfort would likely get them killed sooner than later. She grabbed the girl by the jacket collar and pulled her up to her knees.

"You damn well better!" she barked. Del's place was still a long hike up some steep and rugged ground. The only chance they had of making it was if they kept moving and Sharon prolonged the hunt.

The crack of rifle fire dispelled the second possibility. The bullet slammed into the same tree stump Del had struck the first day Mari had ridden up here. Rotted wood splintered in all directions. Sam screamed, doubling over as if the bullet had passed through her. She pressed her hands over her ears and screamed again. Mari shoved her roughly toward the cover on the hillside, yelling, "Go! Go! Go!" and pushing the girl onward and upward.

From the deep cover of the woods behind them, the eerie sound of laughter floated through the rain, and Mari's blood ran like ice in her veins.

God help them. They were both as good as dead.

CHAPTER 31

"*I*'ll kill her."

Will braced himself on the passenger side of J.D.'s truck with one hand on the dash and one on the door. Explosions of pain went off inside him with every bump and jerk of the truck as it roared up the old logging trail. The fire in his ribs and back and head served only to temper his fury into something as rigid and sharp as a steel blade. Images of the tale Orvis had told kept flashing behind his eyeballs. Sam tied up. Bryce's bitch cousin touching her. His vision misted red. He felt as though a wild animal were in his chest, fighting to get out.

"I'll kill her," he snarled for the tenth time. "If she hurts Sam, I swear, I'll fucking kill her."

J.D. shot him a look across the cab. "There's no chance Sam's there by choice?" he asked carefully. The question left a bad taste in his mouth.

Will gaped at him, looking like a maniac with his battered face and bugging eyes. "If you weren't driving, I'd beat the shit out of you for that! Jesus, J.D., you know Sam better than that!"

"I know she dumped you to hang out with Bryce's crowd."

"Bryce seduced her, that son of a bitch." The truck lurched over a mass of exposed tree roots, and he hissed through his teeth and squeezed his eyes shut for a second, then picked up with his threats. "I oughta kill him too."

J.D. shifted down and gunned the engine. The old Ford screamed up a steep incline, back end sliding sideways. The headlights punched into the gloom of the fading day.

Overhead, the sky had turned the color of gunmetal and lightning broke across it in brilliant spider-web lines. He prayed they would make Del's camp before the deluge came. The old trail only grew steeper and rougher the higher they went. Rain had the same effect as pouring grease down the ruts.

They had agreed the best and quickest route to Bryce's cabin north of Five-Mile Creek was to drive to the summer cow camp and take horses down across Red Bear Basin and over the Forest Service land to Bryce's neck of the woods. J.D. didn't think Will was in any shape to ride, but he didn't want to waste time going the long way around if Sam was in danger.

He stole a glance at his brother out the corners of his eyes and hurt for him. Love-'em-and-leave-'em Will, ever the good-time cowboy, not a care in the world, was frantic with worry, torn up with guilt. It didn't matter that he expected Samantha to divorce him. He loved her. That was plain enough. Loved her enough to rip limb from limb anyone who might hurt her. J.D. had never thought Will capable of feelings that deep, that unselfish.

And what about you, J.D.?

He didn't answer himself. He would have said he had never wanted to care that deeply for a woman, but he didn't want to hear that voice sneering at him again—*liar*. Maybe there was a part of him that longed for something more with Mary Lee, but he had missed his shot and it was for the best for all concerned. That kind of longing had always seemed more like foolishness than necessity.

He negotiated the truck around a curve where the shoulder of the hillside dropped eighty feet almost straight down. The needle on the truck's tachometer was swinging wildly upward toward the red zone. The engine roared. A warning light was glowing red on the dash, and a hot smell rolled out of the air-conditioning vents. The odometer showed 153,189 miles. The trail disappeared over yet another crest. He held his breath and punched the accelerator.

The Ford jumped to meet the challenge, lunging for the

hilltop. At the same instant, over the crest of the rise came Mary Lee's mule. There was no time to react. The mule was flying, long ears back, reins blowing behind him like streamers. He twisted in midair, trying to avoid the truck, but it was too late. They collided with a sickening thump. His front feet skidded up the hood. The cattle guard over the grill caught him in the ribs, and his whole body came up onto the hood, threatening to crash through the windshield. But he slid off on the driver's side as he scrambled in panic, eyes rolling white in his big ugly head.

J.D. swore and slammed the brakes. Every molecule of his body was trembling as he jumped out of the cab and ran for the mule. Clyde had landed heavily on his side, wedged up against the trunk of a fallen tamarack. He thrashed wildly, trying to stand. J.D. caught hold of one rein just as the mule got his feet under him and surged upward.

"Whoa, whoa. Easy, fella." J.D. spoke softly, but he couldn't keep the urgency from his voice. The mule rolled an eye at him and danced in place. His hide was slick with sweat and flecked with lather. His muscles quivered as if an electric current were running through him. The cattle guard had opened a gash in his right side, ugly but not life-threatening. His legs were all intact.

"He all right?" Will demanded as he tried to jog over from the truck. He had pulled a catch rope off the gun rack. His knuckles were white as his hand squeezed around it.

"Doesn't look like he broke anything," J.D. mumbled. His attention was less on the mule than on the mule's empty saddle.

"Where the hell did he come from?" Will groused, slipping the loop over the animal's head and twisting it over his nose into a makeshift halter.

"He belongs to Mary Lee."

"She must have gotten herself dumped," he said, tying the rope around an aspen sapling. "Let's get the hell out of here. If we see Mary Lee on the way up, she can jump in the truck. Let's go."

He started back to the truck, too concerned about Sam to consider anything else. But J.D. stood there and stared at that empty saddle. With fear clenching a fist in his belly, he thought of Mary Lee, the little city girl who liked to act tougher than she was. And he thought of all her suspicions and her determination to find the truth. And he thought of the signs he had seen up on Five-Mile creek, signs of a hunt. He thought of Samantha, who had been seen bound to a bed, and Lucy, who had been found with a bullet blown clean through her.

Above the trees, thunder tumbled through the swollen clouds. A sense of doom descended on him like a shroud.

They scrambled up the hillside, Mari dragging and shoving Samantha along, pushing her own body far beyond its limits. The cover of forest had grown dense again, giving them a small measure of security. Any shot would have to be taken from close range.

Her foot slipped on the trail, and she went down hard, what little breath she had leaving her on a grunt as her right knee cracked against the dome of a rock buried in the soft loam. Gravity and the weight of Samantha hanging on her left arm threatened to pull her backward, and she grabbed wildly to catch hold of a handful of a huckleberry bush.

We're dead. We're dead. The words pulsed through her brain. The expression on Sam's face seemed to confirm them. Her eyes had gone flat and dull, as if there were nothing behind them, as if her soul had already departed. Her mouth hung slack. She was in shock, Mari supposed, her systems shutting down one by one until the only thing left to kill was a body running on autopilot. The plan held a certain appeal. As she sat in the mud, her body on fire with pain, she had to kick herself mentally to keep from succumbing. Her will was flagging, her stamina gone. Del's place was still a distant dream.

We're dead. We're dead!

There was no way on earth they were going to make it. She couldn't drag herself any farther, let alone drag Samantha with her. The sounds of the dogs baying rang in her ears.

We're dead, she thought again. The air sliced in and out of her lungs like the blade of a ripsaw. A million things buzzed through her head—prayers, longings, regrets, images of her family, nebulous thoughts of the children she would never have, J.D. As clearly as anything, she saw J.D., the sexy curve of his mouth set in a frown, his gray eyes stormy with emotions he would never voice. Damn hardheaded cowboy. Too stubborn to know a good thing when he saw it.

Oh, damn, Marilee, this isn't the time.

But the tears rose, despite her inner scolding. She bit her lip hard to keep them from falling. She was going to die soon, and all she could think was that she loved J. D. Rafferty. A hopeless thought for a hopeless situation. She wanted a second chance. She wanted a chance to make him see her for who she really was and love her for who she really was. She wanted a chance to give him something sweet and good and lasting. Her heart. Her love. Her loyalty. Her life.

The life Sharon Russell would take. Soon. The life she would give over meekly if she didn't get up and do something. She thought the old Marilee might have just sat there, complacent. The old Marilee, who had given up dreams and settled for a life that wasn't worth living at all. But that Marilee had ceased to exist. Montana had changed her. She had shed the old life and was emerging new and fresh, alive in a way she was not willing to give up just yet.

From some deep well inside her she dredged up strength she had never imagined possessing and pushed herself to her feet. She propped Samantha up against a tree and scrambled to get a view of their pursuer. She could see the basin they had skirted. The hunting dogs were racing through the high grass. Sharon rode just behind them with a rifle slung across her back. They were moving fast, closing in. Apparently, Sharon didn't find a manhunt nearly as much fun in the rain. She had probably decided to waste them and be done with it. Go home for a soak in the Jacuzzi and relive her glory moments over champagne.

The rain was coming harder, slicing down through the trees, plastering their clothes to their bodies.

"I don't want to die," Samantha mumbled to the world at large. She stared straight ahead as if she were blind.

"Then you have to do what I say," Mari said sharply. She took hold of the girl's shoulders and pulled her around to face her. "Do you understand what I'm saying to you, Sam? You have to listen to me."

Her gaze swept the area for possibilities as her brain did a thumbnail sketch of a plan. It wasn't much, but it was better than being run into the ground and shot in the back. She laid it out for Samantha as quickly and concisely as she could, and prayed that the girl wasn't too deep in shock to comprehend. Then she sent Samantha ahead on the trail and hoisted herself into the branches of a pine tree.

There was no sign of Del at the cabin. J.D. shrugged into a rain slicker and saddled a pair of stout, leggy geldings while Will went to the inner sanctum and procured a pair of rifles.

There had been no sign of Mary Lee along the trail. J.D. couldn't keep his mind off her. Was she lying hurt somewhere? Was she dead? Was her disappearance somehow connected to her search for the truth?

And where the hell did Del fit into this ugly picture? God, he would never forgive himself if Del had done something to Mary Lee. He had allowed his uncle to stew in his own madness up here. If it turned out that Del had gone over the edge, it would be J.D.'s responsibility. What if Del had shot Lucy? What if he had strangled Daggrepont? He didn't want to believe it could happen, but what he wanted to believe and what was true were increasingly two very different things.

He tried unsuccessfully to clear it all from his mind as they mounted up and headed northwest.

• • •

Sharon pulled up at the base of yet another sharp hill, in the shelter of a canopy of ancient pine trees. The rain was turning her mood sour. She had planned to continue riding until the girl turned around and begged her for mercy. But the little bitch was proving to be remarkably resilient and the rain was spoiling everything.

She raised her gun and peered up the trail through the night vision scope. Her quarry was on the ground, lying in a heap, about a hundred and fifty yards up the hill. She could see no sign of the Jennings woman, and assumed she had run on after the girl collapsed. There were no other options for her. She wasn't armed. She couldn't hope to fend off the dogs. She had no way of protecting herself from the rifle except to keep on going after the girl had fallen and hope that Sharon would settle for her original target.

The dogs ran circles around Sharon's horse, frantic for the command to go. She didn't give it. Not just yet. She wanted a moment to savor the anticipation. She smiled wickedly, wishing Bryce could be watching this. She wanted him to see what she could be compelled to do. She wanted him to know the lengths to which she would go. Just imagining his shock brought her a sense of power. He didn't realize her strength. He didn't realize she was *his* strength. Without her, he was nothing. Without her, he would succumb to the tepid pleasures of a girl like Samantha Rafferty or a petty criminal like Lucy MacAdam and his power would shrivel and die.

She would never allow that to happen.

She urged the horse forward.

Mari looked down on her from the branches of the pine tree. A hundred unforeseen complications thundered through her head. What if she missed? What if she landed behind the horse or on one of the dogs? What if the dogs caught her scent? All Sharon had to do was tilt the muzzle of her rifle up and pull the trigger.

She took a breath and held it, waiting. The dogs were

setting up a racket that rivaled the storm, dashing up the trail, then turning back. A memory of the way the dogs had torn into the tiger in the video flashed through her mind, and she shifted uneasily on the branch. Samantha had endured enough horrors without being torn apart by a pack of dogs, but if they weren't diverted soon, they would undoubtedly make a dash for her.

The horse came a step closer and another step closer. Mari crouched down on the limb, wishing she had a weapon of some kind. But there was nothing at hand, and wishing wouldn't save their bacon.

Without allowing herself another thought, she stepped off the branch and hurled herself down on Sharon Russell. She caught the blonde around the shoulders with her arms, tipping her backward in the saddle. The rifle went off with a crack as loud as the lightning that snaked across the sky.

Startled, the horse bolted sideways, ducking out from under Mari and slamming Sharon's right leg into the trunk of a tree. She howled her rage and twisted around in the saddle, swinging the gun in Mari's direction. Mari scrambled to stand and fling herself ahead at the same time, grabbing wildly for the rifle barrel. She caught hold of the fore end of the stock and shoved it aside just as Sharon pulled the trigger.

The rifle cracked again, spitting its load into the soft loam of the hillside. Mari hung on tight to the gun as the horse leapt forward, eyes rolling, hooves scrambling for purchase. Sharon had the choice of giving up her ride or her rifle. She came out of the saddle screaming in fury.

Her momentum drove Mari backward on the steep hillside, and she stumbled and went down, letting go of the gun to try to save herself from rolling down a hundred feet of mountainside. She skidded backward on the rain-slick slope, grabbing for anything she could and catching hold of a broken branch that was three feet long and thicker than a baseball bat. Her fingers gripped it hard as she struggled to get her feet under her, her eyes on Bryce's cousin the whole time.

Sharon came at her with madness flaming in her eyes

and terrible alien cries tearing from her throat. She brought the rifle up against her shoulder. Mari surged upward, swinging the branch, once again knocking the gun to the side. Without wasting a second, she lunged closer and swung again with all her might, catching the woman hard enough in the upper arm to make her lose her grip on the rifle.

The gun dropped and bounced down the hillside, twisting and flipping. Both women scrambled after it, pushing and shoving at each other until they went down in a tangle of arms and legs.

Samantha watched from up the trail, thinking she should do something, but she couldn't think what. Her brain felt numb. The rain pouring down gave the scene a weird, dreamlike quality and separated her from the other women like a wall, like a window she could see through but not move through. She could actually feel her consciousness retreat inside her mind. She wanted to shut down, to black out, to fall into oblivion where she couldn't be hurt and she didn't have to exist in this nightmare. But a small, strident voice inside her shouted for her to hang on, to get up, to do something.

She struggled to her feet and started down the hill. Then the dogs turned and looked right at her with their eyes bright and their teeth showing.

Down the hill, Mari fought to get free of Sharon. They had come to rest on a shelf of treeless ground that jutted out from the hillside. The rifle lay half a yard away, nearer the edge. Mari lunged for it, her fingertips just grazing the butt of the stock as Sharon fell on her. The rifle slipped beyond her grasp. She twisted onto her back and tried to throw her attacker off, but Sharon's hands closed on her throat and squeezed. Those hands were large and strong, as masculine as her face, which was now twisted with madness and rage, distorted into a grotesque mask. The features blurred and melted together as the blackness of unconsciousness crept around the edges of Mari's vision.

She struggled beneath the weight of the larger woman, clawing at Sharon's sinewy forearms to no avail. Flinging her hands out to the side, she scrabbled for anything she could use as a weapon and closed her fingers on a jagged shank of wood. With all the strength she could muster, she swung her arm up and jabbed the shard into Sharon's biceps.

Sharon screamed, twisting to grab the makeshift knife, throwing herself off balance. Mari heaved her hips upward and to the left, and her assailant fell off her, allowing her to scramble to her feet. She jumped up, dizzy, her legs heavy and slow beneath her. Sharon lunged sideways, making another grab for the rifle and catching hold of the sling. She pulled the gun toward her as she slid another five feet toward the edge of the ground. Desperate, Mari flung herself on Bryce's cousin, knocking the gun from her hands and sending it over the edge and down the side of the mountain.

The two of them wrestled and kicked and clawed, sending a hail of loose rock careening down the slope. Mari felt her strength ebb as the initial burst of adrenaline faded. She had been running for miles. Sharon was fresh. Sharon was in shape. Sharon was insane. And as they came to their feet, she discovered one other very important thing about Sharon Russell—she had a knife.

At the sound of the rifle shots, Will kicked his horse into a gallop without regard for the terrain or the animal or his own life. He could think only of Sam and how badly he wanted to hold her safe in his arms.

J.D. was right behind him, his thoughts on Mary Lee. He leaned back hard in the saddle as his gelding skidded down the trail, slipping on the mud and dead vegetation. They crashed through the brush and over fallen logs, dodging trees and boulders, stumbling over roots. The rain came down through the trees as loud as nails on a tin roof. It sluiced over the brims of their hats and obscured vision. They rode on, oblivious of it.

• • •

Del held his position, watching the goings-on through a 36x Unertl scope. The scope nearly ran the length of an all-black Heckler and Koch .308 assault rifle. His meanest, ugliest, ass-kicking gun. He had it tricked out to take a sixty-shot banana clip. It was the siege gun. The gun he would use to protect his family and his land from all comers.

The time had come to use it. He could feel it. His nerves were jumping like live wires beneath his skin. He felt as though he had a swarm of bees inside his head, that if he could uncork the knot of flesh on top of his head, bees would fly out by the hundreds. He wished he could do that to clear his mind. He wished a lot of things. He wished the little blonde—the talker—had not come to his place. She said she had seen the tigers too, but he still wasn't sure she wasn't trying to trick him. The blondes were like that. The one had lured J.D., the dead one, the same one that lured Del during the long nights. They couldn't be trusted.

He had followed the talker a ways out from his place. Not too far, because he didn't feel good about leaving the cabin now that its sanctity had been breached. And then he had picked himself a spider hole and waited. There was something in the air, something akin to the storm that gathered angrily overhead. He lay prone in his spider hole and waited as the anticipation built into a ball of energy at the base of his skull.

He had expected the dog-boys and the hunters. What he saw through the scope were the blondes. Two of them locked in combat. They were perhaps five hundred yards out and sharply down the mountain from him on a lip of ground that had always been called Bald Knob. The lack of trees on Bald Knob afforded him a decent view, but his vision was obscured by the rain and the light was nearly gone. The blondes moved together, like dancers, like sexual mates, writhing and twisting, their bodies melding into a grotesque mutation of the human form.

Del's fingers moved restlessly on the rifle, stretching, limbering. The tip of his trigger finger hummed with energy as it caressed the arc of steel. His heart was running like a generator in his chest. He couldn't seem to slow it. His lungs felt overinflated. Panic filled his throat. He could smell his nerves like smoldering wiring. His stillness had deserted him. Thunder boomed overhead, and he thought of mortar fire and listened to the remembered crackle of radio static as it skated along between the plate and his brain.

He didn't know what to do. Had they come to take the ranch? To taunt him? To drive him mad? To kill one another? He didn't understand. He couldn't calm himself enough to think. Time seemed to be moving at hyperspeed and there was nothing he could do to still even one moment.

Kill them!

But he knew he shouldn't.

Protect the ranch. Make the family proud. Be a hero. Hero.

Behind his eyes he saw the little blonde looking up at him. *You can be a hero, Del . . . J.D. will be so proud of you . . .*

The blondes fought on, their features melting and distorting in the rain until he couldn't tell one from the other.

He had to do something. Do the right thing. Do the hard thing. Save the day. Save the ranch. Save himself.

He tightened the HK-91 against his shoulder and blew out half a breath.

Samantha faced the dogs, holding herself as still as a statue, thinking that if she were still enough, she might somehow become invisible to them. But they had already seen her and they had spent the better part of a day trailing her scent. They took a step toward her and then another. She took a step back, then they all sprang into motion at once—the dogs lunging toward her, Samantha turning and trying to run up the steep slope.

They would be on her in a heartbeat. She looked for a refuge—a boulder she could crawl onto, a tree she could climb. All her brain could tell her was *run*! She had already run too far. Her legs moved as though she were immersed to her waist in mud. She seemed to go no-where. Teeth snapped at her calf, and she screamed just as a horse broke through the cover of brush ahead of her and came flying down the grade.

"Will!"

The sound of her scream went through him like a knife. He had no time to register the damage that had been done to her face or her hair. All he could see was her terror, her arms reaching out to him, the dogs going after her legs as she tried to run toward him.

He never even reined in his horse, but leaned down and caught her around the ribs with one arm and pulled her awkwardly across the saddle in front of him, oblivi-ous of the pain that ripped through his own body.

J.D. blew past them, nearly crashing into a loose horse. He had a clear view of Bald Knob. A clear view of Bryce's cousin as she pulled a knife and swung it high above her head. A clear view of her driving it into Mary Lee as she tried to stumble back out of the way.

At that moment he felt his heart stop dead in his chest. He couldn't get to her in time. There wasn't time for his rifle to clear the scabbard. She fell backward, arms flung out to the side, blood spreading in a stain down the front of her shirt. Sharon fell with her, dropping to her knees, raising the knife again.

He was fifty feet away and he was going to witness the death of the only woman he had ever loved.

It was a terrible epiphany. A terrible irony.

He screamed her name. Jerked at the rifle that caught in its leather sleeve. The knife's arc reached its apex. Lightning split the sky above them. Then the ominous high-pitched crack of a rifle shot split the air, and for a second that sound was the only thing that moved in the universe. The world was held fast in a freeze-frame as the shot echoed and careened from peak to peak.

The force of the hit knocked Sharon's body sideways. She fell to the ground, limp, lifeless, shot cleanly through the head. Her knife bounced over the edge of Bald Knob and down the mountain.

J.D. hauled back savagely on the reins and swung out of the saddle. He hit the ground running, tripping, stumbling, and dropped to his knees beside Mary Lee. She looked up at him through glassy eyes, blinking slowly against the rain that fell steadily in her face.

"Oh, Jesus! Oh, Jesus, baby, hang on," he said breathlessly. He tore off his slicker and threw it over the lower half of her, dug a handkerchief out of his hip pocket, and pressed it hard against the bloody hole in the hollow of her left shoulder. "Hang on, honey. Hang on."

Mari stared at him, feeling pleasantly warm and oddly disembodied, as if she had no arms or legs. She couldn't feel her shoulder, only the heavy pressure he applied to it.

J.D. looked as if he were the one in pain. His face was a mask of anguish, pale and taut, his gray eyes rimmed in red. His mouth quivered as he worked to make her comfortable by pulling off his hat and jamming it beneath her head for a pillow.

"Stay with me, baby," he mumbled, leaning over her, stroking her wet mop of hair back from her face. "Oh, Jesus, baby, please stay with me."

She wanted to ask him if that offer would be good later, but she couldn't form the words, and humor seemed inappropriate at the moment. Turning her head slightly, she could see Sharon Russell lying dead twenty feet away, her eyes and mouth open and expressionless, the back of her head gone.

"Who shot?" she asked weakly.

"I don't know," he mumbled. "Del, I guess. You shouldn't try to talk, sweetheart. Just be still."

She managed a wry smile as she turned her face up to him once more. "Quit bossing me around, Rafferty."

"Boss you around," he grumbled. "I ought to take you over my knee for poking around up here."

"Sadist," she said through her teeth as the first stab of pain went through her. J.D. winced with her. "I'll tell you right now, cowboy, I don't go for that kind of thing."

The cloth beneath his hand was soaked red. Blood oozed up between his fingers as he adjusted the position of his hand and pressed down harder. "Dammit, Mary Lee, be quiet for once in your life," he ordered, terrified that it was her very life leaking out between his fingers.

For once she took his advice, too aware of the weakness stealing through her, too aware of the labored quality of her breathing. J.D. leaned over, sheltering her from the rain, murmuring soft words of comfort, stroking her forehead and cheeks, showing her things he might never say.

She loved him. At that moment, when she knew her life might slip away, everything else became simple and clear. She loved J. D. Rafferty. At that moment everything else was inconsequential—their differences, the fights, the wall he had built around his heart. None of it mattered.

A day late and a dollar short, Marilee. Isn't that just like you?

She had a genuine talent for screwing up. Too bad that wasn't worth anything. How proud her family might have been of her.

She glanced once more at Sharon, wondering what *her* family would think. Did Bryce know his cousin was a killer? Did his depravity go that far?

"J.D.?" she whispered. "There's a videotape. Back at my place. And a book with court reporter's notes. Make sure Quinn gets them."

"Hush," he said, the word barely crawling out around the rock in his throat. He touched her cheek with trembling fingers. "You can give it to him yourself," he said, his voice hoarse and raw at the thought that she may not be able to.

"Just in case." She closed her eyes for a moment, concentrating on the fire that seemed to be spreading down her whole left side. It burned bright, then eased. She let out a breath in relief. "J.D.?"

"What?" he murmured, giving up on the effort to silence her. He wanted to hear her voice. He wanted to hear it every day for the rest of his life, and the fear that he would not have the chance was like a ball of acid in his chest. Tears pressed hard against the backs of his eyes.

"Del is a hero," she whispered. "You tell him I said so. Be proud of him, J.D."

Then she closed her eyes again and the world faded to black as she whispered, "I love you."

J.D. stared down at her, panic tearing through him. "Mary Lee! Mary Lee!" he shouted her name at the top of his lungs as the rain pounded down on them. "Mary Lee!"

She didn't move. She didn't open those huge blue eyes. She lay limp and quiet, her blood warm beneath his hand. And J.D. bent over her, to shield her from the rain, tears scalding his cheeks as he pressed his lips to her forehead and whispered, "I love you. Please don't die. I love you."

CHAPTER 32

Bryce paced along the bank of windows in the living room, moving gracefully and soundlessly across the thick carpet. Outside, the rain that had begun the day before continued, turning the mountainscape shades of gray. Bryce paid no attention to the weather. He had more pressing matters on his mind. He had yet to find Samantha. She had not returned to her home in New Eden. She had not gone back to the Mystic Moose. She had simply vanished.

He didn't like the feel of this situation at all. He had expected her to have second thoughts after their lovemaking; he had not expected her to flee the state. Aside from being concerned about her well-being, he was annoyed. There were plans in the works. The first of his plans for Samantha to take the world by storm. Even as he paced, Brandon Black, the fashion photographer, was on a jet bound for Bozeman. They couldn't very well put into motion the wheels of Samantha's success without her.

He scowled and paced some more, working to hold his temper. Interference in his plans was something he did not tolerate with good grace. Sharon's vanishing act only added to his pique. She knew better than to leave without consulting him.

She was punishing him, of course. Her jealousy was becoming an unmanageable, unpredictable beast. Her little fits had been an irritation while he had been involved with Lucy. But her attitude toward Samantha was intolerable.

The fact that both women were missing simultaneously made him vaguely uneasy.

He checked his watch, slipped his hands back into the pockets of his royal blue linen trousers, and marched on. Ben Lucas sat on one of the leather sofas, sipping scotch and watching him with amusement crinkling the corners of his dark eyes.

"You've really got it for this girl, haven't you?"

Bryce flicked him a glance. "Is that so hard to believe?"

"Not at all. She's a knockout. It's just that you have certain . . . tastes . . . a small town girl might find shocking."

He flashed the Redford smile. It had a sharp edge to it, a hint of warning. "What Samantha doesn't know won't hurt her. She's an innocent. I suppose that's a strong part of her appeal. I have every intention of protecting her, teaching her, eventually she'll learn about the real world in small doses."

"And thank you for your tutelage?"

"That's the plan."

The lawyer raised his eyebrows and his scotch.

Bryce narrowed his gaze at the subtle challenge. "You don't think I can pull it off?"

"I didn't say that. I learned long ago not to underestimate you, friend." Lucas stretched lazily and crossed his Cole-Haan loafers. "I plan to enjoy the show."

"It will be dazzling," Bryce said with a grin that faded quickly. "Provided Samantha turns up to participate."

"Maybe she and Sharon ran away together," Lucas suggested, biting on a smile. "A new twist on the old triangle."

Bryce scowled at him. "That isn't even remotely funny. Sharon has become a loose cannon of late. A situation I won't allow much longer. If I find out she's laid a finger on Samantha, I'll kill her."

The lawyer smiled an evil smile at the prospect. "Can I watch?" he asked sardonically as a doorbell sounded in a distant part of the house.

"I could probably sell tickets," Bryce muttered. "My dear cousin has made enough enemies to fill a stadium."

The housekeeper trundled in, wringing her hands in her apron, her face pinched with concern. "Mr. Bryce—"

"I told you I'm not seeing guests, Reisa," Bryce snapped. "I'm very busy."

"I believe you'll see us, Mr. Bryce," Sheriff Quinn said, stepping into the room behind the housekeeper. He towered over her. His shoulders filled nearly half the archway into the room. The rest of the space was taken up by the men on either side of him. "I'm Sheriff Dan Quinn. This here's Agent Paul Lamm, U.S. Fish and Wildlife Service, and Agent Bob Ware, wildlife agent for the state of Montana. And these," he said, holding up a fistful of papers, "are warrants."

"Warrants?" Ben Lucas unfolded himself from the sofa, rising with his drink still in hand.

"Search warrants, arrest warrants, like that," Quinn explained nonchalantly. Inside his uniform he was sweating like a horse. He was arresting one of the most powerful men in the state, a man who, according to the evidence unearthed by Marilee Jennings, was guilty of a whole lot of sins. "Mr. Evan Bryce," he said as he moved purposefully into the room with the two wildlife agents. "You are under arrest for suspected violations of the Lacey Act and a whole bunch of other state and federal wildlife regulations. You are also under arrest for conspiracy to commit murder as related to the death of Miz Lucy MacAdam."

Bryce gaped at him as the bottom dropped out of his stomach. "This is outrageous!"

Quinn tipped his head and scratched his yellow hair. "No sir, it's a fact. You have the right to remain silent. You have the right to an attorney—"

"I'm his attorney," Lucas interjected.

"Well then," Quinn said, nodding, "let's cut to the chase and take a ride downtown."

· · ·

J.D. walked down the hall of the New Eden Community Hospital with his hat in his hands. His boot heels rang on the hard polished floor, and he scowled at the prospect of drawing attention to himself. He hated this place, the smell of it, the look of it, the air of weakness and despair. It all closed in on him like a blanket drawn over his head until he felt he was smothering. Stopping outside the door to Room 102, he deliberately filled his lungs with air, then pushed open the door and stepped inside.

Mary Lee had her bed tilted up. An IV dripped clear liquid into her veins. The bag of blood that had hung in tandem with the IV solution the last time he had stopped in had since been taken away. She wasn't hooked up to any bleeping, blinking machines, a memory that still haunted him from his mother's last days. Her color was sallow except for the vibrant purple smudges beneath her eyes, but she was managing a weary smile for Nora Davis, who sat on a stool beside her. They were watching a soap opera on the television that stuck out from the wall on a black metal arm. Nora stopped talking in mid-sentence as J.D. made his entrance.

"I'll come back later, honey," she said, patting Mari's leg through the thin white sheet as she slipped down off the stool. "See if I can't sneak you in a piece of chocolate pecan pie."

"Thanks, Nora," Mari murmured.

Nora scooted around the foot of the bed, turning off the TV as she passed by. "J.D.," she said.

He nodded to her, but his eyes were locked on Mari. She blinked at him sleepily.

"Hey, cowboy, how's tricks?"

"Came to see how you're doing."

"So come in and see. Stab wounds aren't contagious."

He moved from the door to the foot of the bed and stood there, staring at her from under his straight, somber brows. He looked drawn and tired beneath his tan. The broad shoulders sloped down as if they bore the weight of the world. And he seemed wary, as if he fully expected her to add to the burden. Not exactly the way she had dreamed of seeing him.

In the half-light of dawn she had floated between memory and wishes and narcotic-induced melancholy, picturing him bent over her, cradling her against him, sheltering her from the rain and stroking her hair. She had imagined tender words and knew she was dreaming, because Rafferty was not a man of tender words.

You sure know how to pick 'em, Marilee.

"How's Samantha doing?" she asked.

"She's pretty rattled. It's gonna take her a while to come out of it, I expect. Doc says her face will scar, but the cut didn't go deep enough to sever any nerves, so I guess that's a blessing. It'll all heal in time."

Except the scars no one could see, Mari thought, hurting for the girl. "Is Will with her?"

"Yeah. He's pretty shaken himself. This put the fear of God in him. He's sworn off drinking and women and honky-tonks and gambling."

"Will he hold to it?"

J.D. thought about that for a minute, thought about the conversation he had shared with Will before the fateful arrival of Orvis Slokum. "I think maybe this time he will."

"I hope so."

Neither of them spoke for several moments as that phantom promise of a clean start hung in the air between them, tempting but unable to penetrate the dense layer of their brief past.

J.D. broke the silence first. "How are you feeling, Mary Lee?"

She found him a wry smile. "Like I been rode hard and put away wet."

"Doc Larimer says you'll be all right," he said quietly.

"Yeah. I won't be throwing the javelin anytime soon, but it's just a flesh wound, as they say in the movies. Larimer is a piece of work. I think you could be hit by a bus and he'd tell you to stop whining and walk it off." She sobered, the gravity of the situation tugging down on the corners of her mouth. "I was very, very lucky. I'd be dead if it weren't for Del."

"He's a hell of a shot."

"I'd be dead if it weren't for you," she said. Just as she expected, he shrugged off his own role in the drama, looking uncomfortable at the prospect of her gratitude. She sighed and let it go for the moment. "Is Del all right?"

Rafferty looked out the window, the muscles in his jaw flexing. "No, he's not. He hasn't been all right in thirty years. I should have faced that a long time ago."

"What will you do?"

"I don't know."

The strain in his voice brought tears to her eyes. She knew how deeply he cared for his uncle. She knew how strong his sense of responsibility was, how he prided himself on taking care of what was his. He thought he had failed. The struggle to deal with the self-recriminations was visible in his face. She wanted to offer him some comfort, but she knew he wouldn't want it, and that hurt.

She also wished there were something she could do for Del. He deserved a medal for fighting past his own fears and mental demons to help her. He deserved a whole box full of medals. She caught a fleeting glimpse of just such a box in her memory, but she was tired and couldn't concentrate on anything more than the moment at hand.

"Quinn arrested Evan Bryce yesterday," he said, turning his attention back to her. "The district attorney and a federal prosecutor are going through the evidence now—what Lucy left and what they got out of Bryce's house. Turns out he had tapes of two dozen or more hunts. Some big people are gonna take big falls. Quinn thinks they'll have enough indictments to fill a wheelbarrow. He sends his apologies for not believing you sooner."

"Yeah, well, there was a lot of that going around. I can't really blame him for choosing the path of least resistance. I probably would have done that too in my past life.

"Come pull up a chair, Rafferty," she said, nodding to the stool Nora had vacated.

Her hair was its usual mess, and it tumbled across her face with the gesture. She swept it back with her right hand. Through the thin fabric of her hospital gown J.D. could see the bandages that swathed her left shoulder and banded across her chest. He felt sick at the memory of her lying on the ground, her blood oozing out between his fingers.

"I should have listened too," he said, easing himself down on the seat.

Mari gave him a wry look. "I was under the impression cowboys are anatomically incapable of listening to women. Tuned in to a different wavelength or something."

He didn't smile. He stared at his old boots and sighed.

"Look, J.D., you had no reason to suspect what was going on. No one could have guessed."

"I knew Lucy was into something," he admitted. "She was always making sly remarks, then watching me, like she was waiting to see if I could figure them out. I ignored her because I didn't want to believe her world had anything to do with mine. And then when she was killed, I just kept thinking—Jesus, what if Del did it? What would I do? How could I turn him in?"

The questions tormented him still. He stared straight ahead as he searched for answers within himself, the muscles in his jaw working, his short thick lashes beating down hard. "After all I said about outsiders coming up here, it would have been my finger on the trigger as much as his. What does that make me?"

"Human," Mari murmured. "Don't beat yourself up, cowboy. Nobody can blame you for wanting to protect what's yours."

She reached out and stroked her fingers along the back of the hand that gripped his thigh. A strong hand. Work and weather-rough. Slowly he turned it palm up and laced his fingers between hers and held her tight. In many ways it was the most intimate act they had shared.

Emotion swelled in her chest and filled her eyes. *I love you.* The words were bittersweet on her tongue. She would not say them. He would not want them any more than he would want her sympathy. Too bad, because after living in a dormant state for so long, she finally felt alive, brimming with life, full of feeling. She needed to give. She needed someone who wanted her love. No more half-life, no more half-love. No more clinging to the wrong things for the wrong reasons.

J.D. looked down at the pale hand twined with his and felt unworthy. He had set out to use her. He had hurt her a dozen times. All in the name of a higher purpose, a clever guise for his own fear. He had accused her of much and given her little, and he was the guilty one. He boasted a code of honor; Mary Lee had lived it. She had risked her life for the truth, for her friend. She had stood up to him and stood up for herself and for justice. She lay in a hospital bed, an escapee from death's door, and yet she reached out to offer *him* comfort.

He had never felt so ashamed of himself.

How long had he told himself he didn't want a woman's love, that it was a burden and a curse, a pernicious thing that fed on a man's weakness and left him less than whole? When the truth of it was, he didn't deserve it. He had spent so long hardening himself against it, he wouldn't have known how to accept it had she offered. And so he let the moment and the opportunity slip past and told himself it was just as well for both of them.

"Well," he murmured after a long while. "There's chores need doing."

He looked up at Mary Lee, his heart squeezing in his chest. She had fallen asleep, her face turned toward him, tears on her cheeks.

Gently, he tucked her hand beneath the covers, leaned down, and kissed her. Then he walked out of her life.

CHAPTER 33

"Darling, are you certain you're feeling up to this?" Drew asked for the ninth time. He slid Mari's guitar case carefully in the back of the Mystic Moose courtesy van and turned to her with one of his concerned-brother looks.

In spite of the tension that lingered between them, Kevin joined forces with Drew in this effort, his brown eyes as hopeful as a spaniel's. "Really, Mari, you can stay as long as you need to. We hate thinking of you way out on that ranch all alone."

In a symbolic gesture, Mari swung the van door shut and gave them both a wry look. "Then you'll have to come out and visit me, guys. It's only nine miles. Besides, I won't be alone. I'll have Spike with me."

At the mention of his name, the black and white rat terrier she had adopted from the Eden Valley Veterinary Clinic jumped out from beneath the shade of the van and set up a yowling that made Drew and Kevin cringe. Mari grinned at him and praised him, leaning down to rub his head with her good hand. Her left arm was still immobilized, though she was due to begin physical therapy soon to rehabilitate the damaged muscles.

Two weeks had passed since that terrible day on the mountain. In that time, she had been visited and pampered and fussed over by her new friends and bullied by Doc Larimer. She had spoken at length with the district attorney and the federal prosecutor and Sheriff Quinn, who brought her a plate piled high with his wife's caramel-fudge brownies as a gesture of apology. She had declined interviews with no less than a dozen newspapers and broadcast news people.

She had spent time with both Will and Samantha, who were working hard at starting their young marriage over. Samantha had a lot of healing to do—emotional as well as physical, and Will had a tough row to hoe beating his drinking problem, but at the heart of the matter their love was real and sweet and tender. Mari wasn't going to bet against them. As far as she was concerned, true love needed all the backers it could get. Too much of what passed for love wasn't real, and too much that was died on the vine. And too many people never got the chance to find out one way or the other.

She had not seen J.D. once since the day they had held hands in silence in her room.

Tucker had come to pay his respects. Chaske came with him and presented her with a Ziploc bag full of powdered rattlesnake skin that was supposed to give her body strength. He told her the recipe was handed down to him from a Sioux medicine man, a claim that made Tucker roll his eyes. The two had entertained her for nearly two hours bickering with each other and telling stories. They had offered her small glimpses of J.D. as a boy, as a teenager, as a young man shouldering the burden of running the ranch after his father died.

Mari had pictured in her mind's eye the events that shaped him into the man he was today, and she felt she understood him a little better than she had, but she couldn't see that the knowledge was going to be of any use to her. J.D. himself didn't come, he didn't call. Nor did she go to him. As much as she ached to see him, to touch him, to have him hold her, she wasn't so sure they weren't better off apart. She had a new life to begin. J.D. had an old way of life that was shifting and changing, leaving him on uncertain ground. It was probably for the best that they let lie what had tried to take root between them. Or so she told herself.

Maybe in time . . . or not. She had to keep reminding herself that J. D. Rafferty was not the reason she had come to Montana in the first place.

She had come for a break. To clear her mind. To get in touch with her soul. She intended to do just that. Permanently. There would be no going back to California. There would be no more living in limbo at the Moose. She felt as if the Marilee Jennings who had first piled her business suits in the back of her Honda and set out from Sacramento had ceased to exist. The false shell of that woman had been shed and the real Mary Lee was just beginning to emerge. What a wonderful feeling that was. A little frightening, a little painful, but so right.

Kevin kissed her cheek and gave her right hand a squeeze. "Promise me you'll come to dinner Wednesday."

"Scout's honor."

She climbed into the passenger seat in the front of the van and Spike promptly launched himself into her lap and propped his feet on the dashboard, ready for adventure.

"You're certain you can manage—" Drew began as he buckled himself into the driver's seat.

"Yes, Drew," Mari said in a tone that was both patient and patronizing, as if she were answering a two-year-old. "I manage very well with one arm. Juggling is a trick, but the day-to-day stuff? No sweat."

He frowned and made a humming noise, as if his brain were stuck in neutral.

They made their way through town at a leisurely pace. The usual wave of summer tourists had swelled with the ranks of the morbidly curious who had seen the town spotlighted on national network news. The sidewalks were busy. All parking spaces were full. The traffic on Main Street was enough to drive the locals to alternate routes. The ranch dogs stayed in the backs of their pickups, guarding their territory and leaving the sidewalks to the strangers.

The businesses were prospering. Still, Mari couldn't help but wonder what J.D. would make of it. She could almost hear his growl of disdain as they passed the Feed and Read, where tourists were emerging licking stick candy and carrying an odd assortment of souvenirs—

eyes. His hands were suddenly nervous. He jammed them at his waist, dropped them, crossed them, wiped the saliva that trailed down his jaw. "No, ma'am," he said, breathing as if he had just run to hell and back. "The fact is, I couldn't tell. I saw blondes and I knew they weren't the same, but then they were, and I couldn't tell—"

He broke off, stared off across the yard, seeing it all again in his fractured mind, image upon image as if he were looking through a prism. The blonde and the blonde, tangled and then apart, their features interchanging. He had wanted to do something. Needed to do the right thing. He couldn't remember anything about the instant he pulled the trigger. That second was gone from his mind as if it had never happened.

Mari closed the distance between them without hesitation and took hold of one of his hands, squeezing it hard. "No," she said strongly. He looked down at her, his gray eyes full of torment. "You knew. In your heart you knew. You saved my life, Del. Don't you let yourself think otherwise."

He stared at her, wanting to believe, wishing he could believe. He knew her now. She was the talker. The good blonde. She had told him he could be a hero; now she claimed he was. Had he known? In that final hairbreadth of a second, had he known? Maybe. He wished so, but wishing wouldn't make it true.

Mari let go his hand and dug her fingers into her shirt pocket, pulling out a small brass star that hung from a red-striped ribbon. She had gone down to Miller Daggrepont's office, dug the medal out of one of his many boxes of "collections," and paid his secretary Inez a dollar for it. It seemed an awfully small price for what it meant.

"I got this for you," she m̲ured, holding it up against his chest. "I found it in an a̲ wes shop in town. I'm not sure where it comes from or was origi- nally meant for, but I mean for you to w̲ because you're my hero."

Del looked down at the little medal she held a̲ him with her small, pale hand. He had some from tṟ war, but he kept them locked in a box with the other mementos of that time because people didn't like that war and they used to make him feel ashamed that he'd gone. He had only meant to do the right thing, but he guessed he didn't always know what that was, even back then.

"You did good, Del," the little blonde whispered. "Please believe that." Her eyes were full of tears. She raised up on her tiptoes and brushed a kiss against his cheek.

Blushing, he took the star and pinned it to his shirt and he felt good about himself for the first time in a long time. "Thank you, ma'am," he murmured. "I'll be proud to wear it."

He tipped his hat to her and without another word went to see about his horse.

Mari watched him walk away with the roan in tow. She could feel J.D.'s gaze on her, but she didn't turn to meet it. Her emotions were running too high. She didn't trust herself not to blurt out that she loved him or some other equally ill-timed revelation. She had to have some pride. Pride was valued here, and she was a part of this place now.

"That's one of the finest things I've ever seen anybody do, Mary Lee," J.D. said softly.

"Well," she said, her voice low and hoarse. "I'm not at all sure he deserved it, but he needed it, and even if he saved my life by accident, I wanted to give him something back."

He hooked a knuckle under her chin and turned her face up to his. Her eyes were like liquid sapphire. Tears left a trail on her cheeks that gleamed in the fading glow of sunset. He had probably known prettier women in his life, but at that moment he could not think of one more beautiful. "You're not who you want to think I am," she what I expect."

"Maybe I'd say you're someone more," he murmured. said. "Or, truer, more honest, stronger, braver. She was everything he would have labeled himself once. Christ, he hated irony. He wasn't so sure anymore that he was any of those things.

"Would you like to find out?" Mari asked. Her heart beat like a fist at the base of her throat, fluttered like a butterfly caught in a net. She could see in his eyes what his answer would be, and even tempered with regret it hurt. "Won't take a chance on a city girl, huh?" she said with a smile more tremulous than wry.

"It's not that," he said as he let his hand drop from her chin. He turned away and faced the west, where the sky was aflame and the mountains were cast in silhouette beneath it. "It's the wrong time and maybe I'm the wrong man. Maybe I'm not who you want to think I am either. I don't know anymore."

"I do," she said, coming to stand beside him. "I know exactly who you are. I know you're proud and stubborn, that you'd do anything for the people you care about. I know you can be pompous and arrogant, and I know there's no one on this planet harder on you than you are on yourself. I know you value integrity and honesty and fair play, and I know you think you violated your own code of honor. I know you're a chauvinist and you'll probably never say the things a woman would like to hear from you.

"I know exactly who you are, Rafferty. And I've managed to fall in love with you anyway."

The word struck him like a ball peen hammer between the eyes. *Love*. The thing he had avoided as judiciously as outsiders. The emotion that had run his father into an early grave. He ___ grown up believing it couldn't be trusted. It would lea___ turn on a man or swallow him whole. He had never wa___ it—

Liar.

He had lain awake nights wa___ never ever naming it. It scared the___ it, aching for it, scared the hell out of him to want it now, out of him. It this woman. She wasn't from his world, a w___ it from disintegrating around him. He couldn't offer ___at was thing but debt and a hard life. That didn't seem lik___ enticement to make a woman stay. He had already seen that it wouldn't make a woman happy. His mind raced ahead to envision her dissatisfaction, then raced back to see his father growing weak as Sondra drained all the pride out of him. He had sworn he wouldn't go through that, not for anyone. He had obligations and responsibilities. He had the land.

Martyr.

The words jabbed him like knives—*love, liar, martyr*—poking at his conscience and his temper. Christ, why couldn't he just be left alone? Why couldn't the world outside his own just keep away? And why did this woman have to complicate something as simple as sex with emotions as volatile as dynamite?

"I can see you're overjoyed," Mari said, channeling her hurt into sarcasm. "You look like you'd rather have jock itch. Thanks, Rafferty, you're a real jerk. And I still love you—how's that for masochism?"

Disgusted, she turned and started for the truck. J.D. reached out and caught her by her good shoulder. "Mary Lee, it couldn't work. Don't you see that?"

"Why?" she challenged.

"We're too different. We don't want the same things—"

"How dare you presume to know what I want," she said angrily. "You don't know anything. You don't know anything about what I want or who I am because you're so damn busy trying to fit me into one of your little pigeonholes—outsider, seductress, troublemaker. Well, here's a news flash for you, Rafferty: I'm more than the sum of your stupid labels. I'm a woman who loves you, and when you decide you can handle that, you know where to find me."

Once again she started for the truck, her feet heavy, her heart squeezing her. "You're staying?"

J.D.'s voice stuck at him and sighed at the suspicion in

She looked eyes. "I'm staying. For good. Forever. I'm not from this place, but that doesn't mean I belong here. You may not like that, but it's how this land was settled. Those Raffertys who came here from

Georgia weren't natives either. They managed to fit in eventually. I will too, on my own terms, in my own way."

She climbed into the cab of the truck and slammed the door just as Tucker walked out of the cabin. The old cowboy looked from the woman to J.D., spat a stream of Red Man into the dirt, and shook his head. He had gladly joined in Mary Lee's conspiracy, but he had hoped for a better outcome than this.

"They don't make steel any harder than your noggin," he muttered irritably as he hobbled across the darkening yard.

J.D. scowled at him. "Stay out of it, Tuck."

"I'll not stay out of it," he snarled. "I stood back and watched your daddy make some big mistakes that you and Will have paid for all your lives. Damned if I'll do it again."

"I'm just avoiding the same mistake."

"No. Your daddy's mistake was looking at Sondra and seeing only what he wanted to see, and what he wanted to see was good things. What you want to see is trouble. Your daddy took a hard road because he loved foolishly. You'd rather take the easy road and avoid it altogether."

"Easy!" J.D. gaped at him, his pride stinging at the accusation.

Tucker didn't bat an eye at his outrage. "You can love the land all you want, J.D., and when you die, they'll bury you in it. But it won't give you comfort and it won't give you children, and it won't stick by you when you're bein' a mule-headed, mean-tempered son of a bitch. It can't give you tenderness and it can't give you love, and I ought to know because I've given my whole life to it and I don't have a damn thing to show for it but rheumatism. I had hoped you might have more sense than to do the same."

He turned on his heel and doddered off toward the pickup on his bandy legs, muttering to himself every step of the way. He clambered into the cab and fired the engine. J.D. turned back to his view and refused to watch as they drove out of the yard.

His appetite had gone. Restless, he climbed back on Sarge and rode down the trail to Bald Knob, where he sat alone and listened to the coyotes sing as the moon came up behind him over the Absarokas.

He had kneeled on this ground and held Mary Lee, knowing that he loved her, knowing that she might die in his arms. Now she offered him her love and he pushed it away.

Because it was best. Because it was smartest.

Because it's easiest and you're a damn coward.

He used to think he knew who he was and what he stood for, what he believed in and what he didn't. He used to pride himself on doing what was right, not what was easiest.

Was it right to cloister himself on this mountain? Was it easier to endure the loneliness of his self-exile than risk the heart he had guarded so jealously since boyhood?

He thought of Mary Lee, risking her life to find the truth because she thought it was the right thing to do, standing up to him because she thought he was wrong. She'd had the courage to abandon the life she knew in order to reach for her dreams. He didn't even have the guts to admit he had dreams.

But he did. When the nights were long and lonely and the days ran together with their endless monotony of duty and labor. Deep, deep inside, where no one could see them or touch them or break them. The dreams had always been there, so secret, they were little more than shadows, even to him. But he never reached for them or spoke of them or thought of them in the light of day.

Now Mary Lee was holding one out to him. A dream. A gift. Her heart. Her love. And he just stood back and waited for her to snatch it away.

What do you have without her, J.D.?
The land.

He looked out across it, moon-silvered and cloaked in shadow, beautiful and wild, rugged and fragile. His first love. His whole life.

His whole empty, lonely life.

CHAPTER 34

$\mathcal{T}$he days found a pleasant, monotonous rhythm. Mari watched the sunrise and ate saltines to fend off nausea. She worked on stripping the house down to its bare essentials and scrubbing away all hints of its former owner. Afternoons were spent on the deck, working on songs and soaking up the beauty of her surroundings. She napped in the Adirondack chair and spent most evenings at the Moose, singing in the lounge.

Once a week she spoke with either Sheriff Quinn or one of the attorneys who were chomping at the bit to take Bryce to court. They couldn't stick him with anything related to Lucy's death, but they were eager to make an example of him on the wildlife charges—twenty-nine counts worth. Ben Lucas was pushing for a plea bargain that involved fines and community service. The U.S. attorney was taking about bigger fines, probation time, and forfeiture of the ranch. Bryce had moved back to his home in L.A. in a show of disdain for the prosecuting attorneys. It was Mari's fondest wish that they throw him in prison for the rest of his unnatural life, but she knew that would never happen. The wheels of justice seldom ran over men like Evan Bryce.

A month had passed since she had challenged J.D. to come find her when he was ready. He had yet to take her up on it. She wondered ten times a day when and how she should tell him that while they had not managed to make their relationship work, they had managed to make a baby. She put it off, thinking that maybe tomorrow he would show up and tell her he loved her.

Foolish hope, but it was better than no hope at all. It was better than thinking about what would happen if he never came back. She would have to go to him, because he had a right to know, but what transpired in her imagination after she made the announcement was most often the fight of the century. He would insist on "doing right by her" because that was the way he thought, and she would tell him to go do the anatomically impossible because she was not about to settle for a marriage based on obligation.

"Here's another fine mess you've got yourself into, Marilee," she muttered on a long, weary sigh. She rubbed a hand absently over her tummy, a gesture that was fast becoming habit. The life inside her was far too small to be felt, but just the knowledge that it was there made her feel less alone. Often she would close her eyes and try to imagine their child—a dark-haired little boy with his daddy's stubborn jaw, a little girl with an unruly mop of hair. Then she would think of raising that child alone and her heart would ache until she cried. And then she would think of J.D., living his life of emotional celibacy, his life pledged to the ranch, his heart pledged to no one because he was afraid of having it broken.

Or so she thought. *Romanticizing again, Marilee . . .*

"Well, at least I'll get a song out of it," she murmured, and jotted down two lines in her court reporter's notebook.

She sat in the Adirondack chair, staring out at the magnificent beauty all around her and pretending to smoke with cut-off lengths of striped plastic drinking straws. The motion was soothing. The deep breathing relaxed her. The beauty of the place healed her and offered a kind of nameless comfort that soothed her heart. In the background, Mary-Chapin Carpenter sang softly through the speakers of a boom box, a voice as familiar and low and smooth and smoky as her own.

The mountains in the distance were deep blue beneath the sky. That big Montana sky, as blue as cobalt in this late part of the day, streaked with mare's-tail clouds. A gentle breeze swept the valley, swirling the tassels of the beargrass and needlegrass and red Indian paintbrush. The heads of the globeflowers along the creek bobbed and swayed. Overhead, an eagle circled lazily for a long while. A pair of antelope wandered out from behind a copse of aspen trees and came down to the creek to drink, casting curious looks at the llamas down the way.

Mari absorbed it all, her mind processing the images into words, snatches of melodies coming to her on the wind. She wrote down desultory lines in the notebook with a felt-tipped pen that leaked. The afternoon slipped away with the slow descent of the sun. From time to time she heard Spike barking, then he would come check on her as if to let her know he had things under control. When he tired of his reconnaissance missions, he curled up beneath her chair and went to sleep.

And so it was he missed his opportunity to prove himself as a watchdog, not rousing until the heavy footfall of boots sounded on the side porch. He darted out from under the chair, then threw his head back and barked so hard, his front paws came up off the deck.

Rafferty stepped around the corner of the house, planted his hands at the waist of his jeans, and scowled down at the terrier. "What the hell is that?"

"Spike. My dog," Mari announced with no small amount of indignation.

She pushed herself up out of her chair and brushed at her wrinkled jeans and baggy purple T-shirt, uncharacteristically self-conscious. Her heart had picked up a couple of extra beats. She could see by her reflection in the glass doors that her hair was a mess. *Your hair is always a mess, Marilee.* She scooped a chunk of it behind her ear.

J.D. snorted as if to say he didn't count anything as small as Spike to be a real dog. Spike glared up at him, not about to back down. A little like his mistress, he thought, chuckling to himself. Slowly, he hunkered down and offered the dog a chance to sniff his hand. A moment later he was fondling the terrier's ears and scratching the back of its muscular little neck.

"What he lacks in size, he makes up in volume," Mari said.

"Takes after you that way."

"Very funny. What are you doing here, Rafferty?" she asked, scowling, cringing a little inwardly at the defensiveness in her tone. In a perfect world she would have been calm and cool. But this was not a perfect world. She knew that better than most people.

J.D. rose slowly and stuck his hands in his pockets. "Came to see to the stock," he said, poker-faced.

Mari nodded slowly, not believing a word of it. "You're about a month late."

"Had a lot on my mind."

"How's Del?" she asked, not certain she wanted to hear what he'd had on his mind. There was no guarantee it was anything good.

"Seeing a psychiatrist in Livingston once a week. Guy was in 'Nam. They go fishing together and talk. He's doing okay."

"I'm glad."

She narrowed her eyes a little and did a head-to-toe assessment of him. He wore a clean blue oxford button-down that had seen an iron recently, dark jeans, boots that still had a little shine on them. No hat. His lean cheeks were freshly shaved. His dark hair was neat except for the little cowlick in front. She wanted to reach up and brush it with her fingers.

"You're not exactly dressed for chores," she said. "Got a hot date in town?"

"Well . . ." he drawled, "that remains to be seen."

Her heart kicked hard against her rib cage. She arched a brow and tried like hell not to look encouraged. "I see."

"How you doin', Mary Lee?" he asked softly, capturing her gaze and holding it steady. He wanted to go to her and touch her face and tangle his fingers in her hair. He wanted to sink his lips down against hers and kiss her for a year. He wanted to lay her down somewhere soft and make love to her forever, but there were things they needed to settle first.

I'm lonely. I miss you. I'm pregnant. "Fine." She raised her hands to show him both were in working order. "My days as a monoplegic are over."

"You're happy here?"

Not without you. "Very."

"You'll stay?"

"Forever."

He spent a moment digesting that, then nodded slowly.

"You're not going to tell me I don't belong here?" she asked.

"No, ma'am."

"You're not going to swear at me for being an outsider?"

"No."

"You're not going to try to run me off?"

He pressed his lips together and shook his head.

She laughed her deep, husky laugh. "That's what I hate about you, cowboy, you just never shut up."

One corner of his mouth tipped up. "You talk enough for both of us."

Mari tipped her head and fought the grin that threatened. "Touché."

She moved to lean back against the deck railing, crossing her ankles as if she felt nonchalant. If there had been a pack of cigarettes on the table, she would have been tempted to light half a dozen simultaneously, but there were only her cut-off straws and the leaky pen. Her nerves were stretched as taut as piano wire. She resisted the urge to rub her hand over her tummy.

"So, you came to see the llamas," she said, her fingernails digging into the railing.

J.D. looked straight at her. "I came to see you."

"What for?" She braced herself for an answer she didn't want to hear. That he wanted to tell her it was officially over between them, that he wouldn't be taking her up on her offer. That he still wanted to buy her land. If he said one word about the land . . .

J.D. glanced down at the table for a moment, rolling a length of plastic straw with his finger. She had some scribbled lines in a notebook. Song lyrics, he supposed.

Her handwriting was as messy as her hair. He stalled, amazed at the amount of courage he was having to dig up for this conversation. He'd spent a month storing it up and losing it, arguing with himself about his future and his motives. He had practiced what he would say on the way down here, and now he stood here, saying nothing.

Mary-Chapin Carpenter sang softly in the background, saving them from an oppressive silence.

Finally, he sighed and faced her. "Well, Will and Sam are starting over. You came here to start over. I thought maybe you and I might start over too."

Mari's breath caught in her throat. "Why?"

Because I love you. "I've spent a lot of time thinking these past few weeks," he said quietly. "I've been wrong. About a lot of things."

"And I'm one of those things?"

"I've been alone all my life, Mary Lee," he whispered.

She knew instantly what he meant. That he had been emotionally abandoned as a child. That he had protected himself ever since. That he was letting down his guard for her.

"I reckon I thought it would be safer, easier," he said. "But it's just lonely and I've grown weary of it."

She had been alone too. Alone inside herself while she went through the motions of fitting in in a world where she didn't belong. She knew the unique ache of that kind of loneliness.

"What do you say, Mary Lee?" he asked, spreading his hands, his heart pounding at the base of his throat. "You gonna give a hardheaded cowboy a second chance?"

She looked at him standing there in his good clothes, clean-shaven, and his hair combed, and her heart nearly overflowed. *You're hopeless, Marilee.* Hardheaded didn't begin to describe him. He was contrary and ornery and they didn't see eye to eye on much of anything. And he was closed and stubborn and opinionated. . . . And he was good and honest and strong and brave, and she loved him. No question that she loved him.

The air went out of J.D.'s lungs when she smiled that wry smile.

"Does this mean you'll actually take me on a date?" she asked suspiciously.

"Dinner and dancing?"

"Dancing?" She sniffed, mischief sparkling like diamonds in her eyes as she pushed herself away from the railing. "You can't dance."

He took a step closer, squaring his shoulders at the challenge. "Can so."

"Cannot."

A smile played at the corners of his mouth. "Come over here and say that, city girl."

Mari stepped up to him with her hands on her hips and looked him in the eye. "Show me."

Carefully he took her in his arms and danced her through a slow two-step around the deck. While Spike looked on from the cushion on the Adirondack chair, they moved in perfect unison to a sweet, pretty song about Halley's comet and innocence and simple joys. He moved with grace and confidence, guiding her, holding her in a way that made her feel safe and protected and small and feminine. Above them the sky turned purple with twilight and the moon rose in the east, a huge white wafer above the jagged teeth of the Absarokas. Down the valley the coyotes began to call.

Mari kept her gaze locked on J.D.'s, searching for a truth she wouldn't count on him speaking. That he could give her his heart. That she could trust him with hers. That the years of wariness hadn't left him permanently isolated.

She caught the slightest whiff of aftershave, and tears of love filled her eyes as she slid her arms around him and pressed her cheek against his chest, slowing their dance to a shuffle. He was a man as hard and unyielding as the land that bred him, and she might spend the next fifty years tearing her hair out over his stubbornness, but she wouldn't trade a second of it for all the gold in California.

She mouthed the words against the soft cotton of his shirt, like a precious secret, like prayer. *I love you.*

J.D. wrapped his arms around her and pressed a kiss to the soft tangle of her hair. His heart felt huge and tender in his chest, beneath her cheek. Looking out across the valley to the mountains beyond, he felt both old and new, strong and vulnerable. He felt as if they were the only two people on earth, alone in paradise, starting fresh. He vowed to do it right this time. No lies, no games, cards on the table, nothing held back.

The music slowed. The sweet harmony of twin fiddles faded away, and the last notes were played on the guitar.

Their feet stilled.

Their hearts beat.

Mari held her breath.

And Rafferty tipped her chin up and gazed down into her blue, blue eyes and whispered, "I love you."

ABOUT THE AUTHOR

Since the publication of her first romance novel in 1988, TAMI HOAG'S romances have regularly appeared on the best-seller lists of America's major booksellers. Her most recent works include the nationally bestselling *Cry Wolf* and the highly acclaimed *Still Waters*. She has won numerous awards for her writing, including a Lifetime Achievement Award from *Romantic Times* magazine. Tami lives with her husband and her menagerie of pets in rural Minnesota.

If you loved DARK PARADISE,
don't miss
Tami Hoag's newest novel of
passion and suspense, scheduled from
Bantam Books in the fall of 1994.

They found the body today. Not nearly as soon as we expected. Obviously we gave them too much credit. The police are not as smart as we are. No one is.

We stood on the sidewalk and watched. What a pitiful scene, grown men in tears and throwing up in the bushes. Hysteria seemed to descend like a cloud, fogging their small minds so they couldn't think. They wandered around and around that corner of the park, trampling the grass and breaking off bits of branches. They called to God, but God didn't answer. Nothing changed. No lightning bolts came down. No one was given knowledge of who or why. Ricky Meyers remained dead, his arms outflung, his sneakers toes-up.

We stood on the sidewalk as the ambulance came with its lights flashing, and more police cars came, and the cars of people from around town. We stood in the crowd, but no one saw us, no one looked at us. They thought we were beneath them, beneath their notice, unimportant. But we are really above them and beyond them and invisible to them. They are blind and stupid and trusting. They would never think to look at us.

We are twelve years old.

Josh Kirkwood and his two best buddies burst out of the locker room, flying into the cold, dark late afternoon, hollering at the tops of their lungs. Their breath billowed out in rolling clouds of steam. They flung themselves off the steps of the ice arena like mountain goats leaping from ledge to ledge and landed hip-deep in the snow on the side of the hill. Down they tumbled, hockey sticks skittering ahead of them, gear bags sliding after; then the Three Amigos, squealing and giggling, tucked themselves into balls of boy and wild-colored ski jackets and bright stocking caps.

The Three Amigos. That was what Brian's dad called them. Brian's family had moved to Deer Lake from Denver, Colorado, and his dad was still a big Broncos fan. He said the Broncos used to have some wide receivers called the Three Amigos and they used to be really good. Josh was a Vikings fan. Every other team was just a bunch of wusses, except maybe the Raiders, 'cause their uniforms were cool. He didn't like the Broncos, but he liked the nickname—the Three Amigos.

"We are the Three Amigos!" Matt yelled as they landed in a heap at the bottom of the hill. He threw back his head and howled like a wolf. Brian and Josh joined in, and the racket was so terrible, it made Josh's ears ring.

Brian fell into a fit of uncontrollable giggles. Matt flopped onto his back and started making a snow angel, swinging his arms and legs in wide arcs, looking as if he were trying to swim back up the hill. Josh pushed himself to his feet and shook like a dog as Coach Olsen came out the main door of the ice arena and started down the steps.

Coach was old—at least forty-five—kind of fat and mostly bald, but he was a good coach. He yelled a lot, but he laughed a lot too. He told them at the beginning of hockey season that if he got too cranky they were supposed to remind him they were only eight years old.

The team had picked Josh for that job. He was one of the co-captains, a responsibility that pleased him a lot even though he would never say so. Nobody liked a bragger, Mom said. If you took your responsibility and did your job well, there wasn't any reason to brag. A good job would speak for itself.

Coach Olsen shuffled down the steps, tugging down the earflaps of his hunting cap. The end of his nose was red from the cold. His breath came out of his mouth and went up around his head like smoke from a chimney. He glanced at Josh and smiled. "You guys all have rides home tonight?"

They answered all at once, scrambling for the coach's attention by being loud and silly. He laughed and held his gloved hands up in surrender. "All right, all right! The rink's still open if you get cold waiting. Olie's inside if you need to use the phone."

Then Coach jumped into the passenger side of his girl-friend's car, the way he did every Wednesday, and off they went to have dinner at Grandma's Attic downtown. Wednesday was Grandma's famous meat loaf night. All-U-Can-Eat, it said on the menu. Josh imagined Coach Olsen could eat a lot.

Cars rumbled around the circular drive in front of the Gordie Knutson Memorial Arena, a parade of minivans and station wagons, doors banging, exhaust pipes coughing. Kids from the various peewee league teams chucked their sticks and equipment in trunks and hatches and climbed into the cars with their moms or dads, talking a mile a minute about the plays and drills they had worked on in practice.

Matt's mom pulled up in their new Transport, a wedge-shaped thing that made Josh think of *Star Trek*. Matt scrambled for his gear and dashed across the side-walk, calling a good-bye over his shoulder. His mother buzzed down the passenger window, looking at Brian and Josh from beneath the thick band of a bright red stocking cap.

"Josh, Brian—you guys have rides coming?"

"My mom's coming," Josh answered, suddenly feeling eager to see her.

She would pick him up on her way home from the hospital and they would stop at the Leaning Tower of Pizza to pick up supper and she would want to hear all about practice. *Really* want to hear. Not like Dad. Dad pretended to listen, but Josh knew his mind was somewhere else. Somewhere bad, if the frown on his face was anything to go by. Sometimes lately on their drives home he even snapped at Josh to be quiet. He always apologized later, when they were sitting in the driveway or when they were hanging up their coats, but it still made Josh feel bad.

"My sister's coming," Brian called. "My sister, Beth Butthead," he added under his breath as Mrs. Conor drove away.

"You're the butthead," Josh teased, shoving him.

Brian shoved back, laughing, three big gaps showing in his mouth where teeth had been. "Butthead!"

"Buttbreath!"

"Buttface!"

Brian scooped up a mittenful of snow and tossed it in Josh's face, then turned and ran up the snowpacked sidewalk, bounded up the steps, and dashed around the side of the brick building. Josh let out a war whoop and bolted after him. Within a minute they were so involved in their game of Attack that the rest of the world ceased to exist. One boy hunted the other down to deliver a snowball up close in the face, in the back, down the neck of the jacket. After a successful attack, the roles reversed and the hunter became the hunted. If the hunter couldn't find the hunted in a count of a hundred, the hunted scored a point.

Josh was good at hiding. He was kind of small for his age and he was smart, a combination that served him well in games like Attack. He smashed Brian in the back of the head with a snowball, whirled, and ran. Before Brian had shaken the snow off his coat, Josh was safely tucked behind the air conditioning units that squatted beside the building. The cylinders were covered with canvas for the winter months and blocked the wind, making it a perfect hiding spot. They sat along the side of the building, where the streetlights didn't quite reach. He watched as Brian ventured cautiously around a Dumpster, snowball in hand, pouncing at a shadow, then drawing back. Josh smiled to himself. He had found the all-time best hiding place. He licked the tip of a gloved forefinger and drew himself a point in the air.

Brian's eyes homed in on a bush at the edge of the parking lot. Tongue sticking out the side of his mouth, he crept toward it. A car horn blared and he swung around, muttering as his sister's Rabbit pulled up to the curve.

Beth Hiatt slammed the transmission into park and climbed halfway out of the car with the motor still running so she could yell at her little brother. "Come on, hurry up, Brian! I've got pageant practice tonight!"

"But—"

"But nothing, twerp!" she snapped. The wind whipped a strand of long blond hair across her face and she snagged it back behind her ear with a bare hand white with cold. "Get your little butt in the car!" She slumped back into the driver's seat and slammed the door, cursing their mother for sending her to play chauffeur when she had a million *important* things to do.

Brian heaved a sigh and dropped his snowball, trudging toward his abandoned gear bag and hockey stick. Beth the Bitch raced the Rabbit's motor, put the car in gear, and let it lurch ahead on the drive, as if she might just leave him behind. She had done exactly that once before and they had both gotten hollered at, but Brian had gotten the worst of it because Beth blamed him for getting her in trouble and spent at least four days tormenting him for it. Instantly forgetting his game and the remaining Amigo, he grabbed his stuff and ran for the car, already plotting ways to get back at his sister for being such a snot.

Behind the air conditioning units, Josh heard Beth Hiatt's voice. He heard the car doors slam and he heard the Rabbit roar around the circle drive. So much for the game.

He crawled out of his hiding spot and went around to the front of the building. The parking lot was empty except for Olie's old rusted-out Chevy van. The circular drive was empty of mom mobiles. The snow that had been packed over the asphalt by countless tires gleamed in the soft pinkish glow of the streetlights, as hard and shiny as ice. Josh tugged off his left glove and shoved up the sleeve of his ski jacket to peer at the watch Uncle Tim had sent him for Christmas. Big and black with lots of dials and buttons, it looked like something a scuba diver might wear—or a commando. Sometimes Josh liked to pretend that he was a commando, a man on a mission, waiting to meet with the world's most dangerous spy. The numbers on the watch face glowed green in the dark. 5:45.

Josh looked down the street, expecting to see headlights, expecting to see the minivan with his mom at the wheel. But the street was dark. The only lights glowed dimly out the windows of houses that lined the block. Inside those houses, people were having supper and watching the news and talking about their day. Outside, the only sound was the buzz of the streetlamps and the wind rattling the dry, bare branches of winter-dead trees. The sky was black.

He was alone.

She nearly escaped. Almost. Not quite. She had her parka halfway on, purse slung over her shoulder, gloves and car keys clutched in one hand. She hurried down the hall toward the west side door of the hospital, staring straight ahead, telling herself if she didn't make eye contact she wouldn't be caught, she would be invisible, she would escape.

I sound like Josh. That's the kind of game he likes—what if we could make ourselves invisible?

A smile curved Hannah's lips. Josh and his imagination. Last night she'd found him in Lily's room, telling his sister an adventure story about Zeek the Meek and Super Duper, characters she had made up in stories for

Josh when he was a toddler. He was passing on the tradition, telling the tale with great enthusiasm while Lily sat in her crib and chewed on her fist, her blue eyes wide with astonishment, as if she were hanging on her brother's every word.

I've got two great kids. Two for the plus column. I'll take what I can get these days.

The smile faded and the knot of tension tightened in Hannah's stomach. She blinked hard, as if she were trying to shake off a trance, and realized she was just standing there at the end of the hall with her coat half on. Rand Bekker, head of maintenance, shouldered his way through the door, letting in a blast of crisp air. A burly man with a full red beard, he pulled off a flame orange hunting cap and shook himself like a big wet ox, as if he could shake off the chill. The fluorescent light gleamed off the bald dome of his skull.

"Hiya, Dr. Garrison. Decent night out there."

"Is it?" She smiled automatically, blankly, as if she were speaking with a stranger. But there were no strangers at Deer Lake Community Hospital. Everyone knew everyone and knew most of their personal lives as well. The hospital was too small for anonymity.

"You bet. It's looking good for Snowdaze."

He grinned, his anticipation for the festival as plain as a child's eagerness for Christmas morning. Snowdaze was big doings in a town the size of Deer Lake, an excuse for the fifteen thousand residents to break the monotony of Minnesota's long winter. Hannah tried to find some matching enthusiasm. She knew Josh was looking forward to Snowdaze, especially the torchlight parade. But it was difficult for her to feel festive these days.

For the most part she felt tired, drained, dispirited. And stretched over it all like plastic wrap was a thin film of desperation, because she couldn't let any of those feelings show. People depended on her, looked up to her, thought of her as some kind of model for working women. Hannah Garrison: doctor, wife, mother, Woman of the Year; juggling all the roles with skill and ease and a

J.D. sighed. "Del—"

"You won't send me away, will you, J.D.?" he asked flat out, then sat there, shaking inside, as he waited for an answer.

He kept his eyes on the view, afraid to look away from it, afraid that if he looked away, it would vanish. His hand crept up against his will and he rubbed his scar as if the smooth disk of flesh were a lucky penny. He wanted to tell his nephew what it had been like for him during that black period in the V.A. hospital, what it had been like to never see the sky or the mountains, to never watch the sunset except through a window with chicken wire imbedded in the glass. He wanted to explain how he couldn't tolerate the lack of space and how the other patients crowded in on him and made it impossible for him to keep his mind together and focused on each individual moment, which was what he needed to do to stay sane. He wanted to tell J.D. what it meant to him to have this place and to have his duties on the Stars and Bars. But when he opened his mouth, all that came out was, "I'd die."

J.D. clenched his jaw against the surge of pain for the old soldier sitting beside him. So much had been taken from him—his youth, his prospects, his face, his mind. All he had left was his job and his place on the land, and a small well of pride in being able to handle those simple responsibilities.

God help me, _____ _'t take that away from him._

But he had shot ____ what was left of his mind man, and he had proved that ____ of stress. What if he happen'd not be trusted in the face and perceived them as a threat ___oss legitimate hunters

His courage running out on him, ____ back around and started up the mou___ng his horse chores need doing."

J.D. followed slowly, accountability weigh___ "There's down like an anchor.

The truck was in the yard when they arrived at th__ cabin, but it wasn't Tucker who sat on the tailgate tossing a Frisbee for the dogs. J.D.'s heart slammed into his sternum as she raised her head and looked right at him.

"Mary Lee . . ." he mumbled.

Her left arm was in a sling. She looked thinner. Her cheekbones were a little more prominent than they had been, the hollows beneath them deeper. Her jewel-blue eyes seemed impossibly large and deep beneath her dark brows. She wore black leggings and hiking boots and an old denim shirt that would have fit him. She eased herself down off the tailgate and swept back a chunk of streaky blond hair that had blown across her face.

"Never fear," she said, her mouth kicking up on one side in a wry smile. "Tucker and your lasagna are inside."

"What are you doing here?" he asked, realizing too late how that sounded.

Her chin came up a little. "I came to see Del."

Del jerked around at the post where he was tying his horse, his eyes open wide, his mouth tugging back on the dead side in a grimace of shock.

Mari offered him the warmest smile she could find. "Hey, Del. I came to thank you."

He narrowed his eyes and looked at her sideways, fussing with his reins. "There's no need."

"Yes, there is," she insisted. "You saved my life."

Del looked down at his boots and rubbed his jaw. He wished she hadn't come back. He wished everyone would just go away and leave him to his shame. He didn't want to have alone about what had happened. Then J.D. would have to say anything about it. If he couldn't take credit if it to put him away for sure. Maybe right.

wasn't his due; that would softly.

"No, ma'am," he sang from Mary Lee to his uncle. He J.D.'s attention to his horse and stood very still, watching stepped down brows tugged together. "Yes, you did, Del. You Del, was woman who was trying to kill me. She would killed me and Samantha too. You saved us both."

He wagged his head from side to side, not meeting her

long time. So why did that last part leave him feeling empty?

J.D. turned his thoughts away from the question and turned his horse toward the southeast. The day was waning. It was Friday, seventeen days since he had seen Mary Lee. Again he ducked the issue and focused on the prospect of lasagna for supper. Tucker brought supplies and lasagna on Friday.

He met Del at the edge of the basin and they rode up toward Bald Knob in silence. Del stared down at his saddle horn as they rode past the knob, the muscles in the shattered side of his face twitching with tension.

"We'll need to talk about it, Del," J.D. said, his heart feeling like a rock in his chest. He had tried to bring the subject up more than once since they had gotten the cattle settled, but Del had dodged it every time and J.D. hadn't had the heart to force it. He couldn't stand to see the sick worry in his uncle's eyes, or the shame.

Del pulled up suddenly and pivoted his roan around so he could look out over the knob to the wide, flower-strewn meadow where the cattle grazed and beyond to the next mountain and the next, their shapes turning hazy and indistinct as the sun slid behind the farthest of them. He stared out at it all from beneath the brim of his hat, stared hard, as if he were memorizing every last detail.

He didn't want to talk about what had happened. He didn't even like to remember it, though the memory was always right there, hovering like a fog just beneath the plate in his head. It descended and tormented him, visions of the blondes, their features melding together until he couldn't one from the other. . . .

He had wanted only to do the right thing, to help save the ranch, to make him proud of him. But he saw the looks his nephew sent him when he didn't think he was paying attention, and they were full of pity and shame

"and I ought to go back down, hadn't you, J.D.?" he said, hoping against hope J.D. would say yes and simply leave, leave him be as if nothing had happened.

excuses. They were wrong for each other. It wasn't meant to be. Just this morning she had tried to tell herself it was best to do nothing. To accept. To settle.

The hell it was.

"Come on, Spike," she said, starting back toward the ranch buildings. "We need a plan."

J.D. slapped his catch rope against the leg of his chaps and shooed the two calves that had wandered back toward their mamas. The youngsters darted to the herd with their skinny tails lifted high. His horse fell out of the canter and dropped to a walk.

He had come up the mountain with the herd three days after the "Incident at Bald Knob," as the newspapers had labeled it, and stayed on. He needed to spend some time with Del, to decide what to do about him. Beyond that, he needed some time to decide what to do about himself. A lot of things had turned around on him and shifted beneath him in the past few weeks—perspectives, philosophies, long-held beliefs. He needed some time to let it all settle into place.

He needed this—long days in the saddle, trailing after cows and calves, days on the mountainside and in the lush meadows with nothing but time to think and reflect. It was a luxury he seldom afforded himself, too busy with running the ranch and protecting the ranch and fighting off the outsiders. But he wasn't the only one capable of doing the work and it wasn't his sole only one capable of doing the land and Will was a Rafferty responsibility. It was Rafferty

J.D. had left him in charge. I seen to and plans made for cutting irrigation had to be first concern was to see to Samantha's rec crop. Will's he had accepted the jobs without complaint. ...ion, but accounts, Will was applying himself with a seri...er's heretofore unknown to him; Samantha was healing; two appeared to be very much in love.

Good news. Something they had been short on for a

the creek to graze and to lie in the shade of the cotton-wood trees. Spike caught sight of them and sent up an alarm that caused the whole herd to raise their heads. He charged toward them, ready to do battle. Mari called him back and explained to him that the llamas were cool and he didn't need to worry about them. The little dog cocked his head and listened to her with perked ears. When the lecture was over, he picked a shady spot and curled up to watch her dig a grave for Mr. Peanut.

The task was awkward and time-consuming because of her temporary handicap, but Mari dug steadily, pushing the spade into the ground with her foot and levering it up with her good arm. The spot she had chosen was far away from the house, on a little knoll of land that over-looked the creek and was shaded by a clump of young aspen trees. An exile of sorts, but a peaceful one.

She buried the box with the peanut tin inside and transplanted wild bitteroot on the grave. When the task was finished, she stood back, leaning on the spade, and stared down at the vibrant pink flowers. Bright, pretty, tough with bitter roots. Like Lucy.

The flood of feelings that came with thoughts of her friend were a muddy mix of loss and hurt and disap-pointment and gratitude. She longed to grab her guitar and try to pick through the tangle with the divining rod of her music. But she couldn't play with one hand, and so she packed the feelings away in her heart to be sorted through another day when time may have given her the gift of perspective.

Turning back toward the house, she looked up the mountain and wondered if time had given J.D. any per-spective.

She missed him. Damned ornery cowboy. She missed his toughness and the tenderness beneath it. She missed his hard opinions and the vulnerability behind them. She missed his arrogance and the rare glimpses of humor that tempered it. She missed his touch. She missed his kiss.

"So what are you gonna do about it, Marilee?" she asked out loud.

In her past life she would have done nothing but make

Drew carried her bags in for her, then headed back to town. Mari didn't invite him to stay. After two weeks of media madness, she wanted some time alone. Time apart from Drew to let the raw feelings fade seemed a good idea as well. They could start over with their friendship in a few days, start fresh.

The house was exactly as she had left it—half restored, half disaster area. Mari walked through, making a mental list of the things she would do in the coming weeks, of the things she would change to make the house her own. Everything that had been Lucy's would go. She couldn't bear to look at a chair or a painting and wonder whose secrets had been used to buy it. She would scavenge through antique shops and flea markets for things of her own. The expensive artwork would go. She would replace it with local folk art. She had already made arrangements for a plumber and a carpenter to come out and repair the damages made by Bryce's people during the search that had passed for vandalism. The cars would be sold and the proceeds, along with the cash Lucy had left behind, would go to pay the inheritance taxes.

When all was said and done, she would have an empty house and an empty bank account, but her new life would not be tainted by the old.

In the great room her eyes landed on the Mr. Peanut tin on the mantel above the fireplace. The peanut regarded her with a cynical, knowing look, as if it had foreseen everything that had happened and was amused with her response to the challenges. With a heavy heart she took it down and packed it in a box.

"You're outta here, Luce," she whispered, blinking back tears.

With Spike scouting the way ahead of her, she walked out to the barn with the box tucked under her bad arm and checked on Clyde. The mule was unimpressed by her return and went on eating grass. The gash in his side was healing nicely. The vet had told her he would be ready to ride before she would be ready to ride him.

Spade in hand, she wandered out into the llama pasture. The llamas had all gone down to the other side of of what Bryce might do to our business if we meddled in his. Then the fear that what happened to Lucy might happen to anyone."

"That wasn't an unreasonable fear," she said, trying to convince herself as much as Drew. She was disappointed in him. She felt let down, betrayed.

"No, but somehow that doesn't make me feel any more a hero," he said. "Perhaps if I'd spoken up earlier, you and Samantha would have been spared your ordeal. Perhaps Lucy would still be alive."

"Sharon killed Lucy out of jealousy. She was after Sam for the same reason. She didn't want another woman getting close to Bryce."

"Still, if Bryce's activities had been revealed sooner, she may never have had the opportunity."

"There's no way of knowing that."

"No, and that's something that will haunt me the rest of my life." He took his eyes off the road long enough to give her his most sincere look of apology. "I'm so sorry, luv."

"This is what you and Kevin were fighting about, isn't it?" Mari said.

He sighed as he let off the gas to negotiate a curve. "Yes. He wanted me to go to the sheriff. I refused. He accused me of condoning what Bryce was doing. In a way, I suppose I was. But I was also trying to keep my friends from getting hurt. Hear no evil, see no evil, and all that."

"Will you work it out?"

"I don't know," he said softly, staring out at the road, then he shot another glance across the cab at her. "Will you and I?"

Mari said nothing for a moment, thinking about the value of friendship and forgiveness. She had nearly lost her life, but Drew's intent had been to save her.

"Let's not be sorry," she said quietly as they started up the switchbacks. "Let's just start over. That's what I came here for."

• • •

seed packets and bottles of horse liniment and stacks of western novels and cookbooks from the Lutheran church ladies' auxiliary. *Outsiders*. Outsiders were becoming the life's blood of his hometown, with or without the permission of J. D. Rafferty. The town would change or the town would die, and Rafferty would stay on his mountain until God or the bankers drove him down.

Stubborn. Unyielding. Uncompromising. Those weren't supposed to be compliments, but she could imagine the hard gleam of pride in his granite-gray eyes when those words were applied to him.

In front of the courthouse Colleen Bentsen had herself an audience as she worked on her pile of twisted metal. M. E. Fralick was giving a one-woman performance of *Evita* under the shade of the bandshell. Her rendition of "Don't Cry for Me, Argentina" carried across the park to clash with strains of Joe Diffie coming from a boom box.

They drove out the ridge road past the Paradise Motel in silence. Since the incident on the mountain, Drew had had little to say about the revelation of Bryce's private game reserve. He had kept their conversations focused on Mari, fussing over her well-being and her state of mind. An obvious diversion, but she had allowed it, too tired and too fresh from the ordeal to want to talk about it any more than she had to. The questions came to mind now, but she didn't ask them. She just sat there, scratching Spike's ears.

Drew glanced at her sideways, trying twice to find the right words. Finally he just plunged in like a penitent in the confessional. "I knew about Bryce's hunts. I pieced it all together from odd bits of conversation I picked up, rumors, that sort of thing. Hints Lucy dropped. She was a great one for leaving a trail of bread crumbs, then standing back to watch who followed it and what they did. I didn't do a bloody thing," he said, his voice sharp with self-loathing.

"Why?" Mari asked evenly.

"Fear, I'm ashamed to say. At first there was the fear

beauty queen smile. Lately the titles had felt as heavy as bowling balls and her arms were growing weary.

"Rough day?"

"What?" She jerked her attention back to Rand and felt a flush of embarrassment warm her cheeks. "I'm sorry, Rand. Yeah, it's been one of those days."

"I better let you go then. I got a hot date with a boiler."

Hannah murmured a good-bye as Bekker pulled open a door marked Maintenance Staff Only and disappeared through it, leaving Hannah alone in the hall. Her inner voice, the voice of the little goblin that kept the cling wrap pulled tight over her emotions, gave a shout.

Go! Go now! Escape while you can! Get away!

She had to pick up Josh. They would stop and get a pizza, then go on to the sitter's for Lily.

But her body refused to bolt in response, and the great escape was lost.

"Dr. Garrison to ER. Dr. Garrison to ER."

That selfish part of her prodded once more, telling her she could still get away. She wasn't on call tonight, had no patients in the hundred-bed facility who were in critical need of her personal attention. There was no one here to see her go. She could leave the work to the doctor on duty, Ben Lomax, who believed he had been put on earth specifically to rush to the aid of mere mortals to comfort them with his coverboy looks. Hannah wasn't even the backup tonight.

But guilt came directly on the heels of those thoughts. She was a doctor. She had taken an oath to serve. It was her responsibility to serve. It didn't matter that she'd seen enough sore throats and bruised bodies to last her for one day. She had a duty—a bigger one now that the hospital board had named her director of the ER. The people of Deer Lake depended on her. Especially the ones who knew Dr. Lomax.

The pings sounded again. Hannah heaved a sigh and felt tears warm the backs of her eyes. She was exhausted —physically, emotionally. She needed this night off, a night with just herself and the kids. Paul was working late, keeping his moods and his sarcasm in his office instead of inflicting them on her.

A wavy strand of honey-blond hair escaped her loose ponytail and fell limply against her cheek. She sighed and brushed it back behind her ear as she stared out the door to the parking lot, which looked sepia-toned beneath the sodium vapor lights.

"Dr. Garrison to ER. Dr. Garrison to ER."

She slipped her parka off and folded it over her arm.

"God, there you are!" Kathleen Casey blurted out as she skidded around the corner and hustled down the hall. The thick, cushioned soles of her running shoes made almost no sound on the polished linoleum. Not a fraction of an inch over five feet, the nurse had a leprechaun's features, a shock of thick red hair, and the tenacity of a pit bull. With small hazel eyes she drew a bead on Hannah that had all the power of a tractor beam.

Hannah tried to muster a wry smile. "Sorry. God may be a woman, but She's not *this* woman."

Kathleen's bow of a mouth twitched up at one corner, and she gave a snort as she curled a hand around Hannah's upper arm. "You'll do."

"Can't Ben handle it?"

"Maybe, but we'd rather have a higher life-form with opposable thumbs."

"Please, Kathleen. I'm not even on call tonight. I have to pick up Josh from hockey. Call Dr. Baskir—"

"We did. He's in bed with your friend and mine, Jurassic Park flu, also known as tracheosaurus phlegmus. That's one butt-kicking virus. Half the staff is down with it, which means I, Kathleen Casey, Queen of the ER, may press you into service against your will. It won't take long, I promise."

"Famous last words," Hannah muttered.

Kathleen ignored her and started to turn as if she had every intention of towing all five feet nine inches of Hannah in her wake. Hannah's feet moved of their own accord as the wail of an ambulance sounded somewhere in the distance.

"What's coming in?" she asked on a sigh of resignation.

"Car accident. Some kid hit a patch of ice on Cedar Lake Road and spun into a car full of grandmas on their way home from a day of bingo and slot machines at Dakota Country Casino."

Their pace picked up with each step, the low heels of Hannah's leather boots pounding a quicker and quicker staccato against the linoleum. Kathleen's hand fell to her side. Hannah felt her fatigue and its companion emotions slip under the surface of duty and her "doctor mode," as Paul called it. The professional armor emerged magically. Power switches were flipped on inside her, filling her brain with light and energy, sending a rush of adrenaline shooting through her. The same thing was happening to Kathleen, she knew. They had talked about the phenomenon once. Kathleen called it her "game face." It settled into place as the ambulance pulled into the hospital drive.

"What's the status?" Hannah asked, even her speech taking on a sharper, harder quality.

"They flew two critical to Hennepin County. We get the leftovers. Two ladies with bumps and bruises and the college kid. Sounds like he's banged up pretty good."

"No seat belt?"

"Why bother when you haven't lived long enough to grasp the concept of mortality?" Kathleen said as they reached the area that served as a combination nurses' station and admissions desk.

Hannah leaned over the counter. "Marge? Could you please call the hockey rink and leave word for Josh that I'll be a little bit late? Maybe he can just stay and practice his skating."

The receptionist smiled without looking up from her typing. "Sure thing, Dr. Garrison."

Dr. Ben Lomax arrived on the scene in immaculate surgical greens, looking like a soap opera doctor. A million-dollar face and a ten-cent brain was Kathleen's description. The nurse shot a look at him and rolled her eyes.

"Jesus," she muttered half under her breath, "he's been watching *Medical Center* reruns again. Get a load of the Chad Everett hair."

Strands of black hair tumbled across his forehead in a careless look he had probably spent fifteen painstaking minutes in front of a mirror to achieve. Lomax was thirty-two, madly in love with himself, and afflicted with an overabundance of confidence in his own talents. He had come to Deer Lake Community in April, a reject from the better medical centers in the Twin Cities—a hard truth that had not managed to put so much as a dent in his ego. Deer Lake was just far enough outstate that they couldn't afford to be choosy. Most doctors preferred the salaries in the metro area over the chance to serve the needy in a small rural college town.

Lomax had arranged his features into a suitably grave expression that cracked a little when he caught sight of Hannah.

"I thought you'd gone home," he said bluntly, planting his hands at his waist.

"Kathleen just caught me."

"In the nick of time," the nurse added.

Lomax sucked in a breath to chastise her for her attitude.

"Save it, Ben," Hannah snapped, tossing her things on a waiting-area couch and moving forward as the doors to the ER slid open.

A stretcher was rolled in, one paramedic at the rear, one bent over the patient, talking to him in a soothing tone. "Hang in there, Mike. The docs'll have you patched up in no time."

The young man on the stretcher groaned and tried to sit up, groaning louder as the chest and head restraints held him down on the backboard. His face was taut and gray with pain above the cervical collar that immobilized his neck. Blood had run down across his temple from a gash on his forehead.

"What have we got here, Arlis?" Hannah asked, shoving up the sleeves of her sweater.

"Mike Chamberlain. Nineteen. He's a little shocky,"

the paramedic at the back of the stretcher said. "Pulse 120. BP 90 over 60. Got a bump on the noggin and some broken bones."

"Is he lucid?"

Lomax cut her off on the way to the stretcher with a move as smooth as glass. He barely spared her a glance over his shoulder. "I'll handle it, Dr. Garrison—you're off-duty. Mavis." He nodded to Mavis Sandstrom. The nurse exchanged a glance with Kathleen, her expression as blank as a cardsharp's.

Hannah bit her tongue and stepped back. There was no point in fighting with Lomax now. Administration frowned on that kind of thing. She didn't want to be here anyway. She had a family to tend to. Let Lomax take the patient who would take the most time.

"Treatment room three, guys," Lomax ordered and ushered them down the hall as a second ambulance pulled into the drive. "Let's start an IV with lactated ringers. . . ."

"Dr. Ben Ego strikes again," Kathleen growled. "He has yet to grasp the notion that you're his boss now."

"No biggie," Hannah said calmly. "If we ignore him long enough, maybe he'll stop trying to mark territory and we can all live happily ever after."

"Or maybe he'll flip out and we'll find him in the parking lot peeing on car tires."

There wasn't time to laugh. A heavyset EMT from the second ambulance charged into the reception area.

"We've got a full arrest," she said breathlessly. "Sixty-nine-year-old lady. We were bringing her in with cuts and bruises, and as we pulled into the drive, *bam!* She grabs her chest and goes—"

The rest of her words were lost as Hannah, Kathleen, and another nurse bolted into response. The emergency room erupted into a whirlwind of sound and action. Orders shouted and relayed. Pages sounding for additional staff. The stretcher wheeling into the reception area and down the hall. The trauma cart and crash cart thundering into the treatment room.

"Standard ACLS procedure, guys," Hannah called out.

"Get me a 6.5 endotracheal tube. Let's get her bagged and get some air into her lungs. Do we have a pulse without CPR?"

"No."

"With CPR?"

"Yes."

"BP 40 over 20 and fading fast."

"Start an IV. Hang bretylium and dopamine and give her a bristoject of epinephrine."

"Goddamn it, I can't get a vein! Come on, baby, come on, come to Mama Kathleen."

"Stop CPR. Angie, run a strip. Is Respiratory coming?"

"Jim's on his way down."

"Gotcha!" Kathleen slipped the line onto the catheter and secured it with tape, her small hands quick and sure. A tech handed her the epinephrine and she injected it into the line.

"Fine v-fib, Dr. Garrison."

"We need to defibrillate. Chris, continue CPR until my word. Charge me up to 320, Allen." Hannah turned and grabbed the paddles, rubbing the heads together to spread the gel across them. "Stand clear!" Paddles in position against the woman's bare chest. "All clear!" Hit the buttons. The old woman's body bucked on the gurney.

"Nothing! No pulse."

"Clear!" She hit the buttons again and her eyes went to the monitor, where a flat green line bisected the screen. "Once more. Clear!"

She hit the buttons. The woman's body convulsed a third time. The flat line snapped like a cracking whip and the monitor began to bleep out an erratic beat. A cheer went up in the room.

They worked on Ida Bergen for forty minutes, pulling her out of the clutches of death only to lose her again ten minutes later. They worked the miracle a second time but not a third.

Hannah delivered the news to Mr. Bergen, who had been called in out of the milking parlor. His chore clothes gave off the warm sweet scent of cows and fresh milk with a pungent undertone of manure. He had the same stoic face she had seen on many a Nordic farmer, but his eyes were bright and moist with worry, and they brimmed with tears when she told him they had done their best but had been unable to save his wife.

She sat with him and led him through some of the cruel rituals of death. Even in this time of grief, decisions had to be made, etc., etc. She went through the routine in a low monotone, feeling on autopilot, numb with exhaustion, crushed by depression. The adrenaline that fueled her through the crisis had vaporized. A crash was imminent. Another familiar part of a routine she hated. As a doctor, she had cheated death time and again, but death wouldn't let her win every time, and she had never learned to be a gracious loser.

After Mr. Bergen had gone, Hannah slipped into her office and sat at the desk with the lights off, her head cradled in her hands. It hurt worse this time. Perhaps because she had never really lost anything in her own life and now felt perilously close to loss for the first time. Her marriage was in trouble. Ed Bergen's marriage was over. Forty-eight years of partnership over in the time it took a car to skid out of control on an icy road. Had they been good years? Loving years? Would he mourn his wife or simply go on?

She thought of Paul, his dissatisfaction, his discontent, his quiet hostility. Ten years of marriage was tearing apart like rotted silk and she felt powerless to stop it. She had never lost anything. She had never developed the skills to fight against an impending loss. She had no point of reference. She felt the tears building—tears for Ida Bergen and Ed and for herself. Tears of grief and confusion and exhaustion. She blinked against them, afraid to let them start falling. She had to be strong. She had to find a solution, smooth over all the rough spots, make everyone happy. But tonight the burdens weighed heavy on her slender shoulders and she couldn't help thinking the only light at the end of the tunnel was the headlight of a big black train.

Knuckles rapped against her door and Kathleen stuck her head in. "Ida had a bad ticker, you know," she said quietly. "She'd been seeing a cardiac specialist at Abbott-Northwestern for years."

Hannah sniffed, reached out and flicked on the desk lamp. "How's Ben's patient?"

The nurse slipped in through the door and into the visitor's chair at the end of the black steel desk. She crossed a sneaker over one knee and rubbed absently at an ink mark on the leg of her white uniform pants. "He'll be fine. A couple of broken bones, a slight concussion, whiplash. He was lucky. I guess his car was turned sideways at the moment of impact. The other car hit him on the passenger side.

"Poor kid. He feels terrible about the accident. He keeps going on and on about how the road was dry and then suddenly there was this big patch of ice and he was out of control."

"I guess life can be that way sometimes," Hannah murmured, fingering the small cube-shaped clock on her desk. The wood was bird's-eye maple, smooth and satiny beneath her fingertips. An anniversary gift from Paul four years ago. A clock so she would always know how long it would be before they could be together again.

"Yeah, well, you've hit your patch of ice for the night. Time to pick yourself up, dust yourself off, and get home to the munchkins."

A chill went through Hannah like a dagger of ice. Her fingers tightened convulsively on the clock and tilted the face up to the light. 6:50.

"Oh my God," she said, shoving to her feet. "Josh. I forgot Josh!"

THE VERY BEST IN CONTEMPORARY
〜❦〜 WOMEN'S FICTION

SANDRA BROWN

___28951-9 Texas! Lucky $6.50/$8.99 in Canada   ___56768-3 Adam's Fall $4.99/$5.99

___28990-X Texas! Chase $6.50/$8.99   ___56045-X Temperatures Rising $5.99/$6.99

___29500-4 Texas! Sage $6.50/$8.99   ___56274-6 Fanta C $5.50/$6.99

___29085-1 22 Indigo Place $5.99/$6.99   ___56278-9 Long Time Coming $4.99/$5.99

___29783-X A Whole New Light $5.99/$6.99   ___57157-5 Heaven's Price $5.50/$6.99

TAMI HOAG

___29534-9 Lucky's Lady $5.99/$7.50   ___29272-2 Still Waters $5.99/$7.50

___29053-3 Magic $5.99/$7.50   ___56160-X Cry Wolf $5.50/$6.50

___56050-6 Sarah's Sin $4.99/$5.99   ___56161-8 Dark Paradise $5.99/$7.50

___09961-2 Night Sins $19.95/$23.95

NORA ROBERTS

___29078-9 Genuine Lies $5.99/$6.99   ___27859-2 Sweet Revenge $5.99/$6.99

___28578-5 Public Secrets $5.99/$6.99   ___27283-7 Brazen Virtue $5.99/$6.99

___26461-3 Hot Ice $5.99/$6.99   ___29597-7 Carnal Innocence $5.99/$6.99

___26574-1 Sacred Sins $5.99/$6.99   ___29490-3 Divine Evil $5.99/$6.99

DEBORAH SMITH

___29107-6 Miracle $5.50/$6.50   ___29690-6 Blue Willow $5.99/$7.99

___29092-4 Follow the Sun $4.99/$5.99   ___29689-2 Silk and Stone $5.99/$6.99

___28759-1 The Beloved Woman $4.50/$5.50

- -

Ask for these books at your local bookstore or use this page to order.

Please send me the books I have checked above. I am enclosing $_____ (add $2.50 to cover postage and handling). Send check or money order, no cash or C.O.D.'s, please.

Name _____

Address _____

City/State/Zip _____

Send order to: Bantam Books, Dept. FN 24, 2451 S. Wolf Rd., Des Plaines, IL 60018

Allow four to six weeks for delivery.

Prices and availability subject to change without notice.   FN 24 1/96